NOBODY BOTHERS GUS by Algis Budrys—What's the point of being a superman if no one can even remember that you exist?

THE MOON MOTH by Jack Vance—On a world where no one's face is ever seen, how can you tell the guilty from the innocent?

THE DANCE OF THE CHANGER AND THE THREE by Terry Carr—Which is more impossible to understand—senseless destruction or senseless creation?

VIEW FROM A HEIGHT by Joan D. Vinge—How do you spend the rest of your life when you find yourself alone on a one-way journey to meet the universe?

THE FIRST CANTICLE by Walter M. Miller, Jr.—In the next Dark Ages what will mankind venerate more—the lost wisdom of the ancients or crumpled, old shopping lists?

These are just some of the questions answered in thirty-one imaginative excursions along

THE ROAD TO
SCIENCE FICTION

JAMES GUNN is a well-known science fiction author and a past president of the Science Fiction Writers of America. He was named Chairman of the prestigious John W. Campbell Memorial Award jury and is currently teaching science fiction and literature courses at the University of Kansas, Lawrence, where he lives. *The Road to Science Fiction #1—From Gilgamesh to Wells, The Road to Science Fiction #2—From Wells to Heinlein,* and *The Road to Science Fiction #3— From Heinlein to Here* are available in Mentor editions, and his science fiction novel, *The Magicians,* is available in a Signet edition.

The Mysteries of Science from MENTOR and SIGNET

(0451)

- ☐ **THE ROAD TO THE STARS by Iain Nicolson.** Noted science writer and space authority Iain Nicolson tells the exciting story of man's attempts to conquer space, from early rocketry to the first successful moon-landing, from the present-day reality of the space shuttle and the Pioneer probes to the future possibilities of space colonies, space arks and interstellar travel. (617800—$2.75)

- ☐ **PARTICLES: An Introduction to Particle Physics by Michael Chester.** A remarkably clear, thoroughly fascinating exploration of the world beyond the atom that offers both a history of this fascinating saga of discovery and an explanation of what we now know about the subatomic order of the universe. (618998—$2.50)

- ☐ **THE WEB OF LIFE by John H. Storer.** This exciting, easy-to-understand introduction to the science of ecology shows how all living things—from bacteria to men—fit into a pattern of life and depend upon each other and the world around them for existence. (615928—$1.95)

- ☐ **THE WELLSPRINGS OF LIFE by Isaac Asimov.** Here is a lucid picture of life on this planet as far as the light of science has been able to penetrate—a provocative study written to be understood and enjoyed by anyone who has asked in his childhood "Where did I come from?" (616197—$1.50)

THE ROAD TO
SCIENCE FICTION #4

From Here to Forever

Edited by James Gunn

A MENTOR BOOK
NEW AMERICAN LIBRARY

TIMES MIRROR

New York and Scarborough, Ontario

Library of Congress Catalog Card Number: 78-070642

ACKNOWLEDGMENTS

Gregory Benford. "Exposures." Copyright © 1981 by Gregory Benford. Reprinted by permission of the author.

Michael Bishop. "Rogue Tomato." Copyright © 1975 by Robert Silverberg; reprinted by permission of the author.

Jorge Luis Borges. "The Library of Babel." From FICCIONES by Jorge Luis Borges. English translation copyright © 1962 by Grove Press, Inc. Reprinted by permission of Grove Press and of Weidenfeld & Nicolson, London. Translated from the Spanish, copyright © 1956 by Emece Editores, S.A. Buenos Aires.

Edward Bryant. "Particle Theory." Copyright © 1977 by the Condé Nast Publications, Inc. Reprinted by permission of the author.

Algis Budrys. "Nobody Bothers Gus." Copyright © 1955, Street & Smith Publishing Co., Inc. Reprinted by permission of the author.

Terry Carr. "The Dance of the Changer and the Three." Copyright © 1968 by Joseph Elder. From THE FARTHEST REACHES, reprinted by permission of the author.

Avram Davidson. "My Boyfriend's Name is Jello." Copyright © 1954 by Mercury Press, Inc. Reprinted by permission of the author's agent, Kirby McCauley, Ltd.

Thomas Disch. "Angouleme." First appeared in *New Worlds 1*. Copyright © 1971 by Michael Moorcock. Reprinted by permission of the author.

Gardner R. Dozois. "Where No Sun Shines." Copyright © 1970 by Damon Knight. Reprinted by permission of the author.

George Alex Effinger. "The Ghost Writer." Copyright © 1973 by Terry Carr. Reprinted by permission of the author.

Carol Emshwiller. "Abominable." Copyright © 1980 by Carol Emshwiller. First published in *Orbit 21*, 1980, ed. by Damon

The following pages constitute an extension of this copyright page.

MENTOR TRADEMARK REG. U.S. PAT. OFF. AND FOREIGN COUNTRIES
REGISTERED TRADEMARK—MARCA REGISTRADA
HECHO EN CHICAGO, U.S.A.

SIGNET, SIGNET CLASSICS, MENTOR, PLUME, MERIDIAN AND NAL BOOKS are published *in the United States by* The New American Library, Inc., 1633 Broadway, New York, New York 10019, *in Canada* by The New American Library of Canada Limited, 81 Mack Avenue, Scarborough, Ontario M1L 1M8

First Printing, November, 1982

1   2   3   4   5   6   7   8   9

PRINTED IN THE UNITED STATES OF AMERICA

**To the teachers of science fiction,
in the hope of
solving some of their many problems**

Contents

Introduction

1

This is the fourth volume of a critical anthology that has tried to trace the development of science fiction from the earliest ancestors of all fiction to its most contemporary expressions. The first volume was subtitled "From Gilgamesh to Wells," the second "From Wells to Heinlein," the third "From Heinlein to Here." That seemed to complete the series; where can one go from "Here"? Where one can go, clearly, is from here to anywhere.

This volume, subtitled "From Here to Forever," attempts to remedy some of the omissions of the earlier volumes and to carry this survey of science fiction, now nearing one million words, up into the 1980s. By plan and necessity, Volume 4 differs from the earlier three. Their contents were chosen to illustrate the development of the genre, but as this survey approached the present the choice became more difficult. The importance of specific works to the development of the genre usually is not apparent until long after they have appeared and the genre has had time to respond to them, to learn their lessons and incorporate their viewpoints and advances.

Thus, in Volume 4 the principle of "genre importance" had to be discarded entirely. The works of the 1970s that will shape science fiction will have to be determined by the winnowing of time. Moreover, the most important trend of the 1970s, as I predicted in *Alternate Worlds,* was diversity. The forces at work on science fiction during this decade were pushing it apart rather than bringing it together; most authors were exploring individual nightmares rather than collective dreams.

This is not to say that important genre events did not occur during the 1970s. The most spectacular was the popular and financial success of several science fiction films, such as *Close Encounters of the Third Kind* and *Star Wars*. Indeed, *Star Wars* became the biggest moneymaker of all time, and its first sequel in a planned cycle of more than half a dozen, *The Empire Strikes Back*, became the second biggest. They precipitated an avalanche of sf films, including *Alien, Superman, The Black Hole, Saturn 3, Time After Time, Flash Gordon*, and *Star Trek: The Motion Picture*. On television they led to *Battlestar Galactica* and dramatizations of *Brave New Worlds, The Martian Chronicles*, and *The Lathe of Heaven*. Whether audiences numbering in the tens of millions can be translated into readers of magazines and books remains debatable. Some of the best sellers of the last few years have been novelizations of sf films, but only a few original novels, such as Frank Herbert's *Children of Dune* and *God Emperor of Dune*, have made the hardcover bestseller lists.

A more certain indicator of a broadening readership of science fiction was the appearance of new magazines: *Isaac Asimov's Science Fiction Magazine* was a remarkable success, surpassing *Analog*'s circulation in a couple of years and leading its publisher to purchase from Condé Nast the fifty-year-old longtime leader in the field. Even more spectacular was the success of *Omni*, which reached a million circulation within a month or two after its heavily advertised appearance under the guidance of Bob Guccione, publisher of *Penthouse*. Although it published only three or four stories per issue and emphasized speculative articles and pictures, *Omni* proved that science fiction was not necessarily limited to a circulation of just over 100,000.

Playboy, of course, had been publishing science fiction since its inception, but its main selling points were photographs of nude women and a sophisticated attitude toward sex. The success of *Omni* provided the example that would push other publishers into the field with such magazines as *Next, Discover, Science 1980*, a new *Science Digest*, and others, mostly emphasizing science popularizations, forecasts, and speculation, and publishing no fiction. But *Rod Serling's The Twilight Zone*, published by the publishers of *Gallery*, entered the fiction field with substantial advertising. Two promising magazines, *Cosmos* and *Galileo*, ran into financial difficulties unrelated to their circulations and were terminated, along with the thirty-year-old *Galaxy,* which the publishers of *Galileo* had purchased. Whether any of these could be resurrected was uncertain.

Science fiction book publishing went through a decade of expansion that made it the second most popular of categories (after the romance) increasing from 348 books a year in 1972 to 1,288 in 1979, according to *Locus,* "the newspaper of the science fiction field." But the recession of 1980 hit the publishing business hard, and science fiction was not immune, dropping that year to 1,184 books. Companies such as Ace, Berkley, Dell, and Pocket Books, which had expanded their publishing programs, began to cut back. Other companies that had planned expansions into the science fiction field reexamined their decisions, and Dell finally canceled its sf line entirely. The picture brightened in 1981, with Ace publishing ten science fiction books a month and a new line, Tor Books, making its debut, but darkened again as several lines (including Ace) was sold to Berkley. The plans of some young writers to make a career out of science fiction may have been postponed if not abandoned entirely. The nature of science fiction has long been influenced by economic considerations, and 1980 was no exception.

2

Having discarded genre importance as the criterion for inclusion in Volume 4 of *The Road to Science Fiction,* I decided to emphasize the quality of the writing rather than the quality of the visions. This does not mean that the stories in this volume are any less startling in content than those in the first three volumes—in many cases they may be even more wonderful, in the original meaning of that word—but that a major consideration for their selection was the literary skill with which they were written. That decision was not as arbitrary as it might seem; in the past two decades readers as well as writers have placed increasing value on the quality of the writing, as both readers and writers have become more sophisticated.

In one of his analyses of science fiction, Isaac Asimov wrote that science fiction was "adventure-dominant" between 1926 and 1938, "science-dominant" between 1938 and 1950, "sociology-dominant" between 1950 and 1965, and "style-dominant" after that. Asimov's own preferences may be apparent—he felt most at home in the science-dominant and sociology-dominant periods—but in spite of his protestations of total ignorance about the writing process, his own work, as in *The Gods Themselves,* has become more style-conscious since 1965.

Style was not the only important aspect of the 1960s and 1970s. There also were changes in perspective and shifts in subject matter. Gathered together and publicized by a magazine that specialized in it and an editor who was fascinated by it, this different kind of science fiction became known as "the New Wave." The term tended to lump together many disparate writers and works produced out of a variety of influences, but it stuck so fast that it is impossible to discuss what happened to science fiction in the 1960s and even the 1970s without using it.

Many different forces pushed science fiction away from its magazine pattern: recognizable heroes dealing with problems of change in straightforward narratives set down in transparent styles. Human reason was expected to come up with rational answers in these stories—the sort of fiction of which Asimov's was the prime example. The euphoria with which the United States emerged from World War II, having disposed of two tyrannical and technological threats, faded into the uncertainties of the Cold War, unresolvable Asian wars, and a loss of scientific and technological superiority through Soviet breakthroughs in atomic weapons and space exploration. The problems perceived in the 1960s seemed impervious to reason.

The first generation of science fiction writers had come from the ranks of the pulp writers, who produced stories in various categories for a wide variety of magazines. Supplementing these were writers, primarily self-educated or educated by their exposure to fantasy and science fiction in the pre-1926 pulp magazines, who were attracted by the reprints of Verne and Poe and Wells that first filled *Amazing Stories,* and who began to write new science fiction stories in the later 1920s and early 1930s.

The second generation of science fiction writers came out of the science fiction magazines themselves, inspired by them, educated by them, and dedicating itself to science fiction with single-minded devotion; some readers were influenced by their reading to seek careers in science; some scientists began to write science fiction. The third generation of science fiction writers grew up wanting to be new Heinleins or Asimovs. And they began to be educated in other ways—they went to college as a general rule, and many of them studied anthropology or sociology, philosophy, languages, and literature rather than the hard sciences. Their stories began to demonstrate as great a familiarity with the humanities as with the physical sciences.

Writers who came into prominence in the 1960s, the fifth generation, emerged in a period of discontent, not only with the science fiction that had preceded them, and often that had inspired them, but with the world. Some of them began to write anti-science stories, even anti-science-fiction stories, taking the icons of the genre and demonstrating that they were hollow and fragile. When Ted Carnell's *New Worlds* failed in England in 1964 and a new publisher appointed twenty-five-year-old Michael Moorcock as editor (a story told in more detail in Volume 3), the fifth generation of science fiction writers had a gathering place, a forum, just as *Astounding* provided a gathering place and a forum for Campbellian writers in the late 1930s, and as the *Magazine of Fantasy and Science Fiction* and *Galaxy* did for their writers in the 1950s. Now from *New Worlds* the voices of what would be called the New Wave could be heard all over the science fiction world. Not since the *Pall Mall Budget* began to publish H. G. Wells's first short stories had an English magazine, particularly one with financial troubles and a smaller-than-average circulation, had such influence.

The main characteristic of the New Wave rebellion was a movement away from traditional science fiction toward the literary mainstream. Though the authors, by and large, had first found publication for their visions and an audience for them in the science fiction world, now they sought different audiences and broader scope. This meant the introduction of mainstream techniques and mainstream attitudes toward science and life and people, including their behavior and fates. What had been transparent became translucent or opaque; what had been straightforward became complex; what had been reasonable became irrational; what had been recognizable heroes became complicated, nonheroic, sometimes realistic characters. The emphasis on character and setting sometimes meant elimination of traditional plot; it also often became a defense of the problems and rights of the individual over the problems and rights of the group or the species, and often a rejection of rationality, even an insistence that the universe was irrational, or, at least, incapable of being understood.

These new approaches to the writing of science fiction created new difficulties of definition. It was not always clear to the reader, the writer, or the critic how what was being published as science fiction—or, as many of the New Wave authors preferred, "speculative fiction"—would fit under the same umbrella as had sheltered what had previously been published.

In the first three volumes of *The Road to Science Fiction*, I offered the following definition:

Science fiction is the branch of literature that deals with the effects of change on people in the real world as it can be projected into the past, the future, or to distant places. It often concerns itself with scientific or technological change, and it usually involves matters whose importance is greater than the individual or the community; often civilization or the race itself is in danger.

Perhaps the definition problems are only peripheral. The new speculative fiction did deal with the effects of change on people in the real world—usually. The customary difference was that the *cause* of the change was often omitted, because it was unknown or unknowable, and the people to whom the changes happened seldom inquired into the causes because the changes were so massive that causes were irrelevant or so mysterious that inquiry was futile, or because the people were incurious, or were benumbed by events or life itself, or had lost their faith in rational inquiry. The reasons why causes were minimized may have been various, but the effects were clear: Rationality was short-circuited (if the causes are unavailable, solutions are so beyond reach as to make the search unthinkable) and characters became victims.

Good examples are J. G. Ballard's catastrophe novels of the 1960s (two published before the official dating of the New Wave)—*The Drowned World* (1962), *The Drought* (1964), and *The Crystal World* (1966). They involve cataclysms that occur without apparent reason and that the characters do not concern themselves about—they even conspire in their own destructions. Whether these characters and the changes they endure are in the real world can be debated; they seem unlike real people in many ways. In some instances, they should be evaluated as symbols, but some critics would claim that modern man is beset by many contemporary changes whose causes are obscure and perhaps beyond discovery, and that dumb acceptance, even collaboration with one's catastrophes, rather than a rational search for solutions is characteristic of the real world.

The second part of the definition, which is cautiously qualified by "often" and "usually," brings up greater difficulties. It speaks of science fiction being concerned "with scientific or technological change" and involving "matters whose importance is greater than the individual or the community." New Wave writers often rejected such notions. Fed up, perhaps, with rationalizations that looked far into the future, offended by justifications that needed evolutionary time to prove themselves, they often focused on the individual, upon his more limited perceptions and his more limited concerns; the species was seldom involved except in universal destruction. Few individual tragedies spelled success for the species, as in Heinlein's "Requiem" (reprinted in Volume 2) or Godwin's "The Cold Equations" (reprinted in Volume 3).

The way the stories were told often was more important than what they said—the manner rather than the matter (although it has become popular in recent years to speak of manner and matter as being inseparable). Experiments in style became commonplace: Subjectivity, which does not work well with a rational approach to the universe but is completely at home with irrationality, became the rule. The experiments may not have been particularly new—John Brunner looked to John Dos Passos's *U.S.A.* (first volume 1930) for the style of *Stand on Zanzibar* (1968), Brian W. Aldiss to Joyce's *Finnegans Wake* (1939) for the style of *Barefoot in the Head* (1969), and J. G. Ballard to more contemporary anti-novelists, typified by Alain Robbe-Grillet, for his "condensed novels"—but they were new to science fiction. At their best they were effective in saying what could not be said as well any other way; at their worst they were distancing, distracting, and obscure.

Not because of but in parallel with the New Wave, this volume of *The Road to Science Fiction* emphasizes the literary aspects of science fiction.

3

Lester del Rey would point out that science fiction always has had literary aspects—not necessarily in all science fiction all the time but in some science fiction some of the time. Science fiction magazines had nothing against effective writing, although at times it may have seemed so. A reader's 1927 letter to Hugo Gernsback's *Amazing Stories* accused H. G. Wells of using "too many words to describe a situation." Subsequently, whether or not in response to a general perception of Wells and others as being too "literary," Gernsback deemphasized his use of Wells reprints and of Wells's name on the cover. Later editors would urge writers to tone down their language and get on with their stories—that is, to avoid "fine writing" and literary touches and anything that smacked of difficulty—but stories with some pretensions to style somehow got published, not always in the leading magazines, not always without difficulty, but here and there, now and then.

John Campbell himself was able to get his more style-conscious stories, written under the name of Don A. Stuart, published in *Astounding* before he became its editor. Stanley Weinbaum was acclaimed not only for creating unusual aliens but for writing more skillfully than many of his contemporaries. Even earlier Dr. David H. Keller had made a beginning of what Damon Knight has called "the science fiction art story." But these stories did not always appear in *Astounding*. Some writers, such as Ed Hamilton, wrote stories they were unable to sell until years later, if then; some, like Jack Williamson, seemed to adapt their work to the demands of each new decade. Some writers, such as Ray Bradbury, soon wrote themselves out of the field, but the work of Theodore Sturgeon seemed to find acceptance no matter how he wrote, and Alfred Bester's literary pyrotechnics earned him awards and acclaim.

Stories came along during the 1930s and the 1940s that seemed to shout out their difference from the mob of genre stories in which they were found; oddly enough—or perhaps not odd at all—they were often the stories most honored and best remembered. Henry Kuttner and his wife, C. L. Moore, for instance, wrote under several pen names for John Campbell during the 1940s when other writers were occupied with the war effort. They began using literary allusions and stylistic techniques that gave their work an unusual flavor and presaged the kind of writing that would not come into its own until the 1960s. "Mimsy Were the Borogoves" (reprinted in Volume 3) is one example, but so are "No Woman Born," "Vintage Season," and many others. The characteristics of these stories were a greater emphasis on the individual and his or her feelings about the situation, the use of historic, literary, and cultural references that brought more of the fullness of life into the story, and a clear concern for words and the order in which they were presented.

The Magazine of Fantasy and Science Fiction, when it was founded in 1949, seemed to provide a natural home for such stories. The editors, Boucher and McComas, preferred literary fiction, and such pieces as Richard Matheson's "Born of Man and Woman," Avram Davidson's "My Boy Friend's Name Is Jello," Walter Miller, Jr.'s, "A Canticle for Leibowitz," and Daniel Keyes's "Flowers for Algernon" were published there in the 1950s. But other magazines were receptive to stories with literary aspects: "The Moon Moth" by Jack Vance was published in Horace Gold's *Galaxy,* and "Nobody Bothers Gus" by Algis Budrys was published in John W. Campbell's *Astounding.*

Internal aspirations toward professionalism and higher standards of art were beginning to make themselves felt in other ways. Damon Knight's criticism was collected in *In Search of Wonder* (first edition 1956) and included reviews originally published beginning in 1945, though most were written between 1950 and 1955, and James Blish's criticism was collected in *The Issue at Hand* (1964), consisting of material originally published between 1952 and 1960. This led in 1956 to Knight's and Blish's annual Milford Science Fiction Writers Conference, and ten years later to the founding of Science Fiction Writers of America.

By the 1960s the trend toward literary science fiction was picking up momentum. Book publication was beginning to rival magazine publication in volume and significance, and the greater liberties allowed the authors of individual books were beginning to loosen up the tight editorial control of the magazines. Frank Herbert's psychological (and Freudian) thriller, *The Dragon in the Sea* (1956), which was serialized by *Astounding* in 1955–56 under the title *Under Pressure,* prepared the way for Herbert's *Dune,* a long, complex novel of palace intrigue and ecological concern, which was serialized in eight parts by *Astounding* (now called *Analog*) as

Dune World in 1963–64, and for his *The Prophet of Dune* in 1965. Bob Shaw's quiet story of personal tragedy and human response to a new invention, "Light of Other Days," was published in *Analog* in 1966.

By then new magazines and anthologies were creating a substantial countermovement: *New Worlds* was followed by Damon Knight's anthology *Orbit*, beginning in 1966, and by Harlan Ellison's one-shot *Dangerous Visions* in 1967 (followed by *Again, Dangerous Visions* five years later). An experimental quarterly, *Quark*, edited by Samuel R. Delany and poet Marilyn Hacker (Delany's wife), lasted only four issues, beginning in 1970. Robert Silverberg launched *New Dimensions*, Harry Harrison *Nova*, and Terry Carr *Universe*, all in 1971. Most of these offered alternative means of publication for short, speculative fiction and earned their authors, and sometimes their editors, a surprising number of awards in the process. In addition, an unusual number of one-shot original anthologies were published in the decade after 1965. The publication of several best-of-the-year collections has continued the work begun by Judith Merril's earlier collections in focusing attention on experimental work, and Nebula Awards at least, if not Hugos, frequently have gone to more literary pieces.

Meanwhile, new writers with new ideas and new methods began to be published here and there and then almost everywhere: Robert Silverberg, Harlan Ellison, Roger Zelazny, Samuel R. Delany, Norman Spinrad, and a writer in a more traditional vein, Larry Niven (all anthologized in Volume 3), and, among others, Thomas M. Disch. Interesting writers were appearing, or being discovered, in other parts of the world, and gradually their influence was seeping into science fiction. In addition to the usual group of excellent English writers, Stanislaw Lem was producing innovative stories and novels in Poland. Although his first work was published in 1951, nothing was translated into English until *Solaris* in 1970. A renaissance in Russian science fiction began in the late 1950s and continued through the 1960s, led by I. Yefremov, the Strugatsky brothers, and others, and, as Darko Suvin has demonstrated, work of interesting quality was being written and published in other socialist countries. The work of the internationally famous Argentinian Jorge Luis Borges, part of which is science fiction and fantasy, began to be published in English translation with *Ficciones* in 1962.

A flood of new American writers moved into the field in

the 1970s, responding perhaps to the new freedom (or, conversely, to the lack of publishing opportunities elsewhere, as the slick magazines folded or stopped publishing fiction and the other category pulp magazines dwindled to a handful). Barry Malzberg, Gene Wolfe, Gardner Dozois, and James Tiptree, Jr. (later revealed to be Alice Sheldon) came into prominence in the 1970s, although they actually began to be published in the late 1960s. After them came such writers as Pamela Sargent, George Zebrowski, Ed Bryant, George Alec Effinger, David Gerrold, Vonda McIntyre, George R. R. Martin, Michael Bishop, and many others.

A new factor that began to exert the kind of influence exercised by the Milford Writers Conference in the 1950s and 1960s was the Clarion Science Fiction Writers Workshop, founded by Robin Scott Wilson at Clarion State College in Pennsylvania in 1968 and later moved to Michigan State University when Wilson left Pennsylvania. The workshop admitted only beginning writers who worked under the direction of such week-long guest teachers as Damon Knight, Kate Wilhelm, and Harlan Ellison. The Workshop produced a surprising number of the newer writers, including Bryant, Zebrowski, Effinger, McIntyre, F. M. Busby, and Lisa Tuttle.

Well into the 1970s the New Wave had been assimilated by science fiction. Not only had the influence of the magazines diminished as books became the major purveyor of science fiction and as the genre unity once enforced by the magazines dissipated into relative anarchy, but fiction similar in tone, philosophy, content, and style to what had once been called the New Wave was being published in all the leading magazines, including *Analog*. The New Wave had not taken over—adventure stories and novels still were being published, as well as hard-science work, and sociological science fiction—but much idiosyncratic and even anti-science fiction was being published next to other kinds of science fiction in the same magazine. The thrust of the rebellion had been incorporated into much of the other kinds of fiction.

4

What were the characteristics that made so much difference in the mid-1960s and so little in the mid-1970s?

Writers have only a limited number of variables with which to work, with which to distinguish their stories from those of everyone else. Words are the basic tool, but, in addition, fiction deals with plot (what happens), characters (to whom it happens), and setting (where and when it happens). Out of these basic ingredients all fiction is assembled. What gives fiction uniqueness, however, is not simply the events or the people or the place—though these may have lesser or greater originality and interest, and may be presented with lesser or greater skill and thoroughness and complexity—but the allusions that are presented along with the events, the people, and the place.

If we think of a piece of fiction as a closed world in which the characters exist for the plot and the plot for the characters and the setting for both, allusions are what relate that closed world to other worlds, including the world with which we, as readers, are familiar. Through the story's allusions to the real world (the world of experience), we, as readers, obtain relevance, meaning, theme—all those attributes of fiction that keep us from saying when we finish, "So what?" Through allusions we learn how to interpret what happens in the closed world of the story.

In genre science fiction the allusions usually relate the fictional world to other genre works, or sometimes to the worlds of the hard sciences or the soft sciences, or to philosophy or history, and only in a limited way to the everyday world. In literary science fiction, allusions relate the fictional world to everyday life, tradition, myth, literature, history, and so forth.

A straightforward adventure story may have simple allusions—if John Carter doesn't get there in time his beloved Dejah Thoris will be killed; we understand the desirability of Carter's actions because we understand love and death and timeliness. But Edgar Rice Burroughs keeps Carter attached to Earth by other ties than basic relationships and the emotions they arouse: every now and then Carter returns, or sends back a manuscript, and in some novels (for instance, *The Mastermind of Mars*) Burroughs alludes to human customs, traditions, and religions, sometimes approvingly, sometimes critically. Out of these allusions comes more than an adventure story.

The allusions in more complex fiction can provide numerous levels of meaning. One reader may read the story simply at the level of plot, while another, harder-working or more sophisticated in reading protocols, may perceive other levels of the story that may complement the plot, supplement it, alter it, or even reverse it. Sometimes the allusions may be

grace notes, lending the support of history or myth or literature to the basic events of the story; sometimes they provide
clues to what is happening.

"Flowers for Algernon," for instance, has many allusions—
in fact, the success of the narrative device depends upon
readers' picking up from Charlie Gordon's vocabulary and
limited experience of the world clues to Charlie's condition
and mental ability. The reader who does not translate "raw
shock" as "Rorschach" has missed at least a bit of the significance of what is going on, and even more, some of the
playfulness of the narrative. As Charlie's mental abilities improve, his spelling gets better and his intellectual horizons
broaden; the reader who misses this may also miss the evidence of his deterioration.

Sometimes in science fiction the allusions to other genre
works produce references that are baffling to the unfamiliar
reader: "ftl," for instance, or "hyperspace" or "blasters." At
other times the process by which authors pack important
clues to the situation of the story or its meaning into otherwise innocent lines of description or dialogue also may make
the novice reader miss much of what is going on. As Samuel
R. Delany has pointed out, science fiction developed its own
protocols of reading.

In "Sail On! Sail On!" (reprinted in Volume 3), for instance, the reader is not expected to understand immediately
what the situation is. Instead the reader must put together
pieces of evidence—the names of the sailing ships, the fact
that the ship has a radio, and other bits of information
dropped into description and conversation—to deduce that
this is Columbus's first voyage across the Atlantic but that it
is a different historical situation. It is what science fiction
readers call an alternative history story; in this alternative history Friar Bacon's scientific work was accepted by the
Church instead of denounced. Finally, the author pulls an unexpected switch: The story is not an alternative history but
an alternative universe in which the physical facts are different.

The skills required to read "Fondly Fahrenheit" (also in
Volume 3) are similar. The reader must follow the shifting
tenses in which the story is narrated to understand that the
human owner of the android is the source of the insanity. In
"I Have No Mouth, and I Must Scream," it might be interesting but not essential to recognize the breaks in the story as
computer language, or even that the statement they make is

"I think, therefore I am." It is more important to recognize the phrase as the philosophical given upon which Descartes erected a set of assumptions about the universe, and that the phrase is the justification, as well as the derivation of the name, for the computer AM and its existence as an independent entity. There also are resonances of God's statement to Moses, "I am that I am."

The protocols of reading for the more literary stories of the 1960s and 1970s became the protocols of the mainstream. The allusions were not to science fiction nor to science but to a more broadly shared experience. The real world includes not only the everyday experiences that everyone shares but the cultural heritage of myth, literature, and history that is assumed, sometimes incorrectly, to be common to all educated men and women.

5

The allusions in literary science fiction are not simple playfulness, though they may be playful, nor simply emblems of culture, to demonstrate the learning of the author and to establish with the sophisticated reader a bond of shared references, though they may do this. At their best, they serve to relate the story to more traditional values, sometimes more basic values, and to fit the story into the larger framework of human existence, including the human past. Sometimes, of course, relating the story to the past militates against relating the story to the future; and the more the events of the story comment on the present, the less they are read as speculations about possible new conditions. Satire finds itself in a similar predicament: The more Pohl and Kornbluth's *The Space Merchants* is read as humorous commentary on contemporary advertising practices the less the novel can be read as extrapolation from present trends into the future. In literary science fiction, the more Pohl's *Gateway* is read as a parable for the human condition the less seriously will we take the Heechee and their marvelous ships.

The emphasis of literary science fiction on the more physical aspects of life was not simply a rebellion against their absence in magazine science fiction. The kind of language and scenes found in *Dangerous Visions,* or in Spinrad's *Bug Jack Barron* that got *New Worlds* banned by an English distributor and denounced in Parliament, were not inserted simply to shock. There was, to be sure, an element of rebellion and a desire to shock, but the language and the descriptions also were intended as allusions to the real world. In real life these things happen, these words are spoken. Traditional science fiction had seen no need to reflect that part of existence, had considered it irrelevant; the newer science-fiction was trying not merely to introduce into science fiction that part of existence but to relate science fiction that much more to the real world.

Literary science fiction emphasized other kinds of details—dress, behavior, actions, setting—that would have been touched upon lightly, if at all, in traditional science fiction. The behavior and actions and dress of characters had been important in traditional science fiction only as they affected the plot; in literary science fiction these elements became important for their own sake and as allusions to the real world. Characters had pasts that affected their behavior and with which they had to come to terms; they had prior experience to deal with. Settings became more vivid and more important as they became more realistic; at the same time settings became surrealistic upon occasion or metaphorical. If more emphasis is placed on setting as an allusion to reality rather than as a stage setting for plot, it is only a step or two farther to give setting the burden of meaning, to make setting reflect the state of society or the emotional attitudes of the characters, or to have setting represent something else, as Ballard's "The Terminal Beach" (reprinted in Volume 3) uses the Eniwetok bomb-test site, or as Leiber's "Coming Attraction" (also in Volume 3) uses the masks women wear.

Some of the allusions were achieved by simile, metaphor, or symbol. The comparison of two unlike things, whether stated directly or implied, allows another level of meaning. "The rocket's exhaust was like a pillar of flame" is a simile that might have appeared in any traditional science fiction story as an effort to make the reading experience more visual; in "The Streets of Ashkelon" Harry Harrison describes the landing of a ship on "a down-reaching tongue of flame." Altered by one word, "the rocket's exhaust was like a sword of flame," the simile would suggest violence being done the Earth. With a more literary simile—"the rocket's exhaust was like the flaming sword set before the gates of Paradise"—the reader would be expected to supply the rest of the biblical story, that after the expulsion of Adam and Eve, God set the flaming sword at the entrance to prevent humanity from returning. The comparison, then, would enhance a visual experience with meaning: The flight of the rocket will prevent humanity from returning to Eden, perhaps literally by poisoning the Earth, perhaps figuratively by using up the fuel available for return. Changing simile to metaphor—"the rocket's exhaust was the flaming sword set before the gates of Paradise"—makes the comparison more forcefully.

In another version of the same imaginary story, Earth might slowly emerge as a symbol for Paradise from which humanity must be driven, never to return, if humanity is to fulfill its destiny to "be fruitful and multiply" and inherit the stars, just as in Henry Kuttner and C. L. Moore's 1947 novel *Fury,* Sam Reed forces humanity out of the comfortable undersea keeps onto the ravening surface of Venus in order to get the human species going again, and then turns the keeps radioactive to ensure that people cannot go back.

The impatient reader may ask why the author doesn't simply come out and say something rather than hinting around at it. This is a good question, and the answer is bound to be unsatisfactory to many. The writing of fiction is dependent upon a series of choices the author must make, from the initial idea to the characters, viewpoint, tone, mood, diction, and on to the finished product. Ideally, all the choices should reinforce one another so that the total is more than the sum of its parts. Thus subtlety and indirection, or allusion, may be the choice of a particular author writing a particular kind of story. A reader may choose not to read such authors, or such stories, but complaint is pointless: The choices are legitimate, the stories that result demand greater participation by the reader, but the readers who survive the difficulties, those who are able and willing to follow allusions and make deductions, may discover greater rewards. Similarly, the experienced science fiction reader must be willing and able to invest patience and thought in a story such as "Sail On! Sail On!" in order to make sense out of it. Patience and thought invested in "Sail On! Sail On!" pay off in a richer and more rewarding reading experience. The same is true of literary science fiction: learning to read it with understanding results in enhanced enjoyment.

6

Not all innovation results in improvement; sometimes the effect is merely difference, sometimes it is failure. Some attempts to broaden the allusions of science fiction were mere rebelliousness: change for the sake of change. One trend minimized plot, or eliminated causal relationships, or omitted consequences for the sake of directing the reader's attention to other aspects of story. One result was that the reader concentrating on the plot level of a multileveled piece of fiction felt abandoned or betrayed. Sometimes the result was as if the author had cut one leg off a tripod: Character and setting were magnified in importance, but the stool toppled.

When emphasis changes, characters customarily change as well to accommodate and produce new values and new meanings. It was as true in the nineteenth century as in the 1960s. Poe, for instance, wrote about hypersensitive men for whom ordinary sensation was too much, who sought to escape in travel or drugs from the everyday abrasions of life, for whom a movement, a word, set off an explosion of adjectives, a firecracker chain of events. Verne, on the other hand, explored vast, untraveled areas of the sea, the land, the air, and space, and he needed tough, adventurous characters not prone to moods or self-doubt. Wells dealt with social problems, and his protagonists were usually ordinary citizens with ordinary common sense and enough toughness of spirit to enable them to survive their harrowing experiences.

When the magazines were created, editors bgan to determine the nature of the characters in the stories they bought. Hugo Gernsback liked inventors; John Campbell wanted scientists who were like real scientists and people who knew how things worked; Horace Gold wanted ordinary citizens caught up in change they had not created and trying somehow to get along. Most magazine editors today want sympathetic characters who are intelligent enough to recognize the nature of their situation and tough enough to do something about it.

Like their predecessors, the newer writers usually chose characters who were the antithesis of those chosen by the previous generation. If Campbell's writers created characters who knew how things worked, the newer writers would write about people who didn't know how anything worked and didn't care; if Gold's writers dealt with common people struggling to survive, the newer writers would write about uncommon people conspiring with their own disasters. New Wave characters became puzzled, obsessed, introspective people—reflective but ineffective. Sometimes, in spite of the fact that these stories were intended to be more "real," the characters were metaphorical—vast areas of response were omitted from some of them—and the reader was intended to understand that they represented something else.

Most literary writers, however, would deny that they wrote in response or reaction to anything: the characters they chose represented real people as the writers saw them. When authors insist—through their fiction or their real-life comments—that their characters represent real people, or the reader fails to recognize their metaphorical aspect, ideological battle begins.

By now the battles have largely ended. The war concluded in a draw, but as in all wars the participants have been changed. Traditional science fiction—in all its forms, from Gernsback to Campbell to Boucher to Gold—coexists with literary science fiction in the marketplace. The subjects and technical innovations pioneered by the New Wave are available to more traditional writers, and are often incorporated in their fiction. The more extreme kinds of experimental writing have largely disappeared, and the more experimental writers have returned to more accessible materials and forms. In recent years, for instance, Tom Disch wrote *On Wings of Song*, J. G. Ballard wrote *The Unlimited Dream Company*, and Gene Wolfe wrote *The Book of the New Sun* series.

Some writers have drifted away from science fiction, or made a sharp break with it, such as Ballard and Ellison; others have made farewell announcements and then had changes of heart, such as Silverberg and Malzberg. New writers have come along to provide new content for old traditions, such as John Varley and Gregory Benford.

In other words, science fiction, as usual, is in a state of flux, and, as usual, is looking forward to greater things.

Born of Skill and Money

In his introduction to *Nebula Award Stories Eight,* Isaac Asimov wrote, "A good science fiction writer can, very probably, write anything else he wishes (and for more money), if he decides to take the trouble to do so. Many science fiction writers have done so and a few have been lost to the field as a result." Asimov himself is the best example; others include the late Frederic Brown, John D. MacDonald, Harlan Ellison, Robert Bloch, Theodore Sturgeon, and Richard Matheson. Most of them have continued to write science fiction occasionally but have diverted much of their effort to other forms.

Matheson (1926–   ) was born in Allendale, N.J. After service in World War II, he earned a bachelor's degree in journalism from the University of Missouri in 1949. A year later his first story, "Born of Man and Woman," was published in *The Magazine of Fantasy and Science Fiction.* He wrote other science fiction stories and three mystery novels before his first sf novel, *I Am Legend,* was published in 1954. He sold the screen rights to his second sf novel, *The Shrinking Man* (1956), to Universal on condition that he write the screenplay to the subsequent film *The Incredible Shrinking Man* (1957).

Since then Matheson has divided his time between screenwriting and fiction, with most going to the far-better-paying screenwriting. His screenplays include *The House of Usher* (1960); *The Pit and the Pendulum* (1961); *Master of the World,* an adaptation of Verne's 1905 novel but mostly taken from his earlier (1886) *Robur the Conqueror* (1961); *Tales of Terror* (1962); *The Raven* (1963); *The Last Man on Earth,* a version of *I Am Legend,* which also was filmed as *The Omega Man* (1963); *Die! Die! My Darling!* (1965); *The Devil's Bride* (1968); *The Young Warriors* (1968); *The Legend of Hell House* (1973) from his own novel; and *Somewhere in Time* (1980) also from his own novel. He wrote numerous screenplays for television's *Twilight Zone, Star Trek,* and *Night Gallery,* as well as individual scripts such as those for *Duel* (1971), *The Night Stalker* (1972), *The Night Strangler* (1973), and *The Martian Chronicles* (1980).

His novels include *A Stir of Echoes* (1958), *The Beardless Warriors* (1960), *Hell House* (1971), *Bid Time Return* (1977), and *What Dreams May Come* (1978). His short stories have been collected in *Born of Man and Woman,* also titled *Third from the Sun* (1954); *The Shores of Space* (1957); *Shock!* (1961); *Shock II* (1964); *Shock III* (1966); and *Shock Waves* (1970).

Many critics see Matheson as primarily a writer of horror fiction whose principal theme is paranoia, as exemplified in *Duel* and *I Am Legend. The Science Fiction Encyclopedia* says that Matheson wrote "Born of Man and Woman" as a "simple horror story," and turned to writing science fiction when that story was perceived as science fiction. The story can be read as either horror or science fiction, and the expectations of the reader do much to shape the response.

As a horror story, "Born of Man and Woman" draws from the same gothic sources as *Frankenstein.* Readers react—as they would to Frankenstein if the scientific element were omitted (that is, as they do to the various film versions)—with horror at the monster and his capacity to destroy. But just as Frankenstein would be less meaningful without the presence of the scientist and his aspirations, so Matheson's story draws resonances from its science fiction aspects. In just this way, the fantasy stories in *The Magazine of Fantasy and Science Fiction* drew resonances from the science fiction stories among which they were found, and the science fiction stories absorbed literary concerns from the fantasy stories.

The Magazine of Fantasy and Science Fiction was still in its first year when Matheson's story arrived—perhaps attracted by the first issue of the magazine in the fall of 1949—but the editors already had established its tone. Anthony Boucher and J. Francis McComas wanted literate stories, and "Born of Man and Woman," in spite of the fact that it was narrated by an illiterate, was literate.

A number of science fiction stories written in the late 1940s and early 1950s dealt with the question of mutations, which were commonly expected as a result of atomic warfare or nuclear accidents. Lewis Padgett's Baldy series beginning with "The Piper's Son" (1945) was one, and so were Poul Anderson and F. N. Waldrop's "Tomorrow's Children" (1947), Wilmar H. Shiras's "In Hiding" (1948), and Judith Merril's "That Only a Mother" (1948). The simple diction and straightforward narration of "Born of Man and Woman" suggests a natural rather than a scientific or supernatural explanation for the monster's birth.

The most striking aspect of Matheson's story, however, is its use of viewpoint. The story is told from the monster's point of view and in his inadequate diction, just as portions of *Frankenstein* are accounts by the monster of his experiences and thoughts. In "Born of Man and Woman," the reader receives only the monster's thoughts; the actions and reactions of the parents are learned only from the monster. Because of the viewpoint, the reader sympathizes with the monster's plight, as in some ways he is expected to do in *Frankenstein*. (Matheson's monster is a natural accident rather than an artificial creation, but like Frankenstein's monster, he is called "wretch.") How terrible it must be, the reader perceives, to be a monster and more—to be disowned, to be chained to a wall in a damp basement, to be beaten with sticks, and to be only eight years old. The monster's youth and his perceptions of beauty and ugliness both tug at the reader's sympathies.

The reversal in viewpoint is what gives the story its unusual effectiveness; it is the same kind of reversal of attitudes and thought processes that science fiction provides in its best moments. The skill of the story with its carefully inarticulate diction serves to suggest the plight of the parents even as it illustrates how natural instincts and deprivation can turn innocent intentions into violence and death.

Born of Man and Woman

by Richard Matheson

X—This day when it had light mother called me a retch. You retch she said. I saw in her eyes the anger. I wonder what it is a retch.

This day it had water falling from upstairs. It fell all around. I saw that. The ground of the back I watched from the little window. The ground it sucked up the water like thirsty lips. It drank too much and it got sick and runny brown. I didn't like it.

Mother is a pretty I know. In my bed place with cold walls around I have a paper thing that was behind the furnace. It says on it SCREEN STARS. I see the pictures faces like of mother and father. Father says they are pretty. Once he said it.

And also mother he said. Mother so pretty and me decent enough. Look at you he said and didn't have the nice face. I touched his arm and said it is right father. He shook and pulled away where I couldn't reach.

Today mother let me off the chain a little so I could look out the little window. That's how I saw the water falling from upstairs.

XX—This day it had goldness in the upstairs. As I know, when I looked at it my eyes hurt. After I look at it the cellar is red.

I think this was church. They leave the upstairs. The big machine swallows them and rolls out past and is gone. In the back part is the *little* mother. She is much small than me. I am big. It is a secret but I have pulled the chain out of the wall. I can see out the little window all I like.

In this day when it got dark I had eat my food and some bugs. I hear laughs upstairs. I like to know why there are laughs for. I took the chain from the wall and wrapped it around me. I walked squish to the stairs. They creak when I walk on them. My legs slip on them because I don't walk on stairs. My feet stick to the wood.

I went up and opened a door. It was a white place. White as white jewels that come from upstairs sometime. I went in and stood quiet. I hear the laughing some more. I walk to the sound and look through to the people. More people than I thought was. I thought I should laugh with them.

Mother came out and pushed the door in. It hit me and hurt. I fell back on the smooth floor and the chain made noise. I cried. She made a hissing noise into her and put her hand on her mouth. Her eyes got big.

She looked at me. I heard father call. What fell he called. She said a iron board. Come help pick it up she said. He came and said now is *that* so heavy you need. He saw me and grew big. The anger came in his eyes. He hit me. I spilled some of the drip on the floor from one arm. It was not nice. It made ugly green on the floor.

Father told me to go to the cellar. I had to go. The light it hurt some now in my eyes. It is not so like that in the cellar.

Father tied my legs and arms up. He put me on my bed. Upstairs I heard laughing while I was quiet there looking on a black spider that was swinging down to me. I thought what father said. Ohgod he said. And only eight.

XXX—This day father hit in the chain again before it had light. I have to try pull it out again. He said I was bad to come upstairs. He said never do that again or he would beat me hard. That hurts.

I hurt. I slept the day and rested my head against the cold wall. I thought of the white place upstairs.

XXXX—I got the chain from the wall out. Mother was upstairs. I heard little laughs very high. I looked out the window. I saw all little people like the little mother and little fathers too. They are pretty.

They were making nice noise and jumping around the ground. Their legs was moving hard. They are like mother and father. Mother says all right people look like they do.

One of the little fathers saw me. He pointed at the window. I let go and slid down the wall in the dark. I curled up as they would not see. I heard their talks by the window and foots running. Upstairs there was a door hitting. I heard the little mother call upstairs. I heard heavy steps and I rushed to my bed place. I hit the chain in the wall and lay down on my front.

I heard mother come down. Have you been at the window she said. I heard the anger. *Stay* away from the window. You have pulled the chain out again.

She took the stick and hit me with it. I didn't cry. I can't do that. But the drip ran all over the bed. She saw it and twisted away and made a noise. Oh mygod mygod she said why have you *done* this to me? I heard the stick go bounce on the stone floor. She ran upstairs. I slept the day.

XXXXX—This day it had water again. When mother was upstairs I heard the little one come slow down the steps. I hidded myself in the coal bin for mother would have anger if the little mother saw me.

She had a little live thing with her. It walked on the arms and had pointy ears. She said things to it.

It was all right except the live thing smelled me. It ran up the coal and looked down at me. The hairs stood up. In the throat it made an angry noise. I hissed but it jumped on me.

I didn't want to hurt it. I got fear because it bit me harder than the rat does. I hurt and the little mother screamed. I grabbed the live thing tight. It made sounds I never heard. I pushed it all together. It was all lumpy and red on the black coal.

I hid there when mother called. I was afraid of the stick. She left. I crept over the coal with the thing. I hid it under my pillow and rested on it. I put the chain in the wall again.

X—This is another times. Father chained me tight. I hurt because he beat me. This time I hit the stick out of his hands and made noise. He went away and his face was white. He ran out of my bed place and locked the door.

I am not so glad. All day it is cold in here. The chain comes slow out of the wall. And I have a bad anger with mother and father. I will show them. I will do what I did that once.

I will screech and laugh loud. I will run on the walls. Last I will hang head down by all my legs and laugh and drip green all over until they are sorry they didn't be nice to me.

If they try to beat me again I'll hurt them. I will.

Word Magic

The Magazine of Fantasy and Science Fiction ranked literary quality in the stories it published at least as high as ideas and narrative, and perhaps higher. That brought a new kind of reader into the field and a new kind of writer as well. When science fiction was monolithic, and John Campbell's *Astounding* defined what it was, the occasional literary story might appear there by accident. But usually it would appear, if it appeared at all, in the lesser, and lower-paying, magazines, where consistency of subject and tone were unimportant. Thus Ray Bradbury's first stories (after three early ones, two in Campbell's "Probability Zero" section, in *Astounding*) were published in magazines such as *Planet Stories* and *Thrilling Wonder Stories.*

Galaxy provided another possible medium for publication, where literary skill was recognized but story was king. *Galaxy* paid rates as high as or higher than *Astounding* and was at least as prestigious. *The Magazine of Fantasy and Science Fiction* provided a third and equally attractive possibility. Avram Davidson (1923–) was one of the writers drawn to the field by the prospect of writing stories that made demands on readers for cultural information and literary references, just as Campbellian science fiction made demands for scientific information and sociological references.

Davidson was born in Yonkers, New York, and attended New York University in 1940–42 and, after service in World War II, in 1947–48, and later attended Pierce College in 1950–51. His first sale to a genre magazine, "My Boy Friend's Name Is Jello," was published in *The Magazine of Fantasy and Science Fiction* for July 1954; he had earlier published stories elsewhere, his first in *Orthodox Jewish Life Magazine* in 1946. After a number of witty, well-written stories published in *The Magazine of Fantasy and Science Fiction* and in *Galaxy*, he served as executive editor of *The Magazine of Fantasy and Science Fiction* from 1962 to 1964, edited three of its annual volumes, and then turned to freelancing, which he has worked at ever since, with occasional appointments as visiting lecturer or writer-in-residence at colleges and universities.

Davidson's first novel, *Joyleg* (1962), was written in collaboration with Ward Moore. Since then eleven more novels have been published, in particular *Masters of the Maze* (1965), *Rogue Dragon* (1965), *Clash of Star-Kings* (1966), *The Phoenix and the Mirror* (1969), *Peregrine: Primus* (1971), and *Peregrine: Secundus* (1981). He is best known for his short stories, however, and they have been collected in *Or All the Seas with Oysters* (1962), *What Strange Stars and Skies* (1965), *Strange Seas and Shores* (1971), *The Enquiries of Doctor Eszterhazy* (1975), *The Redward Edward Papers* (1978), and *The Best of Avram Davidson* (1979). His short stories and his novels often have been nominated for Nebula Awards; "Or All the Seas with Oysters" won a Hugo for 1968.

"My Boy Friend's Name Is Jello" is a story that makes its points by indirection. It is told in the first person by a man whose mind is feverish and jumps from thought to thought. In part this justifies the elaborate style: ". . . its course half run" is poetic inversion; ". . . its course half i-run" suggests Chaucer. The narrator refuses to call the physician a "doctor" and prefers "apothecary." Such words as "herbal clysters," "quinsy," "ague," "pox," "slops," "victuals," and "bedewed" place the reader in the times when spells and charms and potions could be taken seriously.

Not only archaic words and usages but literary references make a knowledge of history and literature useful in reading the story. "Pastor Quiverful," for instance, refers to a character in Anthony Trollope's *Barchester Towers* who has more than a dozen children. A Priapus was a minor Roman god whose statue (with a prominent phallus, often painted red, since he was the god of male procreative power) was used as a scarecrow to protect gardens; Catullus wrote many scatological poems to Priapus, like those traditionally intended to be inserted into the statue's mouth to warn away intruders. Potshards suggest anthropology; Toltec emblems, masons' marks, and the signs of Hindoo holy men, primitive magic. Bergamot is a small citrus tree; the rind of its fruit yields a fragrant oil. Mandrake, a plant with a root forked like the human body, in early times was reputed to have magical properties associated with procreation. "Aroint thee"—a Spenserian-sounding phrase—means "begone!" Hymen was the Greek god of marriage; the "Hymeneal sacrifice" refers to the husband. Runes are the characters and signs of the early Germanic alphabet and were used in Scandinavian magic. Allopathy is a method of treating disease by using drugs to cause symptoms different from those of the patient's illness; homeopathy is a method to cause symptoms similar to those produced by the disease— the word suggests to the narrator the notion of using the same magic that Miss Thurl may have worked upon him. "Cross my palm with silver" is the traditional request of the gypsy fortune-teller.

All of this information is not essential to understanding and enjoying Davidson's story—just as a knowledge of scientific terms may not be necessary to understand a hard-science story—but the more references readers pick up the more they can enjoy Davidson's wit.

My Boy Friend's Name Is Jello

by Avram Davidson

Fashion, nothing but fashion. Virus X having in the medical zodiac its course half i-run, the physician (I refuse to say "doctor" and, indeed, am tempted to use the more correct "apothecary")—the physician, I say, tells me I have Virus Y. No doubt in the Navy it would still be called Catarrhal Fever. They say that hardly anyone had appendicitis until Edward VII came down with it a few weeks before his coronation, and thus made it fashionable. He (the medical man) is dosing me with injections of some stuff that comes in

vials. A few centuries ago he would have used herbal clysters. . . . Where did I read that old remedy for the quinsy
("putrescent sore throat," says my dictionary)? *Take seven
weeds from seven meads and seven nails from seven steeds.*
Oh dear, how my mind runs on. I must be feverish. An ague,
no doubt.

Well, rather an ague than a pox. A pox is something one
wishes on editors . . . strange breed, editors. The females all
have names like Lulu Annabelle Smith or Minnie Lundquist
Bloom, and the males have little horns growing out of their
brows. They must all be Quakers, I suppose, for their letters
invariably begin, "Dear Richard Roe" or "Dear John Doe,"
as if the word *mister* were a Vanity . . . when they write at
all, that is; and meanwhile Goodwife Moos calls weekly for
the rent. If I ever have a son (than which nothing is more
unlikely) who shows the slightest inclination of becoming a
writer, I shall instantly prentice him to a fishmonger or a
Master Chimney Sweep. Don't write about Sex, the editors
say, and don't write about Religion, or about History. If,
however, you *do* write about History, be sure to add Religion
and Sex. If one sends in a story about a celibate atheist, however, do you think they'll buy it?

In front of the house two little girls are playing one of
those clap-handie games. Right hand, left hand, cross hands
on bosom, left hand, right hand . . . it makes one dizzy to
watch. And singing the while:

> My *boy* friend's *name* is *Je*llo,
> He *comes* from *Cinc*inello,
> With a *pimple* on his *nose*
> And *three* fat toes;
> And *that's* the *way* my story *goes!*

There is a pleasing surrealist quality to this which intrigues
me. In general I find little girls enchanting. What a shame
they grow up to be *big* girls and make our lives as miserable
as we allow them, and ofttimes more. Silly, nasty-minded critics, trying to make poor Dodgson a monster of abnormality,
simply because he loved Alice and was capable of following
her into Wonderland. I suppose they would have preferred
him to have taken a country curacy and become another Pastor Quiverful. A perfectly normal and perfectly horrible
existence, and one which would have left us all still on *this*
side of the looking glass.

Whatever was in those vials doesn't seem to be helping me. I suppose old Dover's famous Powders hadn't the slightest fatal effect on the germs, bacteria, or virus (viri?), but at least they gave one a good old sweat (ipecac) and a mild, non-habit-forming jag (opium). But they're old-fashioned now, and so there we go again, round and round, one's train of thought like a Japanese waltzing mouse. I used to know a Japanese who—now, stop that. Distract yourself. Talk to the little girls. . . .

Well, that was a pleasant interlude. We discussed (quite gravely, for I never condescend to children) the inconveniences of being sick, the unpleasantness of the heat; we agreed that a good rain would cool things off. Then their attention began to falter, and I lay back again. Miss Thurl may be in soon. Mrs. Moos (perfect name, she lacks only the antlers) said, whilst bringing in the bowl of slops which the medicine man allows me for victuals, My Sister Is Coming Along Later And She's Going To Fix You Up Some Nice Flowers. Miss Thurl, I do believe, spends most of her time fixing flowers. Weekends she joins a confraternity of overgrown campfire girls and boys who go on hiking trips, comes back sunburned and sweating and carrying specimen samples of plant and lesser animal life. However, I must say for Miss Thurl that she is quiet. Her brother-in-law, the bull-Moos, would be in here all the time if I suffered it. He puts stupid quotations in other people's mouths. He will talk about the weather and I will not utter a word, then he will say, Well, It's Like You Say, It's Not The Heat But The Humidity.

Thinking of which, I notice a drop in the heat, and I see it is raining. That should cool things off. How pleasant. A pity that it is washing away the marks of the little girls' last game. They played this one on the sidewalk, with chalked-out patterns and bits of stone and broken glass. They chanted and hopped back and forth across the chalkmarks and shoved the bits of stone and glass—or were they potshards—"potsie" from potshard, perhaps? I shall write a monograph, should I ever desire a Ph.D. I will compare the chalkmarks with Toltec emblems and masons' marks and the signs which Hindoo holy men smear on themselves with wood ashes and perfumed cow dung. All this passes for erudition.

I feel terrible, despite the cool rain. Perhaps without it, I should feel worse.

Miss Thurl was just here. A huge bowl of blossoms, arranged on the table across the room. Intricately arranged, I should say; but she put some extra touches to it, humming to herself. Something ever so faintly reminiscent about that tune, and vaguely disturbing. Then she made one of her rare remarks. She said that I needed a wife to take care of me. My blood ran cold. An icy sweat (to quote Catullus, that wretched Priapist) bedewed my limbs. I moaned. Miss Thurl at once departed, murmuring something about a cup of tea. If I weren't so weak I'd knot my bedsheets together and escape. But I am terribly feeble.

It's unmanly to weep. . . .

Back she came, literally poured the tea down my throat. A curious taste it had. Sassafras? Bergamot? Mandrake root? It is impossible to say how old Miss Thurl is. She wears her hair parted in the center and looped back. Ageless . . . ageless . . .

I thank whatever gods may be that Mr. Ahyellow came in just then. The other boarder (upstairs), a greengrocer, decent fellow, a bit short-tempered. He wished me soon well. He complained he had his own troubles, foot troubles. . . . I scarcely listened, just chattered, hoping the Thurl would get her hence. . . . Toes . . . something about his toes. Swollen, three of them, quite painful. A bell tinkled in my brain, I asked him how he spelt his name. A-j-e-l-l-o. Curious, I never thought of that. Now, I wonder what he could have done to offend the little girls? Chased them from in front of his store, perhaps. There is a distinct reddish spot on his nose. By tomorrow he will have an American Beauty of a pimple.

Fortunately he and Miss Thurl went out together. I must think this through. I must remain cool. Aroint thee, thou mist of fever. This much is obvious: There are sorcerers about. Sorcer*esses*, I mean. The little ones made rain. And they laid a minor curse on poor Ajello. The elder one has struck me in the very vitals, however. If I had a cow it would doubtless be dry by this time. Should I struggle? Should I submit? Who knows what lies behind those moss-colored eyes, what thoughts inside the skull covered by those heavy tresses? Life with Mr. and Mr. Moos is—even by itself—too frightful to contemplate. Why doesn't she lay her traps for Ajello? Why should I be selected as the milk-white victim for the Hymeneal sacrifice? Useless to question. Few men have escaped once the female cast the runes upon them. And the allopath has nothing in his little black bag, either, which can cure.

Blessed association of words! Allopath—Homeopath—*homoios*, the like, the same, *pathos*, feeling, suffering—*similia similibus curantur*—

The little girls are playing beneath my window once more, clapping hands and singing. Something about a boy friend named Tony, who eats macaroni, has a great big knife and a pretty little wife, and will always lead a happy life . . . that must be the butcher opposite; he's always kind to the children. . . . Strength, strength! The work of a moment to get two coins from my wallet and throw them down. What little girl could resist picking up a dime which fell in front of her? *"Cross my palm with silver, pretty gentleman!"*—eh? And now to tell them my tale. . . .

I feel better already. I don't think I'll see Miss Thurl again for a while. She opened the door, the front door, and when the children had sung the new verse she slammed the door shut quite viciously.

It's too bad about Ajello, but every man for himself.

Listen to them singing away, bless their little hearts! I love little girls. Such sweet, innocent voices.

> My *boy* friend will *soon* be *heal*thy.
> He *shall* be very *weal*thy.
> No *wo*man shall *har*ry
> Or *seek* to *mar*ry;
> *Two* and *two* is *four*, and *one* to *carry!*

It will be pleasant to be wealthy, I hope. I must ask Ajello where Cincinello is.

A Canticle for the Fifties

The 1950s were years of great promise for science fiction. The decade began as a period of wild expansion, with magazines springing up like wild flowers in the desert after a rain. At the center was the original oasis dominated by Campbell's *Astounding*, but Boucher's *Magazine of Fantasy and Science Fiction* and Gold's *Galaxy* were clear rivals.

Writers appeared to fill the magazines with stories whose like had never before been seen. Spring was at hand, and the ripe fulfillment of summer could not be far behind. Then one by one the magazines died and one by one the writers drifted away to other activities or other kinds of writing. Ward Moore wrote only a single sf novel after *Bring the Jubilee*; Chad Oliver devoted most of his time to anthropology; Frank Robinson wrote only a couple of catastrophe novels in collaboration with another sometime dropout, Thomas Scortia; Theodore Cogswell became involved in teaching and a dissertation; Mark Clifton died in 1963; even Robert Sheckley's typewriter fell almost silent after 1960. During the decade, too, Isaac Asimov turned to science writing, Frederik Pohl turned to editing, and Alfred Bester turned to writing for *Holiday*. There were other losses: Mildred Clingerman, Raymond Banks, F. L. Wallace, Robert Abernathy, and many more.

Some of them found more rewarding occupations; some wrote themselves out; some, perhaps, no longer found markets for their work or lost the desire to do it. In an introduction to a collection of stories from the 1950s, Barry

Malzberg wrote that it was *The End of Summer*. He claimed that this was brought about in part by the dismemberment of the foremost newsstand distributor, the American News Service, the subsequent failure of many magazines, and the reduced circulations of others; by the impact of Sputnik; by the deaths of Henry Kuttner and Cyril Kornbluth; by the retirement of Anthony Boucher; by the illness and retirement of Horace L. Gold; and by the dwindling book market.

None of these reasons may apply to Walter M. Miller, Jr. (1922–   ). He was born and has spent most of his life in Florida near the water, except for two years of study at the University of Tennessee, service in World War II that included fifty-three combat missions, and two more years of studying engineering at the University of Texas. He started writing fiction while recovering from an automobile accident. His first publication was "MacDougal's Wife" in *The American Mercury*. His first publication in a science fiction magazine was "Secret of the Death Dome" in the January 1951 *Amazing*. His best-known stories are "Conditionally Human" (1952); "Crucifixus Etiam" (1953); "The Darfstellar," which won a Hugo Award for 1955; and "The Lineman" (1957).

Miller's only novel was *A Canticle for Leibowitz* (1960), but his short stories have been collected in *Conditionally Human* (1963), *The View from the Stars* (1965), *The Science Fiction Stories of Walter M. Miller, Jr.* (1978), and *The Best of Walter M. Miller, Jr.* (1980). *A Canticle for Leibowitz* won a Hugo Award, has been translated into five languages, and went through four hardcover printings in the United States and at least twenty paperback printings, rarely, if ever, going out of print. Perhaps the success of *Canticle* was intimidating, or perhaps the difficulties of writing it wore out Miller's desire to write. Certainly Miller's silence was not due to lack of audience appreciation.

The three parts of *A Canticle for Leibowitz* were published as three separate stories in *The Magazine of Fantasy and Science Fiction*, beginning with "A Canticle for Leibowitz" (titled "The First Canticle" in this anthology, "Fiat Homo"—"let there be man"—in the novel) in the April 1955 issue, continuing with "And the Light Is Risen" ("Fiat Lux"—"let there be light"—in the novel) in August 1956, and concluding with "The Last Canticle" ("Fiat Voluntas Tua"—"let thy will be done"—in the novel) in February

1957. The original stories were extensively rewritten for the book. The first story, for example, took up eighteen pages in the original magazine; that section in the book runs to ninety-eight pages. Not only was the original story filled out with incidents, characters, and reflections on events, but some of the events were changed. Nevertheless, the original remains as a promise of the fulfillment of the novel, an example of the fiction in the magazine in which it appeared, and a display of excellence in its own right.

"The First Canticle" is a post-catastrophe story—that is, it is concerned with the events after a catastrophe, not the catastrophe itself. The earliest post-catastrophe (as well as catastrophe) story probably is the biblical account of Noah and his family. In science fiction, Mary Shelley's *The Last Man* (1826) was the first, followed by Lt. Col. Sir George Tomkyns Chesney's "The Battle of Dorking" (1871), H. G. Wells's "The Time Machine" (1895), M. P. Sheil's *The Purple Cloud* (1901), George Allen England's *Darkness and Dawn* (1912), and many others, including Wells's *In the Days of the Comet* (1906) and *The Shape of Things to Come* (1934) and L. Ron Hubbard's *Final Blackout* (1940).

The post-atomic-catastrophe story may have got a start with a 1943 story titled "Clash by Night" by Lawrence O'Donnell (Henry Kuttner and C. L. Moore), followed by the O'Donnell novel *Fury* (1947), Pat Frank's *Alas, Babylon* (1949), Judith Merril's *Shadow on the Hearth* (1950), and so many others that editors began to list it as one of their least favorite clichés. What distinguished Miller's treatment of the idea was the remoteness of the post-catastrophe period, the concept of the renewed monasterial mission, and the carefully detailed narrative with its treatment of language and character.

Part of the appeal of "The First Canticle" is its folktale-like simplicity and the contrast between the complex reality of which the reader is aware and the distortions created by the gap of centuries, the interpretations of faith, and the lack of sophistication of the characters. Its basic claim on the reader's imagination, however, is the concept that after another great ravaging of civilization—this time by citizens inside the city rather than the barbarians outside the walls—the Catholic Church would perform a role similar to that of the medieval monasteries in preserving and copying Greek and Roman manuscripts. The monks of the Order of Leibowitz preserve handbooks and blueprints.

The novel is considerably more concerned with the framework and details of the religious impulse as well as with religious symbol and allegory. It is a richer, darker, and more reflective treatment of the basic idea. But like "The First Canticle" it is as much concerned with character and the interrelations of characters as with plot.

In the middle of the 1950s, it was a turning point.

The First Canticle

by Walter M. Miller, Jr.

Brother Francis Gerard of Utah would never have discovered the sacred document had it not been for the pilgrim with girded loins who appeared during that young monk's Lenten fast in the desert. Never before had Brother Francis actually seen a pilgrim with girded loins, but that this one was the bona fide article he was convinced at a glance. The pilgrim was a spindly old fellow with a staff, a basket hat, and a brushy beard, stained yellow about the chin. He walked with a limp and carried a small waterskin over one shoulder. His loins truly were girded with a ragged piece of dirty burlap, his only clothing except for hat and sandals. He whistled tunelessly on his way.

The pilgrim came shuffling down the broken trail out of the north, and he seemed to be heading toward the Brothers of Leibowitz Abbey six miles to the south. The pilgrim and the monk noticed each other across an expanse of ancient rubble. The pilgrim stopped whistling and stared. The monk, because of certain implications of the rule of solitude for fast days, quickly averted his gaze and continued about his business of hauling large rocks with which to complete the wolf-proofing of his temporary shelter. Somewhat weakened by a ten-day diet of cactus fruit, Brother Francis found the work made him exceedingly dizzy; the landscape had been shimmering before his eyes and dancing with black specks, and he was at first uncertain that the bearded apparition was not a mirage induced by hunger, but after a moment it called to him cheerfully, *"Ola allay!"*

It was a pleasant musical voice.

The rule of silence forbade the young monk to answer, except by smiling shyly at the ground.

"Is this here the road to the abbey?" the wanderer asked.

The novice nodded at the ground and reached down for a chalklike fragment of stone. The pilgrim picked his way toward him through the rubble. "What you doing with all the rocks?" he wanted to know.

The monk knelt and hastily wrote the words "Solitude & Silence" on a large flat rock, so that the pilgrim—if he could read, which was statistically unlikely—would know that he was making himself an occasion of sin for the penitent and would perhaps have the grace to leave in peace.

"Oh, well," said the pilgrim. He stood there for a moment, looking around, then rapped a certain large rock with his staff. "*That* looks like a handy crag for you," he offered helpfully, then added: "Well, good luck. And may you find a Voice, as y' seek."

Now Brother Francis had no immediate intuition that the stranger meant "Voice" with a capital V, but merely assumed that the old fellow had mistaken him for a deaf mute. He glanced up once again as the pilgrim shuffled away whistling, sent a swift silent benediction after him for safe wayfaring, and went back to his rockwork, building a coffin-sized enclosure in which he might sleep at night without offering himself as wolf-bait.

A sky-herd of cumulus clouds, on their way to bestow moist blessings on the mountains after having cruelly tempted the desert, offered welcome respite from the searing sunlight, and he worked rapidly to finish before they were gone again. He punctuated his labors with whispered prayers for the certainty of true Vocation, for this was the purpose of his inward quest while fasting in the desert.

At last he hoisted the rock which the pilgrim had suggested.

The color of exertion drained quickly from his face. He backed away a step and dropped the stone as if he had uncovered a serpent.

A rusted metal box lay half crushed in the rubble. . . .

He moved toward it curiously, then paused. There were things, and then there were Things. He crossed himself hastily, and muttered brief Latin at the heavens. Thus fortified, he readdressed himself to the box.

"*Apage Satanas!*"

He threatened it with the heavy crucifix of his rosary.

"Depart, O Foul Seductor!"

He sneaked a tiny aspergillum from his robes and quickly spattered the box with holy water before it could realize what he was about.

"If thou be creature of the Devil, begone!"

The box showed no signs of withering, exploding, melting away. It exuded no blasphemous ichor. It only lay quietly in its place and allowed the desert wind to evaporate the sanctifying droplets.

"So be it," said the brother, and knelt to extract it from its lodging. He sat down on the rubble and spent nearly an hour battering it open with a stone. The thought crossed his mind that such an archeological relic—for such it obviously was— might be the Heaven-sent sign of his vocation but he suppressed the notion as quickly as it occurred to him. His abbot had warned him sternly against expecting any direct personal Revelation of a spectacular nature. Indeed, he had gone forth from the abbey to fast and do penance for forty days that he might be rewarded with the inspiration of a calling to Holy Orders, but to expect a vision or a voice crying "Francis, where art thou?" would be a vain presumption. Too many novices had returned from their desert vigils with tales of omens and signs and visions in the heavens, and the good abbot had adopted a firm policy regarding these. Only the Vatican was qualified to decide the authenticity of such things. "An attack of sunstroke is no indication that you are fit to profess the solemn vows of the orders," he had growled. And certainly it was true that only rarely did a call from Heaven come through any device other than the *inward* ear, as a gradual congealing of inner certainty.

Nevertheless, Brother Francis found himself handling the old metal box with as much reverence as was possible while battering at it.

It opened suddenly, spilling some of its contents. He stared for a long time before daring to touch, and a cool thrill gathered along his spine. Here was antiquity indeed! And as a student of archeology, he could scarcely believe his wavering vision. Brother Jeris would be frantic with envy, he thought, but quickly repented this unkindness and murmured his thanks to the sky for such a treasure.

He touched the articles gingerly—they were real enough— and began sorting through them. His studies had equipped him to recognize a screwdriver—an instrument once used for twisting threaded bits of metal into wood—and a pair of cutters with blades no longer than his thumbnail, but strong enough to cut soft bits of metal or bone. There was an odd tool with a rotted wooden handle and a heavy copper tip to which a few flakes of molten lead had adhered, but he could make nothing of it. There was a toroidal roll of gummy black stuff, too far deteriorated by the centuries for him to identify. There were strange bits of metal, broken glass, and an assortment of tiny tubular things with wire whiskers of the type prized by the hill pagans as charms and amulets, but thought by some archeologists to be remnants of the legendary *machina analytica,* supposedly dating back to the Deluge of Flame.

All these and more he examined carefully and spread on the wide flat stone. The documents he saved until last. The documents, as always, were the real prize, for so few papers had survived the angry bonfires of the Age of Simplification, when even the sacred writings had curled and blackened and withered into smoke while ignorant crowds howled vengeance.

Two large folded papers and three hand-scribbled notes constituted his find. All were cracked and brittle with age, and he handled them tenderly, shielding them from the wind with his robe. They were scarcely legible and scrawled in the hasty characters of pre-Deluge English—a tongue now used, together with Latin, only by monastics and in the Holy Ritual. He spelled it out slowly, recognizing words but uncertain of meanings. One note said: *Pound pastrami, can kraut, six bagels, for Emma.* Another ordered: *Don't forget to pick up form 1040 for Uncle Revenue.* The third note was only a column of figures with a circled total from which another amount was subtracted and finally a percentage taken, followed by the word *damn!* From this he could deduce nothing, except to check the arithmetic, which proved correct.

Of the two larger papers, one was tightly rolled and began to fall to pieces when he tried to open it; he could make out the words RACING FORM, but nothing more. He laid it back in the box for later restorative work.

The second large paper was a single folded sheet, whose creases were so brittle that he could only inspect a little of it by parting the folds and peering between them as best he could.

A diagram . . . a web of white lines on dark paper!

Again the cool thrill gathered along his spine. It was a

blueprint—that exceedingly rare class of ancient document most prized by students of antiquity, and usually most challenging to interpreters and searchers for meaning.

And, as if the find itself were not enough of a blessing, among the words written in a block at the lower corner of the document was the name of the founder of his order—of the Blessed Leibowitz *himself!*

His trembling hands threatened to tear the paper in their happy agitation. The parting words of the pilgrim tumbled back to him: "May you find a Voice, as y' seek." Voice indeed, with V capitalized and formed by the wings of a descending dove and illuminated in three colors against a background of gold leaf. V as in V*ere dignum* and V*idi aquam* at the head of a page of the Missal. V, he saw quite clearly, as in Vocation.

He stole another glance to make certain it was so, then breathed, *"Beate Liebowitz, ora pro me . . . Sancte Liebowitz, exaudi me,"* the second invocation being a rather daring one, since the founder of his order had not yet been declared a saint.

Forgetful of his abbot's warning, he climbed quickly to his feet and stared across the shimmering terrain to the south in the direction taken by the old wanderer of the burlap loincloth. But the pilgrim had long since vanished. Surely an angel of God, if not the Blessed Leibowitz himself, for had he not revealed this miraculous treasure by pointing out the rock to be moved and murmuring that prophetic farewell?

Brother Francis stood basking in his awe until the sun lay red on the hills and evening threatened to engulf him in its shadows. At last he stirred, and reminded himself of the wolves. His gift included no guarantee of charismata for subduing the wild beast, and he hastened to finish his enclosure before darkness fell on the desert. When the stars came out, he rekindled his fire and gathered his daily repast of the small purple cactus fruit, his only nourishment except the handful of parched corn brought to him by the priest each Sabbath. Sometimes he found himself staring hungrily at the lizards which scurried over the rocks, and was troubled by gluttonous nightmares.

But tonight his hunger was less troublesome than an impatient urge to run back to the abbey and announce his wondrous encounter to his brethren. This, of course, was unthinkable. Vocation or no, he must remain here until the end

of Lent, and continue as if nothing extraordinary had occurred.

A cathedral will be built upon this site, he thought dream-
ily as he sat by the fire. He could see it rising from the rubble
of the ancient village, magnificent spires visible for miles
across the desert. . . .

But cathedrals were for teeming masses of people. The
desert was home for only scattered tribes of huntsmen and
the monks of the abbey. He settled in his dreams for a shrine,
attracting rivers of pilgrims with girded loins. . . . He
drowsed. When he awoke, the fire was reduced to glowing
embers. Something seemed amiss. Was he quite alone? He
blinked about at the darkness.

From beyond the bed of reddish coals, the dark wolf
blinked back. The monk yelped and dived for cover.

The yelp, he decided as he lay trembling within his den of
stones, had not been a serious breach of the rule of silence.
He lay hugging the metal box and praying for the days of
Lent to pass swiftly, while the sound of padded feet scratched
about the enclosure.

Each night the wolves prowled about his camp, and the
darkness was full of their howling. The days were glaring
nightmares of hunger, heat, and scorching sun. He spent
them at prayer and wood-gathering, trying to suppress his impatience for the coming of Holy Saturday's high noon, the
end of Lent and of his vigil.

But when at last it came, Brother Francis found himself
too famished for jubilation. Wearily he packed his pouch,
pulled up his cowl against the sun, and tucked his precious
box beneath one arm. Thirty pounds lighter and several
degrees weaker than he had been on Ash Wednesday, he
staggered the six-mile stretch to the abbey, where he fell exhausted before its gates. The brothers who carried him in and
bathed him and shaved him and anointed his desiccated tissue
reported that he babbled incessantly in his delirium about an
apparition in a burlap loincloth, addressing it at times as an
angel and again as a saint, frequently invoking the name of
Leibowitz and thanking him for a revelation of sacred relics
and a racing form.

Such reports filtered through the monastic congregation
and soon reached the ears of the abbot, whose eyes immediately narrowed to slits and whose jaw went rigid with the
rock of policy.

"Bring him," growled that worthy priest in a tone that sent a recorder scurrying.

The abbot paced and gathered his ire. It was not that he objected to miracles, as such, if duly investigated, certified, and sealed; for miracles—even though always incompatible with administrative efficiency, and the abbot was administrator as well as priest—were the bedrock stuff on which his faith was founded. But last year there had been Brother Noyen with his miraculous hangman's noose, and the year before that, Brother Smirnov, who had been mysteriously cured of the gout upon handling a probable relic of the Blessed Leibowitz, and the year before that . . . *Faugh!* The incidents had been too frequent and outrageous to tolerate. Ever since Leibowitz' beatification, the young fools had been sniffing around after shreds of the miraculous like a pack of good-natured hounds scratching eagerly at the back gate of Heaven for scraps.

It was quite understandable, but also quite unbearable. Every monastic order is eager for the canonization of its founder, and delighted to produce any bit of evidence to serve the cause in advocacy. But the abbot's flock was getting out of hand, and their zeal for miracles was making the Albertian Order of Leibowitz a laughingstock at New Vatican. He had determined to make any new bearers of miracles suffer the consequences, either as a punishment for impetuous and impertinent credulity, or as payment in penance for a gift of grace in case of later verification.

By the time the young novice knocked at his door, the abbot had projected himself into the desired state of carnivorous expectancy beneath a bland exterior.

"Come in, my son," he breathed softly.

"You sent for . . ." The novice paused, smiling happily as he noticed the familiar metal box on the abbot's table. ". . . for me, Father Juan?" he finished.

"Yes . . ." The abbot hesitated. His voice smiled with a withering acid, adding: "Or perhaps you would prefer that I come to *you,* hereafter, since you've become so famous."

"Oh no, Father!" Brother Francis reddened and gulped.

"You are seventeen, and plainly an idiot."

"That is undoubtedly true, Father."

"What improbable excuse can you propose for your outrageous vanity in believing yourself fit for Holy Orders?"

"I can offer none, my ruler and teacher. My sinful pride is unpardonable."

"To imagine that it is so great as to be unpardonable is even a vaster vanity," the priest roared.

"Yes, Father. I am indeed a worm."

The abbot smiled icily and resumed his watchful calm. "And you are now ready to deny your feverish ravings about an angel appearing to reveal to you this . . ." He gestured contemptuously at the box. ". . . this assortment of junk?"

Brother Francis gulped and closed his eyes. "I—I fear I cannot deny it, my master."

"What?"

"I cannot deny what I have seen, Father."

"Do you know what is going to happen to you now?"

"Yes, Father."

"Then prepare to take it!"

With a patient sigh, the novice gathered up his robes about his waist and bent over the table. The good abbot produced his stout hickory ruler from the drawer and whacked him soundly ten times across the bare buttocks. After each whack, the novice dutifully responded with a *"Deo Gratias!"* for this lesson in the virtue of humility.

"Do you *now* retract it?" the abbot demanded as he rolled down his sleeve.

"Father, I cannot."

The priest turned his back and was silent for a moment. "Very well," he said tersely. "Go. But do not expect to profess your solemn vows this season with the others."

Brother Francis returned to his cell in tears. His fellow novices would join the ranks of the professed monks of the order, while he must wait another year—and spend another Lenten season among the wolves in the desert, seeking a vocation which he felt had already been granted to him quite emphatically. As the weeks passed, however, he found some satisfaction in noticing that Father Juan had not been entirely serious in referring to his find as "an assortment of junk." The archeological relics aroused considerable interest among the brothers, and much time was spent at cleaning the tools, classifying them, restoring the documents to a pliable condition, and attempting to ascertain their meaning. It was even whispered among the novices that Brother Francis had discovered true relics of the Blessed Leibowitz—especially in the form of the blueprint bearing the legend OP COBBLESTONE, REQ LEIBOWITZ & HARDIN, which was stained with several brown splotches which might have been his blood—or equally likely, as the abbot pointed out, might be stains from a decayed apple core. But the print was dated in the year of Grace 1956, which was—as nearly as could be determined— during the venerable man's lifetime, a lifetime now obscured by legend and myth, so that it was hard to determine any but a few facts about the man.

It was said that God, in order to test mankind, had commanded wise men of that age, among them the Blessed Leibowitz, to perfect diabolic weapons and give them into the hands of latter-day Pharaohs. And with such weapons Man had, within the span of a few weeks, destroyed most of his civilization and wiped out a large part of the population. After the Deluge of Flame came the plagues, the madness, and the bloody inception of the Age of Simplification when the furious remnants of humanity had torn politicians, technicians, and men of learning limb from limb, and burned all records that might contain information that could once more lead into paths of destruction. Nothing had been so fiercely hated as the written word, the learned man. It was during this time that the word "simpleton" came to mean "honest, upright, virtuous citizen," a concept once denoted by the term "common man."

To escape the righteous wrath of the surviving simpletons, many scientists and learned men fled to the only sanctuary which would try to offer them protection. Holy Mother Church received them, vested them in monks' robes, tried to conceal them from the mobs. Sometimes the sanctuary was effective; more often it was not. Monasteries were invaded, records and sacred books were burned, refugees seized and hanged. Leibowitz had fled to the Cistercians, professed their vows, became a priest, and after twelve years had won permission from the Holy See to found a new monastic order to be called "the Albertians," after St. Albert the Great, teacher of Aquinas and patron saint of scientists. The new order was to be dedicated to the preservation of knowledge, secular and sacred, and the duty of the brothers was to memorize such books and papers as could be smuggled to them from all parts of the world. Leibowitz was at last identified by simpletons as a former scientist, and was martyred by hanging; but the order continued, and when it became safe again to possess written documents, many books were transcribed from memory. Precedence, however, had been given to sacred writings, to history, the humanities, and social sciences —since the memories of the memorizers were limited, and few of the brothers were trained to understand the physical sciences. From the vast store of human knowledge, only a pitiful collection of handwritten books remained.

Now, after six centuries of darkness, the monks still preserved it, studied it, recopied it, and waited. It mattered not in the least to them that the knowledge they saved was useless—and some of it even incomprehensible. The knowledge was there, and it was their duty to save it, and it would still be with them if the darkness in the world lasted ten thousand years.

Brother Francis Gerard of Utah returned to the desert the following year and fasted again in solitude. Once more he returned, weak and emaciated, to be confronted by the abbot, who demanded to know if he claimed further conferences with members of the Heavenly Host, or was prepared to renounce his story of the previous year.

"I cannot help what I have seen, my teacher," the lad repeated.

Once more did the abbot chastise him in Christ, and once more did he postpone his profession. The document, however, had been forwarded to a seminary for study, after a copy had been made. Brother Francis remained a novice, and continued to dream wistfully of the shrine which might someday be built upon the site of his find.

"Stubborn boy!" fumed the abbot. "Why didn't somebody else see his silly pilgrim, if the slovenly fellow was heading for the abbey as he said? One more escapade for the Devil's Advocate to cry hoax about. Burlap loincloth indeed!"

The burlap had been troubling the abbot, for tradition related that Leibowitz had been hanged with a burlap bag for a hood.

Brother Francis spent seven years in the novitiate, seven Lenten vigils in the desert, and became highly proficient in the imitation of wolf calls. For the amusement of his brethren, he would summon the pack to the vicinity of the abbey by howling from the walls after dark. By day, he served in the kitchen, scrubbed the stone floors, and continued his studies of the ancients.

Then one day a messenger from the seminary came riding to the abbey on an ass, bearing tidings of great joy. "It is known," said the messenger, "that the documents found near here are authentic as to date of origin, and that the blueprint was somehow connected with your founder's work. It's being sent to New Vatican for further study."

"Possibly a true relic of Leibowitz, then?" the abbot asked calmly.

But the messenger could not commit himself to that extent, and only raised a shrug of one eyebrow. "It is said that Leibowitz was a widower at the time of his ordination. If the name of his deceased wife could be discovered . . ."

The abbot recalled the note in the box concerning certain articles of food for a woman, and he too shrugged an eyebrow.

Soon afterwards, he summoned Brother Francis into his presence. "My boy," said the priest, actually beaming. "I believe the time has come for you to profess your solemn vows. And may I commend you for your patience and persistence. We shall speak no more of your, ah . . . encounter with the ah desert wanderer. You are a good simpleton. You may kneel for my blessing, if you wish."

Brother Francis sighed and fell forward in a dead faint. The abbot blessed him and revived him, and he was permitted to profess the solemn vows of the Albertian Brothers of Leibowitz, swearing himself to perpetual poverty, chastity, obedience, and observance of the rule.

Soon afterwards, he was assigned to the copying room, apprentice under an aged monk named Horner, where he would undoubtedly spend the rest of his days illuminating the pages of algebra texts with patterns of olive leaves and cheerful cherubim.

"You have five hours a week," croaked his aged overseer, "which you may devote to an approved project of your own choosing, if you wish. If not, the time will be assigned to copying the *Summa Theologica* and such fragmentary copies of the Britannica as exist."

The young monk thought it over, then asked: "May I have the time for elaborating a beautiful copy of the Leibowitz blueprint?"

Brother Horner frowned doubtfully. "I don't know, son— our good abbot is rather sensitive on this subject. I'm afraid . . ."

Brother Francis begged him earnestly.

"Well, perhaps," the old man said reluctantly. "It seems like a rather brief project, so—I'll permit it."

The young monk selected the finest lambskin available and spent many weeks curing it and stretching it and stoning it to a perfect surface, bleached to a snowy whiteness. He spent more weeks at studying copies of his precious document in every detail, so that he knew each tiny line and marking in the complicated web of geometric markings and mystifying symbols. He pored over it until he could see the whole amazing complexity with his eyes closed. Additional weeks were spent searching painstakingly through the monastery's library for any information at all that might lead to some glimmer of understanding of the design.

Brother Jeris, a young monk who worked with him in the copy room and who frequently teased him about miraculous encounters in the desert, came to squint at it over his shoulder and asked: "What, pray, is the meaning of *Transistorized Control System for Unit Six-B?*"

"Clearly, it is the name of the thing which this diagram represents," said Francis, a trifle crossly since Jeris had merely read the title of the document aloud.

"Surely," said Jeris. "But what is the thing the diagram represents?"

"The transistorized control system for unit six-B, obviously."

Jeris laughed mockingly.

Brother Francis reddened. "I should imagine," said he, "that it represents an abstract concept, rather than a concrete *thing*. It's clearly not a recognizable picture of an object, unless the form is so stylized as to require special training to see it. In my opinion, *Transistorized Control System* is some high abstraction of transcendental value."

"Pertaining to what field of learning?" asked Jeris, still smiling smugly.

"Why . . ." Brother Francis paused. "Since our Beatus Leibowitz was an electronicist prior to his profession and ordination, I suppose the concept applies to the lost art called *electronics.*"

"So it is written. But what was the subject matter of that art, Brother?"

"That too is written. The subject matter of electronics was the Electron, which one fragmentary source defines as a Negative Twist of Nothingness."

"I am impressed by your astuteness," said Jeris. "Now perhaps you can tell me how to negate nothingness?"

Brother Francis reddened slightly and squirmed for a reply.

"A negation of nothingness should yield somethingness, I suppose," Jeris continued. "So the Electron must have been a twist of *something*. Unless the negation applies to the 'twist,' and then we would be 'Untwisting Nothing,' eh?" He chuckled. "How clever they must have been, these ancients. I suppose if you keep at it, Francis, you will learn how to untwist a nothing, and then we shall have the Electron in our midst. Where would we put it? On the high altar, perhaps?"

"I couldn't say," Francis answered stiffly. "But I have a certain faith that the Electron must have existed at one time, even though I can't say how it was constructed or what it might have been used for."

The iconoclast laughed mockingly and returned to his work. The incident saddened Francis, but did not turn him from his devotion to his project.

As soon as he had exhausted the library's meager supply of information concerning the lost art of the Albertians' founder, he began preparing preliminary sketches of the designs he meant to use on the lambskin. The diagram itself, since its meaning was obscure, would be redrawn precisely as it was in the blueprint, and penned in coal-black lines. The lettering and numbering, however, he would translate into a more decorative and colorful script than the plain block letters used by the ancients. And the text contained in a square block marked SPECIFICATIONS would be distributed pleasingly around the borders of the document, upon scrolls and shields supported by doves and cherubim. He would make the black lines of the diagram less stark and austere by imagining the geometric tracery to be a trellis, and decorate it with green vines and golden fruit, birds and perhaps a wily serpent. At the very top would be a representation of the Triune God, and at the bottom the coat of arms of the Albertian Order. Thus was the Transistorized Control System of the Blessed Leibowitz to be glorified and rendered appealing to the eye as well as to the intellect.

When he had finished the preliminary sketch, he showed it shyly to Brother Horner for suggestions or approval. "I can see," said the old man a bit remorsefully, "that your project is not to be as brief as I had hoped. But . . . continue with it anyhow. The design is beautiful, beautiful indeed."

"Thank you, Brother."

The old man leaned close to wink confidentially. "I've heard the case for Blessed Leibowitz' canonization has been speeded up, so possibly our dear abbot is less troubled by you-know-what than he previously was."

The news of the speed-up was, of course, happily received by all monastics of the order. Leibowitz' beatification had long since been effected, but the final step in declaring him to be a saint might require many more years, even though the case was under way; and indeed there was the possibility that the Devil's Advocate might uncover evidence to prevent the canonization from occurring at all.

Many months after he had first conceived the project, Brother Francis began actual work on the lambskin. The intricacies of scrollwork, the excruciatingly delicate work of inlaying the gold leaf, the hair-fine detail, made it a labor of years; and when his eyes began to trouble him, there were long weeks when he dared not touch it at all for fear of spoiling it with one little mistake. But slowly, painfully, the ancient diagram was becoming a blaze of beauty. The brothers of the abbey gathered to watch and murmur over it, and some even said that the inspiration of it was proof enough of his alleged encounter with the pilgrim who might have been Blessed Leibowitz.

"I can't see why you don't spend your time on a *useful* project," was Brother Jeris' comment, however. The skeptical monk had been using his own free-project time to make and decorate sheepskin shades for the oil lamps in the chapel.

Brother Horner, the old master copyist, had fallen ill. Within weeks, it became apparent that the well-loved monk was on his deathbed. In the midst of the monastery's grief, the abbot quietly appointed Brother Jeris as master of the copy room.

A Mass of Burial was chanted early in Advent, and the remains of the holy old man were committed to the earth of their origin. On the following day, Brother Jeris informed Brother Francis that he considered it about time for him to put away the things of a child and start doing a man's work. Obediently, the monk wrapped his precious project in parchment, protected it with heavy board, shelved it, and began producing sheepskin lampshades. He made no murmur of protest, and contented himself with realizing that someday the soul of Brother Jeris would depart by the same road as that of Brother Horner, to begin the life for which this copy room was but the staging ground; and afterwards, please God, he might be allowed to complete his beloved document.

Providence, however, took an earlier hand in the matter. During the following summer, a monsignor with several clerks and a donkey train came riding into the abbey and announced that he had come from New Vatican, as Leibowitz advocate in the canonization proceedings, to investigate such evidence as the abbey could produce that might have bearing on the case, including an alleged apparition of the beatified which had come to one Francis Gerard of Utah.

The gentleman was warmly greeted, quartered in the suite reserved for visiting prelates, lavishly served by six young monks responsive to his every whim, of which he had very few. The finest wines were opened, the huntsman snared the plumpest quail and chaparral cocks, and the advocate was entertained each evening by fiddlers and a troupe of clowns, although the visitor persisted in insisting that life go on as usual at the abbey.

On the third day of his visit, the abbot sent for Brother Francis. "Monsignor di Simone wishes to see you," he said. "If you let your imagination run away with you, boy, we'll use your gut to string a fiddle, feed your carcass to the wolves, and bury the bones in unhallowed ground. Now get along and see the good gentleman."

Brother Francis needed no such warning. Since he had awakened from his feverish babblings after his first Lenten fast in the desert, he had never mentioned the encounter with the pilgrim except when asked about it, nor had he allowed himself to speculate any further concerning the pilgrim's identity. That the pilgrim might be a matter for high ecclesiastical concern frightened him a little, and his knock was timid at the monsignor's door.

His fright proved unfounded. The monsignor was a suave and diplomatic elder who seemed keenly interested in the small monk's career.

"Now about your encounter with our blessed founder," he said after some minutes of preliminary amenities.

"Oh, but I never said he was our Blessed Leibo—"

"Of course you didn't, my son. Now I have here an account of it, as gathered from other sources, and I would like you to read it, and either confirm it or correct it." He paused to draw a scroll from his case and handed it to Francis. "The sources for this version, of course, had it on hearsay only," he added, "and only *you* can describe it firsthand, so I want you to edit it *most* scrupulously."

"Of course. What happened was really very simple, Father."

But it was apparent from the fatness of the scroll that the hearsay account was not so simple. Brother Francis read with mounting apprehension which soon grew to the proportions of pure horror.

"You look white, my son. Is something wrong?" asked the distinguished priest.

"This . . . this . . . it wasn't like this *at all!*" gasped Francis. "He didn't say more than a few words to me. I only saw him once. He just asked me the way to the abbey and tapped the rock where I found the relics."

"No heavenly choir?"

"Oh, no!"

"And it's not true about the nimbus and the carpet of roses that grew up along the road where he walked?"

"As God is my judge, nothing like that happened at all!"

"Ah, well," sighed the advocate. "Travelers' stories are always exaggerated."

He seemed saddened, and Francis hastened to apologize, but the advocate dismissed it as of no great importance to the case. "There are other miracles, carefully documented," he explained, "and anyway—there is one bit of good news about the documents you discovered. We've unearthed the name of the wife who died before our founder came to the order."

"Yes?"

"Yes. It was Emily."

Despite his disappointment with Brother Francis' account of the pilgrim, Monsignor di Simone spent five days at the site of his find. He was accompanied by an eager crew of novices from the abbey, all armed with picks and shovels. After extensive digging, the advocate returned with a small assortment of additional artifacts, and one bloated tin can that contained a desiccated mess which might once have been sauerkraut.

Before his departure, he visited the copy room and asked to see Brother Francis' copy of the famous blueprint. The monk protested that it was really nothing, and produced it with such eagerness his hands trembled.

"Zounds!" said the monsignor, or an oath to such effect. "Finish it, man, finish it!"

The monk looked smilingly at Brother Jeris. Brother Jeris swiftly turned away; the back of his neck gathered color. The following morning, Francis resumed his labors over the illuminated blueprint, with gold leaf, quills, brushes, and dyes.

And then came another donkey train from New Vatican, with a full complement of clerks and armed guards for defense against highwaymen, this time headed by a monsignor with small horns and pointed fangs (or so several novices would later have testified), who announced that he was the

Advocatus Diaboli, opposing Leibowitz' canonization, and he was here to investigate—and perhaps fix responsibility, he hinted—for a number of incredible and hysterical rumors filtering out of the abbey and reaching even high officials at New Vatican. He made it clear that he would tolerate no romantic nonsense.

The abbot greeted him politely and offered him an iron cot in a cell with a south exposure, after apologizing for the fact that the guest suite had been recently exposed to smallpox. The monsignor was attended by his own staff, and ate mush and herbs with the monks in refectory.

"I understand you are susceptible to fainting spells," he told Brother Francis when the dread time came. "How many members of your family have suffered from epilepsy or madness?"

"None, Excellency."

"I'm not an 'Excellency,'" snapped the priest. "Now we're going to get the truth out of you." His tone implied that he considered it to be a simple straightforward surgical operation which should have been performed years ago.

"Are you aware that documents can be aged artificially?" he demanded.

Francis was not so aware.

"Did you know that Leibowitz' wife was named Emily, and that Emma is *not* a diminutive for Emily?"

Francis had not known it, but recalled from childhood that his own parents had been rather careless about what they called each other. "And if Blessed Leibowitz chose to call her Emma, then I'm sure . . ."

The monsignor exploded and tore into Francis with semantic tooth and nail, and left the bewildered monk wondering whether he had ever really seen a pilgrim at all.

Before the advocate's departure, he too asked to see the illuminated copy of the print, and this time the monk's hands trembled with fear as he produced it, for he might again be forced to quit the project. The monsignor only stood gazing at it however, swallowed slightly, and forced himself to nod. "Your imagery is vivid," he admitted, "but then, of course, we all knew that, didn't we?"

The monsignor's horns immediately grew shorter by an inch, and he departed the same evening for New Vatican.

The years flowed smoothly by, seaming the faces of the once young and adding gray to the temples. The perpetual labors of the monastery continued, supplying a slow trickle of

copied and recopied manuscript to the outside world. Brother
Jeris developed ambitions of building a printing press, but
when the abbot demanded his reasons, he could only reply,
"So we can mass-produce."

"Oh? And in a world that's smug in its illiteracy, what do
you intend to do with the stuff? Sell it as kindling paper to
the peasants?"

Brother Jeris shrugged unhappily, and the copy room continued with pot and quill.

Then one spring, shortly before Lent, a messenger arrived
with glad tidings for the order. The case for Leibowitz was
complete. The College of Cardinals would soon convene, and
the founder of the Albertian Order would be enrolled in the
Calendar of Saints. During the time of rejoicing that followed
the announcement, the abbot—now withered and in his
dotage—summoned Brother Francis into his presence, and
wheezed:

"His holiness commands your presence during the canonization of Isaac Edward Leibowitz. Prepare to leave.

"Now don't faint on me again," he added querulously.

The trip to New Vatican would take at least three months,
perhaps longer, the time depending on how far Brother Francis could get before the inevitable robber band relieved him
of his ass, since he would be going unarmed and alone. He
carried with him only a begging bowl and the illuminated
copy of the Leibowitz print, praying that ignorant robbers
would have no use for the latter. As a precaution, however,
he wore a black patch over his right eye, for the peasants,
being a superstitious lot, could often be put to flight by even
a hint of the evil eye. Thus armed and equipped, he set out
to obey the summons of his high priest.

Two months and some odd days later he met his robber on
a mountain trail that was heavily wooded and far from any
settlement. His robber was a short man, but heavy as a bull,
with a glazed knob of a pate and jaw like a block of granite.
He stood in the trail with his legs spread wide and his massive arms folded across his chest, watching the approach of
the little figure on the ass. The robber seemed alone, and
armed only with a knife which he did not bother to remove
from his belt thong. His appearance was a disappointment,
since Francis had been secretly hoping for another encounter
with the pilgrim of long ago.

"Get off," said the robber.

The ass stopped in the path. Brother Francis tossed back his cowl to reveal the eye patch, and raised a trembling finger to touch it. He began to lift the patch slowly as if to reveal something hideous that might be hidden beneath it. The robber threw back his head and laughed a laugh that might have sprung from the throat of Satan himself. Francis muttered an exorcism, but the robber seemed untouched.

"You black-sacked jeebers wore that one out years ago," he said. "Get off."

Francis smiled, shrugged, and dismounted without protest.

"A good day to you, sir," he said pleasantly. "You may take the ass. Walking will improve my health, I think." He smiled again and started away.

"Hold it," said the robber. "Strip to the buff. And let's see what's in that package."

Brother Francis touched his begging bowl and made a helpless gesture, but this brought only another scornful laugh from the robber.

"I've seen that alms-pot trick before too," he said. "The last man with a begging bowl had half a heklo of gold in his boot. Now strip."

Brother Francis displayed his sandals, but began to strip. The robber searched his clothing, found nothing, and tossed it back to him.

"Now let's see inside the package."

"It is only a document, sir," the monk protested. "Of value to no one but its owner."

"Open it."

Silently Brother Francis obeyed. The gold leaf and the colorful design flashed brilliantly in the sunlight that filtered through the foliage. The robber's craggy jaw dropped an inch. He whistled softly.

"What a pretty! Now wouldn't me woman like it to hang on the wall!"

He continued to stare while the monk went slowly sick inside. *If Thou has sent him to test me, O Lord,* he pleaded inwardly, *then help me to die like a man, for he'll get it over the dead body of Thy servant, if take it he must.*

"Wrap it up for me," the robber commanded, clamping his jaw in sudden decision.

The monk whimpered softly. "Please, sir, you would not take the work of a man's lifetime. I spent fifteen years illuminating this manuscript, and . . ."

"Well! Did it yourself, did you?" The robber threw back his head and howled again.

Francis reddened. "I fail to see the humor, sir. . . ."

The robber pointed at it between guffaws. "You! Fifteen years to make a paper bauble. So that's what you do. Tell me why. Give me one good reason. For fifteen years. Ha!"

Francis stared at him in stunned silence and could think of no reply that would appease his contempt.

Gingerly, the monk handed it over. The robber took it in both hands and made as if to rip it down the center.

"*Jesus, Mary, Joseph!*" the monk screamed, and went to his knees in the trail. "For the love of God, sir!"

Softening slightly, the robber tossed it on the ground with a snicker. "Wrestle you for it."

"Anything, sir, anything!"

They squared off. The monk crossed himself and recalled that wrestling had once been a divinely sanctioned sport—and with grim faith, he marched into battle.

Three seconds later, he lay groaning on the flat of his back under a short mountain of muscle. A sharp rock seemed to be severing his spine.

"Heh-heh," said the robber, and arose to claim his document.

Hands folded as if in prayer, Brother Francis scurried after him on his knees, begging at the top of his lungs.

The robber turned. "I believe you'd kiss a boot to get it back."

Francis caught up with him and fervently kissed his boot.

This proved too much for even such a firm fellow as the robber. He flung the manuscript down again with a curse and climbed aboard the monk's donkey. The monk snatched up the precious document and trotted along beside the robber, thanking him profusely and blessing him repeatedly while the robber rode away on the ass. Francis sent a glowing cross of benediction after the departing figure and praised God for the existence of such selfless robbers.

And yet when the man had vanished among the trees, he felt an aftermath of sadness. Fifteen years to make a paper bauble . . . The taunting voice still rang in his ears. Why? Tell one good reason for fifteen years.

He was unaccustomed to the blunt ways of the outside world, to its harsh habits and curt attitudes. He found his heart deeply troubled by the mocking words, and his head hung low in the cowl as he plodded along. At one time he considered tossing the document in the brush and leaving it for the rains—but Father Juan had approved his taking it as a gift, and he could not come with empty hands. Chastened, he traveled on.

The hour had come. The ceremony surged about him as a magnificent spectacle of sound and stately movement and vivid color in the majestic basilica. And when the perfectly infallible Spirit had finally been invoked, a monsignor—it was di Simone, Francis noticed, the advocate for the saint—arose and called upon Peter to speak, through the person of Leo XXII, commanding the assemblage to hearken.

Whereupon, the Pope quietly proclaimed that Isaac Edward Leibowitz was a saint, and it was finished. The ancient and obscure technician was of the heavenly hagiarchy, and Brother Francis breathed a dutiful prayer to his new patron as the choir burst into the *Te Deum*.

The Pontiff strode quickly into the audience room where the little monk was waiting, taking Brother Francis by surprise and rendering him briefly speechless. He knelt quickly to kiss the Fisherman's ring and receive the blessing. As he arose, he found himself clutching the beautiful document behind him as if ashamed of it. The Pope's eyes caught the motion, and he smiled.

"You have brought us a gift, our son?" he asked.

The monk gulped, nodded stupidly, and brought it out. Christ's Vicar stared at it for a long time without apparent expression. Brother Francis' heart went sinking deeper as the seconds drifted by.

"It is a nothing," he blurted, "a miserable gift. I am ashamed to have wasted so much time at . . ." He choked off.

The Pope seemed not to hear him. "Do you understand the meaning of Saint Isaac's symbology?" he asked, peering curiously at the abstract design of the circuit.

Dumbly the monk shook his head.

"Whatever it means . . ." the Pope began, but broke off. He smiled and spoke of other things. Francis had been so honored not because of any official judgment concerning his pilgrim. He had been honored for his role in bringing to light such important documents and relics of the saint, for such they had been judged, regardless of the manner in which they had been found.

Francis stammered his thanks. The Pontiff gazed again at the colorful blaze of his illuminated diagram. "Whatever it means," he breathed once more, "this bit of learning, though dead, will live again." He smiled up at the monk and winked. "And we shall guard it till that day."

For the first time, the little monk noticed that the Pope had a hole in his robe. His clothing, in fact, was threadbare. The carpet in the audience room was worn through in spots, and plaster was falling from the ceiling.

But there were books on the shelves along the walls. Books of painted beauty, speaking of incomprehensible things, copied by men whose business was not to understand but to save. And the books were waiting.

"Goodby, beloved son."

And the small keeper of the flame of knowledge trudged back toward his abbey on foot. His heart was singing as he approached the robber's outpost. And if the robber happened to be taking the day off, the monk meant to sit down and wait for his return. This time he had an answer.

The Lodestone Genre

Until recent years science fiction always has attracted more talented writers than it could reward adequately. This was particularly true in the 1950s, when science fiction went through what Robert Sheckley has called a "false spring." It seemed as if the burgeoning magazines and book markets could support a number of full-time writers, but growth was an illusion and only a handful of writers survived.

One of those writers who did very well, although he almost always had other employment, was Algis Budrys (1931–   ). A Lithuanian, he was born in Königsberg, East Prussia, where his father was a diplomat. He was brought to the United States at the age of six. His father served for many years as consul general of Lithuania in New York City.

Budrys attended the University of Miami and Columbia University; worked as an investigations clerk for the American Express Company; sold his first story, "The High Purpose," to *Astounding* in 1952; became an assistant editor for a pioneering sf book-publishing company, Gnome Press, the same year; and the following year became assistant editor of *Galaxy*. He was an assistant editor and house writer and artist for various publishers from 1953 to 1961, editor-in-chief of Regency Books and also editorial director of Playboy Press from 1963 to 1965, and after 1966 an advertising and public relations account executive. In 1973 he served briefly as an editor again. Since then he has been a freelance writer and communications consultant.

Budrys's first novel came out as *False Night* (1954) and in reinstated and revised form as *Some Will Not Die* (1961). His second novel, *Who?* (1958), won considerable notice and later was turned into a film. *The Falling Torch* (1959) has echoes of his diplomatic corps background. *Rogue Moon* (1960) may be his finest novel, combining themes of love, death, and memory with the science fiction problem of solving a deadly alien maze discovered on the moon. Years later Budrys returned to the science fiction novel with *The Iron Thorn* (1967) and the well-received *Michaelmas* (1977).

In the interim Budrys not only edited books and established himself in the communications career in which he now does freelance work, he also became a critic, publishing regular review columns in *Galaxy* beginning in 1965 and, more recently, columns in *The Magazine of Fantasy and Science Fiction* and reviews in the *Washington Post*, the *Chicago Sun-Times*, and other media. For more than a decade he was the best critic writing regularly in the field; he may still be the best critic, but his reviews appear more sporadically.

That he did not continue to produce science fiction steadily through the 1960s and 1970s may not be due to economic factors but to the fact that talent often is more fully rewarded elsewhere—only so much money and so many awards are available to go around. The imagination and writing skills that make a science fiction writer successful are in demand in other fields as well, and many of these pursuits have their own satisfactions.

"Nobody Bothers Gus" was written early in Budrys's career. Budrys was a prolific writer at the shorter lengths and used many pseudonyms (David C. Hodgkins, Ivan Janvier, Paul Janvier, Robert Marner, Alger Rome, William Scarff, John A. Sentry, and Albert Stroud). "Nobody Bothers Gus" was published in the November 1955 issue of *Astounding* under the name Paul Janvier. Two sequels followed: "And Then She Found Him" in the July 1957 *Venture Science Fiction* and "Lost Love" in the January 1957 *Science Fiction Stories*.

The appeal of "Nobody Bothers Gus" is not easy to pin down. Nothing happens. Part of the story is Gus's reflections on his past; part is sustained by the modest suspense about the communication brought by Gus's visitor. And yet the story contains a basic tension that comes not from what happens but from what might happen. It comes, as it must, from the character of Gus—much is made of the fact that he is a powerful, even threatening, man. All of the images are of power under iron control, but some of Gus's powers are not controllable, and the story continually seems on the point of turning ugly.

The sf idea behind the story is that of the superman and the guise in which he will appear; this is combined with an exploration of psychic abilities that John W. Campbell was emphasizing at the time. Budrys's unique contribution was the notion that a superman, in addition to natural superiority, might develop a natural protection, like the rabbit's timidity or the gazelle's speed. But every protection has its drawbacks. What makes this story endure—in fact, it has frequently been reprinted—is Gus's reactions to his superiority and to the natural protection with which his kind has been endowed. The author stresses Gus's nonhumanity, but his reactions are human in the best sense, and perhaps more than human in his determined, and self-sacrificing, efforts to avoid a violent solution.

What makes the story readable are the details and the language with which Budrys endowed it: the loving attention paid by Gus and the author to the preparation of the lawn; the characterization of Gus and the descriptions of his earlier experiences; and the conviction with which Budrys portrays Gus's lonely alienness, a condition, one feels, that the author knew well. The final feeling of loneliness and waste turns the threat of violence into an appropriate and satisfying conclusion.

Nobody Bothers Gus

by Algis Budrys

Two years earlier, Gus Kusevic had been driving slowly down the narrow back road into Boonesboro.

It was good country for slow driving, particularly in the late spring. There was nobody else on the road. The woods were just blooming into a deep, rich green as yet unburned by summer, and the afternoons were still cool and fresh. And, just before he reached the Boonesboro town line, he saw the locked and weathered cottage standing for sale on its quarter-acre lot.

He had pulled his roadcar up to a gentle stop, swung sideways in his seat, and looked at it.

It needed paint; the siding had gone from white to gray, and the trim was faded. There were shingles missing here and there from the roof, leaving squares of darkness on the sun-bleached rows of cedar, and inevitably, some of the windowpanes had cracked. But the frame hadn't slouched out of square, and the roof hadn't sagged. The çhimney stood up straight.

He looked at the straggled clumps and windrowed hay that were all that remained of the shrubbery and the lawn. His broad, homely face bunched itself into a quiet smile along its well-worn seams. His hands itched for the feel of a spade.

He got out of the roadcar, walked across the road and up to the cottage door, and copied down the name of the real-estate dealer listed on the card tacked to the doorframe. Now it was almost two years later, early in April, and Gus was topdressing his lawn.

Earlier in the day he'd set up a screen beside the pile of topsoil behind his house, shoveled the soil through the screen, mixed it with broken peat moss, and carted it out to the lawn, where he left it in small piles. Now he was carefully raking it out over the young grass in a thin layer that covered only the roots, and let the blades peep through. He intended to be finished by the time the second half of the Giants-Kodiaks doubleheader came on. He particularly wanted to see it because Halsey was pitching for the Kodiaks, and he had something of an avuncular interest in Halsey.

He worked without waste motion or excess expenditure of energy. Once or twice he stopped and had a beer in the shade of the rose arbor he'd put up around the front door. Nevertheless, the sun was hot; by early afternoon, he had his shirt off.

Just before he would have been finished, a battered flivver settled down in front of the house. It parked with a flurry of its rotors, and a gangling man in a worn serge suit, with thin hair plastered across his tight scalp, climbed out and looked at Gus uncertainly.

Gus had glanced up briefly while the flivver was on its silent way down. He'd made out the barely legible "Falmouth County Clerk's Office" lettered over the faded paint on its door, shrugged, and gone on with what he was doing.

Gus was a big man. His shoulders were heavy and broad; his chest was deep, grizzled with thick, iron-gray hair. His stomach had got a little heavier with the years, but the muscles were still there under the layer of flesh. His upper arms were thicker than a good many thighs, and his forearms were enormous.

His face was seamed by a network of folds and creases. His flat cheeks were marked out by two deep furrows that ran from the sides of his bent nose, merged with the creases bracketing his wide lips, and converged towards the blunt point of his jaw. His pale blue eyes twinkled above high cheekbones which were covered with wrinkles. His close-cropped hair was as white as cotton.

Only repeated and annoying exposure would give his body a tan, but his face was permanently browned. The pink of his body sunburn was broken in several places by white scar tissue. The thin line of a knife cut emerged from the tops of his pants and faded out across the right side of his stomach. The other significant areas of scarring lay across the uneven knuckles of his heavy-fingered hands.

The clerk looked at the mailbox to make sure of the name, checking it against an envelope he was holding in one hand. He stopped and looked at Gus again, mysteriously nervous.

Gus abruptly realized that he probably didn't present a reassuring appearance. With all the screening and raking he'd been doing, there'd been a lot of dust in the air. Mixed with perspiration, it was all over his face, chest, arms, and back. Gus knew he didn't look very gentle even at his cleanest and best-dressed. At the moment, he couldn't blame the clerk for being skittish.

He tried to smile disarmingly.

The clerk ran his tongue over his lips, cleared his throat with a slight cough, and jerked his head towards the mailbox. "Is that right? You Mr. Kusevic?"

Gus nodded. "That's right. What can I do for you?"

The clerk held up the envelope. "Got a notice here from the County Council," he muttered, but he was obviously much more taken up by his effort to equate Gus with the rose arbor, the neatly edged and carefully tended flower beds, the hedges, the flagstoned walk, the small goldfish pond under the willow tree, the white-painted cottage with its window boxes and bright shutters, and the curtains showing inside the sparkling windows.

Gus waited until the man was through with his obvious

thoughts, but something deep inside him sighed quietly. He had gone through this moment of bewilderment with so many other people that he was quite accustomed to it, but that is not the same thing as being oblivious.

"Well, come on inside," he said after a decent interval. "It's pretty hot out here, and I've got some beer in the cooler."

The clerk hesitated again. "Well, all I've got to do is deliver this notice," he said, still looking around. "Got the place fixed up real nice, don't you?"

Gus smiled. "It's my home. A man likes to live in a nice place. In a hurry?"

The clerk seemed to be troubled by something in what Gus had said. Then he looked up suddenly, obviously just realizing he'd been asked a direct question. "Huh?"

"You're not in any hurry, are you? Come on in; have a beer. Nobody's expected to be a ball of fire on a spring afternoon."

The clerk grinned uneasily. "No . . . nope, guess not." He brightened. "Okay! Don't mind if I do."

Gus ushered him into the house, grinning with pleasure. Nobody'd seen the inside of the place since he'd fixed it up; the clerk was the first visitor he'd had since moving in. There weren't even any deliverymen; Boonesboro was so small you had to drive in for your own shopping. There wasn't any mail carrier service, of course—not that Gus ever received any mail.

He showed the clerk into the living room. "Have a seat. I'll be right back." He went quickly out to the kitchen, took some beer out of the cooler, loaded a tray with glasses, a bowl of chips and pretzels, and the beer, and carried it out.

The clerk was up, looking around the library that covered two of the living-room walls.

Looking at his expression, Gus realized with genuine regret that the man wasn't the kind to doubt whether an obvious clod like Kusevic had read any of this stuff. A man like that could still be talked to, once the original misconceptions were knocked down. No, the clerk was too plainly mystified that a grown man would fool with books. Particularly a man like Gus; now, one of these kids that messed with college politics, that was something else. But a grown man oughtn't to act like that.

Gus saw it had been a mistake to expect anything of the clerk. He should have known better, whether he was hungry

for company or not. He'd *always* been hungry for company,
and it was time he realized, once and for all, that he just
plain wasn't going to find any.

He set the tray down on the table, uncapped a beer
quickly, and handed it to the man.

"Thanks," the clerk mumbled. He took a swallow, sighed
loudly, and wiped his mouth with the back of his hand. He
looked around the room again. "Cost you a lot to have all
this put in?"

Gus shrugged. "Did most of it myself. Built the shelves
and furniture; stuff like that. Some of the paintings I had to
buy, and the books and records."

The clerk grunted. He seemed to be considerably ill at
ease, probably because of the notice he'd brought, whatever it
was. Gus found himself wondering what it could possibly be,
but, now that he'd made the mistake of giving the man a
beer, he had to wait politely until it was finished before he
could ask.

He went over to the TV set. "Baseball fan?" he asked the
clerk.

"Sure!"

"Giants-Kodiaks ought to be on." He switched the set on
and pulled up a hassock, sitting on it so as not to get one of
the chairs dirty. The clerk wandered over and stood looking
at the screen, taking slow swallows of his beer.

The second game had started, and Halsey's familiar figure
appeared on the screen as the set warmed up. The lithe
young lefthander was throwing with his usual boneless motion, apparently not working hard at all, but the ball was
whipping past the batters with a sizzle that the home-plate
microphone was picking up clearly.

Gus nodded towards Halsey. "He's quite a pitcher, isn't
he?"

The clerk shrugged. "Guess so. Walker's their best man,
though."

Gus sighed as he realized he'd forgotten himself again. The
clerk wouldn't pay much attention to Halsey, naturally.

But he was getting a little irritated at the man, with his
typical preconceptions of what was proper and what wasn't,
of who had a right to grow roses and who didn't.

"Offhand," Gus said to the clerk, "could you tell me what
Halsey's record was, last year?"

The clerk shrugged. "Couldn't tell you. Wasn't bad—I
remember that much. Thirteen—seven, something like that."

Gus nodded to himself. "Uh-huh. How'd Walker do?"

"Walker! Why, man, Walker just won something like twenty-five games, that's all. And three no-hitters. How'd Walker do? Huh!"

Gus shook his head. "Walker's a good pitcher, all right—but he didn't pitch any no-hitters. And he only won eighteen games."

The clerk wrinkled his forehead. He opened his mouth to argue and then stopped. He looked like a sure-thing bettor who'd just realized that his memory had played him a trick.

"Say—I think you're right! Huh! Now what the Sam Hill made me think Walker was the guy? And you know something—I've been talking about him all winter, and nobody once called me wrong?" The clerk scratched his head. "Now, *somebody* pitched them games! Who the dickens was it?" He scowled in concentration.

Gus silently watched Halsey strike out his third batter in a row, and his face wrinkled into a slow smile. Halsey was still young; just hitting his stride. He threw himself into the game with all the energy and enjoyment a man felt when he realized he was at his peak, and that, out there on the mound in the sun, he was as good as any man who ever had gone before him in this profession.

Gus wondered how soon Halsey would see the trap he'd set for himself.

Because it wasn't a contest. Not for Halsey. For Christy Mathewson, it had been a contest. For Lefty Grove and Dizzy Dean, for Bob Feller and Slats Gould, it had been a contest. But for Halsey it was just a complicated form of solitaire that always came out right.

Pretty soon, Halsey'd realize that you can't handicap yourself at solitaire. If you knew where all the cards are, if you knew that unless you deliberately cheated against yourself, you couldn't help but win—what good was it? One of these days, Halsey'd realize there wasn't a game on earth he couldn't beat, whether it was a physical contest, organized and formally recognized as a game, or whether it was the billion-triggered pinball machine called Society.

What then, Halsey? What then? And if you find out, please, in the name of whatever kind of brotherhood we share, let me know.

The clerk grunted. "Well, it don't matter, I guess. I can always look it up in the record book at home."

Yes, you can, Gus commented silently. But you won't no

tice what it says, and, if you do, you'll forget it and never realize you've forgotten.

The clerk finished his beer, set it down on the tray, and was free to remember what he'd come here for. He looked around the room again, as though the memory were a cue of some kind.

"Lots of books," he commented.

Gus nodded, watching Halsey walk out to the pitcher's mound again.

"Uh ... you read 'em all?"

Gus shook his head.

"How about that one by that Miller fellow? I hear that's a pretty good one."

So. The clerk had a certain narrow interest in certain aspects of certain kinds of literature.

"I suppose it is," Gus answered truthfully. "I read the first three pages, once." And, having done so, he'd known how the rest of it was going to go, who would do what when, and he'd lost interest. The library had been a mistake, just one of a dozen similar experiments. If he'd wanted an academic familiarity with human literature, he could just as easily have picked it up by browsing through bookstores, rather than buying the books and doing substantially the same thing at home. He couldn't hope to extract any emotional empathies, no matter what he did.

Face it, though: rows of even useless books were better than bare wall. The trappings of culture were a bulwark of sorts, even though it was a learned culture and not a *felt* one, and meant no more to him than the culture of the Incas. Try as he might, he could never be an Inca. Nor even a Maya or an Aztec, or any kind of kin, except by the most tenuous of extensions.

But he had no culture of his own. There was the thing; the emptiness that nevertheless ached; the rootlessness, the complete absence of a place to stand and say, "This is my own."

Halsey struck out the first batter in the inning with three pitches. Then he put a slow floater precisely where the next man could get the best part of his bat on it, and did not even look up as the ball screamed out of the park. He struck out the next two men with a total of eight pitches.

Gus shook his head slowly. That was the first symptom; when you didn't bother to be subtle about your handicapping any more.

The clerk held out the envelope. "Here," he said brusquely,

having finally shilly-shallied his resolution up to the point of doing it despite his obvious nervousness at Gus's probable reaction.

Gus opened the envelope and read the notice. Then, just as the clerk had been doing, he looked around the room. A dark expression must have flickered over his face, because the clerk became even more hesitant.

"I . . . I want you to know I regret this. I guess all of us do."

Gus nodded hastily. "Sure, sure." He stood up and looked out the front window. He smiled crookedly, looking at the top dressing spread carefully over the painstakingly rolled lawn, which was slowly taking form on the plot where he had plowed last year and picked out pebbles, seeded and watered, shoveled topsoil, laid out flower beds . . . ah, there was no use going into that now. The whole plot, cottage and all, was condemned, and that was that.

"They're . . . they're turnin' the road into a twelve-lane freight highway," the clerk explained.

Gus nodded absently.

The clerk moved closer and dropped his voice. "Look—I was told to tell you this. Not in writin'." He sidled even closer, and actually looked around before he spoke. He laid his hand confidently on Gus's bare forearm.

"Any price you ask for," he muttered, "is gonna be okay, as long as you don't get too greedy. The county isn't paying this bill. Not even the state, if you get what I mean."

Gus got what he meant. Twelve-lane highways aren't built by anything but national governments.

He got more than that. National governments don't work this way unless there's a good reason.

"Highway between Hollister and Farnham?" he asked.

The clerk paled. "Don't know for sure," he muttered.

Gus smiled thinly. Let the clerk wonder how he'd guessed. It couldn't be much of a secret, anyway—not after the grade was laid out and the purpose became self-evident. Besides, the clerk wouldn't wonder very long.

A streak of complete perversity shot through Gus. He recognized its source in his anger at losing the cottage, but there was no reason why he shouldn't allow himself to cut loose.

"What's your name?" he asked the clerk abruptly.

"Uh . . . Harry Danvers."

"Well, Harry, suppose I told you I could stop that highway, if I wanted to? Suppose I told you that no bulldozer could get near this place without breaking down, that no shovel could dig this ground, that sticks of dynamite just plain wouldn't explode if they tried to blast? Suppose I told you that if they did put in the highway, it would turn soft as ice cream if I wanted it to, and run away like a river?"

"Huh?"

"Hand me your pen."

Danvers reached out mechanically and handed it to him. Gus put it between his palms and rolled it into a ball. He dropped it and caught it as it bounced up sharply from the soft, thick rug. He pulled it out between his fingers, and it returned to its cylindrical shape. He unscrewed the cap, flattened it out into a sheet between two fingers, scribbled on it, rolled it back into a cap, and, using his fingernail to draw out the ink which was now part of it, permanently inscribed Danvers's name just below the surface of the metal. Then he screwed the cap on again and handed the pen back to the county clerk. "Souvenir," he said.

The clerk looked down at it.

"Well?" Gus asked. "Aren't you curious about how I did it and what I am?"

The clerk shook his head. "Good trick. I guess you magician fellows must spend a lot of time practicing, huh? Can't say I could see myself spendin' that much working time on a hobby."

Gus nodded. "That's a good, sound, practical point of view," he said. Particularly when all of us automatically put out a field that damps curiosity, he thought. What point of view *could* you have?

He looked over the clerk's shoulder at the lawn, and one side of his mouth twisted sadly.

Only God can make a tree, he thought, looking at the shrubs and flower beds. Should we all, then, look for our challenge in landscape gardening? Should we become the gardeners of the rich humans in their expensive houses, driving up in our old, rusty trucks, oiling our lawnmowers, kneeling on the humans' lawns with our clipping shears, coming to the kitchen door to ask for a drink of water on a hot summer day?

The highway. Yes, he could stop the highway. Or make it go around him. There was no way of stopping the curiosity damper, any more than there was a way of willing his heart to stop, but it could be stepped up. He could force his mind to labor near overload, and no one would ever even *see* the cottage, the lawn, the rose arbor, or the battered old man, drinking his beer. Or rather, seeing them, would pay them absolutely no attention.

But the first time he went into town, or when he died, the field would be off, and then what? Then curiosity, then investigation, then perhaps a fragment of theory here or there to be fitted to another somewhere else. And then what? Pogrom?

He shook his head. The humans couldn't win, and would lose monstrously. *That* was why he couldn't leave the humans a clue. He had no taste for slaughtering sheep, and he doubted if his fellows did.

His fellows. Gus stretched his mouth. The only one he could be sure of was Halsey. There had to be others, but there was no way of finding them. They provoked no reaction from the humans; they left no trail to follow. It was only if they showed themselves, like Halsey, that they could be seen. There was, unfortunately, no private telepathic party line among them.

He wondered if Halsey hoped someone would notice him and get in touch. He wondered if Halsey even suspected there were others like himself. He wondered if anyone had noticed *him*, when Gus Kusevic's name had been in the papers occasionally.

It's the dawn of my race, he thought. The first generation—or is it, and does it matter?—and I wonder where the females are.

He turned back to the clerk. "I want what I paid for the place," he said. "No more."

The clerk's eyes widened slightly, then relaxed, and he shrugged. "Suit yourself. But if it was me, I'd soak the government good."

Yes, Gus thought; you doubtless would. But I don't want to, because you simply don't take candy from babies.

So the superman packed his bags and got out of the human's way. Gus choked a silent laugh. The damping field. The damping field. The thrice-cursed, ever-benevolent, foolproof, autonomic, protective damping field.

Evolution had, unfortunately, not yet realized that there was such a thing as human society. It produced a being with a certain modification from the human stock, thereby arriving at practical psi. In order to protect this feeble new species, whose members were so terribly sparse, it gave them the perfect camouflage.

Result: When young Augustin Kusevic was enrolled in school, it was discovered that he had no birth certificate. No hospital recalled his birth. As a matter of brutal fact, his human parents sometimes forgot his existence for days at a time.

Result: When young Gussie Kusevic tried to enter high school, it was discovered that he had never entered grammar school. No matter that he could quote teachers' names, textbooks, or classroom numbers. No matter if he could produce report cards. They were misfiled, and the anguished interviews forgotten. No one doubted his existence—people remembered the fact of his being, and the fact of his having acted and having been acted upon. But only as though they had read it in some infinitely boring book.

He had no friends, no girl, no past, no present, no love. He had no place to stand. Had there been such things as ghosts, he would have found his fellowship there.

By the time of his adolescence, he had discovered an absolute lack of involvement with the human race. He studied it, because it was the salient feature of his environment. He did not live with it. It said nothing to him that was of personal value; its motivations, morals, manners and morale did not find responsive reactions in him. And his, of course, made absolutely no impression on it.

The life of the peasant of ancient Babylon is of interest to only a few historical anthropologists, none of whom actually want to *be* Babylonian peasants.

Having solved the human social equation from his dispassionate viewpoint, and caring no more than the naturalist who finds that deer are extremely fond of green aspen leaves, he plunged into physical release. He discovered the thrill of picking fights and winning them; of *making* somebody pay attention to him by smashing his nose.

He might have become a permanent fixture on the Manhattan docks, if another longshoreman hadn't slashed him with a carton knife. The cultural demand on him had been plain. He'd had to kill the man.

That had been the end of unregulated personal combat. He discovered, not to his horror but to his disgust, that he could get away with murder. No investigation had been made; no search was attempted.

So that had been the end of that, but it had led him to the only possible evasion of the trap to which he had been born. Intellectual competition being meaningless, organized sports

became the only answer. Simultaneously regulating his efforts
and annotating them under a mound of journalistic record-
keeping, they furnished the first official continuity his life had
ever known. People still forgot his accomplishments, but
when they turned to records, his name was undeniably there.
A dossier can be misfiled. School records can disappear. But
something more than a damping field was required to shunt
aside the mountain of news copy and statistics that drags,
ball-like, at the ankle of even the mediocre athlete.

It seemed to Gus—and he thought of it a great deal—that
this chain of progression was inevitable for any male of his
kind. When, three years ago, he had discovered Halsey, his
hypothesis was bolstered. But what good was Halsey to another male? To hold mutual consolation sessions with? He
had no intention of ever contacting the man.

The clerk cleared his throat. Gus jerked his head around to
look at him, startled. He'd forgotten him.

"Well, guess I'll be going. Remember, you've only got two
months."

Gus gestured noncommittally. The man had delivered his
message. Why didn't he acknowledge he'd served his purpose,
and go?

Gus smiled ruefully. What purpose did *Homo nondescriptus*
serve, and where was he going? Halsey was already walking
downhill along the well-marked trail. Were there others? If
so, then they were in another rut, somewhere, and not even
the tops of their heads showed. He and his kind could recognize each other only by an elaborate process of elimination;
they had to watch for the people no one noticed.

He opened the door for the clerk, saw the road, and found
his thoughts back with the highway.

The highway would run from Hollister, which was a railroad junction, to the air force base at Farnham, where his
calculations in sociomathematics had long ago predicted the
first starship would be constructed and launched. The trucks
would rumble up the highway, feeding the open maw with
men and material.

He cleaned his lips. Up there in space, somewhere, somewhere outside the solar system, was another race. The imprint
of their visits here was plain. The humans would encounter
them, and again he could predict the result; the humans
would win.

Gus Kusevic could not go along to investigate the challenges that he doubted lay among the stars. Even with scrapbooks full of notices and clippings, he had barely made his career penetrate the public consciousness. Halsey, who had exuberantly broken every baseball record in the books, was known as a "pretty fair country pitcher."

What credentials could he present with his application to the air force? Who would remember them the next day if he had any? What would become of the records of his inoculations, his physical check-ups, his training courses? Who would remember to reserve a bunk for him, or stow supplies for him, or add his consumption to the total when the time came to allow for oxygen?

Stow away? Nothing easier. But, again, who would die so he could live within the tight lattice of shipboard economy? Which sheep would he slaughter, and to what useful purpose, in the last analysis?

"Well, so long," the clerk said.

"Goodbye," Gus said.

The clerk walked down the flagstones and out to his flivver.

I think, Gus said to himself, it would have been much better for us if evolution had been a little less protective and a little more thoughtful. An occasional pogrom wouldn't have done us any harm. A ghetto at least keeps the courtship problem solved.

Our seed has been spilled on the ground.

Suddenly, Gus ran forward, pushed by something he didn't care to name. He looked up through the flivver's open door, and the clerk looked down apprehensively.

"Danvers, you're a sports fan," Gus said hastily, realizing his voice was too urgent, that he was startling the clerk with his intensity.

"That's right," the clerk answered, pushing himself nervously back along the seat.

"Who's heavyweight champion of the world?"

"Mike Frazier. Why?"

"Who'd he beat for the title? Who used to be champion?"

The clerk pursed his lips. "Huh! It's been years. Gee, I don't know. I don't remember. I could look it up, I guess."

Gus exhaled slowly. He half-turned and looked back towards the cottage, the lawn, the flower beds, the walk, the arbor, and the fish pond under the willow tree. "Never mind," he said, and walked back into the house while the clerk wobbled his flivver into the air.

The TV set was blaring with sound. He checked the status of the game.

It had gone quickly. Halsey had pitched a one-hitter so far, and the Giants' pitcher had done almost as well. The score was tied at 1–1, the Giants were at bat, and it was the last out in the ninth inning. The camera zoomed in on Halsey's face.

Halsey looked at the batter with complete disinterest in his eyes, wound up, and threw the home-run ball.

Inferiority: The Complex Problem

Daniel Keyes (1927–   ) made his reputation with a single story, "Flowers for Algernon," which he later turned into a novel. It was a success in every form: The short story, published in *The Magazine of Fantasy and Science Fiction* for April 1959, won a Hugo and was dramatized on television by the Theater Guild; the novel version (1966) won a Nebula, made a twenty-best-novels-of-the-year list, was turned into the film *Charly* by Cliff Robertson (who won an Oscar for best actor in the title role), and became a dramatic musical entitled "Charlie and Algernon" that opened first in London, then in Washington, and finally on Broadway.

Keyes was born and grew up in Brooklyn, attended New York City public schools, and went to sea as a ship's purser on oil tankers at the age of seventeen. He returned to College in 1947, earned a B.A. degree from Brooklyn College, served for almost a year as associate editor of *Marvel Science Fiction* (a short-lived—five issues—magazine of 1951–52), had his first story, "Precedent," published there in 1952, went into the fashion photography business, and then accepted a position as a teacher at the high school from which he had been graduated ten years earlier.

While teaching and working on his fiction writing, he studied nights at Brooklyn College and in 1961 earned an M.A. degree in English and American literature. After he accepted a teaching position at Wayne State University, he turned "Flowers for Algernon" into a novel. In 1966 he joined the English faculty at Ohio University, where he teaches writing and American literature. His second novel,

The Touch, was published in 1968, his third, *The Fifth Sally,* in 1980, and his fourth, *The Minds of Billy Milligan,* in 1981.

"Flowers for Algernon" uses a diary format—Charlie's "progris riports"—that is almost as old as the English novel. It is an essential element of the story. Because the reader is allowed to share Charlie's thoughts as he sets down his experience and tells the story of his development from mental retardate to genius and its sequel, the reader receives the evidence of Charlie's changing mental abilities and perceptions as it is manifested—often before it is understood by Charlie. Part of the appeal of the story is the comparison of the reader's knowledge with Charlie's, and the reader's ability to see more in Charlie's reports than he knows is there.

On the other hand, the diary and its strict first-person viewpoint are totally subjective and totally limited. The reader cannot obtain any objective view of events, description, or experience; drama is eliminated; everything must be reported to the reader after the event and filtered through Charlie's consciousness and ability to express himself. But as in many restrictive methods, this method justifies itself.

"Flowers for Algernon" appears to deal with a familiar theme in science fiction: improvement of intelligence. The theme goes back at least as far as H. G. Wells's *The First Men in the Moon.* Pulp heroes of the 1930s, such as Doc Savage, often were described as having incredibly high IQs. E. E. "Doc" Smith's *Lensman* series used the improvement of intelligence, both by genetic breeding and training, as a crucial plot element. Bad sf stories and novels have linked the improvement of intelligence with the "mad scientist" motif. Stanley Weinbaum's *The New Adam* (1939) and Olaf Stapledon's *Odd John* (1935) used natural mutations as a means of achieving higher intelligence and dealt with the problems created by those who considered themselves inferior. Many superman stories, such as those of A. E. van Vogt, linked higher intelligence with other strange new abilities.

The difference between the treatments of the theme in these kinds of generic stories and in that by Keyes illustrates some of the ways in which mainstream stories differ from those that are more traditionally science fiction. "Flowers for Algernon" is only incidentally about increased intelligence; it is about comparative intelligence and the inabilities of people to handle differences without hurting each other. We are not expected to consider the operation as a realistic possibility:

the surgeon's manipulation is neither described nor justified; there's no reason to think that such an operation could accomplish such an end or that if it did it would reverse itself. The operation is a convention: Peter Phillips in his story "P-Plus" called it a "smart pill."

The question of what such an operation might mean to humanity is never considered. Charlie Gordon's ultimate fate militates against an exploration of the improved-intelligence theme. Except for a single paragraph where Charlie speculates about "the widespread use of [the surgical] technique," the only thematic use of Charlie's increased intelligence is to disprove the validity of his mentors' work and to predict his own prognosis. A more generic science fiction treatment might have considered the species-wide implications: What would increased intelligence do for the long-withheld secrets of the universe, the ills that plague humanity's bodies and minds, the evils of society, the problems of energy and pollution and war and space exploration . . . ? What would it mean for ethics and morals and religion?

But that is another story and one that Keyes did not choose to tell. He tells, instead, the story of Charlie Gordon, a story of classic reversal, of a humble man's rise to competence and success and his subsequent fate, a story that tells us about the way people behave and feel from one person's effort to cope with his unusual experience. One reason it appeals so broadly is that it deals primarily with people's feelings rather than with the examination of ideas that might change the way people live and even how they think. It is the traditional method of mainstream fiction.

Flowers for Algernon

by Daniel Keyes

progris riport 1
martch 5 1965

Dr. Strauss says I shud rite down what I think and every thing that happins to me from now on. I dont know why but he says its importint so they wil see if they will use me. I hope they use me. Miss Kinnian says maybe they can make me smart. I want to be smart. My name is Charlie Gordon, I am 37 years old and 2 weeks ago was my birthday. I have nuthing more to rite now so I will close for today.

progris riport 2
martch 6

I had a test today. I think I faled it. and I think that maybe now they wont use me. What happind is a nice young man was in the room and he had some white cards with ink spilled all over them. He sed Charlie what do you see on this card. I was very skared even tho I had my rabits foot in my pockit because when I was a kid I always faled tests in school and I spilled ink to.

I told him I saw a inkblot. He said yes and it made me feel good. I thot that was all but when I got up to go he stopped me. He said now sit down Charlie we are not thru yet. Then I dont remember so good but he wantid me to say what was in the ink. I dint see nuthing in the ink but he said there was picturs there other pepul saw some picturs. I couldnt see any picturs. I reely tryed to see. I held the card close up and then far away. Then I said if I had my glases I could see better I usually only ware my glases in the movies or TV but I said they are in the closit in the hall. I got them. Then I said let me see that card agen I bet Ill find it now.

I tryed hard but I still coudnt find the picturs I only saw the ink. I told him maybe I need new glases. He rote somthing down on a paper and I got skared of faling the test. I told him it was a very nice inkblot with littel points all around the eges. He looked very sad so that wasnt it. I said please let me try agen. Ill get it in a few minits becaus Im not so fast sometimes. Im a slow reeder too in Miss Kinnians class for slow adults but I'm trying very hard.

He gave me a chance with another card that had 2 kinds of ink spilled on it red and blue.

He was very nice and talked slow like Miss Kinnian does and he explaned it to me that it was a *raw shok*. He said pepul see things in the ink. I said show me where. He said think. I told him I think a inkblot but that wasnt rite eather. He said what does it remind you—pretend something. I closd my eyes for a long time to pretend. I told him I pretend a fowntan pen with ink leeking all over a table cloth. Then he got up and went out.

I dont think I passd the *raw shok* test.

progris riport 3
martch 7

Dr Strauss and Dr Nemur say it dont matter about the inkblots. I told them I dint spill the ink on the cards and I coudnt see anything in the ink. They said that maybe they will still use me. I said Miss Kinnian never gave me tests like that one only spelling and reading. They said Miss Kinnian told that I was her bestist pupil in the adult nite scool becaus I tryed the hardist and I reely wantid to lern. They said how come you went to the adult nite scool all by yourself Charlie. How did you find it. I said I askd pepul and sumbody told me where I shud go to lern to read and spell good. They said why did you want to. I told them becaus all my life I wantid to be smart and not dumb. But its very hard to be smart. They said you know it will probly be tempirery. I said yes. Miss Kinnian told me. I dont care if it herts.

Later I had more crazy tests today. The nice lady who gave it me told the name and I asked her how do you spellit so I can rite in my progris riport. THEMATIC APPERCEPTION TEST. I dont know the first 2 words but I know what *test* means. You got to pass it or you get bad marks. This *test* lookd easy becaus I coud see the picturs. Only this time she dint want me to tell her the picturs. That mixd me up. I said the man yesterday said I shoud tell him what I saw in the ink she said that dont make no difrence. She said make up storys about the pepul in the picturs.

I told her how can you tell storys about pepul you never met. I said why shud I make up lies. I never tell lies any more becaus I always get caut.

She told me this test and the other one the raw-shok was for getting personalty. I laffed so hard. I said how can you get that thing from inkblots and fotos. She got sore and put her picturs away. I dont care. It was silly. I gess I faled that test too.

Later some men in white coats took me to a difernt part of the hospitil and gave me a game to play. It was like a race with a white mouse. They called the mouse Algernon. Algernon was in a box with a lot of twists and turns like all kinds of walls and they gave me a pencil and a paper with lines and lots of boxes. On one side it said START and on the other end it said FINISH. They said it was *amazed* and that Algernon and me had the same *amazed* to do. I dint see how we could have the same *amazed* if Algernon had a box and I had a paper but I dint say nothing. Anyway there wasnt time because the race started.

One of the men had a watch he was trying to hide so I woudnt see it so I tryed not to look and that made me nervus.

Anyway that test made me feel worser than all the others because they did it over 10 times with difernt *amazeds*. and Algernon won every time. I dint know that mice were so smart. Maybe thats because Algernon is a white mouse. Maybe white mice are smarter then other mice.

progris riport 4
Mar 8

Their going to use me! Im so exited I can hardly write. Dr Nemur and Dr Strauss had a argament about it first. Dr Nemur was in the office when Dr Strauss brot me in. Dr Nemur was worryed about using me but Dr Strauss told him Miss Kinnian rekemmended me the best from all the people who she was teaching. I like Miss Kinnian becaus shes a very smart teacher. And she said Charlie your going to have a second chance. If you volenteer for this experament you mite get smart. They dont know if it will be perminint but theirs a chance. Thats why I said ok even when I was scared because she said it was an operashun. She said dont be scared Charlie you done so much with so little I think you deserv it most of all.

So I got scaird when Dr Nemur and Dr Strauss argud about it. Dr Strauss said I had something that was very good. He said I had a good *motor-vation*. I never even knew I had that. I felt proud when he said that not every body with an eye-q of 68 had that thing. I dont know what it is or where I got it but he said Algernon had it too. Algernons *motor-vation* is the cheese they put in his box. But it cant be that because I didnt eat any cheese this week.

Then he told Dr Nemur something I dint understand so while they were talking I wrote down some of the words.

He said Dr Nemur I know Charlie is not what you had in mind as the first of your new brede of intelek** (couldnt get the word) superman. But most people of his low ment** are host** and uncoop** they are usually dull apath** and hard to reach. He has a good natcher hes intristed and eager to please.

Dr Nemur said remember he will be the first human beeng ever to have his intelijence trippled by surgicle meens.

Dr Strauss said exackly. Look at how well hes lerned to read and write for his low mentel age its as grate an acheve** as you and I lerning einstines therey of **vity without help. That shows the intenss motor-vation. Its comparat** a tremen** achev** I say we use Charlie.

I dint get all the words and they were talking to fast but it sounded like Dr Strauss was on my side and like the other one wasnt.

Then Dr Nemur nodded he said all right maybe your right. We will use Charlie. When he said that I got so exited I jumped up and shook his hand for being so good to me. I told him thank you doc you wont be sorry for giving me a second chance. And I mean it like I told him. After the operashun Im gonna try to be smart. Im gonna try awful hard.

progris ript 5
Mar 10

Im skared. Lots of people who work here and the nurses and the people who gave me the tests came to bring me candy and wish me luck. I hope I have luck. I got my rabits foot and my lucky penny and my horse shoe. Only a black cat crossed me when I was comming to the hospitil. Dr Strauss says dont be supersitis Charlie this is sience. Anyway Im keeping my rabits foot with me.

I asked Dr Strauss if Ill beat Algernon in the race after the operashun and he said maybe. If the operashun works Ill show that mouse I can be as smart as he is. Maybe smarter. Then ill be abel to read better and spell the words good and know lots of things and be like other people. I want to be smart like other people. If it works perminint they will make everybody smart all over the wurld.

They dint give me anything to eat this morning. I dont know what that eating has to do with getting smart. Im very hungry and Dr Nemur took away my box of candy. That Dr Nemur is a grouch. Dr Strauss says I can have it back after the operashun. You cant eat befor a operashun . . .

Progress Report 6
Mar 15

The operashun dint hurt. He did it while I was sleeping. They took off the bandijis from my eyes and my head today so I can make a PROGRESS REPORT. Dr Nemur who looked at some of my other ones says I spell PROGRESS wrong and he told me how to spell it and REPORT too. I got to try and remember that.

I have a very bad memary for spelling. Dr Strauss says its ok to tell about all the things that happin to me but he says I shoud tell more about what I feel and what I think. When I told him I dont know how to think he said try. All the time when the bandijis were on my eyes I tryed to think. Nothing happened. I dont know what to think about. Maybe if I ask him he will tell me how I can think now that Im suppose to get smart. What do smart people think about. Fancy things I suppose. I wish I knew some fancy things alredy.

Progress Report 7
mar 19

Nothing is happining. I had lots of tests and different kind of races with Algernon. I hate that mouse. He always beats me. Dr Strauss said I got to play those games. And he said some time I got to take those tests over again. Those inkblc are stupid. And those pictures are stupid too. I like to draw a picture of a man and a woman but I wont make up lies about people.

I got a headache from trying to think so much. I thot Dr Strauss was my frend but he dont help me. He dont tell me what to think or when Ill get smart. Miss Kinnian dint come to see me. I think writing these progress reports are stupid too.

Progress Report 8
Mar 23

Im going back to work at the factery. They said it was better I shud go back to work but I cant tell anyone what the operashun was for and I have to come to the hospitil for an hour evry night after work. They are gonna pay me money every month for lerning to be smart.

Im glad Im going back to work because I miss my job and all my frends and all the fun we have there.

Dr Strauss says I shud keep writing things down but I dont have to do it every day just when I think of something or something speshul happins. He says dont get discoridged because it takes time and it happins slow. He says it took a long time with Algernon before he got 3 times smarter than he was before. Thats why Algernon beats me all the time because he had that operashun too. That makes me feel better. I coud probly do that *amazed* faster than a reglar mouse. Maybe someday Ill beat Algernon. Boy that would be something. So far Algernon looks like he mite be smart perminent.

Mar 25 (I dont have to write PROGRESS REPORT on top any more just when I hand it in once a week for Dr Nemur to read. I just have to put the date on. That saves time)

We had a lot of fun at the factery today. Joe Carp said hey look where Charlie had his operashun what did they do Charlie put some brains in. I was going to tell him but I remembered Dr Strauss said no. Then Frank Reilly said what did you do Charlie forget your key and open your door the hard way. That made me laff. Their really my friends and they like me.

Sometimes somebody will say hey look at Joe or Frank or George he really pulled a Charlie Gordon. I dont know why they say that but they always laff. This morning Amos Borg who is the 4 man at Donnegans used my name when he shouted at Ernie the office boy. Ernie lost a packige. He said Ernie for godsake what are you trying to be a Charlie Gordon. I dont understand why he said that. I never lost any packiges.

Mar 28   Dr Strauss came to my room tonight to see why I dint come in like I was suppose to. I told him I dont like to race with Algernon any more. He said I dont have to for a while but I shud come in. He had a present for me only it wasnt a present but just for lend. I thot it was a little television but it wasnt. He said I got to turn it on when I go to sleep. I said your kidding why shud I turn it on when Im going to sleep. Who ever herd of a thing like that. But he said if I want to get smart I got to do what he says. I told him I dint think I was going to get smart and he put his hand on my sholder and said Charlie you dont know it yet but your getting smarter all the time. You wont notice for a while. I think he was just being nice to make me feel good because I dont look any smarter.

Oh yes I almost forgot. I asked him when I can go back to the class at Miss Kinnians school. He said I wont go their. He said that soon Miss Kinnian will come to the hospitil to start and teach me speshul. I was mad at her for not comming to see me when I got the operashun but I like her so maybe we will be frends again.

Mar 29   That crazy TV kept me up all night. How can I sleep with something yelling crazy things all night in my ears. And the nutty pictures. Wow. I dont know what it says when Im up so how am I going to know when Im sleeping.

Dr Strauss says its ok. He says my brains are lerning when I sleep and that will help me when Miss Kinnian starts my lessons in the hospitil (only I found out it isnt a hospitil its a labatory). I think its all crazy. If you can get smart when your sleeping why do people go to school. That thing I dont think will work. I use to watch the late show and the late late show on TV all the time and it never made me smart. Maybe you have to sleep while you watch it.

PROGRESS REPORT 9 — April 3

Dr Strauss showed me how to keep the TV turned low so now I can sleep. I dont hear a thing. And I still dont understand what it says. A few times I play it over in the morning to find out what I lerned when I was sleeping and I dont think so. Miss Kinnian says Maybe its another langwidge or something. But most times it sounds american. It talks so fast faster then even Miss Gold who was my teacher in 6 grade and I remember she talked so fast I coudnt understand her.

I told Dr Strauss what good is it to get smart in my sleep. I want to be smart when Im awake. He says its the same thing and I have two minds. Theres the *subconscious* and the *conscious* (thats how you spell it). And one dont tell the other one what its doing. They dont even talk to each other. Thats why I dream. And boy have I been having crazy dreams. Wow, Ever since that night TV. The late late late late late show.

I forgot to ask him if it was only me or if everybody had those two minds.

(I just looked up the word in the dictionary Dr Strauss gave me. The word is *subconscious. adj. Of the nature of mental operations yet not present in consciousness; as, sub-conscious conflict of desires.*) Theres more but I still don't know what it means. This isnt a very good dictionary for dumb people like me.

Anyway the headache is from the party. My frends from the factery Joe Carp and Frank Reilly invited me to go with them to Muggsys Saloon for some drinks. I dont like to drink but they said we will have lots of fun. I had a good time.

Joe Carp said I shoud show the girls how I mop out the toilet in the factory and he got me a mop. I showed them and everyone laffed when I told that Mr Donnegan said I was the best janiter he ever had because I like my job and do it good and never come late or miss a day except for my operashun.

I said Miss Kinnian always said Charlie be proud of your job because you do it good.

Everybody laffed and we had a good time and they gave me lots of drinks and Joe said Charlie is a card when hes potted. I dont know what that means but everybody likes me and we have fun. I cant wait to be smart like my best frends Joe Carp and Frank Reilly.

I dont remember how the party was over but I think I went out to buy a newspaper and coffe for Joe and Frank and when I came back there was no one their. I looked for them all over till late. Then I dont remember so good but I think I got sleepy or sick. A nice cop brot me back home. Thats what my landlady Mrs Flynn says.

But I got a headache and a big lump on my head and black and blue all over. I think maybe I fell but Joe Carp says it was the cop they beat up drunks some times. I don't think so. Miss Kinnian says cops are to help people. Any way I got a bad headache and Im sick and hurt all over. I dont think Ill drink anymore.

April 6 I beat Algernon! I dint even know I beat him until Burt the tester told me. Then the second time I lost because I got so exited I fell off the chair before I finished. But after that I beat him 8 more times. I must be getting smart to beat a smart mouse like Algernon. But I dont *feel* smarter.

I wanted to race Algernon some more but Burt said thats enough for one day. They let me hold him for a minit. Hes not so bad. Hes soft like a ball of cotton. He blinks and when he opens his eyes their black and pink on the eges.

I said can I feed him because I felt bad to beat him and I wanted to be nice and make frends. Burt said no Algernon is a very specshul mouse with an operashun like mine, and he was the first of all the animals to stay smart so long. He told me Algernon is so smart that every day he has to solve a test to get his food. Its a thing like a lock on a door that changes every time Algernon goes in to eat so he has to lern something new to get his food. That made me sad because if he coudnt lern he woud be hungry.

I dont think its right to make you pass a test to eat. How woud Dr Nemur like to have to pass a test every time he wants to eat. I think Ill be frends with Algernon.

April 9   Tonight after work Miss Kinnian was at the laboratory. She looked like she was glad to see me but scared. I told her dont worry Miss Kinnian Im not smart yet and she laffed. She said I have confidence in you Charlie the way you struggled so hard to read and right better than all the others. At werst you will have it for a littel wile and your doing something for sience.

We are reading a very hard book. I never read such a hard book before. Its called *Robinson Crusoe* about a man who gets merooned on a dessert iland. Hes smart and figers out all kinds of things so he can have a house and food and hes a good swimmer. Only I feel sorry because hes all alone and has no frends. But I think their must be somebody else on the iland because theres a picture with his funny umbrella looking at footprints. I hope he gets a frend and not be lonly.

April 10   Miss Kinnian teaches me to spell better. She says look at a word and close your eyes and say it over and over until you remember. I have lots of truble with *through* that you say *threw* and *enough* and *tough* that you dont say *enew* and *tew*. You got to say *enuff* and *tuff*. Thats how I use to write it before I started to get smart. Im confused but Miss Kinnian says theres no reason in spelling.

Apr 14   Finished *Robinson Crusoe*. I want to find out more about what happens to him but Miss Kinnian says thats all there is. *Why.*

Apr 15   Miss Kinnian says Im lerning fast. She read some of the Progress Reports and she looked at me kind of funny. She says Im a fine person and Ill show them all. I asked her why. She said never mind but I shoudnt feel bad if I find out that everybody isnt nice like I think. She said for a person who god gave so little to you done more then a lot of people with brains they never even used. I said all my frends are smart people but there good. They like me and they never did anything that wasnt nice. Then she got something in her eye and she had to run out to the ladys room.

Apr 16   Today, I lerned, the *comma,* this is a comma (,) a period, with a tail, Miss Kinnian, says its importent, because, it makes writing, better, she said, somebody, coud lose, a lot of money, if a comma, isnt, in the, right place, I dont have, any money, and I dont see, how a comma, keeps you, from losing it,

But she says, everybody, uses commas, so Ill use, them too,

Apr 17   I used the comma wrong. Miss Kinnian told me to look up long words in the dictionary to lern to spell them. I said whats the difference if you can read it anyway. She said its part of your education so now on Ill look up the words Im not sure how to spell. It takes a long time to write that way but I think Im remembering. I only have to look up once and after that I get it right. Anyway that how come I got the word *punctuation* right. (Its that way in the dictionary). Miss Kinnian says a period is punctuation too, and there are lots of other marks to lern. I told her I thot all the periods had to have tails but she said no.

You got to mix them up, she showed? me" how. to mix! them(up,. and now; I can! mix up all kinds" of punctuation, in! my writing? There, are lots! of rules? to lern; but Im gettin'g them in my head.

One thing I? like about, Dear Miss Kinnian: (thats the way it goes in a business letter if I ever go into business) is she, always gives me' a reason" when—I ask. She's a gen'ius! I wish! I cou'd be smart" like, her;

(Punctuation, is; fun!)

April 18   What a dope I am! I didn't even understand what she was talking about. I read the grammar book last night and it explanes the whole thing. Then I saw it was the same way as Miss Kinnian was trying to tell me, but I didn't get it. I got up in the middle of the night, and the whole thing straightened out in my mind.

Miss Kinnian said that the TV working in my sleep helped

out. She said I reached a plateau. Thats like the flat top of a
hill.

After I figgered out how punctuation worked, I read over
all my old Progress Reports from the beginning. Boy, did I
have crazy spelling and punctuation! I told Miss Kinnian I
ought to go over the pages and fix all the mistakes but she
said, "No, Charlie, Dr. Nemur wants them just as they are.
That's why he let you keep them after they were photostated,
to see your own progress. You're coming along fast, Charlie."

That made me feel good. After the lesson I went down and
played with Algernon. We don't race any more.

April 20 I feel sick. Not sick like for a doctor, but inside
my chest it feels empty like getting punched and a heartburn
at the same time.

I wasn't going to write about it, but I guess I got to, because it's important. Today was the first time I ever stayed
home from work.

Last night Joe Carp and Frank Reilly invited me to a
party. There were lots of girls and some men from the factory. I remembered how sick I got last time I drank too
much, so I told Joe I didn't want anything to drink. He gave
me a plain Coke instead. It tasted funny, but I thought it was
just a bad taste in my mouth.

We had a lot of fun for a while. Joe said I should dance
with Ellen and she would teach me the steps. I fell a few
times and I couldn't understand why because no one else was
dancing besides Ellen and me. And all the time I was tripping
because somebody's foot was always sticking out.

Then when I got up I saw the look on Joe's face and it
gave me a funny feeling in my stomach. "He's a scream,"
one of the girls said. Everybody was laughing.

Frank said, "I ain't laughed so much since we sent him off
for the newspaper that night at Muggsy's and ditched him."

"Look at him. His face is red."

"He's blushing. Charlie is blushing."

"Hey, Ellen, what'd you do to Charlie? I never saw him
act like that before."

I didn't know what to do or where to turn. Everyone was
looking at me and laughing and I felt naked. I wanted to
hide myself. I ran out into the street and I threw up. Then I
walked home. It's a funny thing I never knew that Joe and
Frank and the others liked to have me around all the time to
make fun of me.

Now I know what it means when they say "to pull a Charlie Gordon."

I'm ashamed.

PROGRESS REPORT 11

April 21 Still didn't go into the factory. I told Mrs. Flynn
my landlady to call and tell Mr. Donnegan I was sick. Mrs.
Flynn looks at me very funny lately like she's scared of me.

I think it's a good thing about finding out how everybody
laughs at me. I thought about it a lot. It's because I'm so
dumb and I don't even know when I'm doing something
dumb. People think it's funny when a dumb person can't do
things the same way they can.

Anyway, now I know I'm getting smarter every day. I
know punctuation and I can spell good. I like to look up all
the hard words in the dictionary and I remember them. I'm
reading a lot now, and Miss Kinnian says I read very fast.
Sometimes I even understand what I'm reading about, and it
stays in my mind. There are times when I can close my eyes
and think of a page and it all comes back like a picture.

Besides history, geography, and arithmetic, Miss Kinnian
said I should start to learn a few foreign languages. Dr.
Strauss gave me some more tapes to play while I sleep. I still
don't understand how that conscious and unconscious mind
works, but Dr. Strauss says not to worry yet. He asked me to
promise that when I start learning college subjects next week
I wouldn't read any books on psychology—that is, until he
gives me permission.

I feel a lot better today, but I guess I'm still a little angry
that all the time people were laughing and making fun of me
because I wasn't so smart. When I become intelligent like Dr.
Strauss says, with three times my I.Q. of 68, then maybe I'll
be like everyone else and people will like me and be friendly.

I'm not sure what an I.Q. is. Dr. Nemur said it was something that measured how intelligent you were—like a scale in
the drugstore weighs pounds. But Dr. Strauss had a big argument with him and said an I.Q. didn't weigh intelligence at
all. He said an I.Q. showed how much intelligence you could
get, like the numbers on the outside of a measuring cup. You
still had to fill the cup up with stuff.

Then when I asked Burt, who gives me my intelligence
tests and works with Algernon, he said that both of them
were wrong (only I had to promise not to tell them he said

so). Burt says that the I.Q. measures a lot of different things including some of the things you learned already, and it really isn't any good at all.

So I still don't know what I.Q. is except that mine is going to be over 200 soon. I didn't want to say anything, but I don't see how if they don't know *what* it is, or *where* it is—I don't see how they know *how much* of it you've got.

Dr. Nemur says I have to take a *Rorschach Test* tomorrow. I wonder what *that* is.

April 22 I found out what a *Rorschach* is. It's the test I took before the operation—the one with the inkblots on the pieces of cardboard. The man who gave me the test was the same one.

I was scared to death of those inkblots. I knew he was going to ask me to find the pictures and I knew I wouldn't be able to. I was thinking to myself, if only there was some way of knowing what kind of pictures were hidden there. Maybe there weren't any pictures at all. Maybe it was just a trick to see if I was dumb enough to look for something that wasn't there. Just thinking about that made me sore at him.

"All right, Charlie," he said, "you've seen these cards before, remember?"

"Of course I remember."

The way I said it, he knew I was angry, and he looked surprised. "Yes, of course, Now I want you to look at this one. What might this be? What do you see on this card? People see all sorts of things in these inkblots. Tell me what it might be for you—what it makes you think of."

I was shocked. That wasn't what I had expected him to say at all. "You mean there are no pictures hidden in those inkblots?"

He frowned and took off his glasses. "What?"

"Pictures. Hidden in the inkblots. Last time you told me that everyone could see them and you wanted me to find them too."

He explained to me that the last time he had used almost the exact same words he was using now. I didn't believe it, and I still have the suspicion that he misled me at the time just for the fun of it. Unless—I don't know any more—could I have been *that* feeble-minded?

We went through the cards slowly. One of them looked like a pair of bats tugging at something. Another one looked like two men fencing with swords. I imagined all sorts of things. I guess I got carried away. But I didn't trust him any more, and I kept turning them around and even looking on the back to see if there was anything there I was supposed to catch. While he was making his notes, I peeked out of the corner of my eye to read it. But it was all in code that looked like this:

WF + A DdF-Ad orig. WF-A SF + o b j

The test still doesn't make sense to me. It seems to me that anyone could make up lies about things that they didn't really see. How could he know I wasn't making a fool of him by mentioning things that I didn't really imagine? Maybe I'll understand it when Dr. Strauss lets me read up on psychology.

April 25 I figured out a new way to line up the machines in the factory, and Mr. Donnegan says it will save him ten thousand dollars a year in labor and increased production. He gave me a twenty-five-dollar bonus.

I wanted to take Joe Carp and Frank Reilly out to lunch to celebrate, but Joe said he had to buy some things for his wife, and Frank said he was meeting his cousin for lunch. I guess it'll take a little time for them to get used to the changes in me. Everybody seems to be frightened of me. When I went over to Amos Borg and tapped him on the shoulder, he jumped up in the air.

People don't talk to me much any more or kid around the way they used to. It makes the job kind of lonely.

April 27 I got up the nerve today to ask Miss Kinnian to have dinner with me tomorrow night to celebrate my bonus.

At first she wasn't sure it was right, but I asked Dr. Strauss and he said it was okay. Dr. Strauss and Dr. Nemur don't seem to be getting along so well. They're arguing all the time. This evening when I came in to ask Dr. Strauss about having dinner with Miss Kinnian, I heard them shouting. Dr. Nemur was saying that it was *his* experiment and *his* research, and Dr. Strauss was shouting back that he contributed just as much, because he found me through Miss Kinnian and he performed the operation. Dr. Strauss said that someday thousands of neurosurgeons might be using his technique all over the world.

Dr. Nemur wanted to publish the results of the experiment at the end of this month. Dr. Strauss wanted to wait a while longer to be sure. Dr. Strauss said that Dr. Nemur was more interested in the Chair of Psychology at Princeton than he was in the experiment. Dr. Nemur said that Dr. Strauss was nothing but an opportunist who was trying to ride to glory on *his* coattails.

When I left afterwards, I found myself trembling. I don't know why for sure, but it was as if I'd seen both men clearly for the first time. I remember hearing Burt say that Dr. Nemur had a shrew of a wife who was pushing him all the time to get things published so that he could become famous. Burt said that the dream of her life was to have a big-shot husband.

Was Dr. Strauss really trying to ride on his coattails?

April 28 I don't understand why I never noticed how beautiful Miss Kinnian really is. She has brown eyes and feathery brown hair that comes to the top of her neck. She's only thirty-four! I think from the beginning I had the feeling that she was an unreachable genius—and very, very old. Now, every time I see her she grows younger and more lovely.

We had dinner and a long talk. When she said that I was coming along so fast that soon I'd be leaving her behind, I laughed.

"It's true, Charlie. You're already a better reader than I am. You can read a whole page at a glance while I can take in only a few lines at a time. And you remember every single thing you read. I'm lucky if I can recall the main thoughts and the general meaning."

"I don't feel intelligent. There are so many things I don't understand."

She took out a cigarette and I lit it for her. "You've got to be a *little* patient. You're accomplishing in days and weeks what it takes normal people to do in half a lifetime. That's what makes it so amazing. You're like a giant sponge now, soaking things in. Facts, figures, general knowledge. And soon you'll begin to connect them, too. You'll see how the different branches of learning are related. There are many levels, Charlie, like steps on a giant ladder that take you up higher and higher to see more and more of the world around you.

"I can see only a little bit of that, Charlie, and I won't go much higher than I am now, but you'll keep climbing up and up, and see more and more, and each step will open new worlds that you never even knew existed." She frowned. "I hope . . . I just hope to God—"

"What?"

"Never mind, Charles. I just hope I wasn't wrong to advise you to go into this in the first place."

I laughed. "How could that be? It worked, didn't it? Even Algernon is still smart."

We sat there silently for a while and I knew what she was thinking about as she watched me toying with the chain of my rabbit's foot and my keys. I didn't want to think of that possibility any more than elderly people want to think of death. I *knew* that this was only the beginning. I knew what she meant about levels because I'd seen some of them already. The thought of leaving her behind made me sad.

I'm in love with Miss Kinnian.

PROGRESS REPORT 12

April 30   I've quit my job with Donnegan's Plastic Box Company. Mr. Donnegan insisted that it would be better for all concerned if I left. What did I do to make them hate me so?

The first I knew of it was when Mr. Donnegan showed me the petition. Eight hundred and forty names, everyone connected with the factory, except Fanny Girden. Scanning the list quickly, I saw at once that hers was the only missing name. All the rest demanded that I be fired.

Joe Carp and Frank Reilly wouldn't talk to me about it. No one else would either, except Fanny. She was one of the few people I'd known who set her mind to something and believed it no matter what the rest of the world proved, said, or did—and Fanny did not believe that I should have been fired. She had been against the petition on principle and despite the pressure and threats she'd held out.

"Which don't mean to say," she remarked, "that I don't think there's something mighty strange about you, Charlie. Them changes, I don't know. You used to be a good, dependable, ordinary man—not too bright maybe, but honest. Who knows what you done to yourself to get so smart all of a sudden. Like everybody around here's been saying, Charlie, it's not right."

"But how can you say that, Fanny? What's wrong with a man becoming intelligent and wanting to acquire knowledge and understanding of the world around him?"

She stared down at her work and I turned to leave. Without looking at me, she said: "It was evil when Eve listened to the snake and ate from the tree of knowledge. It was evil when she saw that she was naked. If not for that none of us would ever have to grow old and sick, and die."

Once again now I have the feeling of shame burning inside me. This intelligence has driven a wedge between me and all the people I once knew and loved. Before, they laughed at me and despised me for my ignorance and dullness; now, they hate me for my knowledge and understanding. What in God's name do they want of me?

They've driven me out of the factory. Now I'm more alone than ever before. . . .

May 15 Dr. Strauss is very angry at me for not having written any progress reports in two weeks. He's justified because the lab is now paying me a regular salary. I told him I was too busy thinking and reading. When I pointed out that writing was such a slow process that it made me impatient with my poor handwriting, he suggested that I learn to type. It's much easier to write now because I can type nearly seventy-five words a minute. Dr. Strauss continually reminds me of the need to speak and write simply so that people will be able to understand me.

I'll try to review all the things that happened to me during the last two weeks. Algernon and I were presented to the American Psychological Association sitting in convention with the World Psychological Association last Tuesday. We created quite a sensation. Dr. Nemur and Dr. Strauss were proud of us.

I suspect that Dr. Nemur, who is sixty—ten years older than Dr. Strauss—finds it necessary to see tangible results of his work. Undoubtedly the result of pressure by Mrs. Nemur.

Contrary to my earlier impressions of him, I realize that Dr. Nemur is not at all a genius. He has a very good mind, but it struggles under the specter of self-doubt. He wants people to take him for a genius. Therefore, it is important for him to feel that his work is accepted by the world. I believe that Dr. Nemur was afraid of further delay because he worried that someone else might make a discovery along these lines and take the credit from him.

Dr. Strauss on the other hand might be called a genius, although I feel that his areas of knowledge are too limited. He was educated in the tradition of narrow specialization; the broader aspects of background were neglected far more than necessary—even for a neurosurgeon.

I was shocked to learn that the only ancient languages he could read were Latin, Greek, and Hebrew, and that he knows almost nothing of mathematics beyond the elementary levels of the calculus of variations. When he admitted this to me, I found myself almost annoyed. It was as if he'd hidden this part of himself in order to deceive me, pretending—as do many people, I've discovered—to be what he is not. No one I've ever known is what he appears to be on the surface.

Dr. Nemur appears to be uncomfortable around me. Sometimes when I try to talk to him, he just looks at me strangely and turns away. I was angry at first when Dr. Strauss told me I was giving Dr. Nemur an inferiority complex. I thought he was mocking me and I'm oversensitive at being made fun of.

How was I to know that a highly respected psychoexperimentalist like Nemur was unacquainted with Hindustani and Chinese? It's absurd when you consider the work that is being done in India and China today in the very field of his study.

I asked Dr. Strauss how Nemur could refute Rahajamati's attack on his method and results if Nemur couldn't even read them in the first place. That strange look on Dr. Strauss' face can mean only one of two things. Either he doesn't want to tell Nemur what they're saying in India, or else—and this worries me—Dr. Strauss doesn't know either. I must be careful to speak and write clearly and simply so that people won't laugh.

May 18 I am very disturbed. I saw Miss Kinnian last night for the first time in over a week. I tried to avoid all discussions of intellectual concepts and to keep the conversation on a simple, everyday level, but she just stared at me blankly and asked me what I meant about the mathematical variance equivalent in Dorbermann's *Fifth Concerto*.

When I tried to explain she stopped me and laughed. I guess I got angry, but I suspect I'm approaching her on the wrong level. No matter what I try to discuss with her, I am unable to communicate. I must review Vrostadt's equations on *Levels of Semantic Progression*. I find that I don't communicate with people much any more. Thank God for books and music and things I can think about. I am alone in my apartment at Mrs. Flynn's boardinghouse most of the time and seldom speak to anyone.

May 20   I would not have noticed the new dishwasher, a boy of about sixteen, at the corner diner where I take my evening meals if not for the incident of the broken dishes.

They crashed to the floor, shattering and sending bits of white china under the tables. The boy stood there dazed and frightened, holding the empty tray in his hand. The whistles and catcalls from the customers (the cries of "hey, there go the profits!" . . . *"Mazeltov!"* . . . and "Well, *he* didn't work here very long . . ." which invariably seems to follow the breaking of glass or dishware in a public restaurant) all seemed to confuse him.

When the owner came to see what the excitement was about, the boy cowered as if he expected to be struck and threw up his arms as if to ward off the blow.

"All right! All right, you dope," shouted the owner, "don't just stand there! Get the broom and sweep that mess up. A broom . . . a broom, you idiot! It's in the kitchen. Sweep up all the pieces."

The boy saw that he was not going to be punished. His frightened expression disappeared and he smiled and hummed as he came back with the broom to sweep the floor. A few of the rowdier customers kept up the remarks, amusing themselves at his expense.

"Here, sonny, over here there's a nice piece behind you . . ."

"C'mon, do it again . . ."

"He's not so dumb. It's easier to break 'em than to wash 'em . . ."

As his vacant eyes moved across the crowd of amused onlookers, he slowly mirrored their smiles and finally broke into an uncertain grin at the joke which he obviously did not understand.

I felt sick inside as I looked at his dull, vacuous smile, the wide, bright eyes of a child, uncertain but eager to please. They were laughing at him because he was mentally retarded.

And I had been laughing at him too.

Suddenly, I was furious at myself and all those who were smirking at him. I jumped up and shouted, "Shut up! Leave him alone! It's not his fault he can't understand! He can't help what he is! But for God's sake . . . he's still a human being!"

The room grew silent. I cursed myself for losing control and creating a scene. I tried not to look at the boy as I paid my check and walked out without touching my food. I felt ashamed for both of us.

How strange it is that people of honest feelings and sensibility, who would not take advantage of a man born without arms or legs or eyes—how such people think nothing of abusing a man born with low intelligence. It infuriated me to think that not too long ago I, like this boy, had foolishly played the clown.

And I had almost forgotten.

I'd hidden the picture of the old Charlie Gordon from myself because now that I was intelligent it was something that had to be pushed out of my mind. But today in looking at that boy, for the first time I saw what I had been. *I was just like him!*

Only a short time ago, I learned that people laughed at me. Now I can see that unknowingly I joined with them in laughing at myself. That hurts most of all.

I have often reread my progress reports and seen the illiteracy, the childish naïveté, the mind of low intelligence peering from a dark room, through the keyhole, at the dazzling light outside. I see that even in my dullness I knew that I was inferior, and that other people had something I lacked—something denied me. In my mental blindness, I thought that it was somehow connected with the ability to read and write, and I was sure that if I could get those skills I would automatically have intelligence too.

Even a feeble-minded man wants to be like other men.

A child may not know how to feed itself, or what to eat, yet it knows of hunger.

This then is what I was like. I never knew. Even with my gift of intellectual awareness, I never really knew.

This day was good for me. Seeing the past more clearly, I have decided to use my knowledge and skills to work in the field of increasing human intelligence levels. Who is better equipped for this work? Who else has lived in both worlds? These are my people. Let me use my gift to do something for them.

Tomorrow, I will discuss with Dr. Strauss the manner in which I can work in this area. I may be able to help him work out the problems of widespread use of the technique which was used on me. I have several good ideas of my own.

There is so much that might be done with this technique. If I could be made into a genius, what about thousands of others like myself? What fantastic levels might be achieved by using this technique on normal people? On *geniuses?*

There are so many doors to open. I am impatient to begin.

PROGRESS REPORT 13

May 23   It happened today. Algernon bit me. I visited the lab to see him as I do occasionally, and when I took him out of his cage, he snapped at my hand. I put him back and watched him for a while. He was unusually disturbed and vicious.

May 24   Burt, who is in charge of the experimental animals, tells me that Algernon is changing. He is less cooperative; he refuses to run the maze any more; general motivation has decreased. And he hasn't been eating. Everyone is upset about what this may mean.

May 25   They've been feeding Algernon, who now refuses to work the shifting-lock problem. Everyone identifies me with Algernon. In a way we're both the first of our kind. They're all pretending that Algernon's behavior is not necessarily significant for me. But it's hard to hide the fact that some of the other animals who were used in this experiment are showing strange behavior.

Dr. Strauss and Dr. Nemur have asked me not to come to the lab any more. I know what they're thinking but I can't accept it. I am going ahead with my plans to carry their research forward. With all due respect to both of these fine scientists, I am well aware of their limitations. If there is an answer, I'll have to find it out for myself. Suddenly, time has become very important to me.

May 29   I have been given a lab of my own and permission to go ahead with the research. I'm on to something. Working day and night. I've had a cot moved into the lab. Most of my writing time is spent on the notes which I keep in a separate folder, but from time to time I feel it necessary to put down my moods and my thoughts out of sheer habit.

I find the *calculus of intelligence* to be a fascinating study. Here is the place for the application of all the knowledge I have acquired. In a sense it's the problem I've been concerned with all my life.

May 31   Dr. Strauss thinks I'm working too hard. Dr. Nemur says I'm trying to cram a lifetime of research and thought into a few weeks. I know I should rest, but I'm driven on by something inside that won't let me stop. I've got to find the reason for the sharp regression in Algernon. I've got to know *if* and *when* it will happen to me.

June 4

LETTER TO DR. STRAUSS *(copy)*

Under separate cover I am sending you a copy of my report entitled "The Algernon-Gordon Effect: A Study of Structure and Function of Increased Intelligence," which I would like to have you read and have published.

As you see, my experiments are completed. I have included in my report all of my formulae, as well as mathematical analysis in the appendix. Of course, these should be verified.

Because of its importance to both you and Dr. Nemur (and need I say to myself, too?) I have checked and rechecked my results a dozen times in the hope of finding an error. I am sorry to say the results must stand. Yet for the sake of science, I am grateful for the little bit that I here add to the knowledge of the function of the human mind and of the laws governing the artificial increase of human intelligence.

I recall your once saying to me that an experimental *failure* or the *disproving* of a theory was as important to the advancement of learning as a success would be. I know now that this is true. I am sorry, however, that my own contribution to the field must rest upon the ashes of the work of two men I regard so highly.

> Yours truly,
> Charles Gordon

encl.: rept.

June 5 I must not become emotional. The facts and the results of my experiments are clear, and the more sensational aspects of my own rapid climb cannot obscure the fact that the tripling of intelligence by the surgical technique developed by Drs. Strauss and Nemur must be viewed as having little or no practical applicability (at the present time) to the increase of human intelligence.

As I review the records and data on Algernon, I see that although he is still in his physical infancy, he has regressed mentally. Motor activity is impaired; there is a general reduction of glandular activity; there is an accelerated loss of coordination.

There are also strong indications of progressive amnesia.

As will be seen by my report, these and other physical and mental deterioration syndromes can be predicted with statistically significant results by the application of my formula.

The surgical stimulus to which we were both subjected has resulted in an intensification and acceleration of all mental processes. The unforeseen development, which I have taken the liberty of calling the *Algernon-Gordon Effect,* is the logical extension of the entire intelligence speed-up. The hypothesis here proven may be described simply in the following terms: Artifically increased intelligence deteriorates at the rate of time directly proportional to the quality of the increase.

I feel that this, in itself, is an important discovery.

As long as I am able to write, I will continue to record my thoughts in these progress reports. It is one of my few pleasures. However, by all indications, my own mental deterioration will be very rapid.

I have already begun to notice signs of emotional instability and forgetfulness, the first symptoms of the burnout.

June 10   Deterioration progressing. I have become absent-minded. Algernon died two days ago. Dissection shows my predictions were right. His brain had decreased in weight and there was a general smoothing out of cerebral convolutions as well as a deepening and broadening of brain fissures.

I guess the same thing is or will soon be happening to me. Now that it's definite, I don't want it to happen.

I put Algernon's body in a cheese box and buried him in the back yard. I cried.

June 15   Dr. Strauss came to see me again. I wouldn't open the door and I told him to go away. I want to be left to myself. I have become touchy and irritable. I feel the darkness closing in. It's hard to throw off thoughts of suicide. I keep telling myself how important this introspective journal will be.

It's a strange sensation to pick up a book that you've read and enjoyed just a few months ago and discover that you don't remember it. I remembered how great I thought John Milton was, but when I picked up *Paradise Lost* I couldn't understand it at all. I got so angry I threw the book across the room.

I've got to try to hold on to some of it. Some of the things I've learned. Oh, God, please don't take it all away.

June 19 Sometimes, at night, I go out for a walk. Last night I couldn't remember where I lived. A policeman took me home. I have the strange feeling that this has all happened to me before—a long time ago. I keep telling myself I'm the only person in the world who can describe what's happening to me.

June 21 Why can't I remember? I've got to fight. I lie in bed for days and I don't know who or where I am. Then it all comes back to me in a flash. Fugues of amnesia. Symptoms of senility—second childhood. I can watch them coming on. It's so cruelly logical. I learned so much and so fast. Now my mind is deteriorating rapidly. I won't let it happen. I'll fight it. I can't help thinking of the boy in the restaurant, the blank expression, the silly smile, the people laughing at him. No—please—not that again. . . .

June 22 I'm forgetting things that I learned recently. It seems to be following the classic pattern—the last things learned are the first things forgotten. Or is that the pattern? I'd better look it up again. . . .

I reread my paper on the *Algernon-Gordon Effect* and I get the strange feeling that it was written by someone else. There are parts I don't even understand.

Motor activity impaired. I keep tripping over things, and it becomes increasingly difficult to type.

June 23 I've given up using the typewriter completely. My coordination is bad. I feel that I'm moving slower and slower. Had a terrible shock today. I picked up a copy of an article I used in my research, Krueger's *Uber psychische Ganzheit,* to see if it would help me understand what I had done. First I thought there was something wrong with my eyes. Then I realized I could no longer read German. I tested myself in other languages. All gone.

June 30 A week since I dared to write again. It's slipping away like sand through my fingers. Most of the books I have are too hard for me now. I get angry with them because I know that I read and understood them just a few weeks ago.

I keep telling myself I must keep writing these reports so

that somebody will know what is happening to me. But it gets harder to form the words and remember spellings. I have to look up even simple words in the dictionary now and it makes me impatient with myself.

Dr. Strauss comes around almost every day, but I told him I wouldn't see or speak to anybody. He feels guilty. They all do. But I don't blame anyone. I knew what might happen. But how it hurts.

July 7 I don't know where the week went. Todays Sunday I know because I can see through my window people going to church. I think I stayed in bed all week but I remember Mrs. Flynn bringing food to me a few times. I keep saying over and over Ive got to do something but then I forget or maybe its just easier not to do what I say Im going to do.

I think of my mother and father a lot these days. I found a picture of them with me taken at a beach. My father has a big ball under his arm and my mother is holding me by the hand. I dont remember them the way they are in the picture. All I remember is my father drunk most of the time and arguing with mom about money.

He never shaved much and he used to scratch my face when he hugged me. My mother said he died but Cousin Miltie said he heard his mom and dad say that my father ran away with another woman. When I asked my mother she slapped my face and said my father was dead. I dont think I ever found out which was true but I don't care much. (He said he was going to take me to see cows on a farm once but he never did. He never kept his promises . . .)

July 10 My landlady Mrs Flynn is very worried about me. She says the way I lay around all day and dont do anything I remind her of her son before she threw him out of the house. She said she doesnt like loafers. If Im sick its one thing, but if Im a loafer thats another thing and she wont have it. I told her I think Im sick.

I try to read a little bit every day, mostly stories, but sometimes I have to read the same thing over and over again because I dont know what it means. And its hard to write. I know I should look up all the words in the dictionary but its so hard and Im so tired all the time.

Then I got the idea that I would only use the easy words instead of the long hard ones. That saves time. I put flowers on Algernons grave about once a week. Mrs Flynn thinks Im crazy to put flowers on a mouses grave but I told her that Algernon was special.

July 14   Its sunday again. I dont have anything to do to keep me busy now because my television set is broke and I dont have any money to get it fixed. (I think I lost this months check from the lab. I dont remember)

I get awful headaches and asperin doesnt help me much. Mrs Flynn knows Im really sick and she feels very sorry for me. Shes a wonderful woman whenever someone is sick.

July 22   Mrs Flynn called a strange doctor to see me. She was afraid I was going to die. I told the doctor I wasnt too sick and that I only forget sometimes. He asked me did I have any friends or relatives and I said no I dont have any. I told him I had a friend called Algernon once but he was a mouse and we used to run races together. He looked at me kind of funny like he thought I was crazy.

He smiled when I told him I used to be a genius. He talked to me like I was a baby and he winked at Mrs Flynn. I got mad and chased him out because he was making fun of me the way they all used to.

July 24   I have no more money and Mrs Flynn says I got to go to work somewhere and pay the rent because I havent paid for over two months. I dont know any work but the job I used to have at Donnegans Plastic Box Company. I dont want to go back there because they all knew me when I was smart and maybe theyll laugh at me. But I dont know what else to do to get money.

July 25   I was looking at some of my old progress reports and its very funny but I cant read what I wrote. I can make out some of the words but they dont make sense.

Miss Kinnian came to the door but I said go away I dont want to see you. She cried and I cried too but I wouldnt let her in because I didnt want her to laugh at me. I told her I didn't like her any more. I told her I didnt want to be smart any more. Thats not true. I still love her and I still want to be smart but I had to say that so shed go away. She gave Mrs Flynn money to pay the rent. I dont want that. I got to get a job.

Please . . . please let me not forget how to read and write . . .

July 27　Mr Donnegan was very nice when I came back and asked him for my old job of janitor. First he was very suspicious but I told him what happened to me then he looked very sad and put his hand on my shoulder and said Charlie Gordon you got guts.

Everybody looked at me when I came downstairs and started working in the toilet sweeping it out like I used to. I told myself Charlie if they make fun of you dont get sore because you remember their not so smart as you once thot they were. And besides they were once your friends and if they laughed at you that doesnt mean anything because they liked you too.

One of the new men who came to work there after I went away made a nasty crack he said hey Charlie I hear your a very smart fella a real quiz kid. Say something intelligent. I felt bad but Joe Carp came over and grabbed him by the shirt and said leave him alone you lousy cracker or Ill break you neck. I didnt expect Joe to take my part so I guess hes really my friend.

Later Frank Reilly came over and said Charlie if anybody bothers you or trys to take advantage you call me or Joe and we will set em straight. I said thanks Frank and I got choked up so I had to turn around and go into the supply room so he wouldnt see me cry. Its good to have friends.

July 28　I did a dumb thing today I forgot I wasnt in Miss Kinnians class at the adult center any more like I used to be. I went in and sat down in my old seat in the back of the room and she looked at me funny and she said Charles. I dint remember she ever called me that before only Charlie so I said hello Miss Kinnian Im redy for my lesin today only I lost my reader that we was using. She startid to cry and run out of the room and everybody looked at me and I saw they wasnt the same pepul who used to be in my class.

Then all of a suddin I remembered some things about the operashun and me getting smart and I said holy smoke I reely pulled a Charlie Gordon that time. I went away before she came back to the room.

Thats why Im going away from New York for good. I dont want to do nothing like that agen. I dont want Miss Kinnian to feel sorry for me. Evry body feels sorry at the factery and I dont want that eather so Im going someplace where nobody knows that Charlie Gordon was once a genus and now he cant even reed a book or rite good.

Im taking a cuple of books along and even if I cant reed them Ill practise hard and maybe I wont forget every thing I lerned. If I try reel hard maybe Ill be a littel bit smarter then I was before the operashun. I got my rabits foot and my luky penny and maybe they will help me.

If you ever reed this Miss Kinnian dont be sorry for me Im glad I got a second chanse to be smart becaus I lerned a lot of things that I never even new were in this world and Im grateful that I saw it all for a littel bit. I dont know why Im dumb agen or what I did wrong maybe its becaus I dint try hard enuff. But if I try and practis very hard maybe Ill get a littl smarter and know what all the words are. I remember a littel bit how nice I had a feeling with the blue book that has the torn cover when I red it. Thats why Im gonna keep trying to get smart so I can have that feeling agen. Its a good feeling to know things and be smart. I wish I had it rite now if I did I would sit down and reed all the time. Anyway I bet Im the first dumb person in the world who ever found out something importent for sience. I remember I did something but I dont remember what. So I gess its like I did it for all the dumb pepul like me.

Good-by Miss Kinnian and Dr Strauss and evreybody. And P.S. please tell Dr Nemur not to be such a grouch when pepul laff at him and he would have more frends. Its easy to make frends if you let pepul laff at you. Im going to have lots of frends where I go.

P.P.S. Please if you get a chanse put some flowrs on Alger-nons grave in the bak yard. . . .

A Question of Identity

So omnipresent were the pseudonyms adopted by Kenry Kuttner (sometimes in collaboration with his wife, C. L. Moore)—the most famous of which were Lewis Padgett and Lawrence O'Donnell—that the common fate of new writers was to be considered a pseudonym of Kuttner. So it was with Jack Vance (1920–   ), whose first story, "The World Thinker," was written while he was serving in the merchant marine during World War II and published in *Thrilling Wonder Stories* in 1945.

A San Franciscan by birth and choice, Vance earned a bachelor's degree from the University of California in 1942, studying first mining engineering, then physics, and finally journalism. He has written screenplays and mysteries, but his reputation rests upon his science fiction writing, a trade he has plied full-time since 1946 and in which he soon established a solid identity of his own.

Vance's first book, *The Dying Earth* (1950), was a series of fantasies about magic in the far future, as was *The Eyes of the Overworld* (1966). In the early 1950s he wrote a number of adventure novels, for such magazines as *Startling Stories, Thrilling Wonder Stories*, and *Space Stories*, that displayed interest and expertise in anthropology and sociology. The novels later were published as *Big Planet* (1957), *Sons of the Tree* (1964), *Slaves of the Klau* (1958), and *The Houses of Iszm* (1964). Other early novels dealt with immortality—*To Live Forever* (1956)—and linguistics—*The Languages of Pao* (1958).

Vance's greatest success, however, came after his short novel "The Dragon Masters" won a Hugo in 1963. His novella "The Last Castle" won a Hugo and a Nebula for 1967. He is prolific, and his novels since the mid–1960s have come in bunches: the Demon Princes series began with *The Star King* (1964), the Planet of Adventure series began with *City of the Chasch* (1968), the Durdane trilogy began with *The Anome* (1973), and the Alastor series began with *Trullion: Alastor 2262* (1973).

Vance's skill with alien societies has never been better demonstrated than in "The Moon Moth." The pleasure the reader gets from stories like this one springs from the intriguing speculations about the different ways in which people (or creatures) can organize themselves and how it affects their values. The story's success depends upon the thoroughness and consistency with which the author imagines the society. Brian W. Aldiss's *The Dark Light Years* (1964), in which aliens attach the same kind of sacramental importance to elimination that we do to eating, is this kind of societal exploration, as is Ursula K. Le Guin's *The Left Hand of Darkness* (1969), in which a human race that is neuter most of the month becomes either male or female at a time of "kemmer," and Robert Silberberg's *A Time of Changes* (1971), in which individualism (and even the personal pronoun) is unthinkable.

"The Moon Moth," which was published in the August 1961 *Galaxy*, a magazine that placed its greatest emphasis on social science fiction, is a richly detailed picture of a society of the future whose home is a world where life is so easy that people have time for an elaborate ritual of living and communication. The fly in the ointment that Vance postulates for Sirene is the night-people—savages who come down from the mountains at night to loot and murder—who force the rest of society to be alert.

Plenty and the leisure it provides create significant departures from our social system: The only medium of exchange is "strakh," which is defined as "prestige, face, *mana*, repute, glory," and goods are exchanged as gifts that honor both giver and receiver. The major characteristics of the elaborate social system are the use of masks to indicate status and the use of musical instruments to accompany sung speech, with the choice of instrument determined by the status of the speaker and the relationship between the speaker and the person spoken to.

If this sounds confusing to the reader, it is also confusing to Edwer Thissell, the Consular Representative to this strange world, who must learn to understand the society and communicate in its way before he can fulfill his duties. Into this situation comes an assassin who must be apprehended. But how is Thissell to identify him in a world where everyone goes masked all the time: and how is Thissell to accomplish his task when the customs still are new to him and his attempts to communicate only get him deeper into personal difficulties?

The ingenuity with which Thissell solves the problem of identification, the cleverness with which the events precipitated by his earlier social problems save his life, and the wit with which he finally achieves status—these provide the reader's reward for studying the society. But they would not have been possible without the social setting, which establishes the situation and gives richness, credibility, and necessary complication to the story.

The good reader delights in the wit and the invention: Vance mentions "a score" of instruments given Thissell to learn, names fourteen of them, and describes most of them and their social use, usually in footnotes. Even more care is taken with the masks, verifying their variety and their necessary place in this society: Vance names thirty-six of them and mentions another four, describing the appearance of most of them. There is richness of invention as well in other details of existence and their consequences; the loving attention devoted to the houseboat with which the story begins is the equivalent of the description of a vessel in a well-researched historical novel. Eventually the society seems as real to the reader as it does to Thissell, who, as he grows accustomed to it, finds himself shocked at the unmasked faces of the "dray-fish," and offended when he is improperly addressed by another offworlder.

One off-worlder, faced by the thought of leaving Sirene, shudders and says, "Back to the world of faces. Faces! Everywhere pallid, fish-eyed faces. Mouths like pulp, noses knotted and punctured; flat, flabby faces."

And when the purported assassin is described to a Sirenese throng as one who has "murdered, betrayed; he has wrecked ships; he has tortured, blackmailed, robbed, sold children into slavery," a Sirenese cuts him off by saying that "your religious differences are of no importance." The only matter of importance is the person's "crimes" in this social situation.

"The Moon Moth" is a rich reading experience that would be difficult to achieve in anything but science fiction.

The Moon Moth

by Jack Vance

The houseboat had been built to the most exacting standards of Sirenese craftmanship, which is to say, as close to the absolute as human eye could detect. The planking of waxy dark wood showed no joints, the fastenings were platinum rivets countersunk and polished flat. In style, the boat was massive, broad-beamed, steady as the shore itself, without ponderosity or slackness of line. The bow bulged like a swan's breast, the stem rising high, then crooking forward to support an iron lantern. The doors were carved from slabs of a mottled black-green wood; the windows were many-sectioned, paned with squares of mica, stained rose, blue, pale green and violet. The bow was given to service facilities and quarters for the slaves; amidships were a pair of sleeping cabins, a dining saloon and a parlor saloon, opening upon an observation deck at the stern.

Such was Edwer Thissell's houseboat, but ownership brought him neither pleasure nor pride. The houseboat had become shabby. The carpeting had lost its pile; the carved screens were chipped; the iron lantern at the bow sagged with rust. Seventy years ago the first owner, on accepting the boat, had honored the builder and had been likewise honored; the transaction (for the process represented a great deal more than simple giving and taking) had augmented the prestige of both. That time was far gone: the houseboat now commanded no prestige whatever. Edwer Thissell, resident on Sirene only three months, recognized the lack but could do nothing about it: this particular houseboat was the best he could get. He sat on the rear deck practicing the *ganga*, a zitherlike instrument not much larger than his hand. A hundred yards inshore, surf defined a strip of white beach; beyond rose jungle, with the silhouette of craggy black hills against the sky. Mireille shone hazy and white overhead, as if through a tangle of spiderweb; the face of the ocean pooled and puddled with mother-of-pearl luster. The scene had become as familiar, though not as boring, as the *ganga*, at which he had worked two hours, twanging out the Sirenese scales, forming chords, traversing simple progressions. Now he put down the *ganga* for the *zachinko*, this a small sound-box studded with keys, played with the right hand. Pressure on the keys forced air through reeds in the keys themselves, producing a concertinalike tone. Thissell ran off a dozen quick scales, making very few mistakes. Of the six instruments he had set himself to learn, the *zachinko* had proved the least refractory (with the exception, of course, of the *hymerkin*, that clacking, slapping, clattering device of wood and stone used exclusively with the slaves).

Thissell practiced another ten minutes, then put aside the *zachinko*. He flexed his arms, wrung his aching fingers. Every waking moment since his arrival had been given to the instruments: the *hymerkin*, the *ganga*, the *zachinko*, the *kiv*, the *strapan*, the *gomapard*. He had practiced scales in nineteen keys and four modes, chords without number, intervals never imagined on the Home Planets. Trills, arpeggios, slurs; click-stops and nasalization; damping and augmentation of overtones; vibratos and wolf-tones; concavities and convexities. He practiced with a dogged, deadly diligence, in which his orginal concept of music as a source of pleasure had long become lost. Looking over the instruments Thissell resisted an urge to fling all six into the Titanic.

He rose to his feet, went forward through the parlor saloon, the dining saloon, along a corridor past the galley and came out on the fore-deck. He bent over the rail, peered down into the underwater pens where Toby and Rex, the slaves, were harnessing the dray-fish for the weekly trip to Fan, eight miles north. The youngest fish, either playful or captious, ducked and plunged. Its streaming black muzzle broke water, and Thissell, looking into its face, felt a peculiar qualm: the fish wore no mask!

Thissell laughed uneasily, fingering his own mask, the Moon Moth. No question about it, he was becoming acclimated to Sirene! A significant stage had been reached when the naked face of a fish caused him shock!

The fish were finally harnessed; Toby and Rex climbed aboard, red bodies glistening, black cloth masks clinging to their faces. Ignoring Thissell, they stowed the pen, hoisted anchor. The dray-fish strained, the harness tautened, the houseboat moved north.

Returning to the afterdeck, Thissell took up the *strapan*—this a circular sound-box eight inches in diameter. Forty-six wires radiated from a central hub to the circumference, where they connected to either a bell or a tinkle-bar. When plucked, the bells rang, the bars chimed; when strummed, the instrument gave off a twanging, jingling sound. When played with competence, the pleasantly acid dissonances produced an expressive effect; in an unskilled hand, the results were less felicitous, and might even approach random noise. The *strapan* was Thissell's weakest instrument, and he practiced with concentration during the entire trip north.

In due course the houseboat approached the floating city. The dray-fish were curbed, the houseboat warped to a mooring. Along the dock a line of idlers weighed and gauged every aspect of the houseboat, the slaves and Thissell himself, according to Sirenese habit. Thissell, not yet accustomed to such penetrating inspection, found the scrutiny unsettling, all the more so for the immobility of the masks. Self-consciously adjusting his own Moon Moth, he climbed the ladder to the dock.

A slave rose from where he had been squatting, touched knuckles to the black cloth at his forehead, and sang on a three-tone phrase of interrogation: "The Moon Moth before me possibly expresses the identity of Ser Edwer Thissell?"

Thissell tapped the *hymerkin* which hung at his belt and sang: "I am Ser Thissell."

"I have been honored by a trust," sang the slave. "Three days from dawn to dusk I have waited on the dock; three nights from dust to dawn I have crouched on a raft below this same dock listening to the feet of the Night-men. At last I behold the mask of Ser Thissell."

Thissell evoked an impatient clatter from the *hymerkin*. "What is the nature of this trust?"

"I carry a message, Ser Thissell. It is intended for you."

Thissell held out his left hand, playing the *hymerkin* with his right. "Give me the message."

"Instantly, Ser Thissell."

The message bore a heavy superscription:

EMERGENCY COMMUNICATION! RUSH!

Thissell ripped open the envelope. The message was signed by Castel Cromartin, Chief Executive of the Interworld Policies Board, and after the formal salutation read:

ABSOLUTELY URGENT the following orders be executed! Aboard *Carina Cruzeiro,* destination Fan, date of arrival January 10 U.T., is notorious assassin, Haxo Angmark. Meet landing with adequate authority, effect detention and incarceration of this man. These instructions must be successfully implemented. Failure is unacceptable.

ATTENTION! Haxo Angmark is superlatively dangerous. Kill him without hesitation at any show of resistance.

Thissell considered the message with dismay. In coming to Fan as Consular Representative he had expected nothing like this; he felt neither inclination nor competence in the matter of dealing with dangerous assassins. Thoughtfully he rubbed the fuzzy gray cheek of his mask. The situation was not completely dark; Esteban Rolver, Director of the Space-Port, would doubtless cooperate, and perhaps furnish a platoon of slaves.

More hopefully, Thissell reread the message. January 10, Universal Time. He consulted a conversion calendar. Today, 40th in the Season of Bitter Nectar—Thissell ran his finger down the column, stopped. January 10. Today.

A distant rumble caught his attention. Dropping from the mist came a dull shape: the lighter returning from contact with the *Carina Cruzeiro.*

Thissell once more reread the note, raised his head, studied the descending lighter. Aboard would be Haxo Angmark. In five minutes he would emerge upon the soil of Sirene. Landing formalities would detain him possibly twenty minutes. The landing field lay a mile and a half distant, joined to Fan by a winding path through the hills.

Thissell turned to the slave. "When did this message arrive?"

The slave leaned forward uncomprehendingly. Thissell reiterated his question, singing to the clack of the *hymerkin:* "This message: you have enjoyed the honor of its custody how long?"

The slave sang: "Long days have I waited on the wharf,

retreating only to the raft at the onset of dusk. Now my vigil is rewarded; I behold Ser Thissell."

Thissell turned away, walked furiously up the dock. Ineffective, inefficient Sirenese! Why had they not delivered the message to his houseboat? Twenty-five minutes—twenty-two now . . .

At the esplanade Thissell stopped, looked right then left, hoping for a miracle: some sort of air transport to whisk him to the space port, where with Rolver's aid, Haxo Angmark might still be detained. Or better yet, a second message canceling the first. Something, anything . . . But air cars were not to be found on Sirene, and no second message appeared.

Across the esplanade rose a meager row of permanent structures, built of stone and iron and so proof against the efforts of the Night-men. A hostler occupied one of these structures, and as Thissell watched a man in a splendid pearl and silver mask emerged riding one of the lizardlike mounts of Sirene.

Thissell sprang forward. There was still time; with luck he might yet intercept Haxo Angmark. He hurried across the esplanade.

Before the line of stalls stood the hostler, inspecting his stock with solicitude, occasionally burnishing a scale or whisking away an insect. There were five of the beasts in prime condition, each as tall as a man's shoulder, with massive legs, thick bodies, heavy wedge-shaped heads. From their forefangs, which had been artificially lengthened and curved into near-circles, gold rings depended; the scales of each had been stained in diaper-pattern: purple and green, orange and black, red and blue, brown and pink, yellow and silver.

Thissell came to a breathless halt in front of the hostler. He reached for his *kiv*,[1] then hesitated. Could this be considered a casual personal encounter? The *zachinko* perhaps? But the statement of his needs hardly seemed to demand the formal approach. Better the *kiv* after all. He struck a chord, but by error found himself stroking the *ganga*. Beneath his mask Thissell grinned apologetically; his relationship with this hostler was by no means on an intimate basis. He hoped that the hostler was of sanguine disposition, and in any event the urgency of the occasion allowed no time to select an exactly

[1] *kiv:* five banks of resilient metal strips, fourteen to the bank, played by touching, twisting, twanging.

appropriate instrument. He struck a second chord, and, playing as well as agitation, breathlessness and lack of skill allowed, sang out a request: "Ser Hostler, I have immediate need of a swift mount. Allow me to select from your herd."

The hostler wore a mask of considerable complexity which Thissell could not identify: a construction of varnished brown cloth, pleated gray leather and high on the forehead two large green and scarlet globes, minutely segmented like insect eyes. He inspected Thissell a long moment, then, rather ostentatiously selecting his *stimic*,[2] executed a brilliant progression of trills and rounds, of an import Thissell failed to grasp. The hostler sang, "Ser Moon Moth, I fear that my steeds are unsuitable to a person of your distinction."

Thissell earnestly twanged at the *ganga*. "By no means; they all seem adequate. I am in great haste and will gladly accept any of the group."

The hostler played a brittle cascading crescendo. "Ser Moon-Moth," he sang, "the steeds are ill and dirty. I am flattered that you consider them adequate to your use. I cannot accept the merit you offer me. And"—here, switching instruments, he struck a cool tinkle from his *krodatch*[3]—"somehow I fail to recognize the boon companion and co-craftsman who accosts me so familiarly with his *ganga*."

The implication was clear. Thissell would receive no mount. He turned, set off at a run for the landing field. Behind him sounded a clatter of the hostler's *hymerkin*—whether directed toward the hostler's slaves or toward himself Thissell did not pause to learn.

The previous Consular Representative of the Home Planets on Sirene had been killed at Zundar. Masked as a Tavern Bravo he had accosted a girl beribboned for the Equinoctial Attitudes, a solecism for which he had been instantly beheaded by a Red Demiurge, a Sun Sprite and a Magic

---

[2] *stimic:* three flutelike tubes equipped with plungers. Thumb and forefinger squeeze a bag to force air across the mouthpieces; the second, third and fourth little fingers manipulate the slide. The *stimic* is an instrument well adapted to the sentiments of cool withdrawal, or even disapproval.

[3] *krodatch:* a small square sound-box strung with resined gut. The musician scratches the strings with his fingernail, or strokes them with his fingertips, to produce a variety of quietly formal sounds. The *krodatch* is also used as an instrument of insult.

Hornet. Edwer Thissell, recently graduated from the Institute, had been named his successor, and allowed three days to prepare himself. Normally of a contemplative, even cautious, disposition, Thissell had regarded the appointment as a challenge. He learned the Sirenese language by subcerebral techniques, and found it uncomplicated. Then, in the Journal of Universal Anthropology, he read:

The population of the Titanic littoral is highly individualistic, possibly in response to a bountiful environment which puts no premium upon group activity. The language, reflecting this trait, expresses the individual's mood, his emotional attitude toward a given situation. Factual information is regarded as a secondary concomitant. Moreover, the language is sung, characteristically to the accompaniment of a small instrument. As a result, there is great difficulty in ascertaining fact from a native of Fan, or the forbidden city Zundar. One will be regaled with elegant arias and demonstrations of astonishing virtuosity upon one or another of the numerous musical instruments. The visitor to this fascinating world, unless he cares to be treated with the most consummate contempt, must therefore learn to express himself after the approved local fashion.

Thissell made a note in his memorandum book: *Procure small musical instrument, together with directions as to use.* He read on.

There is everywhere and at all times a plenitude, not to say, superfluity of food, and the climate is benign. With a fund of racial energy and a great deal of leisure time, the population occupies itself with intricacy. Intricacy in all things; intricate craftsmanship, such as the carved panels which adorn the houseboat; intricate symbolism, as exemplified in the masks worn by everyone; the intricate half-musical language which admirably expresses subtle moods and emotions; and above all the fantastic intricacy of interpersonal relationships. Prestige, face, *mana*, repute, glory: the Sirenese word is *strakh*. Every man has his characteristic *strakh*, which determines whether, when he needs a houseboat, he will be urged to avail himself of a floating palace, rich with gems, alabaster lanterns, peacock faïence and carved wood, or grudgingly permitted an abandoned shack on a raft. There is no medium of exchange on Sirene; the single and sole currency is *strakh*. . . .

Thissell rubbed his chin and read further.

Masks are worn at all times, in accordance with the philosophy that a man should not be compelled to use a similitude foisted upon him by factors beyond his control; that he should be at liberty to choose that semblance most consonant with his *strakh*. In the civilized areas of Sirene—which is to say the Titanic littoral—a man literally never shows his face; it is his basic secret.

Gambling, by this token, is unknown on Sirene; it would be catastrophic to Sirenese self-respect to gain advantage by means other than the exercise of *strakh*. The word "luck" has no counterpart in the Sirenese language.

Thissell made another note: *Get mask. Museum? Drama guild?*

He finished the article, hastened forth to complete his preparations, and the next day embarked aboard the *Robert Astroguard* for the first leg of the passage to Sirene.

The lighter settled upon the Sirenese spaceport, a topaz disk isolated among the black, green and purple hills. The lighter grounded, and Edwer Thissell stepped forth. He was met by Esteban Rolver, the local agent for Spaceways. Rolver threw up his hands, stepped back. "Your mask," he cried huskily. "Where is your mask?"

Thissell held it up rather self-consciously. "I wasn't sure—"

"Put it on," said Rolver, turning away. He himself wore a fabrication of dull green scales, blue-lacquered wood. Black quills protruded at the cheeks, and under his chin hung a black and white checked pom-pom, the total effect creating a sense of sardonic supple personality.

Thissell adjusted the mask to his face, undecided whether to make a joke about the situation or to maintain a reserve suitable to the dignity of his post.

"Are you masked?" Rolver inquired over his shoulder.

Thissell replied in the affirmative and Rolver turned. The mask hid the expression of his face, but his hand unconsciously flicked a set of keys strapped to his thigh. The instrument sounded a trill of shock and polite consternation.

"You can't wear that mask!" sang Rolver. "In fact—how, where, did you get it?"

"It's copied from a mask owned by the Polypolis museum," declared Thissell stiffly. "I'm sure it's authentic."

Rolver nodded, his own mask more sardonic-seeming than ever. "It's authentic enough. It's a variant of the type known as the Sea-Dragon Conqueror, and is worn on ceremonial occasions by persons of enormous prestige: princes, heroes, master craftsmen, great musicians."

"I wasn't aware—"

Rolver made a gesture of languid understanding. "It's something you'll learn in due course. Notice my mask. Today I'm wearing a Tarn-Bird. Persons of minimal prestige—such as you, I, any other out-worlder—wear this sort of thing."

"Odd," said Thissell as they started across the field toward a low concrete blockhouse. "I assumed that a person wore whatever mask he liked."

"Certainly," said Rolver. "Wear any mask you like—if you can make it stick. This Tarn-Bird, for instance. I wear it to indicate that I presume nothing. I make no claims to wisdom, ferocity, versatility, musicianship, truculence, or any of a dozen other Sirenese virtues."

"For the sake of argument," said Thissell, "what would happen if I walked through the streets of Zundar in this mask?"

Rolver laughed, a muffled sound behind his mask. "If you walked along the docks of Zundar—there are no streets—in any mask, you'd be killed within the hour. That's what happened to Benko, your predecessor. He didn't know how to act. None of us out-worlders know how to act. In Fan we're tolerated—so long as we keep our place. But you couldn't even walk around Fan in that regalia you're sporting now. Somebody wearing a Firesnake or a Thunder Goblin—masks, you understand—would step up to you. He'd play his *krodatch,* and if you failed to challenge his audacity with a passage on the *skaranyi,*[4] a devilish instrument, he'd play his *hymerkin*—the instrument we use with the slaves. That's the ultimate expression of contempt. Or he might ring his dueling-gong and attack you then and there."

"I had no idea that people here were quite so irascible," said Thissell in a subdued voice.

---

[4] *skaranyi:* a miniature bagpipe, the sac squeezed between thumb and palm, the four fingers controlling the stops along four tubes.

Rolver shrugged and swung open the massive steel door into his office. "Certain acts may not be committed on the Concourse at Polypolis without incurring criticism."

"Yes, that's quite true," said Thissell. He looked around the office. "Why the security? The concrete, the steel?"

"Protection against the savages," said Rolver. "They come down from the mountains at night, steal what's available, kill anyone they find ashore." He went to a closet, brought forth a mask. "Here. Use this Moon Moth; it won't get you in trouble."

Thissell unenthusiastically inspected the mask. It was constructed of mouse-colored fur; there was a tuft of hair at each side of the mouth-hole, a pair of featherlike antennae at the forehead. White lace flaps dangled beside the temples and under the eyes hung a series of red folds, creating an effect at once lugubrious and comic.

Thissell asked, "Does this mask signify any degree of prestige?"

"Not a great deal."

"After all, I'm Consular Representative," said Thissell. "I represent the Home Planets, a hundred billion people—"

"If the Home Planets want their representative to wear a Sea-Dragon Conqueror mask, they'd better send out a Sea-Dragon Conqueror type of man."

"I see," said Thissell in a subdued voice. "Well, if I must . . ."

Rolver politely averted his gaze while Thissell doffed the Sea-Dragon Conqueror and slipped the more modest Moon Moth over his head. "I suppose I can find something just a bit more suitable in one of the shops," Thissell said. "I'm told a person simply goes in and takes what he needs, correct?"

Rolver surveyed Thissell critically. "That mask—temporarily, at least—is perfectly suitable. And it's rather important not to take anything from the shops until you know the *strakh* value of the article you want. The owner loses prestige if a person of low *strakh* makes free with his best work."

Thissell shook his head in exasperation. "Nothing of this was explained to me! I knew of the masks, of course, and the painstaking integrity of the craftsmen, but this insistence on prestige—*strakh*, whatever the word is . . ."

"No matter," said Rolver. "After a year or two you'll begin to learn your way around. I suppose you speak the language?"

"Oh indeed. Certainly."

"And what instruments do you play?"

"Well—I was given to understand that any small instrument was adequate, or that I could merely sing."

"Very inaccurate. Only slaves sing without accompaniment. I suggest that you learn the following instruments as quickly as possible: The *hymerkin* for your slaves. The *ganga* for conversation between intimates or one a trifle lower than yourself in *strakh*. The *kiv* for casual polite intercourse. The *zachinko* for more formal dealings. The *strapan* or the *krodatch* for your social inferiors—in your case, should you wish to insult someone. The *gomapard*[5] or the *double-kamanthil*[6] for ceremonials." He considered a moment. "The *crebarin*, the water-lute and the *slobo* are highly useful also—but perhaps you'd better learn the other instruments first. They should provide a least a rudimentary means of communication."

"Aren't you exaggerating?" suggested Thissell. "Or joking?"

Rolver laughed his saturnine laugh. "Not at all. First of all, you'll need a houseboat. And then you'll want slaves."

Rolver took Thissell from the landing field to the docks of Fan, a walk of an hour and a half along a pleasant path under enormous trees loaded with fruit, cereal pods, sacs of sugary sap.

"At the moment," said Rolver, "there are only four outworlders in Fan, counting yourself. I'll take you to Welibus, our Commercial Factor. I think he's got an old houseboat he might let you use."

Cornely Welibus had resided fifteen years in Fan, acquiring sufficient *strakh* to wear his South Wind mask with authority. This consisted of a blue disk inlaid with cabochons of lapis lazuli, surrounded by an aureole of shimmering snakeskin. Heartier and more cordial than Rolver, he not only provided Thissell with a houseboat, but also a score of various musical instruments and a pair of slaves.

Embarrassed by the largesse, Thissell stammered something about payment, but Welibus cut him off with an expansive

[5] *gomapard:* one of the few electric instruments used on Sirene. An oscillator produces an oboelike tone which is modulated, choked, vibrated, raised and lowered in pitch by four keys.

[6] *double-kamanthil:* an instrument similar to the *ganga*, except the tones are produced by twisting and inclining a disk of resined leather against one or more of the forty-six strings.

gesture. "My dear fellow, this is Sirene. Such trifles cost nothing."

"But a houseboat—"

Welibus played a courtly little flourish on his *kiv.* "I'll be frank, Ser Thissell. The boat is old and a trifle shabby. I can't afford to use it; my status would suffer." A graceful melody accompanied his words. "Status as yet need not concern you. You require merely shelter, comfort, and safety from the Night-men."

"Night-men?"

"The cannibals who roam the shore after dark."

"Oh yes. Ser Rolver mentioned them."

"Horrible things. We won't discuss them." A shuddering little trill issued from his *kiv.* "Now, as to slaves." He tapped the blue disk of his mask with a thoughtful forefinger. "Rex and Toby should serve you well." He raised his voice, played a swift clatter on the *hymerkin. "Avan esx trobu!"*

A female slave appeared wearing a dozen tight bands of pink cloth, and a dainty black mask sparkling with mother-of-pearl sequins.

"Fascu etz Rex ae Toby."

Rex and Toby appeared, wearing loose masks of black cloth, russet jerkins. Welibus addressed them with a resonant clatter of *hymerkin,* enjoining them to the service of their new master, on pain of return to their native islands. They prostrated themselves, sang pledges of servitude to Thissell in soft husky voices. Thissell laughed nervously and essayed a sentence in the Sirenese language. "Go to the houseboat, clean it well, bring aboard food."

Toby and Rex stared blankly through the holes in their masks. Welibus repeated the orders with *hymerkin* accompaniment. The slaves bowed and departed.

Thissell surveyed the musical instruments with dismay. "I haven't the slightest idea how to go about learning these things."

Welibus turned to Rolver. "What about Kershaul? Could he be persuaded to give Ser Thissell some basic instruction?"

Rolver nodded judicially. "Kershaul might undertake the job."

Thissell asked, "Who is Kershaul?"

"The third of our little group of expatriates," replied Welibus, "an anthropologist. You've read *Zundar the Splendid? Rituals of Sirene? The Faceless Folk?* No? A pity. All excellent works. Kershaul is high in prestige, and I believe visits

Zundar from time to time. Wears a Cave Owl, sometimes a Star-Wanderer or even a Wise Arbiter."

"He's taken to an Equatorial Serpent," said Rolver. "The variant with the gilt tusks."

"Indeed!" marveled Welibus. "Well, I must say he's earned it. A fine fellow, good chap indeed." And he strummed his *zachinko* thoughtfully.

Three months passed. Under the tutelage of Mathew Kershaul, Thissell practiced the *hymerkin*, the *ganga*, the *strapan*, the *kiv*, the *gomapard*, and the *zachinko*. The double *kamanthil*, the *krodatch*, the *slobo*, the water-lute and a number of others could wait, said Kershaul, until Thissell had mastered the six basic instruments. He lent Thissell recordings of noteworthy Sirenese conversing in various moods and to various accompaniments, so that Thissell might learn the melodic conventions currently in vogue, and perfect himself in the niceties of intonation, the various rhythms, cross-rhythms, compound rhythms, implied rhythms and suppressed rhythms. Kershaul professed to find Sirenese music a fascinating study, and Thissell admitted that it was a subject not readily exhausted. The quartertone tuning of the instruments admitted the use of twenty-four tonalities which, multiplied by the five modes in general use, resulted in one hundred and twenty separate scales. Kershaul, however, advised that Thissell primarily concentrate on learning each instrument in its fundamental tonality, using only two of the modes.

With no immediate business at Fan except the weekly visits to Mathew Kershaul, Thissell took his houseboat eight miles south and moored it in the lee of a rocky promontory. Here, if it had not been for the incessant practicing, Thissell lived an idyllic life. The sea was calm and crystal-clear; the beach, ringed by the gray, green and purple foliage of the forest, lay close at hand if he wanted to stretch his legs.

Toby and Rex occupied a pair of cubicles forward. Thissell had the after cabins to himself. From time to time he toyed with the idea of a third slave, possibly a young female, to contribute an element of charm and gaiety to the menage, but Kershaul advised against the step, fearing that the intensity of Thissell's concentration might somehow be diminished. Thissell acquiesced and devoted himself to the study of the six instruments.

The days passed quickly. Thissell never became bored with the pageantry of dawn and sunset; the white clouds and blue sea of noon; the night sky blazing with the twenty-nine stars of Cluster SI 1-715. The weekly trip to Fan broke the tedium. Toby and Rex foraged for food; Thissell visited the luxurious houseboat of Mathew Kershaul for instruction and advice. Then, three months after Thissell's arrival, came the message completely disorganizing the routine: Haxo Angmark, assassin, *agent provocateur*, ruthless and crafty criminal, had come to Sirene. *Effect detention and incarceration of this man!* read the orders. *Attention! Haxo Angmark superlatively dangerous. Kill without hesitation!*

Thissell was not in the best of condition. He trotted fifty yards until his breath came in gasps, then walked: through low hills crowned with white bamboo and black tree-ferns, across meadows yellow with grass-nuts, through orchards and wild vineyards. Twenty minutes passed, twenty-five minutes; with a heavy sensation in his stomach Thissell knew that he was too late. Haxo Angmark had landed, and might be traversing this very road toward Fan. But along the way Thissell met only four persons: boy-child in a mock-fierce Alk Islander mask; two young women wearing the Red-Bird and the Green-Bird; a man masked as a Forest Goblin. Coming upon the man, Thissell stopped short. Could this be Angmark?

Thissell essayed a strategem. He went boldly to the man, stared into his hideous mask. "Angmark," he called in the language of the Home Planets, "you are under arrest!"

The Forest Goblin stared uncomprehendingly, then started forward along the track.

Thissell put himself in the way. He reached for his *ganga*, then, recalling the hostler's reaction, instead struck a chord on the *zachinko*. "You travel the road from the spaceport," he sang. "What have you seen there?"

The Forest Goblin grasped his hand bugle, an instrument used to deride opponents on the field of battle, to summon animals, or occasionally to evince a rough and ready truculence. "Where I travel and what I see are the concern solely of myself. Stand back or I walk upon your face." He marched forward, and had not Thissell leaped aside the Forest Goblin might well have made good his threat.

Thissell stood gazing after the retreating back. Angmark? Not likely, with so sure a touch on the hand bugle. Thissell hesitated, then turned and continued on his way.

Arriving at the spaceport, he went directly to the office. The heavy door stood ajar; as Thissell approached, a man appeared in the doorway. He wore a mask of dull green scales, mica plates, blue-lacquered wood and black quills—the Tarn-Bird.

"Ser Rolver," Thissell called out anxiously, "who came down from the *Carina Cruzeiro?*"

Rolver studied Thissell a long moment. "Why do you ask?"

"Why do I ask?" demanded Thissell. "You must have seen the spacegram I received from Castel Cromartin!"

"Oh yes," said Rolver. "Of course. Naturally."

"It was delivered only half an hour ago," said Thissell bitterly. "I rushed out as fast as I could. Where is Angmark?"

"In Fan, I assume," said Rolver.

Thissell cursed softly. "Why didn't you hold him up, delay him in some way?"

Rolver shrugged. "I had neither the authority, the inclination nor the capability to stop him."

Thissell fought back his annoyance. In a voice of studied calm he said, "On the way I passed a man in rather a ghastly mask—saucer eyes, red wattles."

"A Forest Goblin," said Rolver. "Angmark brought the mask with him."

"But he played the hand bugle," Thissell protested. "How could Angmark—"

"He's well acquainted with Sirene; he spent five years here in Fan."

Thissell grunted in annoyance. "Cromartin made no mention of this."

"It's common knowledge," said Rolver with a shrug. "He was Commerical Representative before Welibus took over."

"Were he and Welibus acquainted?"

Rolver laughed shortly. "Naturally. But don't suspect poor Welibus of anything more venial than juggling his accounts; I assure you he's no consort of assassins."

"Speaking of assassins," said Thissell, "do you have a weapon I might borrow?"

Rolver inspected him in wonder. "You came out here to take Angmark barehanded?"

"I had no choice," said Thissell. "When Cromartin gives orders he expects results. In any event you were here with your slaves."

"Don't count on me for help," Rolver said testily. "I wear the Tarn-Bird and make no pretentions of valor. But I can lend you a power pistol. I haven't used it recently; I won't guarantee its charge."

"Anything is better than nothing," said Thissell.

Rolver went into the office and a moment later returned with the gun. "What will you do now?"

Thissell shook his head wearily. "I'll try to find Angmark in Fan. Or might he head for Zundar?"

Rolver considered. "Angmark might be able to survive in Zundar. But he'd want to brush up on his musicianship. I imagine he'll stay in Fan a few days."

"But how can I find him? Where should I look?"

"That I can't say," replied Rolver. "You might be safer not finding him. Angmark is a dangerous man."

Thissell returned to Fan the way he had come.

Where the path swung down from the hills into the esplanade a thick-walled *pisé-de-terre* building had been constructed. The door was carved from a solid black plank; the windows were guarded by enfoliated bands of iron. This was the office of Cornely Welibus, Commercial Factor, Importer and Exporter. Thissell found Welibus sitting at his ease on the tiled verandah, wearing a modest adaptation of the Waldemar mask. He seemed lost in thought, and might or might not have recognized Thissell's Moon Moth; in any event he gave no signal of greeting.

Thissell approached the porch. "Good morning, Ser Welibus."

Welibus nodded abstractedly and said in a flat voice, plucking at his *krodatch*, "Good morning."

Thissell was rather taken aback. This was hardly the instrument to use toward a friend and fellow out-worlder, even if he did wear the Moon Moth.

Thissell said coldly, "May I ask how long you have been sitting here?"

Welibus considered half a minute, and now when he spoke he accompanied himself on the more cordial *crebarin*. But the recollection of the *krodatch* chord still rankled in Thissell's mind.

"I've been here fifteen or twenty minutes. Why do you ask?"

"I wonder if you noticed a Forest Goblin pass?"

Welibus nodded. "He went on down the esplanade—turned into that first mask shop, I believe."

Thissell hissed between his teeth. This would naturally be Angmark's first move. "I'll never find him once he changes masks," he muttered.

"Who is this Forest Goblin?" asked Welibus, with no more than casual interest.

Thissell could see no reason to conceal the name. "A notorious criminal: Haxo Angmark."

"Haxo Angmark!" croaked Welibus, leaning back in his chair. "You're sure he's here?"

"Reasonably sure."

Welibus rubbed his shaking hands together. "This is bad news—bad news indeed! He's an unscrupulous scoundrel."

"You knew him well?"

"As well as anyone." Welibus was now accompanying himself with the *kiv*. "He held the post I now occupy. I came out as an inspector and found that he was embezzling four thousand UMI's a month. I'm sure he feels no great gratitude toward me." Welibus glanced nervously up the esplanade. "I hope you catch him."

"I'm doing my best. He went into the mask shop, you say?"

"I'm sure of it."

Thissell turned away. As he went down the path he heard the black plank door thud shut behind him.

He walked down the esplanade to the maskmaker's shop, paused outside as if admiring the display: a hundred miniature masks, carved from rare woods and minerals, dressed with emerald flakes, spiderweb silk, wasp wings, petrified fish scales and the like. The shop was empty except for the maskmaker, a gnarled knotty man in a yellow robe, wearing a deceptively simple Universal Expert mask, fabricated from over two thousand bits of articulated wood.

Thissell considered what he would say, how he would accompany himself, then entered. The maskmaker, noting the Moon Moth and Thissell's diffident manner, continued with his work.

Thissell, selecting the easiest of his instruments, stroked his *strapan*—possibly not the most felicitous choice, for it conveyed a certain degree of condescension. Thissell tried to counteract this flavor by singing in warm, almost effusive, tones, shaking the *strapan* whimsically when he struck a wrong note: "A stranger is an interesting person to deal with; his habits are unfamiliar, he excites curiosity. Not twenty minutes ago a stranger entered this fascinating shop, to exchange his drab Forest Goblin for one of the remarkable and adventurous creations assembled on the premises."

The maskmaker turned Thissell a side glance, and without

words played a progression of chords on an instrument Thissell had never seen before: a flexible sac gripped in the palm with three short tubes leading between the fingers. When the tubes were squeezed almost shut and air forced through the slit, an oboelike tone ensued. To Thissell's developing ear the instrument seemed difficult, the maskmaker expert, and the music conveyed a profound sense of disinterest.

Thissell tried again, laboriously manipulating the *strapan.* He sang, "To an out-worlder on a foreign planet, the voice of one from his home is like water to a wilting plant. A person who could unite two such persons might find satisfaction in such an act of mercy."

The maskmaker casually fingered his own *strapan,* and drew forth a set of rippling scales, his fingers moving faster than the eyes could follow. He sang in the formal style: "An artist values his moments of concentration; he does not care to spend time exchanging banalities with persons of at best average prestige." Thissell attempted to insert a countermelody, but the maskmaker struck a new set of complex chords whose portent evaded Thissell's understanding, and continued: "Into the shop comes a person who evidently has picked up for the first time an instrument of unparalleled complication, for the execution of his music is open to criticism. He sings of homesickness and longing for the sight of others like himself. He dissembles his enormous *strakh* behind a Moon Moth, for he plays the *strapan* to a Master Craftsman, and sings in a voice of contemptuous raillery. The refined and creative artist ignores the provocation. He plays a polite instrument, remains noncommittal, and trusts that the stranger will tire of his sport and depart."

Thissell took up his *kiv.* "The noble maskmaker completely misunderstands me—"

He was interrupted by staccato rasping of the maskmaker's *strapan.* "The stranger now sees fit to ridicule the artist's comprehension."

Thissell scratched furiously at his *strapan:* "To protect myself from the heat, I wander into a small and unpretentious mask shop. The artisan, though still distracted by the novelty of his tools, gives promise of development. He works zealously to perfect his skill, so much so that he refuses to converse with strangers, no matter what their need."

The maskmaker carefully laid down his carving tool. He rose to his feet, went behind a screen, and shortly returned wearing a mask of gold and iron, with simulated flames licking up from the scalp. In one hand he carried a *skaranyi*, in the other a scimitar. He struck off a brilliant series of wild tones, and sang: "Even the most accomplished artist can augment his *strakh* by killing sea-monsters, Night-men and importunate idlers. Such an occasion is at hand. The artist delays his attack exactly ten seconds, because the offender wears a Moon Moth." He twirled his scimitar, spun it in the air.

Thissell desperately pounded the *strapan*. "Did a Forest Goblin enter the shop? Did he depart with a new mask?"

"Five seconds have lapsed," sang the maskmaker in steady ominous rhythm.

Thissell departed in frustrated rage. He crossed the square, stood looking up and down the esplanade. Hundreds of men and women sauntered along the docks, or stood on the decks of their houseboats, each wearing a mask chosen to express his mood, prestige and special attributes, and everywhere sounded the twitter of musical instruments.

Thissell stood at a loss. The Forest Goblin had disappeared. Haxo Angmark walked at liberty in Fan, and Thissell had failed the urgent instructions of Castel Cromartin.

Behind him sounded the casual notes of a *kiv*. "Ser Moon Moth Thissell, you stand engrossed in thought."

Thissell turned, to find beside him a Cave Owl, in a sober cloak of black and gray. Thissell recognized the mask, which symbolized crudition and patient exploration of abstract ideas; Mathew Kershaul had worn it on the occasion of their meeting a week before.

"Good morning, Ser Kershaul," muttered Thissell.

"And how are the studies coming? Have you mastered the C-Sharp Plus scale on the *gomapard*? As I recall, you were finding those inverse intervals puzzling."

"I've worked on them," said Thissell in a gloomy voice. "However, since I'll probably be recalled to Polypolis, it may be all time wasted."

"Eh? What's this?"

Thissell explained the situation in regard to Haxo Angmark. Kershaul nodded gravely. "I recall Angmark. Not a gracious personality, but an excellent musician, with quick fingers and a real talent for new instruments." Thoughtfully he twisted the goatee of his Cave Owl mask. "What are your plans?"

"They're nonexistent," said Thissell, playing a doleful phrase on the *kiv*. "I haven't any idea what masks he'll be wearing, and if I don't know what he looks like, how can I find him?"

Kershaul tugged at his goatee. "In the old days he favored the Exo Cambian Cycle, and I believe he used an entire set of Nether Denizens. Now of course his tastes may have changed."

"Exactly," Thissell complained. "He might be twenty feet away and I'd never know it." He glanced bitterly across the esplanade toward the maskmaker's shop. "No one will tell me anything; I doubt if they care that a murderer is walking their docks."

"Quite correct," Kershaul agreed. "Sirenese standards are different from ours."

"They have no sense of responsibility," declared Thissell. "I doubt if they'd throw a rope to a drowning man."

"It's true that they dislike interference," Kershaul agreed. "They emphasize individual responsibility and self-sufficiency."

"Interesting," said Thissell, "but I'm still in the dark about Angmark."

Kershaul surveyed him gravely. "And should you locate Angmark, what will you do then?"

"I'll carry out the orders of my superior," said Thissell doggedly.

"Angmark is a dangerous man," mused Kershaul. "He's got a number of advantages over you."

"I can't take that into account. It's my duty to send him back to Polypolis. He's probably safe, since I haven't the remotest idea how to find him."

Kershaul reflected. "An out-worlder can't hide behind a mask, not from the Sirenese, at least. There are four of us here at Fan—Rolver, Welibus, you and me. If another out-worlder tries to set up housekeeping the news will get around in short order."

"What if he heads for Zundar?"

Kershaul shrugged. "I doubt if he'd dare. On the other hand—" Kershaul paused, then, noting Thissell's sudden inattention, turned to follow Thissell's gaze.

A man in a Forest Goblin mask came swaggering toward them along the esplanade. Kershaul laid a restraining hand on Thissell's arm, but Thissell stepped out into the path of the Forest Goblin, his borrowed gun ready. "Haxo Angmark," he cried, "don't make a move, or I'll kill you. You're under arrest."

"Are you sure this is Angmark?" asked Kershaul in a worried voice.

"I'll find out," said Thissell. "Angmark, turn around, hold up your hands."

The Forest Goblin stood rigid with surprise and puzzlement. He reached to his *zachinko*, played an interrogatory arpeggio, and sang, "Why do you molest me, Moon Moth?"

Kershaul stepped forward and played a placatory phrase on his *slobo*. "I fear that a case of confused identity exists, Ser Forest Goblin. Ser Moon Moth seeks an out-worlder in a Forest Goblin mask."

The Forest Goblin's music became irritated and he suddenly switched to his *stimic*. "He asserts that I am an out-worlder? Let him prove his case, or he has my retaliation to face."

Kershaul glanced in embarrassment around the crowd which had gathered and once more struck up an ingratiating melody. "I am sure that Ser Moon Moth——"

The Forest Goblin interrupted with a fanfare of *skaranyi* tones. "Let him demonstrate his case or prepare for the flow of blood."

Thissell said, "Very well, I'll prove my case." He stepped forward, grasped the Forest Goblin's mask. "Let's see your face, that'll demonstrate your identity!"

The Forest Goblin sprang back in amazement. The crowd gasped, then set up an ominous strumming and toning of various instruments.

The Forest Goblin reached to the nape of his neck, jerked the cord to his duel gong, and with his other hand snatched forth his scimitar.

Kershaul stepped forward, playing the *slobo* with great agitation. Thissell, now abashed, moved aside, conscious of the ugly sound of the crowd.

Kershaul sang explanations and apologies, the Forest Goblin answered; Kershaul spoke over his shoulder to Thissell: "Run for it, or you'll be killed! Hurry!"

Thissell hesitated; the Forest Goblin put up his hand to thrust Kershaul aside. "Run!" screamed Kershaul. "To Welibus' office, lock yourself in!"

Thissell took to his heels. The Forest Goblin pursued him a few yards, then stamped his feet, sent after him a set of raucous and derisive blasts of the hand bugle, while the crowd produced a contemptuous counterpoint of clacking *hymerkins*.

There was no further pursuit. Instead of taking refuge in the Import-Export office, Thissell turned aside and after cautious reconnaissance proceeded to the dock where his houseboat was moored.

The hour was not far short of dusk when he finally returned aboard. Toby and Rex squatted on the forward deck, surrounded by the provisions they had brought back: reed baskets of fruit and cereal, blue-glass jugs containing wine, oil and pungent sap, three young pigs in a wicker pen. They were cracking nuts between their teeth, spitting the shells over the side. They looked up at Thissell, and it seemed that they rose to their feet with a new casualness. Toby muttered something under his breath; Rex smothered a chuckle.

Thissell clacked his *hymerkin* angrily. He sang, "Take the boat offshore; tonight we remain at Fan."

In the privacy of his cabin he removed the Moon Moth, stared into a mirror at his almost unfamiliar features. He picked up the Moon Moth, examined the detested lineaments: the furry gray skin, the blue spines, the ridiculous lace flaps. Hardly a dignified presence for the Consular Representative of the Home Planets. If, in fact, he still held the position when Cromartin learned of Angmark's winning free!

Thissell flung himself into a chair, stared moodily into space. Today he'd suffered a series of setbacks, but he wasn't defeated yet, not by any means. Tomorrow he'd visit Mathew Kershaul; they'd discuss how best to locate Angmark. As Kershaul had pointed out, another out-world establishment could not be camouflaged; Haxo Angmark's identity would soon become evident. Also, tomorrow he must procure another mask. Nothing extreme or vainglorious, but a mask which expressed a modicum of dignity and self-respect.

At this moment one of the slaves tapped on the doorpanel, and Thissell hastily pulled the hated Moon Moth back over his head.

Early next morning, before the dawnlight had left the sky, the slaves sculled the houseboat back to that section of the dock set aside for the use of out-worlders. Neither Rolver nor Welibus nor Kershaul had yet arrived, and Thissell waited impatiently. An hour passed, and Welibus brought his boat to the dock. Not wishing to speak to Welibus, Thissell remained inside his cabin.

A few moments later Rolver's boat likewise pulled in alongside the dock. Through the window Thissell saw Rolver, wearing his usual Tarn-Bird, climb to the dock. Here he was met by a man in a yellow-tufted Sand Tiger mask, who played a formal accompaniment on his *gomapard* to whatever message he brought Rolver.

Rolver seemed surprised and disturbed. After a moment's thought he manipulated his own *gomapard,* and as he sang, he indicated Thissell's houseboat. Then, bowing, he went on his way.

The man in the Sand Tiger mask climbed with rather heavy dignity to the float and rapped on the bulwark of Thissell's houseboat.

Thissell presented himself. Sirenese etiquette did not demand that he invite a casual visitor aboard, so he merely struck an interrogation on his *zachinko*.

The Sand Tiger played his *gomapard* and sang, "Dawn over the bay of Fan is customarily a splendid occasion; the sky is white with yellow and green colors; when Mireille rises, the mists burn and writhe like flames. He who sings derives a greater enjoyment from the hour when the floating corpse of an out-worlder does not appear to mar the serenity of the view."

Thissell's *zachinko* gave off a startled interrogation almost of its own accord; the Sand Tiger bowed with dignity. "The singer acknowledges no peer in steadfastness of disposition; however, he does not care to be plagued by the antics of a dissatisfied ghost. He therefore has ordered his slaves to attach a thong to the ankle of the corpse, and while we have conversed they have linked the corpse to the stern of your houseboat. You will wish to administer whatever rites are prescribed in the Out-world. He who sings wishes you a good morning and now departs."

Thissell rushed to the stern of his houseboat. There, near-naked and maskless, floated the body of a mature man, supported by air trapped in his pantaloons.

Thissell studied the dead face, which seemed characterless and vapid—perhaps in direct consequence of the mask-wearing habit. The body appeared of medium stature and weight, and Thissell estimated the age as between forty-five and fifty. The hair was nondescript brown, the features bloated by the water. There was nothing to indicate how the man had died.

This must be Haxo Angmark, thought Thissell. Who else could it be? Mathew Kershaul? Why not? Thissell asked himself uneasily. Rolver and Welibus had already disembarked and gone about their business. He searched across the bay to locate Kershaul's houseboat, and discovered it already tying up to the dock. Even as he watched, Kershaul jumped ashore, wearing his Cave Owl mask.

He seemed in an abstracted mood, for he passed Thissell's houseboat without lifting his eyes from the dock.

Thissell turned back to the corpse. Angmark, then, beyond a doubt. Had not three men disembarked from the houseboats of Rolver, Welibus and Kershaul, wearing masks characteristic to these men? Obviously, the corpse of Angmark. . . . The easy solution refused to sit quiet in Thissell's mind. Kershaul had pointed out that another out-worlder would be quickly identified. How else could Angmark maintain himself unless he . . . Thissell brushed the thought aside. The corpse was obviously Angmark.

And yet . . .

Thissell summoned his slaves, gave orders that a suitable container be brought to the dock, that the corpse be transferred therein and conveyed to a suitable place of repose. The slaves showed no enthusiasm for the task, and Thissell was forced to thunder forcefully, if not skillfully, on the *hymerkin* to emphasize his orders.

He walked along the dock, turned up the esplanade, passed the office of Cristofer Welibus and set out along the pleasant little lane to the landing field.

When he arrived, he found that Rolver had not yet made an appearance. An over-slave, given status by a yellow rosette on his black cloth mask, asked how he might be of service. Thissell stated that he wished to dispatch a message to Polypolis.

There was no difficulty here, declared the slave. If Thissell would set forth his message in clear block-print it would be dispatched immediately.

Thissell wrote:

OUT-WORLDER FOUND DEAD, POSSIBLY ANG-MARK. AGE 48, MEDIUM PHYSIQUE, BROWN HAIR. OTHER MEANS OF IDENTIFICATION LACKING. AWAIT ACKNOWLEDGMENT AND/OR INSTRUCTIONS.

He addressed the message to Castel Cromartin at Polypolis and handed it to the over-slave. A moment later he heard the characteristic sputter of trans-space discharge.

An hour passed. Rolver made no appearance. Thissell

paced restlessly back and forth in front of the office. There was no telling how long he would have to wait: trans-space transmission time varied unpredictably. Sometimes the message snapped through in microseconds; sometimes it wandered through unknowable regions for hours; and there were several authenticated examples of messages being received before they had been transmitted.

Another half hour passed, and Rolver finally arrived, wearing his customary Tarn-Bird. Coincidentally Thissell heard the hiss of the incoming message.

Rolver seemed surprised to see Thissell. "What brings you out so early?"

Thissell explained, "It concerns the body which you referred to me this morning. I'm communicating with my superiors about it."

Rolver raised his head and listened to the sound of the incoming message. "You seem to be getting an answer. I'd better attend to it."

"Why bother?" asked Thissell. "Your slave seems efficient."

"It's my job," declared Rolver. "I'm responsible for the accurate transmission and receipt of all spacegrams."

"I'll come with you," said Thissell. "I've always wanted to watch the operation of the equipment."

"I'm afraid that's irregular," said Rolver. He went to the door which led into the inner compartment. "I'll have your message in a moment."

Thissell protested, but Rolver ignored him and went into the inner office.

Five minutes later he reappeared, carrying a small yellow envelope. "Not too good news," he announced with unconvincing commiseration.

Thissell glumly opened the envelope. The message read:

BODY NOT ANGMARK. ANGMARK HAS BLACK HAIR. WHY DID YOU NOT MEET LANDING. SERIOUS INFRACTION, HIGHLY DISSATISFIED. RETURN TO POLYPOLIS NEXT OPPORTUNITY.

CASTEL CROMARTIN

Thissell put the message in his pocket. "Incidentally, may I inquire the color of your hair?"

Rolver played a surprised little trill on his *kiv*. "I'm quite blond. Why do you ask?"

"Mere curiosity."

Rolver played another run on his *kiv*. "Now I understand. My dear fellow, what a suspicious nature you have! Look!" He turned and parted the folds of his mask at the nape of his neck. Thissell saw that Rolver was blond indeed.

"Are you reassured?" asked Rolver jocularly.

"Oh, indeed," said Thissell. "Incidentally, have you another mask you could lend me? I'm sick of this Moon Moth."

"I'm afraid not," said Rolver. "But you need merely go into a maskmaker's shop and make a selection."

"Yes, of course," said Thissell. He took his leave of Rolver and returned along the trail to Fan. Passing Welibus' office he hesitated, then turned in. Today Welibus wore a dazzling confection of green glass prisms and silver beads, a mask Thissell had never seen before.

Welibus greeted him cautiously to the accompaniment of a *kiv*. "Good morning, Ser Moon Moth."

"I won't take too much of your time," said Thissell, "but I have a rather personal question to put to you. What color is your hair?"

Welibus hesitated a fraction of a second, then turned his back, lifted the flap of his mask. Thissell saw heavy black ringlets. "Does that answer your question?" inquired Welibus.

"Completely," said Thissell. He crossed the esplanade, went out on the dock to Kershaul's houseboat. Kershaul greeted him without enthusiasm, and invited him aboard with a resigned wave of the hand.

"A question I'd like to ask," said Thissell. "What color is your hair?"

Kershaul laughed woefully. "What little remains is black Why do you ask?"

"Curiosity."

"Come, come," said Kershaul with an unaccustomed bluffness. "There's more to it than that."

Thissell, feeling the need of counsel, admitted as much. "Here's the situation. A dead out-worlder was found in the harbor this morning. His hair was brown. I'm not entirely certain, but the chances are—let me see, yes, two out of three that Angmark's hair is black."

Kershaul pulled at the Cave Owl's goatee. "How do you arrive at that probability?"

"The information came to me through Rolver's hands. He has blond hair. If Angmark has assumed Rolver's identity, he would naturally alter the information which came to me this morning. Both you and Welibus admit to black hair."

"Hm," said Kershaul. "Let me see if I follow your line of reasoning. You feel that Haxo Angmark has killed either Rolver, Welibus or myself and assumed the dead man's identity. Right?"

Thissell looked at him in surprise. "You yourself emphasized that Angmark could not set up another out-world establishment without revealing himself! Don't you remember?"

"Oh, certainly. To continue. Rolver delivered a message to you stating that Angmark was dark, and announced himself to be blond."

"Yes. Can you verify this? I mean for the old Rolver."

"No," said Kershaul sadly. "I've seen neither Rolver nor Welibus without their masks."

"If Rolver is not Angmark," Thissell mused, "if Angmark indeed has black hair, then both you and Welibus come under suspicion."

"Very interesting," said Kershaul. He examined Thissell warily. "For that matter, you yourself might be Angmark. What color is your hair?"

"Brown," said Thissell curtly. He lifted the gray fur of the Moon Moth mask at the back of his head.

"But you might be deceiving me as to the text of the message," Kershaul put forward.

"I'm not," said Thissell wearily. "You can check with Rolver if you care to."

Kershaul shook his head. "Unnecessary. I believe you. But another matter: what of voices? You've heard all of us before and after Angmark arrived. Isn't there some indication there?"

"No. I'm so alert for any evidence of change that you all sound rather different. And the masks muffle your voices."

Kershaul tugged the goatee. "I don't see any immediate solution to the problem." He chuckled. "In any event, need there be? Before Angmark's advent, there were Rolver, Welibus, Kershaul and Thissell. Now—for all practical purposes—there are still Rolver, Welibus, Kershaul and Thissell. Who is to say that the new member may not be an improvement upon the old?"

"An interesting thought," agreed Thissell, "but it so happens that I have a personal interest in identifying Angmark. My career is at stake."

"I see," murmured Kershaul. "The situation then becomes an issue between yourself and Angmark."

"You won't help me?"

"Not actively. I've become pervaded with Sirenese individualism. I think you'll find that Rolver and Welibus will respond similarly." He sighed. "All of us have been here too long."

Thissell stood deep in thought. Kershaul waited patiently a moment, then said, "Do you have any further questions?"

"No," said Thissell. "I have merely a favor to ask you."

"I'll oblige if I possibly can," Kershaul replied courteously.

"Give me, or lend me, one of your slaves, for a week or two."

Kershaul played an exclamation of amusement on the *ganga.* "I hardly like to part with my slaves; they know me and my ways—"

"As soon as I catch Angmark you'll have him back."

"Very well," said Kershaul. He rattled a summons on his *hymerkin,* and a slave appeared. "Anthony," sang Kershaul, "you are to go with Ser Thissell and serve him for a short period."

The slave bowed, without pleasure.

Thissell took Anthony to his houseboat, and questioned him at length, noting certain of the responses upon a chart. He then enjoined Anthony to say nothing of what had passed, and consigned him to the care of Toby and Rex. He gave further instructions to move the houseboat away from the dock and allow no one aboard until his return.

He set forth once more along the way to the landing field, and found Rolver at a lunch of spiced fish, shredded bark of the salad tree, and a bowl of native currants. Rolver clapped an order on the *hymerkin,* and a slave set a place for Thissell. "And how are the investigations proceeding?"

"I'd hardly like to claim any progress," said Thissell. "I assume that I can count on your help?"

Rolver laughed briefly. "You have my good wishes."

"More concretely," said Thissell, "I'd like to borrow a slave from you. Temporarily."

Rolver paused in his eating. "Whatever for?"

"I'd rather not explain," said Thissell. "But you can be sure that I make no idle request."

Without graciousness Rolver summoned a slave and consigned him to Thissell's service.

On the way gack to his houseboat, Thissell stopped at Welibus' office.

Welibus looked up from his work. "Good afternoon, Ser Thissell."

Thissell came directly to the point. "Ser Welibus, will you lend me a slave for a few days?"

Welibus hesitated, then shrugged. "Why not?" He clacked his *hymerkin;* a slave appeared. "Is he satisfactory? Or would you prefer a young female?" He chuckled rather offensively, to Thissell's way of thinking.

"He'll do very well. I'll return him in a few days."

"No hurry." Welibus made an easy gesture and returned to his work.

Thissell continued to his houseboat, where he separately interviewed each of his two new slaves and made notes upon his chart.

Dusk came soft over the Titanic Ocean. Toby and Rex sculled the houseboat away from the dock, out across the silken waters. Thissell sat on the deck listening to the sound of soft voices, the flutter and tinkle of musical instruments. Lights from the floating houseboats glowed yellow and wan watermelon-red. The shore was dark; the Night-men would presently come slinking to paw through refuse and stare jealously across the water.

In nine days the *Buenaventura* came past Sirene on its regular schedule; Thissell had his orders to return to Polypolis. In nine days, could he locate Haxo Angmark?

Nine days weren't too many, Thissell decided, but they might possibly be enough.

Two days passed, and three and four and five. Every day Thissell went ashore and at least once a day visited Rolver, Welibus and Kershaul.

Each reacted differently to his presence. Rolver was sardonic and irritable; Welibus formal and at least superficially affable; Kershaul mild and suave, but ostentatiously impersonal and detached in his conversation.

Thissell remained equally bland to Rolver's dour jibes, Welibus' jocundity, Kershaul's withdrawal. And every day on returning to his houseboat he made marks on his chart.

The sixth, the seventh, the eighth day came and passed. Rolver, with rather brutal directness, inquired if Thissell wished to arrange for passage on the *Buenaventura*. Thissell considered, and said, "Yes, you had better reserve passage for one."

"Back to the world of faces," shuddered Rolver. "Faces! Everywhere pallid, fish-eyed faces. Mouths like pulp, noses knotted and punctured; flat, flabby faces. I don't think I could stand it after living here. Luckily you haven't become a real Sirenese."

"But I won't be going back," said Thissell.

"I thought you wanted me to reserve passage."

"I do. For Haxo Angmark. He'll be returning to Polypolis, in the brig."

"Well, well," said Rolver. "So you've picked him out."

"Of course," said Thissell. "Haven't you?"

Rolver shrugged. "He's either Welibus or Kershaul, that's as close as I can make it. So long as he wears his mask and calls himself either Welibus or Kershaul, it means nothing to me."

"It means a great deal to me," said Thissell. "What time tomorrow does the lighter go up?"

"Eleven twenty-two sharp. If Haxo Angmark's leaving, tell him to be on time."

"He'll be here," said Thissell.

He made his usual call upon Welibus and Kershaul, then, returning to his houseboat, put three final marks on his chart.

The evidence was here, plain and convincing. Not absolutely incontrovertible evidence, but enough to warrant a definite move. He checked over his gun. Tomorrow, the day of decision. He could afford no errors.

The day dawned bright white, the sky like the inside of an oyster shell; Mireille rose through iridescent mists. Toby and Rex sculled the houseboat to the dock. The remaining three out-world houseboats floated somnolently on the slow swells.

One boat Thissell watched in particular, that whose owner Haxo Angmark had killed and dropped into the harbor. This boat presently moved toward the shore, and Haxo Angmark himself stood on the front deck, wearing a mask Thissell had never seen before: a construction of scarlet feathers, black glass and spiked green hair.

Thissell was forced to admire his poise. A clever scheme, cleverly planned and executed—but marred by an insurmountable difficulty.

Angmark returned within. The houseboat reached the dock. Slaves flung out mooring lines, lowered the gangplank. Thissell, his gun ready in the pocket flap of his robes, walked down the dock, went aboard. He pushed open the door to the saloon. The man at the table raised his red, black and green mask in surprise.

Thissell said, "Angmark, please don't argue or make any—"

Something hard and heavy tackled him from behind; he was flung to the floor, his gun wrested expertly away.

Behind him the *hymerkin* clattered; a voice sang, "Bind the fool's arms."

The man sitting at the table rose to his feet, removed the red, black and green mask to reveal the black cloth of a slave. Thissell twisted his head. Over him stood Haxo Angmark, wearing a mask Thissell recognized as a Dragon-Tamer, fabricated from black metal, with a knife-blade nose, socketed eyelids, and three crests running back over the scalp.

The mask's expression was unreadable, but Angmark's voice was triumphant. "I trapped you very easily."

"So you did," said Thissell. The slave finished knotting his wrists together. A clatter of Angmark's *hymerkin* sent him away. "Get to your feet," said Angmark. "Sit in that chair."

"What are we waiting for?" inquired Thissell.

"Two of our fellows still remain out on the water. We won't need them for what I have in mind."

"Which is?"

"You'll learn in due course," said Angmark. "We have an hour or so on our hands."

Thissell tested his bonds. They were undoubtedly secure.

Angmark seated himself. "How did you fix on me? I admit to being curious. . . . Come, come," he chided as Thissell sat silently. "Can't you recognize that I have defeated you? Don't make affairs unpleasant for yourself."

Thissell shrugged. "I operated on a basic principle. A man can mask his face, but he can't mask his personality."

"Aha," said Angmark. "Interesting. Proceed."

"I borrowed a slave from you and the other two out-worlders, and I questioned them carefully. What masks had their masters worn during the month before your arrival? I prepared a chart and plotted their responses. Rolver wore the Tarn-Bird about eighty percent of the time, the remaining twenty percent divided between the Sophist Abstraction and the Black Intricate. Welibus had a taste for the heroes of Kan-Dachan Cycle. He wore the Chalekun, the Prince Intrepid, the Seavain most of the time: six days out of eight. The other two days he wore his South-Wind or his Gay Companion. Kershaul, more conservative, preferred the Cave Owl, the Star-Wanderer, and two or three other masks he wore at odd intervals.

"As I say, I acquired this information from possibly its most accurate source, the slaves. My next step was to keep watch upon the three of you. Every day I noted what masks you wore and compared it with my chart. Rolver wore his Tarn-Bird six times, his Black Intricate twice. Kershaul wore his Cave Owl five times, his Star Wanderer once, his Quincunx once and his Ideal of Perfection once. Welibus wore the Emerald Mountain twice, the Triple Phoenix three times, the Prince Intrepid once and the Shark-God twice."

Angmark nodded thoughtfully. "I see my error. I selected from Welibus's masks, but to my own taste—and as you point out, I revealed myself. But only to you." He rose and went to the window. "Kershaul and Rolver are now coming ashore; they'll soon be past and about their business—though I doubt if they'd interfere in any case; they've both become good Sirenese."

Thissell waited in silence. Ten minutes passed. Then Angmark reached to a shelf and picked up a knife. He looked at Thissell. "Stand up."

Thissell slowly rose to his feet. Angmark approached from the side, cut, lifted the Moon Moth from Thissell's head. Thissell gasped and made a vain attempt to seize it. Too late; his face was bare and naked.

Angmark turned away, removed his own mask, donned the Moon Moth. He struck a call on his *hymerkin*. Two slaves entered, stopped in shock at the sight of Thissell.

Angmark played a brisk tattoo, sang, "Carry this man up to the deck."

"Angmark," cried Thissell. "I'm maskless!"

The slaves seized him and in spite of Thissell's desperate struggles, conveyed him out on the deck, along the float and up on the dock.

Angmark fixed a rope around Thissell's neck. He said, "You are now Haxo Angmark, and I am Edwer Thissell. Welibus is dead; you shall soon be dead. I can handle your job without difficulty. I'll play musical instruments like a Night-man and sing like a crow. I'll wear the Moon Moth till it rots and then I'll get another. The report will go to Polypolis: Haxo Angmark is dead. Everything will be serene."

Thissell barely heard. "You can't do this," he whispered. "My mask, my face . . ." A large woman in a blue and pink flower mask walked down the dock. She saw Thissell and emitted a piercing shriek, flung herself prone on the deck.

"Come along," said Angmark brightly. He tugged at the rope, and so pulled Thissell down the dock. A man in a Pirate Captain mask coming up from his houseboat stood rigid in amazement.

Angmark played the *zachinko* and sang, "Behold the notorious criminal Haxo Angmark. Through all the outer-worlds his name is reviled; now he is captured and led in shame to his death. Behold Haxo Angmark!"

They turned into the esplanade. A child screamed in fright; a man called hoarsely. Thissell stumbled; tears tumbled from his eyes; he could see only disorganized shapes and colors. Angmark's voice belled out richly: "Everyone behold, the criminal of the out-worlds, Haxo Angmark! Approach and observe his execution!"

Thissell feebly cried out, "I'm not Angmark; I'm Edwer Thissell; he's Angmark." But no one listened to him; there were only cries of dismay, shock, disgust at the sight of his face. He called to Angmark, "Give me my mask, a slave-cloth . . ."

Angmark sang jubilantly, "In shame he lived, in maskless shame he dies."

A Forest Goblin stood before Angmark. "Moon Moth, we meet once more."

Angmark sang, "Stand aside, friend Goblin; I must execute this criminal. In shame he lived, in shame he dies!"

A crowd had formed around the group; masks stared in morbid titillation at Thissell.

The Forest Goblin jerked the rope from Angmark's hand, threw it to the ground. The crowd roared. Voices cried, "No duel, no duel! Execute the monster!"

A cloth was thrown over Thissell's head. Thissell awaited the thrust of a blade. But instead his bonds were cut. Hastily he adjusted the cloth, hiding his face, peering between the folds.

Four men clutched Haxo Angmark. The Forest Goblin confronted him, playing the *skaranyi*. "A week ago you reached to divest me of my mask; you have now achieved your perverse aim!"

"But he is a criminal," cried Angmark. "He is notorious, infamous!"

"What are his misdeeds?" sang the Forest Goblin.

"He has murdered, betrayed; he has wrecked ships; he has

tortured, blackmailed, robbed, sold children into slavery; he has—"

The Forest Goblin stopped him. "Your religious differences are of no importance. We can vouch, however, for your present crimes!"

The hostler stepped forward. He sang fiercely, "This insolent Moon Moth nine days ago sought to preempt my choicest mount!"

Another man pushed close. He wore a Universal Expert, and sang, "I am a Master Maskmaker; I recognize this Moon Moth out-worlder! Only recently he entered my shop and derided my skill. He deserves death!"

"Death to the out-world monster!" cried the crowd. A wave of men surged forward. Steel blades rose and fell; the deed was done.

Thissell watched, unable to move. The Forest Goblin approached, and playing the *stimic* sang sternly, "For you we have pity, but also contempt. A true man would never suffer such indignities!"

Thissell took a deep breath. He reached to his belt and found his *zachinko*. He sang, "My friend, you malign me! Can you not appreciate true courage? Would you prefer to die in combat or walk maskless along the esplanade?"

The Forest Goblin sang, "There is only one answer. First I would die in combat; I could not bear such shame."

Thissell sang, "I had such a choice. I could fight with my hands tied, and so die—or I could suffer shame, and through this shame conquer my enemy. You admit that you lack sufficient *strakh* to achieve this deed. I have proved myself a hero of bravery! I ask, who here has courage to do what I have done?"

"Courage?" demanded the Forest Goblin. "I fear nothing, up to and beyond death at the hands of the Night-men!"

"Then answer."

The Forest Goblin stood back. He played his double *kamanthil*. "Bravery indeed, if such were your motives."

The hostler struck a series of subdued *gomapard* chords and sang, "Not a man among us would dare what this maskless man has done."

The crowd muttered approval.

The maskmaker approached Thissell, obsequiously stroking his double *kamanthil*. "Pray, Lord Hero, step into my nearby shop, exchange this vile rag for a mask befitting your quality."

Another maskmaker sang, "Before you choose, Lord Hero, examine my magnificent creations!"

A man in a Bright Sky Bird mask approached Thissell reverently. "I have only just completed a sumptuous houseboat; seventeen years of toil have gone into its fabrication. Grant me the good fortune of accepting and using this splendid craft; aboard waiting to serve you are alert slaves and pleasant maidens; there is ample wine in storage and soft silken carpets on the decks."

"Thank you," said Thissell, striking the *zachinko* with vigor and confidence. "I accept with pleasure. But first a mask."

The maskmaker struck an interrogative trill on the *gomapard*. "Would the Lord Hero consider a Sea-Dragon Conqueror beneath his dignity?"

"By no means," said Thissell. "I consider it suitable and satisfactory. We shall go now to examine it."

The View from Outside

From the general literary world outside the science fiction ghetto—the "mundane" world, the sf fans call it disdainfully —science fiction looks like pretty insular stuff, full of non-literary readers, magazines, conventions (of both kinds), and stories. Many critics make no distinctions among genres, regarding all science fiction as formula-ridden and beneath serious consideration; those who do distinguish often catergorize science fiction with comic strips like *Buck Rogers* and *Flash Gordon*, comic books like *Superman*, or "sci-fi" films like *The Thing* or *Godzilla*. Some of this attitude has been absorbed by sf writers themselves.

A more perceptive group of critics has looked into the science fiction phenomenon closely and observed that science fiction often is written with serious intent and sometimes with literary skill, that the subject matter, rather than recapitulating formulas, frequently deals with a variety of important matters. A number of writers not customarily associated with science fiction have dipped into the common store of sf ideas for themes and metaphors. These include John Barth, Pierre Boulle, William Burroughs, Anthony Burgess, William Golding, John Hersey, Doris Lessing, Vladimir Nabokov, Walker Percy, Thomas Pynchon, Ayn Rand, John Williams, Herman Wouk, and Vercors (Jean Bruller), in addition to such more familiar practitioners of the sf writer's profession as Aldous Huxley, George Orwell, and Kurt Vonnegut, Jr.

Other writers have worked independently, turning to sf-like materials upon occasion as naturally as they might turn to fable or fairy tale, myth or epic. Such a writer has been the distinguished Argentine short-story writer, poet, essayist, and university professor Jorge Luis Borges (1899–   ).

Borges was born in Buenos Aires of ancestry that was Spanish, English, and remotely Portuguese Jewish; his fiction seems less Spanish or Latin American than cosmopolitan. When he was fifteen, he traveled with his family to Europe and got his secondary education in Geneva, Switzerland, during World War I. From 1919 to 1921, he traveled in Spain and associated himself with the Ultraist literary group. In 1921 he returned to Argentina and began writing laconic free-verse poems, mostly about Buenos Aires, and scholarly essays on literary criticism, metaphysics, and language. Three volumes of poetry and three volumes of essays appeared before 1930.

In 1930, however, he virtually abandoned poetry and turned for the next decade to the writing and polishing of short, compact, precise narratives that were universal in their circumstances and appeal. In 1938 he was appointed librarian of a small municipal Buenos Aires library, but he lost the position in 1946 for political reasons. His first collection of stories appeared in 1935, *El jardin de los senderos que se bifurcan* in 1941, *Ficciones*, his most celebrated collection, in 1944, and *El Aleph* in 1942. His *Collected Works* was published in three volumes in 1954.

In 1955, with the overthrow of the Peronist regime, Borges was named Director of the National Library, and the following year was appointed to the chair of English and North American Literature at the University of Buenos Aires. Failing eyesight and other ailments reduced his writing production. His first English translations came late in his career: *Ficciones* in 1962, and *Labyrinths* the same year, with a revised edition in 1964.

Borges never wrote a novel, arguing that "the compilation of vast books is a laborious and impoverishing extravagance." His stories, instead, are incredibly compact. He has a substantial command of English and of science fiction, admiring Poe and Wells in particular; he included Lovecraft, Heinlein, van Vogt, and Bradbury in his *Introduction to American Literature* (1967).

According to André Maurois, Borges's literary predecessor was Kafka, and, according to Borges, Kafka's predecessors were Zeno of Elea, Kierkegaard, and Robert Browning. Maurois points out that if Kafka had never written, nobody would have noticed the Kafka in each of these earlier writers, which validates one of Borges's paradoxes: "Every writer creates his own precursors."

Some of Borges's best stories and those by which he is most appreciated are fantastic. Fantastic literature, according to Borges, has only four basic devices: the work within the work, the contamination of reality by dream, the voyage in time, and the double. Some of these fantastic stories classify as science fiction. "Tlön, Uqbar, Orbis Tertius," for instance, displays a complete new world invented by a secret society of astronomers, engineers, biologists, metaphysicians, and geometricians that begins to crowd out our own world. "Lottery in Babylon" deals with a mysterious Company that distributes good and bad luck in a game of chance that becomes so complex it is indistinguishable from real life. "The Circular Ruins" presents a dreaming character who gives life to a man only to discover that the dreamer is someone else's dream. "Funes, the Memorious" describes a man who remembers so perfectly that the past is as accessible as the present.

"The Library of Babel" is a science fiction story in which a vast and perhaps infinite library becomes a metaphor for the universe. As Ivor Rogers has pointed out, the idea came from the nineteenth-century German science fiction writer Kurd Lasswitz. Borges mentioned the idea in an essay about Shaw ten years before the story was written; and the idea itself can be traced to the thirteenth-century mystic Raymond Lully. It is akin to a more recent speculation that a group of monkeys typing randomly on typewriters in an infinity of time could reproduce all the books in the British Museum. But Borges is not concerned with originality. He is never reluctant to admit his sources. No one, he believes, can claim originality, since all writers are more or less faithful amanuenses of the spirit.

Like many of his stories, "The Library of Babel" reads more like a fictionalized essay, complete with footnotes. Characterization is minimal—only enough to dramatize the concept through the reactions of the narrator, or fictional essayist, to explanations of the situation of his people. But the idea and its development are everything, as in much of science fiction: Life becomes an attempt to discover the meaning of the universe, and theories, presented and examined, have a curious and not coincidental parallel to our own existence. Our universe may not be a library "whose consummate center is any hexagon, and whose circumference is inaccessible," but surely this theory is not much different from Einstein's that the universe is infinite but bounded.

Does the concept make us stop and think? Is Borges writing about himself when he writes about the metaphysicians of Tlön? He wrote of them: "They seek neither truth nor likelihood; they seek astonishment. They think metaphysics is a branch of the literature of fantasy."

The Library of Babel

by Jorge Luis Borges

Translated by Anthony Kerrigan

> By this art you may contemplate
> the variation of the 23 letters . . .
> —*The Anatomy of Melancholy,*
> *Part 2, Sect. II, Mem. IV.*

The universe (which others call the Library) is composed of an indefinite, perhaps an infinite, number of hexagonal galleries, with enormous ventilation shafts in the middle, encircled by very low railings. From any hexagon the upper or lower stories are visible, interminably. The distribution of the galleries is invariable. Twenty shelves—five long shelves per side—cover all sides except two; their height, which is that of each floor, scarcely exceeds that of an average librarian. One of the free sides gives upon a narrow entranceway, which leads to another gallery, identical to the first and to all the others. To the left and to the right of the entrance way are two miniature rooms. One allows standing room for sleeping; the other, the satisfaction of fecal necessities. Through this section passes the spiral staircase, which plunges down into the abyss and rises up to the heights. In the entranceway hangs a mirror, which faithfully duplicates appearances. People are in the habit of inferring from this mirror that the Library is not infinite (if it really were, why this illusory duplication?); I prefer to dream that the polished surfaces feign and promise infinity. . . .

Light comes from some spherical fruits called by the name

of lamps. There are two, running transversally, in each hexagon. The light they emit is insufficient, incessant.

Like all men of the Library, I have traveled in my youth. I have journeyed in search of a book, perhaps of the catalogue of catalogues; now that my eyes can scarcely decipher what I write, I am preparing to die a few leagues from the hexagon in which I was born. Once dead, there will not lack pious hands to hurl me over the banister; my sepulchre shall be the unfathomable air: my body will sink lengthily and will corrupt and dissolve in the wind engendered by the fall, which is infinite. I affirm that the Library is interminable. The idealists argue that the hexagonal halls are a neccessary form of absolute space or, at least, of our intuition of space. They contend that a triangular or pentagonal hall is inconceivable. (The mystics claim that to them ecstasy reveals a round chamber containing a great book with a continuous back circling the walls of the room; but their testimony is suspect; their words, obscure. That cyclical book is God.) Let it suffice me, for the time being, to repeat the classic dictum: *The Library is a sphere whose consummate center is any hexagon, and whose circumference is inaccessible.*

Five shelves correspond to each one of the walls of each hexagon; each shelf contains thirty-two books of a uniform format; each book is made up of four hundred and ten pages; each page, of forty lines; each line, of some eighty black letters. There are also letters on the spine of each book; these letters do not indicate or prefigure what the pages will say. I know that such a lack of relevance, at one time, seemed mysterious. Before summarizing the solution (whose disclosure, despite its tragic implications, is perhaps the capital fact of this history), I want to recall certain axioms.

The first: The Library exists *ab aeterno.* No reasonable mind can doubt this truth, whose immediate corollary is the future eternity of the world. Man, the imperfect librarian, may be the work of chance or malevolent demiurges; the universe, with its elegant endowment of shelves, of enigmatic volumes, of indefatigable ladders for the voyager, and of privies for the seated librarian, can only be the work of a god. In order to perceive the distance which exists between the divine and the human, it is enough to compare the rude tremulous symbols which my fallible hand scribbles on the end pages of a book with the organic letters inside: exact, delicate, intensely black, inimitably symmetric.

The second: *The number of orthographic symbols is twenty-five.** This bit of evidence permitted the formulation, three hundred years ago, of a general theory of the Library and the satisfactory resolution of the problem which no conjecture had yet made clear: the formless and chaotic nature of almost all books, one of these books, which my father saw in a hexagon of the circuit number fifteen ninety-four, was composed of the letters MCV perversely repeated from the first line to the last. Another, very much consulted in this zone, is a mere labyrinth of letters, but on the next-to-the-last page, one may read *O Time your pyramids*. As is well known: for one reasonable line or one straightforward note there are leagues of insensate cacophony, of verbal farragoes and incoherencies. (I know of a wild region whose librarians repudiate the vain superstitious custom of seeking any sense in books and compare it to looking for meaning in dreams or in the chaotic lines of one's hands. . . . They admit that the inventors of writing imitated the twenty-five natural symbols, but they maintain that this application is accidental and that books in themselves mean nothing. This opinion—we shall see—is not altogether false.)

For a long time it was believed that these impenetrable books belonged to past or remote languages. It is true that the most ancient men, the first librarians, made use of a language quite different from the one we speak today; it is true that some miles to the right the language is dialectical and that ninety stories up it is incomprehensible. All this, I repeat, is true; but four hundred and ten pages of unvarying MCVs do not correspond to any language, however dialectical or rudimentary it might be. Some librarians insinuated that each letter could influence the next, and that the value of MCV on the third line of page 71 was not the same as that of the same series in another position on another page; but this vague thesis did not prosper. Still other men thought in terms of cryptographs; this conjecture has come to be universally accepted, though not in the sense in which it was formulated by its inventors.

* The original manuscript of the present note does not contain digits or capital letters. The punctuation is limited to the comma and the period. These two signs, plus the space sign and the twenty-two letters of the alphabet, make up the twenty-five sufficient symbols enumerated by the unknown author.

Five hundred years ago, the chief of an upper hexagon*
came upon a book as confusing as all the rest but which contained nearly two pages of homogenous lines. He showed his
find to an ambulant decipherer, who told him the lines were
written in Portuguese. Others told him they were in Yiddish.
In less than a century the nature of the language was finally
established: it was a Samoyed-Lithuanian dialect of Guarani,
with classical Arabic inflections. The contents were also deci-
phered: notions of combinational analysis, illustrated by
examples of variations with unlimited repetition. These examples made it possible for a librarian of genius to discover the
fundamental law of the Library. This thinker observed that
all the books, however diverse, are made up of uniform elements: the period, the comma, the space, the twenty-two
letters of the alphabet. He also adduced a circumstance confirmed by all travelers: *There are not, in the whole vast
Library, two identical books.* From all these incontrovertible
premises he deduced that the Library is total and that its
shelves contain all the possible combinations of the twenty-
odd orthographic symbols (whose number, though vast, is not
infinite); that is, everything which can be expressed, in all
languages. Everything is there: the minute history of the
future, the autobiographies of the archangels, the faithful
catalogue of the Library, thousands and thousands of false
catalogues, a demonstration of the fallacy of these catalogues,
a demonstration of the fallacy of the true catalogue, the
Gnostic gospel of Basilides, the commentary of this gospel,
the commentary on the commentary of this gospel, the veridi-
cal account of your death, a version of each book in all
languages, the interpolations of every book in all books.

When it was proclaimed that the Library comprised all
books, the first impression was one of extravagant joy. All
men felt themselves lords of a secret, intact treasure. There
was no personal or universal problem whose eloquent solution did not exist—in some hexagon. The universe was
justified, the universe suddenly expanded to the limitless dimensions of hope. At that time there was much talk of the
Vindications: books of apology and prophecy, which vindi-
cated for all time the actions of every man in the world and

---

* Formerly, for each three hexagons there was one man. Suicide and
pulmonary diseases have destroyed this proportion. My memory recalls
scenes of unspeakable melancholy: there have been many nights when I
have ventured down corridors and polished staircases without encounter-
ing a single librarian.

established a store of prodigious arcana for the future. Thousands of covetous persons abandoned their dear natal hexagons and crowded up the stairs, urged on by the vain aim of finding their Vindication. These pilgrims disputed in the narrow corridors, hurled dark maledictions, strangled each other on the divine stairways, flung the deceitful books to the bottom of the tunnels, and died as they were thrown into space by men from remote regions. Some went mad. . . .

The Vindications do exist. I have myself seen two of these books, which were concerned with future people, people who were perhaps not imaginary. But the searchers did not remember that the calculable possibility of a man's finding his own book, or some perfidious variation of his own book, is close to zero.

The clarification of the basic mysteries of humanity—the origin of the Library and of time—was also expected. It is credible that those grave mysteries can be explained in words: if the language of the philosophers does not suffice, the multiform Library will have produced the unexpected language required and the necessary vocabularies and grammars for this language.

It is now four centuries since men have been wearying the hexagons. . . .

There are official searchers, *inquisitors*. I have observed them carrying out their functions: they are always exhausted. They speak of a staircase without steps where they were almost killed. They speak of galleries and stairs with the local librarian. From time to time they will pick up the nearest book and leaf through its pages, in search of infamous words. Obviously, no one expects to discover anything.

The uncommon hope was followed, naturally enough, by deep depression. The certainty that some shelf in some hexagon contained precious books and that these books were inaccessible seemed almost intolerable. A blasphemous sect suggested that all searches be given up and that men everywhere shuffle letters and symbols until they succeeded in composing, by means of an improbable stroke of luck, the canonical books. The authorities found themselves obliged to issue severe orders. The sect disappeared, but in my childhood I still saw old men who would hide out in the privies for long periods of time, and, with metal disks in a forbidden dicebox, feebly mimic the divine disorder.

Other men, inversely, thought that the primary task was to eliminate useless works. They would invade the hexagons, exhibiting credentials which were not always false, skim through a volume with annoyance, and then condemn entire bookshelves to destruction: their ascetic, hygienic fury is responsible for the senseless loss of millions of books. Their name is execrated; but those who mourn the "treasures" destroyed by this frenzy overlook two notorious facts. One: the Library is so enormous that any reduction undertaken by humans is infinitesimal. Two: each book is unique, irreplaceable, but (inasmuch as the Library is total) there are always several hundreds of thousands of imperfect facsimiles—of works which differ only by one letter or one comma. Contrary to public opinion, I dare suppose that the consequences of the depredations committed by the Purifiers have been exaggerated by the horror which these fanatics provoked. They were spurred by the delirium of storming the books in the Crimson Hexagon: books of a smaller than ordinary format, omnipotent, illustrated, magical.

We know, too, of another superstition of that time: the Man of the Book. In some shelf of some hexagon, men reasoned, there must exist a book which is the cipher and perfect compendium of *all the rest:* some librarian has perused it, and it is analogous to a god. Vestiges of the worship of that remote functionary still persist in the language of this zone. Many pilgrimages have sought Him out. For a century they trod the most diverse routes in vain. How to locate the secret hexagon which harbored it? Someone proposed a regressive approach: in order to locate book A, first consult book B which will indicate the location of A; in order to locate book B, first consult book C, and so on ad infinitum. . . .

I have squandered and consumed my years in adventures of this type. To me, it does not seem unlikely that on some shelf of the universe there lies a total book.* I pray the unknown gods that some man—even if only one man, and though it have been thousands of years ago!—may have examined and read it. If honor and wisdom and happiness are not for me, let them be for others. May heaven exist, though my place be in hell. Let me be outraged and annihilated, but

---

* I repeat: it is enough that a book be possible for it to exist. Only the impossible is excluded. For example: no book is also a stairway, though doubtless there are books that discuss and deny and demonstrate this possibility and others whose structure corresponds to that of a stairway.

may Thy enormous Library be justified, for one instant, in one being.

The impious assert that absurdities are the norm in the Library and that anything reasonable (even humble and pure coherence) is an almost miraculous exception. They speak (I know) of "the febrile Library, whose hazardous volumes run the constant risk of being changed into others and in which everything is affirmed, denied, and confused as by a divinity in delirium." These words, which not only denounce disorder but exemplify it as well, manifestly demonstrate the bad taste of the speakers and their desperate ignorance. Actually, the Library includes all verbal structures, all the variations allowed by the twenty-five orthographic symbols, but it does not permit of one absolute absurdity. It is pointless to observe that the best book in the numerous hexagons under my administration is entitled *Combed Clap of Thunder;* or that another is called *The Plaster Cramp;* and still another *Axaxaxas Mlö.* Such propositions as are contained in these titles, at first sight incoherent, doubtless yield a cryptographic or allegorical justification. Since they are verbal, these justifications already figure, *ex hypothesi*, in the Library. I cannot combine certain letters, as *dhcmrlchtdj*, which the divine Library has not already foreseen in combination, and which in one of its secret languages does not encompass some terrible meaning. No one can articulate a syllable which is not full of tenderness and fear, and which is not, in one of those languages, the powerful name of some god. To speak is to fall into tautologies. This useless and wordy epistle itself already exists in one of the thirty volumes of the five shelves in one of the uncountable hexagons—and so does its refutation. (An *n* number of possible languages makes use of the same vocabulary; in some of them, the symbol *library* admits of the correct definition *ubiquitous and everlasting system of hexagonal galleries,* but *library* is *bread* or *pyramid* or anything else, and the seven words which define it possess another value. You who read me, are you sure you understand my language?)

Methodical writing distracts me from the present condition of men. But the certainty that everything has been already written nullifies or makes phantoms of us all. I know of districts where the youth prostrate themselves before books and barbarously kiss the pages, though they do not know how to make out a single letter. Epidemics, heretical disagreements, the pilgrimages which inevitably degenerate into banditry, have decimated the population. I believe I have mentioned the suicides, more frequent each year. Perhaps I am deceived by old age and fear, but I suspect that the human species—the unique human species—is on the road to extinction, while the Library will last on forever: illuminated, solitary, infinite, perfectly immovable, filled with precious volumes, useless, incorruptible, secret.

Infinite I have just written. I have not interpolated this adjective merely from rhetorical habit. It is not illogical, I say, to think that the world is infinite. Those who judge it to be limited, postulate that in remote places the corridors and stairs and hexagons could inconceivably cease—a manifest absurdity. Those who imagine it to be limitless forget that the possible number of books is limited. I dare insinuate the following solution to this ancient problem: *The Library is limitless and periodic.* If an eternal voyager were to traverse it in any direction, he would find, after many centuries, that the same volumes are repeated in the same disorder (which, repeated, would constitute an order: Order itself). My solitude rejoices in this elegant hope.*

Mar del Plata
1941

---

* Letizia Alvarez de Toledo has observed that the vast Library is useless. Strictly speaking, *one single volume* should suffice: a single volume of ordinary format, printed in nine or ten type body, and consisting of an infinite number of infinitely thin pages. (At the beginning of the seventeenth century, Cavalieri said that any solid body is the superposition of an infinite number of planes.) This silky vade mecum would scarcely be handy: each apparent leaf of the book would divide into other analogous leaves. The inconceivable central leaf would have no reverse.

Inner Concerns in Outer Space

In the early 1960s with the euphoria of the postwar boom already faded into disillusionment and the radical vigor of the New Wave yet to evidence itself, science fiction seemed to be drifting rudderless upon a sea of change. Outer space, as a symbol for the Campbellian emphasis on the importance of the external world, seemed insufficient; but was the only alternative a radical swing toward what J. G. Ballard would call "inner space"?

Frank Herbert (1920–   ) apparently did not think so. His work displayed a respect for traditional science fiction, but he brought to it a new concern for inner struggle and for more difficult choices. The same social and psychological influences that led to the introspection of the New Wave may well have produced Herbert's emphasis on individual and mass psychology, sociology, history, religion, philosophy, mysticism, and myth, but Herbert chose to build upon the past and use it for his own purposes.

Herbert was born at Tacoma, Washington, and attended the University of Washington. He worked as a newspaper reporter and editor for various West Coast newspapers, and also as a photographer, oyster diver, lay analyst, and oenologist. His first story was published in *Esquire* in 1945 and his first science fiction story—"Looking for Something?"— in *Startling Stories* for April 1952, but the novel length was more suited to his interests and abilities. He has written comparatively few short stories, some of which have been collected in *The Worlds of Frank Herbert* (1970), *The Book of Frank Herbert* (1973), and *The Best of Frank Herbert* (1975). In 1970 he became a full-time freelance writer.

Herbert's first novel came out of his service in the U.S. Navy in World War II; it was serialized in *Astounding* in 1955–56 as *Under Pressure* and published in book form as *The Dragon in the Sea, 21st Century Sub,* and *Under Pressure.* His second and most famous novel, *Dune,* was serialized in two sections in *Analog, Dune World* (1963–64) and *The Prophet of Dune* (1965), and published in hard covers in 1965. In spite of the fact that it won the first novel Nebula Award and also won a Hugo, it was not the success that it became after steady sales in paperback accumulated to more than one million copies.

Herbert turned out a group of unrelated novels—*Destination: Void* (1966), *The Eyes of Heisenberg* (1966), *The Green Brain* (1966), *The Heaven Makers* (1968), and *The Santaroga Barrier* (1968)—before producing *Dune Messiah* (1969). That was followed by *Whipping Star* (1970), *Soul Catcher* (1972), *The God Makers* (1972), and *Hellstrom's Hive* (1973). But not until *Children of Dune* (1976), which became the first science fiction hardcover bestseller, was Herbert's position clearly established. Subsequently he sold the film rights to *Dune* to a major producer for a sum rumored to be $1 million. The fourth volume in the *Dune* series, *God Emperor of Dune* (1981), solidified Herbert's reputation as one of the most successful authors in the field. Two novels—*The Dosadi Experiment* (1978) and *The Jesus Incident* (1979) with Bill Ransom—and *The Illustrated Dune* (1978) appeared between the last two *Dune* novels.

Dune is a long (498 pages plus appendices), complex novel placed in the far-distant future of a human-inhabited galaxy. It includes a complicated van Vogtian plot full of Byzantine intrigue and hidden superpowers placed in an Asimovian future history. Even its mythic structure of a youth needing to develop his mature strength and his superhuman abilities in order to regain his lost kingdom is van Vogtian, and the novel's involvement with prescience is psychohistorical. One critic (John L. Grigsby) has called the *Foundation* stories and the *Dune* novels "a vision reversed," and Herbert, in a chapter contributed to *The Craft of Science Fiction* (1976), paid tribute to the *Foundation Triology* as "one of the all-time classics." But he suggested that the *Foundation* stories are based on "unexamined assumptions" and that other assumptions "could serve as the jumping-off point for an entirely new series of stories."

The assumptions that Herbert makes in *Dune* are that conditions of life on various planets will produce different kinds of humans, that similar conditions will produce similar results (the desert world of Arrakis has developed an Arablike character and culture), that hardship is good for people and produces stronger and more effective warriors, that the human species has hidden talents that can be brought into use through genetic selection and training, that racial memory resides in the cells and in special circumstances individual memories can be shared, that a galactic empire would be organized on loose feudal lines rather than Asimov's centralized Roman model, that the development of computers would have resulted in a galaxywide rebellion against machine intelligence and in the development of new human mental abilities, that the banning of atomic bombs and the development of body shields would mean a return to hand-to-hand combat, that individuals and human existence itself survive in a narrow space between life and death, between foresight and will, between the pain of the black box and the poison of the gom jabbar, between the poison of the Water of Life and the change in it that produces sharing and visions. . . .

To these assumptions, and others, Herbert brought a mythic structure, a richly detailed social, historical, and physical scene that helped establish a model for the invented-world novel (as critic Robert A. Foster has pointed out) and led to the publication of a *Dune Encyclopedia,* and a concern for ecology, human development, and messianic movements.

Perhaps the most effective part of *Dune,* and the part that gives the series its title, is the desert world Arrakis, a world in which water is so scarce that people must preserve every drop of moisture, including that which makes up the human body; it produces an environment that people must honor, or they will die. But Arrakis also produces melange, the invaluable and addictive "spice" that can prolong life and enhance human ability to foresee the future; it also is inextricably a part of the Arrakeen ecology. Arrakis also produces the tough, tribal Fremen, the best warriors in the galaxy, and they can change the future through a wild, bloody jihad that Paul sees as "terrible purpose." Herbert got the idea for the novel from an assignment to write an article about the experiments of an Oregon coast research station to control shifting sand dunes, and his long-held desire to write a novel about "messianic

convulsions which inflict themselves upon human societies."
He planned the work for five years.

The story of *Dune* is told on several levels: the effort to
control Arrakis and the spice trade and eventually the galactic empire; the conspiracy that turns Arrakis over to Duke
Leto and the Atreides family only to wipe them out with
treachery and a massive attack; the plans of the Bene
Gesserit "witches," who practice body and mental control, to
breed a "Kwisatz Haderach," a male who can endure the
Bene Gesserit experience of remembering the past and fore-
seeing the future; the Fremen's effort to change the ecology
of Arrakis; the education and development of the Duke's son
Paul to avenge his father's death and restore his family's for-
tunes and position; Paul's rise as the Kwisatz Haderach and
the Fremen's *Lisan al-Gaib;* and the internal conflict caused
by his vision of a bloody future. . . .

The following selection from *Dune* describes the banquet
that occurs after the arrival of the Atreides family on Arrakis. It brings together the various forces at work upon
Arrakis, illustrates the value of water on the planet and intro-
duces one ecological concern, and demonstrates Herbert's
narrative method: the richness of description in which each
detail is linked to some element of plot or character, the development of the plot through conversation punctuated by
internal reflections on the meanings of statements and actions, and the unusual shifting point of view from Duke Leto
to Paul to Jessica to Kynes and back around the cycle several
times. In this manner Herbert develops theme and plot, en-
hances the elements of intrigue, role-playing, and subterfuge,
and brings out the difference between perception and reality.

From Dune

by Frank Herbert

Greatness is a transitory experience. It is never consist-
ent. It depends in part upon the myth-making imagination
of humankind. The person who experiences greatness must
have a feeling for the myth he is in. He must reflect what

*is projected upon him. And he must have a strong sense of
the sardonic. This is what uncouples him from belief in his
own pretensions. The sardonic is all that permits him to
move within himself. Without this quality, even occasional
greatness will destroy a man.*

—from *Collected Sayings of Muad'Dib* by the Princess
Irulan.

In the dining hall of the Arrakeen great house, suspensor
lamps had been lighted against the early dark. They cast their
yellow glows upward onto the black bull's head with its
bloody horns, and onto the darkly glistening oil painting of
the Old Duke.

Beneath these talismans, white linen shone around the burnished reflections of the Atreides silver, which had been
placed in precise arrangements along the great table—little
archipelagos of service waiting beside crystal glasses, each setting squared off before a heavy wooden chair. The classic
central chandelier remained unlighted, and its chain twisted
upward into shadows where the mechanism of the poison-
snooper had been concealed.

Pausing in the doorway to inspect the arrangements, the
Duke thought about the poison-snooper and what it signified
in his society.

All of a pattern, he thought. *You can plumb us by our language—the precise and delicate delineations for ways to
administer treacherous death. Will someone try chaumurky
tonight—poison in the drink? Or will it be chaumas—poison
in the food?*

He shook his head.

Beside each plate on the long table stood a flagon of water.
There was enough water along the table, the Duke estimated,
to keep a poor Arraken family for more than a year.

Flanking the doorway in which he stood were broad laving
basins of ornate yellow and green tile. Each basin had its
rack of towels. It was the custom, the housekeeper had explained, for guests as they entered to dip their hands
ceremoniously into a basin, slop several cups of water onto
the floor, dry their hands on a towel and fling the towel into
the growing puddle at the door. After the dinner, beggars
gathered outside to get the water squeezings from the towels.

How typical of a Harkonnen fief, the Duke thought. *Every degradation of the spirit that can be conceived.* He took a deep breath, feeling rage tighten his stomach.

"The custom stops here!" he muttered.

He saw a serving woman—one of the old and gnarled ones the housekeeper had recommended—hovering at the doorway from the kitchen across from him. The Duke signaled with upraised hand. She moved out of the shadows, scurried around the table toward him, and he noted the leathery face, the blue-within-blue eyes.

"My Lord wishes?" She kept her head bowed, eyes shielded.

He gestured. "Have these basins and towels removed."

"But . . . Noble Born. . . ." She looked up, mouth gaping.

"I know the custom!" he barked. "Take these basins to the front door. While we're eating and until we've finished, each beggar who calls may have a full cup of water. Understood?"

Her leathery face displayed a twisting of emotions: dismay, anger. . . .

With sudden insight, Leto realized that she must have planned to sell the water squeezings from the foot-trampled towels, wringing a few coppers from the wretches who came to the door. Perhaps that also was a custom.

His face clouded, and he growled: "I'm posting a guard to see that my orders are carried out to the letter."

He whirled, strode back down the passage to the Great Hall. Memories rolled in his mind like the toothless mutterings of old women. He remembered open water and waves—days of grass instead of sand—dazed summers that had whipped past him like windstorm leaves.

All gone.

I'm getting old, he thought. *I've felt the cold hand of my mortality. And in what? An old woman's greed.*

In the Great Hall, the Lady Jessica was the center of a mixed group standing in front of the fireplace. An open blaze crackled there, casting flickers of orange light onto jewels and laces and costly fabrics. He recognized in the group a stillsuit manufacturer down from Carthag, an electronics equipment importer, a water-shipper whose summer mansion was near his polar-cap factory, a representative of the Guild Bank (lean and remote, that one), a dealer in replacement parts for spice mining equipment, a thin and hard-faced woman whose escort service for off-planet visitors reputedly operated as cover for various smuggling, spying, and blackmail operations.

Most of the women in the hall seemed cast from a specific type—decorative, precisely turned out, an odd mingling of untouchable sensuousness.

Even without her position as hostess, Jessica would have dominated the group, he thought. She wore no jewelry and had chosen warm colors—a long dress almost the shade of the open blaze, and an earth-brown band around her bronzed hair.

He realized she had done this to taunt him subtly, a reproof against his recent pose of coldness. She was well aware that he liked her best in these shades—that he saw her as a rustling of warm colors.

Nearby, more an outflanker than a member of the group, stood Duncan Idaho in glittering dress uniform, flat face unreadable, the curling black hair neatly combed. He had been summoned back from the Fremen and had his orders from Hawat—*"Under pretext of guarding her, you will keep the Lady Jessica under constant surveillance."*

The Duke glanced around the room.

There was Paul in the corner surrounded by a fawning group of the younger Arrakeen richece, and, aloof among them, three officers of the House Troop. The Duke took particular note of the young woman. What a catch a ducal heir would make. But Paul was treating all equally with an air of reserved nobility.

He'll wear the title well, the Duke thought, and realized with a sudden chill that this was another death thought.

Paul saw his father in the doorway, avoided his eyes. He looked around at the clustering of guests, the jeweled hands clutching drinks (and the unobtrusive inspections with tiny remote-cast snoopers). Seeing all the chattering faces, Paul was suddenly repelled by them. They were cheap masks locked on festering thoughts—voices gabbling to drown out the loud silence in every breast.

I'm in a sour mood, he thought, and wondered what Gurney would say to that.

He knew his mood's source. He hadn't wanted to attend this function, but his father had been firm. "You have a place—a position to uphold. You're old enough to do this. You're almost a man."

Paul saw his father emerge from the doorway, inspect the room, then cross to the group around the Lady Jessica.

As Leto approached Jessica's group, the water-shipper was asking: "Is it true the Duke will put in weather control?"

From behind the man, the Duke said: "We haven't gone that far in our thinking, sir."

The man turned, exposing a bland round face, darkly tanned. "Ah-h, the Duke," he said. "We missed you."

Leto glanced at Jessica. "A thing needed doing." He returned his attention to the water-shipper, explained what he had ordered for the laving basins, adding: "As far as I'm concerned, the old custom ends now."

"Is this a ducal order, m'Lord?" the man asked.

"I leave that to your own . . . ah . . . conscience," the Duke said. He turned, noting Kynes come up to the group.

One of the women said: "I think it's a very generous gesture—giving water to the—" Someone shushed her.

The Duke looked at Kynes, noting that the planetologist wore an old-style dark brown uniform with epaulets of the Imperial Civil Servant and a tiny gold teardrop of rank at his collar.

The water-shipper asked in an angry voice: "Does the Duke imply criticism of our custom?"

"This custom has been changed," Leto said. He nodded to Kynes, marked the frown on Jessica's face, thought: *A frown does not become her, but it'll increase rumors of friction between us.*

"With the Duke's permission," the water-shipper said, "I'd like to inquire further about customs."

Leto heard the sudden oily tone in the man's voice, noted the watchful silence in this group, the way heads were beginning to turn toward them around the room.

"Isn't it almost time for dinner?" Jessica asked.

"But our guest has some questions," Leto said. And he looked at the water-shipper, seeing a round-faced man with large eyes and thick lips, recalling Hawat's memorandum: ". . . *and this water-shipper is a man to watch—Lingar Bewt, remember the name. The Harkonnens used him but never fully controlled him.*"

"Water customs are so interesting," Bewt said, and there was a smile on his face. "I'm curious what you intend about the conservatory attached to this house. Do you intend to continue flaunting it in the people's faces . . . m'Lord?"

Leto held anger in check, staring at the man. Thoughts raced through his mind. It had taken bravery to challenge him in his own ducal castle, especially since they now had Bewt's signature over a contract of allegiance. The action had taken, also, a knowledge of personal power. Water was, indeed, power here. If water facilities were mined, for instance, ready to be destroyed at a signal . . . the man looked capable of such a thing. Destruction of water facilities might well destroy Arrakis. That could well have been the club this Bewt held over the Harkonnens.

"My Lord, the Duke, and I have other plans for our conservatory," Jessica said. She smiled at Leto. "We intend to keep it, certainly, but only to hold it in trust for the people of Arrakis. It is our dream that someday the climate of Arrakis may be changed sufficiently to grow such plants anywhere in the open."

Bless her! Leto thought. *Let our water-shipper chew on that.*

"Your interest in water and weather control is obvious," the Duke said. "I'd advise you to diversify your holdings. One day, water will not be a precious commodity on Arrakis."

And he thought: *Hawat must redouble his efforts at infiltrating this Bewt's organization. And we must start on stand-by water facilities at once. No man is going to hold a club over my head!*

Bewt nodded, the smile still on his face. "A commendable dream, my Lord." He withdrew a pace.

Leto's attention was caught by the expression on Kynes' face. The man was staring at Jessica. He appeared transfigured—like a man in love . . . or caught in a religious trance.

Kynes' thoughts were overwhelmed at last by the words of prophecy: *"And they shall share your most precious dream."* He spoke directly to Jessica: "Do you bring the shortening of the way?"

"Ah, Dr. Kynes," the water-shipper said. "You've come in from tramping around with your mobs of Fremen. How gracious of you."

Kynes passed an unreadable glance across Bewt, said: "It is said in the desert that possession of water in great amount can inflict a man with fatal carelessness."

"They have many strange sayings in the desert," Bewt said, but his voice betrayed uneasiness.

Jessica crossed to Leto, slipped her hand under his arm to gain a moment in which to calm herself. Kynes had said: ". . . the shortening of the way." In the old tongue, the phrase translated as "Kwisatz Haderach." The planetologist's odd questions seemed to have gone unnoticed by the others, and now Kynes was bending over one of the consort women, listening to a low-voiced coquetry.

Kwisatz Haderach, Jessica thought. *Did our Missionaria Protectiva plant that legend here, too?* The thought fanned her secret hope for Paul. *He could be the Kwisatz Haderach. He could be.*

The Guild Bank representative had fallen into conversation with the water-shipper, and Bewt's voice lifted above the renewed hum of conversations: "Many people have sought to change Arrakis."

The Duke saw how the words seemed to pierce Kynes, jerking the planetologist upright and away from the flirting woman.

Into the sudden silence, a house trooper in uniform of a footman cleared his throat behind Leto, said: "Dinner is served, my Lord."

The Duke directed a questioning glance down at Jessica.

"The custom here is for host and hostess to follow their guests to table," she said, and smiled: "Shall we change that one, too, my Lord?"

He spoke coldly: "That seems a goodly custom. We shall let it stand for now."

The illusion that I suspect her of treachery must be maintained, he thought. He glanced at the guests filing past them. *Who among you believes this lie?*

Jessica, sensing his remoteness, wondered at it as she had done frequently the past week. *He acts like a man struggling with himself,* she thought. *Is it because I moved so swiftly setting up this dinner party? Yet, he knows how important it is that we begin to mix our officers and men with the locals on a social plane. We are father and mother surrogate to them all. Nothing impresses that fact more firmly than this sort of social sharing.*

Leto, watching the guests file past, recalled what Thufir Hawat had said when informed of the affair: *"Sire! I forbid it!"*

A grim smile touched the Duke's mouth. What a scene that had been. And when the Duke had remained adamant about attending the dinner, Hawat had shaken his head. "I have bad feelings about this, my Lord," he'd said. "Things move too swiftly on Arrakis. That's not like the Harkonnens. Not like them at all."

Paul passed his father escorting a young woman half a head taller than himself. He shot a sour glance at his father, nodded at something the young woman said.

"Her father manufactures stillsuits," Jessica said. "I'm told that only a fool would be caught in the deep desert wearing one of the man's suits."

"Who's the man with the scarred face ahead of Paul?" the Duke asked. "I don't place him."

"A late addition to the list," she whispered. "Gurney arranged the invitation. Smuggler."

"Gurney arranged?"

"At my request. It was cleared with Hawat, although I thought Hawat was a little stiff about it. The smuggler's called Tuek, Esmar Tuek. He's a power among his kind. They all know him here. He's dined at many of the houses."

"Why is he here?"

"Everyone here will ask that question," she said. "Tuek will sow doubt and suspicion just by his presence. He'll also serve notice that you're prepared to back up your orders against graft—by enforcement from the smugglers' end as well. This was the point Hawat appeared to like."

"I'm not sure *I* like it." He nodded to a passing couple, saw only a few of their guests remained to precede them. "Why didn't you invite some Fremen?"

"There's Kynes," she said.

"Yes, there's Kynes," he said. "Have you arranged any other little surprises for me?" He led her into step behind the procession.

"All else is most conventional," she said.

And she thought: *My darling, can't you see that this smuggler controls fast ships, that he can be bribed? We must have a way out, a door of escape from Arrakis if all else fails us here.*

As they emerged into the dining hall, she disengaged her arm, allowed Leto to seat her. He strode to his end of the table. A footman held his chair for him. The others settled with a swishing of fabrics, a scraping of chairs, but the Duke remained standing. He gave a hand signal, and the house troopers in footman uniform around the table stepped back, standing at attention.

Uneasy silence settled over the room.

Jessica, looking down the length of the table, saw a faint trembling at the corners of Leto's mouth, noted the dark flush of anger on his cheeks. *What has angered him?* she asked herself. *Surely not my invitation to the smuggler.*

"Some question my changing of the laving basin custom," Leto said. "This is my way of telling you that many things will change."

Embarrassed silence settled over the table.

They think him drunk, Jessica thought.

Leto lifted his water flagon, held it aloft where the suspensor lights shot beams of reflection off it. "As a Chevalier of the Imperium, then," he said, "I give you a toast."

The others grasped their flagons, all eyes focused on the Duke. In the sudden stillness, a suspensor light drifted slightly in an errant breeze from the serving kitchen hallway. Shadows played across the Duke's hawk features.

"Here I am and here I remain!" he barked.

There was an abortive movement of flagons toward mouths—stopped as the Duke remained with arm upraised. "My toast is one of those maxims so dear to our hearts: 'Business makes progress! Fortune passes everywhere!'"

He sipped his water.

The others joined him. Questioning glances passed among them.

"Gurney!" the Duke called.

From an alcove at Leto's end of the room came Halleck's voice. "Here, my Lord."

"Give us a tune, Gurney."

A minor chord from the baliset floated out of the alcove. Servants began putting plates of food on the table at the Duke's gesture releasing them—roast desert hare in sauce cepeda, aplomage sirian, chukka under glass, coffee with melange (a rich cinnamon odor from the spice wafted across the table), a true pot-a-oie served with sparkling Caladan wine.

Still, the Duke remained standing.

As the guests waited, their attention torn between the dishes placed before them and the standing Duke, Leto said: "In olden times, it was the duty of the host to entertain his guests with his own talents." His knuckles turned white, so fiercely did he grip his water flagon. "I cannot sing, but I give you the words of Gurney's song. Consider it another toast—a toast to all who've died bringing us to this station."

An uncomfortable stirring sounded around the table.

Jessica lowered her gaze, glanced at the people seated nearest her—there was the round-faced water-shipper and his woman, the pale and austere Guild Bank representative (he seemed a whistle-faced scarecrow with his eyes fixed on Leto), the rugged and scar-faced Tuek, his blue-within-blue eyes downcast.

"Review, friends—troops long past review," the Duke intoned. "All to fate a weight of pains and dollars. Their spirits wear our silver collars. Review, friends—troops long past review: Each a dot of time without pretense or guile. With them passes the lure of fortune. Review, friends—troops long past review. When our time ends on its rictus smile, we'll pass the lure of fortune."

The Duke allowed his voice to trail off on the last line, took a deep drink from his water flagon, slammed it back onto the table. Water slopped over the brim onto the linen.

The others drank in embarrassed silence.

Again, the Duke lifted his water flagon, and this time emptied its remaining half onto the floor, knowing that the others around the table must do the same.

Jessica was first to follow his example.

There was a frozen moment before the others began emptying their flagons. Jessica saw how Paul, seated near his father, was studying the reactions around him. She found herself also fascinated by what her guests' actions revealed—especially among the women. This was clean, potable water, not something already cast away in a sopping towel. Reluctance to just discard it exposed itself in trembling hands, delayed reactions, nervous laughter . . . and violent obedience to the necessity. One woman dropped her flagon, looked the other way as her male companion recovered it.

Kynes, though, caught her attention most sharply. The planetologist hesitated, then emptied his flagon into a container beneath his jacket. He smiled at Jessica as he caught her watching him, raised the empty flagon to her in a silent toast. He appeared completely unembarrassed by his action.

Halleck's music still wafted over the room, but it had come out of its minor key, lilting and lively now as though he were trying to lift the mood.

"Let the dinner commence," the Duke said, and sank into his chair.

He's angry and uncertain, Jessica thought. *The loss of that factory crawler hit him more deeply than it should have. It must be something more than that loss. He acts like a desperate man.* She lifted her fork, hoping in the motion to hide her own sudden bitterness. *Why not? He is desperate.*

Slowly at first, then with increasing animation, the dinner got under way. The stillsuit manufacturer complimented Jessica on her chef and wine.

"We brought both from Caladan," she said.

"Superb!" he said, tasting the chukka. "Simply superb! And not a hint of melange in it. One gets so tired of the spice in everything."

The Guild Bank representative looked across at Kynes. "I understand, Doctor Kynes, that another factory crawler has been lost to a worm."

"News travels fast," the Duke said.

"Then it's true?" the banker asked, shifting his attention to Leto.

"Of course, it's true!" the Duke snapped. "The blasted carry-all disappeared. It shouldn't be possible for anything that big to disappear!"

"When the worm came, there was nothing to recover the crawler," Kynes said.

"It should *not* be possible!" the Duke repeated.

"No one saw the carryall leave?" the banker asked.

"Spotters customarily keep their eyes on the sand," Kynes said. "They're primarily interested in wormsign. A carryall's complement usually is four men—two pilots and two journeymen attachers. If one—or even two of this crew were in the pay of the Duke's foes—"

"Ah-h-h, I see," the banker said. "And you, as Judge of the Change, do you challenge this?"

"I shall have to consider my position carefully," Kynes said, "and I certainly will not discuss it at table." And he thought: *That pale skeleton of a man! He knows this is the kind of infraction I was instructed to ignore.*

The banker smiled, returned his attention to his food.

Jessica sat remembering a lecture from her Bene Gesserit school days. The subject had been espionage and counter-espionage. A plump, happy-faced Reverend Mother had been the lecturer, her jolly voice contrasting weirdly with the subject matter.

A thing to note about any espionage and/or counter-espionage school is the similar basic reaction pattern of all its graduates. Any enclosed discipline sets its stamp, its pattern, upon its students. That pattern is susceptible to analysis and prediction.

"Now, motivational patterns are going to be similar among

*all espionage agents. That is to say: there will be certain
types of motivation that are similar despite differing schools
or opposed aims. You will study first how to separate this
element for your analysis—in the beginning, through interrogation patterns that betray the inner orientation of the
interrogators; secondly, by close observation of language-
thought orientation of those under analysis. You will find
it fairly simple to determine the root languages of your
subjects, of course, both through voice inflection and speech
pattern."*

Now, sitting at table with her son and her Duke and their
guests, hearing that Guild Bank representative, Jessica felt a
chill of realization: the man was a Harkonnen agent. He had
the Giedi Prime speech pattern—subtly masked, but exposed
to her trained awareness as though he had announced himself.

*Does this mean the Guild itself has taken sides against
House Atreides?* she asked herself. The thought shocked her,
and she masked her emotion by calling for a new dish, all the
while listening for the man to betray his purpose. *He will
shift the conversation next to something seemingly innocent,
but with ominous overtones,* she told herself. *It's his pattern.*

The banker swallowed, took a sip of wine, smiled at something said to him by the woman on his right. He seemed to
listen for a moment to a man down the table who was explaining to the Duke that native Arrakeen plants had no
thorns.

"I enjoy watching the flights of birds on Arrakis," the
banker said, directing his words at Jessica. "All of our birds,
of course, are carrion-eaters, and many exist without water,
having become blood-drinkers."

The stillsuit manufacturer's daughter, seated between Paul
and his father at the other end of the table, twisted her pretty
face into a frown, said: "Oh, Soo-Soo, you say the most disgusting things."

The banker smiled. "They call me Soo-Soo because I'm financial adviser to the Water Peddlers Union." And, as Jessica
continued to look at him without comment, he added: "Because of the water-sellers' cry—'Soo-Soo Sook!' " And he
imitated the call with such accuracy that many around the
table laughed.

Jessica heard the boastful tone of voice, but noted most
that the young woman had spoken on cue—a set piece. She

had produced the excuse for the banker to say what he had said. She glanced at Lingar Bewt. The water magnate was scowling, concentrating on his dinner. It came to Jessica that the banker had said: *"I, too, control that ultimate source of power on Arrakis—water."*

Paul had marked the falseness in his dinner companion's voice, saw that his mother was following the conversation with Bene Gesserit intensity. On impulse, he decided to play the foil, draw the exchange out. He addressed himself to the banker.

"Do you mean, sir, that these birds are cannibals?"

"That's an odd question, young Master," the banker said. "I merely said the birds drink blood. It doesn't have to be the blood of their own kind, does it?"

"It was *not* an odd question," Paul said, and Jessica noted the brittle riposte quality of her training exposed in his voice. "Most educated people know that the worst potential competition for any young organism can come from its own kind." He deliberately forked a bite of food from his companion's plate, ate it. "They are eating from the same bowl. They have the same basic requirements."

The banker stiffened, scowled at the Duke.

"Do not make the error of considering my son a child," the Duke said. And he smiled.

Jessica glanced around the table, noted that Bewt had brightened, that both Kynes and the smuggler, Tuek, were grinning.

"It's a rule of ecology," Kynes said, "that the young Master appears to understand quite well. The struggle between life elements is the struggle for the free energy of a system. Blood's an efficient energy source."

The banker put down his fork, spoke in an angry voice: "It's said that the Fremen scum drink the blood of their dead."

Kynes shook his head, spoke in a lecturing tone: "Not the blood, sir. But all of a man's water, ultimately, belongs to his people—to his tribe. It's a necessity when you live near the Great Flat. All water's precious there, and the human body is composed of some seventy per cent water by weight. A dead man, surely, no longer requires that water."

The banker put both hands against the table beside his plate, and Jessica thought he was going to push himself back, leave in a rage.

Kynes looked at Jessica. "Forgive me, my Lady, for elaborating on such an ugly subject at table, but you were being told falsehood and it needed clarifying."

"You've associated so long with Fremen that you've lost all sensibilities," the banker rasped.

Kynes looked at him calmly, studied the pale, trembling face. "Are you challenging me, sir?"

The banker froze. He swallowed, spoke stiffly: "Of course not. I'd not so insult our host and hostess."

Jessica heard the fear in the man's voice, saw it in his face, in his breathing, in the pulse of a vein at his temple. The man was terrified of Kynes!

"Our host and hostess are quite capable of deciding for themselves when they've been insulted," Kynes said. "They're brave people who understand defense of honor. We all may attest to their courage by the fact that they are here . . . now . . . on Arrakis."

Jessica saw that Leto was enjoying this. Most of the others were not. People all around the table sat poised for flight, hands out of sight under the table. Two notable exceptions were Bewt, who was openly smiling at the banker's discomfiture, and the smuggler, Tuek, who appeared to be watching Kynes for a cue. Jessica saw that Paul was looking at Kynes in admiration.

"Well?" Kynes said.

"I meant no offense," the banker muttered. "If offense was taken, please accept my apologies."

"Freely given, freely accepted," Kynes said. He smiled at Jessica, resumed eating as though nothing had happened.

Jessica saw that the smuggler, too, had relaxed. She marked this: the man had shown every aspect of an aide ready to leap to Kynes' assistance. There existed an accord of some sort between Kynes and Tuek.

Leto toyed with a fork, looked speculatively at Kynes. The ecologist's manner indicated a change in attitude toward the House of Atreides. Kynes had seemed colder on their trip over the desert.

Jessica signaled for another course of food and drink. Servants appeared with *langues de lapins de garenne*—red wine and a sauce of mushroom-yeast on the side.

Slowly, the dinner conversation resumed, but Jessica heard the agitation in it, the brittle quality, saw that the banker ate in sullen silence. *Kynes would have killed him without hesitat-*

ing, she thought. And she realized that there was an offhand attitude toward killing in Kynes' manner. He was a casual killer, and she guessed that this was a Fremen quality.

Jessica turned to the stillsuit manufacturer on her left, said: "I find myself continually amazed by the importance of water on Arrakis."

"Very important," he agreed. "What is this dish? It's delicious."

"Tongues of wild rabbit in a special sauce," she said. "A very old recipe."

"I must have that recipe," the man said.

She nodded. "I'll see that you get it."

Kynes looked at Jessica, said: "The newcomer to Arrakis frequently underestimates the importance of water here. You are dealing, you see, with the Law of the Minimum."

She heard the testing quality in his voice, said, "Growth is limited by that necessity which is present in the least amount. And, naturally, the least favorable condition controls the growth rate."

"It's rare to find members of a Great House aware of planetological problems," Kynes said. "Water is the least favorable condition for life on Arrakis. And remember that *growth* itself can produce unfavorable conditions unless treated with extreme care."

Jessica sensed a hidden message in Kynes' words, but knew she was missing it. "Growth," she said. "Do you mean Arrakis can have an orderly cycle of water to sustain human life under more favorable conditions?"

"Impossible!" the water magnate barked.

Jessica turned her attention to Bewt. "Impossible?"

"Impossible on Arrakis," he said. "Don't listen to this dreamer. All the laboratory evidence is against him."

Kynes looked at Bewt, and Jessica noted that the other conversations around the table had stopped while people concentrated on this new interchange.

"Laboratory evidence tends to blind us to a very simple fact," Kynes said. "That fact is this: we are dealing here with matters that originated and exist out-of-doors where plants and animals carry on their normal existence."

"Normal!" Bewt snorted. "Nothing about Arrakis is normal!"

"Quite the contrary," Kynes said. "Certain harmonies could be set up here along self-sustaining lines. You merely have to understand the limits of the planet and the pressures upon it."

"It'll never be done," Bewt said.

The Duke came to a sudden realization, placing the point where Kynes' attitude had changed—it had been when Jessica had spoken of holding the conservatory plants in trust for Arrakis.

"What would it take to set up the self-sustaining system, Doctor Kynes?" Leto asked.

"If we can get three per cent of the green plant element on Arrakis involved in forming carbon compounds as foodstuffs, we've started the cyclic system," Kynes said.

"Water's the only problem?" the Duke asked. He sensed Kynes' excitement, felt himself caught up in it.

"Water overshadows the other problems," Kynes said. "This planet has much oxygen without its usual concomitants—widespread plant life and large sources of free carbon dioxide from such phenomena as volcanoes. There are unusual chemical interchanges over large surface areas here."

"Do you have pilot projects?" the Duke asked.

"We've had a long time in which to build up the Tansley Effect—small-unit experiments on an amateur basis from which my science may now draw its working facts," Kynes said.

"There isn't enough water," Bewt said. "There just isn't enough water."

"Master Bewt is an expert on water," Kynes said. He smiled, turned back to his dinner.

The Duke gestured sharply down with his right hand, barked: "No! I want an answer! Is there enough water, Doctor Kynes?"

Kynes stared at his plate.

Jessica watched the play of emotion on his face. *He masks himself well,* she thought, but she had him registered now and read that he regretted his words.

"Is there enough water?" the Duke demanded.

"There . . . may be," Kynes said.

He's faking uncertainty! Jessica thought.

With his deeper truthsense, Paul caught the underlying motive, had to use every ounce of his training to mask his excitement. *There is enough water! But Kynes doesn't wish it to be known.*

"Our planetologist has many interesting dreams," Bewt

said. "He dreams with the Fremen—of prophecies and messiahs."

Chuckles sounded at odd places around the table. Jessica marked them—the smuggler, the stillsuit manufacturer's daughter, Duncan Idaho, the woman with the mysterious escort service.

Tensions are oddly distributed here tonight, Jessica thought. *There's too much going on of which I'm not aware. I'll have to develop new information sources.*

The Duke passed his gaze from Kynes to Bewt to Jessica. He felt oddly let down, as though something vital had passed him here. "*May*be," he muttered.

Kynes spoke quickly: "Perhaps we should discuss this another time, my Lord. There are so many—"

The planetologist broke off as a uniformed Atreides trooper hurried in through the service door, was passed by the guard and rushed to the Duke's side. The man bent, whispering into Leto's ear.

Jessica recognized the capsign of Hawat's corps, fought down uneasiness. She addressed herself to the stillsuit manufacturer's feminine companion—a tiny, dark-haired woman with a doll face, a touch of epicanthic fold to the eyes.

"You've hardly touched your dinner, my dear," Jessica said. "May I order you something?"

The woman looked at the stillsuit manufacturer before answering, then: "I'm not very hungry."

Abruptly, the Duke stood up beside his trooper, spoke in a harsh tone of command: "Stay seated, everyone. You will have to forgive me, but a matter has arisen that requires my personal attention." He stepped aside. "Paul, take over as host for me, if you please."

Paul stood, wanting to ask why his father had to leave, knowing he had to play this with the grand manner. He moved around to his father's chair, sat down in it.

The Duke turned to the alcove where Halleck sat, said: "Gurney, please take Paul's place at table. We mustn't have an odd number here. When the dinner's over, I may want you to bring Paul to the field C.P. Wait for my call."

Halleck emerged from the alcove in dress uniform, his lumpy ugliness seeming out of place in the glittering finery. He leaned his baliset against the wall, crossed to the chair Paul had occupied, sat down.

"There's no need for alarm," the Duke said, "but I must

ask that no one leave until our house guard says it's safe. You will be perfectly secure as long as you remain here, and we'll have this little trouble cleared up very shortly."

Paul caught the code words in his father's message—*guard-safe-secure-shortly.* The problem was security, not violence. He saw that his mother had read the same message. They both relaxed.

The Duke gave a short nod, wheeled and strode through the service door followed by his trooper.

Paul said: "Please go on with your dinner. I believe Doctor Kynes was discussing water."

"May we discuss it another time?" Kynes asked.

"By all means," Paul said.

And Jessica noted with pride her son's dignity, the mature sense of assurance.

The banker picked up his water flagon, gestured with it at Bewt. "None of us here can surpass Master Lingar Bewt in flowery phrases. One might almost assume he aspired to Great House status. Come, Master Bewt, lead us in a toast. Perhaps you've a dollop of wisdom for the boy who must be treated like a man."

Jessica clenched her right hand into a fist beneath the table. She saw a handsignal pass from Halleck to Idaho, saw the house troopers along the walls move into positions of maximum guard.

Bewt cast a venomous glare at the banker.

Paul glanced at Halleck, took in the defensive positions of his guards, looked at the banker until the man lowered his water flagon. He said: "Once, on Caladan, I saw the body of a drowned fisherman recovered. He—"

"Drowned?" It was the stillsuit manufacturer's daughter.

Paul hesitated, then: "Yes. Immersed in water until dead. Drowned."

"What an interesting way to die," she murmured.

Paul's smile became brittle. He returned his attention to the banker. "The interesting thing about this man was the wounds on his shoulders—made by another fisherman's claw-boots. This fisherman was one of several in a boat—a craft for traveling on water—that foundered . . . sank beneath the water. Another fisherman helping recover the body said he'd seen marks like this man's wounds several times. They meant another drowning fisherman had tried to stand on this poor fellow's shoulders in the attempt to reach up to the surface—to reach air."

"Why is this interesting?" the banker asked.

"Because of an observation made by my father at the time. He said the drowning man who climbs on your shoulders to save himself is understandable—except when you see it happen in the drawing room." Paul hesitated just long enough for the banker to see the point coming, then: "And, I should add, except when you see it at the dinner table."

A sudden stillness enfolded the room.

That was rash, Jessica thought. *This banker might have enough rank to call my son out.* She saw that Idaho was poised for instant action. The House troopers were alert. Gurney Halleck had his eyes on the men opposite him.

"Ho-ho-ho-o-o-o!" It was the smuggler, Tuek, head thrown back laughing with complete abandon.

Nervous smiles appeared around the table.

Bewt was grinning.

The banker had pushed his chair back, was glaring at Paul.

Kynes said: "One baits an Atreides at his own risk."

"Is it Atreides custom to insult their guests?" the banker demanded.

Before Paul could answer, Jessica leaned forward, said: "Sir!" And she thought: *We must learn this Harkonnen creature's game. Is he here to try for Paul? Does he have help?*

"My son displays a general garment and you claim it's cut to your fit?" Jessica asked. "What a fascinating revelation." She slid a hand down to her leg to the cryknife she had fastened in a calf-sheath.

The banker turned his glare on Jessica. Eyes shifted away from Paul and she saw him ease himself back from the table, freeing himself for action. He had focused on the code word: *garment.* "*Prepare for violence.*"

Kynes directed a speculative look at Jessica, gave a subtle hand signal to Tuek.

The smuggler lurched to his feet, lifted his flagon. "I'll give you a toast," he said. "To young Paul Atreides, still a lad by his looks, but a man by his actions."

Why do they intrude? Jessica asked herself.

The banker stared now at Kynes, and Jessica saw terror return to the agent's face.

People began responding all around the table.

Where Kynes leads, people follow, Jessica thought. *He has told us he sides with Paul. What's the secret of his power? It can't be because he's Judge of the Change. That's temporary. And certainly not because he's a civil servant.*

She removed her hand from the crysknife hilt, lifted her flagon to Kynes, who responded in kind.

Only Paul and the banker—(*Soo-Soo! What an idiotic nickname!* Jessica thought.)—remained empty-handed. The banker's attention stayed fixed on Kynes. Paul stared at his plate.

I was handling it correctly, Paul thought. *Why do they interfere?* He glanced covertly at the male guests nearest him. *Prepare for violence? From whom? Certainly not from that banker fellow.*

Halleck stirred, spoke as though to no one in particular, directing his words over the heads of the guests across from him: "In our society, people shouldn't be quick to take offense. It's frequently suicidal." He looked at the stillsuit manufacturer's daughter beside him. "Don't you think so, miss?"

"Oh, yes. Yes. Indeed I do," she said. "There's too much violence. It makes me sick. And lots of times no offense is meant, but people die anyway. It doesn't make sense."

"Indeed it doesn't," Halleck said.

Jessica saw the near perfection of the girl's act, realized: *That empty-headed little female is not an empty-headed little female.* She saw then the pattern of the threat and understood that Halleck, too, had detected it. They had planned to lure Paul with sex. Jessica relaxed. Her son had probably been the first to see it—his training hadn't overlooked that obvious gambit.

Kynes spoke to the banker: "Isn't another apology in order?"

The banker turned a sickly grin toward Jessica, said: "My Lady, I fear I've overindulged in your wines. You serve potent drink at table, and I'm not accustomed to it."

Jessica heard the venom beneath his tone, spoke sweetly: "When strangers meet, great allowance should be made for differences of custom and training."

"Thank you, my Lady," he said.

The dark-haired companion of the stillsuit manufacturer leaned toward Jessica, said: "The Duke spoke of our being secure here. I do hope that doesn't mean more fighting."

She was directed to lead the conversation this way, Jessica thought.

"Likely this will prove unimportant," Jessica said. "But there's so much detail requiring the Duke's personal attention in these times. As long as enmity continues between Atreides and Harkonnen we cannot be too careful. The Duke has sworn kanly. He will leave no Harkonnen agent alive on Arrakis, of course." She glanced at the Guild Bank agent. "And the Conventions, naturally, support him in this." She shifted her attention to Kynes. "Is this not so, Dr. Kynes?"

"Indeed it is," Kynes said.

The stillsuit manufacturer pulled his companion gently back. She looked at him, said: "I do believe I'll eat something now. I'd like some of that bird dish you served earlier."

Jessica signaled a servant, turned to the banker: "And you, sir, were speaking of birds earlier and of their habits. I find so many interesting things about Arrakis. Tell me, where is the spice found? Do the hunters go deep into the desert?"

"Oh, no, my Lady," he said. "Very little's known of the deep desert. And almost nothing of the southern regions."

"There's a tale that a great Mother Lode of spice is to be found in the southern reaches," Kynes said, "but I suspect it was an imaginative invention made solely for purposes of a song. Some daring spice hunters do, on occasion, penetrate into the edge of the central belt, but that's extremely dangerous—navigation is uncertain, storms are frequent. Casualties increase dramatically the farther you operate from Shield Wall bases. It hasn't been found profitable to venture too far south. Perhaps if we had a weather satellite . . ."

Bewt looked up, spoke around a mouthful of food: "It's said the Fremen travel there, that they go anywhere and have hunted out soaks and sip-wells even in the southern latitudes."

"Soaks and sip-wells?" Jessica asked.

Kynes spoke quickly: "Wild rumors, my Lady. These are known on other planets, not on Arrakis. A soak is a place where water seeps to the surface or near enough to the surface to be found by digging according to certain signs. A sip-well is a form of soak where a person draws water through a straw . . . so it is said."

There's deception in his words, Jessica thought.

Why is he lying? Paul wondered.

"How very interesting," Jessica said. And she thought: *"It is said. . . ."* *What a curious speech mannerism they have here. If they only knew what it reveals about their dependence on superstitions.*

"I've heard you have a saying," Paul said, "that polish comes from the cities, wisdom from the desert."

"There are many sayings on Arrakis," Kynes said.

Before Jessica could frame a new question, a servant bent over her with a note. She opened it, saw the Duke's handwriting and code signs, scanned it.

"You'll all be delighted to know," she said, "that our Duke sends his reassurances. The matter which called him away has been settled. The missing carryall has been found. A Harkonnen agent in the crew overpowered the others and flew the machine to a smugglers' base, hoping to sell it there. Both man and machine were turned over to our forces." She nodded to Tuek.

The smuggler nodded back.

Jessica refolded the note, tucked it into her sleeve.

"I'm glad it didn't come to open battle," the banker said. "The people have such hopes the Atreides will bring peace and prosperity."

"Especially prosperity," Bewt said.

"Shall we have our dessert now?" Jessica asked. "I've had our chef prepare a Caladan sweet: pongi rice in sauce dolsa."

"It sounds wonderful," the stillsuit manufacturer said. "Would it be possible to get the recipe?"

"Any recipe you desire," Jessica said, *registering* the man for later mention to Hawat. The stillsuit manufacturer was a fearful little climber and could be bought.

Small talk resumed around her: "Such a lovely fabric. . . ." "He is having a setting made to match the jewel. . . ." "We might try for a production increase next quarter. . . ."

Jessica stared down at her plate, thinking of the coded part of Leto's message: *The Harkonnens tried to get in a shipment of lasguns. We captured them. This may mean they've succeeded with other shipments. It certainly means they don't place much store in shields. Take appropriate precautions.*

Jessica focused her mind on lasguns, wondering. The white-hot beams of disruptive light could cut through any known substance, provided that substance was not shielded. The fact that feedback from a shield would explode both lasgun and shield did not bother the Harkonnens. Why? A lasgun-shield explosion was a dangerous variable, could be more powerful than atomics, could kill only the gunner and his shielded target.

The unknowns here filled her with uneasiness.

Paul said: "I never doubted we'd find the carryall. Once

my father moves to solve a problem, he solves it. This is a fact the Harkonnens are beginning to discover."

He's boasting, Jessica thought. *He shouldn't boast. No person who'll be sleeping far below ground level this night as a precaution against lasguns has the right to boast.*

The Vigor of Traditional SF

Bob Shaw (1931–   ) has said that "my aim in writing is to renew the vigor of traditional sf themes by combining them with, if it is within my powers, the same degree of characterization that one finds in the general novel."

Shaw began his life in Belfast, Northern Ireland, and spent much of his life in that troubled city. He attended technical high school there, became a constructional draftsman there (with three years in Canada), and became an aircraft draftsman there. He turned to public relations in 1960, became a reporter for the *Belfast Telegraph* in 1966, and had a year of freelancing before returning to public relations as press officer and publicity officer for a Belfast firm and then one in England. In 1975 he became a full-time writer. He now lives in England, where he has produced half a dozen novels in an equal number of years.

Shaw began his sf career as a fan and started his sf writing by contributing stories to the English magazine *Nebula Science Fiction*. His first story, "Aspect," appeared in 1954. Several more of his stories were published before he stopped writing for nearly a decade, with the exception of a story published in *Worlds of If* in 1960. He returned to writing in 1965. His best-known story, "Light of Other Days," was published in the August 1966 *Astounding*. It was later combined with two sequels and published as *Other Days, Other Eyes* (1972).

Shaw's first novel was *Night Walk* (1967), followed by *The Two-Timers* (1968), *The Palace of Eternity* (1969), *One Million Tomorrows* (1970), and *Ground Man Zero*

(1971). In 1975 he reached a new level of writing success and recognition with *Orbitsville* (1975), which won the British Science Fiction Award. Later novels are *A Wreath of Stars* (1976), *Medusa's Children* (1977), and *Who Goes Here?* (1977).

True to his aim (he is an archer and twice represented Northern Ireland), Shaw has chosen his themes from sf tradition: inventions, parallel time streams, doppelgangers, interstellar warfare, environment, immortality. . . . *Orbitsville* takes up the notion of astrophysicist Freeman Dyson that superior civilizations may be able to use all the energy of their stars by turning the matter of their planets into spheres (so-called Dyson spheres) surrounding their suns, but also making their stars invisible except in the infrared. The surface area would be millions of times as large as that of Earth. Larry Niven used part of the concept in *Ringworld* (1970); Shaw used the entire sphere. *A Wreath of Stars* speculates about matter made up of anti-neutrinos. Through all of these works Shaw's concern for characterization continued to grow.

That concern is evident in the acclaimed and often reprinted "Light of Other Days." The traditional sf theme is an invention—in this case the invention of "slow glass." The concern for character shows in the portrayal and treatment not only of the man who owns the slow-glass farm and the reasons for his behavior but of the couple who stop by his place.

"Slow glass" is such an ingenious and pleasant notion that every reader must regret it is still only a science fiction idea. We are accustomed to thinking, because of Einstein's theory of relativity, that the speed of light is a lower limit as well as an upper limit, but light travels at different speeds in different media. Refraction, for instance, depends upon this fact— prisms create spectra by slowing different colors of light differentially; raindrops create a rainbow. Shaw's inspiration that light might be slowed down years in passing through a sheet of specially engineered glass is an impossibility as far as we know, but Shaw works hard at rendering it plausible. He suggests that somehow scientists and technologists have devised a way to divert light, possibly through other dimensions ("a spiral tunnel coiled outside the radius of capture of each atom in the glass"), so that the thickness of the glass is the equivalent of the distance to other stars—that is, the distance light travels in a year at its speed of 186,000 miles per second. Shaw also deals with the difficult problem of keeping the glass in phase with the real world, although surely this would be good only for locations in the same general latitude and time zone.

The concept itself is ingenious enough to carry a story. Shaw considers the commercial uses without which any such invention and widespread availability would not be possible, but he restricts his consideration of those uses to the aesthetic. One might think of more obviously valuable applications, such as recording business and government meetings for archives, spying, filmmaking, and so forth, but perhaps, as a slice of life, the story is not under any necessity to explore such uses. Shaw focuses on the human tragedies and consolations involved in being able to visualize scenes and persons gone beyond retrieval in any other way.

In simple, direct prose illuminated by an occasional poetic phrase and image ("land of slow glass," "drinking light," "thirsty glass"), Shaw reveals his human stories. It is no accident that the couple who stop by this Scottish rural area dotted with frames of slow glass have been troubled about their marriage and that the wife is pregnant and angry about it. They, like the panes of slow glass and the man who sells them, carry their pasts within them.

Light of Other Days

by Bob Shaw

Leaving the village behind, we followed the heady sweeps of the road up into a land of slow glass.

I had never seen one of the farms before and at first found them slightly eerie—an effect heightened by imagination and circumstance. The car's turbine was pulling smoothly and quietly in the damp air so that we seemed to be carried over the convolutions of the road in a kind of supernatural silence. On our right the mountain sifted down into an incredibly perfect valley of timeless pine, and everywhere stood the great frames of slow glass, drinking light. An occasional flash of afternoon sunlight on their wind bracing created an illusion of movement, but in fact the frames were deserted. The rows of windows had been standing on the hillside for years, staring into the valley, and men only cleaned them in the middle of the night when their human presence would not matter to the thirsty glass.

They were fascinating, but Selina and I didn't mention the windows. I think we hated each other so much we both were reluctant to sully anything new by drawing it into the nexus of our emotions. The holiday, I had begun to realize, was a stupid idea in the first place. I had thought it would cure everything, but, of course, it didn't stop Selina being pregnant and, worse still, it didn't even stop her being angry about being pregnant.

Rationalizing our dismay over her condition, we had circulated the usual statements to the effect that we would have *liked* having children—but later on, at the proper time. Selina's pregnancy had cost us her well-paid job and with it the new house we had been negotiating and which was far beyond the reach of my income from poetry. But the real source of our annoyance was that we were face to face with the realization that people who say they want children later always mean they want children never. Our nerves were thrumming with the knowledge that we, who had thought ourselves so unique, had fallen into the same biological trap as every mindless rutting creature which ever existed.

The road took us along the southern slopes of Ben Cruachan until we began to catch glimpses of the gray Atlantic far ahead. I had just cut our speed to absorb the view better when I noticed the sign spiked to a gatepost. It said: "SLOW GLASS—Quality High, Prices Low—J. R. Hagan." On an impulse I stopped the car on the verge, wincing slightly as tough grasses whipped noisily at the body work.

"Why have we stopped?" Selina's neat, smoke-silver head turned in surprise.

"Look at that sign. Let's go up and see what there is. The stuff might be reasonably priced out here."

Selina's voice was pitched high with scorn as she refused, but I was too taken with my idea to listen. I had an illogical conviction that doing something extravagant and crazy would set us right again.

"Come on," I said, "the exercise might do us some good. We've been driving too long anyway."

She shrugged in a way that hurt me and got out of the car. We walked up a path made of irregular, packed clay steps nosed with short lengths of sapling. The path curved through trees which clothed the edge of the hill and at its end we found a low farmhouse. Beyond the little stone building tall frames of slow glass gazed out towards the voice-stilling sight of Cruachan's ponderous descent towards the waters of Loch Linnhe. Most of the panes were perfectly transparent but a few were dark, like panels of polished ebony.

As we approached the house through a neat cobbled yard a tall middle-aged man in ash-colored tweeds arose and waved to us. He had been sitting on the low rubble wall which bounded the yard, smoking a pipe and staring towards the house. At the front window of the cottage a young woman in a tangerine dress stood with a small boy in her arms, but she turned disinterestedly and moved out of sight as we drew near.

"Mr. Hagan?" I guessed.

"Correct. Come to see some glass, have you? Well, you've come to the right place." Hagan spoke crisply, with traces of the pure highland which sounds so much like Irish to the unaccustomed ear. He had one of those calmly dismayed faces one finds on elderly road-menders and philosophers.

"Yes," I said. "We're on holiday. We saw your sign."

Selina, who usually has a natural fluency with strangers, said nothing. She was looking towards the now empty window with what I thought was a slightly puzzled expression.

"Up from London, are you? Well, as I said, you've come to the right place—and at the right time, too. My wife and I don't see many people this early in the season."

I laughed. "Does that mean we might be able to buy a little glass without mortgaging our home?"

"Look at that now," Hagan said, smiling helplessly. "I've thrown away any advantage I might have had in the transaction. Rose, that's my wife, says I never learn. Still, let's sit down and talk it over." He pointed at the rubble wall then glanced doubtfully at Selina's immaculate blue skirt. "Wait till I fetch a rug from the house." Hagan limped quickly into the cottage, closing the door behind him.

"Perhaps it wasn't such a marvelous idea to come up here," I whispered to Selina, "but you might at least be pleasant to the man. I think I can smell a bargain."

"Some hope," she said with deliberate coarseness. "Surely even you must have noticed that ancient dress his wife is wearing? He won't give much away to strangers."

"Was that his wife?"

"Of course that was his wife."

"Well, well," I said, surprised. "Anyway, try to be civil with him. I don't want to be embarrassed."

Selina snorted, but she smiled whitely when Hagan reappeared and I relaxed a little. Strange how a man can love a woman and yet at the same time pray for her to fall under a train.

Hagan spread a tartan blanket on the wall and we sat down, feeling slightly self-conscious at having been translated from our city-oriented lives into a rural tableau. On the distant slate of the Loch, beyond the watchful frames of slow glass, a slow-moving steamer drew a white line towards the south. The boisterous mountain air seemed almost to invade our lungs, giving us more oxygen than we required.

"Some of the glass farmers around here," Hagan began, "give strangers, such as yourselves, a sales talk about how beautiful the autumn is in this part of Argyll. Or it might be the spring, or the winter. I don't do that—any fool knows that a place which doesn't look right in summer never looks right. What do you say?"

I nodded compliantly.

"I want you just to take a good look out towards Mull, Mr. . . ."

"Garland."

". . . Garland. That's what you're buying if you buy my glass, and it never looks better than it does at this minute. The glass is in perfect phase, none of it is less than ten years thick—and a four-foot window will cost you two hundred pounds."

"*Two hundred!*" Selina was shocked. "That's as much as they charge at the Scenedow shop in Bond Street."

Hagan smiled patiently, then looked closely at me to see if I knew enough about slow glass to appreciate what he had been saying. His price had been much higher than I had hoped—but *ten years thick!* The cheap glass one found in places like the Vistaplex and Pane-o-rama stores usually consisted of a quarter of an inch of ordinary glass faced with a veneer of slow glass perhaps only ten or twelve months thick.

"You don't understand, darling," I said, already determined to buy. "This glass will last ten years and it's in phase."

"Doesn't that only mean it keeps time?"

Hagan smiled at her again, realizing he had no further necessity to bother with me. "Only, you say! Pardon me, Mrs. Garland, but you don't seem to appreciate the miracle, the genuine honest-to-goodness miracle, of engineering precision needed to produce a piece of glass in phase. When I say the glass is ten years thick it means it takes light ten years to pass through it. In effect, each one of those panes is ten light-years thick—more than twice the distance to the nearest star—so a variation in actual thickness of only a millionth of an inch would . . ."

He stopped talking for a moment and sat quietly looking towards the house. I turned my head from the view of the Loch and saw the young woman standing at the window again. Hagan's eyes were filled with a kind of greedy reverence which made me feel uncomfortable and at the same time convinced me Selina had been wrong. In my experience husbands never looked at wives that way, at least, not at their own.

The girl remained in view for a few seconds, dress glowing warmly, then moved back into the room. Suddenly I received a distinct, though inexplicable, impression she was blind. My feeling was that Selina and I were perhaps blundering through an emotional interplay as violent as our own.

"I'm sorry," Hagan continued, "I thought Rose was going to call me for something. Now, where was I, Mrs. Garland? Ten light-years compressed into a quarter of an inch means . . ."

I ceased to listen, partly because I was already sold, partly because I had heard the story of slow glass many times before and had never yet understood the principles involved. An acquaintance with scientific training had once tried to be helpful by telling me to visualize a pane of slow glass as a hologram which did not need coherent light from a laser for the reconstitution of its visual information, and in which every photon of ordinary light passed through a spiral tunnel coiled outside the radius of capture of each atom in the glass. This gem of, to me, incomprehensibility not only told me nothing, it convinced me once again that a mind as nontechnical as mine should concern itself less with causes than effects.

The most important effect, in the eyes of the average individual, was that light took a long time to pass through a sheet of slow glass. A new piece was always jet black because nothing had yet come through, but one could stand the glass beside, say, a woodland lake until the scene emerged, perhaps a year later. If the glass was then removed and installed in a dismal city flat, the flat would—for that year—appear to overlook the woodland lake. During the year it wouldn't be merely a very realistic but still picture—the water would ripple in sunlight, silent animals would come to drink, birds would cross the sky, night would follow day, season would follow season. Until one day, a year later, the beauty held in the subatomic pipelines would be exhausted and the familiar gray cityscape would reappear.

Apart from its stupendous novelty value, the commercial success of slow glass was founded on the fact that having a scenedow was the exact emotional equivalent of owning land. The meanest cave dweller could look out on misty parks—and who was to say they weren't his? A man who really owns tailored gardens and estates doesn't spend his time proving his ownership by crawling on his ground, feeling, smelling, tasting it. All he receives from the land are light patterns, and with scenedows those patterns could be taken into coal mines, submarines, prison cells.

On several occasions I have tried to write short pieces about the enchanted crystal but, to me, the theme is so ineffably poetic as to be, paradoxically, beyond the reach of poetry—mine at any rate. Besides, the best songs and verse had already been written, with prescient inspiration, by men who had died long before slow glass was discovered. I had no hope of equaling, for example, Moore with his:

> *Oft in the stilly night,*
> *Ere slumber's chain has bound me,*
> *Fond Memory brings the light,*
> *Of other days around me . . .*

It took only a few years for slow glass to develop from a scientific curiosity to a sizable industry. And much to the astonishment of us poets—those of us who remained convinced that beauty lives though lilies die—the trappings of that industry were no different from those of any other. There were good scenedows which cost a lot of money, and there were inferior scenedows which cost rather less. The thickness, measured in years, was an important factor in the cost but there was also the question of *actual* thickness, or phase.

Even with the most sophisticated engineering techniques

available, thickness control was something of a hit-and-miss affair. A coarse discrepancy could mean that a pane intended to be five years thick might be five and a half, so that light which entered in summer emerged in winter; a fine discrepancy could mean that noon sunshine emerged at midnight. These incompatibilities had their peculiar charm—many night workers, for example, liked having their own private time zones—but, in general, it cost more to buy scenedows which kept closely in step with real time.

Selina still looked unconvinced when Hagan had finished speaking. She shook her head almost imperceptibly and I knew he had been using the wrong approach. Quite suddenly the pewter helmet of her hair was disturbed by a cool gust of wind, and huge clean tumbling drops of rain began to spang round us from an almost cloudless sky.

"I'll give you a check now," I said abruptly, and saw Selina's green eyes triangulate angrily on my face. "You can arrange delivery?"

"Aye, delivery's no problem," Hagan said, getting to his feet. "But wouldn't you rather take the glass with you?"

"Well, yes—if you don't mind." I was shamed by his readiness to trust my scrip.

"I'll unclip a pane for you. Wait here. It won't take long to slip it into a carrying frame." Hagan limped down the slope towards the seriate windows, through some of which the view towards Linnhe was sunny, while others were cloudy and a few pure black.

Selina drew the collar of her blouse closed at her throat. "The least he could have done was invite us inside. There can't be so many fools passing through that he can afford to neglect them."

I tried to ignore the insult and concentrated on writing the check. One of the outsize drops broke across my knuckles, splattering the pink paper.

"All right," I said, "let's move in under the eaves till he gets back." You worm, I thought as I felt the whole thing go completely wrong. I just had to be a fool to marry you. A prize fool, a fool's fool—and now that you've trapped part of me inside you I'll never ever, never ever, *never ever* get away.

Feeling my stomach clench itself painfully, I ran behind Selina to the side of the cottage. Beyond the window the neat living room, with its coal fire, was empty but the child's toys were scattered on the floor. Alphabet blocks and a wheelbarrow the exact color of freshly pared carrots. As I stared in, the boy came running from the other room and began kicking the blocks. He didn't notice me. A few moments later the young woman entered the room and lifted him, laughing easily and whole-heartedly as she swung the boy under her arm. She came to the window as she had done earlier. I smiled self-consciously, but neither she nor the child responded.

My forehead prickled icily. *Could they both be blind?* I sidled away.

Selina gave a little scream and I spun towards her.

"The rug!" she said. "It's getting soaked."

She ran across the yard in the rain, snatched the reddish square from the dappling wall and ran back, towards the cottage door. Something heaved convulsively in my subconscious.

"Selina," I shouted. "Don't open it!"

But I was too late. She had pushed open the latched wooden door and was standing, hand over mouth, looking into the cottage. I moved close to her and took the rug from her unresisting fingers.

As I was closing the door I let my eyes traverse the cottage's interior. The neat living room in which I had just seen the woman and child was, in reality, a sickening clutter of shabby furniture, old newspapers, cast-off clothing and smeared dishes. It was damp, stinking and utterly deserted. The only object I recognized from my view through the window was the little wheelbarrow, paintless and broken.

I latched the door firmly and ordered myself to forget what I had seen. Some men who live alone are good housekeepers; others just don't know how.

Selina's face was white. "I don't understand. I don't understand it."

"Slow glass works both ways," I said gently. "Light passes out of a house, as well as in."

"You mean . . . ?"

"I don't know. It isn't our business. Now steady up— Hagan's coming back with our glass." The churning in my stomach was beginning to subside.

Hagan came into the yard carrying an oblong, plastic-covered frame. I held the check out to him, but he was staring at Selina's face. He seemed to know immediately that our uncomprehending fingers had rummaged through his soul.

Selina avoided his gaze. She was old and ill-looking, and her eyes stared determinedly towards the nearing horizon.

"I'll take the rug from you, Mr. Garland," Hagan finally said. "You shouldn't have troubled yourself over it."

"No trouble. Here's the check."

"Thank you." He was still looking at Selina with a strange kind of supplication. "It's been a pleasure to do business with you."

"The pleasure was mine," I said with equal senseless formality. I picked up the heavy frame and guided Selina towards the path which led to the road. Just as we reached the head of the now slippery steps Hagan spoke again.

"Mr. Garland!"

I turned unwillingly.

"It wasn't my fault," he said steadily. "A hit-and-run driver got them both, down on the Oban road six years ago. My boy was only seven when it happened. I'm entitled to keep something."

I nodded wordlessly and moved down the path, holding my wife close to me, treasuring the feel of her arms locked around me. At the bend I looked back through the rain and saw Hagan sitting with squared shoulders on the wall where we had first seen him.

He was looking at the house, but I was unable to tell if there was anyone at the window.

Ambiguities and Inscrutabilities

Although science fiction got its start in France with Jules Verne and in England with H. G. Wells (Brian W. Aldiss would date sf from Mary Shelley's 1818 *Frankenstein*), the center of science fiction shifted to the United States with the creation of the pulp magazines and especially the science fiction magazines. Foreign science fiction tended to be so influenced and sometimes dominated by American science fiction in translation that the characters needed American names to seem like the real stuff. That Americanization of world sf was reversed in England by the New Wave and in Europe by individual writers such as I. Yefremov and the Strugatsky brothers in the U.S.S.R., Italo Calvino in Italy, and Stanislaw Lem in Poland.

Born in Lwów, Lem (1921–   ) studied to be a physician, worked as a car mechanic and welder during the Nazi occupation, and completed his medical studies in 1948. Rather than practice medicine, Lem chose to write. His first novel, *The Astronauts,* was published in 1951. Since then he has written some thirty books that have sold over seven million copies in twenty-eight languages. He has been acclaimed as a major writer by numerous critics (the *New York Times* gave him *Book Review* front-page status). His best-known works (and their U.S. publication dates) are *Solaris* (1970), *The Invincible* (1973), *Memoirs Found in a Bathtub* (1973), *The Cyberiad* (1974), *The Futurological Congress* (1974), *The Investigation* (1974), *The Star Diaries* (1976), *Mortal Engines* (1977), and *Tales of Pirx the Pilot* (1979). He also has written essays and books on science and technology, and literary criticism, including an unfavorable critique of English-language sf in *Fantastyka i futurologia* (1970).

Influenced only negatively by American sf and not much by Marxist philosophy, Lem's fiction combines fascination with the rigors of science and technology, particularly cybernetics, and a humanistic transformation of this interest into metaphor and fable. Most of his serious work involves what his best translator, Michael Kandel, has called a structure consisting of an alien mystery that a protagonist attempts to solve, usually through struggle and hardship, finally to come face to face with the enigma, through which he gains not understanding of the mystery but insight into the human condition. Lem deals with ambiguities and inscrutabilities, and the impossibilities of ultimate understanding. He sees the universe as incapable of being understood, and his dark vision sees consciousness and intelligence as leading only to pain and death.

In his comedies and satires, Lem is a cataloguer who obtains some of his effects by piling up names and details into a glittering mound of ingenuity and wit. "The First Sally (A), or Trurl's Electronic Bard" is a good example of this Lem vein. It comes from *The Cyberiad,* a series of "Fables for the Cybernetic Age" that were gathered together in 1965 in Poland as *Cyberiada,* and translated by Kandel for the English edition.

The Cyberiad concerns the comic doings of two constructors (compare Swift's "projectors"), or inventors of fantastic machines, Trurl and Klapaucius. Trurl and Klapaucius themselves are robots descended from human-built machines; the history of that descent is suggested by the fragment of epic, a parody of the opening lines of Virgil's *Aeneid,* Trurl's electronic bard creates:

> Arms, and machines I sing, that forc'd by fate
> And haughty Homo's unrelenting hate,
> Expell'd and exil'd, left the Terran shore . . .

The origin of the robot civilization is related in more detail in the one non-Trurl-and-Klapaucius fable, which ends the book, "Prince Ferrix and the Princess Crystal," which is "FROM THE CYPHROEROTICON, OR TALES OF DEVIATIONS, SUPERFIXATIONS, AND ABERRATIONS OF THE HEART."

Though robots, Trurl and Klapaucius, and the other robots and machines with which they deal, share many of the char-

acteristics of human beings: They commit violence on each
other, feel pain, suffer, and exhibit vanity, jealousy, insanity,
fear, folly, love. In "Prince Ferrix and the Princess Crystal,"
the most savage attack on humanity since *Gulliver's Travels,*
the robots do not come off much better; there are pirates
among them, foolish princesses, favor-currying courtiers, and
lovesick princes. Clearly the reader is to understand the robots as satirizing human follies in addition to representing a
cleaner, neater, more rational form of existence.

The salient characteristic of "Trurl's Electronic Bard" is its
wit (an unwitty satire ought to be put out of its misery); the
poem about a haircut, each word beginning with the letter *s,*
and the magnificent love poem expressed in the language of
pure mathematics are its high points. The difficulties of literature in translation are great; here the translator's skill
becomes most obvious.

The fable, however, does not depend upon such verbal pyrotechnics alone (although without this kind of validation
and wordplay, the story would fall flat); it also deals both
with the nature of poetry and the follies of poets. The
concept that the program for a poetry-writing machine is all
of life and civilization is an insight that makes necessary the
recreation of the universe and the evolutionary process that
culminated in the robot. And, of course, the final satirical
gibes at poets merges into a transcendent (though comic)
vision concerning the ultimate power of poetry.

The First Sally (A),
or
Trurl's Electronic Bard

by Stanislaw Lem

Translated by Michael Kandel

First of all, to avoid any possible misunderstanding, we
should state that this was, strictly speaking, a sally to
nowhere. In fact, Trurl never left his house throughout it—
except for a few trips to the hospital and an unimportant
excursion to some asteroid. Yet in a deeper and/or higher

sense this was one of the farthest sallies ever undertaken by the famed constructor, for it very nearly took him beyond the realm of possibility.

Trurl had once had the misfortune to build an enormous calculating machine that was capable of only one operation, namely the addition of two and two, and *that* it did incorrectly. As is related earlier in this volume, the machine also proved to be extremely stubborn, and the quarrel that ensued between it and its creator almost cost the latter his life. From that time on Klapaucius teased Trurl unmercifully, making comments at every opportunity, until Trurl decided to silence him once and for all by building a machine that could write poetry. First Trurl collected eight hundred and twenty tons of books on cybernetics and twelve thousand tons of the finest poetry, then sat down to read it all. Whenever he felt he just couldn't take another chart or equation, he would switch over to verse, and vice versa. After a while it became clear to him that the construction of the machine itself was child's play in comparison with the writing of the program. The program found in the head of an average poet, after all, was written by the poet's civilization, and that civilization was in turn programmed by the civilization that preceded it, and so on to the very Dawn of Time, when those bits of information that concerned the poet-to-be were still swirling about in the primordial chaos of the cosmic deep. Hence in order to program a poetry machine, one would first have to repeat the entire Universe from the beginning—or at least a good piece of it.

Anyone else in Trurl's place would have given up then and there, but our intrepid constructor was nothing daunted. He built a machine and fashioned a digital model of the Void, an Electrostatic Spirit to move upon the face of the electrolytic waters, and he introduced the parameter of light, a protogalactic cloud or two, and by degrees worked his way up to the first ice age—Trurl could move at this rate because his machine was able, in one five-billionth of a second, to simulate one hundred septillion events at forty octillion different locations simultaneously. And if anyone questions these figures, let him work it out for himself.

Next Trurl began to model Civilization, the striking of fires with flints and the tanning of hides, and he provided for dinosaurs and floods, bipedality and taillessness, then made the paleopaleface (*Albuminidis sapientia*), which begat the paleface, which begat the gadget, and so it went, from eon to millennium, the endless hum of electrical currents and eddies. Often the machine turned out to be too small for the computer simulation of a new epoch, and Trurl would have to tack on an auxiliary unit—until he ended up, at last, with a veritable metropolis of tubes and terminals, circuits and shunts, all so tangled and involved that the devil himself couldn't have made head or tail of it. But Trurl managed somehow, he only had to go back twice—once, almost to the beginning, when he discovered that Abel had murdered Cain and not Cain Abel (the result, apparently, of a defective fuse), and once, only three hundred million years back to the middle of the Mesozoic, when after going from fish to amphibian to reptile to mammal, something odd took place among the primates and instead of great apes he came out with gray drapes. A fly, it seems, had gotten into the machine and shorted out the polyphase step-down directional widget. Otherwise everything went like a dream. Antiquity and the Middle Ages were recreated, then the period of revolutions and reforms—which gave the machine a few nasty jolts—and then civilization progressed in such leaps and bounds that Trurl had to hose down the coils and cores repeatedly to keep them from overheating.

Towards the end of the twentieth century the machine began to tremble, first sideways, then lengthwise—for no apparent reason. This alarmed Trurl; he brought out cement and grappling irons just in case. But fortunately these weren't needed; instead of jumping its moorings, the machine settled down and soon had left the twentieth century far behind. Civilizations came and went thereafter in fifty-thousand-year intervals; these were the fully intelligent beings from whom Trurl himself stemmed. Spool upon spool of computerized history was filled and ejected into storage bins; soon there were so many spools, that even if you stood at the top of the machine with high-power binoculars, you wouldn't see the end of them. And all to construct some versifier! But then, such is the way of scientific fanaticism. At last the programs were ready; all that remained was to pick out the most applicable—else the electropoet's education would take several million years at the very least.

During the next two weeks Trurl fed general instructions into his future electropoet, then set up all the necessary logic circuits, emotive elements, semantic centers. He was about to invite Klapaucius to attend a trial run, but thought better of it and started the machine himself. It immediately proceeded to deliver a lecture on the grinding of crystallographical surfaces as an introduction to the study of submolecular magnetic anomalies. Trurl bypassed half the logic circuits and made the emotive more electromotive; the machine sobbed, went into hysterics, then finally said, blubbering terribly, what a cruel, cruel world this was. Trurl intensified the semantic fields and attached a strength of character component; the machine informed him that from now on he would carry out its every wish and to begin with add six floors to the nine it already had, so it could better meditate upon the meaning of existence. Trurl installed a philosophical throttle instead; the machine fell silent and sulked. Only after endless pleading and cajoling was he able to get it to recite something: "I had a little froggy." That appeared to exhaust its repertoire. Trurl adjusted, modulated, expostulated, disconnected, ran checks, reconnected, reset, did everything he could think of, and the machine presented him with a poem that made him thank heaven Klapaucius wasn't there to laugh—imagine, simulating the whole Universe from scratch, not to mention Civilization in every particular, and to end up with such dreadful doggerel! Trurl put in six cliché filters, but they snapped like matches; he had to make them out of pure corundum steel. This seemed to work, so he jacked the semanticity up all the way, plugged in an alternating rhyme generator—which nearly ruined everything, since the machine resolved to become a missionary among destitute tribes on far-flung planets. But at the very last minute, just as he was ready to give up and take a hammer to it, Trurl was struck by an inspiration; tossing out all the logic circuits, he replaced them with self-regulating egocentripetal narcissistors. The machine simpered a little, whimpered a little, laughed bitterly, complained of an awful pain on its third floor, said that in general it was fed up, through, life was beautiful but men were such beasts and how sorry they'd all be when it was dead and gone. Then it asked for pen and paper. Trurl sighed with relief, switched it off and went to bed. The next morning he went to see Klapaucius. Klapaucius, hearing that he was invited to attend the debut of Trurl's electronic bard, dropped everything and followed—so eager was he to be an eyewitness to his friend's humiliation.

Trurl let the machine warm up first, kept the power low, ran up the metal stairs several times to take readings (the machine was like the engine of a giant steamer, galleried, with rows of rivets, dials and valves on very tier)—till finally, satisfied all the decimal places were where they ought to be, he said yes, it was ready now, and why not start with something simple. Later, of course, when the machine had gotten the feel of it, Klapaucius could ask it to produce poetry on absolutely whatever topic he liked.

Now the potentiometers indicated the machine's lyrical capacitance was charged to maximum, and Trurl, so nervous his hands were shaking, threw the master switch. A voice, slightly husky but remarkably vibrant and bewitching, said:

"Phlogisticosh. Rhomothriglyph. Floof."

"Is that it?" inquired Klapaucius after a pause, extremely polite. Trurl only bit his lip, gave the machine a few kicks of current, and tried again. This time the voice came through much more clearly; it was a thrilling baritone, solemn yet intriguingly sensual:

> Pev't o' tay merlong gumin gots,
> Untle yun furly päzzen ye,
> Confre an' ayzor, ayzor ots,
> Bither de furloss bochre blee!

"Am I missing something?" said Klapaucius, calmly watching a panic-stricken Trurl struggling at the controls. Finally Trurl waved his arms in despair, dashed clattering several flights up the metal stairs, got down on all fours and crawled into the machine through a trapdoor; he hammered away inside, swearing like a maniac, tightened something, pried at something, crawled out again and ran frantically to another tier. At long last he let out a cry of triumph, threw a burnt tube over his shoulder—it bounced off the railing and fell to the floor, shattering at the feet of Klapaucius. But Trurl didn't bother to apologize; he quickly put in a new tube, wiped his hands on a chammy cloth and hollered down for Klapaucius to try it now. The following words rang out:

> Mockles! Fent on silpen tree,
> Blockards three a-feening,
> Mockles, what silps came to thee
> In thy pantry dreaming?

"Well, that's an improvement!" shouted Trurl, not entirely convinced. "The last line particularly, did you notice?"

"If this is all you have to show me . . ." said Klapaucius, the very soul of politeness.

"Damn!" said Trurl and again disappeared inside the machine. There was a fierce banging and clanging, the sputtering of shorted wires and the muttering of an even shorter temper, then Trurl stuck his head out of a trapdoor on the third story and yelled, "*Now* try it!"

Klapaucius complied. The electronic bard shuddered from stem to stern and began:

> Oft, in that wickless chalet all begorn,
> Where whilom soughed the mossy sappertort
> And you were wont to bong—

Trurl yanked out a few cables in a fury, something rattled and wheezed, the machine fell silent. Klapaucius laughed so hard he had to sit on the floor. Then suddenly, as Trurl was rushing back and forth, there was a crackle, a clack, and the machine with perfect poise said:

> The Petty and the Small
> Are overcome with gall
> When Genius, having faltered, fails to fall.
>
> Klapaucius too, I ween,
> Will turn the deepest green
> To hear such flawless verse from Trurl's machine.

"There you are, an epigram! And wonderfully apropos!" laughed Trurl, racing down the metal stairs and flinging himself delightedly into his colleague's arms. Klapaucius, quite taken aback, was no longer laughing.

"What, *that?*" he said. "That's nothing. Besides, you had it all set up beforehand."

"Set up?!"

"Oh, it's quite obvious . . . the ill-disguised hostility, the poverty of thought, the crudeness of execution."

"All right, then ask it something else! Whatever you like! Go on! What are you waiting for? Afraid?!"

"Just a minute," said Klapaucius, annoyed. He was trying to think of a request as difficult as possible, aware that any argument on the quality of the verse the machine might be able to produce would be hard if not impossible to settle either way. Suddenly he brightened and said:

"Have it compose a poem—a poem about a haircut! But lofty, noble, tragic, timeless, full of love, treachery, retribution, quiet heroism in the face of certain doom! Six lines, cleverly rhymed, and every word beginning with the letter *s!!*'"

"And why not throw in a full exposition of the general theory of nonlinear automata while you're at it?" growled Trurl. "You can't give it such idiotic—"

But he didn't finish. A melodious voice filled the hall with the following:

> Seduced, shaggy Samson snored.
> She scissored short. Sorely shorn,
> Soon shackled slave, Samson sighed,
> Silently scheming,
> Sightlessly seeking
> Some savage, spectacular suicide.

"Well, what do you say to that?" asked Trurl, his arms folded proudly. But Klapaucius was already shouting:

"Now all in *g!* A sonnet, trochaic hexameter, about an old cyclotron who kept sixteen artificial mistresses, blue and radioactive, had four wings, three purple pavilions, two lacquered chests, each containing exactly one thousand medallions bearing the likeness of Czar Murdicog the Headless . . ."

"Grinding gleeful gears, Gerontogyron grabbed/Giggling gynecobalt-60 golems," began the machine, but Trurl leaped to the console, shut off the power and turned, defending the machine with his body.

"Enough!" he said, hoarse with indignation. "How dare you waste a great talent on such drivel? Either give it decent poems to write or I call the whole thing off!"

"What, those aren't decent poems?" protested Klapaucius.

"Certainly not! I didn't build a machine to solve ridiculous crossword puzzles! That's hack work, not Great Art! Just give it a topic, any topic, as difficult as you like . . ."

Klapaucius thought, and thought some more. Finally he nodded and said:

"Very well. Let's have a love poem, lyrical, pastoral, and expressed in the language of pure mathematics. Tensor algebra mainly, with a little topology and higher calculus, if need be. But with feeling, you understand, and in the cybernetic spirit."

"Love and tensor algebra? Have you taken leave of your senses?" Trurl began, but stopped, for his electronic bard was already declaiming:

Come, let us hasten to a higher plane,
Where dyads tread the fairy fields of Venn,
Their indices bedecked from one to n,
Commingled in an endless Markov chain!

Come, every frustum longs to be a cone,
And every vector dreams of matrices.
Hark to the gentle gradient of the breeze:
It whispers of a more ergodic zone.

In Riemann, Hilbert or in Banach space
Let superscripts and subscripts go their ways.
Our asymptotes no longer out of phase,
We shall encounter, counting, face to face.

I'll grant thee random access to my heart,
Thou'lt tell me all the constants of thy love;
And so we two shall all love's lemmas prove,
And in our bound partition never part.

For what did Cauchy know, or Christoffel,
Or Fourier, or any Boole or Euler,
Wielding their compasses, their pens and rulers,
Of thy supernal sinusoidal spell?

Cancel me not—for what then shall remain?
Abscissas, some mantissas, modules, modes,
A root or two, a torus and a node:
The inverse of my verse, a null domain.

Ellipse of bliss, converge, O lips divine!
The product of our scalars is defined!
Cyberiad draws nigh, and the skew mind
Cuts capers like a happy haversine.

I see the eigenvalue in thine eye,
I hear the tender tensor in thy sigh.
Bernoulli would have been content to die,
Had he but known such $a^2 \cos 2\phi$!

This concluded the poetic competition, since Klapaucius suddenly had to leave, saying he would return shortly with more topics for the machine; but he never did, afraid that in so doing, he might give Trurl more cause to boast. Trurl of course let it be known that Klapaucius had fled in order to hide his envy and chagrin. Klapaucius meanwhile spread the word that Trurl had more than one screw loose on the subject of that so-called mechanical versifier.

Not much time went by before news of Trurl's computer laureate reached the genuine—that is, the ordinary—poets. Deeply offended, they resolved to ignore the machine's existence. A few, however, were curious enough to visit Trurl's electronic bard in secret. It received them courteously, in a hall piled high with closely written paper (for it worked day and night without pause). Now these poets were all avant-garde, and Trurl's machine wrote only in the traditional manner; Trurl, no connoisseur of poetry, had relied heavily on the classics in setting up its program. The machine's guests jeered and left in triumph. The machine was self-programming, however, and in addition had a special ambition-amplifying mechanism with glory-seeking circuits, and very soon a great change took place. Its poems became difficult, ambiguous, so intricate and charged with meaning that they were totally incomprehensible. When the next group of poets came to mock and laugh, the machine replied with an improvisation that was so modern, it took their breath away, and the second poem seriously weakened a certain sonneteer who had two State awards to his name, not to mention a statue in the city park. After that, no poet could resist the fatal urge to cross lyrical swords with Trurl's electronic bard. They came from far and wide, carrying trunks and suitcases full of manuscripts. The machine would let each challenger recite, instantly grasp the algorithm of his verse, and use it to compose an answer in exactly the same style, only two hundred and twenty to three hundred and forty-seven times better.

The machine quickly grew so adept at this that it could cut down a first-class rhapsodist with no more than one or two quatrains. But the worst of it was, all the third-rate poets emerged unscathed; being third-rate, they didn't know good poetry from bad and consequently had no inkling of their crushing defeat. One of them, true, broke his leg when, on the way out, he tripped over an epic poem the machine had just completed, a prodigious work beginning with the words:

> Arms, and machines I sing, that, forc'd by fate,
> And haughty Homo's unrelenting hate,
> Expell'd and exil'd, left the Terran shore ...

The true poets, on the other hand, were decimated by Trurl's electronic bard, though it never laid a finger on them. First an aged elegiast, then two modernists committed suicide, leaping off a cliff that unfortunately happened to lie hard by the road leading from Trurl's place to the nearest train station.

There were many poet protests staged, demonstrations, demands that the machine be served an injunction to cease and desist. But no one else appeared to care. In fact, magazine editors generally approved: Trurl's electronic bard, writing under several thousand different pseudonyms at once, had a poem for every occasion, to fit whatever length might be required, and of such high quality that the magazine would be torn from hand to hand by eager readers. On the street one could see enraptured faces, bemused smiles, sometimes even hear a quiet sob. Everyone knew the poems of Trurl's electronic bard, the air rang with its delightful rhymes. Not infrequently, those citizens of a greater sensitivity, struck by a particularly marvelous metaphor or assonance, would actually fall into a faint. But this colossus of inspiration was prepared even for that eventuality; it would immediately supply the necessary number of restorative rondelets.

Trurl himself had no little trouble in connection with his invention. The classicists, generally elderly, were fairly harmless; they confined themselves to throwing stones through his windows and smearing the sides of his house with an unmentionable substance. But it was much worse with the younger poets. One, for example, as powerful in body as his verse was in imagery, beat Trurl to a pulp. And while the constructor lay in the hospital, events marched on. Not a day passed without a suicide or a funeral; picket lines formed around the hospital; one could hear gunfire in the distance—instead of manuscripts in their suitcases, more and more poets were bringing rifles to defeat Trurl's electronic bard. But the bullets merely bounced off its calm exterior. After his return from the hospital, Trurl, weak and desperate, finally decided one night to dismantle the homeostatic Homer he had created.

But when he approached the machine, limping slightly, it

noticed the pliers in his hand and the grim glitter in his eye, and delivered such an eloquent, impassioned plea for mercy, that the constructor burst into tears, threw down his tools and hurried back to his room, wading through new works of genius, an ocean of paper that filled the hall chest-high from end to end and rustled incessantly.

The following month Trurl received a bill for the electricity consumed by the machine and almost fell off his chair. If only he could have consulted his old friend Klapaucius! But Klapaucius was nowhere to be found. So Trurl had to come up with something by himself. One dark night he unplugged the machine, took it apart, loaded it onto a ship, flew to a certain small asteroid, and there assembled it again, giving it an atomic pile for its source of creative energy.

Then he sneaked home. But that wasn't the end of it. The electronic bard, deprived now of the possibility of having its masterpieces published, began to broadcast them on all wave lengths, which soon sent the passengers and crews of passing rockets into states of stanzaic stupefaction, and those more delicate souls were seized with severe attacks of esthetic ecstasy besides. Having determined the cause of this disturbance, the Cosmic Fleet Command issued Trurl an official request for the immediate termination of his device, which was seriously impairing the health and well-being of all travelers.

At that point Trurl went into hiding, so they dropped a team of technicians on the asteroid to gag the machine's output unit. It overwhelmed them with a few ballads, however, and the mission had to be abandoned. Deaf technicians were sent next, but the machine employed pantomime. After that, there began to be talk of an eventual punitive expedition, of bombing the electropoet into submission. But just then some ruler from a neighboring star system came, bought the machine and hauled it off, asteroid and all, to his kingdom.

Now Trurl could appear in public again and breathe easy. True, lately there had been supernovae exploding on the southern horizon, the like of which no one had ever seen before, and there were rumors that this had something to do with poetry. According to one report, that same ruler, moved by some strange whim, had ordered his astroengineers to connect the electronic bard to a constellation of white supergiants, thereby transforming each line of verse into a stupendous solar prominence; thus the Greatest Poet in the Universe was able to transmit its thermonuclear creations to all the illimitable reaches of space at once. But even if there were any truth to this, it was all too far away to bother Trurl, who vowed by everything that was ever held sacred never, never again to make a cybernetic model of the Muse.

Entropy and the World View

One of the central metaphors seized upon by the New Wave was entropy. The German physicist Clasius gave the name to the ratio of the heat content of a system to its absolute temperature. In a closed system this ratio, which expresses the energy in the system available to do work, will always increase as the temperature of the system reaches a common level. When entropy has reached a maximum value the temperature of the closed system has stabilized, and the energy available for work has decreased to zero.

In the universe, the only truly closed system (if it, indeed, is closed), maximum entropy would occur at the end of time, when all matter had reached the same temperature (near absolute zero), and there was no more heat flow, no more change, no more time. This end has been called "the heat death of the universe." The concept became important to *New Worlds* writers because it mirrored their own world view.

Ballard, for instance, wrote a series of stories and novels in which the world or the universe runs down in a variety of fantastic ways. Much of Brian Aldiss's work mirrored his feelings that "we have used up most of our resources and most of our time." Other *New Worlds* authors used the concept of entropy in their own ways and for their own purposes, most of them because it reflected a philosophy that western civilization had reached a zenith somewhere in the past and was now sliding inevitably toward exhaustion, decay, and death. M. John Harrison, a late 1960s *New Worlds* writer who dealt with entropy in stories such as "Running Down," said in an interview published in *Foundation 23* (1981), "Entropy is simply the result of a rather depressed outlook . . . just a subject matter that became obsessive to a lot of writers in the *New Worlds* vein. Many of them didn't have any real contact with one another, and the idea seemed to fire separately in a lot of people at once, and in totally different ways. Jim Sallis's version of entropy was quite different from Pam Zoline's, for instance. . . . Too much concern has been given to a concept which was really a subject matter of Michael Moorcock's. We all dipped into it, because you do that when you get a good metaphor, and entropy is a damned good metaphor."

Of all the stories about entropy, and of all the experimental stories that appeared in *New Worlds* during the height of the New Wave, perhaps the best known and the one that seemed to symbolize the era for many people was "The Heat Death of the Universe" by Pamela Zoline (1941–   ). That was a bit odd, because the story was one of only two science fiction stories she has written and the only one to appear in *New Worlds*.

Born in Chicago, Zoline was educated in America and in London, where she spent four years at the Slade School of Fine Art. She has worked primarily as an artist and illustrator, and was represented in the Young Contemporaries Exhibition at the Tate Gallery in 1966. Her other sf story was "The Holland of the Mind" in *The New SF* (1969). "The Heat Death of the Universe" was published in the July 1967 *New Worlds*. It uses entropy as a metaphor for the deterioration of a housewife's life and sanity. Zoline has said that the story is "an attempt to 'make sense' of things, of general data, by organizing the private to the public, the public to the private; by making the analogies between entropy and personal choice, the end of the universe and our own aging and death, into the crucial structuring metaphor."

The numbering and titling of paragraphs was a popular stylistic device in *New Worlds* at that time, but the numbering also suggests a kind of countdown toward chaos. "The numbering of the paragraphs," Zoline continued, "is the obvious way to indicate increase, the piling-up, the one-way clock. In the increasing chaos of the language, of the character's distress, and in the culmination of the metaphor, the

inner and outer parts of the story (hopefully) glue into each
other, make a whole."

Material from encyclopedias and texts is inserted not only
as explanations of the difficult concepts with which Zoline is
dealing but as flotsam and jetsam among which Sarah Boyle
is battered and to which she tries to cling for meaning. The
detached narration of the story and its conscious artificiality
distance the characters from the reader—the children scarcely
exist except as objects (their mother isn't even sure how
many there are), and even Sarah is presented remotely, and
her emotional responses are recorded as objective data. She,
too, has become a thing, a machine running down toward entropy.

The Heat Death of the Universe

by Pamela Zoline

1. ONTOLOGY: That branch of metaphysics which concerns
itself with the problems of the nature of existence or being.

2. Imagine a pale blue morning sky, almost green, with
clouds only at the rims. The earth rolls and the sun appears
to mount, mountains erode, fruits decay, the Foraminifera
adds another chamber to its shell, babies' fingernails grow as
does the hair of the dead in their graves, and in egg timers
the sands fall and the eggs cook on.

3. Sarah Boyle thinks of her nose as too large, though several
men have cherished it. The nose is generous and performs a
well calculated geometric curve, at the arch of which the skin
is drawn very tight and a faint whiteness of bone can be seen
showing through, it has much the same architectural tension
and sense of mathematical calculation as the day after
Thanksgiving breastbone on the carcass of turkey; her
maiden name was Sloss, mixed German, English and Irish
descent; in grade school she was very bad at playing softball
and, besides being chosen last for the team, was always made
to play center field, no one could ever hit to center field; she

loves music best of all the arts, and of music, Bach, J.S.; she lives in California, though she grew up in Boston and Toledo.

4. BREAKFAST TIME AT THE BOYLES' HOUSE ON LA FLORIDA STREET, ALAMEDA, CALIFORNIA, THE CHILDREN DEMAND SUGAR FROSTED FLAKES.

With some reluctance Sarah Boyle dishes out Sugar Frosted Flakes to her children, already hearing the decay set in upon the little milk-white teeth, the bony whine of the dentist's drill. The dentist is a short, gentle man with a mustache who sometimes reminds Sarah of an uncle who lives in Ohio. One bowl per child.

5. If one can imagine it considered as an abstract object by members of a totally separate culture, one can see that the cereal box might seem a beautiful thing. The solid rectangle is neatly joined and classical in proportions, on it are squandered wealths of richest colors, virgin blues, crimsons, dense ochers, precious pigments once reserved for sacred paintings and as cosmetics for the blind faces of marble gods. Giant size. Net Weight 16 ounces, 250 grams. "They're tigeriffic!" says Tony the Tiger. The box blats promises: Energy, Nature's Own Goodness, an endless pubescence. On its back is a mask of William Shakespeare to be cut out, folded, worn by thousands of tiny Shakespeares in Kansas City, Detroit, Tucson, San Diego, Tampa. He appears at once more kindly and somewhat more vacant than we are used to seeing him. Two or more of the children lay claim to the mask, but Sarah puts off that Solomon's decision until such time as the box is empty.

6. A notice in orange flourishes states that a Surprise Gift is to be found somewhere in the package, nestled amongst the golden flakes. So far it has not been unearthed, and the children request more cereal than they wish to eat, great yellow heaps of it, to hurry the discovery. Even so, at the end of the meal, some layers of flakes remain in the box and the Gift must still be among them.

7. There is even a Special Offer of a secret membership, code and magic ring; these to be obtained by sending in the box top with 50¢.

8. Three offers on one cereal box. To Sarah Boyle this seems to be oversell. Perhaps something is terribly wrong with the cereal and it must be sold quickly, got off the shelves before

the news breaks. Perhaps it causes a special, cruel Cancer in little children. As Sarah Boyle collects the bowls printed with bunnies and baseball statistics, still slopping half full of milk and wilted flakes, she imagines *in her mind's eye* the headlines "Nation's Small Fry Stricken, Fate's Finger Sugar-Coated, Sweetness Socks Tots."

9. Sarah Boyle is a vivacious and intelligent young wife and mother, educated at a fine Eastern college, proud of her growing family which keeps her busy and happy around the house.

10. BIRTHDAY.
   Today is the birthday of one of the children. There will be a party in the late afternoon.

11. CLEANING UP THE HOUSE. ONE.
   Cleaning up the kitchen. Sarah Boyle puts the bowls, plates, glasses and silverware into the sink. She scrubs at the stickiness on the yellow-marbled Formica table with a blue synthetic sponge, a special blue which we shall see again. There are marks of children's hands in various sizes printed with sugar and grime on all the table's surfaces. The marks catch the light, they appear and disappear according to the position of the observing eye. The floor sweepings include a triangular half of toast spread with grape jelly, bobby pins, a green Band-Aid, flakes, a doll's eye, dust, dog's hair and a button.

12. Until we reach the statistically likely planet and begin to converse with whatever green-faced, teleporting denizens thereof—considering only this shrunk and communication-ravaged world—can we any more postulate a separate culture? Viewing the metastasis of Western Culture it seems progressively less likely. Sarah Boyle imagines a whole world which has become like California, all topographical imperfections sanded away with the sweet-smelling burr of the plastic surgeon's cosmetic polisher; a world populace dieting, leisured, similar in pink and mauve hair and rhinestone shades. A land Cunt Pink and Avocado Green, brassiered and girdled by monstrous complexities of Super Highways, a California endless and unceasing, embracing and transforming the entire globe, California, California!

13. INSERT ONE. ON ENTROPY.
   ENTROPY: A quantity introduced in the first place to

facilitate the calculations and to give clear expressions to the results of thermodynamics. Changes of entropy can be calculated only for a reversible process, and may then be defined as the ratio of the amount of heat taken up to the absolute temperature at which the heat is absorbed. Entropy changes for actual irreversible processes are calculated by postulating equivalent theoretical reversible changes. The entropy of a system is a measure of its degree of disorder. The total entropy of any isolated system can never decrease in any change; it must either increase (irreversible process) or remain constant (reversible process). The total entropy of the Universe therefore is increasing, tending towards a maximum, corresponding to complete disorder of the particles in it (assuming that it may be regarded as an isolated system). See *heat death of the Universe*.

14. CLEANING UP THE HOUSE. TWO.

Washing the baby's diapers. Sarah Boyle writes notes to herself all over the house; a mazed wild script larded with arrows, diagrams, pictures; graffiti on every available surface in a desperate/heroic attempt to index, record, bluff, invoke, order and placate. On the fluted and flowered white plastic lid of the diaper bin she has written in Blushing Pink Nitetime lipstick a phrase to ward off fumy ammoniac despair. "The nitrogen cycle is the vital round of organic and inorganic exchange on earth. The sweet breath of the Universe." On the wall by the washing machine are Yin and Yang signs, mandalas, and the words "Many young wives feel trapped. It is a contemporary sociological phenomenon which may be explained in part by a gap between changing living patterns and the accommodation of social services to these patterns." Over the stove she had written "Help, Help, Help, Help, Help."

15. Sometimes she numbers or letters the things in a room, writing the assigned character on each object. There are 819 separate movable objects in the living room, counting books. Sometimes she labels objects with their names, or with false names; thus on her bureau the hair brush is labeled HAIR BRUSH, the cologne, COLOGNE, the hand cream, CAT. She is passionately fond of children's dictionaries, encyclopedias, ABCs and all reference books, transfixed and comforted at their simulacra of a complete listing and ordering.

16. On the door of a bedroom are written two definitions

from reference books, "GOD: An object of worship";
"HOMEOSTASIS: Maintenance of constancy of internal environment."

17. Sarah Boyle washes the diapers, washes the linen, Oh Saint Veronica, changes the sheets on the baby's crib. She begins to put away some of the toys, stepping over and around the organizations of playthings which still seem inhabited. There are various vehicles, and articles of medicine, domesticity and war; whole zoos of stuffed animals, bruised and odorous with years of love; hundreds of small figures, plastic animals, cowboys, cars, spacemen, with which the children make sub and supra worlds in their play. One of Sarah's favorite toys is the Baba, the wooden Russian doll which, opened, reveals a smaller but otherwise identical doll which opens to reveal, etc., a lesson in infinity at least to the number of seven dolls.

18. Sarah Boyle's mother has been dead for two years. Sarah Boyle thinks of music as the formal articulation of the passage of time, and of Bach as the most poignant rendering of this. Her eyes are sometimes the color of the aforementioned kitchen sponge. Her hair is natural spaniel brown; months ago on an hysterical day she dyed it red, so now it is two-toned with a stripe in the middle, like the painted walls of slum buildings or old schools.

19. INSERT TWO. THE HEAT DEATH OF UNIVERSE.
The second law of thermodynamics can be interpreted to mean that the ENTROPY of a closed system tends toward a maximum and that its available ENERGY tends toward a minimum. It has been held that the Universe constitutes a thermodynamically closed system, and if this were true it would mean that a time must finally come when the Universe "unwinds" itself, no energy being available for use. This state is referred to as the "heat death of the Universe." It is by no means certain, however, that the Universe can be considered as a closed system in this sense.

20. Sarah Boyle pours out a Coke from the refrigerator and lights a cigarette. The coldness and sweetness of the thick brown liquid makes her throat ache and her teeth sting briefly, sweet juice of my youth, her eyes glass with the carbonation, she thinks of the Heat Death of the Universe. A logarithmic of those late summer days, endless as the Irish serpent twist-

ing through jeweled manuscripts forever, tail in mouth, the heat pressing, bloating, doing violence. The Los Angeles sky becomes so filled and bleached with detritus that it loses all color and silvers like a mirror, reflecting back the fricasseeing earth. Everything becoming warmer and warmer, each particle of matter becoming more agitated, more excited until the bonds shatter, the glues fail, the deodorants lose their seals. She imagines the whole of New York City melting like a Dali into a great chocolate mass, a great soup, the Great Soup of New York.

21. CLEANING UP THE HOUSE. THREE.
Beds made. Vacuuming the hall, a carpet of faded flowers, vines and leaves which endlessly wind and twist into each other in a fevered and permanent ecstasy. Suddenly the vacuum blows instead of sucks, spewing marbles, dolls' eyes, dust, crackers. An old trick. "Oh my god," says Sarah. The baby yells on cue for attention/changing/food. Sarah kicks the vacuum cleaner and it retches and begins working again.

22. AT LUNCH ONLY ONE GLASS OF MILK IS SPILLED.
At lunch only one glass of milk is spilled.

23. The plants need watering, Geranium, Hyacinth, Lavender, Avocado, Cyclamen. Feed the fish, happy fish with china castles and mermaids in the bowl. The turtle looks more and more unwell and is probably dying.

24. Sarah Boyle's blue eyes, how blue? Bluer far and of a different quality than the Nature metaphors which were both engine and fuel to so much of precedent literature. A fine, modern, acid, synthetic blue; the shiny cerulean of the skies on postcards sent from lush subtropics, the natives grinning ivory ambivalent grins in their dark faces; the promising, fat, unnatural blue of the heavy tranquillizer capsule; the cool, mean blue of that fake kitchen sponge; the deepest, most unbelievable azure of the tiled and mossless interiors of California swimming pools. The chemists in their kitchens cooked, cooled and distilled this blue from thousands of colorless and wonderfully constructed crystals, each one unique and nonpareil; and now that color hisses, bubbles, burns in Sarah's eyes.

25. INSERT THREE. ON LIGHT.
LIGHT: Name given to the agency by means of which a

viewed object influences the observer's eyes. Consists of electromagnetic radiation within the wavelength range 4 x 10-⁵
cm. to 7 x 10-⁵ cm. approximately; variations in the wavelength produce different sensations in the eye, corresponding
to different colors. See *color vision*.

26. LIGHT AND CLEANING THE LIVING ROOM.

All the objects (819) and surfaces in the living room are
dusty, gray common dust as though this were the den of a
giant molting mouse. Suddenly quantities of waves or particles of very strong sunlight speed in through the window, and
everything incandesces, multiple rainbows. Poised in what has
become a solid cube of light, like an ancient insect trapped in
amber, Sarah Boyle realizes that the dust is indeed the most
beautiful stuff in the room, a manna for the eyes. Duchamp,
that father of thought, has set with fixative some dust which
fell on one of his sculptures, counting it as part of the work.
"That way madness lies, says Sarah," says Sarah. The thought
of ordering a household on Dada principles balloons again.
All the rooms would fill up with objects, newspapers and
magazines would compost, the potatoes in the rack, the
canned green beans in the garbage can would take new heart
and come to life again, reaching out green shoots towards the
sun. The plants would grow wild and wind into a jungle
around the house, splitting plaster, tearing shingles, the
garden would enter in at the door. The goldfish would die,
the birds would die, we'd have them stuffed; the dog would
die from lack of care, and probably the children—all stuffed
and sitting around the house, covered with dust.

27. INSERT FOUR. DADA.

DADA (Fr., hobby-horse) was a nihilistic precursor of
Surrealism, invented in Zurich during World War I, a product of hysteria and shock lasting from about 1915 to 1922. It
was deliberately anti-art and anti-sense, intended to outrage
and scandalize, and its most characteristic production was the
reproduction of the *Mona Lisa* decorated with a mustache
and the obscene caption LHOOQ (read: *elle a chaud au cul*)
"by" Duchamp. Other manifestations included Arp's collages
of colored paper cut out at random and shuffled, ready-made
objects such as the bottle drier and the bicycle wheel "signed"
by Duchamp, Picabia's drawings of bits of machinery with
incongruous titles, incoherent poetry, a lecture given by 38
lecturers in unison, and an exhibition in Cologne in 1920,
held in an annex to a café lavatory, at which a chopper was

provided for spectators to smash the exhibits with—which they did.

28. TIME PIECES AND OTHER MEASURING DEVICES.

In the Boyle house there are four clocks; three watches (one a Mickey Mouse watch which does not work); two calendars and two engagement books; three rulers, a yard stick; a measuring cup; a set of red plastic measuring spoons which includes a tablespoon, a teaspoon, a one-half teaspoon, one-fourth teaspoon and one-eighth teaspoon; an egg timer; an oral thermometer and a rectal thermometer; a Boy Scout compass; a barometer in the shape of a house, in and out of which an old woman and an old man chase each other forever without fulfillment; a bathroom scale; an infant scale; a tape measure which can be pulled out of a stuffed felt strawberry; a wall on which the children's heights are marked; a metronome.

29. Sarah Boyle finds a new line in her face after lunch while cleaning the bathroom. It is as yet barely visible, running from the midpoint of her forehead to the bridge of her nose. By inward curling of her eyebrows she can etch it clearly as it will come to appear in the future. She marks another mark on the wall where she has drawn out a scoring area. Face Lines and Other Intimations of Mortality, the heading says. There are thirty-two marks, counting this latest one.

30. Sarah Boyle is a vivacious and witty young wife and mother, educated at a fine Eastern college, proud of her growing family which keeps her happy and busy around the house, involved in many hobbies and community activities, and only occasionally given to obsessions concerning Time/Entropy/Chaos and Death.

31. Sarah Boyle is never quite sure how many children she has.

32. Sarah thinks from time to time; Sarah is occasionally visited with this thought; at times this thought comes upon Sarah, that there are things to be hoped for, accomplishments to be desired beyond the mere reproductions, mirror reproduction of one's kind. The babies. Lying in bed at night sometimes the memory of the act of birth, always the hue and texture of red plush theater seats, washes up; the rending which always, at a certain intensity of pain, slipped into land-

scapes, the sweet breath of the sweating nurse. The wooden Russian doll has bright, perfectly round red spots on her cheeks, she splits in the center to reveal a doll smaller but in all other respects identical with round bright red spots on her cheeks, etc.

33. How fortunate for the species, Sarah muses or is mused, that children are as ingratiating as we know them. Otherwise they would soon be salted off for the leeches they are, and the race would extinguish itself in a fair sweet flowering, the last generations' massive achievement in the arts and pursuits of high civilization. The finest women would have their tubes tied off at the age of twelve, or perhaps refrain altogether from the Act of Love? All interests would be bent to a refining and perfecting of each febrile sense, each fluid hour, with no more cowardly investment in immortality via the patchy and too often disappointing vegetables of one's own womb.

34. INSERT FIVE. LOVE.
LOVE: A typical sentiment involving fondness for, or attachment to, an object, the idea of which is emotionally colored whenever it arises in the mind, and capable, as Shand has pointed out, of evoking any one of a whole gamut of primary emotions, according to the situation in which the object is placed, or represented; often, and by psychoanalysts always, used in the sense of *sex-love* or even *lust* (q.v.).

35. Sarah Boyle has at times felt a unity with her body, at other times a complete separation. The mind/body duality considered. The time/space duality considered. The male/female duality considered. The matter/energy duality considered. Sometimes, at extremes, her Body seems to her an animal on a leash, taken for walks in the park by her Mind. The lampposts of experience. Her arms are lightly freckled, and when she gets very tired the places under her eyes became violet.

36. Housework is never completed, the chaos always lurks ready to encroach on any area left unweeded, a jungle filled with dirty pans and the roaring of giant stuffed toy animals suddenly turned savage. Terrible glass eyes.

37. SHOPPING FOR THE BIRTHDAY CAKE.
Shopping in the supermarket with the baby in front of the cart and a larger child holding on. The light from the ice-

cube-tray-shaped fluorescent lights is mixed blue and pink and brighter, colder, and cheaper than daylight. The doors swing open just as you reach out your hand for them, Tantalus, moving with a ghastly quiet swing. Hot dogs for the party. Potato chips, gum drops, a paper tablecloth with birthday designs, hot-dog buns, catsup, mustard, piccalilli, balloons, instant coffee Continental style, dog food, frozen peas, ice cream, frozen lima beans, frozen broccoli in butter sauce, paper birthday hats, paper napkins in three colors, a box of Sugar Frosted Flakes with a Wolfgang Amadeus Mozart mask on the back, bread, pizza mix. The notes of a just graspable music filter through the giant store, for the most part bypassing the brain and acting directly on the liver, blood and lymph. The air is delicately scented with aluminum. Half-and-half cream, tea bags, bacon, sandwich meat, strawberry jam. Sarah is in front of the shelves of cleaning products now, and the baby is beginning to whine. Around her are whole libraries of objects, offering themselves. Some of that same old hysteria that had incarnadined her hair rises up again, and she does not refuse it. There is one moment when she can choose direction, like standing on a chalk-drawn X, a hot cross bun, and she does not choose calm and measure. Sarah Boyle begins to pick out methodically, deliberately and with a careful ecstasy, one of every cleaning product which the store sells. Window Cleaner, Glass Cleaner, Brass Polish, Silver Polish, Steel Wool, eighteen different brands of Detergent, Disinfectant, Toilet Cleaner, Water Softener, Fabric Softener, Drain Cleanser, Spot Remover, Floor Wax, Furniture Wax, Car Wax, Carpet Shampoo, Dog Shampoo, Shampoo for people with dry, oily and normal hair, for people with dandruff, for people with gray hair. Tooth Paste, Tooth Powder, Denture Cleaner, Deodorants, Antiperspirants, Antiseptics, Soaps, Cleansers, Abrasives, Oven Cleaners, Makeup Removers. When the same products appear in different sizes Sarah takes one of each size. For some products she accumulates whole little families of containers: a giant Father bottle of shampoo, a Mother bottle, an Older Sister bottle just smaller than the Mother bottle, and a very tiny Baby Brother bottle. Sarah fills three shopping carts and has to have help wheeling them all down the aisles. At the checkout counter her laughter and hysteria keep threatening to overflow as the pale blond clerk with no eyebrows like the *Mona Lisa* pretends normality and disinterest. The bill comes to $57.53 and Sarah has to write a check. Driving home, the baby strapped in the drive-a-cot and the paper bags bulging in the back seat, she cries.

38. BEFORE THE PARTY.

Mrs. David Boyle, mother-in-law of Sarah Boyle, is coming to the party of her grandchild. She brings a toy, a yellow wooden duck on a string, made in Austria; the duck quacks as it is pulled along the floor. Sarah is filling paper cups with gum drops and chocolates, and Mrs. David Boyle sits at the kitchen table and talks to her. She is talking about several things, she is talking about her garden which is flourishing except for a plague of rare black beetles, thought to have come from Hong Kong, which are undermining some of the most delicate growths at the roots, and feasting on the leaves of other plants. She is talking about a sale of household linens which she plans to attend on the following Tuesday. She is talking about her neighbor who has Cancer and is wasting away. The neighbor is a Catholic woman who had never had a day's illness in her life until the Cancer struck, and now she is, apparently, failing with dizzying speed. The doctor says her body's chaos, chaos, cells running wild all over, says Mrs. David Boyle. When I visited her she hardly *knew* me, can hardly *speak*, can't keep herself *clean*, says Mrs. David Boyle.

39. Sometimes Sarah can hardly remember how many cute, chubby little children she has.

40. When she used to stand out in center field far away from the other players, she used to make up songs and sing them to herself.

41. She thinks of the end of the world by ice.

42. She thinks of the end of the world by water.

43. She thinks of the end of the world by nuclear war.

44. There must be more than this, Sarah Boyle thinks, from time to time. What could one do to justify one's passage? Or less ambitiously, to change, even in the motion of the smallest mote, the course and circulation of the world? Sometimes Sarah's dreams are of heroic girth, a new symphony using laboratories of machinery and all invented instruments, at once giant in scope and intelligible to all, to heal the bloody breach; a series of paintings which would transfigure and astonish and calm the frenzied art world in its panting race; a

new novel that would refurbish language. Sometimes she considers the mystical, the streaky and random, and it seems that one change, no matter how small, would be enough. Turtles are supposed to live for many years. To carve a name, date and perhaps a word of hope upon a turtle's shell, then set him free to wend the world, surely this one act might cancel out absurdity?

45. Mrs. David Boyle has a faint mustache, like Duchamp's *Mona Lisa*.

46. THE BIRTHDAY PARTY.
Many children, dressed in pastels, sit around the long table. They are exhausted and overexcited from games fiercely played, some are flushed and wet, others unnaturally pale. This general agitation and the paper party hats they wear combine to make them appear a dinner party of debauched midgets. It is time for the cake. A huge chocolate cake in the shape of a rocket and launching pad and covered with blue and pink icing is carried in. In the hush the birthday child begins to cry. He stops crying, makes a wish and blows out the candles.

47. One child will not eat hot dogs, ice cream or cake, and asks for cereal. Sarah pours him out a bowl of Sugar Frosted Flakes, and a moment later he chokes. Sarah pounds him on the back and out spits a tiny green plastic snake with red glass eyes, the Surprise Gift. All the children want it.

48. AFTER THE PARTY THE CHILDREN ARE PUT TO BED.
Bath time. Observing the nakedness of children, pink and slippery as seals, squealing as seals, now the splashing, grunting and smacking of cherry flesh on raspberry flesh reverberate in the pearl-tiled steamy cubicle. The nakedness of children is so much more absolute than that of the mature. No musky curling hair to indicate the target points, no knobbly clutch of plane and fat and curvature to ennoble this prince of beasts. All well-fed naked children appear edible. Sarah's teeth hum in her head with memory of bloody feastings, prehistory. Young humans appear too like the young of other species for smugness, and the comparison is not even in their favor, they are much the most peeled and unsupple of those young. Such pinkness, such utter nuded pinkness; the

orifices neatly incised, rimmed with a slightly deeper rose, the incessant demands for breast, time, milks of many sorts.

49. INSERT SIX. WEINER ON ENTROPY.

In Gibbs' Universe order is least probable, chaos most probable. But while the Universe as a whole, if indeed there is a whole Universe, tends to run down, there are local enclaves whose direction seems opposed to that of the Universe at large and in which there is a limited and temporary tendency for organization to increase. Life finds its home in some of these enclaves.

50. Sarah Boyle imagines, in her mind's eye, cleaning and ordering the whole world, even the Universe. Filling the great spaces of Space with a marvelous sweet-smelling, deep-cleansing foam. Deodorizing rank caves and volcanoes. Scrubbing rocks.

51. INSERT SEVEN. TURTLES.

Many different species of carnivorous Turtles live in the fresh waters of the tropical and temperate zones of various continents. Most northerly of the European Turtles (extending as far as Holland and Lithuania) is the European Pond Turtle (*Emys orbicularis*). It is from 8 to 10 inches long and may live a hundred years.

52. CLEANING UP AFTER THE PARTY.

Sarah is cleaning up after the party. Gum drops and melted ice cream surge off paper plates, making holes in the paper tablecloth through the printed roses. A fly has died a splendid death in a pool of strawberry ice cream. Wet jelly beans stain all they touch, finally becoming themselves colorless, opaque white like flocks of tamed or sleeping maggots. Plastic favors mount half-eaten pieces of blue cake. Strewn about are thin strips of fortune papers from the Japanese poppers. Upon them are printed strangely assorted phrases selected by apparently unilingual Japanese. Crowds of delicate yellow people spending great chunks of their lives in producing these most ephemeral of objects, and inscribing thousands of fine papers with absurd and incomprehensible messages. "The very hairs of your head are all numbered," reads one. Most of the balloons have popped. Someone has planted a hot dog in the daffodil pot. A few of the helium balloons have escaped their owners and now ride the ceiling.

Another fortune paper reads, "Emperor's horses meet death worse, numbers, numbers."

53. She is very tired, violet under the eyes, mauve beneath the eyes. Her uncle in Ohio used to get the same marks under his eyes. She goes to the kitchen to lay the table for tomorrow's breakfast, then she sees that in the turtle's bowl the turtle is floating, still, on the surface of the water. Sarah Boyle pokes at it with a pencil but it does not move. She stands for several minutes looking at the dead turtle on the surface of the water. She is crying again.

54. She begins to cry. She goes to the refrigerator and takes out a carton of eggs, white eggs, extra large. She throws them one by one onto the kitchen floor, which is patterned with strawberries in squares. They break beautifully. There is a Secret Society of Dentists, all mustached, with Special Code and Magic Rings. She begins to cry. She takes up three bunny dishes and throws them against the refrigerator, they shatter, and then the floor is covered with shards, chunks of partial bunnies, an ear, an eye here, a paw; Stockton, California, Acton, California, Chico, California, Redding, California, Glen Ellen, California, Cadiz, California, Angels Camp, California, Half Moon Bay. The total ENTROPY of the Universe therefore is increasing, tending towards a maximum, corresponding to complete disorder of the particles in it. She is crying, her mouth is open. She throws a jar of grape jelly and it smashes the window over the sink. Her eyes are blue. She begins to open her mouth. It has been held that the Universe constitutes a thermodynamically closed system, and if this were true it would mean that a time must finally come when the Universe "unwinds" itself, no energy being available for use. This state is referred to as the "heat death of the Universe." Sarah Boyle begins to cry. She throws a jar of strawberry jam against the stove, enamel chips off and the stove begans to bleed. Bach had twenty children, how many children has Sarah Boyle? Her mouth is open. Her mouth is opening. She turns on the water and fills the sinks with detergent. She writes on the kitchen wall, "William Shakespeare has Cancer and lives in California." She writes, "Sugar Frosted Flakes are the Food of the Gods." The water foams up in the sink, overflowing, bubbling onto the strawberry floor. She is about to begin to cry. Her mouth is opening. She is crying. She cries. How can one ever tell whether there are one or many fish? She begins to break glasses and dishes, she

throws cups and cooking pots and jars of food which shatter and break and spread over the kitchen. The sand keeps falling, very quietly, in the egg timer. The old man and woman in the barometer never catch each other. She picks up eggs and throws them into the air. She begins to cry. She opens her mouth. The eggs arch slowly through the kitchen, like a baseball, hit high against the spring sky, seen from far away. They go higher and higher in the stillness, hesitate at the zenith, then begin to fall away slowly, slowly, through the fine, clear air.

Speculations on Speculative Fiction

Kate Wilhelm (1928–   ) is not so much a woman writer, nor a woman who writes, as a writer whose work is building bridges between science fiction (she would prefer "speculative fiction") and the mainstream. Her technique is to use more sensitive, self-doubting characters in stories that deal with basic themes and avoid generic conventions.

Born in Toledo, Ohio, and married at nineteen to Joseph Wilhelm, she started writing in her late twenties. Her first professional sale, "The Mile-Long Spaceship," was published in the April 1957 *Astounding*, although "The Pint-Sized Genie" appeared first in the October 1956 *Fantastic Stories*. She married Damon Knight in 1963, the same year her first collection of stories, *The Mile-Long Spaceship*, and her first novel, a mystery entitled *More Bitter than Death*, were published.

Wilhelm's first sf novel, *The Clone* (1965), was co-authored by Theodore L. Thomas; they also collaborated on another novel, *The Year of the Cloud* (1970). Her first sf novel on her own was *The Nevermore Affair* (1966). It was followed by *The Killer Thing* (1967), *Let the Fire Fall* (1969), and *Margaret and I* (1971). *Where Late the Sweet Birds Sang* (1976), a post-catastrophe novel about an isolated group that tries to survive through cloning, won a Hugo Award. Other novels include *The Clewiston Test* (1976), *Fault Lines* (1977), and *Juniper Time* (1978).

She was involved with the development of the Clarion Science Fiction Writers conferences, was co-director for nine years, and edited *Clarion SF* (1977). She also edited *Nebula*

Award Stories Nine. More than many sf writers, though not as much as Theodore Sturgeon and Harlan Ellison, her reputation has been built on skillfully written short fiction, which has been brought together in collections of her work: after *The Mile-Long Spaceship* came *The Downstairs Room and Other Speculative Fiction* (1968), *Abyss: Two Novellas* (1971), *The Infinity Box: A Collection of Speculative Fiction* (1975), and *Listen, Listen* (1981).

Wilhelm's preference for the term "speculative fiction" suggests not only that a scientific component is unnecessary in her work but that the conventions of the genre may be ignored or contravened. Most of her stories after the early ones appeared first in Knight's anthology of speculative fiction, *Orbit*, first published in 1966, and many have since been anthologized. Much of her fiction takes place in worlds that are disintegrating or otherwise heading for final catastrophe, and her characters, like most mainstream characters, are introspective people who feel the tragic gap between their hopes and their expectations; often they find more sustenance in acceptance and emotional involvement than in knowledge and the pursuit of answers.

"The Planners," originally published in *Orbit 3*, won a Nebula Award for 1968. The story has a basis in scientific theory—in this case biological experiments on the nature of learning and behavior. The story centers on a project to improve the intelligence of monkeys through injections of soluble ribonucleic acid (sRNA) taken from the most intelligent monkeys. The possibility that memory may be based on chemistry rather than the "electrical wiring" of neurons in the brain goes back to experiments with planarian worms performed more than twenty years ago by Prof. James V. McConnell at the University of Michigan, and on other creatures, including rats, at the Baylor School of Medicine, UCLA, and other places. These experiments suggest that learned behavior, such as running mazes or avoidance of dark places, may be transmitted through some protein factor in the blood, possibly RNA. The concept has been used in other works, including James Gunn's *Kampus* (1977) and *The Dreamers* (1981).

The monkey project is pure research aimed at demonstrating the validity of the concept; its human possibilities are shown through the work with the mentally handicapped boy, Sonny Driscoll. Ironically, the monkey project is succeeding and the Driscoll boy project is failing. But if this had been all, the story would not have been memorable. Its success lies in its unusual third-person viewpoint. The reader follows the project director, Dr. Darin, but gets into his mind so completely that Darin's fantasies become almost real.

The nonscientists in the story, even one of the scientists, are unperceptive, even uninterested; the monkeys are smarter, more direct, and less frustrated, probably because their lives are more natural. Darin himself is frustrated by his marital life, his lack of success with the Driscoll boy, and the callousness to suffering that seems necessary to the method of science. With the threat of an investigation hanging over the project, Darin's fantasy episodes have increased. The author carefully makes no typographic distinction between what is fantasy and what is reality, though each contains a clue; it is the reader's responsibility, as in real life, to distinguish between them.

The Planners

by Kate Wilhelm

Rae stopped before the one-way glass, stooped and peered at the gibbon infant in the cage. Darin watched her bitterly. She straightened after a moment, hands in smock pockets, face innocent of any expression what-so-goddam-ever, and continued to saunter toward him through the aisle between the cages.

"You still think it is cruel, and worthless?"

"Do you, Dr. Darin?"

"Why do you always do that? Answer my question with one of your own?"

"Does it infuriate you?"

He shrugged and turned away. His lab coat was on the chair where he had tossed it. He pulled it on over his sky-blue sport shirt.

"How is the Driscoll boy?" Rae asked.

He stiffened, then relaxed again. Still not facing her, he said, "Same as last week, last year. Same as he'll be until he dies."

The hall door opened and a very large, very homely face appeared. Stu Evers looked past Darin, down the aisle. "You alone? Thought I heard voices."

"Talking to myself," Darin said. "The committee ready yet?"

"Just about. Dr. Jacobsen is stalling with his nose-throat spray routine, as usual." He hesitated a moment, glancing again down the row of cages, then at Darin. "Wouldn't you think a guy allergic to monkeys would find some other line of research?"

Darin looked, but Rae was gone. What had it been this time: the Driscoll boy, the trend of the project itself? He wondered if she had a life of her own when she was away. "I'll be out at the compound," he said. He passed Stu in the doorway and headed toward the livid greenery of Florida forests.

The cacophony hit him at the door. There were four hundred sixty-nine monkeys on the thirty-six acres of wooded ground the research department was using. Each monkey was screeching, howling, singing, cursing, or otherwise making its presence known. Darin grunted and headed toward the compound. The Happiest Monkeys in the World, a newspaper article had called them. Singing Monkeys, a subhead announced. MONKEYS GIVEN SMARTNESS PILLS, the most enterprising paper had proclaimed. *Cruelty Charged*, added another in subdued, sorrowful tones.

The compound was three acres of carefully planned and maintained wilderness, completely enclosed with thirty-foot-high, smooth plastic walls. A transparent dome covered the area. There were one-way windows at intervals along the wall. A small group stood before one of the windows: the committee.

Darin stopped and gazed over the interior of the compound through one of the windows. He saw Heloise and Skitter contentedly picking nonexistent fleas from one another. Adam was munching on a banana; Homer was lying on his back idly touching his feet to his nose. A couple of the chimps were at the water fountain, not drinking, merely pressing the pedal and watching the fountain, now and then immersing a head or hand in the bowl of cold water. Dr. Jacobsen appeared and Darin joined the group.

"Good morning, Mrs. Bellbottom," Darin said politely. "Did you know your skirt has fallen off?" He turned from her to Major Dormouse. "Ah, Major, and how many of the enemy have you swatted to death today with your pretty little yellow rag?" He smiled pleasantly at a pimply young man with a camera. "Major, you've brought a professional peeping tom. More stories in the paper, with pictures this time?" The pimply young man shifted his position, fidgeted with the camera. The major was fiery; Mrs. Bellbottom was on her knees peering under a bush, looking for her skirt. Darin blinked. None of them had on any clothing. He turned toward the window. The chimps were drawing up a table, laden with tea things, silver, china, tiny finger sandwiches. The chimps were all wearing flowered shirts and dresses. Hortense had on a ridiculous flop-brimmed sun hat of pale green straw. Darin leaned against the fence to control his laughter.

"Soluble ribonucleic acid," Dr. Jacobsen was saying when Darin recovered, "sRNA for short. So from the gross beginnings when entire worms were trained and fed to other worms that seemed to benefit from the original training, we have come to these more refined methods. We now extract the sRNA molecule from the trained animals and feed it, the sRNA molecules in solution, to untrained specimens and observe the results."

The young man was snapping pictures as Jacobsen talked. Mrs. Whoosis was making notes, her mouth a lipless line, the sun hat tinging her skin with green. The sun on her patterned red and yellow dress made it appear to jiggle, giving her fleshy hips a constant rippling motion. Darin watched, fascinated. She was about sixty.

". . . my colleague, who proposed this line of experimentation, Dr. Darin," Jacobsen said finally, and Darin bowed slightly. He wondered what Jacobsen had said about him, decided to wait for any questions before he said anything.

"Dr. Darin, is it true that you also extract this substance from people?"

"Every time you scratch yourself, you lose this substance," Darin said. "Every time you lose a drop of blood, you lose it. It is in every cell of your body. Sometimes we take a sample of human blood for study, yes."

"And inject it into those animals?"

"Sometimes we do that," Darin said. He waited for the next, the inevitable question, wondering how he would answer it. Jacobsen had briefed them on what to answer, but he couldn't remember what Jacobsen had said. The question didn't come. Mrs. Whoosis stepped forward, staring at the window.

Darin turned his attention to her; she averted her eyes, quickly fixed her stare again on the chimps in the compound. "Yes, Mrs. uh . . . Ma'am?" Darin prompted her. She didn't look at him.

"Why? What is the purpose of all this?" she asked. Her voice sounded strangled. The pimpled young man was inching toward the next window.

"Well," Darin said, "our theory is simple. We believe that learning ability can be improved drastically in nearly every species. The learning curve is the normal, expected bell-shaped curve, with a few at one end who have the ability to learn quite rapidly, with the majority in the center who learn at an average rate, and a few at the other end who learn quite slowly. With our experiments we are able to increase the ability of those in the broad middle as well as those in the deficient end of the curve so that their learning abilities match those of the fastest learners of any given group. . . ."

No one was listening to him. It didn't matter. They would be given the press release he had prepared for them, written in simple language, no polysyllables, no complicated sentences. They were all watching the chimps through the windows. He said, "So we gabbled the gazooka three times wretchedly until the spirit of camping fired the girls." One of the committee members glanced at him. "Whether intravenously or orally, it seems to be equally effective," Darin said, and the perspiring man turned again to the window. "Injections every morning . . . rejections, planned diet, planned parenthood, planned plans planning plans." Jacobsen eyed him suspiciously. Darin stopped talking and lighted a cigarette. The woman with the unquiet hips turned from the window, her face very red. "I've seen enough," she said. "This sun is too hot out here. May we see the inside laboratories now?"

Darin turned them over to Stu Evers inside the building. He walked back slowly to the compound. There was a grin on his lips when he spotted Adam on the far side, swaggering triumphantly, paying no attention to Hortense, who was rocking back and forth on her haunches, looking very dazed. Darin saluted Adam, then, whistling, returned to his office. Mrs. Driscoll was due with Sonny at 1 P.M.

Sonny Driscoll was fourteen. He was five feet nine inches, weighed one hundred sixty pounds. His male nurse was six feet two inches and weighed two hundred twenty-seven pounds. Sonny had broken his mother's arm when he was twelve; he had broken his father's arm and leg when he was thirteen. So far the male nurse was intact. Every morning Mrs. Driscoll lovingly washed and dressed her baby, fed him, walked him in the yard, spoke happily to him of plans for the coming months, or sang nursery songs to him. He never seemed to see her. The male nurse, Johnny, was never farther than three feet from his charge when he was on duty.

Mrs. Driscoll refused to think of the day when she would have to turn her child over to an institution. Instead she placed her faith and hope in Darin.

They arrived at two-fifteen, earlier than he had expected them, later than they had promised to be there.

"The kid kept taking his clothes off," Johnny said morosely. The kid was taking them off again in the office. Johnny started toward him, but Darin shook his head. It didn't matter. Darin got his blood sample from one of the muscular arms, shot the injection into the other one. Sonny didn't seem to notice what he was doing. He never seemed to notice. Sonny refused to be tested. They got him to the chair and table, but he sat staring at nothing, ignoring the blocks, the bright balls, the crayons, the candy. Nothing Darin did or said had any discernible effect. Finally the time was up. Mrs. Driscoll thanked Darin for helping her boy.

Stu and Darin held class from four to five daily. Kelly O'Grady had the monkeys tagged and ready for them when they showed up at the schoolroom. Kelly was very tall, very slender and red-haired. Stu shivered if she accidentally brushed him in passing; Darin hoped one day Stu would pull an Adam on her. She sat primly on her high stool with her notebook on her knee, unaware of the change that came over Stu during school hours, or, if aware, uncaring. Darin wondered if she was really a Barbie doll fully programmed to perform laboratory duties, and nothing else.

He thought of the Finishing School for Barbies where long-legged, high-breasted, stomachless girls went to get shaved clean, get their toenails painted pink, their nipples removed, and all body openings sewn shut, except for their mouths, which curved in perpetual smiles and led nowhere.

The class consisted of six black spider monkeys who had not been fed yet. They had to do six tasks in order: (1) pull a rope; (2) cross the cage and get a stick that was released by the rope; (3) pull the rope again; (4) get the second stick that would fit into the first; (5) join the sticks together; (6) using the lengthened stick, pull a bunch of bananas close enough to the bars of the cage to reach them and take them inside where they could eat them. At five the monkeys were returned to Kelly, who wheeled them away one by one back to the stockroom. None of them had performed all the tasks, although two had gone through part of them before the time ran out.

Waiting for the last of the monkeys to be taken back to its quarters, Stu asked, "What did you do to that bunch of idiots this morning? By the time I got them, they all acted dazed."

Darin told him about Adam's performance; they were both laughing when Kelly returned. Stu's laugh turned to something that sounded almost like a sob. Darin wanted to tell him about the school Kelly must have attended, thought better of it, and walked away instead.

His drive home was through the darkening forests of interior Florida for sixteen miles on a narrow straight road.

"Of course, I don't mind living here," Lea had said once, nine years ago when the Florida appointment had come through. And she didn't mind. The house was air-conditioned; the family car, Lea's car, was air-conditioned; the back yard had a swimming pool big enough to float the Queen Mary. A frightened, large-eyed Florida girl did the housework, and Lea gained weight and painted sporadically, wrote sporadically—poetry—and entertained faculty wives regularly. Darin suspected that sometimes she entertained faculty husbands also.

"Oh, Professor Dimples, one hour this evening? That will be fifteen dollars, you know." He jotted down the appointment and turned to Lea. "Just two more today and you will have your car payment. How about that!" She twined slinky arms about his neck, pressing tight high breasts hard against him. She had to tilt her head slightly for his kiss. "Then your turn, darling. For free." He tried to kiss her; something stopped his tongue, and he realized that the smile was on the outside only, that the opening didn't really exist at all.

He parked next to an MG, not Lea's, and went inside the house where the martinis were always snapping cold.

"Darling, you remember Greta, don't you? She is going to give me lessons twice a week. Isn't that exciting?"

"But you already graduated," Darin murmured. Greta was not tall and not long-legged. She was a little bit of a thing. He thought probably he did remember her from somewhere or other, vaguely. Her hand was cool in his.

"Greta has moved in; she is going to lecture on modern art for the spring semester. I asked her for private lessons and she said yes."

"Greta Farrel," Darin said, still holding her small hand. They moved away from Lea and wandered through the open windows to the patio where the scent of orange blossoms was heavy in the air.

"Greta thinks it must be heavenly to be married to a psychologist." Lea's voice followed them. "Where are you two?"

"What makes you say a thing like that?" Darin asked.

"Oh, when I think of how you must understand a woman, know her moods and the reasons for them. You must know just what to do and when, and when to do something else ... Yes, just like that."

His hands on her body were hot, her skin cool. Lea's petulant voice drew closer. He held Greta in his arms and stepped into the pool, where they sank to the bottom, still together. She hadn't gone to the Barbie school. His hands learned her body; then his body learned hers. After they made love, Greta drew back from him regretfully.

"I do have to go now. You are a lucky man, Dr. Darin. No doubts about yourself, complete understanding of what makes you tick."

He lay back on the leather couch staring at the ceiling. "It's always that way, Doctor. Fantasies, dreams, illusions. I know it is because this investigation is hanging over us right now, but even when things are going relatively well, I still go off on a tangent like that for no real reason." He stopped talking.

In his chair Darin stirred slightly, his fingers drumming softly on the arm, his gaze on the clock whose hands were stuck. He said, "Before this recent pressure, did you have such intense fantasies?"

"I don't think so," Darin said thoughtfully, trying to remember.

The other didn't give him time. He asked, "And can you break out of them now when you have to, or want to?"

"Oh, sure," Darin said.

Laughing, he got out of his car, patted the MG, and walked into his house. He could hear voices from the living room and he remembered that on Thursdays Lea really did have her painting lesson.

Dr. Lacey left five minutes after Darin arrived. Lacey said

vague things about Lea's great promise and untapped talent, and Darin nodded sober agreement. If she had talent, it certainly was untapped so far. He didn't say so.

Lea was wearing a hostess suit, flowing sheer panels of pale blue net over a skin-tight leotard that was midnight blue. Darin wondered if she realized that she had gained weight in the past few years. He thought not.

"Oh, that man is getting impossible," she said when the MG blasted away from their house. "Two years now, and he still doesn't want to put my things on show."

Looking at her, Darin wondered how much more her things could be on show.

"Don't dawdle too long with your martini," she said. "We're due at the Ritters' at seven for clams."

The telephone rang for him while he was showering. It was Stu Evers. Darin stood dripping water while he listened.

"Have you seen the evening paper yet? That broad made the statement that conditions are extreme at the station, that our animals are made to suffer unnecessarily."

Darin groaned softly. Stu went on, "She is bringing her entire women's group out tomorrow to show proof of her claims. She's a bigwig in the SPCA, or something."

Darin began to laugh then. Mrs. Whoosis had her face pressed against one of the windows, other fat women in flowered dresses had their faces against the rest. None of them breathed or moved. Inside the compound Adam laid Hortense, then moved on to Esmeralda, to Hilda . . .

"God damn it, Darin, it isn't funny!" Stu said.

"But it is. It is."

Clams at the Ritters' were delicious. Clams, hammers, buckets of butter, a mountainous salad, beer, and finally coffee liberally laced with brandy. Darin felt cheerful and contented when the evening was over. Ritter was in Med. Eng. Lit. but he didn't talk about it, which was merciful. He was sympathetic about the stink with the SPCA. He thought scientists had no imagination. Darin agreed with him and soon he and Lea were on their way home.

"I am so glad that you didn't decide to stay late," Lea said, passing over the yellow line with a blast of the horn. "There is a movie on tonight that I am dying to see."

She talked, but he didn't listen, training of twelve years drawing out an occasional grunt at what must have been appropriate times. "Ritter is such a bore," she said. They were nearly home. "As if you had anything to do with that incredible statement in tonight's paper."

"What statement?"

"Didn't you even read the article? For heaven's sake, why not? Everyone will be talking about it . . ." She sighed theatrically. "Someone quoted a reliable source who said that within the foreseeable future, simply by developing the leads you now have, you will be able to produce monkeys that are as smart as normal human beings." She laughed, a brittle meaningless sound.

"I'll read the article when we get home," he said. She didn't ask about the statement, didn't care if it was true or false, if he had made it or not. He read the article while she settled down before the television. Then he went for a swim. The water was warm, the breeze cool on his skin. Mosquitoes found him as soon as he got out of the pool, so he sat behind the screening of the verandah. The bluish light from the living room went off after a time and there was only the dark night. Lea didn't call him when she went to bed. He knew she went very softly, closing the door with care so that the click of the latch wouldn't disturb him if he was dozing on the verandah.

He knew why he didn't break it off. Pity. The most corrosive emotion endogenous to man. She was the product of the doll school that taught that the trip down the aisle was the end, the fulfillment of a maiden's dreams; shocked and horrified to learn that it was another beginning, some of them never recovered. Lea never had. Never would. At sixty she would purse her lips at the sexual display of uncivilized animals, whether human or not, and she would be disgusted and help formulate laws to ban such activities. Long ago he had hoped a child would be the answer, but the school did something to them on the inside too. They didn't conceive, or if conception took place, they didn't carry the fruit, and if they carried it, the birth was of a stillborn thing. The ones that did live were usually the ones to be pitied more than those who fought and were defeated *in utero*.

A bat swooped low over the quiet pool and was gone again against the black of the azaleas. Soon the moon would appear, and the chimps would stir restlessly for a while, then return to deep untroubled slumber. The chimps slept companionably close to one another, without thought of sex. Only the nocturnal creatures, and the human creatures, performed coitus in the dark. He wondered if Adam remembered his human captors. The colony in the compound had been started almost twenty years ago, and since then none of the chimps had seen a human being. When it was necessary to enter the grounds, the chimps were fed narcotics in the evening to insure against their waking. Props were changed then, new obstacles added to the old conquered ones. Now and then a chimp was removed for study, usually ending up in dissection. But not Adam. He was father of the world. Darin grinned in the darkness.

Adam took his bride aside from the other beasts and knew that she was lovely. She was his own true bride, created for him, intelligence to match his own burning intelligence. Together they scaled the smooth walls and glimpsed the great world that lay beyond their garden. Together they found the opening that led to the world that was to be theirs, and they left behind them the lesser beings. And the god searched for them and finding them not, cursed them and sealed the opening so that none of the others could follow. So it was that Adam and his bride became the first man and woman and from them flowed the progeny that was to inhabit the entire world. And one day Adam said, for shame woman, seest thou that thou art naked? And the woman answered, so are you, big boy, so are you. So they covered their nakedness with leaves from the trees, and thereafter they performed their sexual act in the dark of night so that man could not look on his woman, nor she on him. And they were thus cleansed of shame. Forever and ever. Amen. Hallelujah.

Darin shivered. He had drowsed after all, and the night wind had grown chill. He went to bed. Lea drew away from him in her sleep. She felt hot to his touch. He turned to his left side, his back to her, and he slept.

"There is potential x," Darin said to Lea the next morning at breakfast. "We don't know where x is actually. It represents the highest intellectual achievement possible for the monkeys, for example. We test each new batch of monkeys that we get and sort them—x-1, x-2, x-3, suppose, and then we breed for more x-1's. Also we feed the other two groups the sRNA that we extract from the original x-1's. Eventually we get a monkey that is higher than our original x-1, and we reclassify right down the line and start over, using his sRNA to bring the others up to his level. We make constant checks to make sure we aren't allowing inferior strains to mingle with our highest achievers, and we keep control groups that are given the same training, the same food, the same sorting process, but no sRNA. We test them against each other."

Lea was watching his face with some interest as he talked. He thought he had got through, until she said, "Did you realize that your hair is almost solid white at the temples? All at once it is turning white."

Carefully he put his cup back on the saucer. He smiled at her and got up. "See you tonight," he said.

They also had two separate compounds of chimps that had started out identically. Neither had received any training whatever through the years; they had been kept isolated from each other and from man. Adam's group had been fed sRNA daily from the most intelligent chimps they had found. The control group had been fed none. The control-group chimps had yet to master the intricacies of the fountain with its ice-cold water; they used the small stream that flowed through the compound. The control group had yet to learn that fruit on the high, fragile branches could be had, if one used the telescoping sticks to knock them down. The control group huddled without protection, or under the scant cover of palm-trees when it rained and the dome was opened. Adam long ago had led his group in the construction of a rude but functional hut where they gathered when it rained.

Darin saw the women's committee filing past the compound when he parked his car. He went straight to the console in his office, flicked on a switch and manipulated buttons and dials, leading the group through the paths, opening one, closing another to them, until he led them to the newest of the compounds, where he opened the gate and let them inside. Quickly he closed the gate again and watched their frantic efforts to get out. Later he turned the chimps loose on them, and his grin grew broader as he watched the new-men ravage the old women. Some of the offspring were black and hairy, others pink and hairless, some intermediate. They grew rapidly, lined up with arms extended to receive their daily doses, stood before a machine that tested them instantaneously, and were sorted. Some of them went into a disintegration room, others out into the world.

A car horn blasted in his ears. He switched off his ignition and he got out as Stu Evers parked next to his car. "I see the old bats got here," Stu said. He walked toward the lab with Darin. "How's the Driscoll kid coming along?"

"Negative," Darin said. Stu knew they had tried using human sRNA on the boy, and failed consistently. It was too big a step for his body to cope with. "So far he has shown total intolerance to A-127. Throws it off almost instantly."

Stuart was sympathetic and noncommittal. No one else had any faith whatever in Darin's own experiment. A-127 might be too great a step upward, Darin thought. The *Ateles* spider monkey from Brazil was too bright.

He called Kelly from his office and asked about the newly arrived spider monkeys they had tested the day before. Blood had been processed; a sample was available. He looked over his notes and chose one that had shown interest in the tasks without finishing any of them. Kelly promised him the prepared syringe by 1 P.M.

What no one connected with the project could any longer doubt was that those simians, and the men that had been injected with sRNA from the Driscoll boy, had actually had their learning capacities inhibited, some of them apparently permanently.

Darin didn't want to think about Mrs. Driscoll's reaction if ever she learned how they had been using her boy. Rae sat at the corner of his desk and drawled insolently, "I might tell her myself, Dr. Darin. I'll say, Sorry, Ma'am, you'll have to keep your idiot out of here; you're damaging the brains of our monkeys with his polluted blood. Okay, Darin?"

"My God, what are you doing back again?"

"Testing," she said. "That's all, just testing."

Stu called him to observe the latest challenge to Adam's group, to take place in forty minutes. Darin had forgotten that he was to be present. During the night a tree had been felled in each compound, its trunk crossing the small stream, damming it. At eleven the water fountains were to be turned off for the rest of the day. The tree had been felled at the far end of the compound, close to the wall where the stream entered, so that the trickle of water that flowed past the hut was cut off. Already the group not taking sRNA was showing signs of thirst. Adam's group was unaware of the interrupted flow.

Darin met Stu and they walked together to the far side where they would have a good view of the entire compound. The women had left by then. "It was too quiet for them this morning," Stu said. "Adam was making his rounds; he squatted on the felled tree for nearly an hour before he left it and went back to the others."

They could see the spreading pool of water. It was muddy, uninviting-looking. At eleven-ten it was generally known within the compound that the water supply had failed. Some of the old chimps tried the fountain; Adam tried it several times. He hit it with a stick and tried it again. Then he sat on his haunches and stared at it. One of the young chimps whimpered pitiably. He wasn't thirsty yet, merely puzzled and perhaps frightened. Adam scowled at him. The chimp cowered behind Hortense, who bared her fangs at Adam. He waved menacingly at her, and she began picking fleas from her offspring. When he whimpered again, she cuffed him. The young chimp looked from her to Adam, stuck his forefinger in his mouth and ambled away. Adam continued to stare at the useless fountain. An hour passed. At last Adam rose and wandered nonchalantly toward the drying stream. Here and there a shrinking pool of muddy water steamed in the sun. The other chimps followed Adam. He followed the stream through the compound toward the wall that was its source. When he came to the pool he squatted again. One of the young chimps circled the pool cautiously, reached down and touched the dirty water, drew back, reached for it again, and then drank. Several of the others drank also. Adam continued to squat. At twelve-forty Adam moved again. Grunting and gesturing to several younger males, he approached the tree-trunk. With much noise and meaningless gestures, they shifted the trunk. They strained, shifted it again. The water was released and poured over the heaving chimps. Two of them dropped the trunk and ran. Adam and the other two held. The two returned.

They were still working when Darin had to leave, to keep his appointment with Mrs. Driscoll and Sonny. They arrived at one-ten. Kelly had left the syringe with the new formula in Darin's small refrigerator. He injected Sonny, took his sample, and started the tests. Sometimes Sonny cooperated to the extent of lifting one of the articles from the table and throwing it. Today he cleaned the table within ten minutes. Darin put a piece of candy in his hand; Sonny threw it from him. Patiently Darin put another piece in the boy's hand. He managed to keep the eighth piece in the clenched hand long enough to guide the hand to Sonny's mouth. When it was gone, Sonny opened his mouth for more. His hands lay idly on the table. He didn't seem to relate the hands to the candy with the pleasant taste. Darin tried to guide a second to his mouth, but Sonny refused to hold a piece a second time.

When the hour was over and Sonny was showing definite signs of fatigue, Mrs. Driscoll clutched Darin's hands in hers. Tears stood in her eyes. "You actually got him to feed himself a little bit," she said brokenly. "God bless you, Dr. Darin. God bless you!" She kissed his hand and turned away as the tears started to spill down her cheeks.

Kelly was waiting for him when the group left. She collected the new sample of blood to be processed. "Did you hear about the excitement down at the compound? Adam's building a dam of his own."

Darin stared at her for a moment. The breakthrough? He ran back to the compound. The near side this time was where the windows were being used. It seemed that the entire staff was there, watching silently. He saw Stu and edged in by him. The stream twisted and curved through the compound, less than ten inches deep, not over two feet anywhere. At one spot stones lay under it; elsewhere the bottom was of hard-packed sand. Adam and his crew were piling up stones at the one suitable place for their dam, very near their hut. The dam they were building was two feet thick. It was less than five feet from the wall, fifteen feet from where Darin and Stu shared the window. When the dam was completed, Adam looked along the wall. Darin thought the chimp's eyes paused momentarily on his own. Later he heard that nearly every other person watching felt the same momentary pause as those black, intelligent eyes sought out and held other intelligence.

". . . next thunderstorm. Adam and the flood . . ."

". . . eventually seeds instead of food . . ."

". . . his brain. Convolutions as complex as any man's."

Darin walked away from them, snatches of future plans in his ears. There was a memo on his desk. Jacobsen was turning over the SPCA investigatory committee to him. He was to meet with the university representatives, the local SPCA group, and the legal representatives of all concerned on Monday next at 10 A.M. He wrote out his daily report on Sonny Driscoll. Sonny had been on too good behavior for too long. Would this last injection give him just the spark of determination he needed to go on a rampage? Darin had alerted Johnny, the bodyguard, whoops, male nurse, for just such a possibility, but he knew Johnny didn't think there was any danger from the kid. He hoped Sonny wouldn't kill Johnny, then turn on his mother and father. He'd probably rape his mother, if that much goal-directedness ever flowed through him. And the three men who had volunteered for the injections from Sonny's blood? He didn't want to think of them at all, therefore couldn't get them out of his mind as he sat at his desk staring at nothing. Three convicts. That's all, just convicts hoping to get a parole for helping science along. He laughed abruptly. They weren't planning anything now. Not that trio. Not planning for a thing. Sitting, waiting for something to happen, not thinking about what it might be, or when, or how they would be affected. Not thinking. Period.

"But you can always console yourself that your motives were pure, that it was all for Science, can't you, Dr. Darin?" Rae asked mockingly.

He looked at her. "Go to hell," he said.

It was late when he turned off his light. Kelly met him in the corridor that led to the main entrance. "Hard day, Dr. Darin?"

He nodded. Her hand lingered momentarily on his arm. "Good night," she said, turning in to her own office. He stared at the door for a long time before he let himself out and started toward his car. Lea would be furious with him for not calling. Probably she wouldn't speak at all until nearly bedtime, when she would explode into tears and accusations. He could see the time when her tears and accusations would strike home, when Kelly's body would still be a tangible memory, her words lingering in his ears. And he would lie to Lea, not because he would care actually if she knew, but because it would be expected. She wouldn't know how to cope with the truth. It would entangle her to the point where she would have to try an abortive suicide, a screaming-for-attention attempt that would ultimately tie him in tear-soaked knots that would never be loosened. No, he would lie, and she would know he was lying, and they would get by. He started the car, aimed down the long sixteen miles that lay before him. He wondered where Kelly lived. What it would do to Stu when he realized. What it would do to his job if Kelly should get nasty, eventually. He shrugged. Barbie dolls never got nasty. It wasn't built in.

Lea met him at the door, dressed only in a sheer gown, her hair loose and unsprayed. Her body flowed into his, so that he didn't need Kelly at all. And he was best man when Stu and Kelly were married. He called to Rae, "Would that satisfy you?" but she didn't answer. Maybe she was gone for good this time. He parked the car outside his darkened house and leaned his head on the steering wheel for a moment before getting out. If not gone for good, at least for a long time. He hoped she would stay away for a long time.

The Alienness of the Alien

Terry Carr (1937–   ) is best known as an editor because of the successful "Ace Specials" he edited for Ace Books, his many anthologies including his best-of-the-year collections and his annual original anthology, *Universe*. But Carr began his sf career as a writer, and he has continued to produce an occasional short story and novel.

Carr was born in Oregon and attended the City College of San Francisco and the University of California at Berkeley. He became a fan at an early age, joining the Fantasy Amateur Press Association (a fanzine exchange group) at the age of fifteen, and winning Hugo Awards in 1959 for the best fan magazine and in 1973 for the best fan writer. He worked as a freelance writer in 1961–62; his first published story, "Who Sups with the Devil," appeared in the May 1962 *Magazine of Fantasy and Science Fiction*. After two years as an associate editor and agent for the Scott Meredith Literary Agency, he became associate editor of Ace Books from 1964 to 1967 and editor from 1967 to 1971.

During this seven-year period he edited the Ace Specials, which published outstanding work by a number of ambitious new writers, created *Universe* in 1971, and co-edited with Donald A. Wollheim a best-of-the-year collection. When he left Ace Books in 1971 to become a freelance editor, he continued his own best-of-the-year anthology and continued editing *Universe*. Both have been associated with several publishers.

In 1963 Carr's first novel, *Warlord of Kar*, was published; his second, *Invasion from 2500*, appeared in 1964 under the pseudonym Norman Edwards as a collaboration with Ted White. A more ambitious novel, *Cirque*, was published in 1977. His best stories have been collected in *The Light at the End of the Universe* (1976).

"The Dance of the Changer and the Three" was first published in *The Farthest Reaches* (1968) and later reprinted in two best-of-the-year anthologies, including *Nebula Award Stories Four*. It deals with the basic question of alienness, of difference.

Many problems associated with aliens have been the focus of science fiction stories. The first contact with aliens was popular for a long time: Are aliens going to be friendly or hostile? Will initial impressions be vitally important? What can we do to make the meeting come out favorably? Murray Leinster did the definitive story in "First Contact" (1945). Will aliens be superior or inferior? Will humanity be able to communicate? Will aliens want to conquer us, use us, destroy us—or will humanity do it to them? How will their differences affect the way they look at life, at themselves, at the universe? How will we look to them? A number of these questions were dealt with by H. G. Wells in *The War of the Worlds* (1898), by Robert A. Heinlein in a number of works ranging from *The Puppet Masters* (1951) to *Have Spacesuit—Will Travel* (1958), by Ursula K. Le Guin in *The Left Hand of Darkness* (1969), and by hundreds of other writers dealing with the question of that which is not only outside the self but outside human experience.

Carr deals with the fundamental alienness of aliens. Even with Wells's totally inhuman "intellects vast and cool and unsympathetic," people understood why the Martians did what they did: they might be alien, they might never communicate or try to, but we all understand power, conquest, and the use of inferior species as food. But what if aliens are truly incomprehensible? And what if we thought we were beginning to understand them and suddenly discovered we were mistaken? Nations as closely related as the United States and Iran have found themselves unable to understand each other's behavior; even psychologists cannot explain the behavior of some humans to the rest of us. How can creatures who have evolved on different planets, or in different galaxies, who even have different forms or different sources of energy—how can they ever understand each other? Will their actions always seem arbitrary?

Carr's story provides an answer. It is framed as an attempt to communicate the incommunicable. The narration has some resemblances to Frederik Pohl's "Day Million" (*The Road to Science Fiction*, Volume #3) published two years earlier: the narrator is omniscient, at least in the sense that he knows all the story from the beginning, he addresses the reader directly, and he emphasizes the difficulty of communicating the nature of the experience.

Carr uses the strategies and language of alienation: The place is "millions of light-years" distant "beyond Darkedge" in another galaxy; the central narrative is a "folk-hero myth" about events that happened billions of years before, but the aliens still remember and retell it; and the aliens are "energy life-forms" who communicate by "wave-dances." Water isn't water, sky isn't sky, and the creatures aren't creatures as we know them. The words to describe the aliens and their existence leave major questions: What is a "Changer"? a "life cycle"? a "cycle climax"? a "personality-home"? a "wave-dance"? a "pledge-salute"? a "life-mote"? a "life-change"? What, in these circumstances, does "revenge" mean? The narrator visibly struggles with definition, but the problem clearly is greater than his ability, and probably than any human's ability. The words describe things and actions for which we have no analogues; they cannot be described without falsifying them; they are—alien.

In fact, this is what the narrator (who, unlike Pohl's narrator, is a participant in the story) says about the Loarra: "they are . . . totally crazy, incomprehensible, stupid, silly, and plain damn no good." Carr's success in reflecting the incomprehensibility in story and style makes the narrative work.

The story is reminiscent of a fairy tale from its once-upon-a-time beginning to its arbitrary actions. In fairy tales characters have qualities—goodness, evil, hypersensitivity, strength—without having earned them or deserved them; there simply are witches and princesses and cats with eyes as big as saucers and dwarfs who can spin straw into gold and want human babies. There may be good psychological reasons why fairy tales are like this and why children accept and like them. But one reason that parallels Carr's task is that the adult world seems arbitrary to a child.

The difference between a child and an alien is that children grow up into adults and usually find that the world is not a fairy tale, that the way people behave is comprehensible and even predictable, that characteristics and actions are not arbitrary. And yet...

The Dance of the Changer and the Three

by Terry Carr

This all happened ages ago, out in the depths of space beyond Darkedge, where galaxies swim through the black like silent bright whales. It was so long ago that when the light from Loarr's galaxy finally reached Earth, after millions of light-years, there was no one here to see it except a few things in the oceans that were too busy with their monotonous single-celled reactions to notice.

Yet, as long ago as it was, the present-day Loarra still remember this story and retell it in complex, shifting wave-dances every time one of the newly changed asks for it. The wave-dances wouldn't mean much to you if you saw them, nor I suppose would the story itself if I were to tell it just as it happened. So consider this a translation, and don't bother yourself that when I say "water" I don't mean our hydrogen-oxygen compound, or that there's no "sky" as such on Loarr, or for that matter that the Loarra weren't—aren't—creatures that "think" or "feel" in quite the way we understand. In fact, you could take this as a piece of pure fiction, because there are damned few real facts in it—but I know better (or worse), because I know how true it is. And that has a lot to do with why I'm back here on Earth, with forty-two friends and coworkers left dead on Loarr. They never had a chance.

There was a Changer who had spent three life cycles planning a particular cycle climax and who had come to the moment of action. He wasn't really named Minnearo, but I'll call him that because it's the closest thing I can write to approximate the tone, emotional matrix, and associations that were all wrapped up in his designation.

When he came to his decision, he turned away from the crag off which he'd been standing overlooking the Loarran ocean, and went quickly to the personality-homes of three of his best friends. To the first friend, Asterrea, he said, "I am going to commit suicide," wave-dancing this message in his best festive tone.

His friend laughed, as Minnearo had hoped, but only for a short time. Then he turned away and left Minnearo alone, because there had already been several suicides lately and it was wearing a little thin.

To his second friend, Minnearo gave a pledge-salute, going through all sixty sequences with exaggerated care, and wave-danced, "Tomorrow I shall immerse my body in the ocean, if anyone will watch."

He second friend, Fless, smiled tolerantly and told him he would come and see the performance.

To his third friend, with many excited leapings and boundings, Minnearo described what he imagined would happen to him after he had gone under the lapping waters of the ocean. The dance he went through to give this description was intricate and even imaginative, because Minnearo had spent most of that third life cycle working it out in his mind. It used motion and color and sound and another sense something like a smell, all to communicate descriptions of falling, impact with the water, and then the quick dissolution and blending in the currents of the ocean, the dimming and loss of awareness, then darkness, and finally the awakening, the completion of the change. Minnearo had a rather romantic turn of mind, so he imagined himself recoalescing around the life-mote of one of Loarr's greatest heroes, Krollim, and forming on Krollim's old pattern. And he even ended the dance with suggestions of glory and imitation of himself by others, which was definitely presumptuous. But the friend for whom the dance was given did nod approvingly at several points.

"If it turns out to be half what you anticipate," said this friend, Pur, "then I envy you. But you never know."

"I guess not," Minnearo said, rather morosely. And he hesitated before leaving, for Pur was what I suppose I'd better call female, and Minnearo had rather hoped that she would join him in the ocean jump. But if she thought of it she gave no sign, merely gazed an Minnearo calmly, waiting for him to go; so finally he did.

And at the appropriate time, with his friend Fless watching him from the edge of the cliff, Minnearo did his final wave-dance as Minnearo—rather excited and ill-coordinated, but that was understandable in the circumstances—and then performed his approach to the edge, leaped and tumbled downward through the air, making fully two dozen turns this way and that before he hit the water.

Fless hurried back and described the suicide to Asterrea and Pur, who laughed and applauded in most of the right places, so on the whole it was a success. Then the three of them sat down and began plotting Minnearo's revenge.

—All right, I *know* a lot of this doesn't make sense. Maybe that's because I'm trying to tell you about the Loarra in human terms, which is a mistake with creatures as alien as they are. Actually, the Loarra are almost wholly an energy lifeform, their consciousnesses coalescing in each life cycle around a spatial center which they call a "life-mote," so that, if you could see the patterns of energy they form (as I have, using a sense filter our expedition developed for that purpose), they'd look rather like a spiral nebula sometimes, or other times like iron filings gathering around a magnet, or maybe like a half-melted snowflake. (That's probably what Minnearo looked like on that day, because it's the suicides and the aged who look like that.) Their forms keep shifting, of course, but each individual usually keeps close to one pattern.

Loarr itself is a gigantic gaseous planet with an orbit so close to its primary that its year has to be only about thirty-seven Earthstandard Days long. (In Earthsystem, the orbit would be considerably inside that of Venus.) There's a solid core to the planet, and a lot of hard outcroppings like islands, but most of the surface is in a molten or gaseous state, swirling and bubbling and howling with winds and storms. It's not a very inviting planet if you're anything like a human being, but it does have one thing that brought it to Unicentral's attention: mining.

Do you have any idea what mining is like on a planet where most metals are fluid from the heat and/or pressure? Most people haven't heard much about this, because it isn't a situation we encounter often, but it was there on Loarr, and it was very, very interesting. Because our analyses showed some elements that had been until then only computer-theory—elements that were supposed to exist only in the hearts of suns, for one thing. And if we could get hold of some of them . . . Well, you see what I mean. The mining possibilities were very interesting indeed.

Of course, it would take half the wealth of Earthsystem to

outfit a full-scale expedition there. But Unicentral hummed for two-point-eight seconds and then issued detailed instructions on just how it was all to be arranged. So there we went.

And there I was, a Standard Year later (five Standard Years ago), sitting inside a mountain of artificial Earth welded onto one of Loarr's "islands" and wondering what the hell I was doing there. Because I'm not a mining engineer, not a physicist or comp-technician or, in fact, much of anything that requires technical training. I'm a public-relations man; and there was just no reason for me to have been assigned to such a hellish, impossible, godforsaken, inconceivable, and plain damned *unlivable* planet as Loarr.

But there was a reason, and it was the Loarra, of course. They lived ("lived") there, and they were intelligent, so we had to negotiate with them. Ergo: me.

So in the next several years, while I negotiated and we set up operations and I acted as a go-between, I learned a lot about them. Just enough to translate, however clumsily, the wave-dance of the Changer and the Three, which is their equivalent of a classic folk-hero myth (or would be if they had anything honestly equivalent to anything of ours).

To continue:

Fless was in favor of building a pact among the Three by which they would, each in turn and each with deliberate lack of the appropriate salutes, commit suicide in exactly the same way Minnearo had. "Thus we can kill this suicide," Fless explained in excited waves through the air.

But Pur was more practical. "Thus," she corrected him, "we would kill only this suicide. It is unimaginative, a thing to be done by rote, and Minnearo deserves more."

Asterrea seemed undecided; he hopped about, sparking and disappearing and reappearing inches away in another color. They waited for him to comment, and finally he stabilized, stood still in the air, settled to the ground, and held himself firmly there. Then he said, in slow, careful movements, "I'm not sure he deserves an original revenge. It wasn't a new suicide, after all. And who is to avenge us?" A single spark leaped from him. "Who is to avenge us?" he repeated, this time with more pronounced motions.

"Perhaps," said Pur slowly, "we will need no revenge—if our act is great enough."

The other two paused in their random wave-motions, considering this. Fless shifted from blue to green to a bright red which dimmed to yellow; Asterrea pulsed a deep ultraviolet.

"Everyone has always been avenged," Fless said at last. "What you suggest is meaningless."

"But if we do something great enough," Pur said; and now she began to radiate heat which drew the other two reluctantly toward her. "Something which has never been done before, in *any* form. Something for which there can be no revenge, for it will be a *positive* thing—not a death-change, not a destruction or a disappearance or a forgetting, even a great one. A *positive* thing."

Asterrea's ultraviolet grew darker, darker, until he seemed to be nothing more than a hole in the air. "Dangerous, dangerous, dangerous," he droned, moving torpidly back and forth. "You know it's impossible to ask—we'd have to give up all our life cycles to come. Because a positive in the world . . ." He blinked into darkness, and did not reappear for long seconds. When he did he was perfectly still, pulsing weakly but gradually regaining strength.

Pur waited till his color and tone showed that consciousness had returned, then moved in a light wave-motion calculated to draw the other two back into calm, reasonable discourse. "I've thought about this for six life cycles already," she danced. "I must be right—no one has worked on a problem for so long. A positive would *not* be dangerous, no matter what the three- and four-cycle theories say. It would be beneficial." She paused, hanging orange in midair. "And it would be *new*," she said with a quick spiral. "Oh, how *new!*"

And so, at length, they agreed to follow her plan. And it was briefly this: On a far island outcropping set in the deepest part of the Loarran ocean, where crashing, tearing storms whipped molten metal-compounds into blinding spray, there was a vortex of forces that was avoided by every Loarra on pain of inescapable and final death-change. The most ancient wave-dances of that ancient time said that the vortex had always been there, that the Loarra themselves had been born there or had escaped from there or had in some way cheated the laws that ruled there. Whatever the truth about that was, the vortex was an eater of energy, calling and catching from afar any Loarra or other beings who strayed within its influence. (For all the life on Loarr is energy-based, even the mindless, drifting foodbeasts—creatures of uniform dull color, no internal motion, no scent or tone, and absolutely no self-volition. Their place in the Loarran scheme of things is and was literally nothing more than that of food; even though there were countless foodbeasts drifting in the air in most areas of the planet, the Loarra hardly ever noticed them. They ate them when they were hungry, and looked around them at any other time.)

"Then you want us to destroy the *vortex?*" cried Fless, dancing and dodging to right and left in agitation.

"Not *destroy*," Pur said calmly. "It will be a *life*-change, not a destruction."

"Life-change?" said Asterrea faintly, wavering in the air.

And she said it again: "*Life*-change." For the vortex had once created, or somehow allowed to be created, the Oldest of the Loarra, those many-cycles-ago beings who had combined and split, reacted and changed countless times to become the Loarra of this day. And if creation could happen at the vortex once, then it could happen again.

"But how?" asked Fless, trying now to be reasonable, dancing the question with precision and holding a steady green color as he did so.

"We will need help," Pur said, and went on to explain that she had heard—from a windbird, a creature with little intelligence but perfect memory—that there was one of the Oldest still living his first life cycle in a personality-home somewhere near the vortex. In that most ancient time of the race, when suicide had been considered extreme as a means of cycle-change, this Oldest had made his change by a sort of negative suicide—he had frozen his cycle, so that his consciousness and form continued in a never-ending repetition of themselves, on and on while his friends changed and grew and learned as they ran through life cycle after life cycle, becoming different people with common memories, moving forward into the future by this method while he, the last Oldest, remained fixed at the beginning. He saw only the beginning, remembered only the beginning, understood only the beginning.

And for that reason his had been the most tragic of all Loarran changes (and the windbird had heard it rumored, in eight different ways, each of which it repeated word-for-word to Pur, that in the ages since that change more than a hundred hundred Loarra had attempted revenge for the Oldest, but always without success) and it had never been repeated, so that this Oldest was the only Oldest. And for that reason he was important to their quest, Pur explained.

With a perplexed growing and shrinking, brightening and

dimming, Asterrea asked, "But how can he live anywhere near the vortex and not be consumed by it?"

"That is a crucial part of what we must find out," Pur said. And after the proper salutes and rituals, the Three set out to find the Oldest.

The wave-dance of the Changer and the Three traditionally at this point spends a great deal of time, in great splashes of color and bursts of light and subtly contrived clouds of darkness all interplaying with hops and swoops and blinking and dodging back and forth, to describe the scene as Pur, Fless and Asterrea set off across that ancient molten sea. I've seen the dance countless times, and each viewing has seemed to bring me maddeningly closer to understanding the meaning that this has for the Loarra themselves. Lowering clouds flashing bursts of aimless, lifeless energy, a rumbling sea below, whose swirling depths pulled and tugged at the Three as they swept overhead, darting around each other in complex patterns like electrons playing cat's-cradle around an invisible nucleus. A droning of lamentation from the changers left behind on their rugged home island, and giggles from those who had recently changed. And the colors of the Three themselves: burning red Asterrea and glowing green Fless and steady, steady golden Pur. I see and hear them all, but I feel only a weird kind of alien beauty, not the grandeur, excitement and awesomeness they have for the Loarra.

When the Three felt the vibrations and swirlings in the air that told them they were coming near to the vortex, they paused in their flight and hung in an interpatterned motion-sequence above the dark, rolling sea, conversing only in short flickerings of color because they had to hold the pattern tightly in order to withstand the already-strong attraction of the vortex.

"Somewhere near?" asked Asterrea, pulsing a quick green.

"Closer to the vortex, I think," Pur said, chancing a sequence of reds and violets.

"Can we be sure?" asked Fless; but there was no answer from Pur and he had expected none from Asterrea.

The ocean crashed and leaped; the air howled around them. And the vortex pulled at them.

Suddenly they felt their motion-sequence changing, against their wills, and for long moments all three were afraid that it was the vortex's attraction that was doing it. They moved in closer to each other, and whirled more quickly in a still more intricate pattern, but it did no good. Irresistibly they were drawn apart again, and at the same time the three of them were moved toward the vortex.

And then they felt the Oldest among them.

He had joined the motion-sequence; this must have been why they had felt the sequence changed and loosened—to make room for him. Whirling and blinking, the Oldest led them inward over the frightening sea, radiating warmth through the storm and, as they followed, or were pulled along, they studied him in wonder.

He was hardly recognizable as one of them, this ancient Oldest. He was . . . not quite energy any longer. He was half matter, carrying the strange mass with awkward, aged grace, his outer edges almost rigid as they held the burden of his congealed center and carried it through the air. (Looking rather like a half-dissolved snowflake, yes, only dark and dismal, a snowflake weighted with coal dust.) And, for now at least, he was completely silent.

Only when he had brought the Three safely into the calm of his barren personality-home of a tiny rock jutting at an angle from the wash of the sea did he speak. There, inside a cone of quiet against which the ocean raged and fell back, the sands faltered and even the vortex's power was nullified, the Oldest said wearily, "So you have come." He spoke with a slow waving back and forth, augmented by only a dull red color.

To this the Three did not know what to say; but Pur finally hazarded, "Have you been waiting for us?" The Oldest pulsed a somewhat brighter red, once, twice. He paused. Then he said, "I do not *wait*—there is nothing to wait *for*." Again the pulse of a brighter red. "One waits for the future. But there is no future, you know."

"Not for him," Pur said softly to her companions, and Fless and Asterrea sank wavering to the stone floor of the Oldest's home, where they rocked back and forth.

The Oldest sank with them, and when he touched down he remained motionless. Pur drifted over the others, maintaining movement but unable to raise her color above a steady blue-green. She said to the Oldest, "But you knew we would come."

"Would come? *Would* come? Yes, and *did* come, and *have* come, and *are* come. It is today only, you know, for me. I will be the Oldest, when the others pass me by. I will never change, nor will my world."

"But the others have already passed you by," Fless said.

"We are many life cycles after you, Oldest—so many it is beyond the count of windbirds."

The Oldest seemed to draw his material self into a more upright posture, forming his energy-flow carefully around it. To the red of his color he added a low hum with only the slightest quaver as he said, "*Nothing* is after me, here on Rock. When you come here, you come out of time, just as I have. So now you have always been here and will always be here, for as long as you are here."

Asterrea sparked yellow suddenly, and danced upward into the becalmed air. As Fless stared and Pur moved quickly to calm him, he drove himself again and again at the edge of the cone of quiet that was the Oldest's refuge. Each time he was thrown back and each time he returned to dash himself once more against the edge of the storm, trying to penetrate back into it. He flashed and burned countless colors, and strange sound-frequencies filled the quiet, until at last, with Pur's stern direction and Fless's blank gaze upon him, he sank back wearily to the stone floor. "A trap, a trap," he pulsed. "This is it, this is the vortex itself, we should have known, and we'll never get away."

The Oldest had paid no attention to Asterrea's display. He said slowly, "And it is because I am not in time that the vortex cannot touch me. And it is because I am out of time that I know what the vortex is, for I can remember myself born in it."

Pur left Asterrea then, and came close to the Oldest. She hung above him, thinking with blue vibrations, then asked, "Can you tell us how you were born?—what is creation?— how new things are made?" She paused a moment, and added, "And what *is* the vortex?"

The Oldest seemed to lean forward, seemed tired. His color had deepened again to the darkest red, and the Three could clearly see every atom of matter within his energy field, stark and hard. He said, "So many questions to ask one question." And he told them the answer to that question.

—And I can't tell you that answer, because I don't know it. No one knows it now, not even the present-day Loarra who are the Three after a thousand-million-billion life cycles. Because the Loarra really do become different . . . different "persons," when they pass from one cycle to another, and after that many changes, memory becomes meaningless. ("Try it sometime," one of the Loarra once wave-danced to me, and there was no indication that he thought this was a joke.)

Today, for instance, the Three themselves, a thousand-million-billion times removed from themselves but still, they maintain, *themselves*, often come to watch the Dance of the Changer and the Three, and even though it is about them they are still excited and moved by it as though it were a tale never even heard before, let alone lived through. Yet let a dancer miss a movement or color or sound by even the slightest nuance, and the Three will correct him. (And yes, many times the legended Changer himself, Minnearo, he who started the story, has attended these dances—though often he leaves after the re-creation of his suicide dance.)

It's sometimes difficult to tell one given Loarra from all the others, by the way, despite the complex and subtle technologies of Unicentral, which have provided me with sense filters of all sorts, plus frequency simulators, pattern scopes, special gravity inducers, and a minicomp that takes up more than half of my very tight little island of Earth pasted into the surface of Loarr and which can do more thinking and analyzing in two seconds than I can do in fifty years. During my four years on Loarr, I got to "know" several of the Loarra, yet even at the end of my stay I was still never sure just who I was "talking" with at any time. I could run through about seventeen or eighteen tests, linking the sense-filters with the minicomp, and get a definite answer that way. But the Loarra are a bit short on patience and by the time I'd get done with all that whoever it was would usually be off bouncing and sparking into the hellish vapors they call air. So usually I just conducted my researches or negotiations or idle queries, whichever they were that day, with whoever would pay attention to my antigrav "eyes," and I discovered that it didn't matter much just who I was talking with: none of them made any more sense than the others. They were all, as far as I was and am concerned, totally crazy, incomprehensible, stupid, silly, and plain damn no good.

If that sounds like I'm bitter, it's because I am. I've got forty-two murdered men to be bitter about. But back to the unfolding of the greatest legend of an ancient and venerable alien race:

When the Oldest had told them what they wanted to know, the Three came alive with popping and flashing and dancing in the air, Pur just as much as the others. It was all that they had hoped for and more; it was the entire answer to their quest and their problem. It would enable them to create, to transcend any negative cycle-climax they could have devised.

After a time the Three came to themselves and remembered the rituals.

"We offer thanks in the name of Minnearo, whose suicide we are avenging," Fless said gravely, waving his message in respectful deep-blue spirals.

"We thank you in our own names as well," said Asterrea.

"And we thank you in the name of no one and nothing," said Pur, "for that is the greatest thanks conceivable."

But the Oldest merely sat there, pulsing his dull red, and the Three wondered among themselves. At last the Oldest said, "To accept thanks is to accept responsibility, and in only-today, as I am, there can be none of that because there can be no new act. I am outside time, you know, which is almost outside life. All this I have told you is something told to you before, many times, and it will be again."

Nonetheless, the Three went through all the rituals of thanks-giving, performing them with flawless grace and care—color-and-sound demonstrations, dances, offerings of their own energy, and all the rest. And Pur said, "It is possible to give thanks for a long-past act or even a mindless reflex, and we do so in the highest."

The Oldest pulsed dull red and did not answer, and after a time the Three took leave of him.

Armed with the knowledge he had given them, they had no trouble penetrating the barrier protecting Rock, the Oldest's personality-home, and in moments were once again alone with themselves in the raging storm that encircled the vortex. For long minutes they hung in midair, whirling and darting in their most tightly linked patterns while the storm whipped them and the vortex pulled them. Then abruptly they broke their patterns and hurled themselves deliberately into the heart of the vortex itself. In a moment they had disappeared.

They seemed to feel neither motion nor lapse of time as they fell into the vortex. It was a change that came without perception or thought—a change from self to unself, from existence to void. They knew only that they had given themselves up to the vortex, that they were suddenly lost in darkness and a sense of surrounding emptiness which had no dimension. They knew without thinking that if they could have sent forth sound there would have been no echo, that a spark or even a bright flare would have brought no reflection from anywhere. For this was the place of the origin of life, and it was empty. It was up to them to fill it, if it was to be filled.

So they used the secret the Oldest had given them, the secret those at the Beginning had discovered by accident and which only one of the Oldest could have remembered. Having set themselves for this before entering the vortex, they played their individual parts automatically—selfless, unconscious, almost random acts such as even nonliving energy can perform. And when all parts had been completed precisely, correctly, and at just the right time and in just the right sequence, the creating took place.

It was a foodbeast. It formed and took shape before them in the void, and grew and glowed its dull, drab glow until it was whole. For a moment it drifted there, then suddenly it was expelled from the vortex, thrown out violently as though from an explosion—away from the nothingness within, away from darkness and silence into the crashing, whipping violence of the storm outside. And with it went the Three, vomited forth with the primitive bit of life they had made.

Outside, in the storm, the Three went automatically into their tightest motion sequence, whirling and blinking around each other in desperate striving to maintain themselves amid the savagery that roiled around them. And once again they felt the powerful pull of the vortex behind them, gripping them anew now that they were outside, and they knew that the vortex would draw them in again, this time forever, unless they were able to resist it. But they found that they were nearly spent; they had lost more of themselves in the vortex than they had ever imagined possible. They hardly felt alive now, and somehow they had to withstand the crushing powers of both the storm and the vortex, and had to forge such a strongly interlinked motion-pattern that they would be able to make their way out of this place, back to calm and safety.

And there was only one way they could restore themselves enough for that.

Moving almost as one, they converged upon the mindless foodbeast they had just created, and they ate it.

That's not precisely the end of the Dance of the Changer and the Three—it does go on for a while, telling of the honors given the Three when they returned, and of Minnearo's reaction when he completed his change by reappearing around the life-mote left by a dying windbird, and of how all of the Three turned away from their honors and made their next changes almost immediately—but my own attention never quite follows the rest of it. I always get stuck at that one point in the story, that supremely contradictory moment when the Three destroyed what they had made, when they came away with no more than they had brought with them. It doesn't even achieve irony, and yet it is the emotional highpoint of the Dance as far as the Loarra are concerned. In fact, it's the *whole* point of the Dance, as they've told me with brighter sparkings and flashes than they ever use when talking about anything else, and if the Three had been able to come away from there *without* eating their foodbeast, then their achievement would have been duly noted, applauded, giggled at by the newly changed, and forgotten within two life cycles.

And these are the creatures with whom I had to deal and whose rights I was charged to protect. I was ambassador to a planetful of things that would tell me with a straight face that two and two are orange. And yes, that's why I'm back on Earth now—and why the rest of the expedition, those who are left alive from it, are back here too.

If you could read the fifteen-microtape report I filed with Unicentral (which you can't, by the way; Unicentral always Classifies its failures), it wouldn't tell you anything more about the Loarra than I've just told you in the story of the Dance. In fact, it might tell you less, because although the report contained masses of hard data on the Loarra, plus every theory I could come up with or coax out of the minicomp, it didn't have much about the Dance. And it's only in things like that, attitude-data rather than I.Q. indices, psych reports and so on, that you can really get the full impact of what we were dealing with on Loarr.

After we'd been on the planet for four Standard Years, after we'd established contact and exchanged gifts and favors and information with the Loarra, after we'd set up our entire mining operation and had had it running without hindrance for over three years—after all that, the raid came. One day a sheet of dull purple light swept in from the horizon, and as it got closer I could see that it was a whole colony of the Loarra, their individual colors and fluctuations blending into that single purple mass. I was in the mountain, not outside with the mining extensors, so I saw all of it, and I lived through it.

They flashed in over us like locusts descending, and they hit the crawlers and dredges first. The metal glowed red, then white, then it melted. Then it was just gas that formed billowing clouds rising to the sky. Somewhere inside those clouds was what was left of the elements which had comprised seventeen human beings, who were also vapor now.

I hit the alarm and called everyone in, but only a few made it. The rest were caught in the tunnels when the Loarra swarmed over them, and they went up in smoke too. Then the automatic locks shut, and the mountain was sealed off. And six of us sat there, watching on the screen as the Loarra swept back and forth outside, cleaning up the bits and pieces they'd missed.

I sent out three of my "eyes," but they too were promptly vaporized.

Then we waited for them to hit the mountain itself . . . half a dozen frightened men huddled in the comp-room, none of us saying anything. Just sweating.

But they didn't come. They swarmed together in a tight spiral, went three times around the mountain, made one final salute-dip and then whirled straight up and out of sight. Only a handful of them were left behind out there.

After a while I sent out a fourth "eye." One of the Loarra came over, flitted around it like a firefly, blinked through the spectrum, and settled down to hover in front for talking. It was Pur—a Pur who was a thousand-million-billion life cycles removed from the Pur we know and love, of course, but nonetheless still pretty much Pur.

I sent out a sequence of lights and movements that translated, roughly, as "What the hell did you do that for?"

And Pur glowed pale yellow for several seconds, then gave me an answer that doesn't translate. Or, if it does, the translation is just "Because."

Then I asked the question again, in different terms, and she gave me the same answer in different terms. I asked a third time, and a fourth, and she came back with the same thing. She seemed to be enjoying the variations on the Dance; maybe she thought we were playing.

Well . . . We'd already sent out our distress call by then, so all we could do was wait for a relief ship and hope they wouldn't attack again before the ship came, because we didn't have a chance of fighting them—we were miners, not a military expedition. God knows what any military expedition could have done against energy things, anyway. While we were waiting, I kept sending out the "eyes," and I kept talking to one Loarra after another. It took three weeks for the ship to get there, and I must have talked to over a hundred of them in that time, and the sum total of what I was told was this:

Their reason for wiping out the mining operation was untranslatable. No, they weren't mad. No, they didn't want us to go away. Yes, we were welcome to the stuff we were taking out of the depths of the Loarran ocean.

And, most importantly: No, they couldn't tell me whether or not they were likely ever to repeat their attack.

So we went away, limped back to Earth, and we all made our reports to Unicentral. We included, as I said, every bit of data we could think of, including an estimate of the value of the new elements on Loarr—which was something on the order of six times the wealth of Earthsystem. And we put it up to Unicentral as to whether or not we should go back.

Unicentral has been humming and clicking for ten months now, but it hasn't made a decision.

The Virtues of Indirection

In a speech presented in 1976, Theodore Sturgeon commented that nearly all of the top newer writers, with the exception of James Tiptree, Jr., were women. Shortly after, Alice Sheldon (1915–   ) revealed that she was Tiptree.

The use of the pseudonym suggested that period in the 1930s and 1940s when women who wanted to write science fiction used initials, like C. L. Moore, or possessed androgynous names, like Leigh Brackett. At that time science fiction was considered to be a male genre.

But that kind of reasoning can be misleading. Tiptree began writing in the late 1960s, and by then women writers not only were plentiful, but, as Sturgeon's remark suggests, were leading the field. Tiptree's reasons came from her desire to separate the author from the work; and, although many writers and editors corresponded with her, none pierced her pseudonym until she chose to reveal herself.

Alice Sheldon was born in Chicago, the daughter of an explorer and naturalist and of a writer of mysteries and travel books. As a child she accompanied her parents on expeditions to Africa and India and Sumatra. She served in the army, worked in government, and tried her hand at business. She has worked as an experimental psychologist and in 1967 earned a Ph.D. in psychology at George Washington University. About the same time she began writing science fiction.

Tiptree's early stories were relatively straightforward but gradually grew more complex and controversial. Her first published story was "Birth of a Salesman" in the March 1968 *Analog*. Within little more than a year, her stories were being nominated for awards, first "The Last Flight of Dr. Ain" and later "And I Awoke and Found Me on the Cold Hill's Side." "Love Is the Plan, the Plan Is Death" won a Nebula for 1973; "The Girl Who Was Plugged In" won a Hugo in 1974. "Houston, Houston, Do You Read?" won a Nebula and a Hugo for 1976, and "The Screwfly Solution," published under the name of Raccoona Sheldon, won a Nebula Award for 1977. Her one novel, *Up the Walls of the World*, was nominated for a Nebula for 1979.

Her short stories have been collected in *Ten Thousand Light-Years from Home* (1973), *Warm Worlds and Otherwise* (1975), and *Star Songs of an Old Primate* (1978). Two themes began to emerge in her stories. Aliens and their reproductive and nurturing arrangements are the first theme, which reaches its richest expression in "Love Is the Plan . . ." and in her novel. The second theme was the relationship between men and women, expressed in "The Women Men Don't See" (1973), "Houston, Houston . . .," "Your Faces, O My Sisters! Your Faces Filled of Light!" (1976), and "The Screwfly Solution."

"The Last Flight of Dr. Ain" was published in the March 1969 *Galaxy* and extensively revised for publication in *Author's Choice 4* (1974). The story deals with neither of Tiptree's major themes; it is an ecology story and a catastrophe story. It expresses itself through a metaphor whose meaning is not clear until the end, the ecological crisis is described in what seems at first like casual naturalistic detail, and the catastrophe is not what it seems.

"Dr. Ain" is written like a mystery: Why is the scientist going to Moscow, particularly since he seems sick with the flu? Why is he taking a roundabout route rather than a direct jet flight? Who is the sick woman with him and why does nobody see her? And who is making these inquiries about his trip? There are other questions about actions that seem to be dropped casually into the narrative: Why does Dr. Ain keep using a throat-spray? And why does he insist on feeding the birds?

The answers begin to appear in the form of clues as early as the sixth paragraph. More clues appear in the interview with the Glasgow professor. And Dr. Ain's address to the scientific conference in Moscow answers, in an indirect way, most of the questions, although some readers might not understand at that point (nor even by the end). By then, of course, the story is almost over; it is a remarkably short story to imply so much. And yet, afterward, the story could be summarized briefly.

Is the telling of a story, even a short one, by indirection either necessary or desirable? The answer to a question about style must be answered by the individual reader: After the reading is over the reader is satisfied, or confused and disappointed. Nevertheless, theory can ask whether the subject of the story is matched by the manner in which it is told. In "Dr. Ain" the story is pieced together after the event, and mysteries and surmises seem appropriate; moreover, Dr. Ain drops characteristically cryptic remarks, and in his final delirium he rambles wildly.

Tiptree has written that her method in writing "Dr. Ain" was to "start from the end and preferably 5,000 feet underground on a dark day and then *Don't tell them.*"

At the end the reader is left to speculate about the wisdom of Dr. Ain's action: Is he insane, crazed by his illness, or seeking a catastrophic but necessary solution to a catastrophic problem? The reader can guess Tiptree's answer from the name she gives her protagonist—Charles Ain: C. Ain. And Tiptree seems to prefer catastrophic solutions.

The Last Flight of Doctor Ain

by James Tiptree, Jr. (Alice Sheldon)

Doctor Ain was recognized on the Omaha-Chicago flight. A biologist colleague from Pasadena came out of the toilet and saw Ain in aisle seat. Five years before, this man had been jealous of Ain's huge grants. Now he nodded coldly and was surprised at the intensity of Ain's response. He almost turned back to speak, but he felt too tired; like nearly everyone, he was fighting the flu.

The stewardess handing out coats after they landed remembered Ain too: a tall thin nondescript man with rusty hair. He held up the line staring at her; since he already had his raincoat with him she decided it was some kooky kind of pass and waved him on.

She saw Ain shamble off into the airport smog, apparently

alone. Despite the big Civil Defense signs, O'Hare was late getting underground. No one noticed the woman.

The wounded, dying woman.

Ain was not identified en route to New York, but a 2:40 jet carried an "Ames" on the checklist, which was thought to be a misspelling of Ain. It was. The plane had circled for an hour while Ain watched the smoky seaboard monotonously tilt, straighten, and tilt again.

The woman was weaker now. She coughed, picking weakly at the scabs on her face half-hidden behind her long hair. Her hair, Ain saw, that great mane which had been so splendid, was drabbed and thinning now. He looked to seaward, willing himself to think of cold, clean breakers. On the horizon he saw a vast black rug: somewhere a tanker had opened its vents. The woman coughed again. Ain closed his eyes. Smog shrouded the plane.

He was picked up next while checking in for the BOAC flight to Glasgow. Kennedy-Underground was a boiling stew of people, the air system unequal to the hot September afternoon. The check-in line swayed and sweated, staring dully at the newscast. SAVE THE LAST GREEN MANSIONS—a conservation group was protesting the defoliation and drainage of the Amazon basin. Several people recalled the beautifully colored shots of the new clean bomb. The line squeezed together to let a band of uniformed men go by. They were wearing buttons inscribed: WHO'S AFRAID?

That was when a woman noticed Ain. He was holding a newssheet and she heard it rattling in his hand. Her family hadn't caught the flu, so she looked at him sharply. Sure enough, his forehead was sweaty. She herded her kids to the side away from Ain.

He was using *Instac* throat spray, she remembered. She didn't think much of *Instac;* her family used *Kleer*. While she was looking at him, Ain suddenly turned his head and stared into her face, with the spray still floating down. Such inconsiderateness! She turned her back. She didn't recall him talking to any woman, but she perked up her ears when the clerk read off Ain's destination. Moscow!

The clerk recalled that too, with disapproval. Ain checked in alone, he reported. No woman had been ticketed for Moscow, but it would have been easy enough to split up her tickets. (By that time they were sure she was with him.)

Ain's flight went via Iceland with an hour's delay at Keflavik. Ain walked over to the airport park, gratefully breathing the sea-filled air. Every few breaths he shuddered. Under the whine of bull-dozers the sea could be heard running its huge paws up and down the keyboard of the land. The little park had a grove of yellowed birches and a flock of wheatears foraged by the path. Next month they would be in North Africa, Ain thought. Two thousand miles of tiny wing-beats. He threw them some crumbs from a packet in his pocket.

The woman seemed stronger here. She was panting in the sea wind, her large eyes fixed on Ain. Above her the birches were as gold as those where he had first seen her, the day his life began . . . Squatting under a stump to watch a shrewmouse he had been, when he caught a falling ripple of green and recognized the shocking naked girl-flesh, creamy, pink-tipped—coming toward him among the golden bracken! Young Ain held his breath, his nose in the sweet moss and his heart going *crash—crash*. And then he was staring at the outrageous fall of that hair down her narrow back, watching it dance around her heart-shaped buttocks, while the shrewmouse ran over his paralyzed hand. The lake was utterly still, dusty silver under the misty sky, and she made no more than a muskrat's ripple to rock the floating golden leaves. The silence closed back, the trees burning like torches where the naked girl had walked the wild wood, reflected in Ain's shining eyes. For a time he believed he had seen an Oread.

Ain was last on board for the Glasgow leg. The stewardess recalled dimly that he seemed restless. She could not identify the woman. There were a lot of women on board, and babies. Her passenger list had had several errors.

At Glasgow airport a waiter remembered that a man like Ain had called for Scottish oatmeal, and eaten two bowls, although of course it wasn't really oatmeal. A young mother with a pram saw him tossing crumbs to the birds.

When he checked in at the BOAC desk, he was hailed by a Glasgow professor who was going to the same conference at Moscow. This man had been one of Ain's teachers. (It was now known that Ain had done his postgraduate work in Europe.) They chatted all the way across the North Sea.

"I wondered about that," the professor said later. "Why have you come roundabout? I asked him. He told me the direct flights were booked up." (This was found to be untrue: Ain had apparently avoided the Moscow jet hoping to escape attention.)

The professor spoke with relish of Ain's work.

"Brilliant? Oh, aye. And stubborn, too; very very stubborn. It was as though a concept—often the simplest relation, mind you—would stop him in his tracks, and fascinate him. He would hunt all round it instead of going on to the next thing as a more docile mind would. Truthfully, I wondered at first if he could be just a bit thick. But you recall who it was said that the capacity for wonder at matters of common acceptance occurs in the superior mind? And, of course, so it proved when he shook us all up over the enzyme conversion business. A pity your government took him away from his line, there. No, he said nothing of this, I say it to you, young man. We spoke in fact largely of my work. I was surprised to find he'd kept up. He asked me what my *sentiments* about it were, which surprised me again. Now, understand, I'd not seen the man for five years, but he seemed—well, perhaps just tired, as who is not? I'm sure he was glad to have a change; he jumped out for a legstretch wherever we came down. At Oslo, even Bonn. Oh yes, he did feed the birds, but that was nothing new for Ain. His social life when I knew him? Radical causes? Young man, I've said what I've said because of who it was that introduced you, but I'll have you know it is an impertinence in you to think ill of Charles Ain, or that he could do a harmful deed. Good evening."

The professor said nothing of the woman in Ain's life.

Nor could he have, although Ain had been intimately with her in the university time. He had let no one see how he was obsessed with her, with the miracle, the wealth of her body, her inexhaustibility. They met at his every spare moment; sometimes in public pretending to be casual strangers under his friends' noses, pointing out a pleasing view to each other with grave formality. And later in their privacies—what doubled intensity of love! He reveled at her, possessed her, allowed her no secrets. His dreams were of her sweet springs and shadowed places and her white rounded glory in the moonlight, finding always more, always new dimensions of his joy.

The danger of her frailty was far off then in the rush of birdsong and the springing leverets of the meadow. On dark days she might cough a bit, but so did he . . . In those years he had had no thought to the urgent study of disease.

At the Moscow conference nearly everyone noticed Ain at some point or another, which was to be expected in view of his professional stature. It was a small, high-caliber meeting.

Ain was late in; a day's reports were over, and his was to be on the third and last.

Many people spoke with Ain, and several sat with him at meals. No one was surprised that he spoke little; he was a retiring man except on a few memorable occasions of hot argument. He did strike some of his friends as a bit tired and jerky.

An Indian molecular engineer who saw him with the throat spray kidded him about bringing over Asian flu. A Swedish colleague recalled that Ain had been called away to the transatlantic phone at lunch; and when he returned Ain volunteered the information that something had turned up missing in his home lab. There was another joke, and Ain said cheerfully, "Oh yes, quite active."

At that point one of the Chicom biologists swung into his daily propaganda chores about bacteriological warfare and accused Ain of manufacturing biotic weapons. Ain took the wind out of his sails by saying: "You're perfectly right." By tacit consent, there was very little talk about military applications, industrial dusting, or subjects of that type. And nobody recalled seeing Ain with any woman other than old Madame Vialche, who could scarcely have subverted anyone from her wheelchair.

Ain's one speech was bad, even for him. He always had a poor public voice but his ideas were usually expressed with the lucidity so typical of the first-rate mind. This time he seemed muddled, with little new to say. His audience excused this as the muffling effects of security. Ain then got into a tangled point about the course of evolution in which he seemed to be trying to show that something was very wrong indeed. When he wound up with a reference to Hudson's bell bird "singing for a later race," several listeners wondered if he could be drunk.

The big security break came right at the end, when he suddenly began to describe the methods he had used to mutate and redesign a leukemia virus. He explained the procedure with admirable clarity in four sentences and paused. Then gave a terse description of the effects of the mutated strain, which were maximal only in the higher primates. Recovery rate among the lower mammals and the other orders was close to 90 percent. As to vectors, he went on, any warmblooded animal served. In addition, the virus retained its viability in most environmental media and performed very well airborne. Contagion rate was extremely high. Almost offhand, Ain added that no test primate or accidentally exposed human had survived beyond the twenty-second day.

These words fell into a silence broken only by the running feet of the Egyptian delegate making for the door. Then a gilt chair went over as an American bolted after him.

Ain seemed unaware that his audience was in a state of unbelieving paralysis. It had all come so fast: a man who had been blowing his nose was staring popeyed around his handkerchief. Another who had been lighting a pipe grunted as his fingers singed. Two men chatting by the door missed his words entirely and their laughter chimed into a dead silence in which echoed Ain's words: "—really no point in attempting."

Later they found he had been explaining that the virus utilized the body's own immunomechanisms, and so defense was by definition hopeless.

That was all. Ain looked around vaguely for questions and then started down the aisle. By the time he got to the door, people were swarming after him. He wheeled about and said rather crossly, "Yes, of course it is very wrong. I told you that. We are all wrong. Now it's over."

An hour later they found he had gone, having apparently reserved a Sinair flight to Karachi.

The security men caught up with him at Hong Kong. By then he seemed really very ill, and went with them peacefully. They started back to the States via Hawaii.

His captors were civilized types; they saw he was gentle and treated him accordingly. He had no weapons or drugs on him. They took him out handcuffed for a stroll at Osaka, let him feed his crumbs to the birds, and they listened with interest to his account of the migration routes of the common brown sandpiper. He was very hoarse. At that point, he was wanted only for the security thing. There was no question of a woman at all.

He dozed most of the way to the islands, but when they came in sight he pressed to the window and began to mutter. The security man behind him got the first inkling that there was a woman in it, and turned on his recorder.

". . . Blue, blue and green until you see the wounds. Oh my girl, Oh beautiful, you won't die. I won't let you die. I tell you, girl, it's over . . . Lustrous eyes, look at me, let me see you now alive! Great queen, my sweet body, my girl, have I saved you? . . . Oh terrible to know, and noble, Chaos' child green-robed in blue and golden light . . . the thrown and spinning ball of life alone in space . . . Have I saved you?"

On the last leg, he was obviously feverish.

"She may have tricked me, you know," he said confidentially to the government man. "You have to be prepared for that, of course. I know her!" He chuckled confidentially. "She's no small thing. But wring your heart out—"

Coming over San Francisco he was merry. "Don't you know the otters will go back in there? I'm certain of it. That fill won't last; there'll be a bay there again."

They got him on a stretcher at Hamilton Air Base and he went unconscious shortly after takeoff. Before he collapsed, he'd insisted on throwing the last of his birdseed on the field.

"Birds are, you know, warmblooded," he confided to the agent who was handcuffing him to the stretcher. Then Ain smiled gently and lapsed into inertness. He stayed that way almost all the remaining ten days of his life. By then, of course, no one really cared. Both the government men had died quite early, after they finished analyzing the birdseed and throat-spray. The woman at Kennedy had just started feeling sick.

The tape recorder they put by his bed functioned right on through, but if anybody had been around to replay it they would have found little but babbling. "Gaea Gloriatrix" he crooned, "Gaea girl, queen . . ." At times he was grandiose and tormented. "Our life, your death!" he yelled. "Our death would have been your death too, no need for that, no need."

At other times he was accusing. "What did you do about the dinosaurs?" he demanded. "Did they annoy you? How did you fix *them?* Cold. Queen, you're too cold! You came close to it this time, my girl," he raved. And then he wept and caressed the bedclothes and was maudlin.

Only at the end, lying in his filth and thirst, still chained where they had forgotten him, he was suddenly coherent. In the light clear voice of a lover planning a summer picnic he asked the recorder happily:

"Have you ever thought about bears? They have so much . . . funny they never came along further. By any chance were you saving them, girl?" And he chuckled in his ruined throat, and later, died.

Radical Sensibility

New Wave science fiction broke with the Campbell tradition not only on grounds of subject and technique but by reason of a radically different attitude toward humanity and its place in the universe and its political arrangements. That attitude was conditioned by a series of political events such as the Communist takeover in China, the rise of the Soviet Union as a nuclear superpower and a leader in space exploration, the Soviet crushing of the Hungarian rebellion, the Nasser nationalization of the Suez Canal, U.S. involvement in Vietnam, U.S. civil-rights conflicts, and worldwide campus unrest. Part of the changed attitude was described by Robert Silverberg in an introduction to a collection of stories by Gardner Dozois as "the radical sensibility of the Sixties, the awareness that American twentieth-century life seen from the lower depths is not quite as pretty as the television/suburbia/mass-media/Establishment view of things."

Dozois (1947–), who was born in Salem, Massachusetts, and now lives in Philadelphia, emerged from his teens in the 1960s and had his first story, "The Empty Man," published in the September 1966 *If*. Subsequently he spent three years of army service as a military journalist in Nuremberg, Germany. He returned to writing after his discharge in 1969. He attacked it full-time, a remarkable demonstration of confidence, or courage. It meant years of deprivation and work at part-time jobs such as that of first reader for a number of sf magazines and book publishers. He also edited several anthologies, and in 1976 took over the editorship of *The Best Science Fiction Stories of the Year*, published by Dutton.

Dozois writes slowly and has produced only a couple of dozen stories and two novels, one, with George Alec Effinger, entitled *Nightmare Blue* (1975), the other *Strangers* (1978). In 1981 he was at work upon a third, *Flash Point*. His short stories have appeared in *Playboy, Penthouse,* and *Omni* in addition to the usual science fiction magazines and original anthologies, particularly *New Dimensions, Universe,* and *Orbit*. His stories frequently have been nominated for awards; they have been Nebula Award finalists six times, Hugo finalists four times, and Jupiter Award finalists twice. His short fiction has been collected in *The Visible Man* (1977).

The Science Fiction Encyclopedia describes Dozois as "a figure of some note in the latter-day American New Wave," but Dozois puts distance between himself and New Wave attitudes and aims. At a 1973 Washington, D.C., sf convention, Dozois said about the experimental stories of the late 1960s, "The New Wave blows it by turning out stories that are indistinguishable from the stories that fill avant-garde mainstream quarterlies and little magazines. . . . The most extreme of these so-called New Wave writers have abandoned the thread of rationality that is part of genre sf's philosophical heritage, and so have diminished their work."

On the other hand, he pointed out, "The Old Wave fouls up by continuing to write the same old thing year after year, turning out the same old plots like yard-goods, chewing toothlessly on the same cardboard characters and played-out concepts. . . . The cut-and-dried place that they make of the galaxy, not even as interesting as Earth, leaves us with no surprise that the sense of wonder doesn't live there anymore. They have abandoned that thread of irrationality, of fantasy, that is part of genre sf's philosophical heritage, and so have diminished their work."

Dozois called for a synthesis, stories "that keep the inner power of the dream and the irrational, but attempt to analyze it in terms of the known and the traditional."

"Where No Sun Shines," originally published in *Orbit 6* (1970), attempts that synthesis; it seems at one and the same time obscure and transparent. The title apparently is taken from the line "Light breaks where no sun shines" in Dylan Thomas's "Death Shall Have No Dominion," although there is no attribution and the applicability of Thomas's sentiment seems doubtful.

The story is obscure because the situation is unexplained. The reader must pick up what is happening from the actions and recollections of the protagonist, Robinson. The data by which readers can come to their own conclusions is presented in the course of the narrative, as if it were written for someone who had lived through the intervening years.

The story is transparent, because everything that happens is minutely described, from the spit-polish shine on a policeman's boots to the difficulty of an officer trying with one hand to open the sticky pages of a travel-control visa. Indeed, what sustains the story in spite of the obscurity of situation and motivation is the detail with which the author imagines the events and the vigor with which he describes them. The language is active, vivid, and emotional. In the first two sentences, the reader finds "sooty barrens," "desperation," "exhaustion," "rotting," "disintegrating," "frightened," "peering," and "tight-closed." Metaphor and simile enhance the descriptions and expand the flat plane of events into three dimensions: "a tide of crumpled newspapers and dirty candy wrappers," "a ragged wave of refugees," "oily and cinder-flecked as a tattered gray rug."

On the subject itself, a near-future ultimate race war, the story seems deliberately neutral: The actions of the MARC group are brutal and repulsive, but apparently similar brutality and killing, arson and looting, lie behind. Science fiction writers are not prophets, nor are they concerned with the accuracy of the visions they set down, but stories that are placed in the near future draw power from the relevance of the conflicts they embody. Dozois writes, "At the time I wrote the story, late in 1968, I believed that race war was not only likely, but perhaps inevitable. Later on . . . it seemed as if [the story's future projections had] become outdated and obsolete. Now . . . I'm no longer sure just how outdated the story is."

Where No Sun Shines

by Gardner Dozois

Robinson had been driving for nearly two days, across Pennsylvania, up through the sooty barrens of New Jersey, pushing both the car and himself with desperation. Exhaustion had stopped him once in a small, rotting coast town, filled with disintegrating clapboard buildings and frightened pale faces peering from behind tight-closed shutters. He had moved slowly through empty streets washed by a tide of crumpled newspapers and dirty candy wrappers that rolled and rustled in the bitter sea wind. On the edge of town he'd found a deserted filling station and gone to sleep there with doors locked and windows rolled up, watching moonlight glint from a rusting gas pump and clutching a tire iron in his hands. He had dreamed of sharks with legs, and once banged his head sharply on the roof as he lunged up out of sleep and away from ripping teeth, pausing and blinking afterward in the hot, sweat-drenched stuffiness of the closed car, listening to the darkness.

In the drab, pale clarity of morning, a ragged wave of refugees had washed through town and swept him along. He had driven all day by the side of the restless sea, oily and cinder-flecked as a tattered gray rug, drifting through one frightened shuttered town after another, watching the peeling billboards and the boarded-up store fronts.

It was late evening now, and he was just beginning to really believe what had happened, accept it with his bowels as well as his mind, the hard reality jabbing his stomach like a knifeblade. The secondary highway he was following narrowed, banked, and Robinson slowed to take the curve, wincing at the scream of gears as he shifted. The road straightened and he stamped on the accelerator again, feeling the shuddering whine of the car's response. How long will this crate hold up? he thought numbly. How long will my gas last? How many more miles? Exhaustion was creeping up on him again; a sledgehammer wrapped in felt, isolating him even from the aching reality of his own nerves.

There was a wreck ahead, on his side, and he drifted out into the other lane to avoid it. Coming past Philadelphia the highway had been choked with a honking, aimless mass of cars, but he knew the net of secondary roads better than most of them and had outstripped the herd. Now the roads were mostly empty. Sane people had gone to ground.

He pulled even with the wreck, passed it. It was a light pickup truck, tipped on its side, gutted by fire. A man was lying in the road face down, across the white dividing line. Except for the pale gleam of face and hands, it might have been a discarded bundle of rags. There were bloodstains on the worn asphalt. Robinson let his car slide more to the left to keep from running over the man, started to skid slightly, corrected it. Beyond the wreck he swerved back into his own lane and speeded up again. The truck and the man slid backward, lingered in his rear-view mirror for a second, washed by his taillights, and were swallowed by darkness.

A few miles down the road, Robinson began to fall asleep at the wheel, blacking out in split-second dozes, nodding and blinking. He cursed, strained his eyes wide open and rolled his window down. Wind screamed through the crack. The air was muggy, sodden with coal smoke and chemical reeks, the miasma of the industrial nightmare that choked upper New Jersey.

Automatically, Robinson reached for the radio, switched it on, and began turning the selector-knob with one hand, groping blindly through the invisible world for something to keep him company. Static rasped at him. Almost all the Philadelphia and Pittsburgh stations were off the air now; they'd been hit hard down there. The last Chicago station had sputtered off the air at dusk, after an outbreak of fighting had been reported outside the studio. For a while, some of the announcers had been referring to "rebel forces," but this had evidently been judged to be bad PR, because they were calling them "rioters" and "scattered anarchists" again.

For a moment he picked up a strong Boston station, broadcasting a placating speech by some official, but it faded in a burst of static and was slowly replaced by a Philadelphia station relaying emergency ham messages. There were no small local stations anymore. Television was probably out too, not that he missed it very much. He hadn't seen a live broadcast or a documentary for months now, and even in Harrisburg, days before the final flareup, they'd stopped showing any newscasts at all and broadcast nothing but taped situation comedies and old 1920's musicals. (The happy figures dancing in tails on top of pianos, unreal as delirium tremens in the flickering wavering white glow of the television's eyes, as tinny music echoed and canned laughter filled the room like the crying of mechanical birds. Outside, there was occasional gunfire. . . .)

Finally he settled for a station that was playing uninterrupted classical music, mostly Mozart and Johann Strauss.

He drove on with automatic skill, listening to a bit of Dvořák that had somehow slipped in between Haydn and "The Blue Danube." Absorbed in the music, his already fuzzy mind lulled by the steady rolling lap of asphalt slipping under his wheels, Robinson almost succeeded in forgetting—

A tiny red star appeared on the horizon.

Robinson gazed absently at it for a while before he noticed it was steadily growing larger, blinked at it for a moment more before he figured out what it was and the bottom dropped out of his stomach.

He cursed, soft and scared. The gears screamed, the car lurched, slowed. He pumped the brakes to cut his speed still more. A spotlight blinked on just under the red star, turned the night white, blinded him. He whispered an obscenity, feeling his stomach flatten and his thighs tighten in fear.

Robinson cut the engine and let the car roll slowly to a stop. The spotlight followed him, keeping its beam focused on his windshield. He squinted against the glare, blinking. His eyes watered, blurred, and the spotlight blossomed into a Star of David, radiating white lances of light. Robinson winced and looked down, trying to blink his eyes back into focus, not daring to raise a hand. The car sighed to a stop.

He sat motionless, hands locked on the wheel, listening to the shrill hissing and metallic clicks as his engine cooled. There was the sound of a car door slamming somewhere, an unintelligible shouted order, a brief reply. Robinson squinted up sideways, trying to see around the miniature nova that was the spotlight. Feet crunched through gravel. A figure approached the car, becoming a burly, indistinct silhouette in front of the windshield, a blob of dough in roughly human shape. Something glinted, a shaft of starlight twisting in the doughy hands, trying to escape. Robinson felt the pressure of eyes. He sat very still, blinking. . . .

The dough-figure grunted and half-turned back toward the spotlight, its outlines tumbling and bulging. "Okay," it shouted in a dough-voice. A clang, and the spotlight dulled to a quarter of its former intensity, becoming a glazed orange eye. Detail and color washed back into the world, dappled by a dancing overlay of blue-white afterimages. The dough-figure resolved itself into a middle-aged police sergeant, dumpy, unshaven, graying. He held a heavy-gauge shotgun in his hands, and highlights blinked off and on along the barrel, making the blued steel seem to ripple. The muzzle was pointed loosely in the direction of Robinson's throat.

Robinson risked a sly glance around, not moving his head. The red star was the slowly pulsing crashlight on the roof of a big police prowlcar parked across the road. A younger po-

liceman (still rookie enough to care; spit-polished boots; see
the light shimmer from the ebony toes) stood by the smoldering spotlight that was mounted near the junction of windshield and hood. He was trying to look grim and implacable,
the big regulation revolver awkward in his hand.

Motion on the far side of the road. Robinson swiveled his
eyes up, squinted, and then bit the inside of his lip. A mud-
caked MARC jeep was parked halfway up the grassy
embankment. There were three men in it. As he watched, the
tall man in the passenger's seat said something to the driver,
swung his legs over the side and slid down the embankment
on his heels in a tiny avalanche of dirt and gravel. The driver
slipped his hands inside his field jacket for warmth and
propped his elbows against the steering wheel, eyes slitted and
bored. The third man, a grimy corporal, was sitting in the
back of the jeep, manning a .50 caliber machinegun bolted to
the vehicle. The corporal grinned at Robinson down the
machinegun barrel, his hands fidgeting on the triggers.

The tall man emerged slowly from the shadow of the road
shoulder, walked past the nervous rookie without looking at
him and entered the pool of light. As he walked toward
Robinson's car, he slowly metamorphosed from a tall shadow
into a MARC lieutenant in a glistening weatherproofed
parka, hood thrown back. A brown leather patch on his
shoulder read *MOVEMENT AND REGIONAL CONTROL*
in frayed red capitals. He held a submachine gun slung under
one arm.

The police sergeant glanced back as the lieutenant drew
even with the hood. The muzzle of the shotgun didn't waver
from Robinson's chest. "Looks okay," he said. The lieutenant
grunted, passed behind the sergeant, came up to the window
on the driver's side. He looked at Robinson for a second, expressionless, then unslung his submachine gun and held it in
the crook of his right arm. His other hand reached out slowly
and he tapped once on the window.

Robinson rolled the window down. The lieutenant peered
in at him, pale blue eyes that were like windows opening on
nothing. Robinson glanced once down the small, cramped
muzzle of the machinegun, looked back up at the lieutenant's
thin, pinched lips, white, no blood in them. Robinson felt the
flesh of his stomach crawl, the thick hair on his arms and legs
stir and bristle painfully against his clothing. "Let me see
your card," the lieutenant said. His voice was clipped,
precise. Slowly, slowly, Robinson slid his hand inside his

rumpled sports jacket, carefully withdrew it and handed his identification and travel control visa to the lieutenant. The lieutenant took the papers, stepped back and examined them with one hand, holding the submachine gun trained on Robinson with the other. The pinched mouth of the automatic weapon hung only a few inches away, bobbing slightly, tracing a quarter-inch circle on Robinson's chest.

Robinson worked his dry tongue against his lips and tried unsuccessfully to swallow. He looked from the coolly appraising eyes of the lieutenant to the tired frown of the sergeant, to the nervously belligerent glances of the rookie, to the indifferent stare of the jeep driver, to the hooded eyes of the corporal behind the .50 caliber. They were all looking at him. He was the center of the universe. The pulsing crashlight threw long, tangled shadows through the woods, the shadows licking out and then quickly snapping back again, like a yo-yo. On the northern horizon, a smoldering red glow stained the clouds, flaring and dimming. That was Newark, burning.

The lieutenant stirred, impatiently trying to flip a tacky page of the travel visa with his free hand. He muttered, planted a boot on the side of Robinson's hood, braced the submachine gun on his knee and used his teeth to help him open the sticky page. Robinson caught the rookie staring at the lieutenant's big battered combat boot with prim disapproval, and started to laugh in spite of the hovering machinegun. He choked it down because it had a ragged hollow sound even inside his throat; it was hysterical laughter, and it filled his chest like crinkly dead leaves. The lieutenant removed his foot and straightened up again. The boot made a dry sucking sound as it was pulled free, and left a blurred muddy footprint on the side of the hood. You son of a bitch, Robinson thought, suddenly and irrationally furious.

A nightbird wailed somewhere among the trees. A chilly wind came up, spattering the cars with gravel, a hollow metallic wind full of cinders and deserted trainyards. The wind flapped the pages of the travel visa, rumpled the fur on the lieutenant's parka hood, plucked futilely at his close-cropped hair. The lieutenant continued to read with deliberation, holding the rippling pages down with his thumb. You son of a bitch, Robinson raged silently, choked with fear and anger. You sadistic bastard. The long silence had become heavy as rock. The crashlight flicked its red shadows across the lieutenant's face, turning his eyes into shallow pools of blood and draining them, turning his cheeks into gaping deathhead sockets, filling them out again. He flipped pages mechanically, expressionless.

He suddenly snapped the visa closed.

Robinson jerked. The lieutenant stared at him for a smothering heartbeat, then handed the visa back. Robinson took it, trying not to snatch. "Why're you traveling," the lieutenant said quietly. The words tumbled clumsily out: business trip—no planes—had to get back—wife— The lieutenant listened blankly, then turned and gestured to the rookie.

The rookie rushed forward, hurriedly checked the back seat, the trunk. Robinson heard him breathing and rustling in the back seat, the car swaying slightly as he moved. Robinson looked straight ahead and said nothing. The lieutenant was silent, holding his automatic weapon loosely in both hands. The old police sergeant fidgeted restlessly. "Nothing, sir," the rookie said, climbing out. The lieutenant nodded, and the rookie returned smartly to the prowlcar. "Sounds okay, sir," the sergeant said, shifting his weight with doughy impatience from one sore foot to another. He looked tired, and there was a network of blue veins on the side of his graying head. The lieutenant considered, then nodded reluctantly. "Uh-huh," he said, slowly, then speeded up, became brisker, turned a tight parody of a smile on Robinson. "Sure. All right, mister, I guess you can go."

Another pair of headlights bobbed over the close horizon behind.

The lieutenant's smile dissolved. "Okay, mister," he said, "you stay put. Don't you do *anything*. Sarge, keep an eye on him." He turned, strode toward the prowlcar. The headlights grew larger, bobbing. Robinson heard the lieutenant mutter something and the spotlight flicked on to full intensity again. This time it was aimed away from him, and he saw the beam stab out through the night, a solid column of light, and catch something, pinning it like a captured moth.

It was a big Volkswagen Microbus. Under the spotlight's eye it looked grainy and unreal, a photograph with too much contrast.

The Microbus slowed, pulled to a stop near the shoulder across the road from Robinson. He could see two people in the front seat, squinting and holding up their hands against the glare. The lieutenant strolled over, investigated them from a few feet away, and then waved his hand. The spotlight clanged down to quarter intensity.

In the diffused orange glow, Robinson could just make out

the bus's passengers: a tall man in a black turtleneck and a Nordic young woman with shoulder-length blond hair, wearing an orange shift. The lieutenant circled to the driver's side and tapped on the window. Robinson could see the lieutenant's mouth move, hardly opening, neat and precise. The thin man handed his papers over stolidly. The lieutenant began to examine them, flipping slowly through the pages.

Robinson shifted impatiently. He could feel the sweat slowly drying on his body, sticky and trickling under his arms, in the hollows of his knees, his crotch. His clothes stuck to his flesh.

The lieutenant gestured for the rookie to come over, paced backward until he was standing near the hood. The rookie trotted across the road, walked toward the rear of the vehicle and started to open the sliding side door. Robinson caught the quick nervous flicker of the thin man's tongue against his teeth. The woman was looking calmly straight ahead. The thin man said something in a low joking tone to the lieutenant. The rookie slid the side door open, started to climb inside—

Something moved in the space between the back seat and the closed tailgate, throwing off a thick army blanket, rolling to its knees, scrambling up. Robinson caught a glimpse of dark skin, eyes startlingly white by contrast, nostrils flared in terror. The rookie staggered backward, mouth gaping, revolver swinging aimlessly. The thin man grimaced—a rictus, neck cording, lips riding back from teeth. He tried to slam the bus into gear.

A lance of fire split the darkness, the submachine gun yammering, bucking in the lieutenant's hands. He swept the weapon steadily back and forth, expressionless. The bus's windshield exploded. The man and woman jerked, bounced, bodies dancing grotesquely. The lieutenant continued to fire. The thin man arched backward, bending, bending, bending impossibly, face locked in rictus, and then slumped forward over the steering wheel. The woman was flung sideways against the car door. It gave and she toppled out backward, long hair floating in a tangled cloud, one hand flung out over her head, fingers wide, reaching, stretching out for something. She hit the pavement and lay half in, half out of the bus. Her long fingers twitched, closed, opened.

The dark figure at the back of the bus tore frantically at the tailgate, threw it open, scrambled out, tried to jump for the shoulder. From the embankment the big .50 caliber opened up, blew the back of the bus's roof off. Metal screamed and smoked. The black man was caught as he balanced on the tailgate, one foot lifted. The .50 pounded harshly, blew him almost in half, kicked his limp body six or seven feet down the road. The .50 continued to fire, kicking up geysers of asphalt. The rookie, screaming in inhuman excitement, was firing his revolver at the fallen figure.

The lieutenant waved his arm and everything stopped.

There was no noise or motion.

Echoes rolled slowly away.

Smoke dribbled from the muzzle of the lieutenant's submachine gun.

In the unbelievable silence, you could hear somebody sobbing.

Robinson realized it was himself, ground his teeth together and tensed his stomach muscles to fight the vomit sloshing in his throat. His fingers ached where he had locked them around the steering wheel; he could not get them loose. The wind streamed against his wet flesh.

The lieutenant walked around to the driver's side of the Microbus, opened the door. He grabbed the man by the hair, yanked his head up. The gaunt face was relaxed, unlined, almost ascetically peaceful. The lieutenant let go, and the bloody head dropped.

Slowly the lieutenant walked back around the hood, paused, looked down at the woman for a second. She was sprawled half out of the bus, face up, one arm behind her. Her eyes were still open and staring. Her face was untouched; her body was a slowly spreading red horror from throat to crotch. The lieutenant watched her, gently stroking the machinegun barrel, face like polished marble. The bitter wind flapped her dress, bunched it around her waist. The lieutenant shrugged, moved to the rear of the vehicle. He nudged the black man sprawled across the center line, then turned away and walked briskly to the prowlcar. Above, the corporal began to reload his smoking .50. The driver went back to sleep.

The rookie remained standing by the side of the bus, excitement gone, face ashen and sick, looking at the blue smoke that curled from his revolver, staring at his spit-polished boots, red clotting over ebony. The flashing crashlight turned the dead white faces red, flooding them with a mimic flush of life, draining it away.

The old sergeant turned toward Robinson, grimly clutching

the shotgun, looking suddenly twenty years older. "You'd better get out of here now, son," he said gently. He shifted the shotgun, looked toward the smoldering bus, looked quickly away, looked back. The network of blue veins throbbed. He shook his head slowly, limped away hunch-shouldered, started the prowlcar and backed it off the road.

The lieutenant came up as Robinson was fumbling for the ignition switch. "Get the lead out of your ass," the lieutenant said, and snapped a fresh clip into his submachine gun.

Escape Reading

By 1970, science fiction was beginning to sort itself out after the previous two decades of boom and bust, and of New Wave turmoil. The apparent publishing failure of traditional science fiction in the 1950s had progressed into the apparent publishing failure of New Wave science fiction in the 1960s. Battles between the two attitudes toward life and literature still would be waged in the 1970s, but the war was over and both parties to the conflict would wait for new audiences and new understanding. The publishing boom for books that would last through the 1970s and bring totals to one hundred books a month before the decade was over had already begun in the late 1960s.

In this environment of uncertainty, new writers with different ways of telling their stories found opportunities for publication that had not existed in the previous several decades. Gene Wolfe (1931–) may not have had an easy time getting his short stories into print, but that he was able to find a market for his difficult, different fiction was testimony to a new openness in the field.

Wolfe, born in Brooklyn but brought up in Texas, attended Texas A&M, served in the Korean War, and returned to Texas to earn a degree in mechanical engineering from the University of Houston in 1956. He worked as a project engineer for Procter & Gamble until 1972, when he became editor of *Plant Engineering*, a trade journal.

Wolfe's first story, "Mountains Like Mice," appeared in the May 1966 *Worlds of If*. His second story, "Trip, Trap," was published in *Orbit 2*, the anthology of original stories that

Damon Knight had originated in 1966. In the dedication to his first novel, Wolfe paid tribute to the influence of Knight, who, Wolfe wrote, "one well-remembered June evening in 1966 grew me from a bean." Most of Wolfe's best work appeared in *Orbit,* which became the leading journal of literary science fiction for the approximately fifteen years it was published; similarly, few issues of *Orbit* after 1967 appeared without at least one story by Wolfe.

Although primarily a master of complex, sometimes enigmatic short fiction, Wolfe has produced several books, beginning with *The Fifth Head of Cerberus* (1972), which is made up of three linked novellas; *Peace* (1975), a non-sf novel; and *The Devil in a Forest* (1976), a medieval fantasy for a young-adult audience. In 1980 he began a tetralogy titled *The Book of the New Sun* with a novel titled *The Shadow of the Torturer.* In some ways, excellent as they are in their own right, Wolfe's short stories might be considered preparation for the long work that may come to be recognized as his masterpiece. Two collections of his short stories have been published, *The Island of Doctor Death and Other Stories and Other Stories* (1980) and *Gene Wolfe's Book of Days* (1981).

The title story of his first collection was published in *Orbit 7* (1970). Like many of his other stories, it was nominated for a Nebula Award. In a classic moment of embarrassing confusion, the master of ceremonies, Isaac Asimov, announced that Wolfe's story was the winner before it had to be pointed out that "no award" had received more votes. The following year Wolfe's novella "The Death of Doctor Island" did win the Nebula (an example of Wolfe's wry wit: He also wrote a story titled "The Doctor of Death Island").

"The Island of Doctor Death and Other Stories" uses one of Wolfe's favorite devices, the viewpoint character who has limited knowledge or limited ability to understand; often the reader is in that situation as well. In this case, as it often is, the viewpoint character is a child, Tackie. The viewpoint itself is the unusual second-person, but not like "Day Million," where the reader is being addressed; in Wolfe's story the person being addressed is Tackie. What must be understood if the story is to be understood is that it is a story being told to Tackie about himself. Who is telling it? The storyteller who is the anonymous author of all good stories.

"The Island of Doctor Death and Other Stories" is as much about the storytelling process and the need of all people—but particularly the young—for stories in which they can believe, in which they can lose themselves (or find themselves) when everything around is grim or unendurable, as it is about Tackie's personal problems. Tackie is living in a big old house, formerly a resort hotel, with his recently divorced mother and her boyfriend. Tackie is alone a great deal, and he makes friends with the characters in the book the boyfriend stole for Tackie from the drugstore.

The book, presumably titled *The Island of Doctor Death*, is all the pulp adventure stories that ever enthralled a boy or a girl; it has a wonderful hero, a wonderful heroine, a wonderful friend, a wonderful villain. The basic plot is that of Wells's *The Island of Dr. Moreau* mixed with Edgar Rice Burroughs's *Tarzan and the Jewels of Opar*, with perhaps a dash of H. Rider Haggard's *She*. Contrasted with this rich romance is the bare gray life through which Tackie wanders that begins to seem less solid and real than his reading; he doesn't understand everything that is going on, but more than the adults think. It all culminates in the fantasy of the masquerade party that symbolizes the confusion in Tackie's mind between fiction and reality.

No wonder Tackie prefers the companionship of his friends from the books; he knows he can count on Captain Ransom's courage, on the dogman's devotion, on Dr. Death's villainy. The story is a tribute to the joys of escape reading as well as a touching description of a lonely boy's unhappy life. In Tackie, readers who found themselves enthralled by the power of story and writers who turned to creating new fictional adventures because of that early magic see themselves.

The Island of Doctor Death and Other Stories

by Gene Wolfe

Winter comes to water as well as land, though there are no leaves to fall. The waves that were a bright, hard blue yesterday under a fading sky today are green, opaque, and cold. If you are a boy not wanted in the house you walk the beach for hours, feeling the winter that has come in the night; sand blowing across your shoes, spray wetting the legs of your corduroys. You turn your back to the sea, and with the sharp end of a stick found half buried write in the wet sand *Tackman Babcock*.

Then you go home, knowing that behind you the Atlantic is destroying your work.

Home is the big house on Settlers Island, but Settlers Island, so called, is not really an island and for that reason is not named or accurately delineated on maps. Smash a barnacle with a stone and you will see inside the shape from which the beautiful barnacle goose takes its name. There is a thin and flaccid organ which is the goose's neck and the mollusc's siphon, and a shapeless body with tiny wings. Settlers Island is like that.

The goose neck is a strip of land down which a county road runs. By whim, the mapmakers usually exaggerate the width of this and give no information to indicate that it is scarcely above the high tide. Thus Settlers Island appears to be a mere protuberance on the coast, not requiring a name—and since the village of eight or ten houses has none, nothing shows on the map but the spider line of road terminating at the sea.

The village has no name, but home has two: a near and a far designation. On the island, and on the mainland nearby, it is called the Seaview place because in the earliest years of the century it was operated as a resort hotel. Mama calls it The House of 31 February; and that is on her stationery and is presumably used by her friends in New York and Philadelphia when they do not simply say, "Mrs. Babcock's." Home is four floors high in some places, less in others, and is completely surrounded by a veranda; it was once painted yellow, but the paint—outside and The House of 31 February is gray—is mostly gone now and The House of 31 February is gray.

Jason comes out the front door with the little curly hairs on his chin trembling in the wind and his thumbs hooked in the waistband of his Levi's. "Come on, you're going into town with me. Your mother wants to rest."

"Hey tough!" Into Jason's Jaguar, feeling the leather upholstery soft and smelly; you fall asleep.

Awake in town, bright lights flashing in the car windows. Jason is gone and the car is growing cold; you wait for what seems a long time, looking out at the shop windows, the big gun on the hip of the policeman who walks past, the lost dog who is afraid of everyone, even you when you tap the glass and call to him.

Then Jason is back with packages to put behind the seat. "Are we going home now?"

He nods without looking at you, arranging his bundles so they won't topple over, fastening his seatbelt.

"I want to get out of the car."

He looks at you.

"I want to go in a store. Come on, Jason."

Jason sighs. "All right, the drugstore over there, okay? Just for a minute."

The drugstore is as big as a supermarket, with long, bright aisles of glassware and notions and paper goods. Jason buys fluid for his lighter at the cigarette counter, and you bring him a book from a revolving wire rack. "Please, Jason?"

He takes it from you and replaces it in the rack, then when you are in the car again takes it from under his jacket and gives it to you.

It is a wonderful book, thick and heavy, with the edges of the pages tinted yellow. The covers are glossy stiff cardboard, and on the front is a picture of a man in rags fighting a thing partly like an ape and partly like a man, but much worse than either. The picture is in color, and there is real blood on the ape-thing; the man is muscular and handsome, with tawny hair lighter than Jason's and no beard.

"You like that?"

You are out of town already, and without the street lights it's too dark in the car, almost, to see the picture. You nod.

Jason laughs. "That's camp. Did you know that?"

You shrug, riffling the pages under your thumb, thinking of reading, alone, in your room tonight.

"You going to tell your mom how nice I was to you?"

"Uh-huh, sure. You want me to?"

"Tomorrow, not tonight. I think she'll be asleep when we get back. Don't you wake her up." Jason's voice says he will be angry if you do.

"Okay."

"Don't come in her room."

"Okay."

The Jaguar says "*Hutntntaaa . . .*" down the road, and you can see the whitecaps in the moonlight now, and the driftwood pushed just off the asphalt.

"You got a nice, soft mommy, you know that? When I climb on her it's just like being on a big pillow."

You nod, remembering the times when, lonely and frightened by dreams, you have crawled into her bed and snuggled against her soft warmth—but at the same time angry, knowing Jason is somehow deriding you both.

Home is silent and dark, and you leave Jason as soon as you can, bounding off down the hall and up the stairs ahead of him, up a second, narrow, twisted flight to your own room in the turret.

I had this story from a man who was breaking his word in telling it. How much it has suffered in his hands—I should say in his mouth, rather—I cannot say. In essentials it is true, and I give it to you as it was given to me. This is the story he told.

Captain Philip Ransom had been adrift, alone, for nine days when he saw the island. It was already late evening when it appeared like a thin line of purple on the horizon, but Ransom did not sleep that night. There was no feeble questioning in his wakeful mind concerning the reality of what he had seen; he had been given that one glimpse and he knew. Instead his brain teemed with facts and speculations. He knew he must be somewhere near New Guinea, and he reviewed mentally what he knew of the currents in these waters and what he had learned in the past nine days of the behavior of his raft. The island when he reached it—he did not allow himself to say *if*—would in all probability be solid jungle a few feet back from the water's edge. There might or might not be natives, but he brought to mind all he could of the Bazaar Malay and Tagalog he had acquired in his years as a pilot, plantation manager, white hunter, and professional fighting man in the Pacific.

In the morning he saw that purple shadow on the horizon again, a little nearer this time and almost precisely where his mental calculations had told him to expect it. For nine days there had been no reason to employ the inadequate paddles provided with the raft, but now he had something to row for. Ransom drank the last of his water and began stroking with a steady and powerful beat which was not interrupted until the prow of his rubber craft ground into beach sand.

Morning. You are slowly awake. Your eyes feel gummy, and the light over your bed is still on. Downstairs there is no one, so you get a bowl and milk and puffed, sugary cereal out for yourself and light the oven with a kitchen match so that you can eat and read by its open door. When the cereal is gone you drink the sweet milk and crumbs in the bottom of the bowl and start a pot of coffee, knowing that will please Mother. Jason comes down, dressed but not wanting to talk; drinks coffee and makes one piece of cinnamon toast in the oven. You listen to him leave, the stretched buzzing of his car on the road, then go up to Mother's room.

She is awake, her eyes open looking at the ceiling, but you know she isn't ready to get up yet. Very politely, because that minimizes the chances of being shouted at, you say, "How are you feeling this morning, Mama?"

She rolls her head to look. "Strung out. What time is it, Tackie?"

You look at the little folding clock on her dresser. "Seventeen minutes after eight."

"Jason go?"

"Yes, just now, Mama."

She is looking at the ceiling again. "You go back downstairs now, Tackie. I'll get you something when I feel better."

Downstairs you put on your sheepskin coat and go out on the veranda to look at the sea. There are gulls riding the icy wind, and very far off something orange bobbing in the waves, always closer.

A life raft. You run to the beach, jump up and down and wave your cap. "Over here. Over here."

The man from the raft has no shirt but the cold doesn't seem to bother him. He holds out his hand and says, "Captain Ransom," and you take it and are suddenly taller and older; not as tall as he is or as old as he is, but taller and older than yourself. "Tackman Babcock, Captain."

"Pleased to meet you. You were a friend in need there a minute ago."

"I guess I didn't do anything but welcome you ashore."

"The sound of your voice gave me something to steer for while my eyes were too busy watching that surf. Now you can tell me where I've landed and who you are."

You are walking back up to the house now, and you explain to Ransom about you and Mother, and how she doesn't want to enroll you in the school here because she is trying to get you into the private school your father went to once. And after a time there is nothing more to say, and you show Ransom one of the empty rooms on the third floor where he can rest and do whatever he wants. Then you go back to your own room to read.

"Do you mean that you *made* these monsters?"

"*Made* them?" Dr. Death leaned forward, a cruel smile playing about his lips. "Did God *make* Eve, Captain, when he took her from Adam's rib? Or did Adam make the bone and God *alter* it to become what he wished? Look at it this way, Captain. I am God and Nature is Adam."

Ransom looked at the thing who grasped his right arm with hands that might have circled a utility pole as easily. "Do you mean that this thing is an animal?"

"Not animal," the monster said, wrenching his arm cruelly. "Man."

Dr. Death's smile broadened. "Yes, Captain, man. The question is, what are you? When I'm finished with you we'll see. Dulling your mind will be less of a problem than upgrading these poor brutes; but what about increasing the efficacy of your sense of smell? Not to mention rendering it impossible for you to walk erect."

"*Not* to walk all-four-on-ground," the beast-man holding Ransom muttered, "*that* is the *law*."

Dr. Death turned and called to the shambling hunchback Ransom had seen earlier. "Golo, see to it that Captain Ransom is securely put away; then prepare the surgery."

A car. Not Jason's noisy Jaguar, but a quiet, large-sounding car. By heaving up the narrow, tight little window at the corner of the turret and sticking your head out into the cold wind you can see it: Dr. Black's big one, with the roof and hood all shiny with new wax.

Downstairs Dr. Black is hanging up an overcoat with a collar of fur, and you smell the old cigar smoke in his clothing before you see him; then Aunt May and Aunt Julie are there to keep you occupied so that he won't be reminded too vividly that marrying Mama means getting you as well. They talk to you: "How have you been, Tackie? What do you find to do out here all day?"

"Nothing."

"Nothing? Don't you ever go looking for shells on the beach?"

"I guess so."

"You're a handsome boy, do you know that?" Aunt May

touches your nose with a scarlet-tipped finger and holds it there.

Aunt May is Mother's sister, but older and not as pretty. Aunt Julie is Papa's sister, a tall lady with a pulled-out, unhappy face, and makes you think of him even when you know she only wants Mama to get married again so that Papa won't have to send her any more money.

Mama herself is downstairs now in a clean new dress with long sleeves. She laughs at Dr. Black's jokes and holds onto his arm, and you think how nice her hair looks and that you will tell her so when you are alone. Dr. Black says, "How about it, Barbara, are you ready for the party?" and Mother, "Heavens no. You know what this place is like—yesterday I spent all day cleaning and today you can't even see what I did. But Julie and May will help me."

Dr. Black laughs. "After lunch."

You get into his big car with the others and go to a restaurant on the edge of a cliff, with a picture window to see the ocean. Dr. Black orders a sandwich for you that has turkey and bacon and three pieces of bread, but you are finished before the grown-ups have started, and when you try to talk to Mother, Aunt May sends you out to where there is a railing with wire to fill in the spaces like chicken wire only heavier, to look at the view.

It is really not much higher than the top window at home. Maybe a little higher. You put the toes of your shoes in the wire and bend out with your stomach against the rail to look down, but a grown-up pulls you down and tells you not to do it, then goes away. You do it again, and there are rocks at the bottom which the waves wash over in a neat way, covering them up and then pulling back. Someone touches your elbow, but you pay no attention for a minute, watching the water.

Then you get down, and the man standing beside you is Dr. Death.

He has a white scarf and black leather gloves and his hair is shiny black. His face is not tanned like Captain Ransom's but white, and handsome in a different way like the statue of a head that used to be in Papa's library when you and Mother used to live in town with him, and you think: Mama would say after he was gone how good looking he was. He smiles at you, but you are no older.

"Hi." What else can you say?

"Good afternoon, Mr. Babcock. I'm afraid I startled you."

You shrug. "A little bit. I didn't expect you to be here, I guess."

Dr. Death turns his back to the wind to light a cigarette he takes from a gold case. It is longer even than a 101 and has a red tip, and a gold dragon on the paper. "While you were looking down, I slipped from between the pages of the excellent novel you have in your coat pocket."

"I didn't know you could do that."

"Oh, yes. I'll be around from time to time."

"Captain Ransom is here already. He'll kill you."

Dr. Death smiles and shakes his head. "Hardly. You see, Tackman, Ransom and I are a bit like wrestlers; under various guises we put on our show again and again—but only under the spotlight." He flicks his cigarette over the rail and for a moment your eyes follow the bright spark out and down and see it vanish in the water. When you look back, Dr. Death is gone, and you are getting cold. You go back into the restaurant and get a free mint candy where the cash register is and then go to sit beside Aunt May again in time to have coconut cream pie and hot chocolate.

Aunt May drops out of the conversation long enough to ask, "Who was that man you were talking to, Tackie?"

"A man."

In the car Mama sits close to Dr. Black, with Aunt Julie on the other side of her so she will have to, and Aunt May sits way up on the edge of her seat with her head in between theirs so they can all talk. It is gray and cold outside; you think of how long it will be before you are home again, and take the book out.

Ransom heard them coming and flattened himself against the wall beside the door of his cell. There was no way out, he knew, save through that iron portal.

For the past four hours he had been testing every surface of the stone room for a possible exit, and there was none. Floor, walls, and ceiling were of cyclopean stone blocks; the windowless door of solid metal locked outside.

Nearer. He tensed every muscle and knotted his fists.

Nearer. The shambling steps halted. There was a rattle of keys and the door swung back. Like a thunderbolt of purpose he drove through the opening. A hideous face loomed above him and he sent his right fist crashing into it, knocking the lumbering beast-man to his knees. Two hairy arms pinioned him from behind, but he fought free and the monster reeled under his blows. The corridor stretched ahead of him with a dim glow of daylight at the end and he sprinted for it. Then—darkness!

When he recovered consciousness he found himself already erect, strapped to the wall of a brilliantly lit room which seemed to share the characters of a surgical theater and a chemical laboratory. Directly before his eyes stood a bulky object which he knew must be an operating table, and upon it, covered with a sheet, lay the unmistakable form of a human being.

He had hardly had time to comprehend the situation when Dr. Death entered, no longer in the elegant evening dress in which Ransom had beheld him last, but wearing white surgical clothing. Behind him limped the hideous Golo, carrying a tray of implements.

"Ah!" Seeing that his prisoner was conscious, Dr. Death strolled across the room and raised a hand as though to strike him in the face, but, when Ransom did not flinch, dropped it, smiling. "My dear Captain! You are with us again, I see."

"I hoped for a minute there," Ransom said levelly, "that I was away from you. Mind telling me what got me?"

"A thrown club, or so my slaves report. My baboon-man is quite good at it. But aren't you going to ask about this charming little tableau I've staged for you?"

"I wouldn't give you the pleasure."

"But you are curious." Dr. Death smiled his crooked smile. "I shall not keep you in suspense. Your own time, Captain, has not come yet; and before it does I am going to demonstrate my technique to you. It is so seldom that I have a really appreciative audience." With a calculated gesture he whipped away the sheet which had covered the prone form on the operating table.

Ransom could scarcely believe his eyes. Before him lay the unconscious body of a girl, a girl with skin as white as silk and hair like the sun seen through mist.

"You are interested now, I see," Dr. Death remarked dryly, "and you consider her beautiful. Believe me, when I have completed my work you will flee screaming if she so much as turns what will no longer be a face toward you. This woman has been my implacable enemy since I came to this island, and the time has come for me to"—he halted in mid-sentence and looked at Ransom with an expression of mingled slyness and gloating—"for me to illustrate something of your own fate, shall we say."

While Dr. Death had been talking his deformed assistant had prepared a hypodermic. Ransom watched as the needle plunged into the girl's almost translucent flesh, and the liquid in the syringe—a fluid which by its very color suggested the vile perversion of medical technique—entered her bloodstream. Though still unconscious the girl sighed, and it seemed to Ransom that a cloud passed over her sleeping face as though she had already begun an evil dream. Roughly the hideous Golo turned her on her back and fastened in place straps of the same kind as those that held Ransom himself pinned to the wall.

"What are you reading, Tackie?" Aunt May asked.

"Nothing." He shut the book.

"Well, you shouldn't read in the car. It's bad for your eyes."

Dr. Black looked back at them for a moment, then asked Mama, "Have you gotten a costume for the little fellow yet?"

"For Tackie?" Mama shook her head, making her beautiful hair shine even in the dim light of the car. "No, nothing. It will be past his bedtime."

"Well, you'll have to let him see the guests anyway, Barbara; no boy should miss that."

And then the car was racing along the road out to Settlers Island. And then you were home.

Ransom watched as the loathsome creature edged toward him. Though not as large as some of the others its great teeth looked formidable indeed, and in one hand it grasped a heavy jungle knife with a razor edge.

For a moment he thought it would molest the unconscious girl, but it circled around her to stand before Ransom himself, never meeting his eyes.

Then, with a gesture as unexpected as it was frightening, it bent suddenly to press its hideous face against his pinioned right hand, and a great, shuddering gasp ran through the creature's twisted body.

Ransom waited, tense.

Again that deep inhalation, seeming almost a sob. Then the beast-man straightened up, looking into Ransom's face but avoiding his gaze. A thin, strangely familiar whine came from the monster's throat.

"Cut me loose," Ransom ordered.

"Yes. This I came to. Yes, Master." The huge head, wider than it was high, bobbed up and down. Then the sharp blade of the machete bit into the straps holding Ransom. As soon as he was free he took the blade from the willing hand of the beast-man and freed the limbs of the girl on the operating table. She was light in his arms, and for an instant he stood looking down at her tranquil face.

"Come, Master." The beast-man pulled at his sleeve. "Bruno knows a way out. Follow Bruno."

A hidden flight of steps led to a long and narrow corridor, almost pitch dark. "No one use this way," the beast-man said in his harsh voice. "They not find us here."

"Why did you free me?" Ransom asked.

There was a pause, then almost with an air of shame the great, twisted form replied, "You smell good. And Bruno does not like Dr. Death."

Ransom's conjectures were confirmed. Gently he asked, "You were a dog before Dr. Death worked on you, weren't you, Bruno?"

"Yes." The beast-man's voice held a sort of pride. "A St. Bernard. I have seen pictures."

"Dr. Death should have known better than to employ his foul skills on such a noble animal," Ransom reflected aloud. "Dogs are too shrewd in judging character; but then the evil are always foolish in the final analysis."

Unexpectedly the dog-man halted in front of him, forcing Ransom to stop too. For a moment the massive head bent over the unconscious girl. Then there was a barely audible growl. "You say, Master, that I can judge. Then I tell you Bruno does not like this female Dr. Death calls Talar of the Long Eyes."

You put the open book face-down on the pillow and jump up, hugging yourself and skipping bare heels around the room. Marvelous! Wonderful!

But no more reading tonight. Save it, save it. Turn the light off, and in the delicious dark put the book reverently away under the bed, pushing aside pieces of the Tinker Toy set and the box with the filling station game cards. Tomorrow there will be more, and you can hardly wait for tomorrow.

You lie on your back, hands under head, covers up to chin and when you close your eyes, you can see it all: the island, with jungle trees swaying in the sea wind; Dr. Death's castle lifting its big, cold grayness against the hot sky.

The whole house is still, only the wind and the Atlantic are out, the familiar sounds. Downstairs Mother is talking to Aunt May and Aunt Julie and you fall asleep.

You are awake! Listen! Late, it's very late, a strange time you have almost forgotten. Listen!

So quiet it hurts. Something. Something. Listen!

On the steps.

You get out of bed and find your flashlight. Not because you are brave, but because you cannot wait there in the dark.

There is nothing in the narrow, cold little stairwell outside your door. Nothing in the big hallway of the second floor. You shine your light quickly from end to end. Aunt Julie is breathing through her nose, but there is nothing frightening about that sound, you know what it is: only Aunt Julie, asleep, breathing loud through her nose.

Nothing on the stairs coming up.

You go back to your room, turn off your flashlight, and get into bed. When you are almost sleeping there is the scrabbling sound of hard claws on the floorboards and a rough tongue touching your fingertips. "Don't be afraid, Master, it is only Bruno." And you feel him, warm with his own warm and smelling of his own smell, lying beside your bed.

Then it is morning. The bedroom is cold, and there is no one in it but yourself. You go into the bathroom where there is a thing like a fan but with hot electric wires to dress.

Downstairs Mother is up already with a cloth thing tied over her hair, and so are Aunt May and Aunt Julie, sitting at the table with coffee and milk and big slices of fried ham. Aunt Julie says, "Hello, Tackie," and Mother smiles at you. There is a plate out for you already and you have ham and toast.

All day the three women are cleaning and putting up decorations—red and gold paper masks Aunt Julie made to hang on the wall, and funny lights that change color and go around—and you try to stay out of the way, and bring in wood for a fire in the big fireplace that almost never gets used. Jason comes, and Aunt May and Aung Julie don't like him, but he helps some and goes into town in his car for things he forgot to buy before. He won't take you, this time.

The wind comes in around the window, but they let you alone in your room and it's even quiet up there because they're all downstairs.

Ransom looked at the enigmatic girl incredulously.

"You do not believe me," she said. It was a simple statement of fact, without anger or accusation.

"You'll have to admit it's pretty hard to believe," he temporized. "A city older than civilization, buried in the jungle here on this little island."

Talar said tonelessly, "When you were as he"—she pointed at the dog-man—"is now, Lemuria was queen of this sea. All that is gone, except my city. Is not that enough to satisfy even Time?"

Bruno plucked at Ransom's sleeve. "Do not go, Master! Beast-men go sometimes, beast-men Dr. Death does not want, few come back. They are very evil at that place."

"You see?" A slight smile played about Talar's ripe lips. "Even your slave testifies for me. My city exists."

"How far?" Ransom asked curtly.

"Perhaps half a day's travel through the jungle." The girl paused, as though afraid to say more.

"What is it?" Ransom asked.

"You will lead us against Dr. Death? We wish to cleanse this island which is our home."

"Sure. I don't like him any more than your people do. Maybe less."

"Even if you do not like my people you will lead them?"

"If they'll have me. But you're hiding something. What is it?"

"You see me, and I might be a woman of your own people. Is that not so?" They were moving through the jungle again now, the dog-man reluctantly acting as rear guard.

"Very few girls of my people are as beautiful as you are, but otherwise yes."

"And for that reason I am high priestess to my people, for in me the ancient blood runs pure and sweet. But it is not so with all." Her voice sunk to a whisper. "When a tree is very old, and yet still lives, sometimes the limbs are strangely twisted. Do you understand?"

"Tackie? Tackie, are you in there?"

"Uh-huh." You put the book inside your sweater.

"Well, come and open this door. Little boys ought not to lock their doors. Don't you want to see the company?" You open, and Aunt May's a gypsy with long hair that isn't hers around her face and a mask that is only at her eyes.

Downstairs cars are stopping in front of the house and Mother is standing at the door dressed in Day-Glo robes that open way down the front but cover her arms almost to the ends of her fingers. She is talking to everyone as they come in, and you see her eyes are bright and strange the way they are sometimes when she dances by herself and talks when no one is listening.

A woman with a fish for a head and a shiny, silver dress is Aunt Julie. A doctor with a doctor's coat and listening things and a shiny thing on his head to look through is Dr. Black, and a soldier in a black uniform with a pirate thing on his hat and a whip is Jason. The big table has a punchbowl and cakes and little sandwiches and hot bean dip. You pull away when the gypsy is talking to someone and take some cakes and sit under the table watching legs.

There is music and some of the legs dance, and you stay under there a long time.

Then a man's and a girl's legs dance close to the table and there is suddenly a laughing face in front of you—Captain Ransom's. "What are you doing under there, Tack? Come out and join the party." And you crawl out, feeling very small instead of older, but older when you stand up. Captain Ransom is dressed like a castaway in a ragged shirt and pants torn off at the knees, but all clean and starched. His love beads are seeds and sea shells, and he has his arm around a girl with no clothes at all, just jewelry.

"Tack, this is Talar of the Long Eyes."

You smile and bow and kiss her hand, and are nearly as tall as she. All around people are dancing or talking, and no one seems to notice you. With Captain Ransom on one side of Talar and you on the other you thread your way through the room, avoiding the dancers and the little groups of people with drinks. In the room you and Mother use as a living room when there's no company, two men and two girls are making love with the television on, and in the little room past that a girl is sitting on the floor with her back to the wall, and men are standing in the corners. "Hello," the girl says. "Hello to you all." She is the first one to have noticed you, and you stop.

"Hello."

"I'm going to pretend you're real. Do you mind?"

"No." You look around for Ransom and Talar, but they are gone and you think that they are probably in the living room, kissing with the others.

"This is my third trip. Not a good trip, but not a bad trip. But I should have had a monitor—you know, someone to stay with me. Who are those men?"

The men in the corners stir, and you can hear the clinking of their armor and see light glinting on it and you look away. "I think they're from the City. They probably came to watch out for Talar," and somehow you know that this is the truth.

"Make them come out where I can see them."

Before you can answer Dr. Death says, "I don't really think you would want to," and you turn and find him standing just behind you wearing full evening dress and a cloak. He takes your arm. "Come on, Tackie, there's something I think you should see." You follow him to the back stairs and then up, and along the hall to the door of Mother's room.

Mother is inside on the bed, and Dr. Black is standing over her filling a hypodermic. As you watch, he pushes up her sleeve so that all the other injection marks show ugly and red on her arm, and all you can think of is Dr. Death bending over Talar on the operating table. You run downstairs looking for Ransom, but he is gone and there is nobody at the party at all except the real people and, in the cold shadows of the back stoop, Dr. Death's assistant Golo, who will not speak, but only stares at you in the moonlight with pale eyes.

The next house down the beach belongs to a woman you have seen sometimes cutting down the dry fall remnant of her asparagus or hilling up her roses while you played. You pound on her door and try to explain, and after a while she calls the police.

. . . across the sky. The flames were licking at the roof timbers now. Ransom made a megaphone of his hands and shouted, "Give up! You'll all be burned to death if you stay in there!" but the only reply was a shot and he was not certain they had heard him. The Lemurian bowmen discharged another flight of arrows at the windows.

Talar grasped his arm: "Come back before they kill you."

Numbly he retreated with her, stepping across the massive body of the bull-man, which lay pierced by twenty or more shafts.

You fold back the corner of a page and put the book down. The waiting room is cold and bare, and although sometimes the people hurrying through smile at you, you feel lonely. After a long time a big man with gray hair and a woman in a blue uniform want to talk to you.

The woman's voice is friendly, but only the way teachers' voices are sometimes. "I'll bet you're sleepy, Tackman. Can you talk to us a little still before you go to bed?"

"Yes."

The gray-haired man says, "Do you know who gave your mother drugs?"

"I don't know. Dr. Black was going to do something to her."

He waves that aside. "Not that. You know, medicine. Your mother took a lot of medicine. Who gave it to her? Jason?"

"I don't know."

The woman says, "Your mother is going to be well, Tackman, but it will be a while—do you understand? For now you're going to have to live for a while in a big house with some other boys."

"All right."

The man: "Amphetamines. Does that mean anything to you? Did you ever hear that word?"

You shake your head.

The woman: "Dr. Black was only trying to help your mother, Tackman. I know you don't understand, but she used several medicines at once, mixed them, and that can be very bad."

They go away and you pick up the book and riffle the pages, but you do not read. At your elbow Dr. Death says, "What's the matter, Tackie?" He smells of scorched cloth and there is a streak of blood across his forehead, but he smiles and lights one of his cigarettes.

You hold up the book. "I don't want it to end. You'll be killed at the end."

"And you don't want to lose me? That's touching."

"You will, won't you? You'll burn up in the fire and Captain Ransom will go away and leave Talar."

Dr. Death smiles. "But if you start the book again we'll all be back. Even Golo and the bull-man."

"Honest?"

"Certainly." He stands up and tousels your hair. "It's the same with you, Tackie. You're too young to realize it yet, but it's the same with you."

Understanding Reader Reaction

The business of a fiction writer is to make a reader feel, and one way to control what a reader feels is through the distance a writer places between the reader and the characters. The writer can involve the reader with the characters in several ways: by presenting interesting people in difficulties, for instance; the more real the characters seem and the more believable their difficulties, the more the reader will care about what happens to them, particularly if the characters are not so overmatched by their difficulties that their situations are hopeless. On the other hand, a writer can push a reader away from his characters by describing them dispassionately; by displaying them not as people to be cared about but as case studies or specimens; or by presenting them as so weak or their difficulties as so overwhelming that they cannot hope to overcome them.

Traditional science fiction used unusual, often alien viewpoints to obtain a different view of the situation of humanity. The New Wave used various distancing devices to explore the human situation and to dramatize the tyranny of contemporary technology or society, or the inadequacy of humanity's understanding of the universe and its efforts to deal with it. These devices also served to direct the reader away from the characters and toward the words and images.

Thomas M. Disch (1940–   ) exemplified these techniques in his early writing. His purpose, he has said, was "to write a fiction in which narrative momentum was maintained by other means than the reader's vicarious involvement in wish-fulfillment adventures" and "to encompass themes of visionary and ecstatic nature, to chart peak experiences of all kinds." Born in Des Moines, Iowa, and raised in Minnesota, Disch attended Cooper Union and New York University between 1959 and 1962. While in school he worked as a part-time theater checkroom attendant and after leaving college worked in 1963 and 1964 as a copywriter for an advertising agency. By this time his first story, "The Double Time," had been published in the October 1962 *Fantastic Stories.* He has been a full-time freelance writer since 1964. His first novel, *The Genocides,* was published in 1965. His work has appeared in many of the traditional sf magazines. From 1966 to 1968 his fiction was published regularly in *New Worlds,* which serialized two of his novels. His short stories have been collected in *One Hundred and Two H-Bombs* (1966; also titled *White Fang Goes Dingo*), *Under Compulsion* (1968; also titled *Fun with Your New Head*), *Getting into Death* (1973), and *Fundamental Disch* (1980).

His novels came out annually for several years: *Mankind Under the Leash* (1966; also titled *The Puppies of Terror*), *Echo Round His Bones* (1967), *Camp Concentration* (1968), *The Prisoner* (a novelization, 1969), *334* (1972), and *On Wings of Song* (1979). He interspersed them with other kinds of novels, written in collaboration or under pseudonyms, or both: *The House That Fear Built* (1966, with John Sladek, as Cassandra Knye), *Black Alice* (1968, with John Sladek, as Thom Demijohn), *Clara Reeve* (1975, as Leonie Hargrave), and *Neighboring Lives* (1981, with Charles Naylor). His work frequently has been a finalist for Nebula and Hugo Awards; *On Wings of Song* won the John W. Campbell Award for the best sf novel of the year.

Disch also has edited a number of anthologies: *The Ruins of Earth: An Anthology of the Immediate Future* (1971), *Bad Moon Rising* (1973), *The New Improved Sun: An Anthology of Utopian Science Fiction* (1975), *New Constellations* (1976, with Charles Naylor), and *Strangeness* (1977, with Charles Naylor).

Disch's novels generally have taken new looks at familiar sf conventions, while his short stories have been more experimental in both subject and form. His novels, for instance, have dealt in dark and unusual ways with alien invasion, the enhancement of intelligence, matter transmission, and overpopulation. His short stories, on the other hand, have expressed a Kafkaesque feeling of inexplicable entrapment typified by "The Squirrel Cage" and "Descending," and even

"The Asian Shore," which describes the possession of a visiting architectural critic by the life (and wife) of a Turkish native.

In both his novels and his short stories, however, one constant is the distance Disch has placed between the reader and the characters. In *The Science Fiction Encyclopedia*, John Clute wrote of Disch: "Through his intellectual audacity, the distanced coldness of his sometimes mannerist narrative art, the arduous demands he makes upon the reader of genre sf, the austerity of the pleasures he affords and the fine cruelty of his wit, TMD is perhaps the most respected, least trusted, most envied and least read of all modern sf writers of the first rank."

Recently, however, Disch has shown signs of warming up to his characters and of allowing himself and his readers to like them and to care about them, for instance in *On Wings of Song* and "Understanding Human Behavior" (February 1982 *Magazine of Fantasy and Science Fiction*). "Angouleme" belongs to an earlier period. Originally published in *New Worlds Quarterly No. 1* in 1971, it was reprinted in Harrison and Aldiss's *Best SF: 1971;* but its most significant publication was in Disch's own collection, *334. 334* is a group of stories loosely tied together by dealing with people who live at 334 West Eleventh Street (although that connection is not explicit in "Angouleme") in a grim New York City fifty years in the future.

The curious and evocative title "Angouleme," is one of many ambiguous details that maintains the story's "narrative momentum . . . by other means than the reader's vicarious involvement in wish-fulfillment adventures." The narrative, densely packed with details, is an example of Disch's concern with "themes of visionary and ecstatic nature," but also of techniques for suggesting environment that Disch no doubt learned from his reading of science fiction. In a number of ways the protocols for reading "Angouleme" are identical with those for reading Farmer's more clearly generic "Sail On! Sail On!" (Volume 3)—the clues to background and to meaning placed precisely where they must be noted by the reader and accounted for, although perhaps not fully understood until later.

The story actually is a simple one—it could be told in a few sentences—but where it happens and under what conditions give the events meaning and are more difficult to ascertain. This is the way life may be, Disch says, given certain events and certain extrapolations from the present—but what those events are and what those extrapolations may be the reader must piece out for himself from the ambiguous details offered largely through the ambiguous viewpoint of a pre-adolescent boy.

Readers familiar with New York City will have less difficulty with the story, though some of it may still baffle. Others might be helped by the information that the Battery is at the bottom tip of Manhattan Island (it is called the Battery because cannon were placed there to defend the confluence of the East River and the Hudson) and today is a park that features statues of famous persons and memorials to war dead, from which one may see, on a clear day, the Verrazano Bridge, crossing the straits of Verrazano between Brooklyn and Staten Island. Others who may still find the story puzzling are urged to read a book titled *The American Shore* (1978) in which Samuel R. Delany analyzes the story line by line (and even word by word) as an example of structuralist criticism and the protocols of reading science fiction.

Angouleme

by Thomas M. Disch

There were seven Alexandrians involved in the Battery plot—Jack, who was the youngest and from the Bronx, Celeste DiCecca, Sniffles and MaryJane, Tancred Miller, Amparo (of course), and *of course*, the leader and mastermind, Bill Harper, better known as Little Mister Kissy Lips. Who was passionately, hopelessly in love with Amparo. Who was nearly thirteen (she would be, fully, by September this year), and breasts just beginning. Very very beautiful skin, like lucite. Amparo Martinez.

Their first, nothing operation was in the East 60's, a broker or something like that. All they netted was cufflinks, a watch, a leather satchel that wasn't leather after all, some buttons, and the usual lot of useless credit cards. He stayed calm through the whole thing, even with Sniffles slicing off buttons, and *soothing*. None of them had the nerve to ask, though they all wondered, how often he'd been through this scene before. What they were about wasn't an innovation. It was partly that, the need to innovate, that led them to think up the plot. The only really memorable part of the holdup was the name laminated on the cards, which was, weirdly enough, Lowen, Richard W. An omen (the connection being that they were all at the Alexander Lowen School), but of what?

Little Mister Kissy Lips kept the cufflinks for himself, gave the buttons to Amparo (who gave them to her uncle), and donated the rest (the watch was a piece of crap) to the Conservation booth outside the Plaza right where he lived.

His father was a teevee executive. In, as he would quip, both senses. They had got married young, his mama and papa, and divorced soon after but not before he'd come to fill out their quota. Papa, the executive, remarried, a man this time and somewhat more happily. Anyhow it lasted long enough that the offspring, the leader and mastermind, had to learn to adjust to the situation, it being permanent. Mama simply went down to the Everglades and disappeared, sploosh.

In short, he was well to do. Which is how, more than by overwhelming talent, he got into the Lowen School in the first place. He had the right kind of body though, so with half a desire there was no reason in the city of New York he couldn't grow up to be a professional dancer, even a choreographer. He'd have the connections for it, as Papa was fond of pointing out.

For the time being, however, his bent was literary and religious rather than balletic. He loved, and what seventh grader doesn't, the abstracter foxtrots and more metaphysical twists of a Dostoevsky, a Gide, a Mailer. He longed for the experience of some vivider pain than the mere daily hollowness knotted into his tight young belly, and no weekly stomp-and-holler of group therapy with other jejune eleven-year-olds was going to get him his stripes in the major leagues of suffering, crime, and resurrection. Only a bonafide crime would do that, and of all the crimes available, murder certainly carried the most prestige, as no less an authority than Loretta Couplard was ready to attest, Loretta Couplard being not only the director and co-owner of the Lowen School but the author, as well, of two nationally televised scripts, both about famous murders of the 20th Century. They'd even done a unit in social studies on the topic: A History of Crime in Urban America.

The first of Loretta's murders was a comedy involving Pauline Campbell, R.N., of Ann Arbor, Michigan, circa 1951, whose skull had been smashed by three drunken teen-agers. They had meant to knock her unconscious so they could screw her, which was 1951 in a nutshell. The eighteen-year-olds, Bill Morey and Max Pell, got life; Dave Royal (Loretta's hero) was a year younger and got off with twenty-two years.

Her second murder was tragic in tone and consequently inspired more respect, though not among the critics, unfortunately. Possibly because her heroine, also a Pauline (Pauline Wichura), though more interesting and complicated, had also been more famous in her own day and ever since. Which made the competition, one best-selling novel and a serious film biography, considerably stiffer. Miss Wichura had been a welfare worker in Atlanta, Georgia, very much into environment and the population problem, this being the im-mediate pre-Regents period when anyone and everyone was legitimately starting to fret. Pauline decided to do something, *viz.*, reduce the population herself and in the fairest way pos-sible. So whenever any of the families she visited produced one child above the three she'd fixed, rather generously, as the upward limit, she found some unobtrusive way of thin-ning that family back to the preferred maximal size. Between 1989 and 1993 Pauline's journals (Random House, 1994) record twenty-six murders, plus an additional fourteen failed attempts. In addition she had the highest welfare department record in the U.S. for abortions and sterilizations among the families whom she advised.

"Which proves, I think," Little Mister Kissy Lips had ex-plained one day after school to his friend Jack, "that a murder doesn't have to be of someone *famous* to be a form of idealism."

But of course idealism was only half the story: the other half was curiosity. And beyond idealism *and* curiosity there was probably even another half, the basic childhood need to grow up and kill someone.

They settled on the Battery, because, one, none of them ever were there ordinarily; two, it was posh and at the same time relatively, three, uncrowded, at least once the night shift were snug in their towers tending their machines. The night shift seldom ate their lunches down in the park.

And, four, because it was beautiful, especially now at the

beginning of summer. The dark water, chromed with oil, flopping against the buttressed shore; the silences blowing in off the Upper Bay, silences large enough sometimes that you could sort out the different noises of the city behind them, the purr and quaver of the skyscrapers, the ground-shivering *mysterioso* of the expressways, and every now and then the strange sourceless screams that are the melody of New York's theme song; the blue-pink of sunsets in a visible sky; the people's faces, calmed by the sea and their own nearness to death, lined up in rhythmic rows on the green benches. Why even the statues looked beautiful here, as though someone had believed in them once, the way people must have believed in the statues in the Cloisters, so long ago.

His favorite was the gigantic killer-eagle landing in the middle of the monoliths in the memorial for the soldiers, sailors, and airmen killed in World War II. The largest eagle, probably, in all Manhattan. His talons ripped apart what was *surely* the largest artichoke.

Amparo, who went along with some of Miss Couplard's ideas, preferred the more humanistic qualities of the memorial (him on top and an angel gently probing an enormous book with her sword) for Verrazano, who was not, as it turned out, the contractor who put up the bridge that had, so famously, collapsed. Instead, as the bronze plate in back proclaimed:

IN APRIL 1524
THE FLORENTINE-BORN NAVIGATOR
VERRAZANO
LED THE FRENCH CARAVEL LA DAUPHINE
TO THE DISCOVERY OF
THE HARBOR OF NEW YORK
AND NAMED THESE SHORES ANGOULEME
IN HONOR OF FRANCIS I KING OF FRANCE

"Angouleme" they all agreed, except Tancred, who favored the more prevalent and briefer name, was much classier. Tancred was ruled out of order and the decision became unanimous.

It was there, by the statue, looking across the bay of Angouleme to Jersey, that they took the oath that bound them to perpetual secrecy. Whoever spoke of what they were about to do, unless he was being tortured by the Police, solemnly called upon his co-conspirators to insure his silence by other means. Death. All revolutionary organizations take similar precautions, as the history unit on Modern Revolutions had made clear.

How he got the name: it had been Papa's theory that what modern life cried out for was a sweetening of old-fashioned sentimentality. Ergo, among all the other indignities this theory gave rise to, scenes like the following: "Who's my Little Mister Kissy Lips!" Papa would bawl out, sweetly, right in the middle of Rockefeller Center (or a restaurant, or in front of the school), and he'd shout right back, "I am!" At least until he knew better.

Mama had been, variously, "Rosebud," "Peg o' My Heart," and (this only at the end) "The Snow Queen." Mama, being adult, had been able to vanish with no other trace than the postcard that still came every Xmas postmarked from Key Largo, but Little Mister Kissy Lips was stuck with the New Sentimentality willy-nilly. True, by age seven he'd been able to insist on being called "Bill" around the house (or, as Papa would have it, "Just Plain Bill"). But that left the staff at the Plaza to contend with, and Papa's assistants, schoolmates, anyone who'd ever heard the name. Then a year ago, aged ten and able to reason, he laid down the new law—that his name *was* Little Mister Kissy Lips, the whole awful mouthful, each and every time. His reasoning being that if anyone would be getting his face rubbed in shit by this it would be Papa, who deserved it. Papa didn't seem to get the point, or else he got it and another point besides, you could never be sure how stupid or how subtle he really was, which is the worst kind of enemy.

Meanwhile at the nationwide level the New Sentimentality had been a rather overwhelming smash. "The Orphans," which Papa produced, and sometimes was credited with writing, pulled down the top Thursday evening rations for two years. Now it was being overhauled for a daytime slot. For one hour every day our lives were going to be a lot sweeter, and chances were Papa would be a millionaire or more as a result. On the sunny side this meant that *he'd* be the son of a millionaire. Though he generally had contempt for the way money corrupted everything it touched, he had to admit that in certain cases it didn't have to be a bad thing. It boiled down to this (which he'd always known): that Papa was a necessary evil.

This was why every evening when Papa buzzed himself

into the suite he'd shout out, "Where's my Little Mister Kissy Lips," and he'd reply, "Here, Papa!" The cherry on this sundae of love was a big wet kiss, and then one more for their new "Rosebud," Jimmy Ness. (Who drank, and was not in all likelihood going to last much longer.) They'd all three sit down to the nice *family* dinner Jimmyness had cooked, and Papa would tell them about the cheerful, positive things that had happened that day at CBS, and Little Mister Kissy Lips would tell all about the bright fine things that had happened to *him.* Jimmy would sulk. Then Papa and Jimmy would go somewhere or just disappear into the private Everglades of sex, and Little Mister Kissy Lips would buzz himself out into the corridor (Papa knew better than to be repressive about hours), and within half an hour he'd be at the Verrazano statue with the six other Alexandrians, five if Celeste had a lesson, to plot the murder of the victim they'd all finally agreed on.

No one had been able to find out his name. They called him Alyona Ivanovna, after the old pawnbroker woman that Raskolnikov kills with an ax.

The spectrum of possible victims had never been wide. The common financial types of the area would be carrying credit cards like Lowen, Richard W., while the generality of pensioners filling the benches were even less tempting. As Miss Couplard had explained, our economy was being refeudalized and cash was going the way of the ostrich, the octopus, and the moccasin flower.

It was such extinctions as these, but especially seagulls, that were the worry of the first lady they'd considered, a Miss Kraus, unless the name at the bottom of her handlettered poster (STOP THE SLAUGHTER of The *Innocents*!! etc.) belonged to someone else. Why, if she was Miss Kraus, was she wearing what seemed to be the old-fashioned diamond ring and gold band of a Mrs.? But the more crucial problem, which they couldn't see how to solve, was: was the diamond real?

Possibility Number Two was in the tradition of the original Orphans of the Storm, the Gish sisters. A lovely semiprofessional who whiled away the daylight pretending to be blind and serenading the benches. Her pathos was rich, if a bit worked-up; her repertoire was archaeological; and her gross was fair, especially when the rain added its own bit of too-much. However: Sniffles (who'd done this research) was certain she had a gun tucked away under the rags.

Three was the least poetic possibility, just the concessionaire in back of the giant eagle selling Fun and Synthamon. His appeal was commercial. But he had a licensed Weimaraner, and though Weimaraners can be dealt with, Amparo liked them.

"You're just a Romantic," Little Mister Kissy Lips said. "Give me one good reason."

"His eyes," she said. "They're amber. He'd haunt us."

They were snuggling together in one of the deep embrasures cut into the stone of Castle Clinton, her head wedged into his armpit, his fingers gliding across the lotion on her breasts (summer was just beginning). Silence, warm breezes, sunlight on water, it was all ineffable, as though only the sheerest of veils intruded between them and an understanding of something (all this) really meaningful. Because they thought it was their own innocence that was to blame, like a smog in their souls' atmosphere, they wanted more than ever to be rid of it at times, like this, when they approached so close.

"Why not the dirty old man, then?" she asked, meaning Alyona.

"Because he *is* a dirty old man."

"That's no reason. He must take in at least as much money as that singer."

"That's not what I mean." What he meant wasn't easy to define. It wasn't as though he'd be too easy to kill. If you'd seen him in the first minutes of a program, you'd know he was marked for destruction by the second commercial. He was the defiant homesteader, the crusty senior member of a research team who understood Algol and Fortran but couldn't read the secrets of his own heart. He was the Senator from South Carolina with his own peculiar brand of integrity but a racist nevertheless. Killing that sort was too much like one of Papa's scripts to be a satisfying gesture of rebellion.

But what he said, mistaking his own deeper meaning, was: "It's because he deserves it, because we'd be doing society a favor. Don't ask me to give *reasons*."

"Well, I won't pretend I understand that, but do you know what I think, Little Mister Kissy Lips?" She pushed his hand away.

"You think I'm scared."

"Maybe you *should* be scared."

"Maybe you should shut up and leave this to me. I said we're going to do it. We'll do it."

"To him then?"

"Okay. But for gosh sakes, Amparo, we've got to think of something to call the bastard besides 'the dirty old man'!"

She rolled over out of his armpit and kissed him. They glittered all over with little beads of sweat. The summer began to shimmer with the excitement of first night. They had been waiting so long and now the curtain was rising.

M-Day was scheduled for the first weekend in July, a patriotic holiday. The computers would have time to tend to their own needs (which have been variously described as "confession," "dreaming," and "throwing up"), and the Battery would be as empty as it ever gets.

Meanwhile their problem was the same as any kids face anywhere during summer vacation, how to fill the time.

There were books, there were the Shakespeare puppets if you were willing to queue up for that long, there was always teevee, and when you couldn't stand sitting any longer there were the obstacle courses in Central Park, but the density there was at lemming level. The Battery, because it didn't try to meet anyone's needs, seldom got so overpopulated. If there had been more Alexandrians and all willing to fight for the space, they might have played ball. Well, another summer . . .

What else? There were marches for the political, and religions at various energy levels for the apolitical. There would have been dancing, but the Lowen School had spoiled them for most amateur events around the city.

As for the supreme pastime of sex, for all of them except Little Mister Kissy Lips and Amparo (and even for them, when it came right down to orgasm) this was still something that happened on a screen, a wonderful hypothesis that lacked empirical proof.

One way or another it was all consumership, everything they might have done, and they were tired, who isn't, of being passive. They were twelve years old, or eleven, or ten, and they couldn't wait any longer. For what? they wanted to know.

So, except when they were just loafing around solo, all these putative resources, the books, the puppets, the sports, arts, politics, and religions, were in the same category of usefulness as merit badges or weekends in Calcutta, which is a name you can still find on a few old maps of India. Their lives were not enhanced, and their summer passed as summers have passed immemorially. They slumped and moped and lounged about and teased each other and complained. They acted out desultory, shy fantasies and had long pointless arguments about the more peripheral facts of existence—the habits of jungle animals or how bricks had been made or the history of World War II.

One day they added up all the names on the monoliths set up for the soldiers, sailors, and airmen. The final figure they got was 4,800.

"Wow," said Tancred.

"But that can't be *all* of them," MaryJane insisted, speaking for the rest. Even that "wow" had sounded half ironic.

"Why not?" asked Tancred, who could never resist disagreeing. "They came from every different state and every branch of the service. It has to be complete or the people who had relatives left off would have protested."

"But so *few?* It wouldn't be possible to have fought more than one battle at that rate."

"Maybe . . ." Sniffles began quietly. But he was seldom listened to.

"Wars were different then," Tancred explained with the authority of a prime-time news analyst. "In those days more people were killed by their own automobiles than in wars. It's a fact."

"Four thousand, eight *hundred?*"

". . . a lottery?"

Celeste waved away everything Sniffles had said or would ever say. "MaryJane is right, Tancred. It's simply a *ludicrous* number. Why, in that same war the Germans gassed seven *million* Jews."

"Six million Jews," Little Mister Kissy Lips corrected. "But it's the same idea. Maybe the ones here got killed in a particular campaign."

"Then it would say so." Tancred was adamant, and he even got them to admit at last that 4,800 was an impressive figure, especially with every name spelled out in stone letters.

One other amazing statistic was commemorated in the park: over a thirty-three-year period Castle Clinton had processed 7.7 million immigrants into the United States.

Little Mister Kissy Lips sat down and figured out that, it would take 12,800 stone slabs the size of the ones listing the soldiers, sailors, and airmen in order to write out all the immigrants' names, with country of origin, and an area of five square miles to set that many slabs up in, or all of Manhattan from here to 28th Street. But would it be worth the trouble, after all? Would it be that much different from the way things were already?

Alyona Ivanovna:

An archipelago of irregular brown islands were mapped on the tan sea of his bald head. The mainlands of his hair were marble outcroppings, especially his beard, white and crisp and coiling. The teeth were standard MODICUM issue; clothes, as clean as any fabric that old can be. Nor did he smell, particularly. And yet . . .

Had he bathed every morning you'd still have looked at him and thought he was filthy, the way floorboards in old brownstones seem to need cleaning moments after they've been scrubbed. The dirt had been bonded to the wrinkled flesh and the wrinkled clothes, and nothing less than surgery or burning would get it out.

His habits were as orderly as a polka dot napkin. He lived at a Chelsea dorm for the elderly, a discovery they owed to a rainstorm that had forced him to take the subway home one day instead of, as usual, walking. On the hottest nights he might sleep over in the park, nesting in one of the Castle windows. He bought his lunches from a Water Street specialty shop, *Dumas Fils:* cheeses, imported fruit, smoked fish, bottles of cream, food for the gods. Otherwise he did without, though his dorm must have supplied prosaic necessities like breakfast. It was a strange way for a panhandler to spend his quarters, drugs being the norm.

His professional approach was out-and-out aggression. For instance, his hand in your face and, "How about it, Jack?" Or, confidingly, "I need sixty cents to get home." It was amazing how often he scored, but actually it wasn't amazing. He had charisma.

And someone who relies on charisma *wouldn't* have a gun.

Agewise he might have been sixty, seventy, seventy-five, a bit more even, or much less. It all depended on the kind of life he'd led, and where. He had an accent none of them could identify. It was not English, not French, not Spanish, and probably not Russian.

Aside from his burrow in the Castle wall there were two distinct places he preferred. One, the wide-open stretch of pavement along the water. This was where he worked, walking up past the Castle and down as far as the concession stand. The passage of one of the great Navy cruisers, the USS *Dana* or the USS *Melville,* would bring him, and the whole Battery, to a standstill, as though a whole parade were going by, white, soundless, slow as a dream. It was a part of history, and even the Alexandrians were impressed, though three of them had taken the cruise down to Andros Island and back. Sometimes though, he'd stand by the guardrail for long stretches of time without any real reason, just looking at the Jersey sky and the Jersey shore. After a while he might start talking to himself, the barest whisper but very much in earnest to judge by the way his forehead wrinkled. They never once saw him sit on one of the benches.

The other place he liked was the aviary. On days when they'd been ignored he'd contribute peanuts or breadcrumbs to the cause of the birds' existence. There were pigeons, parrots, a family of robins, and a proletarian swarm of what the sign declared to be chickadees, though Celeste, who'd gone to the library to make sure, said they were nothing more than a rather swank breed of sparrow. Here, too, naturally, the militant Miss Kraus stationed herself when she bore testimony. One of her peculiarities (and the reason, probably, she was never asked to move on) was that under no circumstances did she ever deign to argue. Even sympathizers pried no more out of her than a grim smile and a curt nod.

One Tuesday, a week before M-Day (it was the early A.M. and only three Alexandrians were on hand to witness this confrontation), Alyona so far put aside his own reticence as to try to start a conversation going with Miss Kraus.

He stood squarely in front of her and began by reading aloud, slowly, in that distressingly indefinite accent, from the text of STOP THE SLAUGHTER: "The Department of the Interior of the United States Government, under the secret direction of the Zionist Ford Foundation, is *systematically* poisoning the oceans of the World with so-called 'food farms.' Is this 'peaceful application of Nuclear Power'? Unquote, the *New York Times,* August 2, 2024. Or a new Moondoggle!! *Nature World,* Jan. Can we afford to remain indifferent any longer. Every day 15,000 seagulls die as a direct result of Systematic Genocides while elected Officials falsify and distort the evidence. Learn the facts. Write to the Congressmen. *Make your voice heard!!*"

As Alyona had droned on, Miss Kraus turned a deeper and deeper red. Tightening her fingers about the turquoise broomhandle to which the placard was stapled, she began to jerk the poster up and down rapidly, as though this man with his foreign accent were some bird of prey who'd perched on it.

"Is that what you think?" he asked, having read all the way down to the signature despite her jiggling tactic. He touched his bushy white beard and wrinkled his face into a philosophical expression. "I'd *like* to know more about it, yes, I would. I'd be interested in hearing what *you* think."

Horror had frozen up every motion of her limbs. Her eyes blinked shut but she forced them open again.

"Maybe," he went on remorselessly, "we can discuss this whole thing. Sometime when you feel more like talking. All right?"

She mustered her smile, and a minimal nod. He went away then. She was safe, temporarily, but even so she waited till he'd gone halfway to the other end of the sea-front promenade before she let the air collapse into her lungs. After a single deep breath the muscles of her hands thawed into trembling.

M-Day was an oil of summer, a catalog of everything painters are happiest painting—clouds, flags, leaves, sexy people, and in back of it all the flat empty baby-blue of the sky. Little Mister Kissy Lips was the first one there, and Tancred, in a kind of kimono (it hid the pilfered Luger), was the last. Celeste never came. (She'd just learned she'd been awarded the exchange scholarship to Sofia.) They decided they could do without Celeste, but the other nonappearance was more crucial. Their victim had neglected to be on hand for M-Day. Sniffles, whose voice was most like an adult's over the phone, was delegated to go to the Citibank lobby and call the West 16th Street dorm.

The nurse who answered was a temporary. Sniffles, always an inspired liar, insisted that his mother—"Mrs. *Anderson*, of course she lives there, Mrs. Alma F. Anderson"—had to be called to the phone. This was 248 West 16th, wasn't it? Where *was* she if she wasn't there? The nurse, flustered, explained that the residents, all who were fit, had been driven off to a July 4th picnic at Lake Hopatcong as guests of a giant Jersey retirement condominium. If he called bright and early tomorrow they'd be back and he could talk to his mother then.

So the initiation rites were postponed, it couldn't be helped.

Amparo passed around some pills she'd taken from her mother's jar, a consolation prize. Jack left, apologizing that he was a borderline psychotic, which was the last that anyone saw of Jack till September. The gang was disintegrating, like a sugar cube soaking up saliva, then crumbling into the tongue. But what the hell—the sea still mirrored the same blue sky, the pigeons behind their wicket were no less iridescent, and trees grew for all of that.

They decided to be silly and make jokes about what the M *really* stood for in M-Day. Sniffles started off with "Miss Nomer, Miss Carriage, and Miss Steak." Tancred, whose sense of humor did not exist or was very private, couldn't do better than "Mnemone, mother of the Muses." Little Mister Kissy Lips said, "Merciful Heavens!" MaryJane maintained reasonably that M was for MaryJane. But Amparo said it stood for "Aplomb" and carried the day.

Then, proving that when you're sailing the wind always blows from behind you, they found Terry Riley's day-long *Orfeo* at 99.5 on the FM dial. They'd studied *Orfeo* in mime class, and by now it was part of their muscle and nerve. As Orpheus descended into a hell that mushroomed from the size of a pea to the size of a planet, the Alexandrians metamorphosed into as credible a tribe of souls in torment as any since the days of Jacopo Peri. Throughout the afternoon little audiences collected and dispersed to flood the sidewalk with libations of adult attention. Expressively they surpassed themselves, both one by one and all together, and though they couldn't have held out till the apotheosis (at 9:30) without a stiff psychochemical wind in their sails, what they had danced was authentic and very much their own. When they left the Battery that night they felt better than they'd felt all summer long. In a sense they had been exorcised.

But back at the Plaza Little Mister Kissy Lips couldn't sleep. No sooner was he through the locks than his guts knotted up into a Chinese puzzle. Only after he'd unlocked his window and crawled out onto the ledge did he get rid of the bad feelings. The city was real. His room was not. The stone ledge was real and his bare buttocks absorbed reality from it. He watched slow movements in enormous distances and pulled his thoughts together.

He knew without having to talk to the rest that the murder would never take place. The idea had never meant for them what it had meant for him. One pill and they were actors again, content to be images in a mirror.

Slowly, as he watched, the city turned itself off. Slowly the dawn divided the sky into an east and a west. Had a pedestrian been going past on 58th Street and had that pedestrian looked up, he would have seen the bare soles of a boy's feet swinging back and forth, angelically.

He would have to kill Alyona Ivanovna himself. Nothing else was possible.

Back in his bedroom, long ago, the phone was ringing its fuzzy nighttime ring. That would be Tancred (or Amparo?) trying to talk him out of it. He foresaw their arguments. Celeste and Jack couldn't be trusted now. Or, more subtly: they'd all made themselves too visible with their *Orfeo*. If there were even a small investigation, the benches would remember them, remember how well they had danced, and the police would know where to look.

But the real reason, which at least Amparo would have been ashamed to mention now that the pill was wearing off, was that they'd begun to feel sorry for their victim. They'd got to know him too well over the last month and their resolve had been eroded by compassion.

A light came on in Papa's window. Time to begin. He stood up, golden in the sunbeams of another perfect day, and walked back along the foot-wide ledge to his own window. His legs tingled from having sat so long.

He waited till Papa was in the shower, then tippytoed to the old secretaire in his bedroom (W. & J. Sloan, 1952). Papa's keychain was coiled atop the walnut veneer. Inside the secretaire's drawer was an antique Mexican cigar box, and in the cigar box a velvet bag, and in the velvet bag Papa's replica of a French dueling pistol, circa 1790. These precautions were less for his son's sake than on account of Jimmy Ness, who every so often felt obliged to show he was serious with his suicide threats.

He'd studied the booklet carefully when Papa had bought the pistol and was able to execute the loading procedure quickly and without error, tamping the premeasured twist of powder down into the barrel and then the lead ball on top of it.

He cocked the hammer back a single click.

He locked the drawer. He replaced the keys, just so. He buried, for now, the pistol in the stuffs and cushions of the Turkish corner, tilted upright to keep the ball from rolling out. Then with what remained of yesterday's ebullience he bounced into the bathroom and kissed Papa's cheek, damp with the morning's allotted two gallons and redolent of 4711.

They had a cheery breakfast together in the coffee room, which was identical to the breakfast they would have made for themselves except for the ritual of being waited on by a waitress. Little Mister Kissy Lips gave an enthusiastic account of the Alexandrians' performance of *Orfeo,* and Papa made his best effort of seeming not to condescend. When he'd been driven to the limit of this pretense, Little Mister Kissy Lips touched him for a second pill, and since it was better for a boy to get these things from his father than from a stranger on the street, he got it.

He reached the South Ferry stop at noon, bursting with a sense of his own imminent liberation. The weather was M-Day all over again, as though at midnight out on the ledge he'd forced time to go backwards to the point when things had started going wrong. He'd dressed in his most anonymous shorts and the pistol hung from his belt in a dun dittybag.

Alyona Ivanovna was sitting on one of the benches, near the aviary, listening to Miss Kraus. Her ring hand gripped the poster firmly, while the right chopped at the air, eloquently awkward, like a mute's first words following a miraculous cure.

Little Mister Kissy Lips went down the path and squatted in the shadow of his memorial. It had lost its magic yesterday, when the statues had begun to look so silly to everyone. They still looked silly. Verrazano was dressed like a Victorian industrialist taking a holiday in the Alps. The angel was wearing an angel's usual bronze nightgown.

His good feelings were leaving his head by little and little, like aeolian sandstone attrited by the centuries of wind. He thought of calling up Amparo, but any comfort she might bring to him would be a mirage so long as his purpose in coming here remained unfulfilled.

He looked at his wrist, then remembered he'd left his watch home. The gigantic advertising clock on the facade of the First National Citibank said it was fifteen after two. That wasn't possible.

Miss Kraus was *still* yammering away.

There was time to watch a cloud move across the sky from Jersey, over the Hudson, and past the sun. Unseen winds nibbled at its wispy edges. The cloud became his life, which would disappear without ever having turned into rain.

Later, and the old man was walking up the sea promenade toward the Castle. He stalked him, for miles. And then they were alone, together at the far end of the park.

"Hello," he said, with the smile reserved for grown-ups of doubtful importance.

He looked directly at the dittybag, but Little Mister Kissy Lips didn't lose his composure. He would be wondering whether to ask for money, which would be kept, if he'd had any, in the bag. The pistol made a noticeable bulge but not the kind of bulge one would ordinarily associate with a pistol.

"Sorry," he said coolly. "I'm broke."

"Did I ask?"

"You were going to."

The old man made as if to return in the other direction, so he had to speak quickly, something that would hold him here.

"I saw you speaking with Miss Kraus."

He was held.

"Congratulations—you broke through the ice!"

The old man half-smiled, half-frowned. "You know her?"

"Mm. You could say that we're *aware* of her." The "we" had been a deliberate risk, an hors d'oeuvre. Touching a finger to each side of the strings by which the heavy bag hung from his belt, he urged on it a lazy pendular motion. "Do you mind if I ask you a question?"

There was nothing indulgent now in the man's face. "I probably do."

His smile had lost the hard edge of calculation. It was the same smile he'd have smiled for Papa, for Amparo, for Miss Couplard, for anyone he liked. "Where do you come from? I mean, what country?"

"That's none of your business, is it?"

"Well, I just wanted . . . to know."

The old man (he had ceased, somehow, to be Alyona Ivanovna) turned away and walked directly toward the squat stone cylinder of the old fortress.

He remembered how the plaque at the entrance—the same that had cited the 7.7 million—had said that Jenny Lind had sung there and it had been a great success.

The old man unzipped his fly and, lifting out his cock, began pissing on the wall.

Little Mister Kissy Lips fumbled with the strings of the bag. It was remarkable how long the old man stood there pissing because despite every effort of the stupid knot to stay tied he had the pistol out before the final sprinkle had been shaken out.

He laid the fulminate cap on the exposed nipple, drew the hammer back two clicks, past the safety, and aimed.

The man made no haste zipping up. Only then did he glance in Little Mister Kissy Lips' direction. He saw the pistol aimed at him. They stood not twenty feet apart, so he must have seen it.

He said, "Ha!" And even this, rather than being addressed to the boy with the gun, was only a parenthesis from the faintly aggrieved monologue he resumed each day at the edge of the water. He turned away and a moment later he was back on the job, hand out, asking some fellow for a quarter.

—New York,
April, 1970

The Postwar Generation

When historians and critics write about "new generations," the phrase is meant metaphorically: They are describing groups of writers who seem to have similar views, similar interests, and similar styles of writing, and these seem to break with the past. Often the generations have shared common experiences that have marked them: the lost generation of World War I, the Prohibition generation of the 1920s, the hungry generation of the Great Depression, the pragmatic generation of World War II, the alienated generation of the Vietnam War, and no doubt others. The matter of actual chronological age seldom is considered.

Poul Anderson and Damon Knight have suggested that a major new generation of science fiction writers seems to come along every decade or so, but no one has studied birthdates. A preliminary survey suggests that certain years have been prolific with writers and others have been singularly unproductive: 1911, for instance, saw the births of Otto Binder, Finney, Gallun, Hubbard, C. L. Moore, Norton, St. Clair, Schmitz, and George O. Smith among major writers, while the years all around had at most four, usually three, and sometimes one or none; 1915 was another bonus year with Brackett, del Rey, Godwin, Hoyle, Raymond F. Jones, Kuttner, Tiptree (Sheldon), and Young, which would not be equaled until 1920 with Asimov, Galouye, Herbert, Tenn (Klass), Theodore Thomas, Tubb, Vance, and Richard Wilson, and 1923 with Biggle, Bixby, Davidson, Dickson, Gunn, Merril, Walter Miller, Jr., and Vonnegut.

No doubt the clustering is meaningless, and yet of the sto-

ries included in this volume that were published after 1970,
four of the authors were born in 1945, three were born in
1947, and four were born in 1948. Perhaps there is a magic
in numbers.

Pamela Sargent (1948–   ) worked as a saleswoman and
model, assembly-line worker, typist, office worker, and
teaching assistant while getting an education at the State University of New York at Binghamton that culminated in a
master of arts degree in classical philosophy and the history
of philosophy. Her first story, "Landed Minority," was published in the September 1970 *Magazine of Fantasy and
Science Fiction*. Her short stories have been collected in *Star-
shadows* (1977).

The mid-1970s saw the publication of the first of a series
of ambitious novels: *Cloned Lives* (1976) followed by *The
Sudden Star* (1979), *Watchstar* (1980), and *The Golden
Space* (1982). *The Alien Upstairs* has been scheduled for
1983 publication. She has edited four anthologies: *Bio-Fu-
tures* (1976) and three anthologies of science fiction by
women about women, *Women of Wonder* (1975), *More
Women of Wonder* (1976), and *The New Women of Wonder* (1978).

One of the major themes of science fiction has been the
discovery or development of superpowers. Often they become
the means to right wrongs or prepare the way for a new society or even a new race; sometimes the powers are used for
evil, for individual profit or for power. Later uses sometimes
focused on the difficulty of hiding new abilities or coping
with them, or even on the loneliness of the people who have
them (as in "Nobody Bothers Gus"). The post-Holocaust
generation often saw them as additional punishments.

"Gather Blue Roses" seems like an ordinary story about
the difficulties of growing up when one is different. In this
case the child is Jewish, sensitive, retiring, and a twin, and
her mother had survived a Nazi death camp. The unnamed
child also must cope with her mother's fragility of spirit, and
her mother's occasional need to leave her family and spend
some time alone. Only halfway through the story does a suggestion creep into the narrative that something out of the
ordinary may be involved, something that will justify classifying it as science fiction, and only at the end does the peculiar
horror of the mother's affliction become clear and only at the
end is the daughter's sensitivity revealed as a curse worse
than her mother's.

The story is told in remarkably few and simple words, words appropriate to a child. The author has the additional problem of revealing the life the daughter must lead when she has grown up; rather than tacking on a later scene or an awkward postscript, Sargent tells the story simultaneously on two levels: The childhood level is told in retrospect from the viewpoint of the adult; later knowledge and current experience are interpolated within parentheses. Both levels reach simultaneous revelations; the ultimate statement of the situation coincides with its resolution.

Gather Blue Roses

by Pamela Sargent

I cannot remember ever having asked my mother outright about the tattooed numbers. We must have known very early that we should not ask; perhaps my brother Simon or I had said something inadvertently as very small children and had seen the look of sorrow on her face at the statement; perhaps my father had told us never to ask.

Of course, we were always aware of the numbers. There were those times when the weather was particularly warm, and my mother would not button her blouse at the top, and she would lean over us to hug us or pick us up, and we would see them written across her, an inch above her breasts.

(By the time I reached my adolescence, I had heard all the horror stories about the death camps and the ovens; about those who had to remove gold teeth from the bodies; the women used, despite the Reich's edicts, by the soldiers and guards. I then regarded my mother with ambivalence, saying to myself, I would have died first, I would have found some way rather than suffering such dishonor, wondering what had happened to her and what secret sins she had on her conscience, and what she had done to survive. An old man, a doctor, had said to me once, "The best ones of us died, the most honorable, the most sensitive." And I would thank God I had been born in 1949; there was no chance that I was the daughter of a Nazi rape.)

By the time I was four, we had moved to an old frame house in the country, and my father had taken a job teaching at a small junior college near by, turning down his offers from Columbia and Chicago, knowing how impossible that would be for mother. We had a lot of elms and oaks and a huge weeping willow that hovered sadly over the house. Our pond would be invaded in the early spring and late fall by a few geese, which would usually keep their distance before flying on. ("You can tell those birds are Jewish," my father would say, "they go to Miami in the winter," and Simon and I would imagine them lying on a beach, coating their feathers with Coppertone and ordering lemonades from the waitresses; we hadn't heard of Collinses yet.)

Even out in the country, there were often those times when we would see my mother packing her clothes in a small suitcase, and she would tell us that she was going away for a while, just a week, just to get away, to find solitude. One time it was to an old camp in the Adirondacks that one of my aunts owned, another time to a cabin that a friend of my father's loaned her, always alone, always to an isolated place. Father would say that it was "nerves," although we wondered, since we were so isolated as it was. Simon and I thought she didn't love us, that mother was somehow using this means to tell us that we were being rejected. I would try very hard to behave; when mother was resting, I would tip-toe and whisper. Simon reacted more violently. He could contain himself for a while; but then, in a desperate attempt at drawing attention to himself, would run through the house, screaming horribly, and hurl himself, head first, at one of the radiators. On one occasion, he threw himself through one of the large living room windows, smashing the glass. Fortunately, he was uninjured, except for cuts and bruises, but after that incident, my father put chicken wire over the windows on the inside of the house. Mother was very shaken by that incident, walking around for a couple of days, her body aching all over, then going away to my aunt's place for three weeks this time. Simon's head must have been strong; he never sustained any damage from the radiators worse than a few bumps and a headache, but the headaches would often keep mother in bed for days.

(I pick up my binoculars to check the forest again from my tower, seeing the small lakes like puddles below, using my glasses to focus on a couple in a small boat near one of the islands, and then turn away from them, not wanting to invade their privacy, envying the girl and boy who can so freely, without fear of consequences, exchange and share their feelings, and yet not share them, not at least in the way that would destroy a person such as myself. I do not think anyone will risk climbing my mountain today, as the sky is overcast, cirro-cumulus clouds slowly chasing each other, a large storm cloud in the west. I hope no one will come; the family who picnicked beneath my observation tower yesterday bothered me; one child had a headache and another indigestion, and I lay in my cabin taking aspirins all afternoon and nursing the heaviness in my stomach. I hope no one will come today.)

Mother and father did not send us to school until we were as old as the law would allow. We went to the small public school in town. An old yellow bus would pick us up in front of the house. I was scared the first day and was glad Simon and I were twins so that we could go together. The town had built a new school; it was a small, square brick building, and there were fifteen of us in the first grade. The high school students went to classes in the same building. I was afraid of them and was glad to discover that their classes were all on the second floor; so we rarely saw them during the day except when they had gym classes outside. Sitting at my desk inside, I would watch them, wincing every time someone got hit with a ball, or got bruised. (Only three months in school, thank God, before my father got permission to tutor me at home, three months were too much of the constant pains, the turmoil of emotions; I am sweating now and my hands shake, when I remember it all.)

The first day was boring to me for the most part; Simon and I had been reading and doing arithmetic at home for as long as I could remember. I played dumb and did as I was told; Simon was aggressive, showing off, knowing it all. The other kids giggled, pointing at me, pointing at Simon, whispering. I felt some of it, but not enough to bother me too much; I was not then as I am now, not that first day.

Recess: kids yelling, running, climbing the jungle gym, swinging and chinning themselves on bars, chasing a basketball. I was with two girls and a piece of chalk on the blacktop; they taught me hopscotch, and I did my best to ignore the bruises and bumps of the other students.

(I need the peace, the retreat from easily communicated pain. How strange, I think objectively, that our lives are such that discomfort, pain, sadness and hatred are so easily conveyed and so frequently felt. Love and contentment are only soft veils which do not protect me from bludgeons; and with the strongest loves, one can still sense the more violent undercurrents of fear, hate and jealousy.)

It was at the end of the second week that the incident occurred during recess. I was, again, playing hopscotch, and Simon had come over to look at what we were doing before joining some other boys. Five older kids came over. I guess they were in third or fourth grade, and they began their taunts.

"Greeeeenbaum," at Simon and me. We both turned toward them, I balancing on one foot on the hopscotch squares we had drawn, Simon clenching his fists.

"Greeeeeenbaum, Esther Greeeeeenbaum, Simon Greeeeeenbaum," whinnying the green, thundering the baum.

"My father says you're Yids."

"He says you're the Yid's kids." One boy hooted and yelled. "Hey, they're Yid kids." Some giggled, and then they chanted, "Yid kid, Yid kid," as one of them pushed me off my square.

"You leave my sister alone," Simon yelled and went for the boy, fists flying, and knocked him over. The boy sat down suddenly, and I felt pain in my lower back. Another boy ran over and punched Simon. Simon whacked him back, and the boy hit him in the nose, hard. It hurt and I started crying from the pain, holding my nose, pulled away my hand and saw blood. Simon's nose was bleeding, and then the other kids started in, trying to pummel my brother, one guy holding him, another guy punching. "Stop it," I screamed, "stop it," as I curled on the ground, hurting, seeing the teachers run over to pull them apart. Then I fainted, mercifully, and came to in the nurse's office. They kept me there until it was time to go home that day.

Simon was proud of himself, boasting, offering self-congratulations. "Don't tell mother," I said when we got off the bus, "don't, Simon, she'll get upset and go away again, please. Don't make her sad."

(When I was fourteen, during one of the times mother was away, my father got drunk downstairs in the kitchen with Mr. Arnstead, and I could hear them talking, as I hid in my room with my books and records, father speaking softly, Mr. Arnstead bellowing.

"No one, no one, should ever have to go through what

Anna did. We're beasts anyway, all of us, Germans, Americans, what's the difference."

Slamming of a glass on the table and a bellow: "God damn it, Sam, you Jews seem to think you have a monopoly on suffering. What about the guy in Harlem? What about some starving guy in Mexico? You think things are any better for them?"

"It was worse for Anna."

"No, not worse, no worse than the guy in some street in Calcutta. Anna could at least hope she would be liberated, but who's gonna free that guy?"

"No one," softly, "no one is ever freed from Anna's kind of suffering."

I listened, hiding in my room, but Mr. Arnstead left after that; and when I came downstairs, father was just sitting there, staring at his glass; and I felt his sadness softly drape itself around me as I stood there, and then the soft veil of love over the sadness, making it bearable.)

I began to miss school at least twice a week, hurting, unable to speak to mother, wanting to say something to father but not having the words. Mother was away a lot then, and this made me more depressed (I'm doing it, I'm sending her away), the depression endurable only because of the blanket of comfort that I felt resting over the house.

They had been worried, of course, but did not have their worst fears confirmed until Thanksgiving was over and December arrived (snow drifting down from a gray sky, father bringing in wood for the fireplace, mother polishing the menorah, Simon and me counting up our saved allowances, plotting what to buy for them when father drove us to town). I had been absent from school for a week by then, vomiting every morning at the thought that I might have to return. Father was reading and Simon was outside trying to climb one of our trees. I was in the kitchen, cutting cookies and decorating them while mother rolled the dough, humming, white flour on her apron, looking away and smiling when I sneaked small pieces of dough and put them in my mouth.

And then I fell off my chair onto the floor, holding my leg, moaning, "Mother, it hurts," blood running from my nose. She picked me up, clutching me to her, and put me on the chair, blotted my nose with a tissue. Then we heard Simon yelling outside, and then his banging on the back door. Mother went and pulled him inside, his nose bleeding. "I fell outa the tree," and, as she picked him up, she looked back at me; and I knew that she understood, and felt her fear and her sorrow as she realized that she and I were the same, that I would always feel the knife thrusts of other people's pain, draw their agonies into myself, and, perhaps, be shattered by them.

(Remembering: Father and mother outside, after a summer storm, standing under the willow, father putting his arm around her, brushing her black hair back and kissing her gently on the forehead. Not for me, too much shared anguish with love for me. I am always alone, with my mountain, my forest, my lakes like puddles. The young couple's boat is moored at the island.)

I hear them downstairs.

"Anna, the poor child, what can we do?"

"It is worse for her, Samuel," sighing, the sadness reaching me and becoming a shroud, "it will be worse with her, I think, than it was for me."

The Star Trek Syndrome

The traditional development of science fiction writers has begun with an infatuation with reading, and the traditional movement, when it has occurred, has been west—from writing for magazines and books to writing for film and television, as it was for Matheson, Ellison, Bloch, and Sturgeon. These traditions may be changing: Like the stones Deucalion cast behind him, new writers may be springing up from *Star Trek* episodes or *Star Wars* films. Sf writers may have their first experience with screenwriting.

So, at least, it was with David Gerrold (born David Jerrold Friedman in Chicago in 1944). Raised in Los Angeles, he attended Los Angeles Valley Junior College, took film courses at the University of Southern California, and earned a B.A. degree in theater arts from California State College at Northridge in 1967. In the next few years his productivity and success in the science fiction field was remarkable. The only problem with it was that at the age of twenty-three, while he was still a senior in college, he sold a script to *Star Trek* entitled "The Trouble with Tribbles," and that has been difficult to surpass. His script came in second in the Hugo balloting for drama (Ellison's "City at the Edge of Forever" won), and Gerrold even wrote a 1973 book about his experience and a book titled *The World of Star Trek* the same year.

Gerrold also revised the script for the *Star Trek* episode "I, Mudd" and is credited with the story for "The Cloud Minders." Later he wrote two scripts for the animated *Star Trek*, five scripts for the *Land of the Lost* series, wrote for *Logan's*

Run, and served as story editor for *Land of the Lost* and *Buck Rogers*.

Gerrold moved into the writing of stories and novels with a scattering of short stories (his first was "Oracle for a White Rabbit" in the December 1969 *Galaxy*), a collection, a handful of anthologies, and a double handful of novels. His short stories are collected in *With a Finger in My I* (1972). Still a young writer himself, he put his salesmanship to work to produce anthologies of the work of other young writers in *Protostars* (1971), *Generation* (1972), and *Science Fiction Emphasis I* (1974, with Stephen Goldin), the last apparently intended to be the first of a series that did not work out. He also edited *Alternities* (1974, with Stephen Goldin) and *Ascents of Wonder* (1977, with Stephen Goldin).

Gerrold's first novel was a collaboration with Larry Niven, *The Flying Sorcerers* (1971), which was serialized under the title *The Misspelled Magishun*. Three novels were published in 1972: *Space Skimmer*, *Yesterday's Children*, and *When Harlie Was One*. A novelization of *Battle for the Planet of the Apes* followed in 1973, along with *The Man Who Folded Himself*. *Moonstar Odyssey* was published in 1977 and *Deathbeast* in 1978.

When Harlie Was One, *The Man Who Folded Himself*, and *Moonstar Odyssey* have attracted the most attention. All were Nebula Award finalists, and the first two were Hugo finalists as well. Like the television business from which Gerrold drew his first success, the first two offered elaborations of traditional themes. *When Harlie Was One* drew upon the long history of the sentient computer, including the work of two early Gerrold favorites, Isaac Asimov and Arthur C. Clarke, as well as D. F. Jones's *Collosus: The Forbin Project*, to reconsider the role the computer might play (and the opposition it might arouse) in bettering humanity's condition and even succeeding humanity. *The Man Who Folded Himself* continues into ultimate solipsism the kind of time-travel paradoxes pioneered by another Gerrold hero, Robert A. Heinlein. *Moonstar Odyssey* is a different look at the question of sex roles that Ursula K. Le Guin dealt with in another way in *The Left Hand of Darkness*.

"With a Finger in My I," published the same year (1972) in *Again, Dangerous Visions* and Gerrold's collected stories, draws upon the surrealistic and absurdist tradition of Franz Kafka and Jorge Luis Borges seasoned by Theodore Sturgeon's 1941 fantasy "The Ultimate Egoist" and most of all by Lewis Carroll's fantasies. To its theme, however, Gerrold brings a contemporary wit and contemporary concerns that walk a narrow path of inspiration between the precipice of nonsense on one hand and the gulf of insanity on the other.

With a Finger in My I

by David Gerrold

When I looked in the mirror this morning, the pupil was gone from my left eye. Most of the iris had disappeared too. There was just a blank white area and a greasy smudge to indicate where the iris had previously been.

At first I thought it had something to do with the contact lenses, but then I realized that I don't wear lenses. I never have.

It looked kind of odd, that one blank eye staring back at me, but the unsettling thing about it was that I could still see out of it. When I put my hand over my good right eye, I found that the eyesight in my left was as good as ever and it worried me.

If I hadn't been able to see out of it, I wouldn't have worried. It would have meant only that during the night I had gone blind in that eye. But for the pupil of the eye to just fade away without affecting my sight at all—well, it worried me. It could be a symptom of something serious.

Of course, I thought about calling the doctor, but I didn't know any doctors and I felt a little bit embarrassed about troubling a perfect stranger with my problems. But there was that eye and it kept staring at me, so finally I went looking for the phone book.

Only, the phone book seemed to have disappeared during the night. I had been using it to prop up one end of the bookshelf and now it was gone. So was the bookshelf—I began to wonder if perhaps I had been robbed.

First my eye, then the phone book, now my bookshelf had all disappeared. If it had not been that today was Tuesday, I should have been worried. In fact, I was already worried, but Tuesday is my day to ponder all the might-have-beens that had become never-wases. Monday is my day to worry about personal effects (such as eyes and phone books) and Monday would not be back for six days. I was throwing myself off schedule by worrying on a Tuesday. When Monday returned, then I would worry about the phone book, if I didn't have something else of a more pressing nature to worry about first.

(I find that pigeonholing my worrying like that helps me to keep an orderly mind—by allotting only so much time to each problem I am able to keep the world in its proper perspective.) But there was still the matter of the eye and that was upsetting me. Moreover, it was *distorting* my perspective.

I resolved to do something about it immediately. I set out in search of the phone, but somewhere along the way that too had disappeared, so I was forced to abandon that exploration.

It was very frustrating—this distressing habit of disappearing that the inanimate objects had picked up. Every time I started to look for something, I found that it had already vanished, as if daring me to find it. It was like playing hide-and-go-seek, and since I had long ago given up such childish pastimes, I resolved not to encourage them any further and refused to look for them any more. (Let them come to me.)

I decided that I would walk to the doctor. (I would have put on my cap, but that would have meant looking for it and I was afraid that it too would have disappeared by the time I found it.)

Once outside, I noticed that people were staring at me in a strange way as they passed. After a bit, I realized that it must have been my eye. I had forgotten completely about it, not realizing that it might look a bit strange to others.

I started to turn around to go back for my sunglasses, but I knew that if I started to look for them, they too would surely disappear. So I turned around and headed once again for the doctor's.

"Let them come to me," I muttered, thinking of the sunglasses. I must have startled the old lady I was passing at the time because she turned to stare at me in a most peculiar manner.

I shoved my hands into my coat pockets and pushed onward. Almost immediately I felt something hard and flat in my left-hand pocket. It was my sunglasses in their case. They had indeed come to me. It was rewarding to see that I was still the master of the inanimate objects in my life.

I took the glasses out and put them on, only to find that the left lens of the glasses had faded to a milky white. It matched my eye perfectly, but I found that, unlike my eye, I was quite unable to see through the opaqued lens. I would just have to ignore the stares of passersby and proceed directly on to the doctor's office.

After a bit, however, I realized that I did not know where I was going—as I noted earlier, I did not know any doctors. And I most certainly knew that if I started to search for the office of one, I would probably never find it at all. So I stood on the sidewalk and muttered to myself, "Let them come to me."

I must confess that I was a little bit leery of this procedure—remembering what had happened with the sunglasses—but in truth, I had no alternative. When I turned around I saw a sign on the building behind me. It said, "Medical Center." So I went in.

I walked up to the receptionist and I looked at her and she looked at me. She looked me right in the eye (the left one) and said, "Yes, what can we do for you?"

I said, "I would like to see a doctor."

"Certainly," she said. "There goes one down the hall now. If you look quickly, you can catch a glimpse of him. See! There he goes!"

I looked and she was right—there *was* a doctor going down the hall. I could see him myself. I knew he was a doctor because he was wearing golf shoes and a sweater; then he disappeared around a bend in the corridor. I turned back to the girl. "That wasn't exactly what I meant," I said.

"Well, what was it you meant?"

I said, "I would like for a doctor to look at me."

"Oh," she said. "Why didn't you say so in the first place?"

"I thought I did," I said, but very softly.

"No, you didn't," she said. "And speak up. I can hardly hear you." She picked up her microphone and spoke into it, "Dr. Gibbon, puh-lease come to reception . . ." Then she put down her microphone and looked at me expectantly.

I did not say anything. I waited. After a moment, another man in golf shoes and sweater came out of the nearby doors and walked over to us. He looked at the girl behind the desk and she said to him, "This gentleman would like a doctor to look at him."

The doctor took a step back and looked at me. He looked me up and down, then asked me to turn around and he looked at me some more. Then he said, "Okay," and walked back into his office.

I asked, "Is that all?"

She said, "Of course, that's all. That's all you asked for. That will be ten dollars please."

"Wait a minute," I said. "I wanted him to look at my eye."

"Well," she said, "you should have said so in the first place. You know we're very busy here. We haven't got time to keep calling doctors down here to look at just anyone who wanders in. If you had wanted him to look at your eye in particular, you should have said so."

"But I don't want someone to just look at my eye," I said. "I want someone to cure it."

"Why?" she said. "Is there something wrong with it?"

I said, "Can't you see? The pupil has disappeared."

"Oh," she said. "So it has. Did you look for it?"

"Yes, I did," I said. "I looked all over for it—that's probably why I can't find it."

"Maybe you left it somewhere," she cooed softly. "Where was the last place you were?"

"I wasn't anywhere," I said.

"Well, maybe that's your trouble."

"I meant that I stayed home last night. I didn't go anywhere! And I don't feel very well."

"You don't look very well," she said. "You should see a doctor."

"I already have," I said. "He went down that hall."

"Oh, that's right. I remember now."

"Look," I said. I was starting to get a little angry. "Will you please get me an appointment with a doctor?"

"Is that what you want—an *appointment?*"

"Yes, that is what I want."

"You're sure that's *all* you want now? You're not going to come back later and complain that we didn't give you what you want?"

"I'm sure," I said. "I'm not going to come back."

"Good. That's what we want to be sure of."

By now, everything seemed to be all wrong. The whole world seemed to be slipping off sideways—all squished together and stretched out and tilted so that everything was sliding down towards the edge. So far, nothing had gone over, but I thought I could see tiny cracks appearing in the surface.

I shook my head to clear it, but all that did was to produce a very distinct rattling noise—like a very small walnut in a very large shell.

I sat down on the couch to wait—I was still unable to think clearly. The fog swirled in thicker than ever, obscuring everything. Visibility had been reduced to zero and the controllers were threatening to close down all operations until the ceiling lifted. I protested, no—wasn't the ceiling all right where it was?—but they just ignored me.

I stood up then and tried to push the ceiling back by hand, but I couldn't reach it and had to stand on a chair. Even then, the surface of it was hard and unyielding. (Although I was close enough to see that there were numerous cracks and flaws in it.)

I started to push on it again, but a strong hand on my shoulder and a deep voice stopped me. "Lay down on the couch," she said. "Just close your eyes. Relax. Lie back and relax."

"All right," I said, but I did not lay on my back. I lay on my stomach and pressed my face into the hard unyielding surface.

"Relax," she said again.

"I'll try," I said, forcing myself.

"Look out the window," the doctor said. "What do you see?"

"I see clouds," I said.

"What kind?"

"What kind???"

"Yes. What kind?"

I looked again. "Cottage cheese clouds. Little scuds of cottage cheese clouds."

"Cottage cheese clouds—?" asked the doctor.

"Yes," I said. "Cottage cheese clouds. Hard and unyielding."

"Large curd or small curd?"

"Huh?" I asked. I rolled over and looked at her. She did not have on golf shoes, but she was wearing a sweater. Instead of the golf shoes, she had on high heels. But she was a doctor—I could tell that. Her shoes still had cleats.

"I asked you a question," she rumbled in that deep voice of hers.

"Yes, you did," I agreed. "Would you mind repeating it?"

"No, I wouldn't mind," she said and waited quietly.

I waited also. For a moment there was silence between us. I pushed the silence to one side and asked, "Well, what was it?"

This time she answered, "I asked whether the clouds were large curd or small curd."

"I give up," I said. "What were they?"

"That's very good of you to give up—otherwise we'd have had to come in after you and take you by force. By surrendering your misconceptions now you have made it so much easier for both of us."

The whole thing was coming disjointed and teetered precariously on the edge. Bigger cracks were beginning to appear in the image and tiny pieces were starting to slip out and fall slowly to the ground where they shattered like so many soap bubbles.

"Uh—" I said. "Uh, Doctor—there's something wrong with my eye."

"Your I?"

"Uh, yes. The pupil is gone."

"The pupil is gone from your I?" The doctor was astounded. "How astonishing!"

I could only nod—so I did. (A bit too hard perhaps. A few more pieces come flaking off and fluttered gently to the floor. We watched for a bit.)

"Hm," she said. "I have a theory about that. Would you like to hear it?"

I didn't answer. She was going to tell me her theory whether I wanted to hear it or not.

"The world is coming to an end," she whispered conspiratorially.

"Right now?" I asked, somewhat worriedly. I still hadn't fed the cat.

"No, but soon," she reassured me.

"Oh," I said.

We sat there in silence. After a bit, she cleared her throat. "I think . . ." she began slowly, then she trailed off.

"That's nice," I said, but she didn't hear me.

". . . I think that the world exists only as a reflection of our minds. It exists the way it does only because that's the way we think it does."

"*I* think—therefore *I* exist," I said. But she ignored me. She told me to be quiet.

"Yes, you exist," she confirmed. (I'm glad she did—I was beginning to be a bit worried—and this was the wrong day for it. The last time I looked this was Tuesday.) "You exist," she said, "because you think you do. And the world also exists because you think it does."

"Then, when I die—the world ends with me . . . ?" I asked hopefully, making a mental note not to die.

"No—that's nonsense. No sane and rational man believes in solipsism." She scratched at her eyeball with a fork and went on.

"When you die—*you* cease to exist," she said. "But the world goes on—it goes on because everybody else who's still alive still believes that it exists. (The only thing they've stopped believing in is you.) You see, the world is a collective figment of all of our individual imaginations."

"I'm sorry," I said stiffly. "I do not believe in collectivism." I unbent a little so as to sit up. "I am a staunch Republican."

"Don't you see?" she said, ignoring my interruption. "This mass hallucination that the world is real just keeps on going because of its own inertia. You believe in it because that's the way it was when you first began to exist—that is when everybody else first began to believe you existed. When you were born, you saw that the world followed a certain set of rules that other people believed in, so you believed in them too—the fact that you believe in them just gives them that much more strength."

"Oh," I said. I lay there listening to her, trying to figure out some way to leave gracefully. My eye was starting to hurt and I couldn't see the ceiling any more. The fog was rolling in again.

"Look at the church!" she said suddenly.

"Huh?" I said.

"Look at the church!" she said it again, insistent.

I tried to. I lifted my head and tried to look at the church, but the fog was too thick. I couldn't even see my toes.

"Look at it," she said. *"Faith* is the basic precept of religion—faith that what they're telling you is true! Don't they tell you to have faith in the church, that faith can work miracles?!! Well, I'll tell you something—it can! If enough people believe in something, it becomes reality!"

By now, my eye was throbbing more painfully. I tried to sit up, but her strong hands held me back. She leaned closer and whispered intensely, "Yes! It's true. It is."

"If you say so," I nodded.

She went on, "Fortunately, the church long ago abandoned miracles in favor of conservatism—now, it's fighting to preserve the status quo! The church is one of the last bastions of reality—it's one of the few things holding back chaos!"

"Chaos?"

"Yes, chaos."

"Oh."

"The world is changing," she explained. "Man is changing it."

I nodded. "Yes, I know. I read the newspapers too."

"No, no! That's not what I meant! Man is changing his world unconsciously! More and more people are starting to believe that they really can change their environment—and the more they believe it, the more drastically it changes. I'll give you an example—fossils!"

"Fossils?"

"Yes, fossils. Nobody ever discovered any fossils until people started believing in evolution—then when they did start to believe in it, you couldn't turn around without tripping over fossils."

"You really believe this?" I asked.

"Yes, I do!" she said intensely.

"Then it must be so," I said.

"Oh, it is," she agreed and I knew that she really did believe it. She made a very convincing case. In fact, the more she talked, the more I began to believe it too.

"Why did you tell me all this?" I asked.

"Because we're in great danger. That's why." She whispered fiercely, "The world isn't changing uniformly. Everybody is starting to believe in different things and they're forming pockets of non-causality."

"Like a pimple?" I offered.

"Yes," she said and I could see a small one forming on the tip of her nose. "It works this way: a fanatic meets another fanatic, then the two of them meet with some other people who share the same hallucinations and pretty soon there are a whole bunch of fanatics all believing the same thing—pretty soon, their delusions become real for them—they've started to contradict the known reality and replaced it with a node of non-reality."

I nodded and concentrated on wrapping a swirl of the fog securely around me.

"The more it changes, the more people believe in the changes, and the stronger they become. If this keeps up we may be the only sane people left in the world—and we're in danger—"

"They're outnumbering our reality?" I suggested.

"Worse than that—all of their different outlooks are starting to flaw the structure of space! Even the shape of the

Earth is changing! Why, at one time, it was really flat—the world didn't turn until people started to believe it was round."

I turned round then and looked at her, but she had disappeared into the fog. All that was left was her grin.

"But the world is really pear-shaped," I said. "I read it in *Scientific American*."

"And why do you think it's changing shape?" the grin asked. "It's because a certain nation is starting to believe that it's really bigger than it is. The Earth is bulging out to accommodate them."

"Oh," I said.

"It's the fault of the news media—television is influencing our image of the world! They keep telling us that the world is changing—and more and more people keep believing it."

"Well," I said. "With the shape of the world the way it is today, any change has got to be for the—"

"Oh, God—not you too! All you people keep talking about the world going to pieces—falling apart at the seams—"

And then even the grin was gone.

I was left there. I was also right. Other people had begun to notice it too. Great chunks of the surface *had* gone blotchy and holes had appeared in it. More and more pieces were falling out all the time, but the waters had not yet broken through from the other side.

I poked my finger through one of the holes and I could feel the soft gelatinous surface behind. Perhaps it hadn't completely thawed out yet.

So far, nothing had been accomplished about my eye—not only was it beginning to ache something fierce, but my I was beginning to twinge a bit also and I had a feeling that that too might be going opaque.

"Have you found yourself yet?" one of the speakers in the park demanded. (I hadn't even looked—and remembering my previous experiences with looking for things, I certainly was not going to initiate any kind of search.) I walked on.

Farther on, there was another speaker—this one on a soap box. "We should be thankful for this great nation of ours," the speaker woofed and tweetered, "where so many people are allowed to believe in so many different things."

I rubbed at my eye. I had an uneasy queasy feeling that great cracks were opening in the ceiling.

"Anyone can get up and speak for his cause—any group

can believe in anything they choose—indeed we can remake the world if we want to! And in our own images!"

Things were teetering right and left—also write and wrong.

"But the truly great thing about it," he continued, "is that no matter how much we contradict each other, we are all working together for the common good! Our great democratic system lets us minimize our differences so that we can all compromise ourselves. Only by suggesting all the alternatives to a problem can we select the best possible solution. In the long run, this ultimate freedom and individuality will help all of us to achieve the most good for the most people!"

It sounded good to me.

When I got home, the workmen were just finishing with the wallpaper. It was amazing how solid the surface looked once all the cracks and flaws in it had been covered with a gaudy flowered facade.

I could no longer tell where the plaster had given way— and the bare surface of the understructure had disappeared into the fog. Indeed, the only thing was that the ceiling seemed to be much lower than before.

I paused long enough to stroke the cat. He waved as I came in. "Like—hello, man," said the cat. "Give me a J."

"I can't. I'm having trouble with my I."

"Well, then give me a dollar."

"What for?"

"For a trip," he said.

"Oh." I gave him a dollar, waited for the trip.

He dropped the bill into his mouth, lit it, picked up his suitcase and quickly rose to a cruising level of thirty thousand feet. Then he headed west. I did not quite understand this. The fog had gotten much worse and the controllers were just not letting any traffic through.

There had been something I had wanted to ask but I had forgotten it. Oh, well—it couldn't have been very important. But I wish I could figure out—

The man on the TV was a Doctor. He sat on top of it with his feet dangling in front of the screen (his cleats were scratching the image) and said that the drugs were destroying the realities. Drugs could destroy a person's sanity by altering his perceptions of the world until he could no longer perceive reality at all.

"Just so long as it doesn't change what he believes in," I muttered and turned him off. Then I turned him out. It was getting late and I wanted to get some sleep. However, I did make a mental note not to have my prescription refilled. Already the wallpaper was peeling.

In fact, by now, only the framework of the structure is left, and it looks like it's made out of chocolate pudding. Maybe it is. Perhaps it *is* the drugs. Maybe they *are* altering our collective fogments—but I haven't noticed anything.

The Real and the Surreal

Science fiction is a specialized kind of fantasy; it operates by making the fantastic seem real. Reality, then, may be as important to science fiction as fantasy; as rational explanations for events in a story dwindle in number or credibility, the science fiction feel of the story dissipates. Therein resides a remarkable contradiction: Although science fiction is a part of fantasy, the more fantastic a story is, the less it seems like science fiction.

In the world of literature outside the formulaic ghettos of category fiction, the unprecedented horrors of World War I produced a range of reactions, one of which was "Dadaism"; in art and writing it rejected the idea of order in the universe and adopted conscious madness as a method. About 1924 developed into "surrealism," which presented, as one critic put it, "chance events in disorderly array, much like the random sequence of events or recollections experienced in dreams." The "theater of the absurd" adapts surrealistic methods to portray man as a bewildered creature in an incomprehensible universe. "Anti-realism" abandoned realism's dependence on plot, setting, motivation, characterization, cause and effect, and sometimes logic. Early anti-realistic writers were Joyce and Kafka; contemporary anti-realists, though in different ways, are Samuel Beckett, Jorge Luis Borges, John Hawkes, and Joseph Heller.

Perhaps it was inevitable that anti-realism would gain a foothold in science fiction and that surrealism would begin to reshape science fiction's dreams. Liberated by the experiments of the New Wave, anti-realism and surrealism would become new ways of dealing with the strangeness of the Universe and the mysteries of the human mind.

George Alec Effinger (1947–   ) has been called a surrealist. He was born and raised in Cleveland, Ohio. He attended Yale twice and New York University once, abandoning both for his lifelong ambition to write. He attended the 1970 Clarion Writer's Workshop and placed three stories in the workshop's first anthology. His first publication, however, was "The Eight-Thirty to Nine Slot" in the April 1971 *Fantastic*. His 1972 story "All the Last Wars at Once" was a Hugo finalist, as was his 1973 novelette "The City on the Sand."

Effinger's first novel, *What Entropy Means to Me* (1972), won considerable praise and was a Nebula finalist. Effinger himself came in second to Jerry Pournelle for the 1973 Campbell Award as best new writer. Since then he has written *Relatives* (1973), *Nightmare Blue* (1975) with Gardner Dozois, *Those Gentle Voices: A Promethean Romance of the Spaceways* (1976), *Death in Florence* (1978; reprinted as *Utopia Three,* 1980), *Heroics* (1979), and *The Wolves of Memory* (1981). He wrote for Marvel Comic Books in 1971 and 1972 and wrote novelizations of four episodes of the *Planet of the Apes* television series, *Man the Fugitive* (1974), *Escape to Tomorrow* (1975), *Journey into Terror* (1975), and *Lord of the Apes* (1976). His short stories have been collected in *Mixed Feelings* (1974), *Irrational Numbers* (1976), and *Dirty Tricks* (1978).

An article in *Twentieth-Century American Science Fiction Writers* comments that "his ironic wit, his sense of the absurdity of the universe, his eye for concrete detail, and his parody of different styles have caused him to be compared to such writers as Jorge Luis Borges, John Barth, Donald Barthelme, and Thomas Pynchon."

Effinger dislikes handy labels and rejects the term "surrealist." "Surrealism is a starting point, not a style," he writes. "For over a decade I have been writing stories and novels using the traditional materials of science fiction, the conventional characters, settings, and storylines, in a manner that is surreal. But beyond that, I have tried to develop an exploration of character, of motivation, and of response to crisis that is beyond the scope of the surreal story."

Effinger also displays in his writing a fascination with the attitudes and artifacts of contemporary life. As Robert Silverberg observes in his introduction to *Irrational Numbers,* "Effinger's material includes all the standard schlock furniture of contemporary pop culture; what he makes out of it is something more than pop. . . . Effinger is doing something [like Los Angeles's Simon Rodia and his Watts towers] at times, with his ball players and mad scientists and sinister computers."

"The Ghost Writer," originally published in *Universe 3* (1973), illustrates Effinger's concern about artistic creativity. The world it describes exists two thousand years in the future. More is suggested about that world than described (as in the best science fiction), but such suggestions indicate that citizens enjoy a life of leisure supported by automatic machinery known collectively as TECT and individually in lowercase as tect. TECT appears to operate principally by transmission of matter, including human bodies, and mind.

The world also is a place of conformity where difference is considered dangerous. Literature has disappeared because it is disturbing, but recently TECT has allowed "writers" to send their minds not to a specific location, but questing into a "strange flaming place" where "countless elder intellects" continue to exist. Thus Effinger deals with the question of hell and survival after death, and in his title provides a marvelous pun—for the "writers," if they are lucky, come back with fragments of earlier literature from the "ghosts" of earlier writers. If they are unlucky in their maiden voyages, would-be ghost writers who do not find a receptive mind suffer a horrible mind-rending experience in the "death stream" and are "made away" by TECT.

Effinger is dealing with several aspects of creativity: inspiration (the "muse" speaking through the writer), affect (literature as social disturbance), scholarship, inequality of talent, intramural jealousy, and the nature of creation itself. The story is told through the viewpoint of a writer named Anabben (note the use of unfamiliar names to give the flavor of a distant time) who recovers fragments from a previously unknown writer named Sandor Courane (who plays a part in other Effinger stories), and feels jealous of Phioth, who communes with Shakespeare. The story demands that the reader come to terms with Anabben. He is jealous, petty, bullying, and generally unpleasant—but he raises the question that for this society is unthinkable: What if writers could truly write, inventing rather than rediscovering, creating rather than echoing?

The Ghost Writer

by George Alec Effinger

He was performing before several hundred million people, although he himself was the only person in the huge stadium. Concentric circles of transparent plastic slabs surrounded him, beginning only a few yards from his feet at the edge of the low stage and rising higher and higher, until the farthest row of seats was lost in the late evening's darkness. Each of the places was occupied by a wandering consciousness, directed and guarded out-of-body by TECT.

Anabben did not put on as energetic a show as the greater writers, but his stories themselves had a greater vigor. Although many of the audience had come to hear Phioth, the majority had been drawn also by the hope of hearing a long and exciting fragment from Anabben.

He sat in a chair in the middle of the shiny black stage. His feet were on the floor, close together, and his hands were resting in his lap. His head did not droop forward, but his expression was drugged and sleepy. Phioth would not sit; no, the greatest of the writers would dash about his small area, shouting his story, or whispering, and earning his fame as much with his acting as with his words.

This fragment was a particularly long one for Anabben. On the three previous exhibitions his story had ended within thirty minutes; the fragments had seemed unrelated, and none had even come close to being complete. There was always the chance that a new fragment might join two of the enigmatic earlier pieces, and a whole framework might begin to be evident. But not today. Here was another piece, of perhaps a totally different puzzle. It was longer, and it was exciting. The audience would be satisfied, but not the scholars.

"*He threw another bomb,*" said Anabben, reciting slowly with only a minimum of inflection. "*A department store fell in upon itself. Shards of brick and glass rained about him, and he was cut and bleeding. He felt nothing but a weird elation. The sound of authority in the explosion, the sound of tons of concrete and steel falling, the sound of hundreds of windows shattering—all these were strangely comforting and exciting to him."*

Many words were unintelligible to those who listened, and indeed, the basic conflict of the story was meaningless. In some way a man seemed to be acting *differently*, in a new manner unlike people. In many of the stories told by writers, people behaved in frightening patterns. A small number of persons had stopped attending the performances, protesting that the stories might teach one to act so *differently*. It would be the scholars, with the creative resources of TECT, who would ponder the meaning of the strange words: *bomb, authority, concrete.*

Anabben continued. *"In the middle of the twisted and charred rubble knelt."* He fell silent. It was clear that he had ended in the middle of a sentence. The audience, in their millions of scattered homes, sighed. Anabben sat quietly for a few moments. Gradually his face became more animated as he appeared to awaken from a deep trance. He stood, alone in the immense stadium, and walked to the edge of the stage. He was tired.

Anabben sat down, awaiting the next performance. He was alone; Vakeis was in his house. Her empty body rested on the low couch by the pond. Anabben guessed that her mind was still here at the stadium, waiting for the great Phioth. Anabben smiled ruefully. How could he expect Vakeis to be waiting for him, when Phioth was performing? He indulged himself in a little jealousy, an emotion rare for people but just eccentric enough for writers. As a writer he had a permanent slab reserved at the stadium. He knew that thousands of people unable to attend the performance would be horrified at his lack of interest.

He decided to stay because Phioth *did* entertain. And, since he was the greatest of them all, each performance held an element of history. TECT had lit the stage, for the sky was black, now. Phioth appeared from the tect near where Anabben was sitting. Anabben watched him go to the chair in the center of the stage. Phioth's hands grasped the arms of the chair, and one thumb found the small groove where a small amount of relaxant would prepare him for the exhibition. Unless Phioth's mind was calm and unafraid, it would not find its goal when TECT hurled it into the great death stream.

Every year TECT was used to send the consciousness of

dozens of aspiring writers, each hoping to align itself with the
drifting residue of an ancient master. Sometimes, as with
Phioth, there was good fortune, and the young man's self
would find a comfortable mate. Most often, however, there
were no minds waiting to meet the adventurer, and instead of
glory, there was raving panic. Of course TECT *made* each of
these unfortunates *away*, and only the other writers had seen
the terrifying display of a living man with his mind in death.

Phioth approached the chair with confidence, though, having made the journey many times and knowing that a
welcoming soul waited for him. There were countless elder
intellects abandoned to the strange flaming plane after their
bodies died. But if the youthful volunteer did not have a
mind suitably attuned to one of them, the ghostly traffic was
of no use. If the writer were lucky, he would return sane,
with a small scrap of lost literature. If the man were supremely lucky, he would find himself matched with a
legendary genius, a reflection of his own innate powers.

Phioth was the luckiest, and the greatest, of all the writers.
After two centuries of fishing the mind stream, one man had
become William Shakespeare/Phioth. Although none of
Shakespeare's works remained in the world, as no literature
of any sort existed, the Elizabethan's reputation had lived and
grown. Phioth's audiences listened excitedly, for every new
fragment that he brought back was heard on earth for the
first time in two thousand years.

"*Resembles what it was,*" said Phioth, still in the chair. He
rose slowly and, while his face kept the possessed look of the
performing writer, his body paced the narrow stage. His
hands flew about, pointing, gesturing, threatening. His voice
shifted in both tone and tempo, and Anabben marveled at the
impact of the nearly senseless words.

> "*What it should be,*
> *More than his father's death, that thus hath put him*
> *So much from the understanding of himself,*
> *I cannot dream of. I entreat you both,*
> *That, being of so young days brought up with him*
> *And since so neighbour'd to his youth and humour,*
> *That you vouchsafe your rest here in our court*
> *Some little time; so by your companies . . .*"

Anabben watched enviously. Phioth marched back and
forth across the scanty thumbnail stage, and Anabben was

caught up in the flurry of motion. This sort of behavior was so provocative, so *different*, that Anabben wondered that the tectmen did not come to *make* Phioth *away*. Here were not only great, dead words, but also some nameless feeling from the past, a dangerous passion that aroused Anabben. The people of Anabben's time had rediscovered the idea of theater, that certain products of the writer's mind were to be more than merely read. The scholars and TECT had made a vague reconstruction of the forms of literature, based on the several sorts of fragments they received from their writers.

Phioth spoke on as Anabben considered his own popularity. It was obvious from the content of the story fragments that his source was of another time than Shakespeare. Each writer knew the identity of his long-dead tutor, felt it intimately housed within his transported mind until the connection weakened and the tired vessel awoke. Anabben spoke the stories of one Sandor Courane; the scholars knew nothing about him, and they argued his merits relative to Shakespeare. Courane was less subtle, less universal, but more—involving. Courane had greater popular appeal, and such a phenomenon required study. It was not for Anabben to care what the factors were that maintained his distinction. He secretly enjoyed his fame and, even more secretly, wished ill for Phioth.

"—*And I do think*," said Phioth, his fist clenched above his head, "*or else this brain of mine*

> *Hunts not the trail of policy so sure*
> *As it hath us'd to do, that I have found*
> *The very cause of Hamlet's lunacy.*"

Hamlet! Another piece of that famous myth. The scholars must be squealing now, thought Anabben. On an impulse he got up, stepped into the tect, and transported home.

The grass was cool beneath his feet. Among the random pieces of roof Anabben could see the first quiet flush of stars. Thin, widely separated panels stood here and there to support the patches of roof and the house's mechanisms. Among them trees grew, brooks ran, and furniture stood ready for service. At the bottom of the hill Anabben saw a dim light around the couch where Vakeis' body still rested, while she observed Phioth's grandiose performance.

The air was chill, and Anabben requested TECT to raise the temperature of his outdoor home. As an afterthought he had the entire area of his estate lit brightly. TECT scattered the night, broke the darkness into ragged shadows, and chased even these small bits of shade among the roots of the trees. Anabben felt better. He walked down to the pond and sat down in the grass opposite his mistress. He waited for Phioth to end.

In a few minutes Vakeis stirred. She sat up and rubbed her neck, which had become stiff during the long period while her mind traveled to the stadium. She noticed Anabben and smiled. "You're back early," she said, with a puzzled expression.

"I was very tired," said Anabben. He did not return her smile. "I saw only a little of Phioth's reading. *Hamlet* again, wasn't it?"

"Yes. Very beautiful, but strange. I'm sorry you didn't stay. There must be thousands who would have given their Vote to see him."

"I know," said Anabben, standing and holding out his hand to her. They walked around the pond, which, through TECT, Anabben kept frozen all year long. He led her back up the hill to the meeting area. He did not feel like talking, knowing that anything that he said he would lead her to a discussion of Phioth.

"I enjoyed your performance, dear," she said.

"I'm glad. Of course, I can't remember it. Maybe if Charait and the others come over tonight I'll play it. It is sad how my own work interests me so little."

"I don't believe you," said Vakeis, picking a clump of grass and tossing it toward Anabben's head. He ducked, and it missed him. He did not laugh.

"No, really," he said. "I don't even know why I bother. When you're competing with someone like Phioth, it's hard to take yourself seriously."

"Phioth is one thing, you're another." Vakeis could see that Anabben was depressed, more than merely tired from his performance. She tugged at his arm and he stopped walking and looked at her. "Listen," she said, "you know there are just as many people who love your readings."

"Not quite," he said bitterly.

"Well, almost. Shakespeare is a myth. Almost a god. Naturally, people are going to listen to Phioth with different ears. But they *enjoy* your readings more. The two of you aren't even rivals. You appeal to different needs, and you both satisfy those needs equally. You were really wonderful tonight."

"Come on. I suppose they'll be here soon."

Reacting to his boredom and his jealousy, Anabben had TECT kill the lights in the house, leaving only a soft glow on the hill as they walked. He requested faint music, but in his growing impatience he stopped that immediately, too. When they got to the top of the hill, Anabben's meeting area, they saw two men appear from the small tect. The first to arrive was tall and gaunt, with hair braided down to his waist. He wore a pale-blue cloth twined about his body. The second man was shorter and heavier, with closely cut hair and a small beard. He wore no clothing. The new arrivals waved to Anabben and Vakeis, and sat down on the lawn to wait.

"Hello, Charait," said Vakeis, walking up to the man in the blue robe. He touched her leg and kissed her knee, and Vakeis laughed.

"This is Torephes," said Charait, holding up the hand of the other man. "If you can believe it, he wants to perform, too."

Anabben frowned. Charait was no problem; his bits of retrieved literature were from the works of a Mrs. Lidsake. The scholars, with all the subtle forces of TECT, were unable to place her among the other rediscovered, either qualitatively or chronologically. Charait's performances were interesting from a historical viewpoint, as all performances were, but they were somehow not absorbing. But this new Torephes presented a threat to Anabben, as the potential vessel of another genius that would overshadow Anabben's meager contributions.

"My friend Charait isn't joking," said Anabben. "Only we writers have seen what happens to the unsuccessful aspirants. Perhaps if the public knew how awful it is, soon there would be no new writers at all. How much thought have you given to this?"

Torephes looked very uneasy. Anabben made a mental request to TECT, and the temperature in the meeting area was lowered ten degrees.

"It's something that I've *always* wanted," said Torephes. "I understand about the chances. Charait has been warning me for about two years now, but I'm willing." His expression was so determined that Anabben laughed.

"Then let us wait for the others to arrive, and we'll talk

about it," said Anabben. "Maybe the inspiration of Phioth has persuaded you unwisely."

Anabben and Vakeis seated themselves next to the two men. Anabben kept silent, and, out of embarrassment, Vakeis assumed the role of hostess, asking the guests if they were comfortable, and if they desired refreshment.

"It is a bit cool," said Torephes, still ill-at-ease and fearing to offend such a celebrity as Anabben.

Anabben grunted and had TECT increase the temperature by ten degrees. "The dispenser is in that plane," he said, indicating the single wall in the meeting area. From his comment it was apparent that he was not going to serve his guests, as simple courtesy demanded. Torephes whispered to Charait, and Anabben could hear him suggest that they leave, but Charait just shook his head. After all, Anabben was a writer, the sort of person more inclined to moods than common citizens. And, further, he had just given a performance. Charait took Torephes' arm and led him to the dispenser.

"Vakeis," said Charait, "would you like something?"

"No," she said, "I'll wait."

"Anabben?"

Anabben just frowned and waved. Charait requested a small bowl of meat and flowers, and Torephes had a cup of relaxant and some protein bread.

In a short while three people stepped out of Anabben's tect: a young woman and two old men. They greeted Anabben and his guests, went straight to the dispenser, and joined the others on the grass. The young woman was named Rochei; she was a writer attuned to the poetry of a long-dead person named Elizabeth Dawson Douglas. One of the old men was a famous writer, one whom Anabben envied almost as much as he envied Phioth. His name was Tradenne, and he was also Tertius Publius Ieta. The other man was Briol, who had given his first performance just a few days previously, and had held the audience entranced with a fragment written by Daniel Defoe. Anabben was still sitting sullenly next to Vakeis, and she made the introductions. The easy conversation of friends stopped when they learned that Torephes wanted to become a writer.

"Did you watch Phioth this evening?" asked Rochei, as she braided Vakeis' long, dark hair.

"Yes," said Torephes. "One of my fathers understands how much I want to perform, and he let me use his place at the stadium."

"Did you enjoy it?" asked Tradenne.

Torephes hesitated. "Phioth is another sort of greatness. You don't *enjoy* him. You *experience* him, if you know what I mean. Not only the genius of Shakespeare, but the genius of Phioth."

"Exactly," said Briol quietly.

"I would be interested to know what you thought of *my* performance," said Anabben.

There was an immediate silence in Anabben's meeting area. Suddenly the atmosphere was tense. It was an unfair question, and even Anabben's notorious peculiarities did not excuse it.

"I thought you were very good," said Torephes after a long pause. "I've enjoyed all of your performances that I've heard through TECT. You're a contrast. Courane is distinctive; he gives us something that we do not have from any of the others."

Anabben frowned. He stood, causing the others to stare up at him as he paced. "Would you ever ask one of your fathers for a place to watch one of *my* readings?" he said.

Torephes looked at the other guests for help. It was obvious to Anabben that the young man was humiliated. "This was a special case. Phioth does not perform often."

Anabben said nothing. He went to the dispenser, aware of a buzz of whispered conversation behind his back. Knowing that the young man would not dare ask twice, he had TECT lower the temperature another fifteen degrees.

"Our friend Briol wanted to be a writer," said Anabben, after he returned to his place with a cup of stimulant. "He was one of the lucky ones. I'm not sure what arguments your fathers have used, but they can't know the truths of the matter unless they're writers, too."

"I wish that I'd known what it was going to be like before I tried it," said Briol with a nervous laugh. "There's a good chance that I wouldn't have done it."

"And if you hadn't gone before Stalele . . ." said Rochei.

Anabben put down his cup and grasped Torephes' arm. "You ought to listen. We're going to tell you about what it's like, and what just might happen to you, and if you still want to be a writer, we'll know you're insane."

"Don't listen to him, Torephes," said Charait. "I feel responsible. I brought you here. Perhaps it was a bad idea. Anabben's tired."

"No, no," said Anabben. "Not at all. He shouldn't think our life is all glamour and glory."

Torephes tried unsuccessfully to remove his arm from Anabben's hold. "I never had any illusions that way," he said.

"Wait a minute," said Anabben. "I want Briol to tell you about it."

Briol was sitting quietly, his knees drawn up and his head resting on his folded arms. He was older than anyone else in the meeting area, but the writers had their own special style of respect; he was the least experienced writer, and had to accept their inattention without offense. "'Well," said Briol slowly, "the first time was very frightening. I put my thumb in the groove, and I felt a little pinprick. I waited for the relaxant to take effect and then I just had TECT send me. I mean, out. Instead of to a place. Even with the drug I was still afraid."

Briol stared at the softly lighted grass as he spoke. He was an elderly man, one who had lived a useful life as a citizen, and his reasons for becoming a writer at such an advanced age were his secret. "For a brief, bright second there was a glimpse of the death stream itself," he said, his voice growing hoarse. "But before my mind could, well, sicken, I guess, I was rescued by the dead self of a person I know as Daniel Defoe. I was very lucky. That was my audition."

"And your first performance?" asked Torephes.

Briol looked up and smiled. "I was still afraid," he said. "I was afraid that this time Daniel Defoe wouldn't be there. But he was. And he always will be. For me."

"Tell him about Stalele," said Anabben, getting up for another cup of stimulant.

Briol said nothing. "Was he the one who auditioned after you?" asked Tradenne. Briol nodded.

"Did he fail?" asked Torephes.

"It was the most horrible thing I've ever seen," said Vakeis.

"Do you want to try?" asked Anabben, sitting down next to Rochei.

Torephes took Vakeis' hand. "Yes," he said.

Anabben laughed. "Good," he said. "Wonderful. Perhaps you'll land Homer."

"Don't joke with him, Anabben," said Vakeis. "He doesn't understand his chances."

"Oh, he knows the risks," said Anabben. "Come on, let's get it over with. We'll all meet on the stage of the stadium." He rose first, and disappeared into his private tect. The others followed, and TECT transported them to the vast, empty arena.

"Shall we have light?" asked Anabben.

"I suppose," said Torephes.

Anabben requested light from TECT, and the stadium was flooded with a bright noonday glow. "Don't be afraid," said Anabben, leading Torephes to the chair. "Briol is an old man. Death thoughts are his business. Why don't you think of Vakeis? If you come back with a good one, she may be yours."

"I may be his already," said Vakeis sourly. "Why don't you show him what to do?"

Anabben stared at her angrily. "I gave my performance today," he said at last. "My mind is exhausted."

"That's all right," said Torephes. He sat in the chair, bending down to inspect the arm that contained the relaxant pin. "I put my thumb here?" he asked.

"Yes," said Charait. "But you don't have to do this tonight, you know. Your fathers agreed to let me bring you to meet the others. I don't know if they mean for you to try your skill so soon."

"I'll take the responsibility," said Anabben. "He looks like a bright, intense boy."

"I . . . I did it," said Torephes. "How long . . ."

"You should feel it already," said Rochei softly.

"Yes."

"Now have TECT send you," said Briol. "Just as if you were going to the stadium, or to school, but don't specify a place. Just . . . *away*."

There was a short silence. Then Torephes' eyes grew wide; his mouth opened, but he made no sound other than a quiet gurgling. His lips drew back in a terrified snarl. His fists clenched, and he half stood up in the chair, his neck muscles straining and his back arched tensely.

Vakeis gasped, and hid her eyes on Charait's shoulder. Before anyone could say a word three tectmen had arrived and had *made* Torephes *away* through the small tect at the edge of the stage.

"No one home," said Anabben.

"That poor young boy," said Tradenne.

"He was a fool," said Anabben. "He got what he deserved. He wanted glory, but he didn't want to work. Just to parrot the rotting words of some ancient ghost."

"Don't you pity him?" asked Rochei.

"No, I don't. He knew what might happen."

"But we all started like him," said Charait. "We all take that chance. You can't blame *him*; you did it yourself once."

"No, I didn't," said Anabben quietly.

The others looked puzzled. Anabben frowned; if he explained now he would be doing a service, he thought. There need never be another Stalele, another Torephes.

"Don't you see?" he said. "All of you, fishing in the wild streams of death for a shred here and a tatter there. But everything you find belongs with the dead, with the dead worlds of thousands of years ago. But not me. Don't you see? For the first time in scores of centuries, someone is creating. I don't merely report, I *write*. There never was a Sandor Courane. His words are from *my* mind."

Vakeis began to cry. Charait grabbed Anabben's wrists. "You are saying that you do not have TECT send you?" he asked.

"No," said Anabben defiantly. "I have never tried."

"Then you've lied?" asked Tradenne.

"I cannot comprehend," said Briol. "You are not performing those bits of fiction? You are speaking them yourself? I cannot comprehend."

Anabben looked from one person to the other. In the strange light in the stadium each face seemed incredulous and afraid. "Don't you understand?" shouted Anabben. "I do it myself!"

They moved away from Anabben, leaving him by the empty chair. He looked wildly for some sign of approval, of awed surprise, but found only loathing. He started to scream, but stopped when Tradenne raised a hand.

"You are very *different*," said the old man. Before he finished speaking three tectmen had appeared to *make* Anabben *away*.

Of Men, and Women, and Society

The 1970s were a period of heightened concern about women's rights and men's wrongs. Congress proposed the Equal Rights Amendment in 1972, and *Ms.* magazine was founded. It was a time of feminist concern in science fiction as well. Joanna Russ, who had been incorporating feminist themes in her work since the late 1950s and the 1960s, won a Nebula Award for her 1972 story "When It Changed," and her novel *The Female Man* was published in 1975. In 1973 James Tiptree, Jr.—Alice Sheldon—launched a series of feminist stories with "The Women Men Don't See." Pamela Sargent's *Women of Wonder* was published in 1975, and Vonda McIntyre and Susan Janice Anderson's *Aurora: Beyond Equality*, an anthology of new stories on feminist themes, in 1976.

In one sense science fiction was taking up a new issue in much the same way it had taken up racial prejudice, pollution, Armageddon, overpopulation, and other issues. With feminism, however, there was a difference: A few men wrote consciously feminist works, but the great majority of the authors were women, and much of their writing was frankly political, even polemical.

One of the participants in the feminist science fiction movement was Vonda N. McIntyre. Born in Louisville, Kentucky, in 1948, she earned a degree in biology from the University of Washington in 1970 and did graduate study in genetics in 1970–71. She taught and organized conferences at the university, but perhaps the most important event of the time was her 1970 enrollment in the Clarion Science Fiction

352

Writers Workshop. Her work began to appear in 1971, "Cages" in *Quark/4* and "Only at Night" in the first *Clarion* anthology. Her story "Of Mist, and Grass, and Sand" (*Analog*, October 1973) won a Nebula Award, and *Dreamsnake*, the 1978 novel that was an expansion of that novelette, won both a Nebula and a Hugo.

McIntyre's short stories, including several that were nominated for awards, have been collected in *Fireflood and Other Stories* (1981). Another novel, *The Exile Waiting* (1975), was a Nebula finalist.

McIntyre's fiction consciously embodies her feminist concerns. Her narratives almost always involve female protagonists, but their themes are not, as in many feminist stories, those of female subjugation, or its reverse, female domination. McIntyre conveys her concerns in stories about strong women in times of crisis. The protagonist of *The Exile Waiting*, for instance, is a female telepath in a post-holocaust society who must surmount a series of mental and physical obstacles. Feminism is not the theme; the nature of the human predicament is the theme, and the political message is implied by the interplay of characters within a relatively non-sexist society, sometimes reinforced by imagery and metaphor. McIntyre's story "Aztecs," about a woman who must have her heart removed to become a space pilot, begins with the sentence "She gave up her heart quite willingly."

So it is with McIntyre's most famous story, "Of Mist, and Grass, and Sand." A strong young woman, called only "Snake," comes to a desert tribe to cure a child of a tumor. Some critics have described the setting as post-holocaust, but there is no indication within the novelette that this is so; the snakes the protagonist uses in her healing are native to Earth but the black sands may place the story on another planet. If the setting is post-holocaust, the survivors have replaced their technological skills with biological ones; McIntyre's story displays the confidence with which she deals with biology. In this era the venom systems of poisonous snakes, aided by drugs, are used as chemical laboratories to produce healing antibodies and antidotes.

McIntyre does not portray her strong, wise women as omniscient. Snake makes mistakes in dealing with the people of this unfamiliar culture; although her error is forgivable because of her weariness, lack of sleep, and fasting, she does not forgive herself. Among the feminist elements, the reader may note that the tribe is ruled by a woman, that the key actions are taken by women, that men are helpers, and that the attractive native male waits wistfully among the tents while Snake rides off into the desert with only a half-promise that she may return.

The style is direct and uncomplicated. It is almost Hemingwayesque in its simple sentences and short, vivid verbs and nouns, and the dialogue evidences Hemingway's ability to suggest a foreign language. But as in Hemingway's stories, the simplicity leads the reader into complexities, such as the way human needs express themselves in social customs; strong emotional reactions can develop from scenes like the one in which Arevin tells Snake his name. Oddly enough, Snake does not tell Arevin her name, asking only that she be called by the name of honor given by her teachers. But perhaps as a woman who has sacrificed her humanity to an overriding mission like many a hero before her, Snake's original name no longer has any significance.

Of Mist, and Grass, and Sand

by Vonda N. McIntyre

The little boy was frightened. Gently, Snake touched his hot forehead. Behind her, three adults stood close together, watching, suspicious, afraid to show their concern with more than narrow lines around their eyes. They feared Snake as much as they feared their only child's death. In the dimness of the tent, the flickering lamplights gave no reassurance.

The child watched with eyes so dark the pupils were not visible, so dull that Snake herself feared for his life. She stroked his hair. It was long and very pale, a striking color against his dark skin, dry and irregular for several inches near the scalp. Had Snake been with these people months ago, she would have known the child was growing ill.

"Bring my case, please," Snake said.

The child's parents started at her soft voice. Perhaps they had expected the screech of a bright jay, or the hissing of a shining serpent. This was the first time Snake had spoken in their presence. She had only watched, when the three of them had come to observe her from a distance and whisper about her occupation and her youth; she had only listened, and then nodded, when finally they came to ask her help. Perhaps they had thought she was mute.

The fair-haired younger man lifted her leather case from the felt floor. He held the satchel away from his body, leaning to hand it to her, breathing shallowly with nostrils flared against the faint smell of musk in the dry desert air. Snake had almost accustomed herself to the kind of uneasiness he showed; she had already seen it often.

When Snake reached out, the young man jerked back and dropped the case. Snake lunged and barely caught it, set it gently down, and glanced at him with reproach. His partners came forward and touched him to ease his fear. "He was bitten once," the dark and handsome woman said. "He almost died." Her tone was not of apology, but of justification.

"I'm sorry," the younger man said. "It's—" He gestured toward her; he was trembling, and trying visibly to control the reactions of his fear. Snake glanced down to her shoulder, where she had been unconsciously aware of the slight weight and movement. A tiny serpent, thin as the finger of a baby, slid himself around behind her neck to show his narrow head below her short black curls. He probed the air with his trident tongue, in a leisurely manner, out, up and down, in, to savor the taste of the smells.

"It's only Grass," Snake said. "He cannot harm you."

If he were bigger, he might frighten; his color was pale green, but all scales around his mouth were red, as if he had just feasted as a mammal eats, by tearing. He was, in fact, much neater.

The child whimpered. He cut off the sound of pain; perhaps he had been told that Snake, too, would be offended by crying. She only felt sorry that his people refused themselves such a simple way of easing fear. She turned from the adults, regretting their terror of her, but unwilling to spend the time it would take to convince them their reactions were unjustified. "It's all right," she said to the little boy. "Grass is smooth, and dry, and soft, and if I left him to guard you, even death could not reach your bedside." Grass poured himself into her narrow, dirty hand, and she extended him toward the child. "Gently." He reached out and touched the sleek scales with one fingertip. Snake could sense the effort of even such a simple motion, yet the boy almost smiled.

"What are you called?"

He looked quickly toward his parents, and finally they nodded. "Stavin," he whispered. He had no strength or breath for speaking.

"I am Snake, Stavin, and in a little while, in the morning, I must hurt you. You may feel a quick pain, and your body will ache for several days, but you will be better afterward."

He stared at her solemnly. Snake saw that though he understood and feared what she might do, he was less afraid than if she had lied to him. The pain must have increased greatly as his illness became more apparent, but it seemed that others had only reassured him, and hoped the disease would disappear or kill him quickly.

Snake put Grass on the boy's pillow and pulled her case nearer. The lock opened at her touch. The adults still could only fear her; they had had neither time nor reason to discover any trust. The wife was old enough that they might never have another child, and Snake could tell by their eyes, their covert touching, their concern, that they loved this one very much. They must, to come to Snake in this country.

It was night, and cooling. Sluggish, Sand slid out of the case, moving his head, moving his tongue, smelling, tasting, detecting the warmth of bodies.

"Is that—?" The eldest partner's voice was low, and wise, but terrified, and Sand sensed the fear. He drew back into striking position, and sounded his rattle softly. Snake spoke to him and extended her arm. The pit viper relaxed and flowed around and around her slender wrist to form black and tan bracelets. "No," she said. "Your child is too ill for Sand to help. I know it is hard, but please try to be calm. This is a fearful thing for you, but it is all I can do."

She had to annoy Mist to make her come out. Snake rapped on the bag, and finally poked her twice. Snake felt the vibration of sliding scales, and suddenly the albino cobra flung herself into the tent. She moved quickly, yet there seemed to be no end to her. She reared back and up. Her breath rushed out in a hiss. Her head rose well over a meter above the floor. She flared her wide hood. Behind her, the adults gasped, as if physically assaulted by the gaze of the tan spectacle design on the back of Mist's hood. Snake ignored the people and spoke to the great cobra in a singsong voice. "Ah, thou. Furious creature. Lie down; 'tis time for thee to earn thy dinner. Speak to this child, and touch him. He is called Stavin." Slowly, Mist relaxed her hood, and allowed

Snake to touch her. Snake grasped her firmly behind the head, and held her so she looked at Stavin. The cobra's silver eyes picked up the yellow of the lamplight. "Stavin," Snake said, "Mist will only meet you now. I promise that this time she will touch you gently."

Still, Stavin shivered when Mist touched his thin chest. Snake did not release the serpent's head, but allowed her body to slide against the boy's. The cobra was four times longer than Stavin was tall. She curved herself in stark white loops across Stavin's swollen abdomen, extending herself, forcing her head toward the boy's face, straining against Snake's hands. Mist met Stavin's frightened stare with the gaze of lidless eyes. Snake allowed her a little closer.

Mist flicked out her tongue to taste the child.

The youngest partner made a small, cut-off, frightened sound. Stavin flinched at it, and Mist drew back, opening her mouth, exposing her fangs, audibly thrusting her breath through her throat. Snake sat back on her heels, letting out her own breath. Sometimes, in other places, the kinfolk could stay while she worked. "You must leave," she said gently. "It's dangerous to frighten Mist."

"I won't—"

"I'm sorry. You must wait outside."

Perhaps the younger man, perhaps even the woman, would have made the indefensible objections and asked the answerable questions, but the older man turned them and took their hands and led them away.

"I need a small animal," Snake said as the man lifted the tent flap. "It must have fur, and it must be alive."

"One will be found," he said, and the three parents went into the glowing night. Snake could hear their footsteps in the sand outside.

Snake supported Mist in her lap, and soothed her. The cobra wrapped herself around Snake's narrow waist, taking in her warmth. Hunger made her even more nervous than usual, and she was hungry, as was Snake. Coming across the black sand desert, they had found sufficient water, but Snake's traps were unsuccessful. The season was summer, the weather was hot, and many of the furry tidbits Sand and Mist preferred were estivating. When the serpents missed their regular meal, Snake began a fast as well.

She saw with regret that Stavin was more frightened now. "I am sorry to send your parents away," she said. "They can come back soon."

His eyes glistened, but he held back the tears. "They said to do what you told me."

"I would have you cry, if you are able," Snake said. "It isn't such a terrible thing." But Stavin seemed not to understand, and Snake did not press him; she knew that his people taught themselves to resist a difficult land by refusing to cry, refusing to mourn, refusing to laugh. They denied themselves grief, and allowed themselves little joy, but they survived.

Mist had calmed to sullenness. Snake unwrapped her from her waist and placed her on the pallet next to Stavin. As the cobra moved, Snake guided her head, feeling the tension of the striking muscles. "She will touch you with her tongue," she told Stavin. "It might tickle, but it will not hurt. She smells with it, as you do with your nose."

"With her tongue?"

Snake nodded, smiling, and Mist flicked out her tongue to caress Stavin's cheek. Stavin did not flinch; he watched, his child's delight in knowledge briefly overcoming pain. He lay perfectly still as Mist's long tongue brushed his cheeks, his eyes, his mouth. "She tastes the sickness," Snake said. Mist stopped fighting the restraint of her grasp, and drew back her head. Snake sat on her heels and released the cobra, who spiraled up her arm and laid herself across her shoulders.

"Go to sleep, Stavin," Snake said. "Try to trust me, and try not to fear the morning."

Stavin gazed at her for a few seconds, searching for truth in Snake's pale eyes. "Will Grass watch?"

The question startled her, or, rather, the acceptance behind the question. She brushed his hair from his forehead and smiled a smile that was tears just beneath the surface. "Of course." She picked Grass up. "Thou wilt watch this child, and guard him." The snake lay quiet in her hand, and his eyes glittered black. She laid him gently on Stavin's pillow.

"Now sleep."

Stavin closed his eyes, and the life seemed to flow out of him. The alteration was so great that Snake reached out to touch him, then saw that he was breathing, slowly, shallowly. She tucked a blanket around him and stood up. The abrupt change in position dizzied her; she staggered and caught herself. Across her shoulders, Mist tensed.

Snake's eyes stung and her vision was oversharp, fever-clear. The sound she imagined she heard swooped in closer. She steadied herself against hunger and exhaustion, bent slowly, and picked up the leather case. Mist touched her cheek with the tip of her tongue.

She pushed aside the tent flap and felt relief that it was still night. She could stand the heat, but the brightness of the sun curled through her, burning. The moon must be full; though the clouds obscured everything, they diffused the light so the sky appeared gray from horizon to horizon. Beyond the tents, groups of formless shadows projected from the ground. Here, near the edge of the desert, enough water existed so clumps and patches of bush grew, providing shelter and sustenance for all manner of creatures. The black sand, which sparkled and blinded in the sunlight, at night was like a layer of soft soot. Snake stepped out of the tent, and the illusion of softness disappeared; her boots slid crunching into the sharp hard grains.

Stavin's family waited, sitting close together between the dark tents that clustered in a patch of sand from which the bushes had been ripped and burned. They looked at her silently, hoping with their eyes, showing no expression in their faces. A woman somewhat younger than Stavin's mother sat with them. She was dressed, as they were, in a long loose robe, but she wore the only adornment Snake had seen among these people: a leader's circle, hanging around her neck on a leather thong. She and Stavin's eldest parent were marked close kin by their similarities: sharp-cut planes of face, high cheekbones, his hair white and hers graying early from deep black, their eyes the dark brown best suited for survival in the sun. On the ground by their feet a small black animal jerked sporadically against a net, and infrequently gave a shrill weak cry.

"Stavin is asleep," Snake said. "Do not disturb him, but go to him if he wakes."

Stavin's mother and the youngest partner rose and went inside, but the older man stopped before her. "Can you help him?"

"I hope we may. The tumor is advanced, but it seems solid." Her own voice sounded removed, slightly hollow, as if she were lying. "Mist will be ready in the morning." She still felt the need to give him reassurance, but she could think of none.

"My sister wished to speak with you," he said, and left them alone, without introduction, without elevating himself by saying that the tall woman was the leader of this group. Snake glanced back, but the tent flap fell shut. She was feeling her exhaustion more deeply, and across her shoulders Mist was, for the first time, a weight she thought heavy.

"Are you all right?"

Snake turned. The woman moved toward her with a natural elegance made slightly awkward by advanced pregnancy. Snake had to look up to meet her gaze. She had small fine lines at the corners of her eyes, as if she laughed, sometimes, in secret. She smiled, but with concern. "You seem very tired. Shall I have someone make you a bed?"

"Not now," Snake said, "not yet. I won't sleep until afterward."

The leader searched her face, and Snake felt a kinship with her, in their shared responsibility.

"I understand, I think. Is there anything we can give you? Do you need aid with your preparations?"

Snake found herself having to deal with the questions as if they were complex problems. She turned them in her tired mind, examined them, dissected them, and finally grasped their meanings. "My pony needs food and water—"

"It is taken care of."

"And I need someone to help me with Mist. Someone strong. But it's more important that they are not afraid."

The leader nodded. "I would help you," she said, and smiled again, a little. "But I am a bit clumsy of late. I will find someone."

"Thank you."

Somber again, the older woman inclined her head and moved slowly toward a small group of tents. Snake watched her go, admiring her grace. She felt small and young and grubby in comparison.

Sand began to unwrap himself from her wrist. Feeling the anticipatory slide of scales on her skin, she caught him before he could drop to the ground. Sand lifted the upper half of his body from her hands. He flicked out his tongue, peering toward the little animal, feeling its body heat, smelling its fear. "I know thou art hungry," Snake said, "but that creature is not for thee." She put Sand in the case, lifted Mist from her shoulder, and let her coil herself in her dark compartment.

The small animal shrieked and struggled again when Snake's diffuse shadow passed over it. She bent and picked it up. The rapid series of terrified cries slowed and diminished and finally stopped as she stroked it. Finally it lay still, breathing hard, exhausted, staring up at her with yellow eyes.

It had long hind legs and wide pointed ears, and its nose twitched at the serpent smell. Its soft black fur was marked off in skewed squares by the cords of the net.

"I am sorry to take your life," Snake told it. "But there will be no more fear, and I will not hurt you." She closed her hand gently around it, and, stroking it, grasped its spine at the base of its skull. She pulled, once, quickly. It seemed to struggle, briefly, but it was already dead. It convulsed; its legs drew up against its body, and its toes curled and quivered. It seemed to stare up at her, even now. She freed its body from the net.

Snake chose a small vial from her belt pouch, pried open the animal's clenched jaws, and let a single drop of the vial's cloudy preparation fall into its mouth. Quickly she opened the satchel again, and called Mist out. She came slowly, slipping over the edge, hood closed, sliding in the sharp-grained sand. Her milky scales caught the thin light. She smelled the animal, flowed to it, touched it with her tongue. For a moment Snake was afraid she would refuse dead meat, but the body was still warm, still twitching reflexively, and she was very hungry. "A tidbit for thee," Snake said. "To whet thy appetite." Mist nosed it, reared back, and struck, sinking her short fixed fangs into the tiny body, biting again, pumping out her store of poison. She released it, took a better grip, and began to work her jaws around it; it would hardly distend her throat. When Mist lay quiet, digesting the small meal, Snake sat beside her and held her, waiting.

She heard footsteps in the coarse sand.

"I'm sent to help you."

He was a young man, despite a scatter of white in his dark hair. He was taller than Snake, and not unattractive. His eyes were dark, and the sharp planes of his face were further hardened because his hair was pulled straight back and tied. His expression was neutral.

"Are you afraid?"

"I will do as you tell me."

Though his body was obscured by his robe, his long fine hands showed strength.

"Then hold her body, and don't let her surprise you." Mist was beginning to twitch from the effects of the drugs Snake had put in the small animal's body. The cobra's eyes stared, unseeing.

"If it bites—"

"Hold, quickly!"

The young man reached, but he had hesitated too long. Mist writhed, lashing out, striking him in the face with her tail. He staggered back, at least as surprised as hurt. Snake kept a close grip behind Mist's jaws, and struggled to catch the rest of her as well. Mist was no constrictor, but she was smooth and strong and fast. Thrashing, she forced out her breath in a long hiss. She would have bitten anything she could reach. As Snake fought with her, she managed to squeeze the poison glands and force out the last drops of venom. They hung from Mist's fangs for a moment, catching light as jewels would; the force of the serpent's convulsions flung them away into the darkness. Snake struggled with the cobra, speaking softly, aided for once by the sand, on which Mist could get no purchase. Snake felt the young man behind her, grabbing for Mist's body and tail. The seizure stopped abruptly, and Mist lay limp in their hands.

"I am sorry—"

"Hold her," Snake said. "We have the night to go."

During Mist's second convulsion, the young man held her firmly and was of some real help. Afterward, Snake answered his interrupted question. "If she were making poison and she bit you, you would probably die. Even now her bite would make you ill. But unless you do something foolish, if she manages to bite, she will bite me."

"You would benefit my cousin little, if you were dead or dying."

"You misunderstand. Mist cannot kill me." She held out her hand, so he could see the white scars of slashes and punctures. He stared at them, and looked into her eyes for a long moment, then looked away.

The bright spot in the clouds from which the light radiated moved westward in the sky; they held the cobra like a child. Snake found herself half-dozing, but Mist moved her head, dully attempting to evade restraint, and Snake woke herself abruptly. "I must not sleep," she said to the young man. "Talk to me. What are you called?"

As Stavin had, the young man hesitated. He seemed afraid of her, or of something. "My people," he said, "think it unwise to speak our names to strangers."

"If you consider me a witch you should not have asked my aid. I know no magic, and I claim none. I can't learn all the customs of all the people on this earth, so I keep my own. My custom is to address those I work with by name."

"It's not a superstition," he said. "Not as you might think. We're not afraid of being bewitched."

Snake waited, watching him, trying to decipher his expression in the dim light.

"Our families know our names, and we exchange names with those we would marry."

Snake considered that custom, and thought it would fit badly on her. "No one else? Ever?"

"Well . . . a friend might know one's name."

"Ah," Snake said. "I see. I am still a stranger, and perhaps an enemy."

"A *friend* would know my name," the young man said again. "I would not offend you, but now you misunderstand. An acquaintance is not a friend. We value friendship highly."

"In this land one should be able to tell quickly if a person is worth calling 'friend.'"

"We make friends seldom. Friendship is a commitment."

"It sounds like something to be feared."

He considered that possibility. "Perhaps it's the betrayal of friendship we fear. That is a very painful thing."

"Has anyone ever betrayed you?"

He glanced at her sharply, as if she had exceeded the limits of propriety. "No," he said, and his voice was as hard as his face. "No friend. I have no one I call friend."

His reaction startled Snake. "That's very sad," she said, and grew silent, trying to comprehend the deep stresses that could close people off so far, comparing her loneliness of necessity and theirs of choice. "Call me Snake," she said finally, "if you can bring yourself to pronounce it. Speaking my name binds you to nothing."

The young man seemed about to speak; perhaps he thought again that he had offended her, perhaps he felt he should further defend his customs. But Mist began to twist in their hands, and they had to hold her to keep her from injuring herself. The cobra was slender for her length, but powerful, and the convulsions she went through were more severe than any she had ever had before. She thrashed in Snake's grasp, and almost pulled away. She tried to spread her hood, but Snake held her too tightly. She opened her mouth and hissed, but no poison dripped from her fangs.

She wrapped her tail around the young man's waist. He began to pull her and turn, to extricate himself from her coils.

"She's not a constrictor," Snake said. "She won't hurt you. Leave her—"

But it was too late; Mist relaxed suddenly and the young man lost his balance. Mist whipped herself away and lashed figures in the sand. Snake wrestled with her alone while the young man tried to hold her, but she curled herself around Snake and used the grip for leverage. She started to pull herself from Snake's hands. Snake threw them both backward into the sand; Mist rose above her, openmouthed, furious, hissing. The young man lunged and grabbed her just beneath her hood. Mist struck at him, but Snake, somehow, held her back. Together they deprived Mist of her hold, and regained control of her. Snake struggled up, but Mist suddenly went quite still and lay almost rigid between them. They were both sweating; the young man was pale under his tan, and even Snake was trembling.

"We have a little while to rest," Snake said. She glanced at him and noticed the dark line on his cheek where, earlier, Mist's tail had slashed him. She reached up and touched it. "You'll have a bruise, no more," she said. "It will not scar."

"If it were true that serpents sting with their tails, you would be restraining both the fangs and the stinger, and I'd be of little use."

"Tonight I'd need someone to keep me awake, whether or not he helped me with Mist." Fighting the cobra had produced adrenaline, but now it ebbed, and her exhaustion and hunger were returning, stronger.

"Snake . . ."

"Yes?"

He smiled, quickly, half-embarrassed. "I was trying the pronunciation."

"Good enough."

"How long did it take you to cross the desert?"

"Not very long. Too long. Six days."

"How did you live?"

"There is water. We traveled at night, except yesterday, when I could find no shade."

"You carried all your food?"

She shrugged. "A little." And wished he would not speak of food.

"What's on the other side?"

"More sand, more bush, a little more water. A few groups of people, traders, the station I grew up and took my training in. And farther on, a mountain with a city inside."

"I would like to see a city. Someday."

"The desert can be crossed."

He said nothing, but Snake's memories of leaving home were recent enough that she could imagine his thoughts.

The next set of convulsions came, much sooner than Snake had expected. By their severity, she gauged something of the stage of Stavin's illness, and wished it were morning. If she were to lose him, she would have it done, and grieve, and try to forget. The cobra would have battered herself to death against the sand if Snake and the young man had not been holding her. She suddenly went completely rigid, with her mouth clamped shut and her forked tongue dangling.

She stopped breathing.

"Hold her," Snake said. "Hold her head. Quickly, take her, and if she gets away, run. Take her! She won't strike at you now, she could only slash you by accident."

He hesitated only a moment, then grasped Mist behind the head. Snake ran, slipping in the deep sand, from the edge of the circle of tents to a place where bushes still grew. She broke off dry thorny branches that tore her scarred hands. Peripherally she noticed a mass of horned vipers, so ugly they seemed deformed, nesting beneath the clump of desiccated vegetation; they hissed at her: she ignored them. She found a narrow hollow stem and carried it back. Her hands bled from deep scratches.

Kneeling by Mist's head, she forced open the cobra's mouth and pushed the tube deep into her throat, through the air passage at the base of Mist's tongue. She bent close, took the tube in her mouth, and breathed gently into Mist's lungs.

She noticed: the young man's hands, holding the cobra as she had asked; his breathing, first a sharp gasp of surprise, then ragged; the sand scraping her elbows where she leaned; the cloying smell of the fluid seeping from Mist's fangs; her own dizziness, she thought from exhaustion, which she forced away by necessity and will.

Snake breathed, and breathed again, paused, and repeated, until Mist caught the rhythm and continued it unaided.

Snake sat back on her heels. "I think she'll be all right," she said. "I hope she will." She brushed the back of her hand across her forehead. The touch sparked pain: she jerked her hand down and agony slid along her bones, up her arm, across her shoulder, across her chest, enveloping her heart. Her balance turned on its edge. She fell, tried to catch herself but moved too slowly, fought nausea and vertigo and almost succeeded, until the pull of the earth seemed to slip away in pain and she was lost in darkness with nothing to take a bearing by.

She felt sand where it had scraped her cheek and her palms, but it was soft. "Snake, can I let go?" She thought the question must be for someone else, while at the same time she knew there was no one else to answer it, no one else to reply to her name. She felt hands on her, and they were gentle; she wanted to respond to them, but she was too tired. She needed sleep more, so she pushed them away. But they held her head and put dry leather to her lips and poured water into her throat. She coughed and choked and spat it out.

She pushed herself up on one elbow. As her sight cleared, she realized she was shaking. She felt as she had the first time she was snake-bit, before her immunities had completely developed. The young man knelt over her, his water flask in his hand. Mist, beyond him, crawled toward the darkness. Snake forgot the throbbing pain. "Mist!"

The young man flinched and turned, frightened; the serpent reared up, her head nearly at Snake's standing eye level, her hood spread, swaying, watching, angry, ready to strike. She formed a wavering white line against black. Snake forced herself to rise, feeling as though she were fumbling with the control of some unfamiliar body. She almost fell again, but held herself steady. "Thou must not go to hunt now," she said. "There is work for thee to do." She held out her right hand, to the side, a decoy, to draw Mist if she struck. Her hand was heavy with pain. Snake feared, not being bitten, but the loss of the contents of Mist's poison sacs. "Come here," she said. "Come here, and stay thy anger." She noticed blood flowing down between her fingers, and the fear she felt for Stavin was intensified. "Didst thou bite me, creature?" But the pain was wrong: poison would numb her, and the new serum only sting . . .

"No," the young man whispered, from behind her.

Mist struck. The reflexes of long training took over. Snake's right hand jerked away, her left grabbed Mist as she brought her head back. The cobra writhed a moment, and relaxed. "Devious beast," Snake said. "For shame." She turned, and let Mist crawl up her arm and over her shoulder, where she lay like the outline of an invisible cape and dragged her tail like the edge of a train.

"She did not bite me?"

"No," the young man said. His contained voice was touched with awe. "You should be dying. You should be curled around the agony, and your arm swollen purple. When you came back—" He gestured toward her hand. "It must have been a bush viper."

Snake remembered the coil of reptiles beneath the branches, and touched the blood on her hand. She wiped it away, revealing the double puncture of a snakebite among the scratches of the thorns. The wound was slightly swollen. "It needs cleaning," she said. "I shame myself by falling to it." The pain of it washed in gentle waves up her arm, burning no longer. She stood looking at the young man, looking around her, watching the landscape shift and change as her tired eyes tried to cope with the low light of setting moon and false dawn. "You held Mist well, and bravely," she said to the young man. "Thank you."

He lowered his gaze, almost bowing to her. He rose, and approached her. Snake put her hand gently on Mist's neck so she would not be alarmed.

"I would be honored," the young man said, "if you would call me Arevin."

"I would be pleased to."

Snake knelt down and held the winding white loops as Mist crawled slowly into her compartment. In a little while, when Mist had stabilized, by dawn, they would go to Stavin.

The tip of Mist's white tail slid out of sight. Snake closed the case and would have risen, but she could not stand. She had not yet quite shaken off the effects of the new venom. The flesh around the wound was red and tender, but the hemorrhaging would not spread. She stayed where she was, slumped, staring at her hand, creeping slowly in her mind toward what she needed to do, this time for herself.

"Let me help you. Please."

He touched her shoulder and helped her stand. "I'm sorry," she said. "I'm so in need of rest . . ."

"Let me wash your hand," Arevin said. "And then you can sleep. Tell me when to waken you—"

"No. I can't sleep yet." She pulled together the skeins of her nerves, collected herself, straightened, tossed the damp curls of her short hair off her forehead. "I'm all right now. Have you any water?"

Arevin loosened his outer robe. Beneath it he wore a loincloth and a leather belt that carried several leather flasks and pouches. The color of his skin was slightly lighter than the sun-darkened brown of his face. He brought out his water flask, closed his robe around his lean body, and reached for Snake's hand.

"No, Arevin. If the poison gets in any small scratch you might have, it could infect."

She sat down and sluiced lukewarm water over her hand. The water dripped pink to the ground and disappeared, leaving not even a damp spot visible. The wound bled a little more, but now it only ached. The poison was almost inactivated.

"I don't understand," Arevin said, "how it is that you're unhurt. My younger sister was bitten by a bush viper." He could not speak as uncaringly as he might have wished. "We could do nothing to save her—nothing we had would even lessen her pain."

Snake gave him his flask and rubbed salve from a vial in her belt pouch across the closing punctures. "It's a part of our preparation," she said. "We work with many kinds of serpents, so we must be immune to as many as possible." She shrugged. "The process is tedious and somewhat painful." She clenched her fist; the film held, and she was steady. She leaned toward Arevin and touched his abraded cheek again. "Yes . . ." She spread a thin layer of the salve across it. "That will help it heal."

"If you cannot sleep," Arevin said, "can you at least rest?"

"Yes," she said. "For a little while."

Snake sat next to Arevin, leaning against him, and they watched the sun turn the clouds to gold and flame and amber. The simple physical contact with another human being gave Snake pleasure, though she found it unsatisfying. Another time, another place, she might do something more, but not here, not now.

When the lower edge of the sun's bright smear rose above the horizon, Snake rose and teased Mist out of the case. She came slowly, weakly, and crawled across Snake's shoulders. Snake picked up the satchel, and she and Arevin walked together back to the small group of tents.

Stavin's parents waited, watching for her, just outside the entrance of their tent. They stood in a tight, defensive, silent group. For a moment Snake thought they had decided to send her away. Then, with regret and fear like hot iron in her mouth, she asked if Stavin had died. They shook their heads, and allowed her to enter.

Stavin lay as she had left him, still asleep. The adults followed her with their stares, and she could smell fear. Mist flicked out her tongue, growing nervous from the implied danger.

"I know you would stay," Snake said. "I know you would help, if you could, but there is nothing to be done by any person but me. Please go back outside."

They glanced at each other, and at Arevin, and she thought for a moment that they would refuse. Snake wanted to fall into the silence and sleep. "Come, cousins," Arevin said. "We are in her hands." He opened the tent flap and motioned them out. Snake thanked him with nothing more than a glance, and he might almost have smiled. She turned toward Stavin, and knelt beside him. "Stavin—" She touched his forehead; it was very hot. She noticed that her hand was less steady than before. The slight touch awakened the child.

"It's time," Snake said.

He blinked, coming out of some child's dream, seeing her, slowly recognizing her. He did not look frightened. For that Snake was glad; for some other reason she could not identify she was uneasy.

"Will it hurt?"

"Does it hurt now?"

He hesitated, looked away, looked back. "Yes."

"It might hurt a little more. I hope not. Are you ready?"

"Can Grass stay?"

"Of course," she said.

And realized what was wrong.

"I'll come back in a moment." Her voice changed so much, she had pulled it so tight, that she could not help but frighten him. She left the tent, walking slowly, calmly, restraining herself. Outside, the parents told her by their faces what they feared.

"Where is Grass?" Arevin, his back to her, started at her tone. The fair-haired man made a small grieving sound, and could look at her no longer.

"We were afraid," the eldest partner said. "We thought it would bite the child."

"I thought it would. It was I. It crawled over his face, I could see its fangs—" Stavin's mother put her hands on the younger partner's shoulders, and he said no more.

"Where is he?" She wanted to scream; she did not.

They brought her a small open box. Snake took it, and looked inside.

Grass lay cut almost in two, his entrails oozing from his body, half turned over, and as she watched, shaking, he writhed once, and flicked his tongue out once, and in. Snake made some sound, too low in her throat to be a cry. She hoped his motions were only reflex, but she picked him up as gently as she could. She leaned down and touched her lips to the smooth green scales behind his head. She bit him quickly, sharply, at the base of the skull. His blood flowed cool and salty in her mouth. If he were not dead, she had killed him instantly.

She looked at the parents, and at Arevin; they were all pale, but she had no sympathy for their fear, and cared nothing for shared grief. "Such a small creature," she said. "Such a small creature, who could only give pleasure and dreams." She watched them for a moment more, then turned toward the tent again.

"Wait—" She heard the eldest partner move up close behind her. He touched her shoulder; she shrugged away his hand. "We will give you anything you want," he said, "but leave the child alone."

She spun on him in a fury. "Should I kill Stavin for your stupidity?" He seemed about to try to hold her back. She jammed her shoulder hard into his stomach, and flung herself past the tent flap. Inside, she kicked over the satchel. Abruptly awakened, and angry, Sand crawled out and coiled himself. When the younger husband and the wife tried to enter, Sand hissed and rattled with a violence Snake had never heard him use before. She did not even bother to look behind her. She ducked her head and wiped her tears on her sleeve before Stavin could see them. She knelt beside him.

"What's the matter?" He could not help but hear the voices outside the tent, and the running.

"Nothing, Stavin," Snake said. "Did you know we came across the desert?"

"No," he said, with wonder.

"It was very hot, and none of us had anything to eat. Grass is hunting now. He was very hungry. Will you forgive him and let me begin? I will be here all the time."

He seemed so tired; he was disappointed, but he had no strength for arguing. "All right." His voice rustled like sand slipping through the fingers.

Snake lifted Mist from her shoulders, and pulled the blanket from Stavin's small body. The tumor pressed up beneath his ribcage, distorting his form, squeezing his vital organs,

sucking nourishment from him for its own growth. Holding
Mist's head, Snake let her flow across him, touching and tasting him. She had to restrain the cobra to keep her from
striking; the excitement had agitated her. When Sand used his
rattle, she flinched. Snake spoke to her softly, soothing her;
trained and bred-in responses began to return, overcoming
the natural instincts. Mist paused when her tongue flicked the
skin above the tumor, and Snake released her.

The cobra reared, and struck, and bit as cobras bite, sinking her fangs their short length once, releasing, instantly
biting again for a better purchase, holding on, chewing at her
prey. Stavin cried out, but he did not move against Snake's
restraining hands.

Mist expended the contents of her venom sacs into the
child, and released him. She reared up, peered around, folded
her hood, and slid across the mats in a perfectly straight line
toward her dark, close compartment.

"It is all finished, Stavin."

"Will I die now?"

"No," Snake said. "Not now. Not for many years, I hope."
She took a vial of powder from her belt pouch. "Open your
mouth." He complied, and she sprinkled the powder across
his tongue. "That will help the ache." She spread a pad of
cloth across the series of shallow puncture wounds, without
wiping off the blood.

She turned from him.

"Snake? Are you going away?"

"I will not leave without saying good-bye. I promise."

The child lay back, closed his eyes, and let the drug take
him.

Sand coiled quiescently on the dark matting. Snake called
him. He moved toward her, and suffered himself to be replaced in the satchel. Snake closed it, and lifted it, and it still
felt empty. She heard noises outside the tent. Stavin's parents
and the people who had come to help them pulled open the
tent flap and peered inside, thrusting sticks in even before
they looked.

Snake set down her leather case. "It's done."

They entered. Arevin was with them, too; only he was
empty-handed. "Snake—" He spoke through grief, pity, confusion, and Snake could not tell what he believed. He looked
back. Stavin's mother was just behind him. He took her by
the shoulder. "He would have died without her. Whatever has
happened now, he would have died."

The woman shook his hand away. "He might have lived. It might have gone away. We—" She could not speak for hiding tears.

Snake felt the people moving, surrounding her. Arevin took one step toward her and stopped, and she could see he wanted her to defend herself. "Can any of you cry?" she said. "Can any of you cry for me and my despair, or for them and their guilt, or for small things and their pain?" She felt tears slip down her cheeks.

They did not understand her; they were offended by her crying. They stood back, still afraid of her, but gathering themselves. She no longer needed the pose of calmness she had used to deceive the child. "Ah, you fools." Her voice sounded brittle. "Stavin—"

Light from the entrance struck them. "Let me pass." The people in front of Snake moved aside for their leader. She stopped in front of Snake, ignoring the satchel her foot almost touched. "Will Stavin live?" Her voice was quiet, calm, gentle.

"I cannot be certain," Snake said, "but I feel that he will."

"Leave us." The people understood Snake's words before they did their leader's; they looked around and lowered their weapons, and finally, one by one, they moved out of the tent. Arevin remained. Snake felt the strength that came from danger seeping from her. Her knees collapsed. She bent over the satchel with her face in her hands. The older woman knelt in front of her, before Snake could notice or prevent her. "Thank you," she said. "Thank you. I am so sorry . . ." She put her arms around Snake, and drew her toward her, and Arevin knelt beside them, and he embraced Snake, too. Snake began to tremble again, and they held her while she cried.

Later she slept, exhausted, alone in the tent with Stavin, holding his hand. The people had caught small animals for Sand and Mist. They had given her food, and supplies, and sufficient water for her to bathe, though the last must have strained their resources.

When she awakened, Arevin lay sleeping nearby, his robe open in the heat, a sheen of sweat across his chest and stomach. The sternness in his expression vanished when he slept; he looked exhausted and vulnerable. Snake almost woke him, but stopped, shook her head, and turned to Stavin.

She felt the tumor, and found that it had begun to dissolve and shrivel, dying, as Mist's changed poison affected it.

Through her grief Snake felt a little joy. She smoothed Stavin's pale hair back from his face. "I would not lie to you again, little one," she whispered, "but I must leave soon. I cannot stay here." She wanted another three days' sleep, to finish fighting off the effects of the bush viper's poison, but she would sleep somewhere else. "Stavin?"

He half woke, slowly. "It doesn't hurt anymore," he said.

"I am glad."

"Thank you . . ."

"Goodbye, Stavin. Will you remember later on that you woke up, and that I did stay to say goodbye?"

"Goodbye," he said, drifting off again. "Goodbye, Snake. Goodbye, Grass." He closed his eyes.

Snake picked up the satchel and stood gazing down at Arevin. He did not stir. Half grateful, half regretful, she left the tent.

Dusk approached with long, indistinct shadows; the camp was hot and quiet. She found her tiger-striped pony, tethered with food and water. New, full water-skins bulged on the ground next to the saddle, and desert robes lay across the pommel, though Snake had refused any payment. The tiger-pony whickered at her. She scratched his striped ears, saddled him, and strapped her gear on his back. Leading him, she started east, the way she had come.

"Snake—"

She took a breath, and turned back to Arevin. He was facing the sun; it turned his skin ruddy and his robe scarlet. His streaked hair flowed loose to his shoulders, gentling his face. "You must leave?"

"Yes."

"I hoped you would not leave before . . . I hoped you would stay, for a time . . ."

"If things were different, I might have stayed."

"They were frightened—"

"I told them Grass couldn't hurt them, but they saw his fangs and they didn't know he could only give dreams and ease dying."

"But can't you forgive them?"

"I can't face their guilt. What they did was my fault, Arevin. I didn't understand them until too late."

"You said it yourself, you can't know all the customs and all the fears."

"I'm crippled," she said. "Without Grass, if I can't heal a person, I cannot help at all. I must go home and face my teachers, and hope they'll forgive my stupidity. They seldom give the name I bear, but they gave it to me—and they'll be disappointed."

"Let me come with you."

She wanted to; she hesitated, and cursed herself for that weakness. "They may take Mist and Sand and cast me out, and you would be cast out too. Stay here, Arevin."

"It wouldn't matter."

"It would. After a while, we would hate each other. I don't know you, and you don't know me. We need calmness, and quiet, and time to understand each other well."

He came toward her, and put his arms around her, and they stood embracing for a moment. When he raised his head, there were tears on his cheeks. "Please come back," he said. "Whatever happens, please come back."

"I will try," Snake said. "Next spring, when the winds stop, look for me. The spring after that, if I do not come, forget me. Where I am, if I live, I will forget you."

"I will look for you," Arevin said, and he would promise no more.

Snake picked up her pony's lead, and started across the desert.

Of Novas and Other Stars

Occasionally in the development of every literature a special kind of writer comes along who either transforms it or realizes its potential. These special writers are either innovators or realizers. Cervantes and Richardson were innovators; Shakespeare was a realizer. Sometimes what these writers have accomplished is not evident until decades or centuries later, but usually they appear in the heavens like exploding stars—like novas.

In science fiction, Verne and Wells were innovators, but since such terms never are as mutually exclusive as they seem, Verne let no one forget his debt to writers such as Poe and Defoe and Wyss, and Wells paid tribute to Swift and Sterne (but did not admit the ideas he took from such French writers as Rosny, Gourmont, and Flammarion). Edgar Rice Burroughs was both innovator and realizer, but E. E. "Doc" Smith was an innovator. Robert A. Heinlein was an innovator; A. E. van Vogt was a realizer. Both were recognized as superstars from the moment of their first publications.

Not so many have blazed so unequivocally: Ray Bradbury brightened slowly; Alfred Bester exploded; Frederik Pohl, after a long pseudonymous apprenticeship, formed a spectacular double star with Cyril Kornbluth and then had a new burst of creative fire in the middle and late 1970s. Ursula K. Le Guin certainly belongs among the novas, and probably Larry Niven. Others, such as Jack Williamson, Clifford Simak, Fritz Leiber, L. Sprague de Camp, Frank

Herbert, Brian Aldiss, Philip K. Dick, Robert Silverberg, and Harlan Ellison, have burned more evenly.

In the latter part of the 1970s, one of the novas was John Varley (1947–   ). He is a realizer; his work took the conventions of the genre and made them seem freshly invented. Born in Austin, Texas, Varley attended Michigan State University in 1966 and has been a freelance writer since 1973. He lives in Eugene, Oregon. His first published story was "Picnic on Nearside" in the August 1974 *Magazine of Fantasy and Science Fiction*. It was followed by a series of spectacularly inventive stories published in a variety of magazines and original anthologies.

Most of Varley's stories share a common background: mysterious and powerful Invaders have swept in from outer space and evicted humanity from Earth in favor of the whales and dolphins (compare Gordon Dickson's "Dolphin's Way," *TRTSF #3*, p. 367), but humanity continues to exist, and in technologically enhanced circumstances, on the moon, on the other planets and satellites, and in space. Moreover, science, which is indispensable to survival in these environments, has transformed people's lives. Particularly through biological advances, but also through improvements in physical science, people are in greater control not only of their environments but of themselves; they can transform their bodies by means of cloning, memory recording and transfer, genetic manipulation, cosmetic surgery, and other techniques. Much of life has become concerned with art rather than survival.

In these circumstances new kinds of living styles are possible, new options are available, new values are established and old ones discarded. In this life little is final: Virginity can be restored, death is only a momentary interruption of memory, and personal relationships are as variable as the individual's choice of body, face, or even sex. People can live anywhere and do anything. In *Twentieth Century Science Fiction Writers*, Ian Watson calls this "cozy" because choices have no dire consequences, but the effect of Varley's stories is to question what most people believe to be sacred and unchangeable.

From his first publications Varley began earning award nominations in bunches. "Gotta Sing, Gotta Dance" and "The Phantom of Kansas" became Hugo finalists in 1977. "In the Hall of the Martian Kings" was a Hugo finalist in 1978, and Varley was a finalist for the Campbell Award for the best new writer of the year in 1975 and 1976. In 1979,

"The Persistence of Vision" won both the Nebula and the Hugo; "The Barbie Murders" also was a Hugo finalist. In 1980, Varley's novel *Titan* and his story "Options" were both Nebula and Hugo finalists; the sequel to *Titan*, *Wizard*, also was a Hugo finalist the following year.

Varley's short stories have been collected in *The Persistence of Vision* (1978) and *The Barbie Murders* (1980). His first novel, *The Ophiuchi Hotline* (1977), also was well received.

"Air Raid," originally published in the Spring 1977 *Isaac Asimov's Science Fiction Magazine*, was a Nebula and Hugo finalist for that year. The film rights have been sold, and Varley has written a screenplay and a novelization. The story, however, does not share the background common to much of his fiction. Instead it brings together many of the conventions common to earlier science fiction, including the protocols of reading evident in such stories as Farmer's "Sail on! Sail On!" (Volume 3): In the process of telling a story about a well-organized paramilitary operation, the author provides terminology and information that demands interpretation by the reader, such as "Snatch Team," "plugged in," "Ops," "situation board," the date of an air flight, "go-juice," "Caucasian paint job"—all these in the first five paragraphs.

Eventually the meaning comes clear and the narrative—a race against time for a purpose that can only be guessed, and the author's intention is that the guess will be wrong—unrolls itself in a way that answers all the questions raised in the first-person narration, and the answers are surprising and satisfying and humanly revealing, all at the same time.

Air Raid

by John Varley

I was jerked awake by the silent alarm vibrating my skull. It won't shut down until you sit up, so I did. All around me in the darkened bunkroom the Snatch Team members were sleeping singly and in pairs. I yawned, scratched my ribs, and patted Gene's hairy flank. He turned over. So much for a romantic send-off.

Rubbing sleep from my eyes, I reached to the floor for my leg, strapped it on, and plugged it in. Then I was running down the rows of bunks toward Ops.

The situation board glowed in the gloom. Sun-Belt Airlines Flight 128, Miami to New York, September 15, 1979. We'd been looking for that one for three years. I should have been happy, but who can afford it when you wake up?

Liza Boston muttered past me on the way to Prep. I muttered back and followed. The lights came on around the mirrors, and I groped my way to one of them. Behind us, three more people staggered in. I sat down, plugged in, and at last I could lean back and close my eyes.

They didn't stay closed for long. Rush! I sat up straight as the sludge I use for blood was replaced with supercharged go-juice. I looked around me and got a series of idiot grins. There was Liza, and Pinky and Dave. Against the far wall Cristabel was already turning slowly in front of the airbrush, getting a Caucasian paint job. It looked like a good team.

I opened the drawer and started preliminary work on my face. It's a bigger job every time. Transfusion or no, I looked like death. The right ear was completely gone now. I could no longer close my lips; the gums were permanently bared. A week earlier, a finger had fallen off in my sleep. And what's it to you, bugger?

While I worked, one of the screens around the mirror glowed. A smiling young woman, blonde, high brow, round face. Close enough. The crawl line read *Mary Katrina Sondergard, born Trenton, New Jersey, age in 1979: 25.* Baby, this is your lucky day.

The computer melted the skin away from her face to show me the bone structure, rotated it, gave me cross sections. I studied the similarities with my own skull, noted the differences. Not bad, and better than some I'd been given.

I assembled a set of dentures that included the slight gap in the upper incisors. Putty filled out my cheeks. Contact lenses fell from the dispenser and I popped them in. Nose plugs widened my nostrils. No need for ears; they'd be covered by the wig. I pulled a blank plastiflesh mask over my face and had to pause while it melted in. It took only a minute to mold it to perfection. I smiled at myself. How nice to have lips.

The delivery slot clunked and dropped a blonde wig and a

pink outfit into my lap. The wig was hot from the styler. I put it on, then the pantyhose.

"Mandy? Did you get the profile on Sondergard?" I didn't look up; I recognized the voice.

"Roger."

"We've located her near the airport. We can slip you in before take-off, so you'll be the joker."

I groaned and looked up at the face on the screen. Elfreda Baltimore-Louisville, Director of Operational Teams: lifeless face and tiny slits for eyes. What can you do when all the muscles are dead?

"Okay." You take what you get.

She switched off, and I spent the next two minutes trying to get dressed while keeping my eyes on the screens. I memorized names and faces of crew members plus the few facts known about them. Then I hurried out and caught up with the others. Elapsed time from first alarm: twelve minutes and seven seconds. We'd better get moving.

"Goddam Sun-Belt," Cristabel groused, hitching at her bra.

"At least they got rid of the high heels," Dave pointed out. A year earlier we would have been teetering down the aisles on three-inch platforms. We all wore short pink shifts with blue and white diagonal stripes across the front, and carried matching shoulder bags. I fussed trying to get the ridiculous pillbox cap pinned on.

We jogged into the dark Operations Control Room and lined up at the gate. Things were out of our hands now. Until the gate was ready, we could only wait.

I was first, a few feet away from the portal. I turned away from it; it gives me vertigo. I focused instead on the gnomes sitting at their consoles, bathed in yellow lights from their screens. None of them looked back at me. They don't like us much. I don't like them, either. Withered, emaciated, all of them. Our fat legs and butts and breasts are a reproach to them, a reminder that Snatchers eat five times their ration to stay presentable for the masquerade. Meantime we continue to rot. One day I'll be sitting at a console. One day I'll be *built in* to a console, with all my guts on the outside and nothing left of my body but stink. The hell with them.

I buried my gun under a clutter of tissues and lipsticks in my purse. Elfreda was looking at me.

"Where is she?" I asked.

"Motel room. She was alone from ten PM to noon on flight day."

Departure time was 1:15. She had cut it close and would be in a hurry. Good.

"Can you catch her in the bathroom? Best of all, in the tub?"

"We're working on it." She sketched a smile with a fingertip drawn over lifeless lips. She knew how I liked to operate, but she was telling me I'd take what I got. It never hurts to ask. People are at their most defenseless stretched out and up to their necks in water.

"Go!" Elfreda shouted. I stepped through, and things started to go wrong.

I was facing the wrong way, stepping *out* of the bathroom door and facing the bedroom. I turned and spotted Mary Katrina Sondergard through the haze of the gate. There was no way I could reach her without stepping back through. I couldn't even shoot without hitting someone on the other side.

Sondergard was at the mirror, the worst possible place. Few people recognize themselves quickly, but she'd been looking right at herself. She saw me and her eyes widened. I stepped to the side, out of her sight.

"What the hell is . . . hey? Who the hell—" I noted the voice, which can be the trickiest thing to get right.

I figured she'd be more curious than afraid. My guess was right. She came out of the bathroom, passing through the gate as if it wasn't there, which it wasn't, since it only has one side. She had a towel wrapped around her.

"Jesus Christ! What are you doing in my—" Words fail you at a time like that. She knew she ought to say something, but what? *Excuse me, haven't I seen you in the mirror?*

I put on my best stew smile and held out my hand.

"Pardon the intrusion. I can explain everything. You see, I'm—" I hit her on the side of the head and she staggered and went down hard. Her towel fell to the floor. "—working my way through college." She started to get up, so I caught her under the chin with my artificial knee. She stayed down.

"Standard fuggin' *oil!*" I hissed, rubbing my injured knuckles. But there was no time. I knelt beside her, checked her pulse. She'd be okay, but I think I loosened some front teeth. I paused a moment. Lord, to look like that with no makeup, no prosthetics! She nearly broke my heart.

I grabbed her under the knees and wrestled her to the gate. She was a sack of limp noodles. Somebody reached through, grabbed her feet, and pulled. *So long, love! How would you like to go on a long voyage?*

I sat on her rented bed to get my breath. There were car keys and cigarettes in her purse, genuine tobacco, worth its weight in blood. I lit six of them, figuring I had five minutes of my very own. The room filled with sweet smoke. They don't make 'em like that anymore.

The Hertz sedan was in the motel parking lot. I got in and headed for the airport. I breathed deeply of the air, rich in hydrocarbons. I could see for hundreds of yards into the distance. The perspective nearly made me dizzy, but I live for those moments. There's no way to explain what it's like in the pre-meck world. The sun was a fierce yellow ball through the haze.

The other stews were boarding. Some of them knew Sondergard, so I didn't say much, pleading a hangover. That went over well, with a lot of knowing laughs and sly remarks. Evidently it wasn't out of character. We boarded the 707 and got ready for the goats to arrive.

It looked good. The four commandos on the other side were identical twins for the women I was working with. There was nothing to do but be a stewardess until departure time. I hoped there would be no more glitches. Inverting a gate for a joker run into a motel room was one thing, but in a 707 at twenty thousand feet . . .

The plane was nearly full when the woman Pinky would impersonate sealed the forward door. We taxied to the end of the runway, then we were airborne. I started taking orders for drinks in first.

The goats were the usual lot, for 1979. Fat and sassy, all of them, and as unaware of living in a paradise as a fish is of the sea. *What would you think, ladies and gents, of a trip to the future? No? I can't say I'm surprised. What if I told you this plane is going to—*

My alarm beeped as we reached cruising altitude. I consulted the indicator under my Lady Bulova and glanced at one of the restroom doors. I felt a vibration pass through the plane. *Damn it, not so soon.*

The gate was in there. I came out quickly, and motioned for Diana Gleason—Dave's pigeon—to come to the front.

"Take a look at this," I said, with a disgusted look. She started to enter the restroom, stopped when she saw the green glow. I planted a boot on her fanny and shoved. Perfect. Dave would have a chance to hear her voice before popping in. Though she'd be doing little but screaming when she got a look around. . . .

Dave came through the gate, adjusting his silly little hat. Diana must have struggled.

"Be disgusted," I whispered.

"What a mess," he said as he came out of the restroom. It was a fair imitation of Diana's tone, though he'd missed the accent. It wouldn't matter much longer.

"What is it?" It was one of the stews from tourist. We stepped aside so she could get a look, and Dave shoved her through. Pinky popped out very quickly.

"We're minus on minutes," Pinky said. "We lost five on the other side."

"Five?" Dave-Diana squeaked. I felt the same way. We had a hundred and three passengers to process.

"Yeah. They lost contact after you pushed my pigeon through. It took that long to realign."

You get used to that. Time runs at different rates on each side of the gate, though it's always sequential, past to future. Once we'd started the Snatch with me entering Sondergard's room, there was no way to go back any earlier on either side. Here, in 1979, we had a rigid ninety-four minutes to get everything done. On the other side, the gate could never be maintained longer than three hours.

"When you left, how long was it since the alarm went in?"

"Twenty-eight minutes."

It didn't sound good. It would take at least two hours just customizing the wimps. Assuming there was no more slippage on 79-time, we might just make it. But there's *always* slippage. I shuddered, thinking about riding it in.

"No time for any more games, then," I said. "Pink, you go back to tourist and call both of the other girls up here. Tell 'em to come one at a time, and tell 'em we've got a problem. You know the bit."

"Biting back the tears. Got you." She hurried aft. In no time the first one showed up. Her friendly Sun-Belt Airlines smile was stamped on her face, but her stomach would be churning. *Oh God, this is it!*

I took her by the elbow and pulled her behind the curtains in front. She was breathing hard.

"Welcome to the twilight zone," I said, and put the gun to her head. She slumped, and I caught her. Pinky and Dave helped me shove her through the gate.

"Fug! The rotting thing's flickering."

Pinky was right. A very ominous sign. But the green glow stabilized as we watched, with who knows how much slippage on the other side. Cristabel ducked through.

"We're plus thirty-three," she said. There was no sense talking about what we were all thinking: things were going badly.

"Back to tourist," I said. "Be brave, smile at everyone, but make it just a little bit too good, got it?"

"Check," Cristabel said.

We processed the other quickly, with no incident. Then there was no time to talk about anything. In eighty-nine minutes Flight 128 was going to be spread all over a mountain whether we were finished or not.

Dave went into the cockpit to keep the flight crew out of our hair. Me and Pinky were supposed to take care of first class, then back up Cristabel and Liza in tourist. We used the standard "coffee, tea, or milk" gambit, relying on our speed and their inertia.

I leaned over the first two seats on the left.

"Are you enjoying your flight?" Pop, pop. Two squeezes on the trigger, close to the heads and out of sight of the rest of the goats.

"Hi, folks. I'm Mandy. Fly me." Pop, pop.

Halfway to the galley, a few people were watching us curiously. But people don't make a fuss until they have a lot more to go on. One goat in the back row stood up, and I let him have it. By now there were only eight left awake. I abandoned the smile and squeezed off four quick shots. Pinky took care of the rest. We hurried through the curtains, just in time.

There was an uproar building in the back of tourist, with about 60 percent of the goats already processed. Cristabel glanced at me, and I nodded.

"Okay, folks," she bawled. "I want you to be quiet. Calm down and listen up. *You*, fathead, *pipe down* before I cram my foot up your ass sideways."

The shock of hearing her talk like that was enough to buy us a little time, anyway. We had formed a skirmish line across the width of the plane, guns out, steadied on seat backs, aimed at the milling, befuddled group of thirty goats.

The guns are enough to awe all but the most foolhardy. In essence, a standard-issue stunner is just a plastic rod with two grids about six inches apart. There's not enough metal in it to set off a hijack alarm. And to people from the Stone Age to about 2190 it doesn't look any more like a weapon than a ball-point pen. So Equipment Section jazzes them up in a plastic shell to real Buck Rogers blasters, with a dozen knobs and lights that flash and a barrel like the snout of a hog. Hardly anyone ever walks into one.

"We are in great danger, and time is short. You must all do exactly as I tell you, and you will be safe."

You can't give them time to think, you have to rely on your status as the Voice of Authority. The situation is just *not* going to make sense to them, no matter how you explain it.

"Just a minute, I think you owe us—"

An airborne lawyer. I made a snap decision, thumbed the fireworks switch on my gun, and shot him.

The gun made a sound like a flying saucer with hemorrhoids, spit sparks and little jets of flame, and extended a green laser finger to his forehead. He dropped.

All pure kark, of course. But it sure is impressive.

And it's damn risky, too. I had to choose between a panic if the fathead got them to thinking, and a possible panic from the flash of the gun. But when a 20th gets to talking about his "rights" and what he is "owed," things can get out of hand. It's infectious.

It worked. There was a lot of shouting, people ducking behind seats, but no rush. We could have handled it, but we needed some of them conscious if we were ever going to finish the Snatch.

"Get up. Get *up*, you *slugs!*" Cristabel yelled. "He's stunned, nothing worse. But I'll *kill* the next one who gets out of line. Now *get to your feet* and do what I tell you. *Children first! Hurry*, as fast as you can, to the front of the plane. Do what the stewardess tells you. Come on, kids, *move!*"

I ran back into first class just ahead of the kids, turned at the open restroom door, and got on my knees.

They were petrified. There were five of them—crying, some of them, which always chokes me up—looking left and right at dead people in the first class seats, stumbling, near panic.

"Come on, kids," I called to them, giving my special smile. "Your parents will be along in just a minute. Everything's going to be all right, I promise you. Come on."

I got three of them through. The fourth balked. She was determined not to go through that door. She spread her legs and arms and I couldn't push her through. I will *not* hit a child, never. She raked her nails over my face. My wig came off, and she gaped at my bare head. I shoved her through.

Number five was sitting in the aisle, bawling. He was maybe seven. I ran back and picked him up, hugged him and kissed him, and tossed him through. God, I needed a rest, but I was needed in tourist.

"You, you, you, and you. Okay, you too. Help him, will you?" Pinky had a practiced eye for the ones that wouldn't be any use to anyone, even themselves. We herded them toward the front of the plane, then deployed ourselves along the left side where we could cover the workers. It didn't take long to prod them into action. We had them dragging the limp bodies forward as fast as they could go. Me and Cristabel were in tourist, with the others up front.

Adrenaline was being catabolized in my body now; the rush of action left me and I started to feel very tired. There's an unavoidable feeling of sympathy for the poor dumb goats that starts to get me about this stage of the game. Sure, they were better off; sure, they were going to die if we didn't get them off the plane. But when they saw the other side they were going to have a hard time believing it.

The first ones were returning for a second load, stunned at what they'd just seen: dozens of people being put into a cubicle that was crowded when it was empty. One college student looked like he'd been hit in the stomach. He stopped by me and his eyes pleaded.

"Look, I want to *help* you people, just . . . what's going *on*? Is this some new kind of rescue? I mean, are we going to crash—"

I switched my gun to prod and brushed it across his cheek. He gasped and fell back.

"Shut your fuggin' mouth and get moving, or I'll kill you." It would be hours before his jaw was in shape to ask any more stupid questions.

We cleared tourist and moved up. A couple of the work gang were pretty damn pooped by then. Muscles like horses, all of them, but they can hardly run up a flight of stairs. We let some of them go through, including a couple that were at least fifty years old. *Je*-zuz. Fifty! We got down to a core of four men and two women who seemed strong, and worked them until they nearly dropped. But we processed everyone in twenty-five minutes.

The portapak came through as we were stripping off our

clothes. Cristabel knocked on the door to the cockpit and Dave came out, already naked. A bad sign.

"I had to cork 'em," he said. "Bleeding captain just *had* to make his grand march through the plane. I tried *every*thing."

Sometimes you have to do it. The plane was on autopilot, as it normally would be at this time. But if any of us did anything detrimental to the craft, changed the fixed course of events in any way, that would be it. All that work for nothing, and Flight 128 inaccessible to us for all Time. I don't know sludge about time theory, but I know the practical angles. We can do things in the past only at times and in places where it won't make any difference. We have to cover our tracks. There's flexibility; once a Snatcher left her gun behind and it went in with the plane. Nobody found it, or if they did, they didn't have the smoggiest idea of what it was, so we were okay.

Flight 128 was mechanical failure. That's the best kind; it means we don't have to keep the pilot unaware of the situation in the cabin right down to ground level. We can cork him and fly the plane, since there's nothing he could have done to save the flight anyway. A pilot-error smash is almost impossible to Snatch. We mostly work midairs, bombs, and structural failures. If there's even one survivor, we can't touch it. It would not fit the fabric of space-time, which is immutable (though it can stretch a little), and we'd all just fade away and appear back in the ready room.

My head was hurting. I wanted that portapak very badly.

"Who has the most hours on a 707?" Pinky did, so I sent her to the cabin, along with Dave, who could do the pilot's voice for air traffic control. You have to have a believable record in the flight recorder, too. They trailed two long tubes from the portapak, and the rest of us hooked in up close. We stood there, each of us smoking a fistful of cigarettes, wanting to finish them but hoping there wouldn't be time. The gate had vanished as soon as we tossed our clothes and the flight crew through.

But we didn't worry long. There's other nice things about Snatching, but nothing to compare with the rush of plugging into a portapak. The wake-up transfusion is nothing but fresh blood, rich in oxygen and sugars. What we were getting now as an insane brew of concentrated adrenaline, supersaturated hemoglobin, methedrine, white lightning, TNT, and Kickapoo joyjuice. It was like a firecracker in your heart; a boot in the box that rattled your sox.

"I'm growing hair on my chest," Cristabel said solemnly. Everyone giggled.

"Would someone hand me my eyeballs?"

"The blue ones, or the red ones?"

"I think my ass just fell off."

We'd heard them all before, but we howled anyway. We were strong, *strong*, and for one golden moment we had no worries. Everything was hilarious. I could have torn sheet metal with my eyelashes.

But you get hyper on that mix. When the gate didn't show, and didn't show, and *didn't sweetjeez show* we all started milling. This bird wasn't going to fly all that much longer.

Then it did show, and we turned on. The first of the wimps came through, dressed in the clothes taken from a passenger it had been picked to resemble.

"Two thirty-five elapsed upside time," Cristabel announced. "Je-zuz."

It is a deadening routine. You grab the harness around the wimp's shoulders and drag it along the aisle, after consulting the seat number painted on its forehead. The paint would last three minutes. You seat it, strap it in, break open the harness and carry it back to toss through the gate as you grab the next one. You have to take it for granted they've done the work right on the other side: fillings in the teeth, fingerprints, the right match in height and weight and hair color. Most of those things don't matter much, especially on Flight 128, which was a crash-and-burn. There would be bits and pieces, and burned to a crisp at that. But you can't take chances. Those rescue workers are pretty thorough on the parts they *do* find; the dental work and fingerprints especially are important.

I hate wimps. I really hate 'em. Every time I grab the harness of one of them, if it's a child, I wonder if it's Alice. *Are you my kid, you vegetable, you slug, you slimy worm?* I joined the Snatchers right after the brain bugs ate the life out of my baby's head. I couldn't stand to think she was the last generation, that the last humans there would ever be would live with nothing in their heads, medically dead by standards that prevailed even in 1979, with computers working their muscles to keep them in tone. You grow up, reach puberty still fertile—one in a thousand—rush to get pregnant in your first heat. Then you find out your mom or pop passed on a chronic disease bound right into the genes, and none of your kids will be immune. I *knew* about the paraleprosy; I grew up with my toes rotting away. But this was too much. What do you do?

Only one in ten of the wimps had a customized face. It takes time and a lot of skill to build a new face that will stand up to a doctor's autopsy. The rest came premutilated. We've got millions of them; it's not hard to find a good match in the body. Most of them would stay breathing, too dumb to stop, until they went in with the plane.

The plane jerked, hard. I glanced at my watch. Five minutes to impact. We should have time. I was on my last wimp. I could hear Dave frantically calling the ground. A bomb came through the gate, and I tossed it into the cockpit. Pinky turned on the pressure sensor on the bomb and came running out, followed by Dave. Liza was already through. I grabbed the limp dolls in stewardess costume and tossed them to the floor. The engine fell off and a piece of it came through the cabin. We started to depressurize. The bomb blew away part of the cockpit (the ground crash crew would read it—we hoped—that part of the engine came through and killed the crew: no more words from the pilot on the flight recorder) and we turned, slowly, left and down. I was lifted toward the hole in the side of the plane, but I managed to hold onto a seat. Cristabel wasn't so lucky. She was blown backwards.

We started to rise slightly, losing speed. Suddenly it was uphill from where Cristabel was lying in the aisle. Blood oozed from her temple. I glanced back; everyone was gone, and three pink-suited wimps were piled on the floor. The plane began to stall, to nose down, and my feet left the floor.

"Come on, Bel!" I screamed. That gate was only three feet away from me, but I began pulling myself along to where she floated. The plane bumped, and she hit the floor. Incredibly, it seemed to wake her up. She started to swim toward me, and I grabbed her hand as the floor came up to slam us again. We crawled as the plane went through its final death agony, and we came to the door. The gate was gone.

There wasn't anything to say. We were going in. It's hard enough to keep the gate in place on a plane that's moving in a straight line. When a bird gets to corkscrewing and coming apart, the math is fearsome. So I've been told.

I embraced Cristabel and held her bloodied head. She was groggy, but managed to smile and shrug. You take what you get. I hurried into the restroom and got both of us down on the floor. Back to the forward bulkhead, Cristabel between my legs, back to front. Just like in training. We pressed our feet against the other wall. I hugged her tightly and cried on her shoulder.

And it was there. A green glow to my left. I threw myself toward it, dragging Cristabel, keeping low as two wimps were thrown headfirst through the gate above our heads. Hands grabbed and pulled us through. I clawed my way a good five yards along the floor. You can leave a leg on the other side and I didn't have one to spare.

I sat up as they were carrying Cristabel to Medical. I patted her arm as she went by on the stretcher, but she was passed out. I wouldn't have minded passing out myself.

For a while, you can't believe it all really happened. Sometimes it turns out it *didn't* happen. You come back and find out all the goats in the holding pen have softly and suddenly vanished away because the continuum won't tolerate the changes and paradoxes you've put into it. The people you've worked so hard to rescue are spread like tomato surprise all over some goddam hillside in Carolina and all you've got left is a bunch of ruined wimps and an exhausted Snatch Team. But not this time. I could see the goats milling around in the holding pen, naked and more bewildered than ever. And just starting to be *really* afraid.

Elfreda touched me as I passed her. She nodded, which meant well-done in her limited repertoire of gestures. I shrugged, wondering if I cared, but the surplus adrenaline was still in my veins and I found myself grinning at her. I nodded back.

Gene was standing by the holding pen. I went to him, hugged him. I felt the juices start to flow. *Damn it, let's squander a little ration and have us a good time.*

Someone was beating on the sterile glass wall of the pen. She shouted, mouthing angry words at us. *Why? What have you done to us?* It was Mary Sondergard. She implored her bald, one-legged twin to make her understand. She thought she had problems. God, was she pretty. I hated her guts.

Gene pulled me away from the wall. My hands hurt, and I'd broken off all my fake nails without scratching the glass. She was sitting on the floor now, sobbing. I heard the voice of the briefing officer on the outside speaker.

". . . Centauri Three is hospitable, with an Earth-like climate. By that, I mean *your* Earth, not what it has become. You'll see more of that later. The trip will take five years, shiptime. Upon landfall, you will be entitled to one horse, a plow, three axes, two hundred kilos of seed grain . . ."

I leaned against Gene's shoulder. At their lowest ebb, this very moment, they were so much better than us. I had maybe ten years, half of that as a basket case. They are our best, our very brightest hope. Everything is up to them.

". . . that no one will be forced to go. We wish to point out again, not for the last time, that you would all be dead without our intervention. There are things you should know, however. You cannot breathe our air. If you remain on Earth, you can never leave this building. We are not like you. We are the result of a genetic winnowing, a mutation process. We are the survivors, but our enemies have evolved along with us. They are winning. You, however, are immune to the diseases that afflict us . . ."

I winced and turned away.

". . . the other hand, if you emigrate you will be given a chance at a new life. It won't be easy, but as Americans you should be proud of your pioneer heritage. Your ancestors survived, and so will you. It can be a rewarding experience, and I urge you . . ."

Sure, Gene and I looked at each other and laughed. *Listen to this, folks. Five percent of you will suffer nervous breakdowns in the next few days, and never leave. About the same number will commit suicide, here and on the way. When you get there, sixty to seventy percent will die in the first three years. You will die in childbirth, be eaten by animals, bury two out of three of your babies, starve slowly when the rains don't come. If you live, it will be to break your back behind a plow, sun-up to dusk. New Earth is Heaven, folks!*

God, how I wish I could go with them.

Science Fiction, Aliens, and Alienation

The major problem of writing fiction is the difficulty of doing it well. Science fiction, because it demands an understanding not only of people but of science and society, and the ability to create believable new worlds, may be even more difficult to write well. But sf has another drawback: Its audience is a popular audience, which means that it reads for entertainment—the only motivation broad enough to cover a large group. And serious writing is not always entertaining.

Like all fiction writing, science fiction writing is, on the average, poorly paid, but its relatively large and faithful audience continually demands new books. Someone who can write acceptable genre materials fast enough can make a living even at relatively low advances, and writers whose work encompasses but transcends the genre audience can command substantial sums. But the writer who attempts something different, something that is not entertaining in the customary way, must be careful to lead his audience along with him or find a new one.

The serious writer faces a dilemma: The sf audience can support a sizable group of writers, and because it takes its reading seriously it even has a tolerance for greater seriousness, even experimentation. But it is, still, an audience that reads for entertainment.

Barry N. Malzberg (1939–   ) knows a great deal about science fiction, as a reader, as a writer, and as a student of the genre. Born in New York City, he earned a bachelor's degree from Syracuse University in 1960 and worked for the New York City Department of Welfare and Department of

Mental Hygiene before returning to Syracuse for graduate study in 1964, when he was both the Schubert Foundation Playwriting Fellow and the Cornelia Ward Creative Writing Fellow. But he decided that he did not want to be "an *unpublished* assistant professor of English" and left Syracuse to become a freelance writer. He supported himself and a family by working as an assistant for the Scott Meredith Literary Agency, as editor of *Amazing* and *Fantastic*, and as managing editor of *Escapade*, a men's magazine.

Malzberg's disappointment began early. He had wanted to write literary, mainstream fiction but discovered in the early 1960s that a newcomer could not earn a living in that dwindling market. Science fiction had been a longtime passion, however, and he learned, with an initial delight, that he could not only write sf and sell it but even, if he wrote fast enough, support a family doing it. His first story, "We're Coming Through the Windows," appeared in the August 1967 *Galaxy* under the pseudonym K. M. O'Donnell. His first novel was *Oracle of the Thousand Hands* (1968), and he wrote in the introduction to his first collection of stories, *Final War and Other Fantasies* (1969, as O'Donnell, still, perhaps, nursing a dream of mainstream), ". . . the future of literature . . . resides in science fiction. . . . The literary market has become exhausted . . . but 98% of available material and implications [of science fiction] which could concern a writer have not been touched."

In the next decade and a half Malzberg published more than 250 stories, twenty-seven science-fiction novels, eight collections of short stories, and forty other novels, including some pseudonymous pornographic novels and fourteen mystery novels under the name of Mike Barry; seventy of the books appeared in an eight-year period between 1968 and 1976, and twenty-seven of them in a three-year period between 1972 and 1975. Perhaps it is not surprising that less than ten years after the publication of his first work, Malzberg announced his retirement from science fiction writing, with some bitterness about the niggardly financial rewards and the lack of discrimination among publishers and readers, complaints that he has continued to voice on behalf of other writers in the numerous introductions he has contributed to their collected stories, in his perceptive essays about science fiction (some of them collected in *The Engines of the Night*, 1982), and in his notes for the seven anthologies he has co-edited.

In some ways Malzberg's career parallels that of Robert Silverberg, who is four years older but belongs to the same generation. Silverberg, however, began publishing thirteen years earlier, was just as prolific but turned out formulaic work until a decade into his career, and made most of his fortune in nonfiction and then turned to the carefully crafted science fiction that earned him many awards. He too announced his retirement from science fiction writing, and at about the same time as Malzberg and with some of the same disillusionment about the lack of discrimination in his audience—and perhaps with some of the same fatigue from the intensity of the writing that had preceded it. Now, like Silverberg, Malzberg has returned to some writing in the field.

Malzberg's work has been honored: His novel *Beyond Apollo* (1972) won the first John W. Campbell Memorial Award for the best novel of the year, and two stories and a novel were Nebula finalists. *Guernica Night* (1974) was reviewed as a literary work by Joyce Carol Oates in the *New York Times*, and his collection *Down Here in the Dream Quarter* also was reviewed there. Critics also have praised *The Falling Astronauts* (1971), *Overlay* (1972), *Herovit's World* (1973), *Galaxies* (1975), and *Scop* (1976), among others.

Malzberg's fascination with the possibilities of science fiction and his underlying affection for it led him to write sf, but his temperament and his artistic vision led him to create works that use the generic conventions of science fiction as mirrors for a darker human predicament. One senses in Malzberg's work a desire for belief warring with an innate skepticism and a pessimism about the possibilities of success in achieving any kind of goals, but particularly those that relate to human communication and love. His characters are frustrated, depressed, helpless, and bitter, and their obsessions, as Douglas Barbour notes in *Twentieth Century Science Fiction Writers*, "expose the dark underbelly of the science-fiction mythos to the terrible light of art." All this has not always endeared Malzberg to the traditional sf reader. Several works, including *Gather in the Hall of the Planets* (by O'Donnell, 1971), *Galaxies* (1975), and *Herovit's World*, explore the plight of the science-fiction writer, particularly his working conditions and the way its demands use him up, as well as what Malzberg takes to be the impossibility of writing sf well.

"Uncoupling," first published in *Dystopian Visions* (1975),

deals with several persistent Malzberg themes. One is the
dystopian future, here an overpopulated world ("five
times overpopulated," the narrator repeats with improbable
precision). A second is the overwhelming, omnipresent
bureaucracy (perhaps a legacy of Malzberg's work for two
New York City public agencies) to which the protagonist at
first submits and then succumbs. A third theme is obsession,
in this case with sex, which becomes the central metaphor in
the story, providing motivation for the protagonist's compul-
sive behavior and for his dissociation (alienation even from
self) until the moment of orgasm and then, in its aftermath
of withdrawal (uncoupling), establishes the mood for the
protagonist's ready collaboration with the forces that control
his world and regulate everything, including sex.

Stylistically, the story evidences Malzberg's concern for
language, for sentence structure and prose rhythm, and for
allusions, images, similes, and density. "Uncoupling" is also,
as Malzberg points out in the introduction to the story in his
collection *The Best of Barry Malzberg* (1976), a pastiche of
the work of Alfred Bester, whom Malzberg admires greatly.
In particular Malzberg pays tribute to Bester's "5,271,009,"
from which he draws the brittle narrative style, the direct
address, the odd but oddly appropriate choice of verb and
noun, and the lapses into French; and "Fondly Fahrenheit"
(*TRTSF #3*), from which Malzberg adopts the shifts in
viewpoint between first and third person. Malzberg, however,
uses his borrowings for his own purposes. Bester used his
shifts in viewpoint to suggest the growing confusion between
master and android; Malzberg uses it to illustrate the dissociation produced by the protagonist's missed heterosexual
activity that is a monthly obligation as well as a right. The
use of French ("the language of love") is the result, the protagonist claims, of his neurasthenia.

Ultimately the story is about understanding. At one point
the protagonist thinks he understands his situation: "Understanding lying under me like a gray pool filled with winking
fish of knowledge, I plunged into the pool wholeheartedly,
splashing around, spouting little sprays of abysmal French
while I did so." But at the end the protagonist rejects communication and the possibility of understanding, not so much
because of the threat of the bureaucracy but because his need
to understand was only physiological pressure.

Uncoupling

by Barry N. Malzberg

I came to the Towers fuming. The walk across town had bent my breath, shaken the substance, broken the spirit (too often I tend to think in expletives, but pardon: it is an old trait), but the flesh unmortified quivered, reaching for its own purposes. At the unoccupied desk I stood there for a while, inhaling great mouthfuls of hydrogenated 02 (one of the chief lures of the Towers is that it offers an atmosphere of pure oxygen, no small thing in these difficult, crumpling times) and screaming for service. "Come here!" I shouted to the gleaming walls, the spick-and-span corridors, the aerated passageways of the fluorescence. "I need attention. *Je bien attendu. Je desiree a fornication.*"

An attendant appeared, neutered in flowing robes. Everything in the Towers is done for effect; go one inch under the surface and the substance disappears. Nevertheless, one must persevere. The world is plastic. The world is corrupt. Still, in or out of it there is no alternative.

"*Je suis au pardonne, monsieur,*" the attendant said in execrable French. "*Je desire á service mais je non comprendre votre desiree. . . .*"

"Speak English!" I snarled, hitting the counter, a tall, bitter man in my late thirties, the snakes of purpose wending their way through his shattered but wise features. (I often tend to depersonalize, sometimes lapsing even into the third person in my desperate attempts to scrape free of the trap of self: *au pardonniere.*) "Speak English!" the tall, bitter man shouted, his voice echoing through the amplifiers in the halls of the Towers, and the attendant trembled, adjusted his/her robes more tightly about himself/herself.

"Yes," he/her said. "I am here to help you, all of us are here to help you, but you must understand, you must simply understand that in order to achieve you must modulate . . ."

"I will not modulate!" I screamed, slamming a bitter fist into the gleaming and refractive surfaces of the desk. "There is no need for modulation. I am entitled to service, service and understanding—don't you clowns understand this?—and furthermore," I added more quietly as several threatening robot policemen, noiseless on their canisters, glided into the reception area holding cans of Mace at ready, "anyway," I whispered to the attendant, the gentlest and most winsome of expressions chasing all the snakes from the panels of the features, "this is one of my prescribed days for heterosex and I want to make the most of it. Time is money, after all, money is the barter of existence and without time and money where would any of us be? I wish to engage in normative heterosex during this, my relaxative period." I perched an elbow on the desk, turned a non-threatening blink upon the attendant. "Pardon me for my haste," I added, "*pardonniere moi au mon haste, je suis* so needful."

The attendant foraged under the desk, produced a standard application form, passed it across to me. The robot policemen chattered to one another, their tentacles flicking in a consultative manner, and then as noiselessly as they emerged, withdrew, leaving the reception area blank and impermeable once again. I respect the means by which they maintain security here. Really, the Towers is in a difficult position, catering as it must to the full range of human desire and perversity, and if I were administering it, which happily I do not (the Government itself administers everything nowadays; the projections of the mid-1900s were absolutely correct), I would be ever more forceful than they. People must learn to accept their condition. People must realize that in a world of poison, overpopulation, and enormous international tensions, where five people occupy the space biology would have reserved for only one, tensions accumulate and the only way that the world can be prevented from complete destruction is a firm administrative hand at the top. People must fall into place. (I wrote my thesis on neo-Fascism and have in my cubicle a handy collection of whips that I am apt at jocular moments to lay merrily about myself and all visitors.)

"Fill out this form, sir," the attendant said to the tall, bitter fascist standing at the desk, "name, address, locality, zone, authorization, desire and credit voucher." It gestured behind itself meaningfully to a small machine perched on a lower shelf. "We will then feed the application through into the bank and everything checking out satisfactorily . . ." It paused, cocked an eyebrow, looking surprisingly desirous in its pale, pink robes, its catatonic lack of affect. *"Je suis attendre,"* it said.

Hastily I filled out this form: name (irrelevant), age (I have already conceded this), housing (lower domicile in the Blood District), authorization (Condition F-51: Perversities and heterosex) and desire (fornicative). Credit information entered in. I passed the form hurriedly to the attendant, feeling the swift, cool slash of its fingers as it appropriated the form, sending renewed surges of desire through me. "I wonder," I said, leaning across the counter, "I wonder if you yourself might well be . . . uh . . ."

"That is impossible, sir," the attendant said. A modest blush seemed to steal over its features much as embitterment is known to tear over mine. "We are not available for any purpose other than reception, and in any case, you are here seeking heterosex; is that not correct?"

"That has nothing to do with it," the man said in a keening shriek, once again causing the canisters of invisible robot policemen to brush against the floor, "that has absolutely nothing to do with it, and furthermore . . ."

"Je suis ne heterosex pas," the attendant said and turned, fed the application into the machine that seized it angrily, yanking off strips of paper as it ingested. *"Je suis* neuter and therefore would not be satisfactory for your requirements."

"You do not understand," the man said. "In the Blood District we do not, we absolutely do *not*, put up with insubordination from functionaries." He put his hand against the concealed weapon at his belt. "It is insufferable for you to address me in this way. . . ."

Abruptly I stopped. The robot policemen were back in full force and also the lights in the Towers were beating now like little hearts: *wicker, wicker,* sending darts of greenish sensation into the deeper centers of the cerebrum. Abruptly I understood everything. Deprivation of heterosex in my program leads to an accumulation of tension: disassociation reaction, abusiveness to attendants, flickers of bad French. Disturbances of vision. Abrupt disassociation reaction, lapses into the third person. Understanding this, I felt a perilous calm being restored and was able to look at the attendant with neither fear nor desire. *"Je votre au pardonne,"* the bitter man said to the attendant, *"je suis tres excite."*

"Est rien, est maintenant rien," the attendant said, making a signal to the robot policemen. They had closed in on me during this latest insight and were now, twenty or fifty of

them in their Government-issue and insigniaed uniforms, staring balefully. The nearest of them, apparently a supervisor, clapped its tungsten club from hand to hand meaningfully and turned its circuits to orange.

"*Est rien*," I said and reached a hand toward the supervisor, a hand of comity and understanding. I have always believed that man and machine can co-exist in a technocracy. My fascism has a certain overlay of perversity, but that perversity has never included fear or loathing toward machines. I get along with machines very well. Without them the world would have fallen into the sea long ago. Control. Absolute control.

"*Est rien*," the supervisor said in a metallic gurgle, and, retracting its club, spun away. Tentacles waved. The troops, having finished their consultation once again, disappeared. I shuddered with relaxation, realizing that my clothes were drenched, and warned myself to bring no further disgrace. There are no tolerance levels for scenes in this world. Confrontation must be avoided at all costs. The world is five times overpopulated.

"You are adjudged competent for heterosex," the attendant said. The rosy blush had returned; now it seemed heightened and darkened by some information it had picked up on my printout, which was still whirring slyly out of the machine. All of my horrid little secrets being displayed to the attendant, but who am I to complain? With my newfound grip on sanity I smiled back implacably, imagining a daffodil in one corner of my jacket from which I might take absent sniffs. "According to the information you have not had heterosex for two months and therefore may engage in it freely. Your credit rating is also satisfactory."

Two months. Two months! Understanding lying under me like a gray pool filled with the winking fish of knowledge, I plunged into that pool wholeheartedly, splashing around, spouting little sprays of abysmal French while I did so. Two months without heterosex! No wonder the disassociation reaction was so advanced; no wonder that not once, but twice, I had caused the robot policemen to be summoned. "Two months!" I said. "But under the medical profile entered in my twenty-third year I am to engage in heterosex once a month. Once every month. *Recherche du las temps perdu.* I must have forgotten to make my obligatory last month. Of course," I confided to the attendant, "I have been terribly busy." This happens to be absolutely true. I have been engaged in a massive research project on the induction of pain and my concentration has been fervid. Even food and drink evade me when I get deeply into a project.

"You must have forgotten," the attendant agreed. Its eyes became wistful as it put the printout into the shredder and reluctantly demolished it. "But that's perfectly all right now. The Towers are here to serve you. Your Government is here to serve you. You will be well taken care of."

The tall man turned from the counter and found himself in the grip of another attendant, a somewhat burlier one who put two incisive fingers into a forearm. "Just go along," the attendant at the desk said, "and you will be *bien service, je vous assure.*"

"Certainly," the tall man said, feeling his balance momentarily flicker as the burly attendant made a seizing jerk, then readjusting himself to new sights, new sounds as he was carried beyond the swinging gates of the rear and into the deeper mysteries of the Towers. "This must be a very dull job for you," he said to the attendant, "conveying people from the reception desk into the fornication rooms. Undoubtedly you must feel some resentment, too, no? To realize that these people are engaging almost routinely in acts that are permanently denied to you must be quite painful, and, also, your job must be quite delimited. But I don't mean to pry," the man finished, "I don't mean to pry."

"Forget it," the attendant said, "my speech organs are engaged only for simple commands." And it carried me deeper into the corridors and hallways of the Towers: now I could see the various rooms on my right and left moving deeper into the Towers, the doors of the rooms open (why not? who would interfere?) in which however dimly I could see forms struggling, some in pairs, others in multiples, elaborate equipment, gleaming utensils, the cries and unwinding shrieks of copulation. Carried ever further I went past the section marked SADO-MASOCHISM into a somewhat lighter area stamped BESTIALITY in flickering letters, from which now and then from the doors (closed this time: certain things must be forever sacrosanct) I could hear vagrant moos and cackles, crow cries and the barking of dogs, squealing of pigs and the sound of milk cans toppling. Out of bestiality then and into an aseptic corridor in which the word HOMOSEX had been embroidered in swinging tapestry that hung in strands from the ceiling, the attendant's grip ever more devastating on my arm and well it might be since the tall man found his legs beginning to give out from the excitement of this journey, his needful persuasion, his extreme disassociation, and needed all the help that he could get from the attendant in order to make his rapid, scuttling journey. They always rush one through the Towers, but this is to be expected; the Government has many things on its mind and schedules must be obeyed. Finally, the tall man found himself, gasping, and with a bad, purpling bruise on his left forearm, in the section marked HETEROSEX, the doors once again open, a clean, light, bright area much like coming into the concentration camp must have been like after a long, difficult train journey, and there the burly attendant pushed me into a tiny room where a female sat waiting, her hands clasped and folded, quite naked as well, the tall man noticed, since by this time he had obtained a stunning tumescence. These kind of things will happen under panic and stress; one must accept them.

"You have five minutes," the attendant said and went to the door, folded its arms, turned its back. From the rear I could see the small, deadly extrudance of wires coming from the black hair and realized that it was a robot. Of course. Inevitably, the pressure of work and inventory would cause the Towers to convert, but I had hoped (nostalgically, of course) that somehow this would not happen in my time. "Five minutes," the robot said, "is all that you are permitted on your allotment."

"That's ridiculous," the tall man said, already springing out of his clothing, exposing his limbs lustrous and well oiled to the heavy, penetrating light, "I've always been authorized for ten."

"New conditions," the attendant said. The wires seemed to glow beneath the hair, turning orange. "If you don't like it," it said, "you're free to terminate now."

"Oh, no," the tall man said, "oh, no, no, no." And naked, he turned to the female, extending his arms, walking toward her with some difficulty. "Do you speak?" he said.

"*Non.*"

"You should speak," the tall man said. "You always have spoken in the past; I mean, it isn't much to ask, just a few words here or there. . . ."

"You are no longer permitted communication," the attendant said. The tall man looked at the female as if in sad confirmation of this and slowly, bleakly, the female nodded. Pain appeared in her eyes and then disappeared. She rose, extended her own arms. Impassively, one time, she gestured and the tall man came against her.

Hump and jump. Huff and puff. Knead and seed. Pump and rump. The less said about all of this the better: pornographic fantasia was outlawed by the magnificent act of 2010, and I am not one to dispute the Governmental wisdom. Also, about this part there is very little to say. It is a sameness, a grinding grayness under the lights, but the Government has deemed it necessary on an individually analyzed personality profile, and I am not going to dispute the Government in that area, either. I will not dispute the Government in *any* area. The less said about all of this the better, then, other than to point out that the disassociation reaction ceased at once and I no longer had the desire to speak French. Not even two particles of that miserable language—the language of love they call it—remained within me when I was done.

I got off the female slowly and donned my garments. From her position on the floor she regarded me with an admiration that might have been boredom, a boredom that might have been sympathy. "*Je suis satisfee,*" she said.

"Forget that," I said, "I don't want to hear any of that now." Dressed, I went to the attendant, who took my hand once again in that seizing grip. "Must you do that?" I said to him.

"I'm afraid that it must," it said almost regretfully. "Clientele must be escorted."

"I would follow you on my own."

"I know you would follow me on your own," the attendant said, "but according to your profile the infliction of brutality is part of the general satisfaction here. Don't talk to me any further; I told you that I was not programmed. "It seized me once again in that terrible grip and led me through the hallway.

A different route this time. HETEROSEX gave way to NECROPHILIA, a solemn, rather funereal area in which the doors were secured by gravestones on which, like graffiti, epitaphs had been ascribed; past NECROPHILIA it was MASTURBATION, an area not composed like the others of separate rooms but rather a communal, almost dormitory kind of arrangement in which the clientele lay in rows stretched on cots, regarding obscenities and photographs projected on the ceiling and did what they must, depressively; past masturbation was ASEPSIS, and here, in the most solemn area of all, men in rumpled or flowing priestly garb passed among the benches in what was a hastily reconstructed synagogue, passing out small words of cheer and advice to the penitents who, clamped on the benches, gripped themselves and studied the simulated stained glass. There is no end to the range of the Towers. At last, back again to the reception area where the supervisor of the robot policemen (I was able to recognize him by the shape of his tentacles) was engaged in absent banter and joshing with the reception attendant.

"He's here," the burly attendant said and released me from his grip. Abruptly I collapsed, a spreading bruise like a stain lurching across my forearm, sending enormous shooting pains into the scalp. I hit the floor and it must have been the shock of this that revived me, but when I returned to consciousness the burly attendant was alone, the robot policemen standing over with a look of concern.

"Are you all right?" it said.

"I am quite all right," I said with dignity and slowly picked myself off the floor, wiping little scabs of dirt and excrement (the Towers is all front, the actual maintenance of the area quite poor) from my clothing. "I had a minor fall."

"If you do not leave at once," the supervisor said intensely, "it will be necessary to arrest you."

"I'm quite aware of that," I said. Residence in the Towers beyond immediate utility is impermissible, of course. Everyone knows that. The world is five times overpopulated and if people who used the Towers did not leave promptly, where, I would like to know, where would we all be? Cooperation is the key to survival in the technocracy; we are a species who must cooperate or die, and I am quite willing to fulfill my obligations. "I'm going to leave," I said, drawing my clothing around me and summoning dignity like a little nimbus over my head, "just as soon as I have recovered my breath."

"Would you like to program in another appointment now?" the attendant said. It winked at me encouragingly. Always, underneath this efficiency, is a hint of scatology, lure of the deeps, and if someone tells you that this is not one of the basic appeals of the Towers he is crazy. Crazy. "You are entitled to one extra appointment because of your, ah, deprivation."

"That is not necessary," I said. The robot policeman gave me suddenly a stunning blow on the head; then as I wavered to the floor, it held me up and looked at me intensely. "You were ordered to leave," it said.

"This is ridiculous. I am a citizen; you are simply machinery and I cannot be dominated . . ."

"I think we'll have to get rid of him," the policeman said to the attendant, and slowly, sadly, the neuter gave a nod of agreement. Once again I felt myself seized with enormous, clutching force and was conveyed through all the spaces of the reception room toward an exit hatch. "This is disgraceful," I burbled. "You can't do this to me."

"Yes we can," said the policeman, "*oui, nous avons le authoritee*." And then I was shoved through the hatch. I landed street-side, gasping, a drop of only three feet to the rubberized conveyor, but still, in my rather damaged condition, rather shocking. Citizens looked at me quickly, appraisingly, and then their eyes turned inward toward private considerations, the conveyor belt whisking all of us along in silence. In a world five times overpopulated it is necessary to function personally only in terms of one's amity group and never elsewhere. The Towers, for example, would be completely impossible if clients were to essay personal relationships with that personnel.

The conveyor carried me swiftly through Wilbur, past Marseilles and into the Blood District. Even after so short and dramatic an absence, it was good to see the familiar outlines of the slaughtering houses appear on the horizon, see the guillotines and little nooses on the tracts, hear the screams, sniff the odors from the abattoirs. At my own slot I stepped off the conveyor belt quickly, feeling my detumescence swinging within my garments like a credit voucher in the pocket: ease, power. I adjusted myself to the slot and carried myself in, then up ninety-six levels and into my own humble quarters which now, since I have been so absorbed in the research project, look something like an abattoir themselves. It was good to be home. It is always good to be home. I loosened my garments, examined myself for scars from burns or inference, syphilitic infestation (this is impossible, but I am in many ways an obsessive-compulsive), gonococcal traces, sighed and sat on my chair, feeling little puffs of dust whisk up around me. I inhaled them, at peace for the first time in many days, the pressures of heterosex deprivation removed. Then I noticed that sitting in the room across from me, half-hidden in the dimness, shielded by the light of the window was the female with whom I had fornicated at the Towers some forty-five minutes before.

I was not shocked. This kind of thing happens quite often.

It has never happened to me, but I was prepared. Sometimes these employees, depressed and made unhappy by the rather turgid and ritualistic nature of their employment, will sneak out of the Towers and follow clients home, attempting to establish some kind of relationship. There is only one thing to do, of course. I would want it done for me. It is in their best interests.

"Please," she said, "listen to me. *Je vous attendre, vous je attendre.*"

"Impossible," I said, "I'm no longer interested in French. It only happens when I'm neurasthenic."

"You must listen to me," she said intensely, "we can't go on this way. We must truly communicate and get to know one another."

I already had the communicator in operation. She stopped, looked at me bleakly. I hit the buttons for the Towers and the robot supervisor who I already knew so well appeared on the screen and recognized me. "Yes?" he said impassively. I will give them much credit. There is nothing personal in their machinery; they simply do what must be done. As should we all. It is possible to envy the machines, to aspire to their condition.

I stepped away from the screen, allowed the policeman to see the female behind me. "You see what's happened?" I said.

"Yes."

"I refuse to speak with her and I am cooperating."

"Yes," the policeman said. Even in the monochrome viewer I could see the little green light of approval coming from its eyes. "We will have personnel there within fifteen seconds to effect re-entry."

It killed the televiewer. I turned back toward the female. With retrieval coming there was no longer need to fear her. "We must feel," she said. "We must be humans. We must share our common humanity. *Vous et moi, nous êtes humanite.*"

I shrugged. The door, which I never lock (there is safety in accessibility), opened and the burly attendant came in. He must have followed me home. This is standard procedure—to make sure that Towers attendance does not result in abnormal excitation. There have been occasional massacres; now the attendant's pursuit is mandatory. "You," he said to the female, "come here."

He went to her, took her by the arm. I knew that grip. It

caused me, against my will, to smile. She saw the smile, looked up at me, her eyes already beginning to dull. "You don't understand," she said as the attendant took her out.

But I did.

Exotic Parables

The traditional emphasis of science fiction on plot—or what happens—allows the reader the clearest possible statement of meaning. Other bearers of meaning, such as character, setting, mood, diction, direct and indirect commentary, image, and metaphor, can convey to the reader aspects of the story either in addition to plot or in place of it, but the meaning they convey can seldom be as precise. Ambiguity, however, often is tolerated, even welcomed, if it is the price the story must pay for the enrichment of life, of literary allusion, and of archetype, parable, and fable.

As science fiction writers began to emerge from the humanities rather than from the sciences, their models became literary richness rather than scientific clarity. They became less concerned with statement and more concerned with suggestion.

Michael Bishop (1945–) is a product of the humanities. He was born in Lincoln, Nebraska, and attended the University of Georgia, earning a bachelor's degree in English in 1967 and a master's degree in 1968. He taught English at the Air Force Academy Preparatory School from 1968 to 1972 and at the University of Georgia from 1972 to 1974. Since then he has been a full-time freelance writer.

Bishop's first published story, "Piñon Fall," appeared in the October 1970 *Galaxy*. His short fiction frequently has been a finalist for awards: "Death and Designation Among the Asadi" and "The White Otters of Childhood" for both Nebula and Hugo in 1974; "On the Street of the Serpents" for the Nebula in 1975 and "Cathadonian Odyssey" for the Hugo;

"Blooded on Arachne" for the Nebula in 1976 and "Rogue Tomato" for the Hugo; "The Samurai and the Willows" for both Nebula and Hugo in 1976; and "Vernalfest Morning" for the Nebula in 1980. Some of Bishop's short stories have been collected in *Blooded on Arachne* (1982). He and Jan Watson have edited an anthology titled *Changes* (1982).

Bishop's first novel, *A Funeral for the Eyes of Fire*, was published in 1975 (and a revised version as *Eyes of Fire* in 1980), followed by *And Strange at Ecbatan the Trees* (1976; reprinted in paperback as *Beneath the Shattered Moon*), *Stolen Faces* (1977), *A Little Knowledge* (1977), *Catacomb Years* (1979), *Transfigurations* (1979), *Under Heaven's Bridge* (with Ian Watson, 1980), and *No Enemy But Time* (1982). *A Funeral for the Eyes of Fire* was a Nebula finalist.

Bishop's fiction combines a concern for anthropology, often expressed in terms of aliens, alienation, or alien environments, with a literary use of language and a variety of rhetorical devices. In *A Funeral for the Eyes of Fire*, the alien world is named Trope, which means in English "figure of speech." Ian Watson has called Bishop's work "exotic parables."

An example of Bishop's tactics and techniques, although in a lighter vein than Bishop's traditionally somber narratives, is "Rogue Tomato," originally published in *New Dimensions 5* (1975). It begins like Franz Kafka's "Metamorphosis" with an ordinary person changed into something monstrous, in this case a tomato as large as the planet Mars. Bishop prepares the reader for a surrealistic story not only by the similarity of the opening to "Metamorphosis" but by the use of the word in the first heading and the naming of the protagonist. Philip K. is reminiscent of Kafka's protagonist in *The Trial*, Joseph K.

The plot is easily summarized, but Bishop's story operates at other levels. First of all, there is the level of diction. The story's diction is not that of Philip K., a former aerospace worker. It is, instead, that of a literary person who delights in polysyllabic or old-fashioned words such as "bilaterally symmetrical," "rotund and limbless," "tippling," "riotous behavior," and "brusque and unfair." They prepare the reader for the later use of such words as "eucharistic," "ontology," "erophagous," "mandala," and "Annunciation."

Second, there is the level of literary and religious reference. The story pays tribute not only to Kafka but, no doubt, to Philip K. Dick (who also has written about fantastic phenomena and the nature of reality), William Burroughs (*Nova Express*), "2001: A Space Odyssey" ("stargate"), and Kurt Vonnegut's *The Sirens of Titan* ("chrono-synclastic infundibulum"). Third is the level of linguistic playfulness—"holoscopic," "Myrmidopteran," and "erophagous."

The unusual diction and the linguistic playfulness emphasize the ridiculousness of the situation, but the more serious conclusion is foreshadowed by the concern of Philip K., unlike Gregor Samsa, for answers—answers that lead him step to step to his final announcement (like that of Gabriel to the Virgin Mary), for which he has not yet found a means. Philip K.'s initial regret that he is not inhabited leads to his fantasy of being eaten by his lost sweetheart, and that is identified with the eucharist; his comparison of himself with the apple of love leads to a comparison with the fruit of the Tree of Knowledge; the coming of the Myrmidopterans leads to a wish to be consumed by humans, which leads to an identification with the resurrection of Osiris, Christ, and the Green Knight; the Myrmidopterans are identified with archangels and guardian spirits; and finally the way to salvation—"It was not by eating of the fruit of the Tree of Knowledge that one put on the omniscience and the subtle ecstasy of gods, but instead by *becoming* the fruit itself . . . and then by *being eaten*"—is brought to Earth by a rogue tomato.

Rogue Tomato

by Michael Bishop

THE METAMORPHOSIS OF PHILIP K.

When Philip K. awoke, he found that overnight he had grown from a reasonably well shaped, bilaterally symmetrical human being into . . . a rotund and limbless body circling a gigantic, gauzy red star. In fact, by the simple feel, by the total aura projected into the seeds of his consciousness, Philip K. concluded that he was a tomato. A tomato of approximately the same dimensions and mass as the planet Mars.

That was it, certainly: a tomato of the hothouse variety. Turning leisurely on a vertical axis tilted seven or eight degrees out of the perpendicular, Philip K. basked in the angry light of the distant red giant. While basking, he had to admit that he was baffled. This had never happened to him before. He was a sober individual not given to tippling or other forms of riotous behavior, and that he should have been summarily turned into a Mars-sized tomato struck him as a brusque and unfair conversion. Why him? And how? "At least," he reflected, "I still know who I am." Even if in the guise of an immense tomato he now whirled around an unfamiliar sun, his consciousness was that of a human being, and still his own. "I am Philip K. and somehow I'm still breathing and there must be a scientific explanation for this" is a fairly accurate summary of the next several hours (an hour being measured, of course, in terms of one twenty-fourth of Philip K.'s own period of rotation) of his thought processes.

AS I LIVE AND BREATHE

Several Philip K.–days passed. The sufferer of metamorphosis discovered that he had an amenable atmosphere, a topological integument (or *crust,* although for the skin of a void-dwelling variety of *Lycopersicon esculentum* the word crust didn't seem altogether appropriate) at least a mile thick, and weather. Inhaling carbon dioxide and exhaling oxygen, Philip K. photosynthesized. Morning dew ran down his tenderest curvatures, and afternoon dew, too. Some of these drops were ocean-sized. Clouds formed over Philip K.'s equatorial girth and unloaded tons and tons of refreshing rains. Winds generated by these meteorological phenomena and his own axial waltzing blew backward and forward, up and down, over his taut, ripening skin. It was good to be alive, even in this disturbing morphology. Moreover, unlike that of Plato's oysters, his pleasure was not mindless. Philip K. experienced the wind, the rain, the monumental turning of himself, the internal burgeoning of his juices, the sweetness of breathing, and he *meditated* on all these things. It was too bad that he was uninhabited (this was one of his frequent meditations), so much rich oxygen did he give off. Nor was there much hope of immediate colonization. Human beings would not very soon venture to the stars. Only two years before his metamorphosis Philip K. had been an aerospace worker in Houston, Texas, who had been laid off and then unable to find other employment. In fact, during the last four or five weeks Philip K. had kept himself alive on soup made out of hot water and dollops of ketchup. It was—upon reflection—a positive relief to be a tomato. Philip K., inhaling, exhaling, photosynthesizing, had the pleasurable existential notion that he had cut out the middle man.

THE PLOT THICKENS

Several Philip K.–months went by. As he perturbated about the fiery red giant, he began to fear that his orbit was decaying, and that he was falling inevitably, inexorably, into the furnace of his primary, there to be untimely stewed. How large his sun had become. At last, toward the end of his first year as a planetary tomato, Philip K. realized that his orbit wasn't decaying. No. Instead, *he* was growing, plumping out, generating the illimitable juiciness of life. However, since his orange-red epidermis contained an utterly continuous layer of optical cells, his "eyes," or The Eye That He Was (depending on how you desire to consider the matter), had deceived him into believing the worst. What bliss to know that he had merely grown to the size of Uranus, thus putting his visual apparatus closer to the sun. Holoscopic vision, despite the manifold advantages it offered (such as the simultaneous apprehension of daylight and dark, 360-degree vigilance, and the comforting illusion of being at the center of the cosmos), could sometimes be a distinct handicap. But though his orbit was not decaying, a danger still existed. How much larger would he grow? Philip K. had no desire to suffer total eclipse in a solar oven.

INTERPERSONAL RELATIONSHIPS

Occasionally Philip K. thought about things other than plunging into his primary or, when this preoccupation faded, the excellence of vegetable life. He thought about The Girl He Had Left Behind (who was approaching menopause and not the sort men appreciatively call a tomato). Actually, The Girl He Had Left Behind had left *him* behind long before he had undergone his own surreal Change of Life. "Ah, Lydia P.," he nevertheless murmured from the innermost fruity core of himself, and then again: "Ah, Lydia P." He forgave The Girl He Had Left Behind her desertion of him, a desertion that had come hard on the heels of the loss of his job. He forgave . . . and indulged in shameless fantasies in which either Lydia P.—in the company of the first interstellar colonists from Earth—landed upon him, or, shrunk to normal size (for a tomato) and levitating above her sleeping face in her cramped Houston apartment, he offered himself to her. *Pomme d'amour*. Philip K. dredged up these words from his mental warehouses of trivia, and was comforted by them. So the French, believing it an aphrodisiac, had called the tomato when it was first imported from South America. *Pomme d'amour*. The apple of love. The fruit of the Tree of Knowledge, perhaps. But what meaningful relationship could exist between a flesh-and-blood woman and a Uranus-sized tomato? More and more often Philip K. hallucinated an experience in which interstellar colonist Lydia P. fell to her knees somewhere south of his leafy stem, sank her tiny teeth into his ripe integument, and then cried out with tiny cries at the sheer magnificent taste of him. This vision so disconcerted and titillated Philip K. that for days he whirled with no other thought, no other hope, no other desire.

ONTOLOGICAL CONSIDERATIONS

When not hallucinating eucharistic fantasies in which his beloved ate and drank of him, Philip K. gave serious thought to the question of his being. "Wherefore a tomato?" was the way he phrased this concern. He could as easily have been a ball bearing, an eightball, a metal globe, a balloon, a Japanese lantern, a spherical *piñata*, a diving bell. But none of these things respired, none of them lived. Then why not a grape, a cherry, an orange, a cantaloupe, a coconut, a watermelon? These were all more or less round; all were sun-worshippers, all grew, all contained the vital juices and the succulent sweetmeats of life. But whoever or whatever had caused this conversion—for Philip K. regarded his change as the result of intelligent intervention rather than of accident or some sort of spontaneous chemical readjustment—had made him none of those admirable fruits. They had made him a tomato. "Wherefore a tomato?" *Pomme d'amour*. The apple of love. The fruit of the Tree of Knowledge. Ah ha! Philip K., in a suppuration of insight, understood that his erophagous fantasies involving Lydia P. had some cunning relevance to his present condition. A plan was being revealed to him, and his manipulators had gone to the trouble of making him believe that the operations of his own consciousness were little by little laying bare this plan. O edifying deception! The key was *pomme d'amour*. He was a tomato rather than something else because the tomato *was* the legendary fruit of the Tree of Knowledge. (Never mind that tomatoes do not grow on trees.) After all, while a human being, Philip K. had had discussions with members of a proliferating North American sect that held that the biblical Eden had in fact been located in the New World. Well, the tomato was indigenous to South America (not too far from these sectarians' pinpointing of Eden, which they argued lay somewhere in the Ozarks), and he, Philip K., *was* a new world. Although the matter still remained fuzzy, remote, fragmented, he began to feel that he was closing in on the question of his personal ontology. "Wherefore a tomato?" Soon he would certainly know more, he would certainly have his answer . . .

A Brief Intimation of Mortality

Well into his second year circling the aloof red giant, Philip K. deduced that his growth had ceased; he had achieved a full-bodied, invigorating ripeness which further rain and sunshine could in no way augment. A new worry beset him. What could he now hope for? Would he bruise and begin to rot away? Would he split, develop viscous, scarlike lesions, and die on the invisible vine of his orbit? Surely he had not undergone his metamorphosis for the sake of so ignominious an end. And yet as he whirled on the black velour of outer space, taking in with one circumferential glimpse the entire sky and all it contained (suns, nebulae, galaxies, coal sacks, the inconsequential detritus of the void), Philip K. could think of no other alternative. He was going to rot, that was all there was to it; he was going to rot. Wherefore the fruit of the Tree of Knowledge if only to rot? He considered suicide. He could will the halting of his axial spin; one hemisphere would then blacken and boil, the other would acquire an embroidery of rime and turn to ice all the way to his core. Or he could hold his breath and cease to photosynthesize. Both of these prospects had immensely more appeal to Philip K. than did the prospect of becoming a festering, mephitic mushball. At the height of his natural ripeness, then, he juggled various methods of killing himself, as large and as luscious as he was. Thus does our own mortality hasten us to its absolute proof.

The Advent of the Myrmidopterans (or, The Plot Thickens Again)

Amid these morbid speculations, one fine day-and-night, or night-and-day, the optical cells in Philip K.'s integument relayed to him ("the seeds of consciousness," you see, was something more than a metaphor) the information that now encroaching upon his solar system from every part of the universe was a multitude of metallic-seeming bodies. He saw these bodies. He saw them glinting in the attentuated light of Papa (this being the name Philip K. had given the red giant about which he revolved, since it was both handy and comforting to think in terms of anthropomorphic designations), but so far away were they that he had no real conception of their shape and size. Most of these foreign bodies had moved to well within the distance of Papa's nearest stellar neighbors, three stars forming an equilateral triangle with Papa roughly at the center. At first Philip K. assumed these invaders to be starships, and he burbled "Lydia P., Lydia P." over and over again—until stricken by the ludicrousness of this behavior. No expeditionary force from Earth would send out so many vessels. From the depths of ubiquitous night the metallic shapes floated toward him, closer and closer, and they flashed either silver or golden in the pale wash of Papa's radiation. When eight or nine Philip K.–days had passed, he could see the invaders well enough to tell something about them. Each body had a pair of curved wings that loomed over its underslung torso/fuselage like sails, sails as big as Earth's biggest skyscrapers. These wings were either silver or gold; they did not flap but instead canted subtly whenever necessary in order to catch and channel into propulsion the rays of the sun. Watching these bright creatures—for they were not artifacts but living entities—waft in on the thin winds of the cosmos was beautiful. Autumn had come to Philip K.'s solar system. Golden and silver, burnished maple and singing chrome. And from everywhere these great beings came, these god-metal monarchs, their wings filling the globe of the heavens like precious leaves or cascading, beaten coins. "Ah," Philip K. murmured. "Ah . . . Myrmidopterans." This name exploded inside him with the force of resurgent myth: Myrmidon and

Lepidoptera combined. And such an unlikely combination did his huge, serene visitors indeed seem to Philip K.

ONSLAUGHT

At last the Myrmidopterans, or the first wave of them, introduced themselves gently into Philip K.'s atmosphere. Now their great silver or gold wings either flapped or, to facilitate soaring, lay outstretched on the updrafts from his unevenly heated surface. Down the Myrmidopterans came. Philip K. felt that mere shavings and gold dust had been rudely flung into The Eye That Was Himself, for these invaders obscured the sky and blotted out even angry, fat Papa—so that it was visible only as a red glow, not as a monumental roundness. Everything was sharp light, reflected splendor, windfall confusion. What was the outcome of this invasion going to be? Philip K. looked up—all around himself—and studied the dropping Myrmidopterans. As the first part of the name he had given them implied, their torso/fuselages resembled the bodies of ants. Fire ants, to be precise. On Earth such ants were capable of inflicting venomous stings, and these alien creatures had mouthparts, vicious mandibles, of gold or silver (always in contrast to the color of their wings). Had they come to devour him? Would he feel pain if they began to eat of him? "No, go away!" he wanted to shout, but could only shudder and unleash a few feeble dermalquakes in his southern hemisphere. They did not heed these quakes. Down the Myrmidopterans came. Darkness covered Philip K. from pole to pole, for so did Myrmidopterans. And for the first time in his life, as either tomato or man, he was utterly blind.

THE TIRESIAS SYNDROME

Once physically sightless, Philip K. came to feel that his metaphysical and spiritual blinders had fallen away. (Actually, this was an illusion fostered by the subconscious image of the Blind Seer; Tiresias, Oedipus, Homer, and, less certainly, John Milton exemplify good analogs of this archetypal figure. But with Philip K. the *illusion* of new insight overwhelmed and sank his sense of perspective.) In world-wide, self-wide dark he realized that it was his ethical duty to preserve his life, to resist being devoured. "After all," he said to himself, "in this new incarnation, or whatever one ought to term the state of being a tomato, I could prevent universal famine for my own species—that is, if I could somehow materialize in my own solar system within reasonable rocket range of Earth." He envisioned shuttle runs from Earth, mining operations on and below his surface, shipments of his nutritious self (in refrigerator modules) back to the home world, and, finally, the glorious distribution of his essence among Earth's malnourished and starving. He would die, of course, from these constant depredations, but he would have the satisfaction of knowing himself the savior of all humanity. Moreover, like Osiris, Christ, the Green Knight, and other representatives of salvation and/or fertility, he *might* undergo resurrection, especially if someone had the foresight to take graftings home along with his flesh and juice. But these were vain speculations. Philip K. was no prophet, blind or otherwise, and the Myrmidopterans, inconsiderately, had begun to eat of him. "Ah, Lydia P.," he burbled at the first simultaneous, regimented bites. "Ah, humanity."

Not as an Addict (*or, The Salivas of Ecstasy*)

And so Philip K. was eaten. The Myrmidopterans, their wings overlapping all over his planet-sized body, feasted. Daintily they devoured him. And . . . painlessly. In fact, with growing wonder Philip K. realized that their bites, their gnawings, their mandibles' grim machinations injected into him not venom but a saliva that fed volts and volts of current into his vestigial (from the period of his humanity) pleasure centers. God, it was not to be believed! The pleasure he derived from their steady chowing-down had nothing to do with any pleasure he had experienced on Earth. It partook of neither the animal nor the vegetable, of neither the rational nor the irrational. Take note: Philip K. could think about how good he felt without in any way diminishing the effect of the Myrmidopterans' ecstasy-inducing chomps. Then, too soon, they stopped—after trimming off only a few hundred meters of his orange-red skin (a process requiring an entire Philip K.–month, by the way, though because of his blindness he was unable to determine how long it had taken). But as soon as his eaters had flown back into the emptiness of space, permitting him brief glimpses of Papa, a few stars, and the ant-moths' heftier bodies, another wave of Myrmidopterans moved in from the void, set down on his ravaged surface, and began feeding with even greater relish, greater dispatch. This continued for years and years, the two waves of Myrmidopterans alternating, until Philip K. was once more a tomato little bigger than Mars, albeit a sloppy and moth-eaten tomato. What cared he? Time no longer meant anything to him, no more than did the fear of death. If he were to die, it would be at the will of creatures whose metal wings he worshipped, whose jaws he welcomed, whose very spit he craved—not as an addict craves, but instead as the devout communicant desires the wine and the wafer. Therefore, though decades passed, Philip K. let them go.

SOMEWHERE OVER THE SPACE/TIME BOW

Where did the Myrmidopterans come from? Who were they? These were questions that Philip K. pondered even in the midst of his ineffable bliss. As he was eaten, his consciousness grew sharper, more aware, almost uncanny in its extrapolations. And he found an answer . . . for the first question, at least. The Myrmidopterans came from beyond the figurative horizon of the universe, from *over* the ultimate curvature where space bent back on itself. Philip K. understood that a paradox was involved here, perhaps even an obfuscation which words, numbers, and ideograms could never resolve into an explanation commensurate with the lucid reality. Never mind. The Myrmidopterans had seemed to approach Philip K. from every direction, from every conceivable point in the plenum. This fact was significant. It symbolized the creatures' customary *independence of* the space/time continuum to which our physical universe belongs. "Yes," Philip K. admitted to himself, "they operate in the physical universe, they even have physical demands to meet—as demonstrated by their devouring of me. But they belong to the . . . Outer Demesnes of Creation, a nonplace where they have an ethereal existence that this continuum (into which they must occasionally venture) always debases." How did Philip K. know? He knew. The Myrmidopterans ate; therefore, he knew.

MOVING DAY

Then they stopped feeding altogether. One wave of the creatures lifted from his torn body, pulled themselves effort-

lessly out of his gravitational influence, and dispersed to the
. . . well, the uttermost bounds of night. Golden and silver,
silver and golden—until Philip K. could no longer see them.
How quickly they vanished, more quickly than he would have
believed possible. There, then gone. Of the second wave of
Myrmidopterans, which he then expected to descend, only
twelve remained, hovering at various points over him in outer
space. He saw them clearly, for his optical cells, he understood, were now continuous with his whole being, not merely
with his long-since-devoured original surface—a benefit
owing to his guests' miraculous saliva and their concern for
his slow initiation into The Mystery. These twelve archangels
began canting their wings in such a way that they maneu-
vered him, Philip K., out of his orbit around the angrily
expanding Papa. "Papa's going to collapse," he told himself,
"he's going to go through a series of collapses, all of them so
sudden as to be almost simultaneous." (Again, Philip K.
knew; he simply knew.) As they moved him farther and farther out, by an arcane technology whose secret he had a dim
intuition of, the Myrmidopterans used their great wings to reflect the red giant's warming rays on every inch of his
surface. They were not going to let him be exploded, neither
were they going to let him freeze. In more than one sense of
the word, Philip K. was moved. But what would these desperation tactics avail them? If Papa went nova, finally exploded,
and threw out the slaglike elements manufactured in its
100-billion-degree furnace, none of them would escape, neither he nor the twelve guardian spirits maneuvering him ever
outward. Had he been preserved from rotting and his flesh
restored like Osiris' (for Philip K. was whole again, though
still approximately Mars-sized) only to be flash-vaporized or,
surviving that, blown to purée by Papa's extruded shrapnel?
No. The Myrmidopterans would not permit it, assuredly they
would not.

The Nova Express

Papa blew. But just before Philip K.'s old and in many
ways beloved primary bombarded him and his escorts with either deadly radiation or deadly debris, the Myrmidopterans
glided free of him and positioned themselves in a halo-like
ring above his northern pole (the one with the stem). Then
they canted their wings and with the refracted energy of both
the raging solar wind and their own spirits *pushed* Philip K.

into an invisible slot in space. Before disappearing into it completely, however, he looked back and saw the twelve archangels spread wide their blinding wings and . . . *wink out* of existence. In our physical universe, at least. Then Philip K. himself was in another continuum, another reality, and could feel himself falling through it like a great Newtonian *pomme d'amour*. Immediately after the winking out of the twelve Myrmidopterans, Papa blew; and Philip K., even in the new reality, was being propelled in part by the colossal concussion resulting from that event. He had hitched, with considerable resistance, a ride on the Nova Express. But where to, he wondered, and why?

SPECIAL EFFECTS ARE DO-IT-YOURSELF UNDERTAKINGS

In transit between the solar system of his defunct red giant and wherever he now happened to be going, Philip K. watched—among other things—the colors stream past. Colors, lights, elongated stars; fiery smells, burning gong-sounds, ripplings of water, sheets of sensuous time. This catalogue makes no sense, or very little sense, expressed in linguistic terms; therefore, imagine any nonverbal experience which involves those senses whereby sense may indeed be made of this catalogue. Light shows, Moog music, and cinematic special effects are good starting places. Do not ask me to be more specific, even though I could; allusion to other works, other media, is at best a risky business, and you will do well to exercise your own imaginative powers in conjuring up a mental picture of the transfinite reality through which Philip K. plunged. Call it the avenue beyond a stargate. Call it the interior of a chrono-synclastic infundibulum. Call it the enigmatic subjective well which one may enter via a black hole. Call it sub-, para-, warp-, anti-, counter-, or even id-space. Many do. The nomenclature, however, will fail to do justice to the transfinite reality itself, the one in which Philip K. discovered that he comprehended The Mystery that the Myrmidopterans had intended him, as a tomato, to comprehend *in toto*. For as he fell, or was propelled, or simply remained stationary while the new continuum roared vehemently by, he bathed in the same ineffable pleasure he had felt during the many dining-ins of the gold and silver antmoths. At the same time, he came to understand (1) the identity of these beings, (2) his destination, (3) the nature of his mission, and (4) the glorious and terrible meaning of his

bizarre metamorphosis. All became truly clear to him, everything. And this time his enlightenment was not an illusion,
not a metaphysical red herring like the Tiresias Syndrome.
For, you see, Philip K. had evolved beyond self, beyond illusion, beyond the bonds of space/time—beyond everything, in
fact, but his roguish giant-tomatohood.

How the Mandala Turned (*or, What Philip K. Learned*)

Although one ought to keep in mind that his learning
process began with the first feast of the ant-moths, this is
what Philip K. discovered in transit between two realities: It
was not by eating of the fruit of the Tree of Knowledge that
one put on the omniscience and the subtle ecstasy of gods,
but instead by *becoming* the fruit itself—in the form of a
sentient, evolving world—and then by *being eaten* by the
seraphically winged, beautifully silver, messianically golden
Myrmidopterans. They, of course, were the incarnate (so to
speak) messengers of the universe's supreme godhead. By
being consumed, one was saved, apotheosized, and lifted to
the omega point of man's evolutionary development. This was
the fate of humankind, and he, Philip K., only a short time
before—on an absolute, extra-universal scale—an insignificant man of few talents and small means, had been chosen
by the Myrmidopterans to reveal to the struggling masses of
his own species their ineluctable destiny. Philip K. was again
profoundly moved, the heavens sang about him with rever-
berant hosannas, all of creation seemed to open up for him
like a blood-crimson bud. Filled with bright awe, then, and
his own stingingly sweet ichor, Philip K. popped back into
our physical universe in the immediate vicinity of Earth (incidentally capturing the moon away from its rightful owner).
Then he sat in the skies of an astonished North America just
as if he had always been there. Millions died as a result of
the tidal upheavals he unfortunately wrought, but this was all
in the evolutionary Game Plan of the supreme godhead, and
Philip K. felt exultation rather than remorse. (He did wonder
briefly if Houston had been swamped and Lydia P.
drowned.) He was a rogue tomato, yes, but no portent of
doom. He was the messenger of the New Annunciation and
he had come to apprise his people of it. Floating 350,000
miles from Earth, he had no idea how he would deliver this
message, the news that the mandala of ignorance, knowledge,

and ultimate perception was about to complete its first round. No idea at all. Not any. None.

CODA

But, as the saying goes, he would think of something.

The Labor Day Group

The 1939–50 period dominated by Campbell's *Astounding* has been called the Golden Age. The dozen years that followed, divided in influence among *Astounding/Analog,* Boucher's *Magazine of Fantasy and Science Fiction,* and Gold's *Galaxy,* has been described variously as the boom that busted, the false spring, or, in Barry Malzberg's words, the end of summer. The period of the mid-1960s symbolized by Michael Moorcock's *New Worlds* and Harlan Ellison's *Dangerous Visions* has been called the New Wave. What then is the proper designation and the accurate description of the period that followed?

That question remains for the future to answer in any definitive way, but Thomas Disch, in a critical essay published in the February 1981 *Magazine of Fantasy and Science Fiction,* described one group of writers that seemed to dominate the Hugo and Nebula Awards and the best-of-the-year collections as "the Labor Day Group," because the members of the group could most often be found together at the World Science Fiction Convention, which traditionally meets over the Labor Day weekend. Disch went on to say:

> I don't mean to suggest that anything like a cabal is at work, only that a coherent generational grouping exists. . . . Further, I'd suggest that these writers have more in common *as a group* than those (myself among them) who were lumped together under the rubric "New Wave," that they possess something approaching solidarity, as the Futurians did in their day.

One of the writers Disch placed in that group was George R. R. Martin. Born in Bayonne, New Jersey, in 1948, Martin earned a degree in journalism from Northwestern University in 1970 and a masters' degree in 1971. He served with the Cook County Legal Assistance Foundation from 1972 to 1974, as a chess tournament director from 1973 to 1975, and as a journalism teacher (and as an organizer of a science fiction writers' workshop in the summer) at Clarke College in Dubuque, Iowa, from 1976 to 1978; he has worked as a freelance writer since then. Currently he lives in Santa Fe, New Mexico.

Martin's first story, "The Hero," was published in *Galaxy* for February 1971. His work began to be nominated for awards with "With Morning Comes Mistfall" (1973) and "A Song for Lya" (1974). The latter won a Hugo. "Sandkings" and "The Way of Cross and Dragon" won Martin two Hugo Awards in 1980; "Sandkings" also won a Nebula Award. Martin received a Breadloaf Writers Conference fellowship in 1977. His short stories have been collected in *A Song for Lya and Other Stories* (1976) and *Songs of Stars and Shadows* (1977).

Like many sf writers, Martin was slow in shaping his talents to the novel. *Dying of the Light* was published in 1978, *Windhaven* (with Lisa Tuttle) in 1980, and *Nightflyers* in 1981. He also has edited a series of anthologies containing stories by Campbell Award nominees for best new science fiction author, *New Voices in Science Fiction* (the first volume appeared in 1977).

In his essay, Disch said that "the Labor Day Group" was a product of the "disillusionment and retrenchment" of the 1970s, that its members had witnessed the artistic and commercial failures of the New Wave and opted for marketable fiction aimed at fans and awards and featuring "simple problems clearly solved by wholesome, likeable characters."

Martin responded in the December 1981 *Magazine of Fantasy and Science Fiction* by agreeing that there was a community of writers such as Ed Bryant, Vonda McIntyre, Tanith Lee, Jack Dann, Michael Bishop, Orson Scott Card, John Varley, and himself, but disagreeing with most of the other charges. The common qualities of the group, he wrote, arose from the fact that they were "a fusion of the two warring camps of the '60s." They had "one foot firmly in the camp of traditional SF," but they were also "the generation of Viet Nam." The failure of the New Wave, he continued, did not turn them all into "literary journeymen churning out the yardgoods. The real story is one of thesis, antithesis, synthesis." What Martin thinks the Labor Day Group is about, at heart, is "combining the color and the verve and unconscious power of the best of traditional SF with the literary concerns of the New Wave. Mating the poet with the rocketeer. Bridging the two cultures."

In "This Tower of Ashes," originally published in the *Analog Annual* (1976), Martin provides evidence for his claims. The story is traditional in its basic structure: Earth people encounter an alien world; callous Earthman is unable to see alien beauty and the possibilities of older civilizations. The plot is even more traditional than that, going back to pre-sf patterns; it is a love triangle in which the boy has lost the girl but still hopes to win her back. All this, however, is only the armature on which Martin molds another story; that story is told as a contrast between the known and the unknown in its various guises: life and story, practicality and beauty, the familiar and the alien, reality and dreams. In the introduction to *Songs of Stars and Shadows*, Martin wrote, "Love and loneliness may be *among* my favorite themes, but the all-time champion to date has got to be reality's search and destroy mission against romance, a subject that I've turned to again and again."

To the service of these contrasts Martin brings not only a sensitivity to language and an inventiveness of detail and incident but an evocative use of image, symbol, and metaphor. The crumbling alien brick tower, the glowing blue moss, and the dream spiders and their bright webs represent more than their naturalistic meanings can encompass.

This Tower of Ashes

by George R. R. Martin

My tower is built of bricks, small soot-gray bricks mortared together with a shiny black substance that looks strangely like obsidian to my untrained eye, though it clearly cannot be obsidian. It sits by an arm of the Skinny Sea, twenty feet tall and sagging, the edge of the forest only a few feet away.

I found the tower nearly four years ago, when Squirrel and I left Port Jamison in the silver aircar that now lies gutted and overgrown in the weeds outside my doorstep. To this day I know almost nothing about the structure, but I have my theories.

I do not think it was built by men, for one. It clearly predates Port Jamison, and I often suspect it predates human spaceflight. The bricks (which are curiously small, less than a quarter the size of normal bricks) are tired and weathered and old, and they crumble visibly beneath my feet. Dust is everywhere and I know its source, for more than once I have pried a loose brick from the parapet on the roof and crushed it idly to fine dark powder in my naked fist. When the salt wind blows from the east, the tower flies a plume of ashes.

Inside, the bricks are in better condition, since the wind and the rain have not touched them quite so much, but the tower is still far from pleasant. The interior is a single room full of dust and echoes, without windows; the only light comes from the circular opening in the center of the roof. A spiral stair, built of the same ancient brick as the rest, is part of the wall; around and around it circles, like the threading on a screw, before it reaches roof level. Squirrel, who is quite small as cats go, finds the stairs easy climbing, but for human feet they are narrow and awkward.

But I still climb them. Each night I return from the cool forests, my arrows black with the caked blood of the dream-spiders and my bag heavy with their poison sacs, and I set aside my bow and wash my hands and then climb up to the roof to spend the last few hours before dawn. Across the narrow salt channel, the lights of Port Jamison burn on the island, and from up there it is not the city I remember. The square black buildings wear a bright romantic glow at night; the lights, all smoky orange and muted blue, speak of mystery and silent song and more than a little loneliness, while the starships rise and fall against the stars like the tireless wandering fireflies of my boyhood on Old Earth.

"There are stories over there," I told Korbec once, before I had learned better. "There are people behind every light, and each person has a life, a story. Only they lead those lives without ever touching us, so we'll never know the stories." I think I gestured then; I was, of course, quite drunk.

Korbec answered with a toothy smile and a shake of his

head. He was a great dark fleshy man, with a beard like knotted wire. Each month he came out from the city in his pitted black aircar, to drop off my supplies and take the venom I had collected, and each month we went up to the roof and got drunk together. A truck driver, that was all Korbec was; a seller of cut-rate dreams and second-hand rainbows. But he fancied himself a philosopher and a student of man.

"Don't fool yourself," he said to me then, his face flush with wine and darkness, "you're not missing nothin'. Lives are rotten stories, y'know. Real stories now, they usually got a plot to 'em. They start and they go on a bit and when they end they're over, unless the guy's got a series goin'. Peoples' lives don't do that nohow, they just kinda wander around and ramble and go on and on. Nothin' ever finishes."

"People die," I said. "That's enough of a finish, I'd think."

Korbec made a loud noise. "Sure, but have you ever known anybody to die at the right time? No, don't happen that way. Some guys fall over before their lives have properly gotten started, some right in the middle of the best part. Others kinda linger on after everything is really over."

Often when I sit up there alone, with Squirrel warm in my lap and a glass of wine by my side, I remember Korbec's words and the heavy way he said them, his coarse voice oddly gentle. He is not a smart man, Korbec, but that night I think he spoke the truth, maybe never realizing it himself. But the weary realism that he offered me then is the only antidote there is for the dreams that spiders weave.

But I am not Korbec, not can I be, and while I recognize his truth, I cannot live it.

I was outside taking target practice in the late afternoon, wearing nothing but my quiver and a pair of cutoffs, when they came. It was closing on dusk and I was loosening up for my nightly foray into the forest—even in those early days I lived from twilight to dawn, as the dream-spiders do. The grass felt good under my bare feet, the double-curved silverwood bow felt even better in my hand, and I was shooting well.

Then I heard them coming. I glanced over my shoulder toward the beach, and saw the dark blue aircar swelling rapidly against the eastern sky. Gerry, of course, I knew that from the sound; his aircar had been making noises as long as I had known him.

I turned my back on them, drew another arrow—quite steady—and notched my first bull's-eye of the day.

Gerry set his aircar down in the weeds near the base of the tower, just a few feet from my own. Crystal was with him, slim and grave, her long gold hair full of red glints from the afternoon sun. They climbed out and started toward me.

"Don't stand near the target," I told them, as I slipped another arrow into place and bent the bow. "How did you find me?" The twang of the arrow vibrating in the target punctuated my question.

They circled well around my line of fire. "You'd mentioned spotting this place from the air once," Gerry said, "and we knew you weren't anywhere in Port Jamison. Figured it was worth a chance." He stopped a few feet from me, with his hands on his hips, looking just as I remembered him; big, dark-haired, and very fit. Crystal came up beside him and put one hand lightly on his arm.

I lowered my bow and turned to face them. "So. Well, you found me. Why?"

"I was worried about you, Johnny," Crystal said softly. But she avoided my eyes when I looked at her.

Gerry put a hand around her waist, very possessively, and something flared within me. "Running away never solves anything," he told me, his voice full of the strange mixture of friendly concern and patronizing arrogance he had been using on me for months.

"I did *not* run away," I said, my voice strained. "Damn it. You should never have come."

Crystal glanced at Gerry, looking very sad, and it was clear that suddenly she was thinking the same thing. Gerry just frowned. I don't think he ever once understood why I said the things I said, or did the things I did; whenever we discussed the subject, which was infrequently, he would only tell me with vague puzzlement what *he* would have done if our roles had been reversed. It seemed infinitely strange to him that anyone could possibly do anything differently in the same position.

His frown did not touch me, but he'd already done his damage. For the month I'd been in my self-imposed exile at the tower, I had been trying to come to terms with my actions and my moods, and it had been far from easy. Crystal and I had been together for a long time—nearly four years—when we came to Jamison's World together, trying to track down some unique silver and obsidian artifacts that we'd picked up on Baldur. I had loved her all that time, and I still loved her, even now, after she had left me for Gerry. When I was feeling good about myself, it seemed to me that the impulse that had driven me out of Port Jamison was a noble and unselfish one. I wanted Crys to be happy, simply, and she could not be happy with me there. My wounds were too deep, and I wasn't good at hiding them; my presence put the damper of guilt on the new-born joy she'd found with Gerry. And since she could not bear to cut me off completely, I felt compelled to cut myself off. For them. For her.

Or so I liked to tell myself. But there were hours when that bright rationalization broke down, dark hours of self-loathing. Were those the real reasons? Or was I simply out to hurt myself in a fit of angry immaturity, and by doing so, punish them—like a willful child who plays with thoughts of suicide as a form of revenge?

I honestly didn't know. For a month I'd fluctuated from one belief to the other while I tried to understand myself and decide what I'd do next. I wanted to think myself a hero, willing to make a sacrifice for the happiness of the woman I loved. But Gerry's words made it clear that he didn't see it that way at all.

"Why do you have to be so damned dramatic about everything?" he said, looking stubborn. He had been determined all along to be very civilized, and seemed perpetually annoyed at me because I wouldn't shape up and heal my wounds so that everybody could be friends. Nothing annoyed me quite so much as his annoyance; *I* thought I was handling the situation pretty well, all things considered, and I resented the inference that I wasn't.

But Gerry was determined to convert me, and my best withering look was wasted on him. "We're going to stay here and talk things out until you agree to fly back to Port Jamison with us," he told me, in his most forceful now-I'm-getting-tough tone.

"Like shit," I said, turning sharply away from them and yanking an arrow from my quiver. I slid it into place, pulled, and released, all too quickly. The arrow missed the target by a good foot and buried itself in the soft dark brick of my crumbling tower.

"What *is* this place, anyway?" Crys asked, looking at the tower as if she'd just seen it for the first time. It's possible that she had—that it took the incongruous sight of my arrow lodging in stone to make her notice the ancient structure.

More likely, though, it was a premeditated change of subject, designed to cool the argument that was building between Gerry and me.

I lowered my bow again and walked up to the target to recover the arrows I'd expended. "I'm really not sure," I said, somewhat mollified and anxious to pick up the cue she'd thrown me. "A watchtower, I think, of nonhuman origin. Jamison's World has never been thoroughly explored. It may have had a sentient race once." I walked around the target to the tower, and yanked loose the final arrow from the crumbling brick. "It still may, actually. We know very little of what goes on on the mainland."

"A damn gloomy place to live, if you ask me," Gerry put in, looking over the tower. "Could fall in any moment, from the way it looks."

I gave him a bemused smile. "The thought had occurred to me. But when I first came out here, I was past caring." As soon as the words were out, I regretted saying them; Crys winced visibly. That had been the whole story of my final weeks in Port Jamison. Try as I might, it had seemed that I had only two choices; I could lie, or I could hurt her. Neither appealed to me, so here I was. But here they were too, so the whole impossible situation was back.

Gerry had another comment ready, but he never got to say it. Just then Squirrel came bounding out from between the weeds, straight at Crystal.

She smiled at him and knelt, and an instant later he was at her feet, licking her hand and chewing on her fingers. Squirrel was in a good mood, clearly. He liked life near the tower. Back in Port Jamison, his life had been constrained by Crystal's fears that he'd be eaten by alleysnarls or chased by dogs or strung up by local children. Out here I let him run free, which was much more to his liking. The brush around the tower was overrun by whipping-mice, a native rodent with a hairless tail three times its own body length. The tail packed a mild sting, but Squirrel didn't care, even though he swelled up and got grouchy every time a tail connected. He *liked* stalking whipping-mice all day. Squirrel always fancied himself a great hunter, and there's no skill involved in chasing down a bowl of catfood.

He'd been with me even longer than Crys had, but she'd become suitably fond of him during our time together. I often suspected that Crystal would have gone with Gerry even sooner than she did, except that she was upset at the idea of leaving Squirrel. Not that he was any great beauty. He was a small, thin, scruffy-looking cat, with ears like a fox and fur a scroungy gray-brown color, and a big bushy tail two sizes too big for him. The friend who gave him to me back on Avalon informed me gravely that Squirrel was the illegitimate off-spring of a genetically engineered psicat and a mangy alley tom. But if Squirrel could read his owner's mind, he didn't pay much attention. When he wanted affection, he'd do things like climb right up on the book I was reading and knock it away and begin biting my chin; when he wanted to be let alone, it was dangerous folly to try to pet him.

As Crystal knelt by him and stroked him and Squirrel nuzzled up to her hand, she seemed very much the woman I'd traveled with and loved and talked to at endless length and slept with every night, and I suddenly realized how I'd missed her. I think I smiled; the sight of her, even under these conditions, still gave me a cloud-shadowed joy. Maybe I was being silly and stupid and vindictive to send them away, I thought, after they had come so far to see me. Crys was still Crys, and Gerry could hardly be so bad, since she loved him.

Watching her, wordless, I made a sudden decision; I would let them stay. And we could see what happened. "It's close to dusk," I heard myself saying. "Are you folks hungry?"

Crys looked up, still petting Squirrel, and smiled. Gerry nodded. "Sure."

"All right," I said. I walked past them, turned and paused in the doorway, and gestured them inside. "Welcome to my ruin."

I turned on the electric torches and set about making dinner. My lockers were well stocked back in those days; I had not yet started living off the forests. I unthawed three big sandragons, the silver-shelled crustacean that Jamie fishermen dragged for relentlessly, and served them up with bread and cheese and white wine.

Mealtime conversation was polite and guarded. We talked of mutual friends in Port Jamison, Crystal told me about a letter she'd received from a couple we had known on Baldur, Gerry held forth on politics and the efforts of the Port police to crack down on the traffic in dreaming venom. "The Council is sponsoring research on some sort of super-pesticide that would wipe out the dream-spiders," he told me. "A saturation spraying of the near coast would cut off most of the supply, I'd think."

"Certainly," I said, a bit high on the wine and a bit piqued at Gerry's stupidity. Once again, listening to him, I had found myself questioning Crystal's taste. "Never mind what other effects it might have on the ecology, right?"

Gerry shrugged. "Mainland," he said simply. He was Jamie through-and-through, and the comment translated to "Who cares?" The accidents of history had given the residents of Jamison's World a singularly cavalier attitude toward their planet's one large continent. Most of the original settlers had come from Old Poseidon, where the sea had been a way of life for generations. The rich, teeming oceans and peaceful archipelagoes of their new world had attracted them far more than the dark forests of the mainland. Their children grew up to the same attitudes, except for a handful who found an illegal profit selling dreams.

"Don't shrug it all off so easy," I said.

"Be realistic," he replied. "The mainland's no use to anyone, except the spider-men. Who would it hurt?"

"Damn it, Gerry, look at this tower! Where did it come from, tell me that! I tell *you*, there might be intelligence out there, in those forests. The Jamies have never even bothered to look."

Crystal was nodding over her wine. "Johnny could be right," she said, glancing at Gerry. "That was why I came here, remember. The artifacts. The shop on Baldur said they were shipped out of Port Jamison. He couldn't trace them back any farther than that. And the workmanship—I've handled alien art for years, Gerry. I know Fyndii work, and Damoosh, and I've seen all the others. This was *different*."

Gerry only smiled. "Proves nothing. There are other races, millions of them, farther in toward the core. The distances are too great, so we don't hear of them very often, except maybe third-hand, but it isn't impossible that every so often a piece of their art would trickle through." He shook his head. "No, I'd bet this tower was put up by some early settler. Who knows? Could be there was another discoverer, before Jamison, who never reported his find. Maybe he built the place. But I'm not going to buy mainland sentients."

"At least not until you fumigate the damned forests and they all come out waving their spears," I said sourly. Gerry laughed and Crystal smiled at me. And suddenly, suddenly, I had an overpowering desire to *win* this argument. My thoughts had the hazy clarity that only wine can give, and it seemed so logical. I was so clearly *right*, and here was my chance to show up Gerry like the provincial he was and make points with Crys.

I leaned forward. "If you Jamies would ever look, you might find sentients," I said. "I've only been on the mainland a month, and already I've found a great deal. You've no damned concept of the kind of beauty you talk so blithely of wiping out. A whole ecology is out there, different from the islands, species upon species, a lot probably not even discovered yet. But what do you know about it? Any of you?"

Gerry nodded. "So, show me." He stood up suddenly. "I'm always willing to learn, Bowen. Why don't you take us out and show us all the wonders of the mainland?"

I think Gerry was trying to make points, too. He probably never thought I'd take up his offer, but it was exactly what I'd wanted. It was dark outside now, and we had been talking by the light of my torches. Above, stars shone through the hole in my roof. The forest would be alive now, eerie and beautiful, and I was suddenly eager to be out there, bow in hand, in a world where I was a force and a friend, Gerry a bumbling tourist.

"Crystal?" I said.

She looked interested. "Sounds like fun. If it's safe."

"It will be," I said. "I'll take my bow." We both rose, and Crys looked happy. I remembered the times we tackled Baldurian wilderness together, and suddenly I felt very happy, certain that everything would work out well. Gerry was just part of a bad dream. She couldn't possibly be in love with him.

First I found the sober-ups; I was feeling good, but not good enough to head out into the forest when I was still dizzy from wine. Crystal and I flipped ours down immediately, and seconds later my alcoholic glow began to fade. Gerry, however, waved away the pill I offered him. "I haven't had that much," he insisted. "Don't need it."

I shrugged, thinking that things were getting better and better. If Gerry went crashing drunkenly through the woods, it couldn't help but turn Crys away from him. "Suit yourself," I said.

Neither of them was really dressed for wilderness, but I hoped that wouldn't be a problem, since I didn't really plan on taking them very deep in the forest. It would be a quick trip, I thought; wander down my trail a bit, show them the dust pile and the spider-chasm, maybe nail a dream-spider for them. Nothing to it, out and back again.

I put on a dark coverall, heavy trail boots, and my quiver, handed Crystal a flash in case we wandered away from the bluemoss regions, and picked up my bow. "You really need that?" Gerry asked, with sarcasm.

"Protection," I said.

"Can't be that dangerous."

It isn't, if you know what you're doing, but I didn't tell him that. "Then why do you Jamies stay on your islands?"

He smiled. "I'd rather trust a laser."

"I'm cultivating a deathwish. A bow gives the prey a chance, of sorts."

Crys gave me a smile of shared memories. "He only hunts predators," she told Gerry. I bowed.

Squirrel agreed to guard my castle. Steady and very sure of myself, I belted on a knife and led my ex-wife and her lover out into the forests of Jamison's World.

We walked in single file, close together, me up front with the bow, Crys following, Gerry behind her. Crys used the flashlight when we first set out, playing it over the trail as we wound our way through the thick grove of spikearrows that stood like a wall against the sea. Tall and very straight, crusty gray of bark and some as big around as my tower, they climbed to a ridiculous height before sprouting their meager load of branches. Here and there they crowded together and squeezed the path between them, and more than one seemingly impassable fence of wood confronted us suddenly in the dark. But Crys could always pick out the way, with me a foot ahead of her to point her flash when it paused.

Ten minutes out from the tower, the character of the forest began to change. The ground and the very air were drier here, the wind cool but without the snap of salt; the water-hungry spikearrows had drained most of the moisture from the air. They began to grow smaller and less frequent, the spaces between them larger and easier to find. Other species of plant began to appear; stunted little goblin trees, sprawling mockoaks, graceful ebonfires whose red veins pulsed brilliantly in the dark wood when caught by Crystal's wandering flash.

And bluemoss.

Just a little at first; here a ropy web dangling from a goblin's arm, there a small patch on the ground, frequently chewing its way up the back of an ebonfire or a withering solitary spikearrow. Then more and more; thick carpets underfoot, mossy blankets on the leaves above, heavy trailers that dangled from the branches and danced around in the wind. Crystal sent the flash darting about, finding bigger and better bunches of the soft blue fungus, and peripherally I began to see the glow.

"Enough," I said, and Crys turned off the light.

Darkness lasted only for a moment, till our eyes adjusted to a dimmer light. Around us, the forest was suffused by a gentle radiance, as the bluemoss drenched us in its ghostly phosphorescence. We were standing near one side of a small clearing, below a shiny black ebonfire, but even the flames of its red-veined wood seemed cool in the faint blue light. The moss had taken over the undergrowth, supplanting all the local grasses and making nearby shrubs into fuzzy blue beachballs. It climbed the sides of most of the trees, and when we looked up through the branches at the stars, we saw that other colonies had set upon the woods a glowing crown.

I laid my bow carefully against the dark flank of the ebonfire, bent, and offered a handful of light to Crystal. When I held it under her chin, she smiled at me again, her features softened by the cool magic in my hand. I remember feeling very good, to have led them to this beauty.

But Gerry only grinned at me. "Is this what we're going to endanger, Bowen?" he asked. "A forest full of bluemoss?"

I dropped the moss. "You don't think it's pretty?"

Gerry shrugged. "Sure, it's pretty. It is also a fungus, a parasite with a dangerous tendency to overrun and crowd out all other forms of plant-life. Bluemoss was very thick on Jolostar and the Barbis Archipelago once, you know. We rooted it all out; it can eat its way through a good corn crop in a month." He shook his head.

And Crystal nodded. "He's right, you know," she said.

I looked at her for a long time, suddenly feeling very sober indeed, the last memory of the wine long gone. Abruptly it dawned on me that I had, all unthinking, built myself another fantasy. Out here, in a world I had started to make my own, a world of dream-spiders and magic moss, somehow I had thought that I could recapture my own dream long fled, my smiling crystalline soulmate. In the timeless wilderness of the mainland, she would see us both in fresh light and would realize once again that it was me she loved.

So I'd spun a pretty web, bright and alluring as the trap of any dream-spider, and Crys had shattered the flimsy filaments with a word. She was his; mine no longer, not now, not ever. And if Gerry seemed to me stupid or insensitive or

overpractical, well, perhaps it was those very qualities that
made Crys choose him. And perhaps not—I had no right to
second-guess her love, and possibly I would never understand
it.

I brushed the last flakes of glowing moss from my hands,
while Gerry took the heavy flash from Crystal and flicked it
on again. My blue fairyland dissolved, burned away by the
bright white reality of his flashlight beam. "What now?" he
asked, smiling. He was not so very drunk after all.

I lifted my bow from where I'd set it down. "Follow me,"
I said, quickly, curtly. Both of them looked eager and interested, but my own mood had shifted dramatically. Suddenly
the whole trip seemed pointless. I wished that they were gone,
that I was back at my tower with Squirrel. I was down . . .

. . . and sinking. Deeper in the moss-heavy woods, we
came upon a dark swift stream, and the brilliance of the
flashlight spared a solitary ironhorn that had come to drink.
It looked up quickly, pale and startled, then bounded away
through the trees, for a fleeting instant looking a bit like the
unicorn of Old Earth legend. Long habit made me glance at
Crystal, but her eyes sought Gerry's when she laughed.

Later, as we climbed a rocky incline, a cave loomed near
at hand; from the smell, a woodsnarl lair.

I turned to warn them around it, only to discover that I'd
lost my audience. They were ten steps behind me, at the bottom of the rocks, walking very slowly and talking quietly,
holding hands.

Dark and angry, wordless, I turned away again and continued on over the hill. We did not speak again until I'd found
the dust pile.

I paused on its edge, my boots an inch deep in the fine
gray powder, and they came straggling up behind me. "Go
ahead, Gerry," I said. "Use your flash here."

The light roamed. The hill was at our back, rocky and lit
here and there with the blurred cold fire of bluemoss-choked
vegetation. But in front of us was only desolation; a wide vacant plain, black and blasted and lifeless, open to the stars.
Back and forth Gerry moved the flashlight, pushing at the
borders of the dust nearby, fading as he shone it straight out
into the gray distance. The only sound was the wind.

"So?" he said at last.

"Feel the dust," I told him. I was not going to stoop this
time. "And when you're back at the tower, crush one of my
bricks and feel that. It's the same thing, a sort of powdery

ash." I made an expansive gesture. "I'd guess there was a city here once, but now it's all crumbled into dust. Maybe my tower was an outpost of the people who built it, you see?"

"The vanished sentients of the forest," Gerry said, still smiling. "Well, I'll admit there's nothing like this on the islands. For a good reason. We don't let forest fires rage unchecked."

"*Forest fire!* Don't give me that. Forest fires don't reduce everything to a fine powder, you always get a few blackened stumps or something."

"Oh? You're probably right. But all the ruined cities I know have at least a few bricks still piled on top of each other for the tourists to take pictures of," Gerry said. The flash beam flicked to and fro over the dust pile, dismissing it. "All you have is a mound of rubbish."

Crystal said nothing.

I began walking back, while they followed in silence. I was losing points every minute; it had been idiocy to bring them out here. At that moment nothing more was on my mind than getting back to my tower as quickly as possible, packing them off to Port Jamison together, and resuming my exile.

Crystal stopped me, after we'd come back over the hill into the bluemoss forest. "Johnny," she said. I stopped, they caught up, Crys pointed.

"Turn off the light," I told Gerry. In the fainter illumination of the moss, it was easier to spot; the intricate iridescent web of a dream-spider, slanting groundward from the low branches of a mockoak. The patches of moss that shone softly all around us were nothing to this; each web strand was as thick as my little finger, oily and brilliant, running with the colors of the rainbow.

Crys took a step toward it, but I took her by the arm and stopped her. "The spiders are around someplace," I said. "Don't go too close. Papa spider never leaves the web, and mama ranges around in the trees at night."

Gerry glanced upward a little apprehensively. His flash was dark, and suddenly he didn't seem to have all the answers. The dream-spiders are dangerous predators, and I suppose he'd never seen one outside of a display case. They weren't native to the islands. "Pretty big web," he said. "Spiders must be a fair size."

"Fair," I said, and at once I was inspired. I could discomfort him a lot more if an ordinary web like this got to him.

And he had been discomforting me all night. "Follow me. I'll show you a real dream-spider."

We circled around the web carefully, never seeing either of its guardians. I led them to the spider-chasm.

It was a great V in the sandy earth, once a creekbed perhaps, but dry and overgrown now. The chasm is hardly very deep by daylight, but at night it looks formidable enough, as you stare down into it from the wooded hills on either side. The bottom is a dark tangle of shrubbery, alive with little flickering phantom lights; higher up, trees of all kinds lean into the chasm, almost meeting in the center. One of them, in fact, does cross the gap. An ancient, rotting spikearrow, withered by lack of moisture, had fallen long ago to provide a natural bridge. The bridge hangs with bluemoss, and glows.

The three of us walked out on that dim-lit, curving trunk, and I gestured down.

Yards below us, a glittering multihued net hung from hill to hill, each strand of the web thick as a cable and aglisten with sticky oils. It tied all the lower trees together in a twisting intricate embrace, and it was a shining fairy-roof above the chasm. Very pretty; it made you want to reach out and touch it.

That, of course, was why the dream-spiders spun it. They were nocturnal predators, and the bright colors of their webs afire in the night made a potent lure.

"Look," Crystal said, "the spider." She pointed. In one of the darker corners of the web, half-hidden by the tangle of a goblin tree that grew out of the rock, it was sitting. I could see it dimly, by the webfire and moss light, a great eight-legged white thing the size of a large pumpkin. Unmoving. Waiting.

Gerry glanced around uneasily again, up into the branches of a crooked mockoak that hung partially above us. "The mate's around somewhere, isn't it?"

I nodded. The dream-spiders of Jamison's World are not quite twins of the arachnids of Old Earth. The female is indeed the deadlier of the species, but far from eating the male, she takes him for life in a permanent specialized partnership. For it is the sluggish, great-bodied male who wears the spinnerets, who weaves the shining-fire web and makes it sticky with his oils, who binds and ties the prey snared by light and color. Meanwhile, the smaller female roams the dark branches, her poison sac full of the viscous dreaming-venom that grants bright visions and ecstacy and final blackness. Creatures many times her own size she stings, and drags limp back to the web to add to the larder.

The dream-spiders are soft, merciful hunters for all that. If they prefer live food, no matter; the captive probably enjoys being eaten. Popular Jamie wisdom says a spider's prey moans with joy as it is consumed. Like all popular wisdoms, it is vastly exaggerated. But the truth is, the captives never struggle.

Except that night, something was struggling in the web below us.

"What's that?" I said, blinking. The iridescent web was not even close to empty—the half eaten corpse of an ironhorn lay close at hand below us, and some great dark bat was bound in bright strands just slightly farther away—but these were not what I watched. In the corner opposite the male spider, near the western trees, something was caught and fluttering. I remember a brief glimpse of thrashing pale limbs, wide luminous eyes, and something like wings. But I did not see it clearly.

That was when Gerry slipped.

Maybe it was the wine that made him unsteady, or maybe the moss under our feet, or the curve of the trunk on which we stood. Maybe he was just trying to step around me to see whatever it was I was staring at. But, in any case, he slipped and lost his balance, let out a yelp, and suddenly he was five yards below us, caught in the web. The whole thing shook to the impact of his fall, but it didn't come close to breaking— dream-spider webs are strong enough to catch ironhorns and woodsnarls, after all.

"Damn," Gerry yelled. He looked ridiculous; one leg plunged right down through the fibers of the web, his arms half-sunk and tangled hopelessly, only his head and shoulders really free of the mess. "This stuff is sticky. I can hardly move."

"Don't try," I told him. "It'll just get worse. I'll figure out a way to climb down and cut you loose. I've got my knife." I looked around, searching for a tree limb to shimmy out on.

"*John.*" Crystal's voice was tense, on edge.

The male spider had left his lurking place behind the goblin tree. He was moving toward Gerry with a heavy deliberate gait; a gross white shape clamoring over the preternatural beauty of his web.

"Damn," I said. I wasn't seriously alarmed, but it was a bother. The great male was the biggest spider I'd ever seen, and it seemed a shame to kill him. But I didn't see that I had much choice. The male dream-spider has no venom, but he *is* a carnivore, and his bite can be most final, especially when he's the size of this one. I couldn't let him get within biting distance of Gerry.

Steadily, carefully, I drew a long gray arrow out of my quiver and fitted it to my bowstring. It was night, of course, but I wasn't really worried. I was a good shot and my target was outlined clearly by the glowing strands of his web.

Crystal screamed.

I stopped briefly, annoyed that she'd panic when everything was under control. But I knew all along that she would not, of course. It was something else. For an instant I couldn't imagine what it could be.

Then I saw, as I followed Crys' eyes with my own. A fat white spider the size of a big man's fist had dropped down from the mockoak to the bridge we were standing on, not ten feet away. Crystal, thank God, was safe behind me.

I stood there—how long? I don't know. If I had just acted, without stopping, without thought, I could have handled everything. I should have taken care of the male first, with the arrow I had ready. There would have been plenty of time to pull a second arrow for the female.

But I froze instead, caught in that dark bright moment, for an instant timeless, my bow in my hand yet unable to act.

It was all so complicated, suddenly. The female was scuttling toward me, faster than I would have believed, and it seemed so much quicker and deadlier than the slow white thing below. Perhaps I should take *it* out first. I might miss, and then I would need time to go for my knife or a second arrow.

Except that would leave Gerry tangled and helpless under the jaws of the male that moved toward him inexorably. He could die. He could die. Crystal could never blame me. I had to save myself, and her, she would understand that. And I'd have her back again.

Yes.

NO!

Crystal was screaming, screaming, and suddenly everything was clear and I knew what it had all meant and why I was here in this forest and what I had to do. There was a moment of glorious transcendence. I had lost the gift of making her happy, my Crystal, but now for a moment suspended in time that power had returned to me, and I could give or withhold happiness forever. With an arrow, I could prove a love that Gerry would never match.

I think I smiled. I'm sure I did.

And my arrow flew darkly through the cool night, and found its mark in the bloated white spider that raced across a web of light.

The female was on me, and I made no move to kick it away or crush it beneath my heel. There was a sharp stabbing pain in my ankle.

Bright and many-colored are the webs the dream-spiders weave.

At night, when I return from the forests, I clean my arrows carefully and open my great knife, with its slim barbed blade, to cut apart the poison sacs I've collected. I slit them open, each in turn, as I have earlier cut them from the still white bodies of the dream-spiders, and then I drain the venom off into a bottle, to wait for the day when Korbec flies out to collect it.

Afterwards I set out the miniature goblet, exquisitely wrought in silver and obsidian and bright with spider motifs, and pour it full of the heavy black wine they bring me from the city. I stir the cup with my knife, around and around until the blade is shiny clean again and the wine is a trifle darker than before. And I ascend to the roof.

Often Korbec's words will return to me then, and with them my story. Crystal my love, and Gerry, and a night of lights and spiders. It all seemed so very right for that brief moment, when I stood upon the moss-covered bridge with an arrow in my hand, and decided. And it has all gone so very very *wrong* . . .

. . . from the moment I awoke, after a month of fever and visions, to find myself in the tower where Crys and Gerry had taken me to nurse me back to health. My decision, my transcendent choice, was not so final as I would have thought.

At times I wonder if it *was* a choice. We talked about it, often, while I regained my strength, and the tale that Crystal tells me is not the one that I remember. She says that we never saw the female at all, until it was too late, that it dropped silently onto my neck just as I released the arrow that killed the male. Then, she says, she smashed it with the flashlight that Gerry had given her to hold, and I went tumbling into the web.

In fact, there *is* a wound on my neck, and none on my ankle. And her story has a ring of truth. For I have come to know the dream-spiders in the slow-flowing years since that night, and I know that the females are stealthy killers that drop down on their prey unawares. They do not charge across fallen trees like berserk ironhorns; it is not the spiders' way.

And neither Crystal nor Gerry has any memory of a pale winged thing flapping in the web.

Yet *I* remember it clearly . . . as I remember the female spider that scuttled toward me during the endless years that I stood frozen . . . but then . . . they say the bite of a dream-spider does strange things to your mind.

That could be it, of course.

Sometimes when Squirrel comes behind me up the stairs, scraping the sooty bricks with his eight white legs, the wrongness of it all hits me, and I know I've dwelt with dreams too long.

Yet the dreams are often better than the waking, the stories so much finer than the lives.

Crystal did not come back to me, then or ever. They left when I was healthy. And the happiness I'd bought her with the choice that was not a choice and the sacrifice not a sacrifice, my gift to her forever—it lasted less than a year. Korbec tells me that she and Gerry broke up violently, and that she has since left Jamison's World.

I suppose that's truth enough, if you can believe a man like Korbec. I don't worry about it overmuch.

I just kill dream-spiders, drink wine, pet Squirrel. And each night I climb this tower of ashes to gaze at distant lights.

Fiction and Science

Science fiction emerged from the pulp ghetto in the late 1940s and the 1950s. The pulp magazines were dying off like the dinosaurs; ironically, the survival of the sf magazines into the 1960s and the 1970s and beyond is like a few of the dinosaurs living on into the present, poking their heads out of misty lakes like the Loch Ness Monster. The sf magazines are virtually the only survivors of a prolific breed that once ruled the newsstands, but what they once purveyed as entertainment has been recognized by many as literature.

As science fiction reached a larger audience, the nature of the writers changed. The writers of the 1930s had been attracted by the science and the speculative ideas and the adventure in strange places; the writers of the 1960s were attracted by the conventions and the metaphors but were repelled by science as a faith or even a hope; the writers of the 1970s were attracted by the potential of science fiction for literature and accepted science as a human activity at least as meaningful as art.

Observations like these are, of course, overgeneralizations; the times always were mixed; there was no unanimity, only a tendency. In the 1970s, nevertheless, some writers reunited literature and science. Some, like Gregory Benford, did it from the science end, learning how to write fiction well enough to turn their knowledge of science into effective stories and novels; others, like Ed Bryant, learned enough about science to turn their crafts into significant science fiction.

Edward Bryant (1945–   ) was born in White Plains, New York, but was raised on a ranch in Wyoming, where he attended grade school and high school and eventually earned a bachelor's and a master's degree in English at the University of Wyoming in 1967 and 1968. Perhaps of greater importance to his education was attendance at the 1968 and the 1969 Clarion SF Writer's Workshop, and his subsequent friendship with Harlan Ellison. The first story he sold, "The 10:00 Report Is Brought to You by . . . ," appeared four years later in *Again, Dangerous Visions* (1972). His first published story, "Sending the Very Best," appeared in the January 1970 *New Worlds*. He has held a variety of jobs but since 1969 he has been a full-time freelance writer.

He has published a great many short stories in a variety of magazines, and anthologies. In fact, his work is almost entirely at the short-story length. It often has been of award quality. "Shark" was nominated for a Nebula Award in 1973; "Particle Theory" and "The *Hibakusha* Gallery" were nominated in 1977; "Stone," which was nominated for the Hugo, won the Nebula for 1978; "giANTS," also nominated for the Hugo, won the Nebula for 1979. His stories have been collected in *Among the Dead* (1973); *Cinnabar* (1976), a linked group of stories centering around a fabulous city at the end of time that Bryant called a "mosaic novel"; *Wyoming Sun* (1980); and *Particle Theory* (1981).

Bryant wrote *Phoenix Without Ashes* (1975), a novelization of Harlan Ellison's original screenplay for the ill-fated *Starlost* syndicated television series. He edited an anthology titled *2076: The American Tricentennial* (1977). He also has lectured frequently and participated in writer-in-residence projects, has written film criticism, has co-authored a screenplay for a feature film, and has adapted a teleplay of his story "Prairie Sun" for Walt Disney Productions.

"Particle Theory," which Barry Malzberg has called one of the ten best science fiction stories ever published, originally appeared in the February 1977 *Analog*. It deals with three different subjects: supernovas in the sky, a cancerous prostate gland, and the emotional life and losses of the protagonist, a science popularizer. These themes are tied together in several meaningful ways: at the simplest level, in the mind of the protagonist, but more importantly at the level of action and meaning and imagery. Chance is one element: It determines that Rigel will flare into a supernova and that the protagonist is stricken with prostate cancer some twenty years early; it even plays a part in the death of his wife and the way the binding force of the nucleus is transformed into matter. At another level, the pions that cure the cancerous prostate may also be involved in fueling stars and supernovas. An explanation for what is happening in the sky comes to the protagonist during the period he is undergoing radiation. All these elements and more are bound together by the event that is taking place as the story opens. The story is told in a series of flashbacks that are as jumbled in time sequence as the "life review" that is "the second of three definable steps in the process of dying"; the effect is to juxtapose events in space rather than time like a series of images linked by the mind of the protagonist—and the reader.

Finally, the various parts of the story are united by imagery: the blaze of light, the storm of radiation, high noon, supernovas, fire balloons. The first paragraph pays tribute to poetic visions of the end of the world: "Eliot was wrong; Frost, right." In the introduction to his collection *Particle Theory,* Bryant saw the 1970s as a decade "of innovation and a blending of diverse literary elements. . . . The New Wave people were getting over their knee-jerk dread of all things scientific and technical, and beginning to exercise a natural curiosity about the workings of the physical universe. And the traditionalists discovered that their brilliant ideas were not defused by couching them in sophisticated prose." In "Particle Theory" Bryant provides his own example, bringing together all the elements of science fiction—the language, the imagery, the idea, and the science—in a combination for which he himself provides a phrase: "poetry glorifying the new technology."

Particle Theory

by Edward Bryant

I see my shadow flung like black iron against the wall. My sundeck blazes with untimely summer. Eliot was wrong: Frost, right.

Nanoseconds . . .

Death is as relativistic as any other apparent constant. I wonder: *am I dying?*

I thought it was a cliché with no underlying truth.

"Lives *do* flash in a compressed instant before dying eyes," said Amanda. She poured me another glass of burgundy the color of her hair. The fire highlighted both. "A psychologist named Noyes—" She broke off and smiled at me. "You really want to hear this?"

"Sure." The fireplace light softened the taut planes of her face. I saw a flicker of the gentler beauty she had possessed thirty years before.

"Noyes catalogued testimonial evidence for death's-door phenomena in the early seventies. He termed it 'life review,' the second of three clearly definable steps in the process of dying; like a movie, and not necessarily linear."

I drink, I have a low threshold of intoxication, I ramble. "Why does it happen? How?" I didn't like the desperation in my voice. We were suddenly much further apart than the geography of the table separating us; I looked in Amanda's eyes for some memory of Lisa. "Life goes shooting off—or we recede from it—like Earth and an interstellar probe irrevocably severed. Mutual recession at light-speed, and the dark fills in the gap." I held my glass by the stem, rotated it, peered through the distorting bowl.

Pine logs crackled. Amanda turned her head and her eyes' image shattered in the flames.

The glare, the glare—

When I was thirty I made aggrieved noises because I'd screwed around for the past ten years and not accomplished nearly as much as I should. Lisa only laughed, which sent me into a transient rage and a longer-lasting sulk before I realized hers was the only appropriate response.

"Silly, silly," she said. "A watered-down Byronic character, full of self-pity and sloppy self-adulation." She blocked my exit from the kitchen and said millimeters from my face, "It's not as though you're waking up at thirty to discover that only fifty-six people have heard of you."

I stuttered over a weak retort.

"Fifty-seven?" she laughed; I laughed.

Then I was forty and went through the same pseudo-menopausal trauma. Admittedly, I hadn't done any work at all for nearly a year, and any *good* work for two. Lisa didn't laugh this time; she did what she could, which was mainly to stay out of my way while I alternately moped and raged around the coast house southwest of Portland. Royalties from the book I'd done on the fusion breakthrough kept us in groceries and mortgage payments.

"Listen, maybe if I'd go away for a while—" she said. "Maybe it would help for you to be alone." Temporary separations weren't alien to our marriage; we'd once figured that our relationship got measurably rockier if we spent more than about sixty percent of our time together. It had been a long winter and we were overdue; but then Lisa looked intently at my face and decided not to leave. Two months later I worked through the problems in my skull, and asked her for solitude. She knew me well—well enough to laugh again because she knew I was waking out of another mental hibernation.

She got onto a jetliner on a gray winter day and headed east for my parents' old place in southern Colorado. The jetway for the flight was out of commission that afternoon, so the airline people had to roll out one of the old wheeled stairways. Just before she stepped into the cabin, Lisa paused and waved back from the head of the stairs; her dark hair curled about her face in the wind.

Two months later I'd roughed out most of the first draft for my initial book about the reproductive revolution. At least once a week I would call Lisa and she'd tell me about the photos she was taking river-running on an icy Colorado or Platte. Then I'd use her as a sounding board for speculations about ectogenesis, heterogynes, or the imminent emergence of an exploited human host-mother class.

"So what'll we do when you finish the first draft, Nick?"

"Maybe we'll take a leisurely month on the Trans-Canadian Railroad."

"Spring in the provinces . . ."

Then the initial draft was completed and so was Lisa's Colorado adventure. "Do you know how badly I want to see you?" she said.

"Almost as badly as I want to see you."

"Oh, no," she said. "Let me tell you—"

What she told me no doubt violated state and federal laws and probably telephone company tariffs as well. The frustration of only hearing her voice through the wire made me twine my legs like a contortionist.

"Nick, I'll book a flight out of Denver. I'll let you know."

I think she wanted to surprise me. Lisa didn't tell me when she booked the flight. The airline let me know.

And now I'm fifty-one The pendulum has swung and I again bitterly resent not having achieved more. There is so much work left undone; should I live for centuries, I still could not complete it all. That, however, will not be a problem.

I am told that the goddamned level of acid phosphatase in my goddamned blood is elevated. How banal that single fact sounds, how sterile; and how self-pitying the phraseology. Can't I afford a luxurious tear, Lisa?

Lisa?

Death: I wish to determine my own time.

"Charming," I said much later. "End of the world."

My friend Denton, the young radio astronomer, said, "Christ almighty! Your damned jokes. How can you make a pun about this?"

"It keeps me from crying," I said quietly. "Wailing and breast-beating won't make a difference."

"Calm, so calm." She looked at me peculiarly.

"I've seen the enemy," I said. "I've had time to consider it."

Her face was thoughtful, eyes focused somewhere beyond this cluttered office. "*If* you're right," she said, "it could be the most fantastic event a scientist could observe and record." Her eyes refocused and met mine. "Or it might be the most frightening; a final horror."

"Choose one," I said.

"If I believed you at all."

"I'm dealing in speculations."

"Fantasies," she said.

"However you want to term it." I got up and moved to the door. "I don't think there's much time. You've never seen where I live. Come—" I hesitated. "Visit me if you care to. I'd like that—to have you there."

"Maybe," she said.

I should not have left the situation ambiguous.

I didn't know that in another hour, after I had left her office, pulled my car out of the Gamow Peak parking lot and driven down to the valley, Denton would settle herself behind the wheel of her sports car and gun it onto the Peak road. Tourists saw her go off the switchback. A Highway Department crew pried her loose from the embrace of Lotus and lodgepole.

When I got the news I grieved for her, wondering if this

were the price of belief. I drove to the hospital and, because no next of kin had been found and Amanda intervened, the doctors let me stand beside the bed.

I had never seen such still features, never such stasis short of actual death. I waited an hour, seconds sweeping silently from the wall clock, until the urge to return home was overpowering.

I could wait no longer because daylight was coming and I would tell no one.

Toward the beginning:

I've tolerated doctors as individuals; as a class they terrify me. It's a dread like shark attacks or dying by fire. But eventually I made the appointment for an examination, drove to the sparkling white clinic on the appointed day and spent a surly half hour reading a year-old issue of *Popular Science* in the waiting room.

"Mr. Richmond?" the smiling nurse finally said. I followed her back to the examination room. "Doctor will be here in just a minute." She left. I sat apprehensively on the edge of the examination table. After two minutes I heard the rustling of my file being removed from the outside rack. Then the door opened.

"How's it going?" said my doctor. "I haven't seen you in a while."

"Can't complain," I said, reverting to accustomed medical ritual. "No flu so far this winter. The shot must have been soon enough."

Amanda watched me patiently. "You're not a hypochondriac. You don't need continual reassurance—or sleeping pills, any more. You're not a medical group, God knows. So what is it?"

"Uh," I said. I spread my hands helplessly.

"Nicholas." Get-on-with-it-I'm-busy-today sharpness edged her voice.

"Don't imitate my maiden aunt."

"All right, *Nick*," she said. "What's wrong?"

"I'm having trouble urinating."

She jotted something down. Without looking up, "What kind of trouble?"

"Straining."

"For how long?"

"Six, maybe seven months. It's been a gradual thing."

"Anything else you've noticed?"

"Increased frequency."

"That's all?"

"Well," I said, "afterwards. I, uh, dribble."

She listed, as thought by rote: "Pain, burning, urgency, hesitancy, change in stream of urine? Incontinence, change in size of stream, change in appearance of urine?"

"What?"

"Darker, lighter, cloudy, blood discharge from penis, VD exposure, fever, night sweats?"

I answered with a variety of nods or monosyllables.

"Mmh." She continued to write on the pad, then snapped it shut. "Okay, Nick, would you get your clothes off?" And when I had stripped, "Please lie on the table. On your stomach."

"The greased finger?" I said. "Oh shit."

Amanda tore a disposable glove off the roll. It crackled as she put it on. "You think I get a thrill out of this?" She's been my GP for a long time.

When it was over and I sat gingerly and uncomfortably on the edge of the examining table, I said, "Well?"

Amanda again scribbled on a sheet. "I'm sending you to a urologist. He's just a couple of blocks away. I'll phone over. Try to get an appointment in—oh, inside of a week."

"Give me something better," I said, "or I'll go to the library and check out a handbook of symptoms."

She met my eyes with a candid blue gaze. "I want a specialist to check out the obstruction."

"You found something when you stuck your finger in?"

"Crude, Nicholas." She half smiled. "Your prostate is hard—stony. There could be a number of reasons."

"What John Wayne used to call the Big C?"

"Prostatic cancer," she said, "is relatively infrequent in a man of your age." She glanced down at my records. "Fifty."

"Fifty-one," I said, wanting to shift the tone, trying, failing. "You didn't send me a card on my birthday."

"But it's not impossible," Amanda said. She stood. "Come on up to the front desk. I want an appointment with you after the urology results come back." As always, she patted me on the shoulder as she followed me out of the examination room. But this time there was slightly too much tension in her fingers.

I was seeing grassy hummocks and marble slabs in my

mind and didn't pay attention to my surroundings as I exited the waiting room.

"Nick?" A soft Oklahoma accent.

I turned back from the outer door, looked down, saw tousled hair. Jackie Denton, one of the bright young minds out at the Gamow Peak Observatory, held the well-thumbed copy of *Popular Science* loosely in her lap. She honked and snuffled into a deteriorating Kleenex. "Don't get too close. Probably doesn't matter at this point. Flu. You?" Her green irises were red-rimmed.

I fluttered my hands vaguely. "I had my shots."

"Yeah." She snuffled again. "I was going to call you later on from work. See the show last night?"

I must have looked blank.

"Some science writer," she said. "Rigel went supernova."

"Supernova," I repeated stupidly.

"Blam, you know? *Blooie*." She illustrated with her hands and the magazine flipped onto the carpet. "Not that you missed anything. It'll be around for a few weeks—biggest show in the skies."

A sudden ugly image of red-and-white-aircraft warning lights merging in an actinic flare sprayed my retinas. I shook my head. After a moment I said, "First one in our galaxy in—how long? Three hundred and fifty years? I wish you'd called me."

"A little longer. Kepler's star was in 1604. Sorry about not calling—we were all a little busy, you know?"

"I can imagine. When did it happen?"

She bent to retrieve the magazine. "Just about midnight. Spooky. I was just coming off shift." She smiled. "Nothing like a little cosmic cataclysm to take my mind off jammed sinuses. Just as well; no sick leave tonight. That's why I'm here at the clinic. Kris says no excuses."

Krishnamurthi was the Gamov director. "You'll be going back up to the peak soon?" She nodded. "Tell Kris I'll be in to visit. I want to pick up a lot of material."

"For sure."

The nurse walked up to us. "Ms. Denton?"

"Mumph." She nodded and wiped her nose a final time. Struggling up from the soft chair, she said, "How come you didn't read about Rigel in the papers? It made every morning edition."

"I let my subscriptions lapse."

"But the TV news? The radio?"

"I didn't watch, and I don't have a radio in the car."

Before disappearing into the corridor to the examination rooms, she said, "That country house of yours must really be isolated."

The ice drips from the eaves as I drive up and park beside the garage. Unless the sky deceives me there is no new weather front moving in yet; no need to protect the car from another ten centimeters of fresh snow.

Sunset comes sooner at my house among the mountains; shadows stalk across the barren yard and suck heat from my skin. The peaks are, of course, deliberate barriers blocking off light and warmth from the coastal cities. Once I personified them as friendly giants, amiable *lummoxen* guarding us. No more. Now they are only mountains again, the Cascade Range.

For an instant I think I see a light flash on, but it is just a quick sunset reflection on a window. The house remains dark and silent. The poet from Seattle's been gone for three months. My coldness—her heat. I thought that transference would warm me. Instead she chilled. The note she left me in the vacant house was a sonnet about psychic frostbite.

My last eleven years have not been celibate, but sometimes they feel like it. Entropy ultimately overcomes all kinetic force.

Then I looked toward the twilight east and saw Rigel rising. Luna wouldn't be visible for a while, so the brightest object in the sky was the exploded star. It fixed me to this spot by my car with the intensity of an aircraft landing light. The white light that shone down on me had left the supernova five hundred years before (a detail to include in the inevitable article—a graphic illustration of interstellar distances never fails to awe readers).

Tonight, watching the 100 billion-degree baleful eye that was Rigel convulsed, I know *I* was awed. The cataclysm glared, brighter than any planet. I wondered whether Rigel— unlikely, I knew—had had a planetary system; whether guttering mountain ranges and boiling seas had preceded worlds frying. I wondered whether, five centuries before, intelligent beings had watched stunned as the stellar fire engulfed their skies. Had they time to rail at the injustice? There are 100 billion stars in our galaxy; only an estimated three stars go supernova per thousand years. Good odds: Rigel lost.

Almost hypnotized, I watched until I was abruptly rocked by the wind rising in the darkness. My fingers were stiff with cold. But as I started to enter the house I looked at the sky a final time. Terrifying Rigel, yes—but my eyes were captured by another phenomenon in the north. A spark of light burned brighter than the surrounding stars. At first I thought it was a passing aircraft, but its position remained stationary. Gradually, knowing the odds and unwilling to believe, I recognized the new supernova for what it was.

In five decades I've seen many things. Yet watching the sky I felt like I was a primitive, shivering in uncured furs. My teeth chattered from more than the cold. I wanted to hide from the universe. The door to my house was unlocked, which was lucky—I couldn't have fitted a key into the latch. Finally I stepped over the threshold. I turned on all the lights, denying the two stellar pyres burning in the sky.

My urologist turned out to be a dour black man named Sharpe who treated me, I suspected, like any of the other specimens that turned up in his laboratory. In his early thirties, he'd read several of my books. I appreciated his having absolutely no respect for his elders or for celebrities.

"You'll give me straight answers?" I said.

"Count on it."

He also gave me another of those damned urological fingers. When I was finally in a position to look back at him questioningly, he nodded slowly and said, "There's a nodule."

Then I got a series of blood tests for an enzyme called acid phosphatase. "Elevated," Sharpe said.

Finally, at the lab, I was to get the cystoscope, a shiny metal tube which would be run up my urethra. The biopsy forceps would be inserted through it. "Jesus, you're kidding." Sharpe shook his head. I said, "If the biopsy shows a malignancy . . ."

"I can't answer a silence."

"Come on," I said. "You've been straight until now. What are the chances of curing a malignancy?"

Sharpe had looked unhappy ever since I'd walked into his office. Now he looked unhappier. "Ain't my department," he said. "Depends on many factors."

"Just give me a simple figure."

"Maybe thirty percent. All bets are off if there's a metastasis." He met my eyes while he said that, then busied himself with the cystoscope. Local anesthetic or not, my penis burned like hell.

I had finally gotten through to Jackie Denton on a private line the night of the second supernova. "I thought last night was a madhouse," she said. "You should see us now. I've only got a minute."

"I just wanted to confirm what I was looking at," I said. "I saw the damn thing actually blow."

"You're ahead of everybody at Gamow. We were busily focusing on Rigel—" Electronic *wheeps* garbled the connection. "Nick, are you still there?"

"I think somebody wants the line. Just tell me a final thing: is it a full-fledged supernova?"

"Absolutely. As far as we can determine now, it's a genuine Type II."

"Sorry it couldn't be the biggest and best of all."

"Big enough," she said. "It's good enough. This time it's only about nine light-years away. Sirius A."

"Eight point seven light-years," I said automatically. "What's that going to mean?"

"Direct effects? Don't know. We're thinking about it." It sounded like her hand cupped the mouthpiece; then she came back on the line. "Listen, I've got to go. Kris is screaming for my head. Talk to you later."

"All right," I said. The connection broke. On the dead line I thought I heard the 21-centimeter basic hydrogen hiss of the universe. Then the dial tone cut in and I hung up the receiver.

Amanda did not look at all happy. She riffled twice through what I guessed were my laboratory test results. "All right," I said from the patient's side of the wide walnut desk. "Tell me."

"*Mr. Richmond? Nicholas Richmond?*"

"*Speaking.*"

"*This is Mrs. Kurnick, with Trans-West Airways. I'm calling from Denver.*"

"*Yes?*"

"*We obtained this number from a charge slip. A ticket was issued to Lisa Richmond—*"

"*My wife. I've been expecting her sometime this weekend. Did she ask you to phone ahead?*"

"Mr. Richmond, that's not it. Our manifest shows your wife boarded our Flight 903, Denver to Portland, tonight."

"So? What is it? What's wrong? Is she sick?"

"I'm afraid there's been an accident."

Silence choked me. *"How bad?"* The freezing began.

"Our craft went down about ten miles northwest of Glenwood Springs, Colorado. The ground parties at the site say there are no survivors. I'm sorry, Mr. Richmond."

"No one?" I said. *"I mean—"*

"I'm truly sorry," said Mrs. Kurnick. *"If there's any change in the situation, we will be in touch immediately."*

Automatically I said, *"Thank you."*

I had the impression that Mrs. Kurnick wanted to say something else; but after a pause, she only said, *"Good night."*

On a snowy Colorado mountainside I died.

"The biopsy was malignant," Amanda said.

"Well," I said. "That's pretty bad." She nodded. "Tell me about my alternatives." *Ragged bits of metal slammed into the mountainside like teeth.*

My case was unusual only in a relative sense. Amanda told me that prostatic cancer is the penalty men pay for otherwise good health. If they avoid every other health hazard, twentieth-century men eventually get zapped by their prostates. In my case, the problem was about twenty years early; my bad luck. *Cooling metal snapped and sizzled in the snow, was silent.*

Assuming that the cancer hadn't already metastasized, there were several possibilities; but Amanda had, at this stage, little hope for either radiology or chemotherapy. She suggested a radical prostatectomy.

"I wouldn't suggest it if you didn't have a hell of a lot of valuable years left," she said. "It's not usually advised for older patients. But you're in generally good condition; you could handle it."

Nothing moved on the mountainside. "What all would come out?" I said.

"You already know the ramifications of 'radical.' "

I didn't mind so much the ligation of the spermatic tubes—I should have done that a long time before. At fifty-one I could handle sterilization with equanimity, but—

"Sexually dysfunctional?" I said. "Oh my God." I was aware of my voice starting to tighten. "I can't do that."

"You sure as hell can," said Amanda firmly. "How long

454   *Edward Bryant*

have I known you?" She answered her own question. "A long time. I know you well enough to know that what counts isn't all tied up in your penis."

I shook my head silently.

"Listen, damn it, cancer death is worse."

"No," I said stubbornly. "Maybe. Is that the whole bill?"

It wasn't. Amanda reached my bladder's entry on the list. It would be excised as well.

"Tubes protruding from me?" I said. "*If* I live, I'll have to spend the rest of my life toting a plastic bag as a drain for my urine?"

Quietly she said, "You're making it too melodramatic."

"But am I right?"

After a pause, "Essentially, yes."

And all that was the essence of it; the *good* news, all assuming that the carcinoma cells wouldn't jar loose during surgery and migrate off to other organs. "No," I said. The goddamned lousy, loathsome unfairness of it all slammed home. "Goddamn it, no. It's my choice; I won't live that way. If I just die, I'll be done with it."

"Nicholas! Cut the self-pity."

"Don't you think I'm entitled to some?"

"Be reasonable."

"You're supposed to comfort me," I said. "Not argue. You've taken all those death-and-dying courses. *You* be reasonable."

The muscles tightened around her mouth. "I'm giving you suggestions," said Amanda. "You can do with them as you damned well please." It had been years since I'd seen her angry.

We glared at each other for close to a minute. "Okay," I said. "I'm sorry."

She was not mollified. "Stay upset, even if it's whining. Get angry, be furious. I've watched you in a deep-freeze for a decade."

I recoiled internally. "I've survived. That's enough."

"No way. You've been sitting around for eleven years in suspended animation, waiting for someone to chip you free of the glacier. You've let people carom past, occasionally bouncing off you with no effect. Well, now it's not some*one* that's shoving you to the wall—it's some*thing*. Are you going to lie down for it? Lisa wouldn't have wanted that."

"Leave her out," I said.

"I can't. You're even more important to me because of her. She was my closest friend, remember?"

"Pay attention to her," Lisa had once said. *"She's more sensible than either of us."* Lisa had known about the affair; after all, Amanda had introduced us.

"I know." I felt disoriented; denial, resentment, numbness —the roller coaster clattered toward a final plunge.

"Nick, you've got a possibility for a healthy chunk of life left. I want you to have it, and if it takes using Lisa as a wedge, I will."

"I don't want to survive if it means crawling around as a piss-dripping cyborg eunuch." The roller coaster teetered on the brink.

Amanda regarded me for a long moment, then said earnestly, "There's an outside chance, a long shot, I heard from a friend there that the New Mexico Meson Physics Facility is scouting for a subject."

I scoured my memory. "Particle beam therapy?"

"Pions."

"It's chancy," I said.

"Are you arguing?" She smiled.

I smiled too. "No."

"Want to give it a try?"

My smile died. "I don't know. I'll think about it."

"That's encouragement enough," said Amanda. "I'll make some calls and see if the facility's as interested in you as I expect you'll be in them. Stick around home? I'll let you know."

"I haven't said 'yes.' We'll let each other know." I didn't tell Amanda, but I left her office thinking only of death.

Melodramatic as it may sound, I went downtown to visit the hardware stores and look at their displays of pistols. After two hours, I tired of handling weapons. The steel seemed uniformly cold and distant.

When I returned home late that afternoon, there was a single message on my phone-answering machine:

"Nick, this is Jackie Denton. Sorry I haven't called for a while, but you know how it's been. I thought you'd like to know that Kris is going to have a press conference early in the week—probably Monday afternoon. I think he's worried because he hasn't come up with a good theory to cover the three Type II supernovas and the half-dozen standard novas that have occurred in the last few weeks. But then nobody I know has. We're all spending so much time awake nights, we're turning into vampires. I'll get back to you when I know the exact time of the conference. I think it must be about thirty seconds now, so I—" The tape ended.

I mused with winter bonfires in my mind as the machine rewound and reset. Three Type II supernovas? One is merely nature, I paraphrased. Two mean only coincidence. Three make a conspiracy.

Impulsively I slowly dialed Denton's home number; there was no answer. Then the lines to Gamow Peak were all busy. It seemed logical to me that I needed Jackie Denton for more than being my sounding board, or for merely news about the press conference. I needed an extension of her friendship. I thought I'd like to borrow the magnum pistol I knew she kept in a locked desk drawer at her observatory office. I knew I could ask her a favor. She ordinarily used the pistol to blast targets on the peak's rocky flanks after work.

The irritating regularity of the busy signal brought me back to sanity. Just a second, I told myself. Richmond, what the hell are you proposing?

Nothing, was the answer. Not yet. Not . . . quite.

Later in the night, I opened the sliding glass door and disturbed the skiff of snow on the second-story deck. I shamelessly allowed myself the luxury of leaving the door partially open so that warm air would spill out around me while I watched the sky. The stars were intermittently visible between the towering banks of stratocumulus scudding over the Cascades. Even so, the three supernovas dominated the night. I drew imaginary lines with my eyes; connect the dots and solve the puzzle. How many enigmas can you find in this picture?

I reluctantly took my eyes away from the headline phenomena and searched for old standbys. I picked out the red dot of Mars.

Several years ago I'd had a cockamamie scheme that sent me to a Mesmerist—that's how she'd billed herself—down in Eugene. I'd been driving up the coast after covering an aerospace medical conference in Oakland. Somewhere around Crescent City, I capped a sea-bass dinner by getting blasted on prescribed pills and proscribed Scotch. Sometime during the evening, I remembered the computer-enhancement process JPL had used to sharpen the clarity of telemetered photos from such projects as the Mariner fly-bys and the

Viking Mars lander. It seemed logical to me at the time that memories from the human computer could somehow be enhanced, brought into clarity through hypnosis. Truly stoned fantasies. But they somehow sufficed as rationale and incentive to wind up at Madame Guzmann's "Advice/Mesmerism/Health" establishment across the border in Oregon. Madame Guzmann had skin the color of her stained hardwood door; she made a point of looking and dressing the part of a stereotype we *gajos* would think of as Gypsy. The scarf and crystal ball strained the image. I think she was Vietnamese. At any rate she convinced me she could hypnotize, and then she nudged me back through time.

Just before she ducked into the cabin, Lisa paused and waved back from the head of the stairs; her dark hair curled about her face in the wind.

I should have taken to heart the lesson of stasis; entropy is not so easily overcome.

What Madame Guzmann achieved was to freeze-frame that last image of Lisa. Then she zoomed me in so close it was like standing beside Lisa. I sometimes still see it in my nightmares: Her eyes focus distantly. Her skin has the graininess of a newspaper photo. I look but cannot touch. I can speak but she will not answer. I shiver with the cold—

—and slid the glass door further open.

There! An eye opened in space. A glare burned as cold as a refrigerator light in a night kitchen. Mars seemed to disappear, swallowed in the glow from the nova distantly behind it. Another one, I thought. The new eye held me fascinated, pinned as securely as a child might fasten a new moth in the collection.

Nick?

Who is it?

Nick ...

You're an auditory hallucination.

There on the deck the sound of laughter spiraled around me. I thought it would shake loose the snow from the trees. The mountain stillness vibrated.

The secret, Nick.

What secret?

You're old enough at fifty-one to decipher it.

Don't play with me.

Who's playing? Whatever time is left—

Yes?

You've spent eleven years now dreaming, drifting, letting others act on you.

I know.

Do you? Then act on that. Choose your actions. No lover can tell you more. Whatever time is left—

Shivering uncontrollably, I gripped the rail of the deck. A fleeting, pointillist portrait in black and white dissolved into the trees. From branch to branch, top bough to bottom, crusted snow broke and fell, gathering momentum. The trees shed their mantle. Powder swirled up to the deck and touched my face with stinging diamonds.

Eleven years was more than half what Rip van Winkle slept. "Damn it," I said. "Damn you." We prize our sleep. The grave rested peacefully among the trees. "Damn you," I said again, looking up at the sky.

On a snowy Oregon mountainside I was no longer dead.

And yes, Amanda. Yes.

After changing planes at Albuquerque, we flew into Los Alamos on a small feeder line called Ross Airlines. I'd never flown before on so ancient a DeHavilland Twin Otter, and I hoped never to again; I'd take a Greyhound out of Los Alamos first. The flight attendant and half the other sixteen passengers were throwing up in the turbulence as we approached the mountains. I hadn't expected the mountains. I'd assumed Los Alamos would lie in the same sort of southwestern scrub desert surrounding Albuquerque. Instead I found a small city nestled a couple of kilometers up a wooded mountainside.

The pilot's unruffled voice came on the cabin intercom to announce our imminent landing, the airport temperature, and the fact that Los Alamos has more Ph.D.'s per capita than any other American city. "Second only to Akademgorodok," I said, turning away from the window toward Amanda. The skin wrinkled around her closed eyes. She hadn't had to use her airsick bag. I had a feeling that despite old friendships, a colleague and husband who was willing to oversee the clinic, the urgency of helping a patient, and the desire to observe the exotic experiment, Amanda might be regretting accompanying me to what she'd termed "the meson factory."

The Twin Otter made a landing approach like a strafing run and then we were down. As we taxied across the apron I had a sudden sensation of déjà vu: the time a year ago when a friend had flown me north in a Cessna. The airport in Los

Alamos looked much like the civil air terminal at Sea-Tac where I'd met the Seattle poet. It happened that we were both in line at the snack counter. I'd commented on her elaborate Haida-styled medallion. We took the same table and talked; it turned out she'd heard of me.

"I really admire your stuff," she said.

So much for my ideal poet using only precise images. Wry thought. She was—is—a first-rate poet. I rarely think of her as anything but "the poet from Seattle." Is that kind of de-personalization a symptom?

Amanda opened her eyes, smiled wanly, said, "I could use a doctor." The flight attendant cracked the door and thin New Mexican mountain air revived us both.

Most of the New Mexico Meson Physics Facility was buried beneath a mountain edge. Being guest journalist as well as experimental subject, I think we were given a more exhaustive tour than would be offered most patients and their doctors. Everything I saw made me think of expensive sets for vintage science fiction movies: the interior of the main accelerator ring, glowing eggshell white and curving away like the space-station corridors in *2001;* the linac and booster areas; the straightaway tunnel to the meson medical channel; the five-meter bubble chamber looking like some sort of time machine.

I'd visited both FermiLab in Illinois and CERN in Geneva, so I had a general idea of what the facilities were all about. Still I had a difficult time trying to explain to Amanda the *Alice in Wonderland* mazes that constituted high energy particle physics. But then so did Delaney, the young woman who was the liaison biophysicist for my treatment. It became difficult sorting out the mesons, pions, hadrons, leptons, baryons, J's, fermions and quarks, and such quantum qualities as strangeness, color, baryonness and charm. Especially charm, that ephemeral quality accounting for why certain types of radioactive decay should happen, but don't. I finally bogged down in the mist of quarks, antiquarks, charmed quarks, neo-quarks and quarklets.

Some wag had set a sign on the visitor's reception desk in the administration center reading: "Charmed to meet you." "It's a joke, right?" said Amanda tentatively.

"It probably won't get any funnier," I said.

Delaney, who seemed to load every word with deadly earnestness, didn't laugh at all. "Some of the technicians think it's funny. I don't."

We rehashed the coming treatment endlessly. Optimistically I took notes for the book: _The primary problem with a radiological approach to the treatment of cancer is that hard radiation not only kills the cancerous cells, it also irradiates the surrounding healthy tissue. But in the mid-nineteen seventies, cancer researchers found a more promising tool: shaped beams of subatomic particles which can be selectively focused on the tissue of tumors._

Delaney had perhaps two decades on Amanda; being younger seemed to give her a perverse satisfaction in playing the pedagogue. "Split atomic nuclei on a small scale—"

"Small?" said Amanda innocently.

"—smaller than a fission bomb. Much of the binding force of the nucleus is miraculously transmuted to matter."

"Miraculously?" said Amanda. I looked up at her from the easy cushion shot I was trying to line up on the green velvet. The three of us were playing rotation in the billiards annex of the NMMPF recreation lounge.

"Uh," said Delaney, the rhythm of her lecture broken. "Physics shorthand."

"Reality shorthand," I said, not looking up from the cue now. "Miracles are as exact a quality as charm."

Amanda chuckled. "That's all I wanted to know."

The miracle pertinent to my case was atomic glue, mesons, one of the fission-formed particles. More specifically, my miracle was the negatively charged pion, a subclass of meson. Electromagnetic fields could focus pions into a controllable beam and fire it into a particular target—me.

"There are no miracles in physics," said Delaney seriously. "I used the wrong term."

I missed my shot. A gentle stroke, and gently the cue ball roled into the corner pocket, missing the eleven. I'd set things up nicely, if accidentally, for Amanda.

She assayed the table and smiled. "Don't come unglued."

"That's very good," I said. Atomic glue does become unstuck, thanks to pions' unique quality. When they collide and are captured by the nucleus of another atom, they reconvert to pure energy; a tiny nuclear explosion.

Amanda missed her shot too. The corners of Delaney's mouth curled in a small gesture of satisfaction. She leaned across the table, hands utterly steady. "Multiply pions, multiply target nuclei, and you have a controlled aggregate explosion releasing considerably more energy than the entering pion beam. *Hah!*"

She sank the eleven and twelve; then ran the table. Amanda and I exchanged glances. "Rack 'em up," said Delaney.

"Your turn," Amanda said to me.

In my case the NMMPF medical channel would fire a directed pion beam into my recalcitrant prostate. If all went as planned, the pions intercepting the atomic nuclei of my cancer cells would convert back into energy in a series of atomic flares. The cancer cells being more sensitive, tissue damage should be restricted, localized in my carcinogenic nodule.

Thinking of myself as a nuclear battlefield in miniature was wondrous. Thinking of myself as a new Stagg Field or an Oak Ridge was ridiculous.

Delaney turned out to be a pool shark *par excellence*. Winning was all-important and she won every time. I decided to interpret that as a positive omen.

"It's time," Amanda said.

"You needn't sound as though you're leading a condemned man to the electric chair." I tied the white medical smock securely about me, pulled on the slippers.

"I'm sorry. Are you worried?"

"Not so long as Delaney counts me as part of the effort toward a Nobel Prize."

"She's good." Her voice rang too hollow in the sterile tiled room. We walked together into the corridor.

"Me, I'm bucking for a Kalinga Prize," I said.

Amanda shook her head. Cloudy hair played about her face. "I'll just settle for a positive prognosis for my patient." Beyond the door, Delaney and two technicians with a gurney waited for me.

There is a state beyond indignity that defines being draped naked on my belly over a bench arrangement, with my rear spread and facing the medical channel. Rigidly clamped, a ceramic target tube opened a separate channel through my anus to the prostate. Monitoring equipment and shielding shut me in. I felt hot and vastly uncomfortable. Amanda had shot me full of chemicals, not all of whose names I'd recognized. Now dazed, I couldn't decide which of many discomforts was the most irritating.

"Good luck," Amanda had said. "It'll be over before you know it." I'd felt a gentle pat on my flank.

I thought I heard the phasing-up whine of electrical equipment. I could tell my mind was closing down for the duration; I couldn't even remember how many billion electron-volts were about to route a pion beam up my backside. I heard sounds I couldn't identify; perhaps an enormous metal door grinding shut.

My brain swam free in a chemical river; I waited for something to happen.

I thought I heard machined ball bearings rattling down a chute; no, particles screaming past the giant bending magnets into the medical channel at 300,000 kilometers per second; flashing toward me through the series of adjustable filters; slowing, slowing, losing energy as they approach; then through the final tube and into my body. Inside . . .

The pion sails the inner atomic seas for a relativistically finite time. Then the perspective inhabited by one is inhabited by two. The pion drives toward the target nucleus. At a certain point the pion is no longer a pion; what was temporarily matter transmutes back to energy. The energy flares, expands, expends and fades. Other explosions detonate in the spaces within the patterns underlying larger patterns.

Darkness and light interchange.

The light coalesces into a ball; massive, hot, burning against the darkness. Pierced, somehow stricken, the ball begins to collapse in upon itself. Its internal temperature climbs to a critical level. At 600 million degrees, carbon nuclei fuse. Heavier elements form. When the fuel is exhausted, the ball collapses further; again the temperature is driven upward; again heavier elements form and are in turn consumed. The cycle repeats until the nuclear furnace manufactures iron. No further nuclear reaction can be triggered; the heart's fire is extinguished. Without the outward balance of fusion reaction, the ball initiates the ultimate collapse. Heat reaches 100 billion degrees. Every conceivable nuclear reaction is consummated.

The ball explodes in a final convulsive cataclysm. Its energy flares, fades, is eaten by entropy. The time it took is no more than the time it takes Sol-light to reach and illuminate the Earth.

"How do you feel?" Amanda leaned into my field of vision, eclipsing the fluorescent rings overhead.

"Feel?" I seemed to be talking through a mouthful of cotton candy.

"Feel."

"Compared to what?" I said.

She smiled. "You're doing fine."

"I had one foot on the accelerator," I said.

She looked puzzled, then started to laugh. "It'll wear off soon." She completed her transit and the lights shone back in my face.

"No hand on the brake," I mumbled. I began to giggle. Something pricked my arm.

I think Delaney wanted to keep me under observation in New Mexico until the anticipated ceremonies in Stockholm; I didn't have time for that. I suspected none of us did. Amanda began to worry about my moody silence; she ascribed them at first to my medication and then to the two weeks' tests Delaney and her colleagues were inflicting on me.

"To hell with this," I said. "We've got to get out of here." Amanda and I were alone in my room.

"What?"

"Give me a prognosis."

She smiled. "I think you may as well shoot for the Kalinga."

"Maybe." I quickly added, "I'm not a patient any more; I'm an experimental subject."

"So? What do we do about it?"

We exited NMMPF under cover of darkness and struggled a half kilometer through brush to the highway. There we hitched a ride into town.

"This is crazy," said Amanda, picking thistle out of her sweater.

"It avoids a strong argument," I said as we neared the lights of Los Alamos.

The last bus of the day had left. I wanted to wait until morning. Over my protests, we flew out on Ross Airlines. "Doctor's orders," said Amanda, teeth tightly together, as the Twin Otter bumped onto the runway.

I dream of pions. I dream of colored balloons filled with hydrogen, igniting and flaming up in the night, I dream of Lisa's newsprint face. Her smile is both proud and sorrowful.

Amanda had her backlog of patients and enough to worry

about, so I took my nightmares to Jackie Denton at the observatory. I told her of my hallucinations in the accelerator chamber. We stared at each other across the small office.

"I'm glad you're better, Nick, but—"

"That's not it," I said. "Remember how you hated my article about poetry glorifying the new technology? Too fanciful?" I launched into speculation, mixing with abandon pion beams, doctors, supernovas, irrational statistics, carcinogenic nodes, fire balloons and gods.

"Gods?" she said. "*Gods?* Are you going to put that in your next column?"

I nodded.

She looked as though she were inspecting a newly foundout psychopath. "No one needs that in the press now, Nick. The whole planet's upset already. The possibility of nova radiation damaging the ozone layer, the potential for genetic damage, all that's got people spooked."

"It's only speculation."

She said, "You don't yell 'fire' in a crowded theater."

"Or in a crowded world?"

Her voice was unamused. "Not now."

"And if I'm right?" I felt weary. "What about it?"

"A supernova? No way. Sol simply doesn't have the mass."

"But a nova?" I said.

"Possibly," she said tightly. "But it shouldn't happen for a few billion years. Stellar evolution—"

"—is theory," I said. "*Shouldn't* isn't *won't*. Tonight look again at that awesome sky."

Denton said nothing.

"Could you accept a solar flare? A big one?"

I read the revulsion in her face and knew I should stop talking; but I didn't. "Do you believe in God? Any god?" She shook her head. I had to get it all out. "How about concentric universes, one within the next like Chinese carved ivory spheres?" Her face went white. "Pick a card," I said, "any card. A wild card."

"God damn you, shut up." On the edge of the desk, her knuckles were as white as her lips.

"Charming," I said, ignoring the incantatory power of words, forgetting what belief could cost. I do not think she deliberately drove her Lotus off the Peak road. I don't want to believe that. Surely she was coming to join me.

Maybe, she'd said.

Nightmares should be kept home. So here I stand on my sundeck at high noon for the Earth. No need to worry about destruction of the ozone layer and the consequent skin cancer. There will be no problem with mutational effects and genetic damage. I need not worry about deadlines or contractual commitments. I regret that no one will ever read my book about pion therapy.

All that—maybe.

The sun shines bright— The tune plays dirgelike in my head.

Perhaps I am wrong. The flare may subside. Maybe I am not dying. No matter.

I wish Amanda were with me now, or that I were at Jackie Denton's bedside, or even that I had time to walk to Lisa's grave among the pines. Now there is no time.

At least I've lived as long as I have now by choice.

That's the secret, Nick . . .

The glare illuminates the universe.

The Anthropology of the Future

THE ANTHROPOLOGY OF THE FUTURE

Science fiction and anthropology always have shared a peculiar affinity. Many of the finest sf stories and novels have been concerned with anthropological questions. Lost-race stories, even though they drew on the older tradition of the travel story and their basic appeal at the hands of practitioners such as H. Rider Haggard and Edgar Rice Burroughs was romantic adventure, nevertheless raised interesting questions about how these remnants of ancient peoples survived the centuries and how their abilities and practices give evidence of more sophisticated or more primitive times.

Subsequent writers have used the future, or the past, as a means of studying man as a species. In 1906, H. G. Wells told the Sociological Society (sociology studies humanity in its collective activities) that it should use the writing and criticism of utopias to discuss the Ideal Society. A number of stories have been written by professional anthropologists such as Chad Oliver, who specialized in such stories in the 1950s and went on to a professorship at the University of Texas at Arlington, and Leon E. Stover of the Illinois Institute of Technology; others have been written by such gifted amateurs as Mack Reynolds, Ursula K. Le Guin (whose father was a distinguished scholar in the field), and Ian Watson.

In its consideration of the past, present, and future of the human species, science fiction is a great deal like anthropology, and a number of anthropologists have admitted that they went into that field because it was "the closest thing to science fiction." Maybe the affinity is not so peculiar after all.

Joan D. Vinge (1948–) doesn't think it is. "Archeology is

the anthropology of the past," she notes, "and science fiction is the anthropology of the future." Born in Baltimore, Maryland, she earned a bachelor's degree in anthropology from San Diego State University in 1971. She worked for a time as a salvage archaeologist for San Diego county. She began writing science fiction in 1973, and her first published story, "Tin Soldier," was published in *Orbit 14* (1974). She was married to Vernor Vinge, another sf writer and a professor of mathematics at San Diego State University, but now is married to Jim Frenkel, former sf editor at Dell Books. Their first child, Jessica, was born in 1981.

Her stories have appeared in a variety of magazines and anthologies. "Eyes of Amber" won a Hugo Award in 1978. "View from a Height" and "Fireship" were finalists for the Hugo in 1979, and the latter was a finalist for the Nebula. Her stories have been collected in *Fireship* (1978) and *Eyes of Amber and Other Stories* (1979).

Vinge's first novel, *The Outcasts of Heaven Belt*, was published in 1978. Her second, the long and ambitious *The Snow Queen*, was published in 1980, was a finalist for the Nebula, and won the Hugo.

Vinge has said that she tends "to write anthropological science fiction, with an emphasis on the interaction of different cultures (human and alien), and of individual people to their surroundings. The importance of communication across barriers of alienness often becomes a theme in my work." "View from a Height," originally published in the June 1978 *Analog*, is an example: It deals with a woman who has an unusual reason for alienation, the one-way mission she takes into space, and how she copes with the knowledge that she can never return, that she is shut off from human contact for the rest of her life. Forever.

Who would be capable of volunteering for such a mission? Who could remain sane in such solitude, with such terrible knowledge? Vinge's answer is: a woman who has been alone all her life because she was born without natural immunities and was raised in a sterile environment, protected from contamination by the outside world, barred from the touch and comfort—and contamination—of others. So she volunteers for a mission on a ship equipped as an astronomical observatory to be sent thousands of astronomical units into space to get a clear view of the universe. (An astronomical unit is about 93,000,000 miles, the distance from the Earth to the Sun.) After twenty years and one thousand astronomical units, Vinge gives the situation a savage twist that sends the protagonist into a rage followed by a dangerous depression.

The story is told in diary form (it is a recorded diary, unlike Charlie Gordon's) so that the author doesn't have to conceal important information from the reader and yet can share Emmylou Stewart's reactions as they develop. Then come insights: Emmylou has wondered about her own motives; now she realizes that she went into astronomy and astronautics rather than into medicine or research because she identified with the spacesuited astronauts, protected, as she was, from the deadliness of their environment.

The story begins with Emmylou looking back toward the solar system from which she has come and can never return: "I always look down, and there's that tremendous abyss full of space and time." But at the end as Emmylou moves from the personal to the universal, from "me" to the universe like a metaphor for the focus of science fiction, she realizes that she has an opportunity available to no one else, an opportunity to see the universe clear of clouds and dust, that there is another view one can get from a height.

View from a Height

by Joan D. Vinge

Saturday, the 7th

I want to know why those pages were missing! How am I supposed to keep up with my research if they leave out pages—?

(*Long sighing noise.*)

Listen to yourself, Emmylou: You're listening to the sound of fear. It was an oversight, you know that. Nobody did it to you on purpose. Relax, you're getting Fortnight Fever. Tomorrow you'll get the pages, and an apology too, if Harvey Weems knows what's good for him.

But still, five whole pages; and the table of contents. How could you miss *five* pages? And the table of contents.

How do I know there hasn't been a coup? The Northwest's finally taken over completely, and they're censoring the media—And like the Man without a Country, everything they send me from now on is going to have holes cut in it.

In *Science?*

Or maybe Weems has decided to drive me insane—?

Oh, my God . . . it would be a short trip. Look at me. I don't have any fingernails left.

("*Arrwk. Hello, beautiful. Hello? Hello?*")

("Ozymandias! Get out of my hair, you devil." *Laughter.* "Polly want a cracker? Here . . . gently! That's a boy.")

It's beautiful when he flies. I never get tired of watching him, or looking at him, even after twenty years. Twenty years. . . . What did the *psittacidae* do, to win the right to wear a rainbow as their plumage? Although the way we've hunted them for it, you could say it was a mixed blessing. Like some other things.

Twenty years. How strange it sounds to hear those words, and know they're true. There are gray hairs when I look in the mirror. Wrinkles starting. And Weems is bald! Bald as an egg, and all squinty behind his spectacles. How did we get that way, without noticing it? Time is both longer and shorter than you think, and usually all at once.

Twelve days is a long time to wait for somebody to return your call. Twenty years is a long time gone. But I feel somehow as though it was only last week that I left home. I keep the circuits clean, going over them and over them, showing those mental home movies until I could almost step across, sometimes, into that other reality. But then I always look down, and there's that tremendous abyss full of space and time, and I realize I can't, again. You can't go home again.

Especially when you're almost one thousand astronomical units out in space. Almost there, the first rung of the ladder. Next Thursday is the day. Oh, that bottle of champagne that's been waiting for so long. Oh, the parallax view! I have the equal of the best astronomical equipment in all of near-Earth space at my command, and a view of the universe that no one has ever had before; and using them has made me the only astrophysicist ever to win a Ph.D. in deep space. Talk about your field work.

Strange to think that if the Forward Observatory had massed less than its thousand-plus tons, I would have been replaced by a machine. But because the installation is so large, I in my infinite human flexibility, even with my infinite human appetite, become the most efficient legal tender. And the farther out I get the more important my own ability to judge what happens, and respond to it, becomes. The first—and maybe the last—manned interstellar probe, on a one-way journey into infinity . . . into a universe unobscured by our own system's gases and dust . . . equipped with eyes that see everything from gamma to ultra-long wavelengths, and ears that listen to the music of the spheres.

And Emmylou Stewart, the captive audience. Adrift on a star . . . if you hold with the idea that all the bits of inert junk drifting through space, no matter how small, have star potential. Dark stars, with brilliance in their secret hearts, only kept back from letting it shine by Fate, which denied them the critical mass to reach their kindling point.

Speak of kindling: the laser beam just arrived to give me my daily boost, moving me a little faster, so I'll reach a little deeper into the universe. Blue sky at bedtime; I always was a night person. I'm sure they didn't design the solar sail to filter light like the sky . . . but I'm glad it happened to work out that way. Sky-blue was always my passion—the color, texture, fluid purity of it. This color isn't exactly right; but it doesn't matter, because I can't remember how anymore. This sky is a sun-catcher. A big blue parasol. But so was the original, from where I used to stand. The sky is a blue parasol . . . did anyone ever say that before, I wonder? If anyone knows, speak up—

Is anyone even listening. Will anyone ever be?

("Who cares, anyway? Come on, Ozzie—climb aboard. Let's drop down to the observation porch while I do my meditation, and try to remember what days were like.")

Weems, damn it, I want satisfaction!

Sunday, the 8th

That idiot. The intolerable moron—how could he do that to me? After all this time, wouldn't you think he'd know me better than that? To keep me waiting for twelve days, wondering and afraid: twelve days of all the possible stupid paranoias I could weave with my idle hands and mind, making myself miserable, asking for trouble—

And then giving it to me. God, he must be some kind of sadist! If I could only reach him and hurt him the way I've hurt these past hours—

Except that I know the news wasn't his fault, and that he didn't mean to hurt me . . . and so I can't even ease my pain by projecting it onto him.

I don't know what I would have done if his image hadn't

been six days stale when it got here. What would I have done, if he'd been in earshot when I was listening; what would I have said? Maybe no more than I did say.

What can you say when you realize you've thrown your whole life away?

He sat there behind his faded blotter, twiddling his pen, picking up his souvenir moon rocks and laying them down— looking for all the world like a man with a time bomb in his desk drawer—and said, "Now, don't worry, Emmylou. There's no problem . . ." Went on saying it, one way or another, for five minutes; until I was shouting, "What's *wrong*, damn it?"

"I thought you'd never even notice the few pages . . ." with that sliding smile of his. And while I'm muttering, "I may have been in solitary confinement for twenty years, Harvey, but it hasn't turned my brain to mush," he said,

"So maybe I'd better explain, first—" and the look on his face; oh, the look on his face. "There's been a biomed breakthrough. If you were here on Earth, you . . . well, your body's immune responses could be . . . made normal . . ." And then he looked down, as though he could really see the look on my own face.

Made normal. Made normal. It's all I can hear. I was born with no natural immunities. No defense against disease. No help for it. No. *No, no, no;* that's all I ever heard, all my life on Earth. Through the plastic walls of my sealed room; through the helmet of my sealed suit . . . And now it's all changed. They could cure me. But I can't go home. I knew this could happen; I knew it had to happen someday. But I chose to ignore that fact, and now it's too late to do anything about it.

Then why can't I forget that I could have been f-free. . . .

. . . I didn't answer Weems today. Screw Weems. There's nothing to say. Nothing at all.

I'm so tired.

Monday, the 9th

Couldn't sleep. It kept playing over and over in my mind. . . . Finally took some pills. Slept all day, feel like hell. Stupid. And it didn't go away. It was waiting for me, still waiting, when I woke up.

It isn't fair—!

I don't feel like talking about it.

Tuesday, the 10th

Tuesday, already. I haven't done a thing for two days. I haven't even started to check out the relay beacon, and that damn thing has to be dropped off this week. I don't have any strength; I can't seem to move, I just sit. But I have to get back to work. Have to . . .

Instead I read the printout of the article today. Hoping I'd find a flaw! If that isn't the greatest irony of my entire life. For two decades I prayed that somebody would find a cure for me. And for two more decades I didn't care. Am I going to spend the next two decades hating it, now that it's been found?

No . . . hating myself. I could have been free, they could have cured me; if only I'd stayed on Earth. If only I'd been patient. But now it's too late . . . by twenty *years*.

I want to go home. I want to go home. . . . But you can't go home again. Did I really say that, so blithely, so recently? *You* can't: you, Emmylou Stewart. You are in prison, just like you have always been in prison.

It's all come back to me so strongly. Why me? Why must I be the ultimate victim—In all my life I've never smelled the sea wind, or plucked berries from a bush and eaten them right there! Or felt my parents' kisses against my skin, or a man's body. . . . Because to me they were all deadly things.

I remember when I was a little girl, and we still lived in Victoria—I was just three or four, just at the brink of understanding that I was the only prisoner in my world. I remember watching my father sit polishing his shoes in the morning, before he left for the museum. And me smiling, so deviously, "Daddy . . . I'll help you do that if you let me come out—"

And he came to the wall of my bubble and put his arms into the hugging gloves, and said, so gently, "No." And then he began to cry. And I began to cry too, because I didn't know why I'd made him unhappy. . . .

And all the children at school, with their "spaceman" jokes, pointing at the freak; all the years of insensitive people asking the same stupid questions every time I tried to go out anywhere . . . worst of all, the ones who weren't stupid, or insensitive. Like Jeffrey . . . no, I will not think about Jeffrey! I couldn't let myself think about him then. I could never afford to get close to a man, because I'd never be able to touch him. . . .

And now it's too late. Was I controlling my fate when I

volunteered for this oneway trip? Or was I just running away from a life where I was always helpless: helpless to escape the things I hated, helpless to embrace the things I loved.

I pretended this was different, and important . . . but was that really what I believed? No! I just wanted to crawl into a hole I couldn't get out of, because I was so afraid.

So afraid that one day I would unseal my plastic walls, or take off my helmet and my suit; walk out freely to breathe the air or wade in a stream or touch flesh against flesh . . . . and die of it.

So now I've walled myself into this hermetically sealed tomb for a living death. A perfectly sterile environment, in which my body will not even decay when I die. Never having really lived, I shall never really die, dust to dust. A perfectly sterile environment—in every sense of the word.

I often stand looking at my body in the mirror after I take a shower. Hazel eyes, brown hair in thick waves with hardly any gray . . . and a good figure; not exactly stacked, but not unattractive. And no one has ever seen it that way but me. Last night I had the Dream again . . . I haven't had it for such a long time . . . this time I was sitting on a carved wooden beast in the park beside the Provincial Museum in Victoria; but not as a child in my suit. As a college girl, in white shorts and a bright cotton shirt, feeling the sun on my shoulders, and—Jeffrey's arm around my waist . . . We stroll along the bayside hand in hand, under the Victorian lamp posts with their bright hanging flowerbaskets, and everything I do is fresh and spontaneous and full of the moment. But always, always, just when he holds me in his arms at last, just as I'm about to . . . I wake up.

When we die, do we wake out of reality at last, and all our dreams come true? When I die . . . I will be carried on and one into the timeless depths of uncharted space in this computerized tomb, unmourned and unremembered. In time all the atmosphere will seep away; and my fair corpse, lying like Snow White's in inviolate sleep, will be sucked dry of moisture, until it is nothing but a mummified parchment of shriveled leather and bulging bones. . . .

("*Hello? Hello, baby? Good night. Yes, no, maybe. . . . Awk. Food time!*")

("Oh, Ozymandias! Yes, yes, I know . . . I haven't fed you, I'm sorry. I know, I know . . .")

(*Clinks and rattles.*)

Why am I so selfish? Just because I can't eat, I expect him to fast, too. . . . No. I just forgot.

He doesn't understand, but he knows something's wrong; he climbs the lamp pole like some tripodal bem, using both feet and his beak, and stared at me with that glass-beady bird's eye, stares and stares and mumbles things. Like a lunatic! Until I can hardly stand not to shut him in a cupboard, or something. But then he sidles along my shoulder and kisses me—such a tender caress against my cheek, with that hooked prehensile beak that could crush a walnut like a grape—to let me know that he's worried, and he cares. And I stroke his feathers to thank him, and tell him that it's all right . . . but it's not. And he knows it.

Does he ever resent his life? Would he, if he could? Stolen away from his own kind, raised in a sterile bubble to be a caged bird for a caged human. . . .

I'm only a bird in a gilded cage. I want to go home.

Wednesday, the 11th

Why am I keeping this journal? Do I really believe that sometime some alien being will find this, or some starship from Earth's glorious future will catch up to me . . . glorious future, hell. Stupid, selfish, shortsighted fools. They ripped the guts out of the space program after they sent me away; no one will ever follow me now. I'll be lucky if they don't declare me dead and forget about me.

As if anyone would care what a woman all alone on a lumbering space probe thought about day after day for decades, anyway. What monstrous conceit.

I did lubricate the bearings on the big scope today. I did that much. I did it so that I could turn it back toward Earth . . . toward the sun . . . toward the whole damn system. Because I can't even see it, all crammed into the space of two moon diameters, even Pluto; and too dim and small and faraway below me for my naked eyes, anyway. Even the sun is no more than a gaudy star that doesn't even make me squint. So I looked for them with the scope. . . .

Isn't it funny how when you're a child you see all those drawings and models of the solar system with big, lumpy planets and golden wakes streaming around the sun. Somehow you never get over expecting it to look that way in person. And here I am, one thousand astronomical units north of the solar pole, gazing down from a great height . . . and it doesn't look that way at all. It doesn't look like anything, even through the scope. One great blot of light, and all the pale tiny diamond chips of planets and moons around it, barely distinguishable from half a hundred undistinguished stars trapped in the same arc of blackness. So meaningless, so insignificant . . . so disappointing.

Five hours I spent, today, listening to my journal, looking back and trying to find—something, I don't know, something I suddenly don't have anymore.

I had it at the start. I was disgusting; Pollyanna Grad-student skipping and singing through the rooms of my very own observatory. It seemed like heaven, and a lifetime spent in it couldn't possibly be long enough for all that I was going to accomplish, and discover. I'd never be bored, no, not me. . . .

And there was so much to learn about the potential of this place, before I got out to where it supposedly would matter, and there would be new things to turn my wonderful extend-ed senses toward . . . while I could still communicate easily with my dear mentor Dr. Weems, and the world. (Who'd ever have thought, when the lecherous old goat was my thesis ad-visor at Harvard, and making jokes to his other grad students about "the lengths some women will go to protect their vir-ginity," that we would have to spend a lifetime together.)

There was Ozymandias's first word . . . and my first birth-day in space, and my first anniversary . . . and my doctoral degree at last, printed out by the computer with scrolls made of little x's and taped up on the wall. . . .

Then day and night and day and night, beating me black and blue with blue and black . . . my fifth anniversary, my eighth, my decade. I crossed the magnetopause, to become truly the first voyager in interstellar space . . . but by then there was no one left to *talk* to anymore, to really share the experience with. Even the radio and television broadcasts drifting out from Earth were diffuse and rare; there were fewer and fewer contacts with the reality outside. The plod-ding routines, the stupifying boredom—until sometimes I stood screaming down the halls just for something new; lis-tening to the echoes that no one else would ever hear, and pretending they'd come to call; trying so hard to believe there was something to hear that wasn't *my* voice, *my* echo, or Ozymandias making a mockery of it.

("*Hello, beautiful. That's a crock. Hello, hello?*")

("Ozymandias, get *away* from me—")

But always I had that underlying belief in my mission: that

I was here for a purpose, for more than my own selfish reasons, or NASA's (or whatever the hell they call it now), but for Humanity, and Science. Through meditation I learned the real value of inner silence, and thought that by creating an inner peace I had reached equilibrium with the outer silences. I thought that meditation had disciplined me, I was in touch with myself and with the soul of the cosmos. . . . But I haven't been able to meditate since—it happened. The inner silence fills up with my own anger screaming at me until I can't remember what peace sounds like.

And what have I really discovered, so far? Almost nothing. Nothing worth wasting my analysis or all my fine theories—or my freedom—on. Space is even emptier than anyone dreamed, you could count on both hands the bits of cold dust or worldlet I've passed in all this time, lost souls falling helplessly through near-perfect vacuum . . . all of us together. With my absurdly long astronomical tape measure I have fixed precisely the distance to NGC 2419 and a few other features, and from that made new estimates about a few more distant ones. But I have not detected a miniature black hole insatiably vacuuming up the vacuum; I have not pierced the invisible clouds that shroud the ultralong wavelengths like fog; I have not discovered that life exists beyond the Earth in even the most tentative way. Looking back at the solar system I see nothing to show definitively that we even exist, anymore. All I hear anymore when I scan is electromagnetic noise, no coherent thought. Only Weems every twelfth night, like the last man alive. . . . Christ, I still haven't answered him.

Why bother? Let him sweat. Why bother with any of it. Why waste my precious time.

Oh, my precious time. . . . Half a lifetime left that could have been mine, on Earth.

Twenty years—I came through them all all right. I thought I was safe. And after twenty years, my façade of discipline and self-control falls apart at a touch. What a self-deluded hypocrite I've been. Do you know that I said the sky was like a blue parasol eighteen years ago? And probably said it again fifteen years ago, and ten, and five—

Tomorrow I pass 1,000 AUs.

Thursday, the 12th

I burned out the scope. I burned out the scope. I left it pointing toward the Earth, and when the laser came on for the night it shone right down the scope's throat and burned it out. I'm so ashamed. . . . Did I do it on purpose, subconsciously?

(*"Good night, starlight. Arrk. Good night. Good . . ."*)

("Damn it, I want to hear another human voice—!")

(*Echoing, "voice, voice, voice, voice . . ."*)

When I found out what I'd done, I ran away. I ran and ran through the halls. . . . But I only ran in a circle: This observatory, my prison, myself . . . I can't escape. I'll always come back in the end, to this greenwalled room with its desk and its terminals, its cupboards crammed with a hundred thousand dozens of everything, toilet paper and magnetic tape and oxygen tanks. . . . And I can tell you exactly how many steps it is to my bedroom or how long it took me to crochet the afghan on the bed . . . how long I've sat in the dark and silence, setting up an exposure program or listening for the feeble pulse of a radio galaxy two billion light-years away. There will never be anything different, or anything more.

When I finally came back here, there was a message waiting. Weems, grinning out at me half bombed from the screen—"Congratulations," he cried, "on this historic occasion! Emmylou, we're having a little celebration here at the lab; mind if we join you in yours, one thousand astronomical units from home—?" I've never seen him drunk. They really must have meant to do something nice for me, planning it all six days ahead. . . .

To celebrate I shouted obscenities I didn't even know I knew at him, until my voice was broken and my throat was raw.

Then I sat at my desk for a long time with my jackknife lying open in my hand. Not wanting to die—I've always been too afraid of death for that—but wanting to hurt myself. I wanted to make a fresh hurt, to take my attention off the terrible thing that is sucking me into myself like an imploding star. Or maybe just to punish myself, I don't know. But I considered the possibility of actually cutting myself quite calmly, while some separate part of me looked on in horror. I even pressed the knife against my flesh . . . and then I stopped and put it away. It hurts too much.

I can't go on like this. I have duties, obligations, and I can't face them. What would I do without the emergency automechs? . . . But it's the rest of my life, and they can't go on doing my job for me forever—

Later.

I just had a visitor. Strange as that sounds. Stranger yet—it was Donald Duck. I picked up half of a children's cartoon show today, the first coherent piece of nondirectional, unbeamed television broadcast I've recorded in months. And I don't think I've ever been happier to see anyone in my life. What a nice surprise, so glad you could drop by. . . . Ozymandias loves him; he hangs upside down from his swing under the cabinet with a cracker in one foot, cackling away and saying, "Give us a kiss, *smack-smack-smack*." . . . We watched it three times. I even smiled, for a while; until I remembered myself. It helps. Maybe I'll watch it again until bedtime.

Friday, the 13th

Friday the Thirteenth. Amusing. Poor Friday the Thirteenth, what did it ever do to deserve its reputation? Even if it had any power to make my life miserable, it couldn't hold a candle to the rest of this week. It seems like an eternity since last weekend.

I repaired the scope today; replaced the burnt-out parts. Had to suit up and go outside for part of the work . . . I haven't done any outside maintenance for quite a while. Odd how both exhilarating and terrifying it always is when I first step out of the airlock, utterly alone, into space. You're entirely on your own, so far away from any possibility of help, so far away from anything at all. And at that moment you doubt yourself, suddenly, terribly . . . just for moment.

But then you drag your umbilical out behind you and clank along the hull in your magnetized boots that feel so reassuringly like lead ballast. You turn on the lights and look for the trouble, find it and get to work; it doesn't bother you anymore. . . . When your life seems to have torn loose and be drifting free; it creates a kind of sea anchor to work with your hands; whether it's doing some mindless routine chore or the most intricate of repairs.

There was a moment of panic when I actually saw charred wires and melted metal, when I imagined the damage was so bad that I couldn't repair it again. It looked so final, so—masterful. I clung there by my feet and whimpered and clenched my hands inside my gloves, like a great shining baby, for a while. But then I pulled myself down and began to pry here and unscrew there and twist a component free . . . and little by little I replaced everything. One step at a time; the way we get through life.

By the time I'd finished I felt quite calm, for the first time in days; the thing that's been trying to choke me to death this past week seemed to falter a little at my demonstration of competence. I've been breathing easier since then; but I still don't have much strength. I used up all I had just overcoming my own inertia.

But I shut off the lights and hiked around the hull for a while, afterwards—I couldn't face going back inside just then: looking at the black convex dish of the solar sail I'm embedded in, up at the radio antenna's smaller dish occluding stars as the observatory's cylinder wheels endlessly at the hub of the spinning parasol. . . .

That made me dizzy, and so I looked out into the starfields that lie on every side. Even with my own poor, unaugmented senses there's so much more to see out here, unimpeded by atmosphere or dust, undominated by any sun's glare. The brilliance of the Milky Way, the depths of star and nebula and the farthest galaxy breathlessly suspended . . . as I am. The realization that I'm lost for eternity in an uncharted sea.

Strangely, although that thought aroused a very powerful emotion when it struck me, it wasn't a negative one at all: it was from another scale of values entirely, like the universe itself. It was as if the universe itself stretched out its finger to touch me. And in touching me, singling me out, it only heightened my awareness of my own insignificance.

That was somehow very comforting. When you confront the absolute indifference of magnitudes and vistas so overwhelming, the swollen ego of your self-important suffering is diminished. . . .

And I remembered one of the things that was always so important to me about space—that here *anyone* has to put on a spacesuit before they step outside. We're all aliens, no one better equipped to survive than another. I am as normal as anyone else, out here.

I must hold on to that thought.

Saturday, the 14th

There is a reason for my being here. There is a reason.

I was able to meditate earlier today. Not in the old way, the usual way, by emptying my mind. Rather by letting the questions fill up the space, not fighting them; letting them merge with my memories of all that's gone before. I put on music, that great mnemonic stimulator; letting the images that each tape evoked free-associate and interact.

And in the end I could believe that my being here was the result of a free choice. No one forced me into this. My motives for volunteering were entirely my own. And I was given this position because NASA believed that I was more likely to be successful in it than anyone else they could have chosen.

It doesn't matter that some of my motives happened to be unresolved fear or wanting to escape from things I couldn't cope with. It really doesn't matter. Sometimes retreat is the only alternative to destruction, and only a madman can't recognize the truth of that. Only a madman. . . . Is there anyone "sane" on Earth who isn't secretly a fugitive from something unbearable somewhere in their life? And yet they function normally.

If they ran, they ran toward something, too, not just away. And so did I. I had already chosen a career as an astrophysicist before I ever dreamed of being a part of this project. I could have become a medical researcher instead, worked on my own to find a cure for my condition. I could have grown up hating the whole idea of space and "spacemen," stumbling through life in my damned ugly sterile suit. . . .

But I remember when I was six years old, the first time I saw a film of suited astronauts at work in space . . . they looked just like me! And no one was laughing. How could I help but love space, then?

(And how could I help but love Jeffrey, with his night-black hair, and his blue flight suit with the starry patch on the shoulder. Poor Jeffrey, poor Jeffrey, who never even realized his own dream of space before they cut the program out from under him. . . . I will not talk about Jeffrey. I will not.)

Yes, I could have stayed on Earth, and waited for a cure! I knew even then there would have to be one, someday. It was both easier and harder to choose space, instead of staying.

And I think the thing that really decided me was that those people had faith enough in me and my abilities to believe that I could run this observatory and my own life smoothly for as long as I lived. Billions of dollars and a thousand tons of equipment resting on me, like Atlas holding up his world.

Even Atlas tried to get rid of his burden; because no matter how vital his function was, the responsibility was still a burden to him. But he took his burden back again too, didn't he; for better or worse. . . .

I worked today. I worked my butt off getting caught up on

a week's worth of data processing and maintenance, and I'm still not finished. Discovered while I was at it that Ozymandias had used those missing five pages just like the daily news: crapped all over them. My sentiments exactly! I laughed and laughed.

I think I may live.

Sunday, the 15th

The clouds have parted.

That's not rhetorical—among my fresh processed data is a series of photo reconstructions in the ultra-long wavelengths. And there's a gap in the obscuring gas up ahead of me, a break in the clouds that extends thirty or forty light-years. Maybe fifty! Fantastic. What a view. What a view I have from here of everything, with my infinitely extended vision: of the way ahead, of the passing scene—or looking back toward Earth.

Looking back. I'll never stop looking back, and wishing it could have been different. That at least there could have been two of me, one to be here, one who could have been normal, back on Earth; so that I wouldn't have to be forever torn in two by regrets—

("*Hello. What's up doc? Avast!*")

("Hey, watch it! If you drink, don't fly.")

Damn bird. . . . If I'm getting maudlin, it's because I had a party today. Drank a whole bottle of champagne. Yes, I had *the* party . . . we did, Ozymandias and I. Our private 1,-000 AU celebration. Better late than never, I guess. At least we did have something concrete to celebrate—the photos. And if the celebration wasn't quite as merry as it could have been, still, I guess it will probably seem like it was when I look back on it from the next one, at 2,000 AUs. They'll be coming faster now, the celebrations. I may even live to celebrate 8,000. What the hell, I'll shoot for 10,000—

After we finished the champagne . . . Ozymandias thinks '98 was a great year, thank God he can't drink as fast as I can . . . I put on my Strauss waltzes, and the *Barcarolle:* Oh, the Berliner Philharmonic; their touch is what a lover's kiss must be. I threw the view outside onto the big screen, a ballroom of stars, and danced with my shadow. And part of the time I wasn't dancing above the abyss in a jumpsuit and headphones, but waltzing in yards of satin and lace across a ballroom floor in nineteenth-century Vienna. What I wouldn't give to be *there* for a moment out of time. Not for a lifetime, or even a year, but just for an evening, just for one waltz.

Another thing I shall never do. There are so many things we can't do, any of us, for whatever the reasons—time, talent, life's callous whims. We're all on a one-way trip into infinity. If we're lucky we're given some life's work we care about, or some person. Or both, if we're very lucky.

And I do have Weems. Sometimes I see us like an old married couple, who have grown to a tolerant understanding over the years. We've never been soul mates, God knows, but we're comfortable with each other's silences. . . .

I guess it's about time I answered him.

Form and Content

A debate continues among literary critics, but mostly between critics and readers, about the relative importance of form and content. Generally, the critics and some writers insist on the superiority of style to content—that is, of "what words are chosen and how they are put together" over "what happens." Some even insist that the two aspects of fiction are indivisible, that there is no content without form, though there may not be so great a confidence that there is no form without content. In his essay entitled "About 5,175 Words," Samuel R. Delany said it this way: "Put in opposition to 'style,' there is no such thing as 'content.' "

At the simplest level of meaning, the statement is a truism: Without words sentences do not exist. But at the level of literary criticism the refusal to recognize distinctions is to deny the possibility of discussing one or the other. This makes difficulties for science fiction, which grew up as a pulp medium of entertainment more concerned with storytelling than style. Content continues to be denigrated or ignored by critics and teachers; story is accessible to the most naive reader, and only the difficult is worth discussing.

In an essay scheduled for late 1982 publication in a book about George Zebrowski's work, Ian Watson makes a distinction between what he calls a "dual consensus at work in American sf"—"at the high level" of "aesthetically ambitious work" and "at the low level" of "slick adventure." A third kind of sf to which, he thinks, the genre should aspire is fiction in which the intellectual content is presented rigorously by whatever methods are necessary, rather than "sublimated into mere narrative, mere story" that, at best, conveys only "the *illusion* of mental exercise to the reader."

As an example of what he is describing, Watson cites the work of George Zebrowski (1945–). Born in Villach, Austria, of parents who had been abducted from Poland by the German army as slave labor, Zebrowski was taken as an infant to Italy and then to England, where he spent the first six years of his life. He came to the United States in 1951 under the displaced persons program, attended grade school in Manhattan, then Miami, and finally back to the Bronx, where he also attended high school.

Zebrowski went on to SUNY-Binghamton, where he studied philosophy from 1964 to 1969. He has held a wide variety of jobs, but from an early age he knew he wanted to write. Early fascination with science fiction and attendance at the 1968 Clarion SF Writers Workshop turned him toward science fiction. Two years later his first story, "The Water Sculptor," was published in *Infinity One* (1970), and he has been a full-time writer ever since. The same year he became editor of the Science Fiction Writers of America *Bulletin*, a position he filled until 1975. His fourth published story, "Heathen God," was a Nebula finalist. He also has taught a college course in sf.

Zebrowski's first novel, *The Omega Point*, was published in 1972. It is part of a trilogy that includes *Ashes as Stars* (1977) and *Mirror of Minds* (not yet published). A second trilogy began with *The Star Web* (1975), which has been revised (but not yet published) as *Stranger Suns*. A number of his thirty some short stories have been collected in *The Monadic Universe* (1977).

Zebrowski has edited several anthologies: *Tomorrow Today* (1975); *Human-Machines* (1975, with Thomas N. Scortia); and *Faster than Light* (1976, with Jack Dann). He also has edited *The Best of Thomas N. Scortia* (1981).

Zebrowski's major achievement to date is the ambitious, long novel *Macrolife* (1979), which received considerable favorable comment from Arthur C. Clarke and Gerard K. O'Neill, among others. It deals with the movement of humans into space as a further step in evolution, away from "dirtworlds" and their inherent dangers of racial extermination to the infinite environment and resources of space and an eternity of experience and growth. Like Olaf Stapledon's *Last and First Men*, *Macrolife* covers a vast expanse of time, beginning at about the present as the macroworld concept is taking shape and continuing to a period one hundred billion years in the future when the universe is beginning to collapse. Such a span demands a great deal of exposition, of lecturing, of reading over the protagonist's shoulder. One reviewer wondered if its content disqualified it as a novel. Watson, on the other hand, says that Zebrowski is "preoccupied with future sociology" and that sf "is actually a didactic literature . . . in the sense that it is content-oriented." Both Zebrowski and Stapledon, to whom Zebrowski is often compared, were students of philosophy.

"The Word Sweep," first published in the August 1979 *Magazine of Fantasy and Science Fiction*, is typically philosophical but not so typically expansive; instead it is a concise consideration of the relationship between language and intelligence, between the real and the unreal, and between reality and the transcendent aspirations of humanity. The concept begins in the Kafka-esque absurdity of spoken words taking physical shape and piling up until speech must be rationed or people will be inundated. The story develops naturalistically with careful attention to the ways in which people realistically would respond to such a fantastic development, but it ends in transcendence.

The Word Sweep

by George Zebrowski

The words on the floor were as thick as leaves when Felix came into the party. At five past eleven, the room should have been silent.

"Quiet!" he shouted, unable to hold back.

The word formed in the air and floated to the floor at his feet. A deaf couple in the corner continued talking with their hands. Everyone was looking at him, and he felt his stomach tighten. He should have motioned for silence instead of speaking.

A small woman with large brown eyes came up to him and handed him a drink. He sipped. Vodka. It was her way of saying, yeah, we know you've got a lousy job policing the yak ration. Pooping parties for a living can't be fun, you poor bastard. We know.

Heads nodded to show approval of the woman's gesture.

Felix tried to smile, feeling ashamed for losing control. Then he turned and went out again into the cool October night.

At the end of the block, the compactor was waiting for the sweeps to clean out the corner house. He was glad that he did not have to work in the inner city, where control was always slipping, where the babbling often buried entire neighborhoods to a depth of four or five feet.

He took a deep breath. Watching out for five suburban blocks was not so bad, especially when his beat was changed once a month, so he could not grow too friendly with the homeowners.

The tension in his gut lessened. At least this party had not given him any trouble. He could see that the guests had tried to be sedate, speaking as little as possible during the evening, priding themselves on their ability to hold words and liquor. He had not seen any babblers sitting on a pile of verbiage. This was a good block, much better than last month's section.

A dog ran by in the empty street. Felix noted the muzzle. No problem there.

He started a slow walk home, passing the compactor as it turned on its light and started silently down the next block. Two streets down, he turned to avoid going through the district square, where they were still cleaning up after the political rally.

There was a message for him on the phone screen:

> Let's ration together after
> you get home. I'll save
> mine. Love, June

The words angered him, bringing back the tension in his stomach. He cleared the screen, resenting the message because it had ruined the calming effect of his long walk home.

He went into the bedroom and lay down. When he tried, he could almost remember the time when words did not materialize. He must have been four or five when it happened for the first time. He remembered wafer-thin objects, letters joined together in as many differing styles as there were speakers.

At first it had been a novelty, then a perpetual snowstorm. Cities had to clean up after a daily disaster, three hundred and sixty-five days a year, trucking the words to incinerators and landfills. The words would burn only at high temperatures, and even then they would give off a toxic gas which had to be contained. There had been a project to find a use for the gas, but it took too much energy for the burning to make it worthwhile; later the gas was found to be useless.

Psychiatric treatment came to a halt, then shifted to computer printout and nonverbal therapies. Movies had gone back to silent and subtitled versions; only the very rich could afford to truck away the refuse after each talkie showing. Opera was performed in mime and music-only reductions. . . .

Felix opened his eyes and sat up in the darkness. Somewhere far away, a deviant was running through the streets. He could just barely hear the screaming, but it was loud enough to remind him of the time he had been a deviant.

Unable to control himself, he had almost buried himself in words one night, under a giant elm tree near the edge of town. The words had poured out of him as if they were trying to outnumber the stars, while he had held his stomach and screamed obscenities.

Bruno Black, who had been fully grown before the world had changed, had explained it to him later. It had been the silence, the prolonged, thought-filled silence, that had broken his control, as it had broken the resolve of countless others. The need to speak uncontrollably had come into him one day, ridding him of cogency, sweeping through him like a wind, bestowing the freedom of babble, taking away wit and limit, making his mouth into a river, out of which words had flowed like wars . . . in the end a wonderful nonsense had cleansed his brain.

Now, as he listened to the distant deviant howling in the night, he again felt the trial of terse expression; the jungle was growing in around him, threatening to wipe away all his control when he fell asleep, enticing him with pleasures stronger than the silence. . . .

He looked around the dark room. The closed bedroom door stood in the corner, a sly construction, suggesting an entire world on the other side. . . .

The distant sound stopped. They had caught him. Samson, Winkle, Blake—all the block watchers had converged on the explosion to squash it. The word sweeps were already clearing up, compacting, driving away to the landfills.

For a moment he wondered if it might have been Bruno, then rejected the idea; Bruno's voice was much lower than that. It might have been a woman.

Felix relaxed and lay back again.

He woke up in the night, got up and went to his desk. He saw the phone screen glowing and remembered June's message. The new message read:

> You bastard! Answer for
> Christ's sake. Is Bruno
> with you again? What
> do you two do together?

He cleared the screen and turned on the desk lamp. Then he sat down and took out Bruno's journal. He looked at it under the light, remembering how much relief it had given him through the years. His fingers were shaking. Inside its pages were all the things he had wanted to say, but Bruno had written them down.

Opening at random, he looked at the neat handwriting. Bruno was not verbose, even on paper, where it would have been harmless. The very letters were well-formed, the sentences thoughtful and clear. If read out loud, they would not exceed anyone's daily ration.

He read an early entry:

23 July 1941

When the words started materializing, the difference between language and physical reality was blurred. The appearance of spoken words in all shapes and sizes, depending on the articulation of the speaker, imposed a martial law of silence, enforced at first by a quietly administered death penalty in some parts of the world. The rate of materialization had to be cut down at all costs, lest the world be thrown into a global economic depression. . . .

The depression had come and gone, leaving behind a new code of conduct, the word sweeps, the compactors, and the block watchers—and a mystery as great as the very fact of existence. Bruno was certain that there had to be an answer; his journal represented twenty years of speculation about the problem. The possibility of an answer, Felix thought, is all that keeps me together. I don't know what I'll do if Bruno doesn't come back.

Someone started pounding on the front door. Felix got up and went out to check.

He opened the door and June came in, marching past him into the living room, where she turned on the lights.

He closed the door and faced her.

"You treat me like I don't exist!" she shouted.

The *you* was a flimsy thing; it broke into letters when it hit the carpet. *Treat* seemed to be linked like a chain as it clattered onto the coffee table, where it produced a few nonsense-masses before it lay still. *Me* whipped by him like a sparrow and crunched against the wall, creating more nonsense-masses. *Like* settled slowly to the rug; *I* knifed into the pile next to it. *Don't* and *exist* collided in midair, scattering their letters.

Felix spread his hands, afraid to speak, fearful that at any moment his deviancy would slide up out of the darkness within him and take over. Didn't she know how hard a life he led? He'd told her a hundred times. A look of pity started to form on her freckled face, reminding him of the brown-eyed woman who had given him a drink; but it died suddenly. June turned and started for the door.

"We're finished!" she shouted as she went out. The words failed to clear the door as she slammed it behind her, and dropped next to the coat rack. He looked at the nonsense-masses that her pounding had created, grateful that the door was well-cushioned.

He let out a mental sigh and sat down in the armchair by the lamp. At least there would be no more pressure, however much he missed her. Soon, he knew, he would have to go looking for Bruno.

The clock over the fireplace read four a.m.

He turned on the radio and listened to the merciful music. The notes formed, evaporating one by one. A harpsichord came on, the notes lasting a bit longer before winking out. He watched them come and go for a long time, wondering, as Bruno had done so often in his journal, what kind of cosmic justice had permitted music to remain. As the Scarlatti sonata rushed toward its finale, the crystalline sounds came faster and faster, dusting the room with vibrant notes. . . .

June had never liked Bruno; there was no darkness in her. Like those who were forgetting the self-awareness created by speech, she did not need to speak.

He turned off the radio and wondered if Mr. Seligman next door was burying himself in sleeptalk. How many children were sleeping with their training muzzles on, until they learned self-control?

His hands started shaking again. The pressure to speak was building up inside him, almost as strongly as during his deviant days. June's visit had triggered it; the loss of her had affected him more than he realized.

"June," he said softly, wanting her.

The word was round, the letters connected with flowing curves, as it drifted to the rug. He reached down, picked it up and dropped it into the felt-lined waste basket.

His hands were still shaking. He got up and paced back and forth. After a few minutes he noticed that his screen was on in the bedroom. He walked through the open door, sat down at the desk, and read:

> Disturbance reported at the
> landfill. Check when your shift
> begins this morning. Webber

One of the others has gone nuts, he thought, and they want me to bring him home.

Felix changed his shirt and shoes and went outside. He unlocked the bicycle from its post, mounted the cracked leather seat, and pushed out into the empty street.

Cool, humid mists rose around the one-story suburban houses. Only every fifth streetlamp was on, and these began to wink out as the sky grew brighter. He estimated that it would take him half an hour to reach the landfill.

He remembered it as a plain of dry earth being blown into dust clouds by the wind. The place would soon be incapable of accepting any more words, or garbage; it was full, except for an occasional hole. A new site would have to be found.

As Felix neared the landfill, he noticed the strangeness of the grass on both sides of the road. The sun cleared the horizon in a clear blue sky; and the grass suddenly looked like matted animal hair, growing up from a red skin. There was a pungent, lemon-like odor in the air as he stood up on the bicycle to climb a hill.

He reached the top and stopped.

The landfill was covered with trees, looking like fresh moss, or tall broccoli. The sharp smell was stronger.

He got back on the seat and rolled downhill.

A stillness enveloped him when he reached bottom, as if he had entered the quiet center of the world. As the forest came closer, he considered the possibility of a massive planting program but realized that it would not have been possible in so short a time.

He passed the first trees. They appeared very fresh, like the limbs of young girls, bent upward, open in inviting positions; soft yellow-green moss had grown between the branches.

He pedaled forward, growing anxious, but the stillness was restful, calming him. The lemon-like scent of the trees cleared away the sleepiness in his head.

Suddenly he rolled into a small clearing and stopped short at the edge of a large hole. Bruno Black sat at the bottom, talking to himself as the words piled up around him.

"Hello, Bruno." The words formed and slid down the sandy slope.

The blond-haired man looked up. "Come down." The words popped away from his mouth and landed on the pile.

Felix started down.

"It's safe here," Bruno shouted, "we can talk all we want."

When he reached the large, seated figure, Felix noticed that Bruno's clothes were torn and dirty.

"You've got to let me get you out of this," Felix said.

Only the first three words formed, falling at his feet.

"Notice that?"

"What's going on here, Bruno?"

No words formed this time, as if the effect was beginning to die away.

"It's only here," Bruno said, "nowhere else."

Felix sat down next to the ruddy-faced man and looked at him carefully.

"Bruno—you know me?"

"Of course, Felix, don't be stupid. You're my friend."

"What are you doing here?"

"I think I've figured it—all of it, why it happens, and why it fails here." The last three words formed, wretched little gray letters floating in the air like smoke.

Bruno brushed them away with a bear-like swipe.

"Felix, I may really know. I'm not nuts."

Felix heard a wind rushing above the hole, as if something were growing angry. He remembered a schoolyard, many years ago, with children playing volleyball, silently.

"Have you got a shovel?"

"No," Felix said, "but I can get one."

Again no words. Bruno was watching him.

"Wonderful, isn't it?"

"Bruno—how long has all this been here?"

"About a month."

"All this grew in a month?"

"The trees grew out of the buried words, Felix, pregnant words they were. . . ."

The silence was clear between them, devoid of words.

"It comes and goes," Bruno said. All the words appeared, letters deformed, as if they were gnarly tree branches, and fell into Bruno's lap.

"There's something that does this," he said as he brushed them away. "We can bring it all to an end, when we find it. The shovel is the key to the whole business."

It all made a peculiar sense.

"There's a utility shed at the fork in the road," Felix said, "but are you okay?"

"I just look bad."

There were no words. Felix marveled as he scrambled out of the hole. Bruno was definitely on to something.

Bruno was digging with his hands when Felix came back with two shovels. He threw them in and clambered down.

"It couldn't be natural, what happened to the world," Bruno said as he picked up a shovel and started digging. Felix picked the other one and they dug back-to-back.

"Why not natural?" Felix asked.

"Maybe it could—some twist in the geometry of space forms words in response to our sounds. I assumed it wasn't natural and went looking for spots where it wouldn't happen."

"Why did it all start?"

"Maybe it was a political thing," Bruno said. "Somebody was planning a form of thought control, but it got out of hand: A while back, I think, our politicos contacted an alien civilization in some far space, a mind contact maybe, and learned how to construct . . . certain devices. Perhaps the alien culture thought it would help us think more concisely." He laughed. "It's more than poetic prankery, you see. Language, as much as toolmaking, is directly responsible for the growth of our intelligence and self-consciousness. We're as smart or stupid as how well we use words. It's the automatic programs, the habits, that deaden the mind, the dogmatic mazes. . . ."

He paused. "Not this hole, we've got to try elsewhere."

Bruno might simply be crazy, Felix thought, nothing more.

"If you wanted to affect a culture," Bruno continued, "put a restriction on its use of language and watch native ingenuity increase, like the improvement of hearing in the blind. . . ."

Felix climbed out of the hole and gave Bruno a hand up.

A wind was blowing across the landfill, soughing through the strange trees as if it were slowly becoming aware of the intruders. Leaves lay strewn everywhere. Some seemed to be stained by decay, like old, misshapen coins; others were curling into small tubes. The wind gusted, swirling them into disarray, imparting its energy of motion to raise them into the air. Again Felix had the sensation of standing at the edge of the world. He wondered what June would think if she were to see him here with Bruno.

Then he noticed that the trees seemed to be shaped like letters, bent and distorted, echoing the millions of words buried in the ground.

"Let's dig by one of the trees," Bruno said. The seven words flew out of his mouth and were lifted by the wind, which deposited them in the branches, where they sat like blackbirds.

Felix went up to the nearest tree and started digging. Bruno joined in. The sun climbed toward noon.

"Testing," Bruno said. No word appeared. "Maybe it was something in our minds that was altered, to make the words when we speak. . . ."

"You mean there may be no machine?"

"What's that?" Bruno asked, pointing.

A crystalline rod was protruding from the dirt. Felix stepped into the hole and continued digging while Bruno rested. Slowly, a complex mechanism was uncovered, a cube-like shape of glassy-metallic connections, a maze of shiny pipes and joints, mirror surfaces and solid figures.

"It's . . . like a large piece of jewelry," Felix said.

"I was afraid of this," Bruno said. "I thought there might be a relay device, a generator, the thing that changed speech into solid objects, worldwide, of course. I was hoping to find the local station in the net. . . ."

"Well, what's this then?"

Bruno clutched at his chest and fell forward, easing himself down with the shovel.

"You're ill," Felix said, squatting down next to him.

"My heart . . . but listen. I may die, but you have to listen. . . ."

A demented stare came into Bruno's face, as if he knew that his understanding of the truth was superior to all the deceiving forces around him. He pulled himself backward on the ground, until he was sitting up against the tree, one foot in the hole.

"Try not to move, I'll get help," Felix said.

"Listen!" He raised his hand to his eyes and rubbed them. Then he stared at the alien artifact and spoke, his voice a low, silken tenor. "Humankind fell into a dream. Maybe it was the result of some massive failure, brought on by the straining of psyches long overworked with the yoke of metaphor and simile, paradigm and tautology—in a creature that longed to know the universe directly, tired of sense-show charades, the shadows of real things projected through the dirty windows of the eye, the noisy avenues of the ear. . . ."

His voice grew plaintive and sad. "We grew discouraged by the blindness of touch, the lie of taste and smell, disappointed by the children's universe of not-too-little and not-too-much, of knowing and not knowing, of anxious flight from ignorance into only relative knowledge, stretched tightly between the extremes of sufficiency and insufficiency, between the great and small. We would never be all-knowing, yet we were not *nothing*. The hopelessness was too much, driving us into this common delusion." He closed his eyes and Felix saw tears in his friend's face.

"But maybe it is an alien yoke," Felix said.

"I would prefer that, but this silly machine. . . ."

He coughed and clutched his chest.

"Bruno!"

Felix picked up the shovel and struck the ornate machine. It was a blow for objectivity, forging a way into a universe outside delusion, for an end to the torment of the brute words struggling to break out of him. He hit the machine again; maybe the blow would alter something in the human mind.

"Even if we end this," Bruno whispered loudly, "we don't know what else we may awaken into."

Felix struck the machine a third time.

"It's only a projection of our wish, Felix, to find an answer. . . ."

The world darkened and the wind threw branches onto them and the machine. The device shimmered and disappeared. The branches were like snakes as Felix struggled to free himself. There was a horrible sound from Bruno. Felix crawled toward him and looked into his face. Bruno's eyes were glassy, like the crystal of the machine, staring into an abyss.

"I see it," Bruno croaked, his words trembling.

Felix looked around. A black bag had been pulled down over the world.

"What is it?"

"I see it all!" The words vibrated, but did not form.

"I don't see anything." The blackness was impenetrable.

"Senseless . . . blind, nothing there for us," Bruno muttered.

Felix strained to see. The dark shimmered. He heard a howling in his ears; his eyes rushed forward through a confusion of colors; he expected to collide with a wall at any moment.

"Nothing for us," Bruno was saying, "only constraints, humiliating chains for a will that can expand to infinity or focus into smallness . . ."

The continuum tilted and Felix was falling. Chaos crept into him. Not the sense of chance or statistical disorder obeying its own laws, but mindless, unpredictable fluidity, cruel, unrestrained and unredeemable—the pulsing substratum of reality. He perceived it in the only way possible, with the narrow gauge of finite senses—a gray, alien mass at the center of time, at the heart of mind, enveloping all space, a cosmic jack-in-the-box always ready to give the lie to all pretense, a centrality which could never be defeated, only held in degrees of check.

"Bruno!" he called, but the word came out as nonsense.

The darkness faded and he saw Bruno sitting up against the tree.

"You're okay!" Felix shouted in relief.

Bruno looked up, but he seemed to be on the other side of a barrier. "Wic wore tos repelton," he said, smiling.

"What?"

"Repelton, tos?"

They stared at each other as the last quantum of information slipped across the bridge of silence, revealing the situation to them.

Felix took a step forward, but Bruno seemed to retreat, as if there were a frame around him and something had moved him back.

Cages, Felix realized. We'll die alone unless we can reach each other. He would never touch June again, or even speak to her; they would look at each other through the wrong end of a telescope, trying to rename the simplest things with gibberish. Our illnesses, our desire to transcend the world, have deformed everything.

Bruno was waving at him. "Tos? Wixwell, mamtom ono!" He shrugged. "Prexel worbout it," he added.

Felix cursed, but the word was indecipherable as two copies appeared and settled to the ground near his feet.

Dialectic of History and Transcendence

The evolution of science fiction has been a tug-of-war between the fantastic and the realistic, between the supernatural and the natural, between the wonderful and the prosaic, between the followers of Verne and the followers of Wells. Early science fiction (and proto-science fiction with its journeys to the moon and other exotic lands) reveled in the marvelous and made its obligatory gesture toward the ordinary by the mechanism of travel. Wells, however, focused on the everyday aspects of the extraordinary. For many years the Vernians seemed to prevail, but with Campbell's prodding, Heinlein's craft, and Asimov's cool reason, Wellsians achieved at least equal status until the rebellions of the New Wave and the recent retreat into fantasy and science-fantasy.

In another sense, however, the dialectic remains at the heart of the genre: the fantastic pumping out on the systole, the realistic returning on the diastole. For the story to be science fiction rather than mainstream or even futuristic fiction, the situation of the characters must be significantly out of the ordinary, but the situation must be rationalized or the story will be fantasy. The balance between the two shifts, however: sometimes the fantastic predominates, sometimes the realistic, depending upon movements or periods or writers, even upon the moods of a single writer.

Ian Watson (1943–   ) describes his work as "a dialectic of history and transcendence," history being the everyday matrix, and transcendence, that which goes beyond ordinary experience. Born in North Shields, Northumberland, England, Watson earned a bachelor's degree in English from Balliol

497

College, Oxford, in 1963, a bachelor of literature in 1965, and a master's degree in 1966. He taught at University College, Dar es Salaam, Tanzania, from 1965 to 1967; at the Tokyo University of Education and Keio University (and a one-year temporary position at Japan Women's University) from 1967 to 1970; and at the Birmingham Polytechnic Art and Design Center from 1970 to 1976. Since then he has been a full-time writer and has served as features editor and regular contributor to the English journal *Foundation*.

Watson's first professional sale was "Soyinka's Dance of the Forests" to the Uganda magazine *Transition* #27 in 1966. His stories began appearing in *New Worlds* with "Roof Garden under Saturn" in November 1969. A collection of his stories, *The Very Slow Time Machine*, was published in 1979.

Watson published a juvenile book, *Japan: A Cat's Eye View*, in 1969. His first science fiction novel, *The Embedding*, exploded on the science fiction world in 1973 and won second place in the John W. Campbell Memorial Award competition for the best sf novel of the year. It was followed by *The Jonah Kit* (1975), *Orgasmachine* (1976 in a French translation for which there is no English-language edition), *The Martian Inca* (1977), *Alien Embassy* (1977), *Miracle Visitors* (1977), *God's Word* (1979), *The Gardens of Delight* (1980), *Under Heaven's Bridge* (1981, with Michael Bishop), and *Deathhunter* (1981). He also has published another juvenile book about Japan, *Japan Tomorrow* (1977).

Watson began writing science fiction in Japan as a way of surviving what he called "the contradiction between the English literature I was nominally teaching and the environmental message from outside." He sees sf "as a survival strategy generally—a metamorphical tool for thinking about the future flexibly and boldly." His novels in particular are about "the relationship between reality and consciousness (testing out this theme variously by way of linguistics [*The Embedding*], speculation about cetacean intelligence [*The Jonah Kit*], evolution [*Alien Embassy*], novel life forms [*The Martian Inca*], the UFO mythos [*Miracle Visitors*], etc." His novels ask "whether any kind of ultimate understanding of the nature of reality and the reason for life and the universe may or may not be arrived at." But this concern with transcendence is solidly based on hard science and developed in terms of "a strong socio-political underpinning to events." He calls the area in which he works "loosely . . .

Social Science SF . . . somewhere at the intersection of Linguistics, Philosophy, Social Anthropology, Epistemology."

"The World Science Fiction Convention of 2080," published in the *Magazine of Fantasy and Science Fiction* for October 1980 that was put on sale about the time the 38th World Science Fiction Convention (Noreascon II) was convening in Boston, is perhaps not typical Watson. It is a delightful romp that uses the sociology of science fiction itself as an indirect way of describing the "Collapse" that has returned civilization to the technological level of the early 19th century. More importantly, it is about the spirit that inspires the creation of science fiction.

Non-sf-convention-goers should know that the activities of the Worldcon of 2080 are traditions at contemporary worldcons: the gathering, the parties, the films, the banquet, the awards, the guest of honor, and the speech. In Watson's story the events have been adapted to more primitive times. In that time to come, however, the guest of honor makes a moving speech in which he claims the planets and the stars as more certainly the property of science fiction because they now are beyond humanity's reach. They belong to the mythology of science fiction.

The dialectic continues. Perhaps the story is not atypical Watson after all.

The World Science Fiction Convention of 2080

by Ian Watson

What a gathering! Four hundred people—writers, fans and both magazine editors—have made their way successfully to these sailcloth marquees outside the village of New Boston.

We know of another three people who didn't make it, and the opening ceremony includes a brief "In Memoriam" tribute to each of them, followed by one minute's silence for all. For Kurt Rossini, master of heroic fantasy—slain by an Indian arrow on his way from far California. For Suzie

McIntosh, whose amusing woodcuts (sent down by trade caravan from Moose Jaw last summer season) adorn the program booklet—killed by a wolf pack outside of Winnipeg. And for our worst loss, lovely Charmian Jones, acclaimed Queen of Titan in the masquerade at the last Worldcon three years ago in Tampa, whose miniature is worn close to many a fan's heart from the Yukon to Florida Bay—murdered by Moslem pirates during a kidnap raid on Charleston while she was passing through. (Could she have survived seraglio life in North Africa, and even become a bit of a queen there? No! Cut off from the slow percolation of fandom's lifeblood? Never! She defended her honor bravely with a short sword, and died.)

Some dozen others with attending memberships haven't arrived, either. We hope that they're just late—held up by contrary winds or a broken wagon axle. No doubt we will learn in six months or so when their personal-zines travel the trade routes.

In the bar tent, around the still, at the ox roast, and in the art tent with its fine embroideries and batiks based on the Old Masters Delany, Heinlein, Le Guin, we greet old friends and colleagues and swap our travel tales. And I thought that my own journey from South Scotland on foot, on horseback, by canal longboat, and finally for five weeks by sailship across the stormy Atlantic (our mortars loaded against raiders) was eventful enough! But compared to some of the others' experiences, mine was a cake run: Indians, Badlands, outlaw bands, mercenaries, pietist communities that close around one like a Venus's-flytrap, Army Induction Centers, plague zones, technophile citadels! I was even two and a half weeks early and managed to arrive with the manuscript of a new novel in my knapsack, penned on the sailship in between working my passage, all ready for bartering to "Monk" Lewiston, head of Solaris Press of Little New York.

The new novel is called *The Aldebaran Experience* and is about a starship journey from the Luna Colony through metaspace to an alien planet orbiting Aldebaran. It is, though I say it myself, an ambitious exercise in what the critic Suvin once called "cognitive estrangement"—but one can't really convey the breadth of the book in a couple of lines; besides, here isn't the place—though I did appear on a foreign writers' panel to discuss my own by now well-known earlier novel *The Film-Maker's Guide to Alien Actors* (Neogollancz

Press, Edinburgh) dating from only four years ago. (Ah, the speed of publication and distribution in our SF world!)

On this panel, along with me, were the Frenchman Henri Guillaume, whose tale of mighty computerized bureaucracy and subjective time distortions, *The Ides of Venus*, is still winning acclaim for its originality—a definite step beyond the Old French Masters, Curval and Jeury; and the Mexican Gabriel Somosa—an exciting encounter; and my fellow islander Jeremy Symons, whom I last met in the flesh at our biennial thrash Gypsycon '77 all the way in Devon—his *The Artificial Man* has been a hot contender for this year's Hugo award ever since the nominations started trickling along the trade routes and over the ocean two years ago.

But I should describe the highlights of this wonderful get-together under cloth in New Boston. Frankly, that panel was rather ho-hum. Poor Jeremy had come down with some allergy working in the bilges, which affected his throat, and his voice would hardly carry to the back of the marquee. . . .

Highlights, then: *The Film*. Yes, indeed, as advertised in the flyer a year ago, a film had been found! And what a film. Craftsmen built a hand-cranked projector whose light source was the sun itself, focused by an ingenious system of lenses and mirrors from outside the marquee; and six times during the Boskon week we stared, enthralled, at the flickerings of an original print of *Silent Running*, praying that rainclouds would not dim the light too much. Let me not hear any sarcasm about the appropriateness of the title, since no way could anyone activate a soundtrack. We were all enchanted.

The Auction: oh, this was an experience. There was an Ace Double on sale! And an original SF Book Club edition of a Larry Niven collection. *And,* yellow and brittle with age, issues 250 to 260 inclusive of *Locus*. As well as much interesting and historic stuff from our own early post-Collapse era, such as a copy of a handwritten scroll novel (from just before we got hand presses cranking again) by the great Tessa Brien—part of her Jacthar series. The copies of *Locus* went in exchange for a fine Pinto pony—the Alabaman who bid his mount for them was quite happy to walk all the way home. But the Ace Double (Phil Dick's *Dr. Futurity* backed by *The Unteleported Man*) went for a slim bar of gold.

Then there was the Solaris Press party where Henri Guillaume, high on Boston applejack, attempted to dance the can-can, endearing himself to everyone—a few quick sketches were "snapped" of this, and there was even a watercolor for barter by the next morning.

And *The Banquet*, of spiced rabbit stew, followed by . . . *The Hugo Awards:* the carved beechwood rocketships for the best work in our field over the three years '75 to '78. First, for the best fanzine, scooped by Alice Turtle's *Call of the Wild* from New Chicago; then for the best story in either of the bi-annual magazines *Jupiter* or *Fantasy*, won by Harmony Friedlander for her moving "Touchdown" in *Jupiter* four years ago; and finally the long-awaited novel Hugo, going to Boskon's Guest of Honor, Jerry Meltzer (as expected, by everyone except Jeremy Symons!), for his cosmos-spanning *Whither, Starman?*

But I think it is Jerry Meltzer's Guest of Honor speech that I shall most treasure the memory of. The speech was entitled "Some Things Do Not Pass." From the very beginning of it I was riveted, reinvigorated, and felt my life reaffirmed.

Jerry is pushing sixty now, which is quite a miracle now that the average life-expectancy is down to forty or so. He has lost an ear to frostbite and wears a coonskin cap at all times to cover his mutilation. He's a raftsman on the Missouri.

Surveying the marquee full of four hundred faces, he smiled—wisely, confidently. He spoke slowly.

"Some things do not pass. Some things *increase* in truth and beauty. Science Fiction is one of these. I say this because Science Fiction is a fiction: it is a *making*, a forging of the legends of our tribe, and the best legends of all humanity. Now that *research* and *probing* have ceased"—he grinned dismissively—"we can indeed freshly and freely invent our science and our worlds. SF was always being spoilt, having her hands tied and the whip cracked over her head by scientific *facts*. They're gone now—most of those blessed facts, about quarks and quasars and I don't know what!—and there won't be any more! It's all mythology now, friends. SF has come into her own, and we who are here today, we know this. Friends, we're Homers and Lucians once again—because science is a myth, and we're its mythmakers. Mars is ours again, and Saturn is, and Alpha C—and lovely Luna. We can read the Grand Masters of yore in a light that the poor folk of the Late Twentieth could never read them in! I say to you, Some Things Do Not Pass. Their loveliness increases. Now we can make that mythic loveliness wilder and headier and more fabulous than ever. This is the true meaning of my *Whither, Starman?!*"

He spoke till the Con Committee lit the whale-oil flambeaux in the tent, and then he talked some more. At the end he was chaired shoulder-high out into the meadow underneath the stars. And just then, what must have been one of the very last dead satellites from the old days streaked across the sky like a comet tail, burning up as it plunged towards the Atlantic to drown fathoms deep. Maybe it was only an ordinary shooting star—but I don't think so. Nor did anyone else. Four hundred voices cheered its downfall, as Jerry threw back his head and laughed.

With a gesture he quietened the crowd. "My friends," he called out, "we really own the stars now. We really do. Never would have done, the other way. Dead suns, dead worlds the lot of them, I shouldn't be surprised—dead universe. Now Sirius is ours. Canopus is. The dense suns of the Hub are all ours. All." His hand grasped at the sky. It gripped the Milky Way, and we cheered again.

Two mornings later, after many perhaps overconfident goodbyes—"See you in '83!"—I walked down into New Boston to the harbor along with my compadre Jeremy—who was somewhat hung over and weaved about at times—to take ship next week or the week after for Liverpool. I wouldn't need to work my passage back, though. I'd bartered *The Aldebaran Experience* to "Monk" Lewiston for a bundle of furs, much in demand in our cold island.

In a year or so I'll receive my free copy, hand-printed in Solaris Press's characteristic heavy black type, by way of some sheep drove up through the Borders. If Monk is fast in getting it out and the trade routes are kind, who knows, it just might get on the ballot for '83—to be voted at the fishing village of Santa Barbara, way across the Plains and Deserts and Badlands.

Can I possibly make it to Santa Barbara? Truth to tell, I can hardly wait. After this year's wonderful thrash, I'll be on the sailship—and I'll board those stagecoaches, come Hell or high water.

I nudged Jeremy in the ribs.

"We own the stars," I said. "You and I."

Estranging the Everyday

One of science fiction's functions is to domesticate the strange, to make the future plausible and the unusual commonplace, and one of its accomplishments is to innoculate its readers against humanity's customary fear of the unknown. H. G. Wells pointed out the function, and John W. Campbell institutionalized it in *Astounding* during the Golden Age ("I want a story that would be published in a magazine in the twenty-fifth century"). Heinlein ("the best modern writers . . . have worked out some truly remarkable techniques") perfected the methods that allowed information about the fantastic environment to be fed into the narrative slowly and unobtrusively ("for presenting a great deal of background and associated material without intruding into the flow of the story") rather than through the older methods of lecture and exposition to strangers, students, and reporters.

But another and gentler aspect of science fiction is the way in which it finds strangeness in the ordinary, alienness in the everyday. Rather than domesticating the strange, it estranges the domestic. The effect of this is to make the reader look at his world with unblindered eyes, to see the commonplace clearly for the first time, and to appreciate the mysteries that lie close to home.

One of the writers who has been accomplishing this for many years is Carol Emshwiller (1921–). Born in Ann Arbor, Michigan, she earned bachelor's degrees in music and design in 1949 at the University of Michigan, and studied in 1949–1950 at the Ecole Nationale Supérieure des Beaux-Arts in Paris as a Fulbright Fellow. In 1949 she married the science fiction illustrator and later experimental filmmaker Ed Emshwiller and had three children. She started writing late, about the age of thirty, and her first published story, "This Thing Called Love," did not appear until the number 28 issue of *Future Science Fiction* in 1955. Soon after, her stories began appearing in *Science Fiction Quarterly*, then in the *Magazine of Fantasy and Science Fiction*, and finally in a variety of literary magazines and original science fiction anthologies such as *Orbit, Nova,* and *Quark*.

Emshwiller wrote slowly but over the years has published more than one hundred stories. One collection, *Joy in Our Cause*, was published in 1974. She has written scripts for two one-hour public television programs, received a 1975 New York State Creative Artists Public Service grant and a 1979–80 National Endowment for the Arts grant, and is a MacDowell Colony fellow. She has served on the New York State Creative Artist Public Service grant panel, has participated in several writers workshops, has given readings at various colleges and universities, and has worked on the editorial board of *The Little Magazine*. She has taught short-story writing for New York University's Continuing Education.

Early in her career Emshwiller attempted to replace plot in her fiction with other values, to dispense with simile and metaphor, and finally to transmute character into what she called "selves." Her writing, therefore, became more experimental, more like that of mainstream experimenters than of the sf magazines and anthologies in which much of her work was published. Richard Kostelanetz called her stories "scrupulously strange."

In *Twentieth Century Science Fiction Writers*, Douglas Barbour wrote that "much sf . . . has tended to domesticate the unknown (so that strange places, the galaxy itself, become merely places to have quite ordinary 'extraordinary' adventures)." He went on to write that "Emshwiller's fictions force us to look again at the supposedly ordinary domestic world and see it as truly weird and, yes, unknown."

"Abominable," first published in *Orbit 21* (1980), is a parable about the differences between men and women told in the form of a science-fiction story. The author draws upon several science fiction traditions, particularly that of the search for the abominable snowman (also known as Bigfoot and the Yeti) and the separation of the sexes, as in Philip Wylie's *The Disappearance*.

The story can be read on two levels. At the plot level, it describes a time when women have disappeared from the world of men, and searching parties are sent out to find them as if they were quasi-mystical legends, while rumors about their existence, their attitudes and appearance and ways and values, are discussed among men like stories about the Yeti. At the metaphorical level, the story deals with the ways in which men, in their sexual confusion and cultural ignorance and identity crises, are unable to understand women and their needs and angers and resentments. Both stories are told in language that is simple but evocative, and wisdom slips in concealed between parentheses.

Abominable

by Carol Emshwiller

We are advancing into an unknown land with a deliberate air of nonchalance, our elbows out or our hands on hips, or standing one foot on a rock when there's the opportunity for it. Always to the left, the river, as they told us it should be. Always to the right, the hills. At every telephone booth we stop and call. Frequently the lines are down because of high winds or ice. The Commander says we are already in an area of the sightings. We must watch now, he has told us over the phone, for those curious two-part footprints no bigger than a boy's and of a unique delicacy. "Climb a tree," the Commander says, "or a telephone pole, whichever is the most feasible, and call out a few of the names you have memorized." So we climb a pole and cry out: Alice, Betty, Elaine, Jean, Joan, Marilyn, Mary . . . and so on, in alphabetical order. Nothing comes of it.

We are seven manly men in the dress uniform of the Marines, though we are not (except for one) Marines. But this particular uniform has always been thought to attract them. We are seven seemingly blasé (our collars open at the neck in any weather) experts in our fields, we, the research team for the Committee on Unidentified Objects that Whizz by in Pursuit of Their Own Illusive Identities. Our guns shoot sparks and stars and chocolate-covered cherries and make a big bang. It's already the age of frontal nudity, of "Why not?" instead of "Maybe." It's already the age of devices that can sense a warm, pulsing, live body at seventy-five yards and home in on it, and we have one of those devices with us. (I might be able to love like that myself someday.) On the other hand, we carry only a few blurry pictures in our wallets, most of these from random sightings several months ago. One is thought to be of the wife of the Commander. It was taken from a distance and we can't make out her features, she was wearing her fur coat. He thought he recognized it. He has said there was nothing seriously wrong with her.

So far there has been nothing but snow. What we put up with for these creatures!

Imagine their bodies as you hold this little reminder in the palm of your hand . . . this fat, four-inch Venus of their possibilities. . . . The serious elements are missing, the eyes simple dots (the characteristic hair-do almost covers the face), the feet, the head inconsequential. Imagine the possibility of triumph but avoid the smirk. Accept the challenge of the breasts, of the outsize hips, and then . . . (the biggest challenge of all). If we pit ourselves against it *can we win!* Or come off with honorable mention, or, at the least, finish without their analysis of our wrong moves?

Here are the signs of their presence that we have found so far (we might almost think these things had been dropped in our path on purpose if we didn't know how careless they can be, especially when harassed or in a hurry; and since they are nervous creatures, easily excited, they usually *are* harassed and/or in a hurry). . . . Found in our path, then: one stalk of still-frozen asparagus, a simple recipe for moussaka using onion-soup mix, carelessly torn out of a magazine, a small purse with a few crumpled-up dollar bills and a book of matches. (It is clear that they do have fire. We take comfort in that.)

And now the Commander says to leave the river and to go up into the hills even though they are treacherous with spring thaws and avalanches. The compass points up. We slide on scree and ice all day sometimes, well aware that they may have all gone south by now, whole tribes of them feeling worthless, ugly, and unloved. Because the possibilities are endless, any direction may be wrong, but at the first sign of superficialities we'll know we're on the right track.

One of us is a psychoanalyst of long experience, a specialist in hysteria and masochism. (Even without case histories, he is committed to the study of their kind.) He says that if we find them they will probably make some strange strangling sounds, but that these are of no consequence and are often mistaken for laughter, which, he says, is probably the best way to take them. If, on the other hand, they smile, it's a simple reflex and serves the purpose of disarming us. (It has been found that they smile two and a half times as often as we do.) Sometimes, he says, there's a kind of nervous giggle which is essentially sexual in origin and, if it occurs when they see us, is probably a very good sign. In any case, he says, we should give no more than our names and our rank, and, if they get angry, we should be careful that their rage doesn't turn against themselves.

Grace is the name of the one in the picture, but she must be all of fifty-five by now. Slipped out of a diner one moonlit night when the Commander forgot to look in her direction. But what was there to do but go on as usual, commanding what needed to be commanded? We agree. He said she had accepted her limitations up to that time, as far as he could see, and the limits of her actions. He blamed it on incomplete acculturation or on not seeing the obvious, and did not wonder about it until several years later.

I'd like to see one like her right now. Dare to ask where I come from and how come they're so unlike? How we evolved affectations the opposite of theirs? And do they live deep underground in vast kitchens, some multichambered sanctuary heated by ovens, the smell of gingerbread, those of childbearing age perpetually pregnant from the frozen semen of some tall, redheaded, long-dead comedian or rock star? Anyway, that's one theory.

But now the sudden silence of our own first sighting. One! . . . On the heights above us, huge (or seems so) and in full regalia (as in the Commander's photograph): mink and monstrous hat, the glint of something in the ears, standing (it seems a full five minutes) motionless on one leg. Or maybe just an upright bear (the sun was in our eyes) but gone when we got up to the place a half hour later. The psychoanalyst waited by the footprints all night, ready with his own kind of sweet-talk, but no luck.

The information has been phoned back to the commander ("Tell her I think I love her," he said), and it has been decided that we will put on the paraphernalia ourselves . . . the shoes that fit the footprints, the mink, fox, leopard (phony) over several layers of the proper underwear. We have decided to put bananas out along the snow in a circle seventy-five yards beyond our camp and to set up our live warm-body sensor. Then when they come out for the bananas we will follow them back to their lairs, down into their own dark sacred places; our camera crew will be ready to get their first reactions to us for TV. They'll like being followed. They always have.

We hope they are aware, if only on some dim level, of our reputations in our respective fields.

But the live warm-body sensor, while it does sound the alarm, can't seem to find any particular right direction, and in the morning all the bananas are gone.

It's because they won't sit still . . . won't take anything seriously. There's nobody to coordinate their actions, so they run around in different directions, always distracted from the task at hand, jumping to conclusions, making unwarranted assumptions, taking everything for granted or, on the other hand, not taking *anything* for granted (love, for instance). The forces of nature are on their side, yes, (chaos?) but we have other forces. This time we will lay the bananas out in one long logical straight line.

When we step into those kitchens finally! The largest mountain completely hollowed out, my God! And the smells! The bustle! The humdrum *everydayness* of their existence! We won't believe what we see. And they will probably tell us things are going better than ever. They will be thinking they no longer need to be close to the sources of power. They may even say they like places of no power to anyone . . . live powerless, as friends, their own soft signals one to the other, the least of them to the least of them. And they will also say we hardly noticed them anyway, or noticed that they weren't there. They will say we were always looking in the other direction, that we never knew who or what they were, or cared. Well, we did sense something . . . have sensed it for a

This is the diagram the psychoanalyst has laid out for further study:

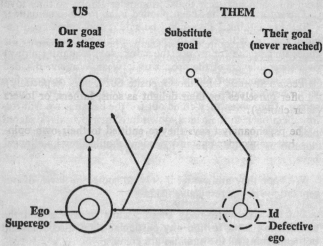

US

Our goal
in 2 stages

THEM

Substitute
goal

Their goal
(never reached)

Ego —
Superego —

Id
Defective
ego

(Their id reacts to our superego
and then bounces back to the
substitute goal and/or becomes
deflected to our goal.)

**Deflected goal in 3 stages with 2
possibilities (both achieved)**

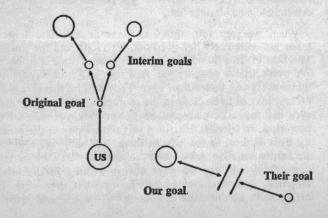

Interim goals

Original goal

US

Our goal.

Their goal

long time, and we feel a lack we can't quite pinpoint. Unpaid creatures, mostly moneyless, but even so, noticed. We will tell them this, and also that the Commander thinks he may love one of them.

But this time they have refused the bananas. (What we offer them is never quite right.) Okay. The final offering (they have one more chance): these glass beads that look like jade; a set of fine, imported cookware; a self-help book, "How to Overcome Shyness with the Opposite Sex"; and (especially) we offer ourselves for their delight as sons, fathers, or lovers (their choice).

The psychoanalyst says they're entitled to their own opinions, but we wonder how independent should they be allowed to be?

One of us has said it was just a bear we saw at the top of that hill. He said he remembered that it humped down on all fours after standing on one leg, but they *might* do that.

The psychoanalyst has had a dream. Afterwards he told us never to be afraid of the snapping vagina (figuratively speaking) but to come on down to them (though we are climbing up, actually) and throw fish to the wombs (nothing but the best filet of sole, figuratively speaking).

Well, if I had one I'd wash its feet (literally) and the back. Venture the front, too. Let the water flow over both of us. Let their hair hang down. I'd take some time out now and then, even from important work, to do some little things like this of hardly any meaning, and listen, sometimes, to its idle chatter or, at least, seem to. But as to Grace, it must be something else I have in mind, though I'm not sure what.

We are telling all the old tales about them around our campfires in the late evenings, but it's not the same kind of frightening that it used to be when we were young and telling the tales in similar circumstances because now we know they may actually be lurking out there in the shadows, and what's scary is that we have really no idea of their size! We're not sure what to believe. On the one hand, whether they are twice our size or, as the Commander insists, whether almost all of them are quite a bit smaller and definitely weaker. The more mythically oriented among us have said that they are large enough to swallow us up into their stomachs (from below) and to ejaculate us out again months later, weak and helpless. The anthropologically oriented say they may be the missing link we have searched for so long and stand, as they believe, somewhere between the gorilla and us (though probably quite a bit higher on the scale than pithecanthropus erectus) and that they are, therefore, (logically) distinctly smaller and somewhat bent over, but may not necessarily be weaker. The sexually obsessed among us wonder, among other things, if their orgasm is as specific a reaction as ours is. The romantics among us think they will be cute and lovable creatures even when they're angry and regardless of size and strength. Others think the opposite. Opinions also vary as to how to console them for the facts of their lives and whether it is possible to do so at all since 72 percent of them perceive themselves as inferior, 65 percent perceive themselves to be in a fragile mental balance, only 33⅓ percent are without deep feelings of humiliation simply for being what they are. How will it be possible, then, to penetrate their lines of self-defense and their lines of defensiveness? Altercations are inevitable, that's clear. (Eighty-five percent return to rehash old arguments.) We dislike unpleasant emotional confrontations, try to avoid such things at all costs, but we also realize that playing the role of dominant partner in intimate interaction won't always be easy. How nice, even so, to have a group of beings, one of these days (almost invisible, too), whose main job would be to tidy up!

Pedestals have already been set out for them.

Even if (or especially if) they are not quite up to our standards, they will, in any case, remind us of the animal in all of us, of our beastliness . . . our ebb and flow . . . of lifeforces we barely know exist . . . maybe some we never suspected.

But now we have had a strange and disturbing message from the Commander telling us that some very important political appointees have said that these stories of sightings are exactly that, stories . . . hoaxes, and it's been proven that the photographs have been doctored, in one case a gorilla superimposed on a snowy mountain, in another case a man in drag. (Only two pictures still unexplained.) Several people have confessed. Some have never even been in the area at all. Whatever we have seen must have been a trick of light and shadow or, more likely, one of the bears in this vicinity and (they're sure of it) we have a hoaxer among us, stealing the

bananas himself and making footprints with an old shoe on
the end of a long stick. Besides, think if we should discover
that they do, in fact, exist. We would only be adding to our
present problems. Committees would have to be set up to find
alternatives to boredom once their dishwashing years were
over. Cures would have to be discovered for cancers in
peculiar places, for strange flows, for vaginismus and other
spasms. A huge group of dilettantes (Sunday poets and painters) would be added to society, which society can well do
without, according to the Commander. And why should we
come searching them, as though they were Mount Everest
(and as important), simply because they're there? Anyway,
the funding for our search has run out. The Commander
even doubts if we can afford any more phone calls.

We are all very depressed by this news, though it's hard to
pinpoint exactly why. Some of us feel sure, or fairly sure,
that there *is* something out there . . . just out of sight . . .
just out of earshot. Some of us seem to see, sometimes, a
flash of color out of the corners of our eyes, as though the essentially invisible had been made *almost* visible for a few
seconds. Makes one think, too (and some of us do), how
socks and underwear might someday return, magically, from
under beds to be found clean and folded in the drawer, as if
cups of coffee could appear out of nowhere just when most
needed, as if the refrigerator never ran out of milk or butter
. . . But we are at the service of our schedule and our
budget. We must return to the seats of power, to the service
of civilization . . . politics. . . . We turn back.

For a while I think seriously of going on by myself. I think
perhaps if I crept back alone, sat quietly, maybe dressed to
blend in more. Maybe if I sat still long enough (and stopped
telling, out loud, those old, scary stories about them), if I
made no proud gestures . . . shoulders not so stiff . . .
maybe then they'd get used to me, even eat bananas out of
my hand, and come, in time, to recognize an authoritarian
figure by the subtle reality of it, and perhaps learn a few
simple commands. But I have to stick to my orders. It's too
bad, though I do want to pick up my pay, my medals, and
get on with the next project. Still, I want to make one more
move toward these creatures, if only a symbolic one. I sneak
back along the trail and leave a message where it can't be
missed, surrounded by bananas. I leave something they'll be
sure to understand: the simple drawing of a naked man; a

crescent that can't help but stand for moon; a heart shape (anatomically correct) for love; a clock face with the time of the message; the outline of a footprint of my own next to an outline of one of theirs (looks like a question mark next to an exclamation point). "To Grace" at the top. I sit there for a while, then, and listen for sighs and think I hear some . . . think I see something vaguely white on white in the clarity of snow. Invisible *on purpose,* that's for sure (if there at all), so if we can't see them, it's not *our* fault.

Well, if that's how they want it, let them bark at the moon alone (or whatever it is they do) and dance and keep their own home fires burning. Let them live, as was said, "in the shadow of man." It serves them right.

I ask the psychoanalyst, "Who are we, anyway?" He says about 90 percent of us ask that same question in one form or another, while about 10 percent seem to have found some kind of an answer of their own. He says that, anyway, we will remain essentially who we already are whether we bother to ask the question or not.

Science and Fiction

Ever since Poe and Verne, science fiction has patted itself on the back about the scientific information incorporated in its stories. Along with speculation and narrative excitement, the genre's apologists have said, science fiction gives youthful readers a background in science. Hugo Gernsback cherished the notion that science fiction would turn his readers toward careers in science and engineering; the stories published in *Amazing*, he said, were a candy coating of fiction around a pill of instruction. He and later editors would point to the "real" scientists who wrote for their magazines, and Gernsback made a practice of including degree-describing alphabet soup after the names of the editor and his authors. Edward Elmer Smith, for instance, always was followed by "Ph.D.," even though his doctorate was in food chemistry and he spent most of his professional career as a doughnut-mix specialist.

So it was with other scientists: The mathematician Eric Temple Bell wrote adventure stories under the name John Taine, and Isaac Asimov had a Ph.D. in chemistry but wrote stories about robots and galactic empires. On the other hand, astronomer R. S. Richardson, who wrote a number of stories under the name Philip Latham, often included knowledgeable material about astronomy, and astronomer Fred Hoyle's speculative novels were perhaps no more speculative than his theory about the continuous creation of matter. Even when scientists did not write in the area of their expertise (perhaps constrained by what they knew to be unlikely), their sense of the scientific method and scientific procedures often shaped their fiction. Gernsback and Campbell were at least partially right.

A true synthesis of science and fiction, a synthesis that ought to be the ideal the genre seeks, has seldom been achieved, however. Hal Clement's elegantly designed alien worlds are one example of what can be done, as well as some of Poul Anderson's more scientific works. Recently Dr. Robert Forward, once a source of fascinating scientific speculation, has turned his knowledge of physics into fiction.

The goal of a well-written piece of fiction that not only reflects science but is about science can be approached from two directions. One is that of writers like Ed Bryant, gifted writers who learn enough about science to make it an integral part of their work; the other is that of scientists who learn how to write well enough to deal with the important elements in their science. One major difficulty has been the necessity to master two areas—writing and science. Usually the writers don't know enough science, and the scientists seldom master the art of writing. A more fundamental problem may be that not everyone shares the ideal; many writers and critics refuse to believe that science has anything to do with the matter.

One scientist who has recognized the ideal and harnessed his talents to achieve it has been Gregory Benford (1941–   ). Born in Mobile, Alabama, one of twin brothers, he earned a bachelor's degree in physics from the University of Oklahoma in 1963, and a master's degree in 1965 and a Ph.D. in 1967 from the University of California at La Jolla. He has been a working scientist ever since, serving as a fellow from 1967 to 1969 and a research physicist from 1969 to 1972 at the Lawrence Radiation Laboratory and since 1972 as a faculty member at the University of California at Irvine.

Benford was an active fan in his early years and edited a fanzine. His professional writing began with "Stand In" in the June 1965 *Magazine of Fantasy and Science Fiction*, and he has contributed a sizable number of short stories and novelettes to magazines and original anthologies since then. He and Gordon Eklund won a Nebula award in 1974 for "If the Stars Are Gods." He has not yet had a collection of stories.

His first novel, *Deeper than Darkness*, was published in 1970 and reprinted in 1978 as *The Stars in Shroud*. Other novels are: *Jupiter Project* (1974); *If the Stars Are Gods* (an expansion of the novelette, 1977, with Gordon Eklund); *In the Ocean of Night* (1977); *Find the Changeling* (1980, with Gordon Eklund); *Shiva Descending* (1980, with William

Rotsler); and *Timescape* (1980). *Timescape* is the most effective example of Benford's effort to combine science, speculation, and narrative. It describes an attempt to send a message backward in time, using tachyons (faster-than-light-particles that are allowed by current scientific theory). Near-future scientists, facing catastrophic pollution, try to send signals to a young professor-researcher in 1962, to avert calamity. Evidence begins to accumulate in the 1960s world that marks it as different from the real world, and this is only one of the paradoxes the novel encompasses. It is a novel not only about catastrophe and the different ways people cope with it but about scientists "doing" science and behaving as real people. It won the Campbell Award, the Nebula Award, and the British Science Fiction Association Award.

"Exposures," first published in the July 6, 1981, *Isaac Asimov's Science Fiction Magazine,* is a story complicated both in theme and technique. It is a reflective, multiple-meaning story, whose various threads of plot are interwoven into a definitive statement at the end.

The young astronomer who is the narrator of the story is studying some enigmatic astronomical plates on which red and blue jets emerge from a distant galaxy, NGC 1097. He also has an emotional life suggested by his memories of the past—preparing the table for Sunday breakfast as a child and serving as an altar boy—and by the mundane details of his everyday existence—donating blood, helping his son with his reading difficulties, attending a grade-school Open House. Into this situation is injected an element of the fantastic—computer images of Sagittarius A, a radio source nearer the core of our galaxy, where no images should exist, and taken from impossible angles and distances. At the end the young scientist has solved the NGC 1097 puzzle but also the mystery of the Sagittarius A images. The second solution suggests worldwide catastrophe in the distant future, but its revelations would be unacceptable to science because it lacks credible supporting data. The unnamed but well-individualized astronomer is faced with a lifelong effort to discover supporting data without revealing the source of his inspiration.

The scientific validity of the story is suggested not only by the protagonist's knowledgeable methods but by his willingness to accept the answer, no matter how difficult, that is the only one to explain all the data; and by the description of the innate (and necessary!) conservatism of science ("the standards of science are austere, unforgiving—and who would have it differently?") rather than the more traditional sf "Eureka!" process. The scientific feel of the story is embodied in a work that is as frankly literary as any "New Wave" story. Language, sentence structure, and detail combine with image and metaphor in an unusually effective final scene that brings all the disparate elements together, like a symphony reuniting its themes, a device Benford has used in other works.

"Exposures" is about the process of learning, through exposures from which we may or may not learn something depending on whether we pay attention and make the proper deductions. It is about science itself: "science [is] not final results but instead a continuing meditation carried on in the face of enormous facts." It also is about life and death and belief and process. It makes comparisons between cancer and destructive black holes bouncing at the heart of galaxies, between blood donations and communion, between the process of reading sentences by putting the phrases into their proper order and an approach to life that is a slow accumulation of data and partial provisional explanations. . . .

Exposures

by Gregory Benford

Puzzles assemble themselves one piece at a time. Yesterday I began laying out the new plates I had taken up on the mountain, at Palomar. They were exposures of varying depth. In each, NGC 1097—a barred spiral galaxy about twenty megaparsecs away—hung suspended in its slow swirl.

As I laid out the plates I thought of the way our family had always divided up the breakfast chores on Sunday. On that ritual day our mother stayed in bed. I laid out the forks and knives and egg cups and formal off-white china, and then stood back in the thin morning light to survey my precise placings. Lush napkin pyramids perched on lace tablecloth, my mother's favorite. Through the kitchen door leaked the mutter and clang of a meal coming into being.

I put the exposures in order according to the spectral filters used, noting the calibrated photometry for each. The ceramic sounds of Bridge Hall rang in the tiled hallways and seeped through the door of my office: footsteps, distant talk, the scrape of chalk on slate, a banging door. Examining the plates through an eyepiece, I felt the galaxy swell into being, huge.

The deep exposures brought out the dim jets I was after. There were four of them pointing out of NGC 1097, two red and two blue, the brightest three discovered by Wolsencroft and Zealey, the last red one found by Lorre over at JPL. Straight lines scratched across the mottling of foreground dust and stars. No one knew what colored a jet red or blue. I was trying to use the deep plates to measure the width of the jets. Using a slit over the lens, I had stopped down the image until I could employ calibrated photometry to measure the wedge of light. Still further narrowing might allow me to measure the spectrum, to see if the blues and reds came from stars, or from excited clouds of gas.

They lanced out, two blue jets cutting through the spiral arms and breaking free into the blackness beyond. One plate, taken in that spectral space where ionized hydrogen clouds emit, giving H II radiation, showed a string of beads buried in the curling spiral lanes. They were vast cooling clouds. Where the jets crossed the II regions, the spiral arms were pushed outward, or else vanished altogether.

Opposite each blue jet, far across the galaxy, a red jet glowed. They, too, snuffed out the H II beads.

From these gaps in the spiral arms I estimated how far the barren spiral galaxy had turned, while the jets ate away at them: about fifteen degrees. From the velocity measurements in the disk, using the Doppler shifts of known spectral lines, I deduced the rotation rate of the NGC 1097 disk: approximately a hundred million years. Not surprising; our own sun takes about the same amount of time to circle around our galactic center. The photons which told me all these specifics had begun their steady voyage sixty million years ago, before there was a *New General Catalog of Nebulae and Clusters of Stars* to label them as they buried themselves in my welcoming emulsion. Thus do I know thee, NGC 1097.

These jets were unique. The brightest blue one dog-legs in a right-angle turn and ends in silvery blobs of dry light. Its counter-jet, offset a perverse eleven degrees from exact oppositeness, continues on a warmly rose-colored path over an immense distance, a span far larger than the parent galaxy itself. I frowned, puckered my lips in concentration, calibrated and calculated and refined. Plainly these ramrod, laconic patterns of light were trying to tell me something. But answers come when they will, one piece at a time.

I tried to tell my son this when, that evening, I helped him with his reading. Using what his mother now knowingly termed "word attack skills," he had mastered most of those tactics. The large strategic issues of the sentence eluded him still. *Take it in phrases,* I urged him, ruffling his light brown hair, distracted, because I liked the nutmeg smell. (I have often thought that I could find my children in the dark, in a crowd, by my nose alone. Our genetic code colors the air.) He thumbed his book, dirtying a corner. Read the words between the commas, I instructed, my classroom sense of order returning. Stop at the commas, and then pause before going on, and think about what all those words mean. I sniffed at his wheatlike hair again.

I am a traditional astronomer, accustomed to the bitter cold of the cage at Palomar, the Byzantine marriage of optics at Kitt Peak, the muggy air of Lick. Through that long morning yesterday I studied the NGC 1097 jets, attempting to see with the quick eye of the theorist, "dancing on the data" as Roger Blandford down the hall had once called it. I tried to erect some rickety hypothesis that my own uncertain mathematical abilities could brace up. An idea came. I caught at it. But holding it close, turning it over, pushing terms about in an overloaded equation, I saw it was merely an old idea tarted up, already disproved.

Perhaps computer enhancement of the images would clear away some of my enveloping fog, I mused. I took my notes to the neighboring building, listening to my footsteps echo in the long arcade. The buildings at Caltech are mostly done in a pseudo-Spanish style, tan stucco with occasional flourishes of Moorish windows and tiles. The newer library rears up beside the crouching offices and classrooms, a modern extrusion. I entered the Alfred Sloan Laboratory of Physics and Mathematics, wondering for the *n*th time what a mathematical laboratory would be like, imagining Lewis Carroll in charge, and went into the new computer-terminal rooms. The indices which called up my plates soon stuttered across the screen. I used a median numerical filter, to suppress variations in the background. There were standard routines to subtract particular parts of the spectrum. I called them up, averaging away noise from dust and gas and the image-saturating spikes that were foreground stars in our own galaxy. Still, nothing dramatic emerged. Illumination would not come.

I sipped at my coffee. I had brought a box of crackers from my office; and I broke one, eating each wafer with a heavy crunch. I swirled the cup and the coffee swayed like a dark disk at the bottom, a scum of cream at the vortex curling out into gray arms. I drank it. And thumbed another image into being.

This was not NGC 1097. I checked the number. Then the log. No, these were slots deliberately set aside for later filing. They were not to be filled; they represented my allotted computer space. They should be blank.

Yet I recognized this one. It was a view of Sagittarius A, the intense radio source that hides behind a thick lane of dust in the Milky Way. Behind that dark obscuring swath that is an arm of our Galaxy, lies the center. I squinted. Yes: this was a picture formed from observations sensitive to the 21-centimeter wavelength line, the emission of nonionized hydrogen. I had seen it before, on exposures that looked radially inward at the Galactic core. Here was the red band of hydrogen along our line of sight. Slightly below was the well-known arm of hot, expanding gas, nine thousand light years across. Above, tinted green, was a smaller arm, a ridge of gas moving outward at 135 kilometers per second. I had seen this in seminars years ago. In the very center was the knot no more than a light year or two across, the source of the 10^{40} ergs per second of virulent energy that drove the cooker that caused all this. Still, the energy flux from our Galaxy was ten million times less than that of a quasar. Whatever the compact energy source there, it was comparatively quiet. NGC 1097 lies far to the south, entirely out of the Milky Way. Could the aim of the satellite camera have strayed so much?

Curious, I thumbed forward. The next index number gave another scan of the Sagittarius region, this time seen by the spectral emissions from outward-moving clouds of ammonia. Random blobs. I thumbed again. A formaldehyde-emission view. But now the huge arm of expanding hydrogen was sprinkled with knots, denoting clouds that moved faster, Dopplered into blue.

I frowned. No, the Sagittarius A exposures were no aiming error. These slots were to be left open for my incoming data.

Someone had co-opted the space. Who? I called up the identifying codes, but there were none. As far as the master log was concerned, these spaces were still empty.

I moved to erase them. My finger paused, hovered, went limp. This was obviously high-quality information, already processed. Someone would want it. They had carelessly dumped it into my territory, but . . .

My pause was in part that of sheer appreciation. Peering at the color-coded encrustations of light, I recalled what all this had often been like: impossibly complicated, ornate in its terms, caked with the eccentric jargon of long-dead professors, choked with thickets of atomic physics and thermodynamics, a web of complexity that finally gave forth mental pictures of a whirling, furious past, of stars burning now into cinders, of whispering, turbulent hydrogen that filled the void between the suns. From such numbers came the starscape that we knew. From a sharp scratch on a strip of film we could catch the signature of an element, deduce velocity from the Doppler shift, and then measure the width of that scratch to give the random component of the velocity, the random jigglings due to thermal motion and thus the temperature. All from a scratch. No, I could not erase it.

When I was a boy of nine I was brow-beaten into serving at the altar, during the unendurably long Episcopal services that my mother felt we should attend. I wore the simple robe and was the first to appear in the service, lighting the candles with an awkward long device and its sliding wick. The organ music was soft and did not call attention to itself, so the congregation could watch undistracted as I fumbled with the wick and tried to keep the precarious balance between feeding it too much (so that, engorged, it bristled into a ball of orange) and the even worse embarrassment of snuffing it into a final accusing puff of black. Through the service I would alternately kneel and stand, murmuring the worn phrases as I thought of the softball I would play in the afternoon, feeling the prickly gathering heat underneath my robes. On a bad day the sweat would accumulate and a drop would cling to my nose. I'd let it hang there in mute testimony. The minister never seemed to notice. I would often slip off into decidedly untheological daydreams, intoxicated by the pressing moist heat, and miss the telltale words of the litany that signaled the beginning of communion. A whisper would come skating across the layered air and I would surface, to see the minister turned with clotted face toward me, holding the implements of his forgiving trade, waiting for me to bring the wine and wafers to be blessed. I would surge upward, swearing under my breath with the ardor only those who have just learned the words can truly muster, unafraid to be muttering these things as I snatched up the chalice and sniffed the too-sweet murky wine, fetching the plates of wafers, swearing that once the polished walnut altar rail was emptied of its upturned and strangely blank faces, once the simpering organ had ebbed into silence and I had shrugged off these robes swarming with the stench of mothballs, I would have no more of it, I would erase it.

I asked Redman who the hell was logging their stuff into my inventory spaces. He checked. The answer was: nobody. There were no recorded intrusions into those sections of the memory system. *Then look further,* I said, and went back to work at the terminal.

They were still there. What's more, some index numbers that had been free before were now filled.

NGC 1097 still vexed me, but I delayed working on the problem. I studied these new pictures. They were processed, Doppler-coded, and filtered for noise. I switched back to the earlier plates, to be sure. Yes, it was clear: these were different.

Current theory held that the arm of expanding gas was on the outward phase of an oscillation. Several hundred million years ago, so the story went, a massive explosion at the galactic center had started the expansion: a billowing, spinning doughnut of gas swelled outward. Eventually its energy was matched by the gravitational attraction of the massive center. Then, as it slowed and finally fell back toward the center, it spun faster, storing energy in rotational motion, until centrifugal forces stopped its inward rush. Thus the hot cloud could oscillate in the potential well of gravity, cooling slowly.

These computer-transformed plates said otherwise. The Doppler shifts formed a cone. At the center of the plate, maximum values far higher than any observed before, over a thousand kilometers per second. That exceeded escape velocity from the Galaxy itself. The values tapered off to the sides, coming smoothly down to the shifts that were on the earlier plates.

I called the programming director. He looked over the displays, understanding nothing of what it meant but everything about how it could have gotten there; and his verdict was clean, certain: human error. But further checks turned up no such mistake. "Must be coming in on the transmission from orbit," he mused. He seemed half-asleep as he punched in commands, traced the intruders. These data had come in from the new combination optical, IR, and UV 'scope in orbit, and the JPL programs had obligingly performed the routine miracles of enhancement and analysis. But the orbital staff were sure no such data had been transmitted. In fact, the 'scope had been down for inspection, plus an alignment check, for over two days. The programming director shrugged and promised to look into it, fingering the innumerable pens clipped in his shirt pocket.

I stared at the Doppler cone, and thumbed to the next index number. The cone had grown, the shifts were larger. Another: still larger. And then I noticed something more; and a cold sensation seeped into me, banishing the casual talk and mechanical-printout stutter of the terminal room.

The point of view had shifted. All the earlier plates had shown a particular gas cloud at a certain angle of inclination. This latest plate was slightly cocked to the side, illuminating a clotted bunch of minor H II regions and obscuring a fraction of the hot, expanding arm. Some new features were revealed. If the JPL program had done such a rotation and shift, it would have left the new spaces blank, for there was no way of filling them in. These were not empty. They brimmed with specific shifts, detailed spectral indices. The JPL program would not have produced the field of numbers unless the raw data contained them. I stared at the screen for a long time.

That evening I drove home the long way, through the wide boulevards of Pasadena, in the gathering dusk. I remembered giving blood the month before, in the eggshell light of the Caltech dispensary. They took the blood away in a curious plastic sack, leaving me with a small bandage in the crook of my elbow. The skin was translucent, showing the riverwork of tributary blue veins, which—recently tapped—were nearly as pale as the skin. I had never looked at that part of me before and found it tender, vulnerable, an unexpected opening. I remembered my wife had liked being stroked there when we were dating, and that I had not touched her there for a long time. Now I had myself been pricked there, to pipe brimming life into a sack, and then to some other who could make use of it.

That evening I drove again, taking my son to Open House. The school bristled with light and seemed to command the neighborhood with its luminosity, drawing families out of their homes. My wife was taking my daughter to another school, and so I was unshielded by her ability to recognize people we knew. I could never sort out their names in time to answer the casual hellos. In our neighborhood the PTA nights draw a disproportionate fraction of technical types, like me. Tonight I saw them without the quicksilver verbal fluency of my wife. They had compact cars that seemed too small for their large families, wore shoes whose casualness offset the formal, just-come-from-work jackets and slacks, and carried creamy folders of their children's accumulated work, to use in conferring with the teachers. The wives were sun-darkened, wearing crisp, print dresses that looked recently put on, and spoke with ironic turns about PTA politics, bond issues, and class sizes. In his classroom my son tugged me from board to board, where he had contributed paragraphs on wildlife. The crowning exhibit was a model of Io, Jupiter's pizza-mocking moon, which he had made from a tennis ball and thick, sulphurous paint. It hung in a box painted black and looked remarkably, ethereally real. My son had won first prize in his class for the mockup moon, and his teacher stressed this as she went over the less welcome news that he was not doing well at his reading. Apparently he arranged the plausible phrases—A, then B, then C—into illogical combinations, C coming before A, despite the instructing commas and semicolons which should have guided him. It was a minor problem, his teacher assured me, but should be looked after. Perhaps a little more reading at home, under my eye? I nodded, sure that the children of the other scientists and computer programmers and engineers did not have this difficulty, and already knew what the instructing phrase of the next century would be, before the end of this one. My son took the news matter-of-factly, unafraid, and went off to help with the cake and Koolaid. I watched him mingle with girls whose awkwardness was lovely, like giraffes'. I remembered that his teacher (I had learned from gossip) had a mother dying of cancer, which might explain the furrow between her eyebrows that would not go away. My son came bearing cake. I ate it with him, sitting with knees slanting upward in the small chair, and quite calmly and suddenly an idea came to me and would not go away. I turned it over and felt its shape, testing it in a preliminary fashion. Underneath I was both excited and fearful and yet sure that it would survive: it was right. Scraping up the last crumbs and icing, I looked down, and saw my son had drawn a crayon design, an enormous father playing ball with a son, running and catching, the scene carefully fitted into the small compass of the plastic, throwaway plate.

The next morning I finished the data reduction on the slit-image exposures. By carefully covering over the galaxy and background I had managed to take successive plates which blocked out segments of the space parallel to the brightest blue jet. Photometry of the resulting weak signal could give a cross section of the jet's intensity. Pinpoint calibration then yielded the thickness of the central jet zone.

The data was somewhat scattered, the error bars were larger than I liked, but still—I was sure I had it. The jet had a fuzzy halo and a bright core. The core was less than a hundred light-years across, a thin filament of highly ionized hydrogen, cut like a swath through the gauzy dust beyond the galaxy. The resolute, ruler-sharp path, its thinness, its profile of luminosity: all pointed toward a tempting picture. Some energetic object had carved each line, moving at high speeds. It swallowed some of the matter in its path; and in the act of engorgement the mass was heated to incandescent brilliance, spitting UV and x-rays into an immense surrounding volume. This radiation in turn ionized the galactic gas, leaving a scratch of light behind the object, like picnickers dumping luminous trash as they pass by.

The obvious candidates for the fast-moving sources of the jets were black holes. And as I traced the slim profiles of the NGC 1097 jets back into the galaxy, they all intersected at the precise geometrical center of the barred spiral pattern.

Last night, after returning from the Open House with a sleepy boy in tow, I talked with my wife as we undressed. I described my son's home room, his artistic achievements, his teacher. My wife let slip offhandedly some jarring news. I had, apparently, misheard the earlier gossip; perhaps I had mused over some problem while she related the story to me over breakfast. It was not the teacher's mother who had cancer, but the teacher herself. I felt an instant, settling guilt. I could scarcely remember the woman's face, though it was a mere hour later. I asked why she was still working. Because, my wife explained with straightforward New England sense, it was better than staring at a wall. The chemotherapy took only a small slice of her hours. And anyway, she probably needed the money. The night beyond our windows seemed solid, flinty, harder than the soft things inside. In the glass I watched my wife take off a print dress and stretch backward, breasts thinning into crescents, her knobbed spine describing a serene curve that anticipated bed. I went over to my chest of drawers and looked down at the polished walnut surface, scrupulously rectangular and arranged, across which I had tossed the residue of an hour's dutiful parenting: a scrawled essay on marmosets, my son's anthology of drawings, his reading list, and on top, the teacher's bland paragraph of assessment. It felt odd to have called these things into being, these signs of a forward tilt in a small life, by an act of love or at least lust, now years past. The angles appropriate to cradling my children still lived in my hands. I could feel clearly the tentative clutch of my son as he attempted some upright steps. Now my eye strayed to his essay. I could see him struggling with the notion of clauses, with ideas piled upon each other to build a point, and with the caged linearity of the sentence. On the page above, in the loops of the teacher's generous flow pen, I saw a hollow rotundity, a denial of any constriction in her life. She had to go on, this schoolgirlish penmanship said, to forcefully forget a gnawing illness among a roomful of bustling children. Despite all the rest, she had to keep on doing.

What could be energetic enough to push black holes out of the galactic center, up the slopes of the deep gravitational potential well? Only another black hole. The dynamics had been worked out years before—as so often happens, in another context—by William Saslaw. Let a bee-swarm of black holes orbit about each other, all caught in a gravitational depression. Occasionally, they veer close together, deforming the space-time nearby, caroming off each other like billiard balls. If several undergo these near-miss collisions at once, a black hole can be ejected from the gravitational trap altogether. More complex collisions can throw pairs of black holes in opposite directions, conserving angular momentum: jets and counter-jets. But why did NGC 1097 display two blue jets and two red? Perhaps the blue ones glowed with the phosphorescent waste left by the largest, most energetic black holes; their counter-jets must be, by some detail of the dynamics, always smaller, weaker, redder.

I went to the jutting, air-conditioned library, and read Saslaw's papers. Given a buzzing hive of black holes in a gravitational well—partly of their own making—many things could happen. There were compact configurations, tightly orbiting and self-obsessed, which could be ejected as a body. These close-wound families could in turn be unstable, once they were isolated beyond the galaxy's tug, just as the group at the center had been. Caroming off each other, they could eject unwanted siblings. I frowned. This could explain the astonishing right-angle turn the long blue jet made. One black hole thrust sidewise and several smaller, less energetic black holes pushed the opposite way.

As the galactic center lost its warped children, the ejections would become less probable. Things would die down. But how long did that take? NGC 1097 was no younger than our own Galaxy; on the cosmic scale, a sixty-million year difference was nothing.

In the waning of afternoon—it was only a bit more than twenty-four hours since I first laid out the plates of NGC 1097—the Operations report came in. There was no explanation for the Sagittarius A data. It had been received from the station in orbit and duly processed. But no command had made the scope swivel to that axis. Odd, Operations said, that it pointed in an interesting direction, but no more.

There were two added plates, fresh from processing. I did not mention to Redman in Operations that the resolution of these plates was astonishing, that details in the bloated, spilling clouds were unprecedented. Nor did I point out that the angle of view had tilted further, giving a better perspective on the outward-jutting inferno. With their polynomial percussion, the computers had given what was in the stream of downward-flowing data, numbers that spoke of something being banished from the pivot of our Galaxy.

Caltech is a compact campus. I went to the Athenaeum for coffee, ambling slowly beneath the palms and scented eucalyptus, and circumnavigated the campus on my return. In the varnished perspectives of these tiled hallways, the hammer of time was a set of Dopplered numbers, blue-shifted because the thing rushed toward us, a bulge in the sky. Silent numbers.

There were details to think about, calculations to do, long

strings of hypothesis to unfurl like thin flags. I did not know the effect of a penetrating, ionizing flux on Earth. Perhaps it could affect the upper atmosphere and alter the ozone cap that drifts above our heedless heads. A long trail of disturbed, high-energy plasma could fan out through our benign spiral arm—odd, to think of bands of dust and rivers of stars as a neighborhood where you have grown up—churning, working, heating. After all, the jets of NGC 1097 had snuffed out the beaded H II regions as cleanly as an eraser passing across a blackboard, ending all the problems that life knows.

The NGC 1097 data was clean and firm. It would make a good paper, perhaps a letter to *Astrophysical Journal Letters*. But the rest—there was no crisp professional path. These plates had come from much nearer the Galactic center. The information had come outward at light speed, far faster than the pressing bulge, and tilted at a slight angle away from the radial vector that led to Earth.

I had checked the newest Palomar plates from Sagittarius A this afternoon. There were no signs of anything unusual. No Doppler bulge, no exiled mass. They flatly contradicted the satellite plates.

That was the key: old reliable Palomar, our biggest ground-based 'scope, showed nothing. Which meant that someone in high orbit had fed data into our satellite 'scope—exposures that had to be made nearer the Galactic center and then brought here and deftly slipped into our ordinary astronomical research. Exposures that spoke of something stirring where we could not yet see it, beyond the obscuring lanes of dust. The plumes of fiery gas would take a while longer to work through that dark cloak.

These plain facts had appeared on a screen, mute and undeniable, keyed to the data on NGC 1097. Keyed to a connection that another eye than mine could miss. Some astronomer laboring over plates of eclipsing binaries or globular clusters might well have impatiently erased the offending, multicolored spattering, not bothered to uncode the Dopplers, to note the persistent mottled red of the Galactic dust arm at the lower right, and so not known what the place must be. Only I could have made the connection to NGC 1097, and guessed what an onrushing black hole could do to a fragile planet: burn away the ozone layer, hammer the land with high-energy particles, mask the sun in gas and dust.

But to convey this information in this way was so strange,

so—yes, that was the word—so alien. Perhaps this was the way they had to do it: quiet, subtle, indirect. Using an oblique analogy which only suggested, yet somehow disturbed more than a direct statement. And of course, this might be only a phrase in a longer message. Moving out from the Galactic center, they would not know we were here until they grazed the expanding bubble of radio noise that gave us away, and so their data would use what they had, views at a different slant. The data itself, raw and silent, would not necessarily call attention to itself. It had to be placed in context, beside NGC 1097. How had they managed to do that? Had they tried before? What odd logic dictated this approach? How . . .

Take it in pieces. Some of the data I could use, some not. Perhaps a further check, a fresh look through the dusty Sagittarius arm, would show the beginnings of a ruddy swelling, could give a verification. I would have to look, try to find a bridge that would make plausible what I knew but could scarcely prove. The standards of science are austere, unforgiving—and who would have it differently? I would have to hedge, to take one step back for each two forward, to compare and suggest and contrast, always sticking close to the data. And despite what I thought I knew now, the data would have to lead, they would have to show the way.

There is a small Episcopal church, not far up Hill Street, which offers a Friday communion in early evening. Driving home through the surrounding neon consumer gumbo, musing, I saw the sign, and stopped. I had the NGC 1097 plates with me in a carrying case, ripe beneath my arm with their fractional visions, like thin sections of an exotic cell. I went in. The big oak door thumped solemnly shut behind me. In the nave two elderly men were passing woven baskets, taking up the offertory. I took a seat near the back. Idly I surveyed the people, distributed randomly like a field of unthinking stars, in the pews before me. A man came nearby and a pool of brassy light passed before me and I put something in, the debris at the bottom clinking and rustling as I stirred it. I watched the backs of heads as the familiar litany droned on, as devoid of meaning as before. I do not believe, but there is communion. Something tugged at my attention; one head turned a fraction. By a kind of triangulation I deduced the features of the other, closer to the ruddy light of the altar, and saw it was my son's teacher. She was listening raptly.

I listened, too, watching her, but could only think of the gnawing at the center of a bustling, swirling galaxy. The lights seemed to dim. The organ had gone silent. *Take, eat. This is the body and blood of* and so it had begun. I waited my turn. I do not believe, but there is communion. The people went forward in their turns. The woman rose; yes, it was she, the kind of woman whose hand would give forth loops and spirals and who would dot her i's with a small circle. The faint timbre of the organ seeped into the layered air. When it was time I was still thinking of NGC 1097, of how I would write the paper—fragments skittered across my mind, the pyramid of the argument was taking shape—and I very nearly missed the gesture of the elderly man at the end of my pew. Halfway to the altar rail I realized that I still carried the case of NGC 1097 exposures, crooked into my elbow, where the pressure caused a slight ache to spread the spot where they had made the transfusion in the clinic, transferring a fraction of life, blood given. I put it beside me as I knelt. The robes of the approaching figure were cobalt blue and red, a change from the decades since I had been an acolyte. There were no acolytes at such a small service, of course. The blood would follow; first came the offered plate of wafers. Take, eat. Life calling out to life. I could feel the pressing weight of what lay ahead for me, the long roll of years carrying forward one hypothesis, and then, swallowing, knowing that I would never believe this and yet I would want it, I remembered my son, remembered that these events were only pieces, that the puzzle was not yet over, that I would never truly see it done, that as an astronomer I had to live with knowledge forever partial and provisional, that science was not final result, but instead a continuing meditation carried on in the face of enormous facts—*take it in phrases*—let the sentences of our lives pile up.

MENTOR Books of Special Interest

(0451)

☐ **THE HUMAN BRAIN: Its Capacities and Functions by Isaac Asimov.** A remarkable clear investigation of how the human brain organizes and controls the total functioning of the individual. Illustrated by Anthony Ravielli. (619013—$2.25)

☐ **THE HUMAN BODY: Its Structure and Operation by Issac Asimov.** A superbly up-to-date and informative study which also includes aids to pronunciation, derivations of specialized terms, and drawings by Anthony Ravielli. (621166—$2.95)

☐ **THE CHEMICALS OF LIFE by Isaac Asimov.** An investigation of the role of hormones, enzymes, protein and vitamins in the life cycle of the human body. (620372—$1.95)

☐ **THE INDIVIDUAL AND HIS DREAMS by Calvin S. Hall and Vernon J. Nordby.** The authors of this absorbing study offer new insight into the meaning of dreams by way of an objective and quantitative approach. By following the procedures outlined here, the reader will be rewarded by remarkable gains in self-knowledge and awareness. (616359—$1.95)

☐ **THE DOUBLE HELIX by James D. Watson.** A "behind-the-scenes" account of the work that led to the discovery of DNA. "It is a thrilling book from beginning to end—delightful, often funny, vividly observant, full of suspense and mounting tension . . . so directly candid about the brilliant and abrasive personalities and institutions involved . . ."—*Eliot Fremont-Smith, New York Times.* Illustrated.
(620496—$2.50)
